JUDGMENT ROAD

CHRISTINE FEEHAN

JOVE
New York

A JOVE BOOK
Published by Berkley
An imprint of Penguin Random House LLC
375 Hudson Street, New York, New York 10014

Copyright © 2018 by Christine Feehan
Excerpt from *Covert Game* copyright © 2018 by Christine Feehan
Penguin Random House supports copyright. Copyright fuels creativity, encourages
diverse voices, promotes free speech, and creates a vibrant culture. Thank you for
buying an authorized edition of this book and for complying with copyright laws by not
reproducing, scanning, or distributing any part of it in any form without permission.
You are supporting writers and allowing Penguin Random House to continue to publish
books for every reader.

A JOVE BOOK and BERKLEY are registered trademarks and the B colophon is a
trademark of Penguin Random House LLC.

ISBN: 9780451488510

First Edition: January 2018

Printed in the United States of America
1   3   5   7   9   10   8   6   4   2

Cover art © Cliff Nielsen / Shannon Associates
Cover design by Judith Lagerman
Torpedo Ink logo design by Patrick J. Mears
Book design by Kelly Lipovich

For my beloved grandson and wild child, Mason Stottsberry. I'm certain you're riding a Harley across the sky, surfing the longest comet and teaching the angels to dance. You'll always be in our hearts. As promised, this one is for you!

FOR MY READERS

Be sure to go to christinefeehan.com/members/ to sign up for my private book announcement list and download the free ebook of *Dark Desserts*. Join my community and get firsthand news, enter the book discussions, ask your questions and chat with me. Please feel free to email me at Christine@christinefeehan.com. I would love to hear from you.

ACKNOWLEDGMENTS

As with any book, there are so many people to thank. First, Nancy Rich, who was gracious enough to talk to me at length about clubs. Ed, my go-to man, who answers my questions when needed. A huge shout-out to Patrick J. Mears from Spread Eagle Tattoo for working so closely with me to create my vision and concept of the Torpedo Ink graphics. Brian and Sheila, for competing with me during power hours for top word count when I wanted to move fast on this one. And Domini, for always editing, no matter how many times I ask her to go over the same book before we send it for additional editing.

TORPEDO INK MEMBERS

Viktor Prakenskii aka *Czar*—President

Lyov Russak aka *Steele*—Vice President

Savva Pajari aka *Reaper*—Sergeant at Arms

Savin Pajari aka *Savage*—Sergeant at Arms

Isaak Koval aka *Ice*—Secretary

Dmitry Koval aka *Storm*

Alena Koval aka *Torch*

Luca Litvin aka *Code*—Treasurer

Maksimos Korsak aka *Ink*

Kasimir Popov aka *Preacher*

Lana Popov aka *Widow*

Nikolaos Bolotan aka *Mechanic*

Pytor Bolotan aka *Transporter*

Andrii Federoff aka *Maestro*

Gedeon Lazaroff aka *Player*

Kir Vasiliev aka *Master*

Lazar Alexeev aka *Keys*

Aleksei Solokov aka *Absinthe*

NEWER PATCHED MEMBERS

Gavriil Prakenskii

Casimir Prakenskii

PROSPECTS

Fatei

Glitch

Hyde

ONE

The wind blew off the sea as the three Harleys made their way through the last series of snaking turns and hit the straight stretch on Highway 1 running parallel to the ocean. The night was well under way, a fact that Savva "Reaper" Pajari was well aware of. He had to report to the president of his club, Czar, the moment they arrived back in Caspar, but time didn't matter for that. Even if Czar was at his home in Sea Haven, tucked in close to his wife, Reaper'd just hit the roof and climb in through the bedroom window. He'd done it more than once.

He lived for two things: riding free and fighting. He needed to feel solid muscle under his knuckles. He needed to feel fists hitting his body, tapping into that well of ice that covered every emotion. That swift explosion of violence and sweet pain as fists connected was his life, and had been his life since he was five. Now, he needed to stay sharp somehow, in this new bullshit direction the club had taken.

He rode along the highway, aware of the others on either side of him. Brothers, some for over thirty years. Men he counted on. Men he called family. Still, he was apart from them and he knew it, even if they didn't. He turned his head toward the ocean. Waves sprayed up into the air, rushing over rocks and battering at the cliffs. Sometimes he felt those battered rocks were him, time wearing him away, little by little.

His soul had been gone so long ago that he couldn't remember having one. Now, his heart was slowly disappearing. There wasn't a place on his body without a scar. He had another to add from this last trip. He also would have to have Ink tat his back, three more skulls to add to the collection of those resting in the roots of the tree on his back.

Viktor Prakenskii, the man known as Czar, was the best man he knew. Reaper's job was to stand in front of Czar, his self-appointed task from the time he was a little boy. He'd been doing it for so long now, he didn't know any other way of life. He stood in front of all his brothers and sisters—in Torpedo Ink, his club. He was proud to wear the club colors. He'd die for those colors and still detested any mission he ran if he had to take them off.

They turned off the main highway onto Caspar Road leading to the town of Caspar, where they'd set up home. They'd designed their compound around the old paymaster's building for the Caspar logging company. They had spent the first few months working on the building, turning it into their clubhouse. It housed multiple bedrooms, a bar, their meeting room—known as the chapel—and a kitchen. They shared bathrooms, whichever was closest to their assigned sleeping room. Czar had insisted each of them purchase a home nearby. He wanted those roots put down deep.

Reaper didn't give a damn where they all slept. As long as he could defend his club and their president, he was fine. The compound had a bed and right now, he needed one. He was forty-eight hours without sleep. He'd stitched up the wound in his side himself, making a piss-poor job of it too, but all he'd had was a little whiskey to disinfect it, and that had burned like hell. It still did.

They rode up to the compound, and Storm and Keys parked their bikes while he scanned the lot. Either Czar was home or at the bar. Reaper was fairly certain he'd be at the bar waiting for a report. He didn't like to disturb his wife, Blythe, or their four adopted children. Reaper didn't shut his bike down and waited for the others to turn to him.

"Goin' to find Czar," he said, unnecessarily, but they were looking at him like he should say something. He didn't like stupid shit, like the formalities that seemed so important to others. He didn't care if people liked him; in fact, he preferred they stay the hell away, except for his brothers, who understood him and made it clear they expected him to at least talk once in a while.

"I can report in," Keys offered. "You could use the downtime."

Reaper shook his head. "Won't be able to sleep right away. I have to check on him anyway. You know how I am."

"Want company?" Storm asked.

He shook his head. "Not necessary. Savage will be with him, probably a few others. Get some sleep. We all earned it." Savin "Savage" Pajari was his birth brother. Like Reaper, he acted as sergeant at arms, protecting Czar at all times. Between the two men, they had their president covered whether he liked it or not around the clock. "I already texted Czar we were comin' in when we were an hour out."

He was certain if he did that, Czar would go to the bar rather than have Reaper come to his home—exactly what Reaper wanted. It was the new bartender. Reaper didn't like anything out of the ordinary. He didn't trust it. The woman was definitely something out of the ordinary. Code could find dirt on anyone, but he hadn't found a single trace of her anywhere. She worked for cash, under the table. She wore designer jeans, but she drove a beat-up car on its last leg, rust breaking through the paint. The fucking thing smoked every time she turned the engine over.

Torpedo Ink had a garage up and running. Did she take her car there to get it fixed? Hell no. She drove off every night thinking no one knew where she was going. That was the hell of it. She drove back toward Fort Bragg, took Highway 20 and turned off at the Egg Taking Station, a campground in the Jackson Demonstration Forest. Why the fuck would a classy woman be bartending in a biker bar, drive a beat-up Honda Civic older than she was and be camping? It made no sense. He didn't like puzzles, and Anya Rafferty was not only a puzzle, but one big headache.

Reaper had watched her for over a month. Five weeks and three days to be precise. He'd learned she was a hard worker. She listened to people, remembered their names and what they liked to drink. She flirted just enough to get good tips, but not enough to cause fights. She was generous with the waitresses, sharing tips she didn't have to share. She was careful and guarded yet gave the illusion she was open. She was kind to those less fortunate.

He'd watched her give a homeless man a blanket she carried in her car, and twice she'd brought him coffee and a meal. Twice she'd spent money he was certain she didn't have to get food or shoes for someone living on the streets. She seemed to have an affinity for the homeless, and he was certain she knew all of them by name. She volunteered in the soup kitchen Saturday mornings even though she couldn't have had more than a couple of hours of sleep.

She didn't flinch around the bikers, but it was obvious she wasn't from their world and didn't have a clue how to fit in. She took her cues from Czar and sometimes asked him questions. She'd never asked Reaper a single question, but she sent him a few shy smiles, which he didn't return. He'd spent more time in the bar in the five weeks she'd been there than he'd ever spent in a bar in his life.

Reaper glanced away from the compound, up toward the

THE DECISION IS UNANIMOUS— SCOTT TUROW'S
PLEADING GUILTY
IS THE GUILTY PLEASURE OF THE YEAR!

★

"Scott Turow's linear forebears are not the manufacturers of assembly-line entertainments but the likes of Theodore Dreiser and James Gould Cozzens."
—*Washington Post Book World*

"An uncommonly skilled writer, and an uncommonly eloquent one." —*Christian Science Monitor*

"Scott Turow is about to condemn another summer's worth of beachgoers to addictive page turning. . . . An irresistible tale and a dark, moral thriller." —*TIME*

"Mr. Turow's effects hold one enthralled until the last page." —*New York Times*

"Turow's novels are not mere entertainments. They transcend their genre. They are literature that will last. . . . The cadences of Turow's prose as well as the substance of his stories are as urban as the sound of a jazz saxophone at 2 A.M. . . . Turow's Kindle County is acquiring a reality as a convincing moral landscape comparable to that of Faulkner's Yoknapatawpha County."
—**George F. Will**
"The Last Word," *Newsweek*

★

more . . .

★

"A page-turner."
—*Cosmopolitan*

"A classy tale, superbly told."
—*USA Weekend*

"Lean, tough, tightly plotted . . . a deceptively quick read, a cliffhanger that keeps you racing through the pages, matching wits with its twists and turns right up to the deft, startling conclusion. . . . PLEADING GUILTY has the freshness and energy of a confident writer reaching out. His readers have more thrills and fun— and it feels as if Turow did, too."
—*Playboy*

"Irresistible . . . Turow is worthy to be ranked with Dashiell Hammett or Raymond Chandler."
—*New York Times Book Review*

"Well plotted and well written. . . . Again, Turow demonstrates that he is unequaled in portraying the intricacies and duplicities of the law."
—*Detroit News*

"The suspense never flags . . . Mack Malloy is one of recent fiction's great characters. . . . You'll root for him."
—*New Woman*

"Another surefire hit."
—*Booklist*

★

★

"Mr. Turow has proved beyond a shadow of a doubt what a brilliant novelist he is."
—*Atlanta Journal & Constitution*

"Authentic and mature . . . first rate, full of well-earned, head-turning surprises."
—*Mirabella*

"The pulsing, carnal appeal of Turow's dramatic narrative is irresistible."
—*Glamour*

"A narrative tour de force."
—*San Jose Mercury News*

"Wise, surefooted. . . . Though every element of the novel is polished and professional, the charisma of Mack Malloy's narration is its triumph. Add to this a taut, twist-filled plot, expert pacing, colorful and well-rendered supporting characters, and an appealing whiff of larceny, and Turow surpasses Grisham hands down."
—*Publishers Weekly*

"Turow aspires to greater literary heights than do the John Grishams or Richard North Pattersons, and with PLEADING GUILTY, he succeeds admirably. . . . Turow skillfully moves the reader through well-placed plot twists and nicely triggered surprises."
—*Houston Chronicle*

★

more . . .

★

"Turow's prose is clear, his dialogue real, and his characters sympathetic."
—*American Bar Association Journal*

"Combines the best of *Presumed Innocent* and *Burden of Proof*. . . complex and compelling."
—*Seattle Times*

"One of the great virtues of PLEADING GUILTY is the skill with which Turow moves from intricate and rarefied legal technicality to the bare-bones business of a chilled corpse. . . . Mack is the kind of character who matters, whose actions are freighted with moral significance."
—*New York Newsday*

"A compelling story that draws its strength more from rich characterizations than suspense . . . a thoughtfully conceived, perceptively well-written novel that should deeply satisfy readers with its insight."
—*The State* (Columbia, S.C.)

"The extrememly entertaining PLEADING GUILTY is faster paced, more plot driven, and less self-consciously introspective than his previous bestsellers. . . . The verdict? Get your copy now. . . He easily proves he is the best in the business."
—*Providence Sunday Journal*

★

★

"Turow's great strength—the dialogue that rings as true as an overheard phone conversation—comes shining through here. . . . He knows human nature, how people talk, how they think and feel. And he's marvelously savvy about *fin de siècle* urban life. In fact, Turow is just plain good at the whole writing game."

—*Buffalo News*

"Turow is utterly convincing in the picture he paints. . . . His quick, intimate word pictures reveal a stunningly fluid and perceptive writing style. . . . PLEADING GUILTY is a trip you shouldn't miss."

—*Arizona Daily Star*

"A good deal more than a standard whodunit: It is a novel in the full sense of the word in which character and style are essential factors in the finished product . . . a rattling good yarn that you will long remember."

—*John Barkham Reviews*

"Sure, John Grisham can spin a yarn, but if we're weighing psychological acuity and pure literary talent, the scales of justice tip easily in favor of counselor Turow. . . . Mack Malloy isn't the first outsider Turow has created, but he's the most ambiguous, the most dissipated, the most secretive, and, in some ways, the most intriguing."

—*Hartford Courant*

★

more . . .

★

"Lyric and almost romatic at surprising moments, PLEADING GUILTY simmers nicely in its own plot."
—*Washington Times*

"Compelling . . . a taut, twisting tale of greed. . . . The book's real surprises relate to revelations of character.... Turow is a master at proving hidden motives and emotions."
—*Orlando Sentinel*

"Turow is back, better than ever, and he has brought Malloy with him. We can only hope the two will return in the future."
—*Sunday Oregonian*

"Displays the same impressive narrative abilities and whiplash plotting that marked *Presumed Innocent* . . . characters are deftly drawn . . .plot twists are numerous and effective, right up to the last turn of the screw."
—*Wall Street Journal*

"Turow joins the ranks of that very special group of authors—Jane Austen, Tolstoy, Rex Stout, among others—who, by knowing how to keep our attention, have caused more sleepless nights than caffeine." —*Vogue*

"One of the summer's big reads."
—*Entertainment Weekly*

★

★

"Stunningly realistic. . . . Turow establishes Mack Malloy's character so brilliantly that Mack becomes one of modern literature's genuinely tragic figures. . . . Turow, as usual, keeps us guessing until the end."
—*Arkansas Democrat Gazette*

"Perhaps Turow's most riveting novel. . . . The most compelling of Turow's fictional realms is the mind of protagonist Mack Malloy . . . a refreshingly complex guy."
—*Independent Reader* (Durham, N.C.)

"Expertly crafted, and intelligent and insightful book that is also a great read."
—*St. Petersburg Times*

"The story has the virtues of Turow's best books: clear-headed intelligence, a sense of the perilous nature of every person's moral universe, and some good puzzles."
—*Milwaukee Journal*

"No one writes better mystery suspense novels than Scott Turow."
—*Los Angeles Times*

"Fascinating . . . mesmerizing . . . memorable."
—*Chicago Tribune*

★

Also by Scott Turow

THE BURDEN OF PROOF (1990)
PRESUMED INNOCENT (1987)
ONE L (1977)

Published by
WARNER BOOKS

PLEADING GUILTY

SCOTT TUROW

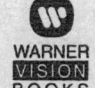

WARNER
VISION
BOOKS

A Time Warner Company

WARNER BOOKS EDITION

Copyright © 1993 by Scott Turow
All rights reserved.

Cover design by Neil Stuart

This Warner Books Edition is published by arrangement with Farrar, Straus and Giroux, New York.

Warner Vision is a trademark of Warner Books, Inc.

Warner Books, Inc.
1271 Avenue of the Americas
New York, NY 10020

Ⓦ A Time Warner Company

Printed in the United States of America

First Warner Books Printing: June, 1994

10 9 8 7 6 5 4 3 2 1

For seven years now, my colleagues at Sonnenschein Nath & Rosenthal—lawyers and non-lawyers alike, but especially my partners—have provided me with unflagging support in a variety of circumstances which have occasionally surprised us all. Only I know better than they how little the law firm described in the following pages either resembles our firm or shares its atmosphere of sustained decency. In gratitude for their comradeship, their kindness—and their tolerance—this novel is affectionately dedicated to the many persons at Sonnenschein to whom my deepest thanks are due.

Where was my heart to flee for refuge from my heart?
Whither was I to fly, where I would not follow? In what
place should I not be prey to myself?

The Confessions of St. Augustine
BOOK FOUR, CHAPTER VII

The secret self—
ever more secret,
unhappy,
misled.

TO: Management Oversight Committee
FROM: McCormack A. Malloy
RE: Our Missing Partner

Attached, pursuant to your assignment, please find my report.

(Dictated but not read)

TAPE 1

Dictated January 24, 4:00 a.m.

I. MY ASSIGNMENT

The Management Oversight Committee of our firm, known among the partnership simply as "the Committee," meets each Monday at 3:00 p.m. Over coffee and chocolate brioche, these three hotshots, the heads of the firm's litigation, transactional, and regulatory departments, decide what's what at Gage & Griswell for another week. Not bad guys really, able lawyers, heady business types looking out for the greatest good for the greatest number at G&G, but since I came here eighteen years ago the Committee and their austere powers, freely delegated under the partnership agreement, have tended to scare me silly. I'm forty-nine, a former copper on the street, a big man with a brave front and a good Irish routine, but in the last few years I've heard many discouraging words from these three. My points have been cut, my office moved to something smaller, my hours and billing described as far too low. Arriving this afternoon, I steadied myself, as ever, for the worst.

"Mack," said Martin Gold, our managing partner, "Mack, we need your help. Something serious." He's a sizable man, Martin, a wrestler at the U. three decades ago, a middleweight with a chest broad as the map of America. He has a dark, shrewd face, a little like those Mongol warriors of Genghis Khan's, and the venerable look of somebody who's mixed it up with life. He is, no question, the best lawyer I know.

The other two, Carl Pagnucci and Wash Thale, were eating at the walnut conference table, an antique of Continental origin with the big heavy look of a cuckoo clock. Martin invited me to share the brioche, but I took only coffee. With these guys, I needed to be quick.

"This isn't about you," said Carl, making a stark appraisal of my apprehensions.

"Who?" I asked.

"Bert," said Martin.

For going on two weeks, my partner Bert Kamin has not appeared at the office. No mail from him, no calls. In the case of your average baseline human being who has worked at Gage & Griswell during my time, say anyone from Leotis Griswell to the Polish gal who cleans the cans, this would be cause for concern. Not so clearly Bert. Bert is a kind of temperamental adolescent, big and brooding, who enjoys the combat of the courtroom. You need a lawyer who will cross-examine opposing party's CEO and claw out his intestines in the fashion of certain large cats, Bert's your guy. On the other hand, if you want someone who will come to work, fill out his time sheets, or treat his secretary as if he recollected that slavery is dead, then you might think about somebody else. After a month or two on trial, Bert is liable to take an absolute powder. Once he turned up at the fantasy camp run by the Trappers, our major league baseball team. Another time he was gambling in Monte Carlo. With his dark moods, scowls, and hallway tantrums, his macho stunts and episodic schedule, Bert has survived at Gage & Griswell largely through the sufferance of Martin, who is a champion of tolerance and seems to enjoy the odd ducks like Bert. Or, for that matter, me.

"Why don't you talk to those thugs down at the steam bath where he likes to hang out? Maybe they know where he is." I meant the Russian Bath. Unmarried, Bert is apt to follow the Kindle County sporting teams around the country on weekends, laying heavy bets and passing time in sports bars or places like the Bath where people talk about the players with an intimacy they don't presume with their relations. "He'll show up," I added, "he always does."

Pagnucci said simply, "Not this time."

"This is very sensitive," Wash Thale told me. "Very sensitive." Wash tends to state the obvious in a grave, portentous manner, the self-commissioned voice of wisdom.

"Take a look." Martin shot a brown expandable folder across the glimmer of the table. A test, I feared at once, and felt a bolt of anxiety quicken my thorax, but inside all I found were eighteen checks. They were drawn on what we call the 397 Settlement Account, an escrow administered by G&G which contains $288 million scheduled to be paid out shortly to various plaintiffs in settlement of a massive air crash case brought against TransNational Air.

TN, the world's biggest airline and travel concern, is G&G's largest client. We stand up for TN in court; we help TN buy and deal and borrow. With its worldwide hotels and resorts, its national catering business, its golf courses, airport parking lots, and rent-a-car subsidiaries, TN lays claim to some part of the time of almost every lawyer around here. We live with the company like family in the same home, tenanted on four floors of the TN Needle, just below the world corporate headquarters.

The checks inside the folder had all been signed by Bert, in his flourishing maniac hand, each one cut to something called Litiplex Ltd., in an amount of several hundred thousand dollars. On the memo lines of the drafts Bert had written "Litigation Support." Document analyses, computer models, expert witnesses—the engineers run amok in air crash cases.

"What's Litiplex?" I asked.

Martin, to my amazement, rifled a finger as if I'd said something adroit.

"Not incorporated or authorized to do business in any of the fifty states," he said. "Not in any state's Assumed Names registry. Carl checked."

Nodding, Carl added like an omen, "Myself."

Carl Pagnucci—born Carlo—is forty-two, the youngest of three, and stingy with words, a lawyer's lawyer who holds his own speech in the same kind of suspicion with which Woody Hayes viewed the forward pass. He is a pale little guy with a mustache like one of those round brushes that comes with your electric shaver. In his perfect suits, somber and tasteful, with a flash of gold from his cuff links, he reveals nothing.

Assessing the news that Bert, my screwball colleague, had written millions of dollars of checks to a company that didn't exist, I felt some peculiar impulse to defend him, my own longtime alliance with the wayward.

"Maybe somebody asked him to do it," I said.

"That's where *we* started," Wash replied. He'd taken his stout figure back to the brioche. This had come up initially, Wash said, when Glyndora Gaines, our staff supervisor in Accounting, noticed these large disbursements with no backup.

"Glyndora's searched three times for any paper trail," Wash told me. "Invoices. Sign-off memo from Jake." Under our procedures, Bert was allowed to write checks on the 397 account only after receiving written approval from Jake Eiger, a former partner in this firm, who is now the General Counsel at TN.

"And?"

"There is none. We've even had Glyndora make inquiries upstairs with her counterparts at TN, the folks who handle the accounting on 397. Nothing to alarm them. You understand. 'We had some stray correspondence for this Litiplex. Blah, blah, blah.' Martin tried the same approach with one or two of the plaintiffs' lawyers in the hope they knew something we didn't. There's nothing," he said, "not a scrap. Nobody's ever heard the name." Wash is more shifty than smart, but looking at him—his liver spots and wattles, his discreet twitches and the little bit of mouse gray hair he insists on pasting across his scalp—I detected the feckless expression he has when he is sincere. "Not to mention," he added, "the endorsement."

I'd missed that. Now I took note on the back of each

check of the bilingual green block stamp of the International Bank of Finance in Pico Luan. Pico, a tiny Central American nation, a hangnail on the toe of the Yucatán, is a pristine haven of fugitive dollars and absolute bank secrecy. There were no signatures on the checks' backs, but what I took for the account number was inscribed on each beneath the stamp. A straight deposit.

"We tried calling the bank," said Martin. "I explained to the General Manager that we were merely trying to confirm that Robert Kamin had rights of deposit and withdrawal on account 476642. I received a very genial lecture on the bank secrecy laws in Pico in reply. Quite a clever fellow, this one. With that beautiful accent. Just the piece of work you'd expect in that business. Like trying to grab hold of smoke. I asked if he was familiar with Mr. Kamin's name. Not a word I could quote, but I thought he was saying yes. God knows, he didn't say no."

"And what's the total?" I thumbed the checks.

"Over five and a half million," said Carl, who was always quickest with figures. "Five point six and some change actually."

With that, we were all briefly silent, awed by the gravity of the number and the daring of the feat. My partners writhed in further anguish, but on closer inspection of myself I found I was vibrating like a bell that had been struck. What a notion! Grabbing all that dough and hieing out for parts unknown. The wealth, the freedom, the chance to start anew! I wasn't sure if I was more shocked or thrilled.

"Has anybody talked to Jake?" That seemed like the next logical step to me, tell the client they'd been had.

"God, no," said Wash. "There's going to be hell to pay with TN. A partner in the firm lies to them, embezzles, steals. That's just the kind of thing that Krzysinski has been waiting for to leverage Jake. We will be dead. Dead," he said.

There was a lot that was beyond me going on among the three of them—the Big Three, as they are called behind their backs—but I now thought I could see why I was here. Through most of my career at G&G I have been viewed as Jake Eiger's proxy. We grew up in the same neighborhood and Jake was also a third or fourth cousin of my former wife. Jake was the person responsible for bringing me to the firm when he left to become Senior Division Counsel of TransNational Air. That is a long tradition at Gage & Griswell. For over four decades now, our former partners have dominated the law department at TN, becoming rich on stock options and remembering their old colleagues with the opportunity for lavish billing. Jake, however, has been under pressure from Tad Krzysinski, TN's new CEO, to spread TN's legal business around, and Jake, unsure of his own ground with Krzysinski, has given troubling signs that he will respond. In fact, in my case he seems to have responded some time ago, although I can't tell you if that's because I divorced his cousin, used to drink my lunch, or remain afflicted by something you might politely call "malaise."

"We wanted your advice, Mack, on what we should do," said Martin. "Before we went any further." He eyed me levelly beneath his furry brows. Behind him, out the broad windows of the thirty-seventh story of the TN Needle, Kindle County stretched—the shoebox shapes of Center City and, beyond that, upraised brick smokestack arms. On the west bank of the river, suburban wealth spread beneath the canopy of older trees. All of it was forlornly sullied by the dingy light of winter.

"Call the FBI," I offered. "I'll give you a name." You'd expect a former city cop to recommend his own department, but I left some enemies on the Force. Reading my partners' looks, you could see that I'd missed their mood anyway. Law enforcement was not on the agenda.

Wash finally said it: "Premature."

I admitted that I didn't see the alternatives.

"This is a business," said Carl, a credo from which all further premises devolved. Carl worships what he calls the market with an ardor which in former centuries was reserved for religion. He has a robust securities practice, making the markets work, and a jet-lagged life, zooming back here to Kindle County at least twice a week from D.C., where he heads our Washington office.

"What we were thinking," said Wash, who laid his elderly hands daintily on the dark table, "some of us, anyway, is what if we could find Bert..Reason with him." Wash swallowed. "Get him to give the money back."

I stared.

"Perhaps he's had second thoughts," Wash insisted. "Something like this—he's impulsive. He's been running now, hiding. He might like another chance."

"Wash," I said, "he has five and a half million reasons to say no. And a little problem about going to jail."

"Not if we don't tell," said Wash. He swallowed again. His sallow face was wan with hope above his bow tie.

"You wouldn't tell TN?"

"If they didn't ask, no. And why should they? Really, if this works out, what is there to tell them? There was *almost* a problem? No, no," said Wash, "I don't believe that's required."

"And what would you do with Bert? Just kiss and make up?"

Pagnucci answered. "It's a negotiation," he said simply, a deal maker who believes that willing parties always find a way.

I pondered, slowly recognizing how artfully this could be engineered. The usual false faces of the workplace, only more so. They'd let Bert come back here and say it was all a bad dream. Or withdraw from the practice for a while and pay him—severance, purchase of equity, call it what you'd like. A person feeling either frightened or remorseful might find these offers attractive. But I wasn't sure Bert would see this as much of a deal. In fact, for three smart guys they seemed to have little idea of what had happened. They'd been flipped the bird and were still acting as if it was sign language for the deaf.

Wash had gotten out his pipe, one of his many props, and was waving it around.

"Either we find some way to solve this problem— privately—or the doors here will be shut in a year. Six months. That's my firm prediction." Wash's sense of peril no doubt was greatest for himself, since he had been the billing partner for TN for nearly three decades, his only client worth mentioning and the linchpin of what would otherwise have been a career as mediocre as mine. He has been an *ex officio* member of TN's board for twenty-two years now and is so closely attuned to the vibrations of the company that he can tell you when someone on TN's "Executive Level," seven floors above, has broken wind.

"I still don't understand how you think you'll find Bert."

Pagnucci touched the checks. I didn't understand at first. He was tapping the endorsement.

"Pico?"

"Have you ever been down there?"

I'd first been to Pico when I was assigned to Financial Crimes more than twenty years ago—sky of blue, round and perfect as a cereal bowl above the Mayan Mountains; vast beaches long and lovely as a suntanned flank. Most of the folks around here are down there often. TN was one of the first to despoil the coast, erecting three spectacular resorts. But I hadn't taken the trip in years. I told Carl that.

"You think that's where Bert is?"

"That's where his money is," Pagnucci said.

"No, sir. That's where it went. Where it is now is anybody's guess. The beauty of bank secrecy is that it ends the trail. You can send the money anywhere from Pico. It could be back here, frankly. If it was in the right municipal bonds, he wouldn't even have to pay taxes."

"Right," Pagnucci quickly said. He took this setback, like most things, in silence, but his precise, mannerly good looks clouded with vexation.

"And who's going to do the looking?" I asked. "I don't know many private investigators I'd trust with this one."

"No, no," said Wash. "No one outside the family. We weren't thinking of a private investigator." He was looking somewhat hopefully at me. I actually laughed when I finally got it.

"Wash, I know more about writing traffic tickets than how to find Bert. Call Missing Persons."

"He trusts you, Mack," Wash told me. "You're his friend."

"Bert has no friends."

"He'd respect your opinion. Especially about his prospects of escaping without prosecution. Bert's childish. We all know that. And peculiar. With a familiar face, he'd consider this in a new light."

Anybody who's survived for more than two decades in a law firm or a police department knows better than to say no to the boss. Around here it's team play—yes, sir, and salute smartly. No way I could refuse. But there was a reason I was going to law school at night while I was on the street. I was never one of these lamebrains who thought cop work was glamorous. Kicking doors in, running down dark alleys—that stuff tended to terrify me, especially afterwards when I got to thinking about what I'd done.

"I have a hearing Wednesday," I said. This took them all back for a moment. No one, apparently, had considered the prospect that I might be working. "Bar Admissions and Discipline still wants to punch Toots Nuccio's ticket."

There was a moment's byplay as Wash proposed alternatives—a continuance, perhaps, or allowing another G&G lawyer to handle the case; there were, after all, 130 attorneys here. Martin, the head of litigation, eventually suggested I find another partner to join me at the hearing, someone who could take over down the road if need be. Even with that settled, I was still resisting.

"Guys, this doesn't make sense. I'm never going to find Bert. And you'll only make them angrier at TN once they realize we waited to tell them."

"Not so," said Wash. "Not so. We needed time to gather facts so that we could advise them. You'll prepare a report, Mack," he said, "something we can hand them. Dictate it as you go along. After all, this is a significant matter. Something that can badly embarrass them, as well as us. They'll understand. We'll say you'll take no more than two weeks." He looked to Martin and Carl for verification.

I repeated that there was no place to look.

"Why don't you ask those thugs down at the steam bath where he likes to hang out?" Pagnucci asked. Talking to Carl is often even less satisfying than his silence. He is stubbornly, subtly, but inalterably contrary. Pagnucci regards agreement as a failure of his solemn obligation to exercise critical intelligence. There is always a probing question, a sly jest, a suggested alternative, always a way for him to put an ax to your tree. The guy is more than half a foot shorter than me and makes me feel no bigger than a flea.

"Mack, you would be the savior of this firm," said Wash. "Imagine if it did work out. Our gratitude would be"—Wash waved—"unspeakable."

It all looked perfect from their side. I'm a burnt-out case. No big clients. Gun-shy about trials since I stopped drinking. A fucked-up wreck with the chance to secure my position. And all of this coming up at the most opportune time. The firm was in its annual hysteria with the approaching conclusion of our fiscal year on January 31. All the partners were busy choking overdue fees out of our clients and positioning themselves for February 2, a week and a half from now, when the profits would be divided.

I considered Wash, wondering how I ever ended up working for anybody in a bow tie.

"I say the same thing to you I've said to Martin and Carl," Wash told me. "It's ours, this place, our lives as lawyers are here. What do we lose if we take a couple of weeks trying to save it?"

With that, the three were silent. If nothing else, I had their attention. In high school I used to play baseball. I'm big—six three—and never a lightweight. I have good eye-hand, I could hit the ball a long way, but I'm slow, what people call lumbering when they're trying to be polite, and the coaches had to find someplace to play me, which turned out to be the outfield. I've never been the guy you'd want on your team. If I wasn't batting, I wasn't really in the game. Three hundred feet away from home plate you can forget. The wind comes up; you smell the grass, the perfume from some girl in the stands. A wrapper kicks across the field, followed by a ghost of dust. You check the sun, falling, even with all the yelling to keep you awake, into a kind of trance state, a piece of meditation or dreams. And then, somehow, you feel the eyes of everybody in the park suddenly shifted toward you—the pitcher looking back, the batter, the people in the stands, somebody someplace has yelled your name. It's all coming to you, this dark circle hoving through the sky, changing size, just the way you've seen it at night when you're asleep. I had that feeling now, of having been betrayed by my dreams.

Fear, as usual, was my only real excuse.

"Listen, guys. This was carefully planned. By Mr. Liti-plex or Kamin or whoever. Bert's three sheets to the wind with his sails nowhere in sight. And even if I do find him, by some miracle, what do you think happens when he opens the door and sees that he's been tracked down by one of his partners, who undoubtedly is going to speak to him about going to prison? What do you think he'll do?"

"He'll talk to you, Mack."

"He'll shoot me, Wash. If he's got any sense."

Bereft of a response, Wash looked on with limpid blue eyes and a guttering soul—an aging white man. Martin, a step ahead as ever, smiled in his subtle way because he knew I'd agreed.

Pagnucci as usual said nothing.

II. MY REACTION

Privately, my partners would tell you I'm a troubled individual. Wash and Martin are polite enough to murmur some fainthearted denial as they read this, but, guys, we all know the truth. I am, I admit, kind of a wreck from all directions—overweight even by the standards of big men who seem to get some latitude, gimpy on rainy days because I ruined my knee while I was a copper, jumping off a fence to chase some bum who never was worth catching. My skin, from two decades of drinking hard, has got that reddened look, as if someone took a Brillo pad to my forehead and my cheeks. Worse is what goes on inside. I have a sad heart, stomped on, fevered and corrupted, and a brain that boils at night in a ferment of awful dreams. I hear like far-off music the harsh voices of my mother and my former wife, both of them tough Irishwomen who knew that the tongue, for the right occasion, can be made an instrument of pain.

But now I was excited. After the Committee broke, I lit out from the Needle for the Russian Bath, eager and actually somewhat jealous of Bert. Imagine! I thought as I bounced along in the taxi taking me west. Just imagine. A guy who worked down the hall. A foul ball. Now he was off roistering with a stolen fortune while I was still landlocked in my squalid little life.

Reading this, my partners probably are squinting. What kind of jealous? they say. What envy? Fellas, let's not kid ourselves, especially at 4:00 a.m. It is the hour of the wolf, quiet as doom, and I, the usual insomniac mess, am murmuring into my Dictaphone, whispering in fact, in case my nosy teenaged son actually returns from his night of reprobate activity. When I finish, I'll hide the tape in the strongbox beneath my bed. That way, in the event of second thoughts, I can drop the cassette into the trash.

Before I began dictating the cover memo, I actually figured I would do it just as Wash requested. A report. Something anesthetized and lawyerly, prose in a straitjacket, and many footnotes. But you know me—as the song goes, I've done it my way. Say what you like, this is quite a role. I talk, you listen. I know. You don't. I tell you what I want—when I want. I discuss you like the furniture, or address you now and then by name. Martin, you are smiling in spite of yourself. Wash, you are wondering how Martin will react. Carl, you'd like it all in no more than three sentences and are bristling already.

The bottom line, then: I didn't find Bert this afternoon. I tried. The cab got me to the right place and I stood outside the Bath, looking over the run-down commercial street, one of DuSable's many played-out neighborhoods, with

the gritty restaurants and taverns, storefronts and tene-
ments, windows dulled by dust. The brick buildings are
permanently darkened from the years when this city burned
coal. The masonry seemed to gather weight against the
sky, which had been galvanized by winter, heavy-bellied
clouds, gray and lusterless as zinc.

I actually grew up not far from here on the West End of
the city, near the Callison Street Bridge, a phenomenal
structure of enormous brownish stones and concrete filigree, designed, I believe, by H. H. Richardson himself.
A mighty thing, it cast a shadow for blocks over our
gloomy little Irish village, a neighborhood really, but a
place as closed off as if there were a drawbridge and walls.
The dads were all firemen, like my father, or policemen
or public-payroll hacks or guys who worked in factories.
A tavern on every corner and two lovely large churches,
St. Joe's and St. Viator's, where the parish, to my ma's
constant regret, was half Italian. Lace curtains. Rosary
beads. Until I was twelve, I did not know a kid who
went to public school. My mother named me for John
McCormack, the famous Irish tenor, whose sad ballads
and perfect diction left her trembling over the sadness of
life and the forlorn hope of love.

"Seedy" is not the word for the Russian Bath; better
"prehistoric." Inside, the place was vintage Joe McCar-
thy—exposed pipes overhead, with the greenish lacquered
walls darkened by oil and soot, and split by an old mahogany chair rail. The motif here was Land That Time Forgot,
where was and would-be were the same, an Ur region of
male voices, intense heat, and swinging dicks. Time would
wear it down but ne'er destroy it: the sort of atmosphere

that the Irish perpetuate in every bar. I paid fourteen dollars to an immigrant Russian behind a cage, who gave me a towel, a sheet, a locker key, and a pair of rubber shoes I purchased as an afterthought to shield my tootsies. The narrow corridor back was lined with photos in cheap black frames, all the great ones—sports stars, opera singers, politicians, and gangsters, a few of whom fit in more than one of these categories. In the locker room where I undressed, the carpet was the gray of dead fish and smelled of chlorine and mildew.

This Russian Bath is a notorious spot in Kindle County. I'd never set foot inside before, but when I was working Financial Crimes, the FBI always had somebody sitting on a surveillance here. Pols, union types, various heavy-browed heavyweights like to take a meet in this place to talk their dirty business, because even the Feebies can't hide a transmitter under a wet sheet. Bert is down here, relishing the unsavory atmosphere, whenever he can break free—lunchtime, after work, even for an hour after court when he's in trial.

Inside his head, Bert seems to live in his own Boys Town. Most of my partners are men and women with fancy degrees—Harvard, Yale, and Easton—intellectuals for a few minutes in their lives, the types who keep *The New York Review of Books* in business, reading all those carping articles to put themselves to sleep. But Bert is sort of the way people figure me, smart but basic. He'd been law review at the U., and before that an Air Force Academy grad and a combat pilot in Nam in the last desperate year of war, but the events of his later life don't seem to penetrate. He's caught up in the fantasies that preoccupied him at age eleven. Bert thinks it's nifty to hang out with guys who hint about hits and scores, who can give you the line on tomorrow's game before they've seen the papers. What these fellas are actually doing, I suspect, is the same thing as Bert—talking trash and feeling dangerous. After their steam bath, they sit around card tables in the locker room in their sheets, eating pickled herring served at a little stand-up bar and telling each other stories about scores they've settled, jerks that they've set straight. For a grown-up, this sort of macho make-believe is silly. For a guy whose daytime life is devoted to making the world safe for airlines, banks, and insurance companies, it is, frankly, delusional.

The bath was down the stairs and I held tight to the rail, full of the usual doubts about exactly what I was up to, including going someplace I didn't know without my clothes on, but it proved to be a spot of well-worn grace, full of steam and smoke, a breath of heat that rushed to meet you. The men sat about, young guys shamelessly naked, with their dongs hanging out, and older fellas, fat and withered, who'd slopped a sheet across their middles or slung it toga-like over their shoulders.

The bath was a wood construction, not your light color like a sauna that reminds you of Scandinavian furniture, but dark planks, blackened by moisture. A large room rising fifteen feet or more, its scent was like a wet forest floor. Tiers of planked benches stepped up in ranks on all sides and in the center was the old iron oven, jacketed in cement, indomitable and somehow insolent, like a 300-pound mother-in-law. At night the fires burned there, scalding the rocks that sit within the oven's belly, a brood of dinosaur eggs, granite boulders scraped from the bottoms of the Great Lakes, now scarred white from the heat.

Every now and then some brave veteran struggled to his feet with a heavy, indigenous grunt and shoved a pitcher of hot water in there. The oven sizzled and spit back in fury; the steam rose at once. The higher up you sat, the more you felt, so that even after a few minutes at the third level you could feel your noggin cooking. Sitting, steaming, the men spoke episodically, talking gruff half-sentences to one another, then stood and poured a bucket of icy water, drained from flowing spigots in the boards, over their heads. Watching this routine, I wondered how many guys the paramedics have carried out. Occasionally someone lay down on the benches and another fella, in a bizarre ceremony, soaped him from head to toe, front and back, with callus sponges and sheaves of oak leaves frothing heavy soap.

These days, of course, a bunch of naked men rubbing each other leads to a thought or two, and frankly, exactly what gives with Bert is not a matter I'd put money on. But these guys looked pretty convincing—big-bellied old-world types, fellas like Bert who've been coming here since they were kids, ethnics with a capital E. Slavs. Jews. Russians. Mexicans. People steeped in peasant pleasures, their allegiance to the past in their sweat.

From time to time I could catch the sideward glances. Many gay blades, I suspected, had to be stomped into recognizing that Kindle County isn't San Francisco. This crowd looked like they made fast judgments about new-comers.

"Friend of Bert Kamin's," I muttered, trying to explain

myself to a solid old lump who sat in his sheet across from me. His graying hair was soapy and deviled up, going off in three or four different directions so he looked mostly like a hood ornament. "He's always talked about it. Had to give it a try."

The fella made a sound. "Who's that?" he asked.

"Bert," I said.

"Oh, Bert," he said. "What's with him? Big trial or somethin? Where all's he gone to?"

I took a beat with that. I had figured that would be my line. I could feel the heat now, agitating my blood and drying my nostrils, and I moved down a level. Where does a fellow go with five and a half million dollars? I wondered. What are the logical alternatives? Plastic surgery? The jungles of Brazil? Or just a small town where nobody you'd know would ever appear? You'd think it's easy, but try the question on yourself. Personally, I figured I'd favor a simple agenda. Swim a lot. Read good books. Play some golf. Find one of those women looking for a fellow who's honest and true.

"Maybe he's got someplace with Archie and them," said the old lump. "I ain't seen him too much neither."

"Archie?"

"Don't you know Archie? He's a character for you. Got a big position. Whosiewhasit. Whadda they call it. Hey. Lucien. Whatta you call what Archie does with that insurance company?" He addressed a guy sitting near the oven, a man who looked more or less like him, with a sloping belly and fleshy breasts pink from the heat.

"Actuary," answered Lucien.

"There you go," said the guy, sending suds flying as

he gestured. He went on talking about Archie. He was here every day, the guy said. Clockwork. Five o'clock. Him and Bert always together, two professional fellas.

"I bet that's where-all he's gone, Bert. Hey, Lucien. Bert and Archie, they together or what?"

This time Lucien moved. "Who's asking?"

"This guy."

I made some demurrer that they both ignored.

"Name of?" asked Lucien, and squinted in the steam. He'd come in without his glasses and he stepped down to get a better look at me, clearly sizing me up, one of these guys too old to apologize anymore for anything. I gave my name and offered a hand, which Lucien limply grabbed backhanded, his right paw holding fast to the bedsheet around his middle. He took a breath or two through his open mouth, red as a pomegranate.

"You lookin for Kam Roberts, too?" he asked finally. Kam Roberts. Robert Kamin. I was sure it was a joke.

"Yeah," I said, and brought out some blarney smile. "Yeah, Kam Roberts," I repeated. Don't ask me why I do these things—I'm always pretending to know more than I do. Since I was a naughty kid, I've been like that, faking one thing or another; there are so many selves rollicking around in here and it is a harmful indulgence for a man often out of control. I had the thought that "Kam Roberts" was like the secret password, I could ask a few more questions once I'd said it, but something, the peculiarity of the name or my odd tone of enthusiasm, seemed to deaden the air in the room.

In response, Lumpy and Lucien more or less withdrew. Lucien said he wanted to play cards and nudged his pal along, both of them shoving off with only a bare goodbye and a quick look back in my direction.

I stayed put in the steam, blanching like some vegetable and considering my prospects. Heat has its odd effects. In time, the limbs grow heavy and the mind is slower, as if gravity's increased, as if you'd taken a seat on Jupiter. This thing of men being men amid the intense heat revived some lost thought of my old man and the firehouse where all those guys spent so much of their lives together, bunking down in that single large room in which they dreamt uneasily, awaiting the hoarse call of the alarm, the summons to danger. We always knew when there'd been fires. You could hear the engines tearing out of the little firehouse four blocks away, the clanging of the bells, 'the sireens,' as my father said, the enormous roaring motors that sounded big enough to power rocket ships. My dad came home sometimes still carrying the fire with him, a penetrating scent that hung around him like a cloud. 'Smellin like the sinners down in hell' was how he put it, weary and beaten in by physical exertion and fear, waiting for The Black Rose to open so he could have a snoot before he slept. My dreams since are full of fire, though I can't say for sure if that's from my pa or the way my ma, when she was scolding, would pinch my ear and tell me I was in league with Satan and would need to be buried in britches of asbestos.

Cooked out, I stumbled back up to the seedy locker room. I was trying to squint up the number from my key when I heard a voice behind me.

"Hey, yo, mister, you. Jorge wants to see you." It was a kid with a bucket and a mop. I wasn't sure he was talking to me, but he tossed his head of sleek jet hair and waved for me to follow, which I did, clip-clopping after him in my thongs and wet sheet, leaving the locker area for something a hand-drawn sign called "The Club Room." Maybe somebody wanted me to buy a membership, I figured. Or to tell me about Bert.

Here again the furnishings were the latest, if the year happened to be 1949. Cheap mahogany paneling. Brown, speckled asbestos floor tiles such as would give any OSHA inspector an instant coronary. Red vinyl furniture with the stuffing oozing out the corners and, in one case, a black spring so long exposed it was beginning to rust. At a gray Formica table, with one of those old designs of vague forms like the sight through an unfocused microscope, four men were seated, playing pinochle. The youngest of them, a smooth-looking Mexican, nodded, and behind me the kid with the bucket scooted a chair.

"You lookin for Kam Roberts?" the Mexican asked. His eyes were on his cards. Lucien and Lumpy were nowhere in sight.

"I'm a friend of Bert Kamin."

"I asked you 'Kam Roberts.' " He considered me now. This fella, Jorge, was a thin guy, one of those unshaved stringy-looking Mexicans who make such amazing lightweights, always whipping the fannies of these sleek black guys with bulging muscles. Unforeseen strength like that always impresses me. "You got some I.D.?"

I looked at my sheet, heavy and almost translucent from the steam.

"Give me two minutes."

"How far you think you get in two minutes?" he asked and threw down a card. I took a while on that.

"My name is Mack Malloy. Bert's my partner. I'm a lawyer." I offered my hand.

"No, you ain," said Jorge. Story of my life. Lie and I make you smile. The truth, you only wonder.

"Who are you?" I asked.

"Who am I? I'm a guy sittin here talkin to you, okay? You're lookin for Kam Roberts, that's who I am. Okay?" Jorge studied me with what you might call Third World anger—this thing that really goes beyond skin color and echoes back across the epochs, some gene-encoded memory of the syphilis that Cortez's men spread, of the tribal chieftains that the helmeted European troops tossed into the steaming volcanic crevices. "Mr. Roberts here, that's Mr. Shit. You know what I mean?"

"I hear you."

He turned to a guy beside him, a thick old brute who was still holding his cards.

"He hears me." They exchanged a laugh.

Overall, this was not a good situation, being naked with four angry men. Jorge put both hands down on the table.

"I say you're a cop." He wet his lips. "I *know* you're a cop." Those dark Hispanic eyes had irises like caves and emitted no light, and I was lost in there; it was a second before I heartened with the thought that a copper was unlikely to end up beaten in the alley. "I'd make you nine days a week. You got a star tattooed on your tushy."

The three guys watching thought this was a terrific line.

I smiled faintly, that primate fear-flight thing, still trying to figure what it was this guy thought he knew about me. It had been more than twenty years, but I would bet I could remember every guy I cracked. Sort of like the kids from grade school. Some faces you don't forget.

"Whatever you lookin for, *hombre*, you don' find here. You check with Hans over in Six, you'll find out."

"I'm looking for Bert."

Jorge closed his eyes, heavy-lidded like a lizard's.

"Wouldn't know him. Don' know him and don' know nobody he knows. I tole the first copper what come around askin Kam Roberts, I tole him straight up, I don' want none of this shit. I tole him, see Hans, and now we got some fucker here playin What's My Line. Don' fuck with me." He worked his head around completely as if it were on a string, so that I knew I'd had it right to start: a former boxer.

I got it now, why he thought I was a cop, because the cops had already been here looking for Kam Roberts. I wanted to ask more, of course—which coppers, which unit, what they thought Bert had done—but I knew better than to press my luck.

Jorge had leaned in his confidential way across the table once again.

"I'm not supposed to have any this shit." That's what he paid Hans for, that's what he was telling me. I knew Hans too, a watch commander in the Sixth District, two, three years from retirement, Hans Gudrich, real fat these days, with very clear blue eyes, quite beautiful actually, if you could say that about the eyes on a fat old cop.

"I was on my way out," I said.

"See, that's what I thought."

"You were right." I stood up, my sheet wetting the floor beneath me. "We all have a job to do." My impression of an honest policeman didn't sell. Jorge pointed.

"Nobody got no jobs to do here. You want to sweat, that's fine. You come here runnin any scams, Mr. Roberts or whatever, we'll take a piece of your candy-ass, I don' care what kind of star you carry. To me, Mr. Roberts, man, I better not hear no Mr. Roberts again, you know?"

"Got it."

I was gone fast. Bert may have been a fake tough guy; these fellas knew a thing or two about making hard choices, and I was dressed and on the street in a jiffy, bombing down the walk, my insides still melted down in fear. Nice crowd, I told Bert, and, once I'd started this conversation, asked a few more questions like why he was calling himself Kam Roberts.

I was now up to the intersection of Duhaney and Shields, one of these grand city neighborhoods, the league of nations, four blocks with eleven languages, all of them displayed on the garish signs flogging bargains that are pasted in the store windows. Taxis here are at best occasional, and I stomped around near the bus stop, where a little bit of the last snow remained in a dirty crusted hump, my cheeks stinging in the cold and my soul still seething from the trip into that inferno of tough men and intense heat. Near my native ground, I found myself in the thick grip of time and the stalled feelings that forty years ago seemed to bind my spirit like glue. I was hopelessly at odds with everyone—my ma, the Church, the nuns at school, the entire claustrophobic community with its million rules. I took no part in the joy that everybody here seemed to feel

in belonging. Instead, I felt I was a spy, a clandestine
agent from somewhere else, an outsider who took them all
as objects, surfaces, things to see.

Now this last couple of years, since Nora scooted, I
seem to be back here more and more, my dreams set in
the dim houses beneath the Callison Street Bridge, where
I am searching. Four decades later, it turns out it was me
who was secretly infiltrated. Sometimes in these dreams I
think I'm looking for my sister, sweet Elaine, dead three
years now, but I cannot find her. Outside, the wash flags
in the sunshine which is bright enough to purify, but I am
inside, the wind shifting in the curtains and the papers
down the hall as I prowl the grim interior corridors to find
some lost connection. What did I care about back then?
Desperately, in the nights now, I sit up, concentrating,
trying to recall the source of all of these errors, knowing
that somewhere in this dark house, in one room or another,
I will sweep aside a door and feel the rush of light and
heat, the flames.

III. MY LAWYER

It was about seven-thirty when I got back to the office, and Brushy, as usual, was still there. Near as I can tell, none of my partners believes that money is the most important thing in the world—they just work as if they did. They are decent folks, my partners, men and women of refined instinct, other-thinking, many of them lively company and committed to a lot of do-good stuff, but we are joined together, like the nucleus of an atom, by the dark magnetic forces of nature—a shared weakness for our own worst desires. Get ahead. Make money. Wield power. It all takes time. In this life you're often so hard-pressed that scratching your head sometimes seems to absorb an instant you're sure will be precious later in the day.

Brush, like many others, felt best here, burning like some torch in the dark hours. No phone, no opposing counsel or associates, no fucking management meetings. Her fierce intelligence could be concentrated on the tasks at hand, writing letters, reviewing memos, seven little things in sixty minutes, each one billable as a quarter of an hour. My own time in the office was a chain of aimless spells.

I stuck my head in, feeling the need for someone sensible.

"Got a minute?"

Brushy has the corner office, the glamour spot. I'm ten years older, with smaller digs next door. She was at her desk, a plane of glass engulfed at either end by green standing plants whose fronds languished on her papers.

"Business?" she asked. "Who's the client?" She had reached for her time sheet already.

"Old one," I said. "Me." Brushy was my attorney in my wars with Nora. An absolutely ruthless trial lawyer, Emilia Bruccia is one of G&G's great stars. On deposition, I've seen her reform the recollections of witnesses more dramatically than if they had ingested psychoactive drugs, and she's also gifted with that wonderful, devious, clever cast of mind by which she can always explain away the opposition's most damaging documents as something not worth using to wrap fish. She's become a mainstay of our relationship with TN, while developing a dozen great clients of her own, including a big insurance company in California.

Not only does she bill a million bucks a year, but this is a terrific person. I mean it. I would no sooner try to get a jump on Brushy than I would a hungry panther. But she is not dim to feelings. She has plenty of her own, which she exhausts in work and sexual plunder, having a terminal case of hot pants that makes her personal life, behind her back, the object of local sport. She is loyal; she is smart; she has a long memory for kindnesses done. And she is a great partner. If I had to find someone on an hour's notice to go take a dep for me a hundred miles from Tulsa in the middle of the night, I'd call Brushy first. It was her dependability, in fact, which inspired my visit. When I told her I needed a favor, she didn't even flinch.

"I'd love it if you could grab the wheel on Toots's disciplinary hearing at BAD," I said. "I'll be there for the first session on Wednesday, but after that I may be on the loose." BAD—the Bar Admissions and Disciplinary Commission—is a sagging bureaucracy ministering over entrances, exits, and timeouts from the practice of law. I spent my first four years as a lawyer there, struggling to remain afloat in the tidal crest of complaints regarding lawyerly feasance, mis, mal, and non.

Brushy objected that she'd never handled a hearing at BAD and it took a second to persuade her she was up to it. Like many great successes, Brushy has her moments of doubt. She flashes the world a winning smile, then wrings her hands when she is alone, not sure she sees what everybody else does. I promised to have Lucinda, the secretary whose services we shared, copy the file, to let Brushy look it over.

"Where will you be?" she asked.

"Looking for Bert."

"Yeah, where in the world is he?"

"That's what the Committee wants to know."

"The Committee?"

Brushy warmed to my account. The Big Three tend to be tight-vested and most of my partners relish any chance to peek behind the curtains. Brushy savored each detail until she suddenly grasped the problem.

"Just like that? Five million, six?" Her small mouth hanging open, Brushy looked dimly toward the future— the lawsuits, the recriminations. Her investment in the law firm was in jeopardy. "How could he do that to us?"

"There are no victims," I told her. She didn't get it. "Cop talk," I said, "it's a thing we'd say. Guy walks down a dark street alone in the wrong neighborhood and gets mugged. Some shmo cries a river cause he lost a hundred-thousand-bucks hoping some con artist could make a car run on potato chips. People get what they're asking for. There are no victims."

She looked at me with concern. Brushy sat here tonight in a trim suit and a blouse with a big orange bow. Her short hair was cut close, a little butch, and showed off two or three prominent acne scars that pitted her left cheek, like the dimples of the moon. Her teenaged years had to have been tough.

"It's a saying," I said.

"Meaning what? Here?"

Shrugging, I went to the pencil drawer in the gunmetal credenza behind her to find a cigarette. We both sneak butts. Gage & Griswell is now a smoke-free environment, but we sit in Brushy's office or mine with the door closed. From the drawer I also removed a little makeup mirror, which I asked to borrow. Brushy couldn't have cared less. She was chewing on her thumb, still wrought up with the prospect of disaster.

"Should you be telling me this?" Brushy asked. She

always had a better sense than me for the value of a confidence.

"Probably not," I admitted. "Call it attorney-client." Privileged, I meant. Forever secret. Another of those witless jokes lawyers make about the law. Brushy wasn't really my lawyer here; I wasn't really her client. "Besides, I need to ask you something about Bert."

She was still pondering the situation. She said again she couldn't believe it.

"It's a nice idea, *n'est-ce pas*? Fill your pocket with some new I.D.'s and several million dollars and jet off to be someone else for the rest of your life." I made a sound. "It gives me the shivers just to think of it."

"What kind of new I.D.'s?" she asked.

"Oh, he seems to be using some screwy alias. You ever hear him call himself Kam Roberts for any reason—even just kidding around?"

Never. I told her a little about my visit to the Russian Bath, watching these guys built like refrigerators flail each other with oak branches and soap.

"Weird," she said.

"That's how it struck me. Here's the thing, Brush. These birds around there seem to think Bert has gone off with some man. He ever mention anyone named Archie?"

"Nope." She eyed me through the smoke. She already knew I was up to something.

"It made me think, you know. It's been years since I saw Bert with a woman." When Bert got here more than a decade ago, he was still squiring Doreen, his high-school honey, to firm functions. He'd made vague promises to marry this woman, a sweet schoolteacher, and in the years she waited she turned into a kind of sports-bar bimbo, with a drinking problem like mine and skirts the size of handkerchiefs and blond hair so ravaged by chemicals that it stuck out from her head like raffia. One day at lunch Bert announced she was marrying her principal. No further comment. Ever. And no replacement.

Always live to nuance, Brushy had perked up. "Are you asking what I think?"

"You mean something dirty and indiscreet? Right. I'm not asking you to speculate. I just thought you might be able to contribute pertinent information." I sort of scratched my ear lamely but it wasn't fooling her a bit. Pugnacious, you would call her look. She's not big— short, broad, and but for tireless health-club hours tending to the stout—but her jaw was set meanly.

"Who are you now? The Public Health Service?"

"Spare me the details. Yes or no will do to start."

"No."

I wasn't sure she was answering. Brushy is touchy about personal lives, since hers is always the subject of sniggering. Every office deserves a Brushy, a stalwartly single, sexually predatory female. She subscribes to a feminism of her own vision, which seems to be inspired by piracy on the high seas, regarding it as an achievement to board every passing male ship. She does not recognize any common boundary: marital status, age, social class. When she decides on a man, either for the position he occupies, the promise he radiates, or the good looks that stimulate other females to mere fancy, she is unambiguous in making her desires known. Over the years she has been seen in the company of judges and politicians, journalists, opponents, guys from the file room, a couple of former jurors—and many of her partners, including, should you be wondering, for one fitful afternoon, me. Big and good-looking, Bert had undoubtedly fallen within the circled sights of Brushy's up-periscope.

"It's not prurient interest, Brush. It's professional. Just give me a wink. I need your opinion: Is it he's or she's when Bert dances the hokey-pokey?"

"I don't *believe* you," she said and looked off with a sour scowl. In her pursuits, Brushy, in her own way, is discreet. She generally wouldn't talk under torture, and her advances, while relentless, always recognize the proprieties of the workplace. But for her sexual follies, Brushy still pays a heavy price. Her commitment to appetites that most of us are busy trying to suppress leads folks to regard her as odd, even dangerous; other females are often downright hostile. And among her peers, the younger partners, the men and women who started together as associates and survived those years together—the giddy all-nighters in the library, the one thousand carry-in meals—Brushy is on the outs anyway. They envy her advancement in the firm, and when they gather privately for gossip, it's often about her.

She is, in her own way, alone here, a fact which I suppose has drawn us together. Our one misfiring encounter is never a topic. After Nora, my volcano seems more or less extinct, and we both know that afternoon belongs to my wackiest period—right after my sister, Elaine, had died and I had stopped drinking, just when the recognition that my wife was busy with other sexual pursuits was beginning to assume the form of what we might call an idea, sort of the way all that swirling gas and dust in the remote regions of the cosmos starts to zero in on being a planet. For Brush and me our interlude served its purpose, nonetheless. In the aftermath, we became good pals, schmoozing, smoking, and playing racquetball once a week. On court, she is as vicious as a mink.

"How's the Loathsome Child?" Brushy asked. She eyed me in strict warning. We both knew she'd changed the subject.

"Living up to his name," I assured her. Lyle was Nora's and my only kid, and his insular ways as a little boy had led me to refer to him with what I thought was tenderness as the Lonesome Child. When adolescence set in, however, the consonants migrated.

"What's the latest?"

"Oh, please. Let me count the ways. I find muddy footprints on the sofa. Dried soda pop on the kitchen floor. He comes home at 4:00 a.m. and rings the doorbell because he forgot the keys. The PDR doesn't list half the drugs he takes. Nineteen years old. And he doesn't flush the toilet."

At that last item, Brushy made a face. "Isn't it time for him to grow up? Doesn't that happen with children?"

"Not so as you'd notice with Lyle. I'll tell you, whatever you saved me on alimony, Brushy, she got even with that shrink. All that crap about how an adolescent male was too vulnerable to be without his father in these circumstances."

Brushy said what she always said: the first custody fight she'd seen where the dispute was over who had to take the child.

"Well, she got even," I repeated.

"What did she have to get even for?"

"Jesus Christ," I said, "you really haven't been married, have you? The world went to hell and I went with it. I don't know."

"You stopped drinking."

I shrugged. I am seldom as impressed by this feat as other people, who like to think it shows I have something, some element which if not unique is still special to the human condition. Courage. I don't know. But I was aware of the secret and it never left me. I'm still hooked. Now I depend on the pain of not drinking, on the craving, on the denial. Especially the denial. I get up in the morning and it strikes me that I'm not going to drink and I actually wonder why I have to do this to myself, same as I used to think waking from a bender. And inside there's the same little harpy telling me that I deserve it.

I had taken another cigarette and wandered to the big windows. The trail of headlamps and brake lights stippled the strip of highway, and an occasional building window was lit up by the isolated sparks of somebody else's life being squandered in evening toil. Stepping back, I caught a glimpse of my own reflection decaled over the night: the weary warrior, hair gone gray and so much ruddy flesh beneath my chin that I can never button my collar.

"You know," I said, "you get divorced, it's like being hit by a truck. You walk around in a fucking fog. You're not even sure you're alive. Maybe the last year, I've realized when I stopped drinking was probably what pushed her out the door."

Brushy had removed her pumps and crossed her feet on

the desktop. With my remark she stopped wiggling her short toes against the orange mesh of her panty hose and asked what I was talking about.

"Nora liked me better when I drank. She didn't like me much, but she liked me better. I left her alone. She could conduct her international experiment in living. The last thing she wanted was my attention. They have a word for this now. What is it?"

" 'Co-dependent.' "

"There you go." I smiled, but we were both rendered silent. It hadn't taken Brushy many guesses. As usual, the mess in my life was its own dead end.

I sat down on her sofa, black leather trimmed with metal rails. It was twenty-first-century decorating in here, "high-tech," so that the place had the warmth of a hospital operating room. Every partner furnishes as he or she likes, inasmuch as our offices are otherwise the same, three walls of union Sheetrock and a glamour view, all plate glass framed by piers of stressed concrete. We have been here in the TN Needle, a forty-four-story stiletto looming prominently against Center City and the prairie landscape, since it opened six years ago, keeping cozy with our biggest client. Our phones and electronic mail intersect with TN's; half our lawyers have stationery of the General Counsel, Jake Eiger, so they can dash off letters in his name. Visitors to the building often say they cannot tell where TN ends and Gage & Griswell starts, which is just how we like it.

"So you're really going to do this, look for Bert?"

"The Big Three didn't think I had a choice. We all know my story. I'm too old to learn to do something else, too greedy to give up the money I make, and too burnt out to deserve it. So I take on Mission Impossible and buy myself a job.''

"That sounds like the kind of deal somebody could forget about. Have you thought of that?''

I had, but it was humiliating as hell to think it was so obvious. I just shrugged.

"Besides,'' I said, "the cops'll probably find Bert before me.''

She became rigid at the mention of the police. I took some time to tell her the rest of the story, about Jorge, the lightweight, and his three mean friends.

"Are you telling me the cops know about this? The money?''

"No chance. It's gone out of our escrow account and we haven't heard word one from them. It's not that.''

"Then what?''

I shook my head sadly. I didn't have a clue.

"Actually,'' I said, "from the drift I got, I think they've been asking about Kam Roberts.''

"I'm lost,'' she said.

"Me too.''

"Well, I don't understand why you're willing to do this,'' Brushy told me. "Didn't you say he'd shoot you?''

"I was negotiating. I'll fend him off. I'll tell him I didn't believe it, I took it on to defend his honor.''

"*Do* you believe it?''

I raised my hands: who knows? Who ever knows? I spent a moment with the wonder of it all. What is it really, this life? You're shoulder to shoulder with a guy eight hours a day, try cases with him, go to lunch, sit in the back row and make wisecracks at partners' meetings, stand beside him in the men's room and watch him shake his thing, and what the hell do you know? Zippity-do. You haven't got a clue about the inner regions. You don't know what he regards as dirty thoughts or the place he dreams of as a haven. You don't know if he constantly feels close to the Great Spirit or if anxiety is always nibbling inside him like some famished rat. Really—what *is* this? You never know with people, I thought, another phrase I picked up on the street and have been repeating to myself for twenty years. I repeated it to Brushy now.

"I can't accept it," she said. "This is so calculating. And Bert's impulsive. If you told me he'd signed up to be an astronaut last week and was already halfway to the moon, that would sound more like him."

"We'll see. I figure if I actually track him down, I'll always have a great alternative to turning him in or bringing him back."

She stared, green eyes hopped up with all her wily curiosity.

"And what alternative is that?"

"Bert and I can split the money right down the middle." I put out the cigarette and winked. I said to her again, "Attorney-client."

IV. BERT AT HOME

A. His Apartment

My partner Bert Kamin is not an everyday-type guy. Angular and swarthy, with a substantial athletic build and long dark hair, he looks good enough, but there is something wild in his eye. Until she passed away, five or six years ago, Bert—former combat ace, trial shark, hotshot gambler and hoodlum hanger-on—lived with his mother, a demanding old witch by the name of Mabel. He didn't have a shortcoming she failed to mention. Slothful. Irresponsible. Ungrateful. Mean. She'd let him have it, and Bert, with his macho jaw set, tough talk, and chewing gum, just sat there.

The man left after this thirty-five-year mortar assault is a sort of heaping dark mystery, one of those vague paranoiacs who defends his odd habits in the name of individuality. Food's one of his specialties. He is sure America is

43

out to poison him. He subscribes to a dozen obscure health newsletters—"Vitamin B Update" and "The Soluble Fiber Wellness Letter"—and he is regularly reading books by goofballs just like him which convince him that something new should not be ingested. I have unwillingly absorbed his opinions over many meals. He lives in mortal fear of tap water, which he figures has everything deadly in it—fluoride, chlorine, and lead—and will drink nothing from the city pipes; over the protests of the Committee, he's even had one of those big green bottled water coolers installed in his office. He won't eat cheese ("junk food"), sausage ("nitrites"), chicken ("DES"), or milk (he still worries about strontium 90). On the other hand, he believes that cholesterol is an AMA-sponsored fiction and has no brief against red meat. And he never ate green vegetables. He will tell you they are overrated, but in fact, he just never got to like them as a kid.

I was feeling Bert's presence pretty strongly now, all his screwball intensity, as I stood outside his place. It was about eleven and I'd decided to check out his digs on my way home. Last time I looked, break and enter was still a crime and I figured I'd just keep this visit to myself.

Bert lives—or lived—in a little freestanding two-flat in a rehabbed area near Center City. As I recalled the story, he'd wanted to stay in his ma's house in the South End, but he got into one of those coffin-side spats with his sister and had to sell to make her happy. Here, he was pretty much at loose ends. I arrived with my briefcase, which had nothing in it but two coat hangers, a screwdriver which I'd borrowed from the maintenance closet on my way out of the office, and the Dictaphone, which I took on the bet that my dreams would wake me, as they have, and leave me grateful for something to do in these awful, still hours.

Twenty-some years ago, before they shipped me off to Financial Crimes to give me time to finish law school, I worked in the tactical unit with a good street cop name of Gino Dimonte, who everybody called Pigeyes. Tac guys are plainclothes, the sort of roving linebackers of the Force who'll do further investigation on what the beat cop reports—stake out an arrest, round up a suspect. I learned a lot from Pigeyes, which is one of the things that ticked him off when I testified about him before a federal grand jury; these days he's backwatered in Financial Crimes and, as the legend goes, always looking for me, the same way Captain Hook had an eye out for the crocodile and Ahab for the whale. Anyway, Pigeyes taught me a million tricks. How to sneak the cruiser down an alley, headlights out, using the emergency brake to stop so that your suspect doesn't even see the red glow of the rear lamps. I watched him get into apartments without a warrant by making calls, saying he was UPS and had left a package downstairs, or that he lived across the street and thought there was a fire on the roof, so that our man would come rushing out and leave his door wide open. I even heard him phone and say there were suspicious guys around, and have a high old time when the dip stuck his mug out with an unregistered pistol in his hand and got his ass arrested and his front room tossed incident to arrest.

This was another of Gino's little bits, just a makeup mirror that a lady would carry in her purse or keep in the drawer in her office, as Brushy had. In most old buildings, the front door on an apartment has been trimmed at the foot to fit the carpeting, and with the mirror, if you get used to looking upside down, you can see a lot. I knelt there in the vestibule, putting my ear to the door to the upstairs apartment now and then to make sure the neighbor wasn't shaking around. As I remembered it, she was a flight attendant. I figured on trying her sometime, after I'd seen what was what in Bert's apartment.

It sure looked like Bert was gone. In the mirror I could see the mail piled up on the floor in heaps—*Sports Illustrated* and health and muscle magazines and flyers, and of course a bunch of bills. I rumbled around a little bit against the door, enough noise so that if there was anyone inside I'd get them moving, then after a while I used the coat hangers. I straightened them out, all but the hook, and joined them at the crimps. Using the mirror, I could see the chain lock hanging open. I must have spent five minutes trying to get a decent purchase on the knob of the dead bolt, and then it turned out the damn thing wasn't set. The old skeleton-keyed door lock and knob came off with the screwdriver in twenty seconds. I always told Nora: If they want to get in, they're coming in.

Maybe it was that thought of Nora, but as soon as the door swung open, I was attacked by the loneliness of it all, Bert's life. I felt like I'd gone hollow, unfilled space aching with the absence. It scares me to see the way single guys live. When Nora bolted for the great outdoors, she left most everything behind. A lot of the furniture is broken and torn, what with the Loathsome Child, but it's there, it's still a house. Bert's living room didn't even have a rug on the floor. He had a sofa, a 30-inch TV, and a huge green plant that I bet somebody sent him as a gift. In one corner, housed on its packing box, was an entire computer setup—box, keyboard, monitor, printer—with a folding chair in front of it. I had a sudden vision of goofy old Bert lost inside the machine, spending the dead hours of the night with his mind tracing the circuits of a chip, whizzing from one bulletin board to the next or playing complex computer war games, wiping out little green people with a death ray from space. Crazy guy.

I walked right through the mail as I came in, then thought better of it and plunked myself down on the hardwood floor among the gathered dustballs. The oldest items were postmarked about ten days ago, which seemed to fit Bert's suspected date of departure. One envelope had a footprint on it, maybe mine, or someone else's, or Bert's when he took off. The last thought seemed to make the most sense, since I found another envelope which had been opened. Inside was a bank card—one only—tucked into the little two-sided cardboard holder used to send out new cards annually. Maybe Bert had taken the other card to travel? The one that was there was embossed with the name Kam Roberts.

In the scattered mail I found another envelope addressed to Kam Roberts. I held it up to the light, then just ripped it open. A monthly statement for the bank card. It was pretty much what you'd expect with Bert during basketball season, charges run up in every town in the Mid-Ten. Bert thought nothing of flashing to the airport at five and getting in one of those flying buckets so he could arrive in some Midwestern college town in time to witness the walloping of the U.'s team, the Bargehands, known for generations as the Hands. There were a number of local charges, too, but I stashed all of it, the card and the bill, in my inside suit pocket, figuring I'd study the details later.

The only other item in Bert's mail that struck me was *The Advisor*, Kindle County's gay newspaper, with its sizzling personals section and some pretty embarrassing ads for underwear. Was he or wasn't he? Bert might tell me that he subscribed for the classifieds or film criticism, but to me it figured that Bert was in the closet. He's of my place in history, when sex was dirty and desire a hidden misery that each of us kept steeled within our own Pandora's Box and released only in clandestine darkness where we were promptly enslaved. Bert's inclinations are a deep-dark secret. He isn't telling anybody, maybe even himself. That's where Kam Roberts comes in; it's his drag. If he's meeting boys in the men's room of the Kindle County Public Library or visiting leather bars in another city where he's supposedly gone to watch the Hands, Kam is his name. All of this is surely what the TN engineers refer to as a WAG—a wild-assed guess. Yet standing in the apartment, I thought it made sense. No, he never put his hand on my knee or cast lascivious glances at the Loathsome Child either. But I'd bet the farm anyway that all Bert's twitches and costumes and lonely moods came out of which way his pecker was pointing. Which is his business, not mine. I really mean it. Frankly, I've always admired people with secrets worth keeping, having, of course, one or two of my own.

Which is not to pretend on the other hand that scoping

all this out did not give me a combo of the creeps and some little thrill of kinky curiosity. So talk to me about my tendencies. But don't you wonder sometimes, really, what these guys are up to? I mean, who does what to whom. You know, tab A, slot B. They've got this weird secret thing, like the Masons or the Mormons.

I wondered if it was problems in his life as Kam that had the coppers looking for Bert. When I was on the street, there were always the sorriest scams with these fellows— a prisoner in the Rudyard penitentiary who somehow got a bunch of guys he'd found through the personals to pay him fifty bucks apiece with a letter promising he was "going to put a liplock on your love-muscle" as soon as he was released. There was one restaurant owner who installed a hidden camera behind one of the urinals and had a private photo gallery of Kindle County's most prominent penises. And you'd hear of plenty of outright extortion, boy-toys who threatened to tell the wife or the employer. There were a billion ways Bert could have gotten himself in trouble, and tossing all this around, big bluff old Mack felt pretty sorry for Bert, who wasn't trying to hurt a soul.

I made a tour of the apartment. Bert's bedroom wasn't much better than the living room—a cheap dresser set, his bed unmade. There wasn't a picture in the entire place. His suits hung neatly in his closet but his other stuff was thrown around the room in the familiar fashion of Lyle.

I went to the kitchen to check out the fridge, still trying to see how long our hero had been gone, another old cop move, smell the milk, check the pull date. When I opened the fridge, there was a dead guy staring back.

B. His Refrigerator

The dead, like the rich, are different from you and me. I was racing with that crazy bursting feeling as if I was going to pop out of my own skin. Not that I couldn't acknowledge a macabre interest. I actually pulled one of the kitchen chairs around and was sitting, say, three feet away, staring at him. In my time on the street I'd seen my share of corpses, suicides hanging from the basement pipes or in a bathtub full of blood, a couple of murder victims, and lots of folks who just plain expired, and I'm at the age now where every couple of weeks it seems like I'm going to a wake. However it is, I'm always impressed by the way a human being looks stripped of that fundamental vitality, like a tree without its leaves. Death always takes something away, nothing you could really name, but life somehow is a visible thing.

It wasn't Bert. This guy was about Bert's size, but he was older, maybe sixty. He had been folded into the refrigerator like a garment bag. His feet went one way, his legs were squashed down under him, his head was forced to about ninety degrees to make him fit. His eyes were bugged out unbelievably; they were that very light green you might as well call gray. He was wearing a suit and a tie, and around the collar of his shirt, the blood had soaked in and dried like a kind of batik. Eventually I noticed the black line dug into his neck and tied to a shelf hook to hold him up. Fishing tackle. Deep-sea stuff. One-hundred-pound test. The refrigerator light glowed like a bald head and threw a little orange into his gray face. Alive, he must have been a respectable-looking fellow.

I sat there trying to figure out what to do. I had to be good and careful, I knew that much. Still, I kept wondering what had happened. Bert's motives for disappearing seemed clearer. The most obvious reason to chill the remains would be to get some time to run. But there was no blood anywhere in the apartment. Unless there'd been a rug or a little more furniture before. Did wonky old Bert have murder in him? The Jesuits in high school told me nobody did, then the police force gave me a gun and told me to shoot and I was in enough basements looking for some slug who'd vanished down a gangway, ready to piss my trousers every time I heard the furnace creak, so that I knew I would have. Bert, in his own way, was pretty tightly wound. So maybe.

Option 2 was that this was somebody else's handiwork. Before Bert left or after? Before appeared unlikely. Not too many people are going to break into your apartment with a stiff and leave him in your refrigerator without your permission. After was possible. If somebody knew Bert was gone.

I really didn't want to call the cops. If I did, everything was going to come out. Missing Bert. Missing money. So long, client. So long, Mack and G&G. Worse yet, the way things work, murder suspect number one for a while would be me. That could be a real pain, given the number of coppers, pals of Pigeyes, who are laying for me, one of whom in time would realize he could charge me for the break-in. Sooner or later the police would have to hear about this. This poor bastard, after all, probably had a family. But the best way to tip them was anonymously, after I'd had some time to think things through.

I went about putting the place back together as best I could, wiped the refrigerator handle down, swept the kitchen floor to clear my footprints. I couldn't get the lock in the front door without opening it, since the outer plate screwed in from the other side. So I stood there on the threshold, upright, in plain view, fumbling for five minutes, fixing up the apartment I'd just broken into. I tried to imagine what the hell I'd say if the stew came home or if I raised the curiosity of somebody passing on the street, how I'd get myself out of trouble. Still, as I fooled around with the last screw, I liked it, my minute dangling over the cliff. Sometimes in life, things just happen. No planning. Out of control. That's one of those things guys like about being cops. I'd liked it too, just not the way I woke up in the night, with my heart galloping and my mouth like glue and the fears, the fears, licking me all over like some cat getting ready to do it to a mouse. It drove me to drink, was one of the things, and off the Force, though it has never stopped.

But nothing happened, not now. The stew never showed, nobody on the street even looked my way. I went through the outer door with my scarf pulled up to my nose, and down the city walk, safe and happy, just like I am with daybreak coming now, knowing I can stop talking into this thing, having slipped away for one more night.

TAPE 2

Dictated January 24, 11 p.m.

V. A WORKING LIFE

A. The Mind of the Machine

Now and then everybody wants to be somebody else, Elaine. There are all these secret people rolling around inside—ma and pa, killers and cops and various prime-time heroes, and all of them at times reaching for the throttle. There's no way to stop it, and who's to say we should. What seemed sweeter yesterday than the thought of nabbing Bert and running with the money? It's just your brother, the old copper, explaining how it is that folks go wrong. Every guy I cracked said it: I didn't mean to, I didn't want to. As if it were somebody else who'd scored the smack or kicked the coins out of the vending machine. And it is in a way. That's what I'm saying.

I sat in my office this morning, venturing this two-bit commentary for the benefit of my dead sister, as I do a couple of times each day, and noodling over the statement that I'd pocketed from the Kam Roberts credit card. The thought of Bert being someone else impromptu still drilled me with that little secret jolt, but the particulars of his hidden life remained elusive. Besides the charges for air tickets and restaurants and motels in little Mid-Ten towns, there were items, five to fifteen dollars each, posted almost daily for some something called "Infomode," and there was also a series of cash advances totaling about three grand. Bert made more dough than me, maybe 275K, and I'd have figured he'd write a check to cash in Accounting if he needed folding money, rather than pay interest. Then we got really strange: a single credit item, over nine thousand bucks for something called Arch Enterprises. Maybe this was pal Archie, the wayward actuary, but what-for nine thousand dollars credit? I was writing comedy making up the explanations. *E.g.*, Bert returned a big insurance policy? And then we had the small-time peculiar, two nights' charges last month at U Inn, a kind of run-down hotel/motel right across from the university's main quadrangle, an odd spot for Bert to be checking in since his apartment was only a mile away.

I was pushing around these puzzle pieces when my phone rang.

"We have a serious problem." It was Wash.

"We do?"

"Very serious." He sounded undone, but Wash is not the fellow we turn to in crisis. There are people, like Martin, who talk about Wash as a legend, but I suspect he was one of those young men who was admired for his bright future and now is forgiven his lapses due to the supposed achievements of his past. Aged sixty-seven,

Wash by my reckoning lost interest in the practice of law at least a decade ago. You could say the same of me, but I'm not an icon. This life can make you soft. There are always younger lawyers, agile-minded and bristling with ambition, to think for you, to write the opinion letters and draft the contracts. Wash has capitulated to that. He is, for the most part, a ceremonial lawyer, a soothing presence to old clients to whom he is connected by club affiliations and schooling.

"I just spoke with Martin," Wash said. "He ran into Jake Eiger in the elevator."

"So?"

"Jake was asking about Bert."

"Uh-oh." Ticklish inquiries from the client. I felt the usual moment of private gratitude that I wasn't in charge.

"We have to figure out what to tell Jake. Martin had to jump onto a conference call—we only spoke for a second. But he should be through soon. He suggested we all get together."

I told Wash I'd stand by.

In the interval I resumed my routine endeavor these days at G&G—trying to find something to do. When I came here eighteen years ago, it was with the promise that Jake Eiger would have lots of work for me, and for a number of years his word held true. I rewrote TN's Employees' Code of Conduct, I conducted a number of internal investigations—flight attendants selling drinks out of their own bottles, a hotel manager whose hiring standard for chambermaids was whether they swallowed after fellating him. Eventually that stuff tapered off, and in the last two years has stopped cold. I'm left doing odds and ends for Bert

and Brushy and some of my other partners who remain on
Jake's main menu, trying cases they are too busy for, doing
firm committee work, still hoping, after eighteen years in
private practice, that somehow, somewhere there's some
million-dollar client who wants an ex-drunk former copper
for its principal outside counsel. Between slouching work
habits and a lack of clientele, my economic value to this
enterprise is dwindling toward zero. True, I cash a hefty
draw check every quarter, notwithstanding three straight
years of reductions; and there are folks, like Martin, who
seem inclined to support me as an act of enduring sentiment. But I have to worry about when someone like Pagnucci will call time's up—and then there's the matter of
my pride, assuming I have any left.

   Not happy thoughts as I looked over the Blue Sheet, our
daily bulletin, and the remainder of the lost forest of
memos and mail that are generated within G&G each day.
I had some desultory work to do on 397, the air crash
disaster that has provided nearly full-time employment for
Bert and more than occasional toil for me in the last three
years. There were letters to sign and a draft of payout
documents which were due over with Peter Neucriss, the
lead plaintiff's lawyer, an exacting prick who'd force me
to rewrite them four times. Today's letters purported to be
from TN, written on TN stationery—various proclama-
tions regarding the settlement fund that we were supposed
to safeguard and which TN controlled—and I applied my
flawless imitation of Jake Eiger's signature, then went back
to the Blue Sheet, shifting for interesting news. Only the
usual. A corporate department luncheon to discuss interest
rate swaps; time sheets due by 5:00 or we'd get fined; and,

my favorite, mystery mail, a photocopy of a check payable to the firm for $275 with a note from Glyndora in Accounting asking if anybody knew who sent it and why. There was once a check for about 750 grand that ran for three days straight which I very nearly claimed. Carl and various subalterns had also sent four separate memos to the partners, hard copy and E-mail, telling us to giddy up and get our clients to pay their fees before the fiscal year ended next week on January 31.

This thought of bills coming due reminded me of the Kam Roberts credit card. I told Lucinda where I'd be when Wash called and rambled through the halls to the law library, a floor above on 38. Three associates, all in their initial year of practice, were yakking around a table. At the rare sight of a partner in these surroundings, they embarked on a silent, quailed departure from each other's company to resume making profit of their time.

"Not so fast," I said. I had recruited each of them. A large law firm is basically organized on the same principles as a Ponzi scheme. The only sure ingredients of growth are new clients, bigger bills, and—especially—more people at the bottom, each a little profit center, toiling into the wee hours and earning more for the partnership than they take home. Thus we have a lecher's interest in new talent and are always wooing. In the summers we give fifteen law students a tryout on terms that make overnight camp look like hard labor. Twelve hundred a week to go to baseball games and concerts and fancy lunches, an experience that is a better introduction to life as royalty than the practice of law. And who's in charge of sucking up to these children this way? Yours truly.

When I was assigned to the recruiting subcommittee, Martin tried to explain it as a tribute to my raffish charm. Young people would relate to my offhand ways, he suggested, my casual eccentricities. I knew that with his native bureaucratic dexterity he'd struck on some last-hope way to demonstrate my usefulness to our partners. The fact is I do not particularly care for younger people. Ask my son. I resent their youth—their opportunities, the zillion ways they are inherently better off than I am. Nor, frankly, are they particularly taken with me. But nineteen times each fall I sit in some desolate hotel room near a premier law school and watch them, in their lawyer costumes, strut their stuff, twenty-five-year-olds, a few so self-impressed you want to stick a pin in and watch them blow around the room. Jesus.

"I got this guy's bank card statement in discovery," I said, "and I'm trying to figure what he was spending money on. What's Infomode?" Amid the library's lavish surroundings, the three listened to me with the studied solemnity reserved to the young and ambitious. This was a comfortable, old-fashioned place with club chairs and oak bookcases and tables, and a second-floor balcony rimmed with gold-trimmed volumes that ran the circumference of the room. Leotis Griswell, the firm's late founder, had spent generously here, sort of on the same theory by which Catholics like to glorify their churches.

It was Lena Holtz who knew about Infomode.

"It's a modem information service. You know. You dial up and can go shopping or get stock-market quotes, the wire services. Anything."

"You dial up what?"

"Here." She walked me over to a laptop computer in one of the carrels. Lena was my touchdown for the year, law review at the U., from a rich family out in the West Bank suburbs. She'd had some rough times prior to law school and they left her with an appealing determination to use herself well. Five feet tall, with those teensy thin limbs so there always seems to be extra room in her clothes, she's not much to look at, not when you looked closely, but the pieces fit well. Hair, cosmetics, clothes—Lena has what is generally called style.

I had given her Kam Roberts's bill and she was already punching at the computer. A phone was ringing inside.

"See?" she said as the screen brightened with color proclaiming INFOMODE!

"And what kind of information can you get?" I asked.

"You name it—flight schedules, the prices of antiques, weather reports. They have two thousand different libraries."

"So how do I figure out what he was doing?"

"You could look at his billing information. It would come right up on the screen."

"Great!"

"But you'd need his password," she told me.

Naturally I was blank.

"See, this isn't free," she said. "They charge your credit card every time you enter a library. Like now, I logged on into his account."

"How?"

"The account number's right here on the bank card

statement. But to make sure that I'm really authorized to use it, we need his password.''

"What's the password? 'Rosebud'?''

"A kid's name. Birthday. Anniversary.''

"Great,'' I said again. I sat hunched, watching little iridescent squiggles radiate on the screen, as if the letters were burning, fascinated as ever by the thought of fire. This might be why Bert had the card, so he could rack up Infomode charges in another name. I grabbed her arm.

"Try Kam Roberts.'' I spelled it.

The screen lit up again: WELCOME TO INFOMODE!

"Whoa,'' I said. Once an art student, always an art student. How I love color.

"Do Billing,'' she typed. The listing that scrolled up looked like the bank card statement, a log of charges incurred every day or two, which included the length of use and the cost. It was just what you'd expect of Bert. It was all for something called "Sportsline,'' or for another service they referred to as "Mailbox.'' I figured Sportsline reported the scores of games. I asked about Mailbox.

"It's what it sounds like. Get messages from people who are on-line. Like electronic mail.''

Or, it turned out, you could leave messages behind, little memos to yourself or to someone who logged into your account with your permission. That was what Bert had done. The note we found was dated three weeks ago and seemed to make no sense.

It read:

Hey Arch—

SPRINGFIELD
Kam's Special 1.12—U. five, five
  Cleveland.
1.3—Seton five, three Franklin.
1.5—SJ five, three Grant.

NEW BRUNSWICK
1.2—S.F. eleven, five Grant.

Lena grabbed a yellow pad out of another carrel and wrote it down.

"Does this mean anything to you?" she asked.

Not a thing. Baseball scores in January? Map readings? The combination for a safe? We both stared desolately at the screen.

I heard my name from the P.A.s in the ceiling: "Mr. Malloy, please go to Mr. Thale's office." The announcement was repeated twice, somehow more ominous with each rendition. I felt trouble darken my heart. What were we going to tell Jake? I rose, thanking Lena. She clicked off the machine so that Bert's message, whatever it was, vanished in a little star of light that lingered on the dull screen.

B. Washing

Relieved to have found me, Wash welcomed me to his office with a warmth you'd expect if you were entering his home. George Washington Thale III has the sort of charm meant to reflect breeding, a steady geniality he radiates even with the secretaries. When he turns all his attention and smooth manners on you, you feel like you've met somebody out of Fitzgerald, scion of an old rich world to which all Americans once aspired. Still, I never can forget the term "stuffed shirt." He has this big bag belly that seems to push up to his chest when he is seated. With his bow ties and his horn-rimmed glasses, his liver-spotted face and his pipe, he is a type, one of those used-up emblems of prosperity whose very sight makes you think that somewhere there's a kid waiting for his inheritance.

Wash asked after my well-being, but he was still fretting about Jake, and he promptly dialed Martin's extension on his speakerphone. In Wash's grand corner office, decorated in dark woods, with colonial objects brightened by dabs of gold or red, the practice of law generally has an easy, elegant air, a world where men of importance make decisions and minions at a distance carry them out. He has filled this space with memorabilia of George Washington—portraiture and busts, little mementos, things that G.W. was alleged to have touched. Wash is some ninth- or twelfth-hand relation, and his hapless attachment to this stuff always seems secretly pitiful to me, as if his own life will never measure up.

"I'm with Mack," Wash said when Martin came on.

"Good," he replied. "Just the men I'm looking for." I could tell from Martin's tone, a quart over on oil, that he too was in the company of someone else. "Mack, I just bumped into Jake and we began to talk about the progress on some of the 397 cases Bert's been handling. I invited him to stop in. I thought we all might want to talk about this together.''

"Jake's *with* you?'' Wash asked. He only now grasped what Martin had meant when he said we all should get together.

"Right here,'' Martin answered. Upbeat. Strong tone. Martin is like Brushy—like Pagnucci—like Leotis Griswell in his day, like many others who do it well, a lawyer every waking hour. He manages the firm; he plans the renewal of the river and the buildings on the shore. He counsels clients and gets fourteen younger attorneys in a room and plays war games on all his big-time cases. He flies here and there and engages in endless conference calls with parties strung out across most of the world's time zones, during which he listens, opines, edits briefs, and reads his mail. Something in the law is always at hand and on his mind. And he adores it—he is like a gourmet gorging down an endless meal, eating every goody on his plate. With Jake there, with crisis looming, he sounded chipper and self-confident, raring to go. But when Wash looked back, his aging, pale face was stricken and he looked more scared than me.

C. Introducing the Victim of the Crime

If you've ever seen *The Birth of Venus* with the goddess on the half-shell and all the seraphim bent back with the vapors because she is so great, then you've seen big-firm lawyers when the General Counsel of their major client arrives. During our first few minutes with Jake Eiger in

Martin's vast corner office, getting coffee and waiting as Martin quelled the usual urgent calls, about half a dozen partners stuck their heads in to tell Jake how fit he looked, or that his latest letter on the Suchandsuch matter reflected the same pith and sensibility as the Gettysburg Address; they threw out offhand invitations to dinner, theater, and basketball games. Jake, as ever, accepted this attention with grace. His father was a politician and he knows the way, waving, laughing, parrying with various skillful jests.

I have known Jake Eiger most of my life. We went to high school together at Loyola, Jake two years ahead. You and I, Elaine, we were the kind of Catholics who grew up thinking we were a minority group, the mackerel snappers who ate fish on Friday and wore ash on our foreheads and made way for the ladies in black sheets; we knew we were regarded by Protestants as a clandestine organization with foreign loyalties, like the Freemasons or the KGB. Jack Kennedy of course was our hero, and in his aftermath America for Catholics, I think, truly was different. But you are ever the child, and I'll never really be sure there is a place at the table for me.

But Jake was a Catholic boy, German-Irish, who thought he'd joined the white man's country club. I envied him that and many other things, that his father was rich and that Jake was easy with people. Very good-looking, a movie-star type, he has smooth coppery blond hair that never leaves its place and is only now, with Jake a year or two past fifty, beginning to show less of the radiance that always made you think he was under a spotlight. He has prepossessing eyes—the kind of abundant lashes that you seldom see on a man and which gave Jake, since an otherwise unimpressive childhood, the misleading look of a worldly adult depth. There were always lots of girls after him, and I suspected him of treating them cruelly, wooing them in his soft way and rebuffing them once he'd gotten between their legs.

Still, when I was on my fourteenth version of who I would be, having decided against Vincent Van Gogh, Jack Kerouac, and Dick Tracy, and figured I'd give my dad's idea, law school, a try, Jake, of all people, became a kind of ideal. Our paths had split after high school but my role as Nora's intended brought us back in contact at little family dos, and Jake took it on himself to give me pointers and advice about law school and practice. Then when I got started at BAD he called upon me for a rather auspicious favor which he felt obliged to repay years later by bringing me here.

A rational person would be grateful to Jake Eiger for that. I made $228,168 last year, and that was after they cut my points for the third time in a row. Without Jake, I'd probably be in some interior office space with cheap paneling, practicing on my own, scrambling around to the police courts and otherwise looking hungrily at the silent telephone. But Jake flies and I float. He's still soaring for the stars and on his way has cut me loose to go to cinders as I plummet back through the atmosphere. A lesser type might be bitter, because without me Jake Eiger would be a handsome middle-aged guy looking for ways to explain why he gave up the practice of law many years ago.

"Wash, Mack—" Martin had clapped down the phone, dispensing with the last interruption, and his secretary had finally closed the door. "About Brother Kamin."

"Ah yes." I smiled brightly and waited to watch Martin dance this tightrope.

"Jake's aware, of course, that Bert is on another of his self-declared sabbaticals."

"Right." Smiles. Wash laughed out loud. Martin's such a card.

"And I thought, frankly, that it would make more sense just to share with Jake everything that we've been concerned about. Everything. I don't want any misunderstandings down the line."

Martin went on in a mood of impressive gravity. The room was quiet as he spoke, windowed on three sides, full of abstract paintings and the kind of kooky objets d'art that Martin adores—funny clocks, a side table whose glass top overlay an entire city carved of exotic woods, a shaman's crook that makes the sound of a waterfall when you turn it upside down. Rather than the standard photo of the family, a small soft-sculpture that rendered Martin and his wife and three kids in the mode of Cabbage Patch Kids was perched on his credenza. Martin was behind the desk toward which all the room's furnishings subtly angle, a broad barely finished burl from the trunk of some thousand-year-old oak.

I saw where Martin was going long before Wash, who was in one of the Barcelona chairs that form a proscenium about Martin's desk. When Wash finally realized that Martin was detailing our suspicions about Bert, he made a vague move to object. But Wash clearly had no time to think it through and instead contained himself.

Martin removed his credenza key—he had it hidden in the rubber belly of a clock set in a hula dancer—and displayed the folder of documents I'd seen yesterday. He explained to Jake that we had found no paper trail authorizing these checks. As Jake began to sense that something had gone wrong, he started to fidget. But Martin, the man of principles and solid commitments, showed no wavering. It couldn't have been easy for him. G&G has been life to Martin since his days at Leotis Griswell's right hand, and he adores the hurly-burly, the business of bringing everyone together. That's his faith, that the team is greater than the sum of the parts. He's my Chinaman here, the man I admire, and he was being admirable now. Only yesterday the Committee had made its decision to wait before the client was informed. Yet Martin was manifesting his allegiance to something more significant than law firm Hoyle: Values. Duty. The lawyer's code. The client, unexpectedly, had asked a question which clearly invited the truth and Martin would not be party to withholding it.

By now Martin was explaining the Committee's plan, how I was searching for Bert in the hope he could be persuaded to relent. From Jake, Martin asked brief forbearance, a couple of weeks, with the promise that at the end I'd provide a full report. To sum up, he came and sat on the forward edge of his desk.

"If we can tell Bert that you, that TN, is looking at this in an understanding way," he said to Jake, "I think there's a chance, a real chance, to get the money back. If we do, we can, perhaps, avoid the scandal. That truly strikes me as best for everyone.''

He stopped. Martin had made his appeal, all his formidable charm and powers turned on Jake. Now we waited. It was, on the whole, a moment of high daring. Gage & Griswell was probably about to join the lost city of Atlantis as a civilization that fell into the sea. I thought Wash might black out, and even my skin was crawling, anticipating Jake's reaction. Jake, for his part, looked worse than I'd ever seen him, the fatal gray of a man in shock.

"Unbelievable." That was the first thing Jake said. He got to his feet and walked a circle one way and then the other around his chair. "How am I ever going to handle this upstairs?" He asked this question mostly of himself, fingertips at his lips, and it was clear he did not know the answer. He stood there, visibly pained, not quite willing to discuss the repercussions, as if they were lexically beyond him, like a man who could not bear to utter dirty words.

"We're here to help you," Wash said.

"Oh, you've helped a lot," said Jake and winced at the thought.

TN lately had been on hard times, if a company with gross earnings of four billion every year can be described that way. Almost everything they own—the hotels, the rent-a-car companies, the airlines—is sensitive to fluctuations in travel, of which there had been damn little since our warlette against Sodamn Insane. No surprise either, since anybody with a college business course could have told you that covey of enterprises would move cyclically. To diversify, TN a decade ago bought a traveler's check business and from that made an entry into the world of Sunbelt banking, just in time to watch their loan portfolio go to hell. After the suicidal fare wars of last summer, the company lost about 600 million bucks, the third bad year in a row. To stem the bleeding, the outside directors brought in Tadeusz Krzysinski as CEO, the first person ever to advance above the level of vice-president who was not homegrown. Among many reforms, Tad has cracked the whip on expenses and by all accounts has been prodding Jake about his relationship with G&G, on the theory that there should be more competition for TN's legal work. Krzysinski has been heard to speak warmly of a 200-lawyer firm in Columbus he grew to like when he was in his last incarnation, as president of Red Carpet Rental Car.

This, to say the least, is a subject of concern at Gage & Griswell, since TN has never been less than 18 percent of our revenues. Martin and Wash have been trying to convert Krzysinski, lunching with him, inviting him to meetings, reminding him repeatedly how expensive it would be to replace our knowledge of TN's structure and past legal affairs. In response, Krzysinski has emphasized that the decision is Jake's—his General Counsel, like most, must have free rein to choose the outside lawyers he works with—a deft move since both Jake and G&G have their supporters on TN's board. But Jake has a seasoned corporate bureaucrat's lust for terrain. He covets a seat on the board, the title of Vice-Chairman, which only Krzysinski can award him, and evinces a toadying willingness to please his new Chairman, with whom in truth he seems frequently ill at ease. As often happens in corporation land, there's been more talk than action. Jake has sent only a few morsels to Columbus, as he does with many other firms. But in business, like baseball, senior management is often behind you right up to the day you get the ax.

Jake by now had turned to me. "This is very sensitive. Mack, I want to know about everything you're doing. And for God's sake," he added, "be discreet."

Jake is accustomed to being an executive. He stood a moment, medium height and lean, a hand placed over his eyes. He was wearing a smart double-breasted suit, a subtle glen plaid, and his initials—J.A.K.E.: John Andrew Kenneth Eiger—a favored decorative element, had showed on his shirtsleeve when he pointed at me. "Jesus Christ," Jake said in final reflection and with nothing further left.

Wash rose in his wake. In extremis his aging face had taken on the texture of a gourd, and he hung there, a mystery to himself, torn between remonstrating with Martin and comforting Jake, and finally chose the latter. A grade-schooler knew what he was going to say: Give us time. Don't be rash. Once we find Kamin, this can be worked out.

Behind the thousand-year oak, Martin watched them vanish and asked me, "So what do you think?" He had his hands across his tummy, his face tucked down shrewdly between the matching braces, so that his chin rested on his fancy handmade shirt of jazzy vertical stripes.

"I'll let you know as soon as I get feeling again in my limbs." My heart was still flapping. "I thought we weren't going to say anything."

Martin is one of those men who abound in the legal profession whose brains seem to make them a quarter larger than life. His mind is always zipping along at the speed of an electron. You sit down with him and feel surrounded on all sides. Jesus Christ, you wonder, what is this fellow thinking? I know he's turned over every word I've said three times before I get another one out of my mouth. Accompanying this kind of intellectual hand-speed is a canny grasp of human nature. To what uses all of this is put is not necessarily clear. Martin would not be mistaken for Mother Teresa. Like anybody else who has whizzed along the fast track in the practice of law, he can cut your heart out if need be. And talking to him, as I say, is a kind of contest, in which his clever, warm remarks, his conveyed sense that he knows just what you mean, is somehow never mutual. I know you; you don't know me. His true residence is out-of-bounds, somewhere in the neighborhood of Mount Olympus. But Martin was rarely as mystifying as he was now. He seemed unshaken by anything that had occurred here. He met my inquiry with an inscrutable little tip of the hand, as if he could not alter bygones.

"What do you think Krzysinski's going to say when Jake tells him about this?" I asked.

Martin closed his eyes to weigh the inquiry, as if it had not occurred to him yet, and when he looked back a little wrinkle of something close to humor, an embracing irony, briefly crossed his worn face. He stood to regard me, as another of his funny clocks began to chatter like a chipmunk somewhere in the room.

"I think you'd better find Bert," he told me.

VI . THE SECRET LIFE
OF KAM ROBERTS

A. Good News

Most of the time as I am recording this, talking it through, I do not see the faces of Carl and Wash and Martin. I can't really imagine them with the pages in their hands. So there must be someone else I mean to talk to, sitting here in my rummage-sale bedroom late at night. In the stillness the voice seems to be the spirit, the way a candle is best represented by a flame. Maybe the Dictaphone's a medium, then, a way to enhance communication with the dear departed. Maybe this is really an extended message to sweet Elaine, with whom I used to speak three times a day. Today I've felt her absence starkly, the willing ear to whom I've muttered stray remarks, even as I sat in my office, shiftless and sour, feeling perplexed by the hunt for Bert.

I stared again at the statement from the Kam Roberts

bank card. My feet were on my desk, a large period piece with the formidable tiered look of a steamship, its rosy surface lost in a patchwork of discarded telephone messages, throwaway memos, and various briefs and transcripts that I was yet to file. When I came in at G&G with Jake Eiger's backing and made partner during those initial years when Jake drowned me in work, I had the option to redecorate this room but never got around to it, too drunk to care I guess. I've lived all this time with what is in reality secondhand stuff, the big walnut desk, the glass-paned bookcases, two leather gooseneck chairs with brass studs, a nice, if worn, Oriental rug, a personal computer, and my own clutter. The only object I care much about is on the wall, a terrific Beckmann print—the usual dissipated people in a café. By daylight I have a fine view of the river and the west edge of Center City, girded by the Interstate, U.S. 843.

I thought sullenly about how I was going to make Martin happy and find Bert. I still wanted to talk to the flight attendant in the apartment above his, but I didn't have her name—she hadn't left it on the mailbox—and the notion of putting myself in the vicinity of that stiff again gave me the willies. I phoned long-distance information for Scottsdale and after two calls found Bert's sister, Mrs. Cheryl Moeller, whom I'd met when the ma was buried. She didn't know where her brother was and had not heard from him in months, which was par for the course. She couldn't remember any pal of Bert's named Archie either. She didn't sound as if she liked her brother any better than she ever had and ended up reassuring me that Bert was going to turn up, as usual.

Fellas, Elaine—whoever I'm talking to—I have to tell you, your investigator was stumped. I went over the statement one more time. Why was Bert booking hotel rooms on game nights when he had an empty apartment a mile away? Purely on a flyer, I called U Inn. I got the hotel operator and did what we used to refer to in Financial as a pretext call. I said I was trying to get information on a guy I'd had a business meeting with at U Inn on December 18. I'd lost my entire file in a taxi and was hoping maybe they had a forwarding address or phone for him.

"What's this gentleman's name?" the hotel operator asked.

"Kam Roberts." I was looking for any clue to Bert's present whereabouts. I heard a few computer keys click, then spent most of eternity on hold, but finally got a fellow named Trilby who said he was the Associate Manager. He asked first thing for my name and number, which I gave him.

"I'll check our records, Mr. Malloy, and ask Mr. Roberts to call you."

Wrong idea. Bert didn't figure to stick around for an encounter with any of his partners.

"I'm on vacation after today. I really need to reach him. Any chance of that?"

"Just a moment." It was a good deal longer than that, but Trilby sounded quite pleased with himself when he returned. "Mr. Malloy, you must have ESP. He's a guest in the hotel."

My heart stopped.

"Kam Roberts is? You're sure?"

He laughed. "Well, I wouldn't say that anybody here knows him, but there's a gentleman by that name checked in to Room 622. Should I have him call you? Or can we tell him when you'll be coming by?"

I thought. "Can I talk to him?"

He returned after I'd heard an extended symphonic version of "Raindrops Keep Falling On My Head."

"There's no answer there, Mr. Malloy. Why don't you stop by at the end of the day and we'll get him a message you'll be here."

"Sure," I said. "Or I'll call."

"Call or come by," said Trilby. He was writing a note.

After I put down the phone, I sat a long time looking at the river. There was one building across the way, still wearing Yuletide festoonery, lights and a skirt of holly across the roof. It didn't make much sense. Bert had reason to be laying low—his partners, the police, and maybe even whoever had stuffed that bug-eyed businessman in his refrigerator were all after him. But why hide in Kindle, where sooner or later he'd run into somebody he knew? Whatever, I had to get down there fast, before Bert got this lamebrained message in which I'd used my actual factual name, the sight of which undoubtedly would lead him to scoot once more.

I took the elevator down and crossed the street to the health club where I play racquetball with Brushy. I jumped into my sweats and shoved my wallet in a pocket, then started jogging. It was 28 degrees so I hauled my broad Irish backside down the avenues with some dispatch, but I ran out of wind after about four blocks and went back and forth, running till my smoked-up lungs felt like I'd breathed in bleach, then stopping and letting sweat freeze up on my nose.

I cruised out of Center City into the neighborhoods where the two-family houses roosted like hens behind the frozen lawns and the leafless trees, stark and black, loomed above the parkways. Lured by my mood, I jogged a few blocks out of my way into the edges of the ghetto, so I could pass St. Bridget's School. It is a stucco building split by long cracks the shape of lightning. There, for more than thirty-one years, Elaine was the school librarian— "feeding the starving," as she put it. This was a person of iron convictions. With our ma, I turned myself into a sort of human tetherball, always close enough to be pounded back in another direction when she'd go off her nut and rage about one thing or another, but Elaine was smarter and held her distance. She developed, through this exercise, I suppose, a strongly contrary temperament. When everyone was sitting, Elaine was standing; she wandered around the kitchen when the family dined. She preferred her solitary self to any company, and that never seemed to change.

She ended up one of those Catholic spinsters, a spiritual type who never quite joined the secular world, at 5:00 a.m. Mass every morning, always palling around with the nuns and identifying people, and even store locations, throughout the tri-cities by their parish. She had her worldly moments, some gentlemen friends with whom she sinned, and she was a terrific card too, one of these clever old Irish gals with a bracing wit. All Ma's sharpness was still resident in her, but where Bess took to the cudgel of spiteful words and judgments, Elaine's humor was aimed principally at herself. These little muttered cracks as you left your seat, turned your back, and always an arrow to the heart. Her only failing she came by naturally—she drank a bit. The night she left our house, goofy from plum brandies, and turned up the off ramp and headed onto U.S. 843 was the final drunken evening of my life.

In AA, where I've lapsed just like I have in the Church, impressed by the faith but unwilling to engage in the required daily rituals—in AA they told me to submit myself to a power outside myself. Don't count on beating the demon on your own. The help I ask for, Elaine, is yours. And sometimes as I do it, as I ran down the bleak streets toward the U Inn or sit here in the night whispering into the Dictaphone, I puzzle on what strikes me as a piece of nasty truth.

I miss you ten times more than Nora.

B. Bad News

Eventually I reached the outskirts of the U., with its handsome progressive neighborhood, integrated since early in the century, its bookstores and vague bohemian air. U Inn was at the corner of Calvert and University, and I did a long tour of the parking lot, then jogged right through the front door, waving to the doorman, playing today's role as another hotel guest, a traveling business type living on snacks from the mini-bar and morning aerobics. I ran all the way to the elevator, hopped in with a fat woman who was whistling to herself, and rode up to 6.

Room 622 was quiet. I stuck my ear to the door and rattled the knob. As I figured, there were not going to be any of Pigeyes's tricks in a mid-city hotel. The doors were reinforced and the locks had been replaced with those solid-state electronic gizmos, little brass boxes with lights that required sliding in some plastic card they give you these days instead of a key. I knocked hard. Nothing doing. A suspect fellow in a lizard-skin jacket came by and I kept my eye on him until he got some ice and disappeared under the exit sign at the other end of the dim hall. The hotel corridor was quiet, except for the whine of a vacuum inside one of the rooms.

I'd planned the next move. The guy on the phone had told me nobody here knew Kam on sight. I had some second thoughts, but I had to count on sliding by. That was the point of leading a perilous life. I needed to find what in the hell Bert'd been up to. And I'd be a lot better off sneaking up on him than announcing myself. I took the Kam Roberts credit card out of my wallet.

At the reception desk in the lobby, I talked to a cute blonde, a student, I imagined, like many of the employees.

"I'm Mr. Roberts in 622. I went out for a little trot and like a fool I grabbed my credit card when I left instead of my room pass." I showed her the credit card casually, tapping an edge on the counter. "If you could just get me another."

She disappeared in back. This was frankly a pretty rummy place, especially after the big-bucks life where you get used to going first class. The shabbiness of course was excused by a convenient location—there wasn't another hotel within a mile of the university—and an atmosphere of self-conscious boosterism. The U Inn, as you would expect, is pretty rah-rah. Everything was roped in U. colors, vermilion and white, and near the desk there were pennants and pom-poms and U. sweatshirts tacked to the walls. The Hands basketball schedule, a cardboard poster featuring a color photo of Bobby Adair, this year's wanna-be star, was pinned up on either side of the desk, and as I studied it I realized that a Hands basketball game probably would have brought Bert back to town no matter what.

But there was none today. Not even last night. Or tomorrow. In fact, a lot of things didn't fit. The home games were set on the schedule in vermilion, the away games in black. I didn't have Kam's bank card bill with me, but I'd been staring holes in it for eighteen hours and I was pretty sure that I had committed most of the entries to memory. What bothered me was that the days didn't match. December 18, the last time Kam was here, the Hands were at home. But according to the schedule, they'd been in Bloomington and Lafayette and Kalamazoo since then, and on different dates than the ones when Kam had rung up charges in the same towns.

"Mr. Roberts?" The blonde had returned. "Can I see your credit card again for a moment?" I'd kept it out and she removed it from my hand. I had some instinct to start running, but the girl looked like she'd rolled in off a haywagon, with those sweet eyes the color of cornflowers. One of America's twenty million blondes with looks too standard to conceal any scam. She disappeared again into the office, but was gone just a second.

"Mr. Roberts," she said when she returned, "Mr. Trilby would like to see you for one minute in back." She

opened a door for me and pointed to the small rear office,
but I hung on the threshold, heart fluttering like a moth.

"Is there a problem?"

"I think he said he had a message."

Ah yes. Me old bud Mack Malloy had called. A perceptive fellow, Trilby probably wanted to tell me that Mack
sounded like a phony. There were three men in back, a
black man behind a desk whom I took to be Trilby and the
wormy-looking guy I'd seen upstairs in the hall. The third
one turned to face me last.

Pigeyes.

I was in deep.

C. Would You Care If Your Partner Did This to You?

This is not an especially pretty story, Elaine. Pigeyes and
I worked tac nearly two years, life and death and plenty
of whiskey, lots of laughs, I'm the former college-boy art
student, wet behind the ears, he's the guy who's been
street-smart since he was seven. I'm talking out loud about
Edward Hopper and Edvard Munch when we drive down
city streets at night and he's feeling up every hooker. Some
team.

Working with this guy was always an adventure. Pigeyes was one of those cops in the old style, who think
parents take care of kids, you go to church and pray to
God to save your soul, and everything after that sort of
depends on where you stand, how you look at it, right and
wrong, you know, sometimes you have to squint. I'd been

riding with him about eighteen months when we hit a dope house, just a small packaging factory in a dismal apartment building. We had followed some little shitbum off the street, pretty sure we'd seen him swapping packages, and then, afraid we'd got made, decided to go through the door in the name of hot pursuit before any backup arrived. Pigeyes was always that kind of cowboy—he thought he was in the movies, strung out on the rush of danger as bad as if he were sticking a spike in his arm.

Anyway, you've seen the next scene at the Odeon: We come through with guns drawn, a lot of yelling and carrying on in two or three different languages, people jumping out the windows and onto the fire escapes, and some poor bastard running first one way, then the other with a seal-a-meal under one arm and a scale under the other. I kick in the door of the john and there's a gal sitting on the can with her print skirt around her belly, holding a baby in one hand, using the other to push a baggy full of powder up herself.

We got four people facedown on the floor. Pigeyes did his usual raging, sticking his service revolver in their ears and saying various terrible things until somebody whimpered or literally shit their trousers, then he turned his attention to a little card table in the corner of the living room which was covered with money, I mean a lot, lying there in heaps like it was just paper. Pigeyes had radioed for the narcs to come help us with the arrest, but without skipping a beat he counted out two piles of bills, three or four grand each, and handed me one. I took it but handed the money back in the car, after Narcotics had shown up.

'What's this?' he asked.

'I'm goin to law school.' I'd been accepted by then.
'So?'
'So I shouldn't be doin this shit.'
'Hey, get real.' He read me out then. He beat me up
with the truth. Did I think the narc guys wouldn't take a
nibble out of this? What were we supposed to do, leave it
in a nice pile so that the shitface beaners could have it all
back when Judge Nowinski decided we weren't in hot
pursuit? Were we gonna wait around and hope that the
mopes in the Forfeiture Unit actually took some time off
from the golf course to try to get a writ, in which case the
cash'd get lost in the clerk's office or maybe in some
judge's chambers? Did I think the beaners were gonna say
something? Every one of them didn't know nothin, man.
They were wet and waitin for a trip across the river. 'Or
do you just want to be able to go tell Momma?' he asked.
'Hey, give me a break.' We'd sort of been down this
pass before. What he did, he did, I figured, he wasn't the
only one and he made some effort not to involve me. Now
he wanted me aboard. 'You do what you wanna, I'll do
what I wanna. I got a rest-of-my-life to think about. That's
all.'
He sat there watching me, a nasty-looking fellow normally, with a sullen face going to jowls and those little
whiteless eyes, his expression now slackened and mis-
trustful. This was what they call a delicate situation. Like
being with the Yakuza. You got to cut off a finger to prove
you're in. What was he up to? I think, in retrospect, he
had a point to make, that before I departed for the world
I ought to know that there's no judging, that everybody
has their moments. So I brought the money home and

showed it to my wife and, after leaving it in my sock drawer for three weeks, gave it to my sister for St. Bridget's. Yeah, Elaine, that's where it came from, it wasn't, like I said, a stationhouse collection. I got a note back from the eighth-grade class president which I've kept for all these years, a pointless thing to do, since I wasn't going to tell anyone the real story, inasmuch as I was a policeman who was supposed to arrest Pigeyes's unlawful ass right on the spot, not sing "Que Sera, Sera," or make a charitable donation of what was, in law, money I'd stolen.

Two months later I started law school and a few weeks after that I was Form 60'd to Financial. Pigeyes threw a nice bash when I left. Everything for the best.

The police, any city you go to, are kind of a sneak fraternity. The Force. Close-knit. Trust each other first and most and nobody very much. There are lots of reasons, maybe the most important being that no one really likes the police. Who should? All these types looking sidewise and waiting for you to slip. I was a cop myself, but when I see a black-and-white just sitting on the corner, the first thing I think is, Why's this bastard got his eye on me?

Also, cops are really by themselves. This retinue of lawyers, prosecutors, judges, wardens, that whole world of rules, they're as far away as Pago Pago when you're in that basement looking for the robbery suspect Mrs. Washington saw running. You go through the basement door and wait there on the threshold, come out five minutes later shaking your head in disappointment, just can't find him, that whole crew, lawyers, wardens, so on and so forth, they have nobody to chew on. It's only you—not

just your life on the line, but you're the only reason this
guy is going to get caught. There's no system. That's why
it's so easy to whack the mouthy bastard when he's cuffed
in the back of the black-and-white and is still talking about
your mother or the violation of his constitutional fucking
rights, never mind the seventy-seven-year-old guy he just
hit in the head with a paving stone the better to steal his
T-check. Because it was only you. And he's yours. And
only other cops really understand that.

Which is how come, even forgetting everything else—
that you're a sneak fraternity, that nobody likes you—
even forgetting all that, coppers don't do it to coppers.
When you're there, when it's only you, you do your best.
And if some days you're not up to your best, then you're
no worse than anybody else, are you? Tomorrow you can
try again. Who's to judge? You start that game, I saw you
be bad, shit, it's the whole Force tellin tales.

Shift scene: Two years later I'm coming out of Constitutional Law II, here's two Feebies, real types, drawls and
polyester suits and white shoes, who want to talk to me—
did I work with Gino Dimonte, la-di-da, a few warm-up
pitches, then the hard stuff—was I on a dope bust three
years ago April? I do the arithmetic real fast. One of
the dopers has finally gotten cracked federally rather than
stateside and has found some Ivy League AUSA happy to
cut him a few months in summer camp if he'll talk about
Kindle coppers with their hands on dirty money, and the
doper naturally doesn't give him everybody he has on the
pad who he might need again, he gives him Pigeyes, who
used self-help. I know all this at once, I see just where
they're going, and I'm like 'Yeah, okay, yeah, I think I

remember that one, oh yeah, that one, there was money on the table.' A bubble in the brain. What am I thinking? It was the weirdest goddamned thing. Five seconds in the law school hallway and I've changed my freaking life. There was not a cop who heard about this—and believe me, they all heard about it before the ink was dry on the 302s, the FBI agents' reports—who didn't think I'd done it because I felt with law school I was now a cut above. Coppers are very sensitive about class and have always got it on the brain, they just can't get over the fact that they make forty grand to keep the world safe for millionaires, eat a bullet for Daddy Warbucks, who'll use your corpse to wipe his shoes. But it wasn't that, I wasn't trying to make new friends, and in point of fact, I never much liked snitches. And it wasn't my sterling character for the truth. Who am I kidding? I've fibbed for worse reasons than to help a pal. It's just that, at that moment, I was standing there in the law school, with its wainscotted walls, and something came over me, that thing going back to when I was a kid when I'd realize I didn't belong, that feeling that the world was objects. That's where I was, I guess, the smartass fourth-grader looking at his life as Something in This Picture Does Not Fit and always thinking the Something was me.

Anyway, I got about three-quarters through the story when it hit me like a bolt that this would not work out. The agents had come on with the usual street immunity, just be straight and you're okay, you won't even get lint on your new suit, but I realized suddenly that the feds were not my only problem. I would have to explain this to Bar Admissions and Discipline, to BAD, and they were pretty

tough on the new recruits. Immunity. Felonies. Breach of
trust. I was not going to make a good impression with this
story of stolen dope money in my sock drawer. So the tale
ended with me and Pigeyes in the car and me telling him
to inventory my end and his end too, handing the money
back so he could turn it all in to the evidence room.

Things sort of went in natural sequence after that. I
testified in the grand jury, just what I'd said in my statement to the agents, nothing more. The last six months I
was a policeman, I was assigned behind a file cabinet, I
didn't get near the street, and even the khaki crew, the
unsworn personnel, would spit in my coffee when I turned
my back. Then Pigeyes got indicted and I went to court
and testified against him. He had paid about thirty grand
to Sandy Stern, who a few years ago I would have described as a Jew defense lawyer, and Sandy made it look
like the government did not have much of a case. They
had a couple of the shitbum dopers who had to admit
they'd had their faces planted on the floor; a narcotics
officer's inventory of two grand in cash on the table when
the beaners said there had been forty; and they had me. Of
course, I was up there only sort of telling the truth, with
my old pal Pigeyes giving me the death look, and something uneasy came to the surface, like bones bubbling up
in tar. Stern asked if I was jealous of Pigeyes, felt he was
a better cop than me, and I said yes to that, and I agreed
that I never checked with Evidence to see what Pigeyes
had inventoried. I allowed as how there were beaners who
didn't know one Anglo cop from another, and I even said
yes when Stern asked if Yours Truly was in fact the only
police officer who admitted having received money re-

moved from that table. The AUSA got this look like he needed Preparation H and the jury came back not guilty in two hours. When I walked out of the courtroom I had really lit the scoreboard: I don't think there was a soul there, not the judge, not even the toothless buffs out in the peanut gallery, who didn't think I was lower than pond slime. Nora, never one to miss a point of vulnerability, put it nicely: 'So, Mack, now do you think you got what you want?'

Did I? There were a few strange turns, I admit. One of the strangest was that BAD publicly embraced me. They thought ratting out your friend was a mark of character and gave me a job, since I'd demonstrated such fidelity to the rules of upstanding conduct in another calling. As for Pigeyes, he was ruined. For the jury it's always opening night, but the cops had all seen Stern's act before and they didn't need a trial to know that Pigeyes was dirty. All his buddies in the department, and there are a million, they'll do him favors day to day, get him twice as much for uniform allowance, but as far as going higher, he smelled bad, to the brass he was wearing lead boots. He's been on his unhappy trail down the hill ever since, getting the kind of discipline they practice out of Rome, sending the pederast priest to dwell at a convent. Pigeyes's punishment is Financial Crimes. Personally, I'd always liked the intricacy of Financial, the fact that there was more to investigating a case than finding the perp's girlfriend and sitting on her house until he came by for a cha-cha, but for Pigeyes, a proof mark will never take the place of drawing his gun.

From what I hear he has a sad life now. These days the rare dope bust he horns in on, he's picking powder off the table, not money. Behind his back, guys call him G-Nose or Snowman, and it's not cause he likes winter weather. He was always a copper's copper, full of twitches and complexes, sort of hated everyone, so there never was a Mrs. Pig, just the usual copper-bar girls and chickies on the edge of trouble who thought it was a good idea to give a cop a screw. He did not have much. Until now. Now he had me.

D. Pigeyes and I Renew Acquaintances

"Didn't I *tell* you this guy was gonna turn up? Didn't I *fucking* tell you?" Pigeyes was so happy, gloating like some cock who'd gotten every hen in the coop, that I thought he was going to fall over and give himself a hug. I had, I admit, some glum thoughts about my partners who had set me off blind on a path that led straight to my life's greatest enemy—even counting my former wife—a man who, judging by his comments, was clearly expecting me.

"Refresh me," he said, "memory serves, this ain't you." He was holding the credit card.

"I'm sorry, Officer?"

"Detective, shitface."

"Detective Shitface, I'm sorry." Personally, I didn't believe I'd done it. But there you have it. Chasing Bert and teasing myself with the notion of another life, I was becoming a new man. By the door, the younger cop in lizard, in his longhair do with shiny sidewalls, grimaced and turned a full pirouette. I was looking for it. But he didn't know the history. If Pigeyes kicked the bejesus out of me, he could never fit a story good enough. He stared at me with those little black eyes without any visible whites, while this reality crowded in on both of us. Then he extended one finger, thick as a stake, and gave me his own unique look, a laser right to the heart.

"Not again," he said.

Trilby spoke up at that point, a pudgy black man of middle years, sitting behind his desk. He and his sidekick out front had done a nice job of setting me up. The coppers obviously had been here long ago looking for Kam and had left instructions to get in touch if anybody connected with him ever reappeared. While I was on hold, Trilby was probably on the line with Pigeyes, who gleefully thanked whatever idol he worshipped as soon as he heard my name. To this point, Trilby had watched our exchange out of one eye, face sort of averted, so he could claim he hadn't seen it, if anything bad happened. Now he stuck up his courage to ask who I was.

"A drunk," said Pigeyes.

It's always strange how that shot can reach me.

"I'm a lawyer, Mr. Trilby."

"Quiet," said Pigeyes. He wasn't that tall, probably lying when he said he was five ten, but he was built like your freezer, no neck, no waist, a lot of slack flesh on a real solid structure. His anger gave him a kind of aura, an impression of heat. You knew he was there. He was dressed in a sport jacket and a knit shirt, beneath which his undershirt showed. He was wearing cowboy boots.

His partner could see he was hot and edged past him; Gino sunk back toward the door. With the second cop, we started again.

"Dewey Phelan." He pulled his badge from his pocket and we actually shook hands. Good cop, bad cop. Mutt and Jeff. Fuck, I invented this game, but still I was relieved to be talking to skinny young Dewey here, maybe he's twenty-three, with pale skin, a lumped-up complexion like custard, and that greasy black hair falling into his eyes.

"Now the question, Mr. Malloy, you understand what it is, is we kind of think you were trying to go into a hotel room that isn't yours. See? So maybe you could explain that." Dewey wasn't really great at this yet. He shifted between feet like a five-year-old who had to go tinkle. Pigeyes was back near the door, arm on a filing cabinet, just taking this in with a sour expression.

"I'm looking for a partner of mine, Officer." Better the truth. There was only so much I could bluff, and right now everything was concentrated on looking chipper.

"Uh-huh," said Dewey. He nodded and tried to think of what to ask next. "Your partner, what's his name? What kind of partner is he?"

I spelled Kamin. Dewey wrote in his little pocket spiral, which he rested on his thigh.

"False personation," said Pigeyes. Back at the filing cabinets he gestured at the credit card which Dewey was now holding. Pigeyes was going to charge me with the crime of pretending to be someone else. I had forgotten up to now that the state claimed any interest in who I was or wanted to be.

I looked to Dewey almost as if he were a friend. "You know, Gino and me," I said, "there's some history. But you can explain this to him. It's not false personation when you use somebody's name with their permission. That credit card belongs to Kamin. See?''

Dewey didn't. ''You got this card from him, is that what you're saying? From Kamin?'' He looked back to Pigeyes for a second, maybe to check how he was doing. I had the sense, though, I had told them something. There was a little of that light-bulb look in both faces. Bert was Kam, or vice versa. They hadn't known that. ''It's Kamin's card?'' Dewey asked.

''Right.''

''And he gave it to you?''

''It's Kamin's card, I came here to look for him, as far as I know it's Kamin's hotel room. I'm sure he'll tell you I had his permission.''

''Well, we'll have to ask him.''

''Natch,'' I said.

''So what's his address?''

I'd raised him one too many. I saw that, but not quick enough. Sooner or later, when Bert didn't answer their phone calls, they'd turn up at his place. And the shit would fly when they opened the refrigerator. I tried momentarily to figure how many days it would be until we got to that point and what would happen then.

Dewey, in the meantime, had written down Bert's address and stepped away to chew things over with Pigeyes. Dewey, no doubt, was telling Gino they didn't have any real good reason to hold me and Pigeyes was saying, Like hell, he had me in sweatpants using someone else's name. But even Pigeyes would realize that, given our colorful past, if he pinched me and it didn't hold up, the civil suit

I'd file for retaliatory arrest would lead to his immediate retirement.

All in all, I was beginning to figure I'd come out okay, when I heard Gino say, "I'm gonna get her." He was back in a blink with the sweet-looking student who'd been at the front desk. I imagined he wanted to review my antics out there with the card, see if maybe she'd give him some handhold on me he had missed. I was wrong.

"This isn't the guy, right?" he asked her.

This office was small and getting crowded, five of us now and most of the space to begin with occupied by Trilby's desk, which was clean but for pictures of his children, all grown, and his wife. There was a U. pennant on the paneled walls and a clock. The girl looked around.

"No, of course not," she said.

"Describe him."

"Well, for one thing he was black."

"Who's that?" I asked.

Dewey gave me a warning look, a minute shake of the head: Don't interrupt. Pigeyes told the girl to go on.

"Late twenties, I'd say. Twenty-seven. Kind of receding hair. Athletic build. Nice-looking," she added, and shrugged, maybe by way of apology for the frank observations of a white girl.

"And how many times have you seen him?"

"Six times. Seven. He's been here a lot."

I spoke up again. "What is this, a show-up? What'd I do supposedly, steal this guy's wallet?" I was guessing now, earnest if confused.

"Hey, dude," said Dewey. "I think it's time for you to be quiet."

"You're questioning me, you're talking about someone in my presence. Come on, I want to know who."

"Oh my God, can you believe this guy?" Pigeyes turned away and bit his knuckle.

"Hey, so tell him," said Dewey. He hitched a slight shoulder. What was it to them? Gino eventually caught the drift. A glimmer struck home.

"Here, fine," said Pigeyes, "knock yourself out." He moved his hammy paw toward the girl. "Tell Mr. Malloy here who we been talking about."

The girl did not get any of this. She shrugged, farmplain, a little thick in her white blouse.

"Mr. Roberts," she said. "Kam Roberts."

"Your pal." Across the room, Pigeyes's hard little eyes glowed like agates. "So now tell us something smart."

VII. WHERE I LIVE

The house in which Nora Goggins and I made our married life was a little square thing, brick with vinyl siding and black shutters, three bedrooms, in a sort of middle-of-the-middle suburb called Nearing. Nora always said we could afford more, but I didn't want it; we had a summer place out on Lake Fowler and that was plunge enough for me. There were so many extraneous expenses—the Beemer, my suits and hers, the frigging clubs. I suppose, in retrospect, it means something that our home wasn't much. Ivy clings to the bricks, plantings that went in when we bought and now have vines thick as tree branches which are beginning to develop bark and sinister tendrils that have found the cracks in the mortar and are gradually pulling the entire place down. When I got the kid, I got the house. Nora cashed out. Nearing will never be glamorous and Nora knows a thing or two about value anyway.

Nora is a Real Estate Lady, you've seen them before,

suburban gals dressed to kill at lunch. She could not stand it at home. She limped to the finish line with Lyle, got him into high school, but I could tell that she had done a calculation on some scratch paper somewhere and figured what percentage of her brain cells were dying every day. Even drunk, I sensed a wild, unhappy thing in her that was not going to be tamed. I remember seeing her once; she was in the garden. She had a different homebound passion each year and that summer it was vegetables. All the green things abounded: the cornstalks with their broad leaves like graceful hands, the jungle density of the peas, the ferny tops of asparagus spread like lace. She stood in our tiny suburban back yard with Lyle at her knee and looked toward the distance, a mind full of lonely visions like Columbus, who saw round when everybody else saw flat.

Eventually she tore off into the land of open houses, showings, new on the market, with a ruthless glee, lit up like a rocket—she loved it, being back in the grown-up world. She was like twenty-one again—regrettably in all ways. When I figured out something was doing, a year or two along, I was more or less immobilized. I was no longer drinking, so I'd sit at home with painful fantasies, thinking about the guys relocating from Kansas City who got something special off Nora's own Welcome Wagon. She was pointing out the features of her inner sanctum and I, the former sot who'd done more wandering than a minstrel, was at home conducting a perverse and private romance with Mary Fivefingers. Isn't that the worst part of sex, that we *think* about it? Guys especially. You know how that goes, we don't have babies so we only have one way to prove the point. "You gettin any?" It's like asking a fat person if they've had a chance to eat. I swear, I was depressed for days after my last physical, when the doctor asked, in the modern way, if I was sexually active and I had to answer no. But then, I digress.

In her roaming, Nora was joined by her manager, a gal named Jill Horwich with whom she was always having a drink or sneaking off to a convention. Jill was like a good number of the Real Estate Ladies, divorced, the main support of a passel of kids, and I figured she liked screwing around because it was low-stress, some tomcat in a bar better than a fellow making himself a fixture in the kitchen, one more mouth to feed. Nora somehow seemed impressed by Jill's way of life.

But it was hardly news that Nora was adventurous. Soon after I met her, on date number two, it was Nora Goggins who gave me my first blow job. I still count the moment when she peeled back my zipper and greeted John Peter eye to eye, taking hold with the confidence of some nightclub vocalist grabbing the mike, as among the most exciting instants of my life. It was not a boy's thrill I'm talking about either. I knew I'd found a rare one, somebody braver than I was, a trait that I found irresistible, especially in a Catholic girl. I figured this was someone to follow through the jungle, who'd show no fear of the wild creatures and had the inner strength to clear a path of her own. Instead, it meant that she was a person of strong opinions who would feel thwarted by our life. She picked on me, told me regularly how I failed her emotionally, and apparently conceived of secret yearnings that I could never satisfy.

The noise I made coming in tonight brought the Loathsome Child in person bouncing off the staircase, rubbing his eyes, shirtless but wearing his jeans, looking as if he had been foraged on by some roaming beast. He is a scrofulous creature, frankly, my size but still not well developed, with a few errant hairs that crop up along his breastbone amid the acne. His peculiar haircut, which looks like a golf green cut onto an overgrown hillside, was disheveled. We ended up together at the kitchen table, both of us making a meal on Cheerios.

"Tough night?"

He made a vaguely affirmative sound. His hand was across his face and he rested his arm on the cereal box as if it was the only thing keeping him from collapse. He had put a shirt on by now, some chic rayon chemise I'm sure I paid for. The red stripe on it, I decided, was not design but ketchup.

"What time did you get home?"

"One."

He meant afternoon, not morning. I checked the clock: 7:48 p.m. Lyle was just rising. He pretty much lives backward. He and his pals consider it uncool to get started anytime this side of midnight. Nora, of course, attributes Lyle's libertine existence to the poor example his drunken father set when he was growing up.

"You should try reading St. Augustine. He has much cautionary advice about a life of excess."

"Oh, shut up, Dad."

Maybe if there were just a trace of humor in this I wouldn't have been so hot to smack him. As it was, I had to contain myself with the thought that if I hit him he would tell his mother, who'd tell her lawyer, who'd tell the judge. If I believed they'd take the kid away I'd have

knocked him cold, but it would only end in more re-
straining orders and restrictions on me.

According to that splendid education I received out at
the U., it was Rousseau who began in Western culture the
worship of the child, innocent and perfect in nature. Anyone who has raised a human from scratch knows this is a
lie. Children are savages—egocentric little brutes who by
the age of three master every form of human misconduct,
including violence, fraud, and bribery, in order to get what
they want. The one who lived in my house never improved.
Last fall it turned out that the community college, for which
I'd dutifully given him a tuition check at the beginning of
each quarter, did not have the bastard registered. A month
ago I took him out to dinner and caught him trying to
pocket the waitress's tip.

About three times a week I threaten to throw him out,
but his mother has told him the divorce decree provides
that I will support him until he's twenty-one—Brushy and
I had assumed that meant paying for college—and Nora,
who thinks the boy needs understanding, especially since
she doesn't have to provide much, would doubtless find
this an occasion for yet another principled disagreement
and probably seek an order requiring Lyle and me to get
some counseling—another five hundred bucks a month.
Thus, the thought often stabs me with the ugly starkness
of a rusty knife: I am afraid of him now too.

Believe me, I am not as cheerful as I sound.

Rising for another bowl of cereal, my son asked where
I had been.

"I was dealing with uncomfortable aspects of my past,"
I told him.

"Like Mom, you mean?" He thought he was funny.

"I ran into a cop I used to know. Over at U Inn."

"Really?" Lyle thinks it's neat that I was a policeman, but he couldn't pass up the opportunity for role reversal. "You aren't in trouble are you, Dad?"

"If I ever need to be bailed out, chum, I know where I can find an expert." I gave him a meaningful look, which sent Lyle at once across the kitchen.

It had killed Pigeyes to let me go. He and Dewey had talked it over for about fifteen minutes and apparently decided that they had better check out my story about Bert Gino gave me back the credit card and told me to hold on to it because I'd hear from him soon. It didn't sound like he'd be bringing a bouquet.

Slurping up my dinner now, I wished I hadn't been so hasty with Bert's name. The problem, slowly dawning on me, was that when Pigeyes and Dewey open Bert's refrigerator, the next stop would be G&G. They'd want to know everything about Kamin. At that point—probably within the next week—it would be hard to keep the missing money out of our answers. And once this was a police matter, everybody would be posturing. Even if Krzysinski kept his cool now when Jake gave him the lowdown, there'd be no hush-hush after the cops arrived, no diplomatic solutions. It'd be sayonara, G&G. I needed to get going.

Still, the news that there is a living breathing human named Kam Roberts has left me feeling like an astronomer who just discovered that there's a second planet in our orbit, also called Earth. If he wasn't Bert—and Bert wasn't twenty-seven, black, or losing his hair when I last saw him twelve days ago—then why is Kam Roberts using Bert's name upside down and getting his mail at Bert's house?

I'd been carrying the note that Lena had copied off Infomode in my shirt pocket. I studied it for a second and in total desperation even showed it to Lyle. I told him it seemed like Bert had written it.

"That dude? One who took us to a couple Trappers games? Got to be sports with him, man."

"Thank you, Sherlock. What sport in particular? Safecracking?"

Lyle was blank. I might as well have asked him about Buddhism. The kid had left a pack of cigarettes on the table and I took one as a garnish.

"Hey." He pointed. "Buy your own."

"I'm saving you," I said. "I'm conserving your health and future."

The kid didn't think I was funny. He never did. If I start counting the endeavors in this life at which I have failed, I'll burn out the batteries on this thing. But somehow Lyle and I stand on our own plateau. When I was an active drunkard, there were moments while I was crocked that my love for this child would come over me with breathtaking intensity. It was always the same image, this chubby two-year-old running to beat all hell, his laughter free as a waterfall and sweeter than music, and I loved him so dearly, with such heartsore tenderness, that I'd sit over my highball glass shameless at my tears. These were the most intimate moments I had with my kid, this kind of imaginary contact while he was fast asleep and I was in some barroom half a dozen miles from home. Practically speaking, I did him little good. Near as I can figure, that makes me the same as three-quarters of the dads I know who just sort of phone it in as fathers. But somewhere along the line Lyle recognized my vulnerability, that when it comes to him I am wholly paralyzed by regret. Call it what you like, getting even or being nuts together, we both know that him pushing my buttons and me refusing to jump has the same screwed-up emotional dynamic as, say, ritual torture or some family form of S and M. Lyle by his behavior berates me, while I cry out by suffering this punishment that I love, if not him, then something he alone represents.

With the cigarette I retreated and knocked around the living room. I had gone back to the health club to dress and to the office to pick up the file for Toots Nuccio's hearing tomorrow and I read at it a bit. Eventually I wandered upstairs, doing my nightly usual, trying to sneak up sidelong on sleep. Should I describe my bedroom, site of my nighttime dictation? Hiroshima after the bomb. Books and newspapers and cigarette butts. Scattered highbrow journals and law reviews read in my brainier moods. A brass colonial lamp with a broken shade. Beside my cherry highboy, there is a rectangle of carpeting less faded than the rest, dimpled at each corner by the casters from Nora's dresser, one of the few pieces of furniture she took. With Lyle around, there is not much point in cleaning anywhere, and my little corner of the world now seems crushed and flattened on all sides.

Next to my bed is a dropcloth and a half-finished canvas on an easel, upon whose ledge sit many tubes of paint, thumb-dented and fingerprinted with the bright pigments. Artist at work. When I was eighteen, I was going to be Monet. As a child in my mother's house, as a victim of her shrill tirades, I took a certain comfort in concentrating on what did not change, on the permanence of a line and the silence of the page. I don't know how many times, in how many schoolrooms, I drew the people from the funnies, Batman, Superman, Dagwood. I was good too. Teachers praised my work, and nights when I was sitting around The Black Rose with my old man I'd amuse his cronies by faultlessly rendering a photo from the paper. 'Boy's great, Tim.' He took the usual bar-time pleasure from this, man among men, letting others boast about his son, but at home he would not cross my ma, who took a dim view of this vocation. 'Drawin flippin pictures,' she'd mutter whenever the subject was raised. It was not until I got a D in a drawing class in my first year at the U. that I began to see she had a point.

Here's the problem: I see well only in two dimensions. I don't know if it's depth perception or something in the brain. I envision the picture but not the figure it is drawn from. If counterfeiting were a legitimate profession, I would be its Pablo Fucking Picasso. I can reproduce anything on paper as if it were traced. But real life somehow defeats me. Foreshortened, distorted—it never comes out right. My career as an artist, I had realized shortly before I joined the Force, would be a sort of secondhand hell in which I'd never do anything original. So I became a lawyer. Another of those jokes, though when I make it, my partners flinch.

At home, in private, I like to pretend. Normally, when I jolt awake at 3:00 a.m., it's not Wash's report or the Dictaphone that occupies me. Instead, I repaint Vermeer and imagine the thrill of being the man who so saucily transfigured reality. I am here often in the middle of the night, the light intense, the glare from the shiny art book page and the wet acrylics somehow dazzling, as I try to avoid thinking too much about the image that leapt up from the flames to wake me.

And what image is that? you ask. It's a man, actually. I see him stepping out of the blaze, and when I start awake, heart banging and mouth dry, I am looking for him, this guy who's got my number. He's around the corner, always behind me. Wearing a hat. Carrying a blade. In dreams sometimes I catch the gleam winking as he treads through the path of blue light from a streetlamp. This is an always thing, all my life, me and this guy, Mr. Stranger Danger, as the coppers put it, the guy who's out there and gonna do you bad. He's the one that mothers warn their daughters to watch out for on a deserted street. He's the mugger in the park, the home invader who strikes at 3:00 a.m. I became a copper, maybe, because I thought I'd catch him, but it turns out he still gets the drop on me at night.

Jesus, what is it I have to be so scared of? Five years on the streets and still with all my fingers and toes, a job that I'm busy trying to make secure, and skills of one kind or another. But I am looking at the big 5–0, and the numbers still stir something in me, as if they were the caliber of a gun that is pointed at my head. It gets a body down. I lie here in the bed in which I screwed several thousand times a woman who I figure now never really cared much about what I was doing; I listen to the phlegmy report from the rotted muffler of what I used to call my car and desolately hold to the departing sounds of that roaming creature who was once a tender child. What is there to be so scared of, Elaine, except this, my one and only life?

Tonight I woke only once. It was not as bad as sometimes. No dreams. No knives or flames. Just a single thought, and the horror of it for a change was not too large to name.

Bert Kamin is probably dead.

TAPE 3

Dictated January 26, 9:00 p.m.

VIII. MEN OF THE CITY

A. Archie Was a Cool Operator

When I got to the office on Wednesday morning, Lena was waiting for me.

"Is this guy a gambler?" You could see she already knew the answer was yes.

"Show me." I followed her toward the library.

When I interviewed Lena on campus at the U. last year, I noticed there was a hole in her résumé—seven years to finish college. I asked if she'd been working.

'Not really.' She had grasped her briefcase, a little redhead with a worldly eye. 'I went through a rough spell.'

'How rough?'

'Rough.' We scrutinized one another in the interview room, a soundproofed spot no bigger than a closet; it would have done well for torture. 'I thought I was in love with a guy,' she said. 'But I was in love with the dope. I'm

NarcAnon. That whole thing. Once a week.' She awaited my reaction. There were a half dozen other good firms in the city and we were interviewing early. If candor didn't work, she could lie to the next bunch, or hope she'd make it through someplace before anybody asked. She'd had A's. Somebody would take a chance. You could read all these calculations in her strong features.

'AA,' I said and shook her hand. She'd done well here. Brilliantly. She had taken control of her life with an athlete's determination, which, whenever I witnessed it, colored me from the same palette of murky feelings—envy, admiration, the ever-present conviction that I am a phony and she the real thing.

In the library she stationed me by a p.c. and went through the codes to bring Bert's message up on the screen. I stared at it again:

```
Hey Arch—


          SPRINGFIELD
Kam's Special 1.12—U. five, five
    Cleveland.
1.3—Seton five, three Franklin.
1.5—SJ five, three Grant.


          NEW BRUNSWICK
1.2—S.F. eleven, five Grant.
```

"See," she said, "I looked in Sportsline. It's not only scores. They also have a sports book. From Las Vegas? It shows the odds and spreads. Here." The list went on for pages: basketball, college and pro, and hockey, with a point spread for every game, each one listed on a separate line. "Then I asked myself," she said, "do any of these sports have anything to do with Springfield or New Brunswick?"

There was some kind of basketball shrine in Springfield, Massachusetts, but I drew a blank on New Jersey.

"Football," she said, "that's where they played the first college football game. In New Brunswick. And the first basketball game was in Springfield."

I made her flip the screen back so I could look again at Bert's message. Three weeks ago, the NFL playoffs had laid waste to my weekend.

"These are games," she said. "I think he's betting one side of the spread or the other." She looked at me to see how she was doing, which was fine. "It makes sense," she told me. "Franklin and Grant—they're on money, right? I mean bills. I don't quite get Cleveland."

"Grover Cleveland's on the thousand."

"He *is* betting," she said. "Heavy too. How's he covering his losses?" An addict, Lena had an ingrained view: For sin you pay sometime.

I considered her question. Betting between five and ten grand a day, Bert had the look of a man likely to steal.

"I can't figure what this means," she said, "Kam's Special?"

I had no idea.

"And who's Arch?" she asked.

That one was more obvious to me.

"A bookie." Actuaries, of course, are oddsmakers in white shirts. Archie, I guess, couldn't resist plotting probabilities on something more amusing than mortality tables.

It was a funny thought, some buttoned-down type making book in one of these steel towers.

"Look," I said to Lena, "if this character Archie had my guy's account number and the name Kam Roberts, he could call in and take bets out of the mailbox. Right? And he could do that with dozens of other people too, if he had the same kind of arrangement with them."

"Why would he want to?"

"Because bookmaking is illegal and it's a better business if he doesn't get caught." Even when I was on the street, before wiretapping got so big, guys kept a book on the run. Somebody with no nose would knock on a door in a poor neighborhood and offer to rent an apartment for a month, three grand, no questions asked. They'd use the place for four weeks, then go somewhere else, hoping to stay ahead of the feds. But these days, no matter how they do it, when they're taking bets over the phone there's the chance the G is listening. Archie took calls from no one. You could scout out the Sportsline and leave your bets for Archie in your Infomode mailbox. Archie was an electronic tout, man of his times.

Which also explained the reference to Arch Enterprises on the Kam Roberts bank card statement. Archie had solved the bookie's age-old dilemma—how do I collect without giving the legbreakers a call to knock 6 for 5 out of you by Friday? This was clean, professional. It was all charged to the credit card. Wins and losses. Probably once a month a debit or credit memo went through. For a winner, it was as good as cash—you could wash your airline tickets, dinners out, a suit, a tie, everything you charged. If you lost, Arch got paid by the bank. No doubt everybody employed intermediate devices. In all likelihood Arch Enterprises was the subsidiary of some holding company owned in turn by a trust. Maybe created in Pico Luan?

"What's this case about?" Lena asked. "Can I work on it?" Better than bond indentures and coverage claims.

I thanked her at length, then took the bill back to my office, somewhat saddened by myself. As usual, I had let my lurid imagination get the better of me. Archie was not Bert's lover. He was a bookie. Even so, there was a lot of this that didn't fit. I still didn't know what Bert had to do with Kam, and I couldn't figure why Pigeyes and his pals were chasing him. It wasn't for gambling, which would be a vice investigation. Pigeyes and Dewey were working this out of Financial Crimes. But this information did do one thing. It made my wee-hours theory look even better, and I said it to myself again out loud, if quietly: "Bert's dead."

Icicles of steely light drifted out on the river. You had to consider Bert's situation with what I call cop logic. Look for the simple explanation. The gentleman in the Amana had not tied a fishing line around his neck by himself. Bad People had a point to make. And given the location of the body, it seemed that point had something to do with Bert. And now Bert had disappeared, and I find out, to boot, that he was in the middle of some off-the-wall gambling scheme, just the kind of scene where people end up sore over money and who shorted who, subterranean disputes that get settled with bloodshed, since you can't file a lawsuit. I wondered if Bert had another fridge in his basement.

One thing for sure, I wasn't going back to check, especially now that I'd sent Pigeyes in that direction. It would have been enlightening to take a peek at what was on the computer I'd seen in Bert's living room, to see if there were more references to Kam, his specials and his life. Settling for second best, I visited Bert's office down the hall. The door was locked—that was Bert, manic and jealous of his clients' secrets, not to mention his own. They'd moved his secretary to another station while her boss was AWOL, but I knew where she kept the key and I let myself in.

Bert's home had that fly-about look, but fitting his compulsions, the office was crazy clean. Every object dusted and in its place. Lawyers' furnishings are pretty standard: diplomas on the walls, pictures of the family, and a few discreet mementos that nod toward the high points of their legal career and are likely to impress clients. Wash, for example, keeps the reminders of certain big deals in one bookcase—announcements from the *Journal* preserved in little Lucite blocks; deal "bibles" in which the thousands of closing documents, all on foolscap, are bound in leather with the name and date of the transaction etched in gold on the binding. Even I have a framed sketch, done by one of the local TV station's artists, of me arguing a big jury case for TN concerning their firing of a pilot who'd been hired as John and later took on the name and genitalia of Juanita.

Looking around Bert's office, all you'd know is this guy's sports-crazy—game memorabilia were wall-to-wall: autographed baseballs, a Hands jersey, signed in indelible marker by every member of the '84 championship team, which was framed and hung from one of the concrete pilasters. Nothing else was visible he cared about, except the huge goofy water cooler in the corner.

Working on 397, I learned all Bert's passwords on the network, and I popped on the computer and cruised through the directories, pressing the buttons to glimpse different documents in the hope that there'd be more signs here of what was doing with Kam Roberts and Archie. But there was nothing. Instead, I started looking over Bert's endless correspondence, sort of idly poking for clues but also, I admit, enjoying some of the twisted thrill of the snoop, surveying old Bert's life as a lawyer.

His odd ways have held Bert back with clients and he's brought in few of his own. He is what they call a "service lawyer," like me, somebody who does the work that one of our hotshot partners has been hired for. But with that limit, the Committee loves him. Bert clocks a good twenty-five hundred hours every year, and with his own fierce methods gets great results in court. Every case is a full-bore commitment. Got a client with a small problem, say, falsely representing that night is day, Bert will defend him without blinking. He is one of those lawyers who agrees with the other side about nothing. Everything leads to correspondence. Move the dep from two to one, Bert will send you a letter. Which bears no resemblance, by the way, to the conversation it claims to record. I say my client's having open-heart and Bert's letter says the guy can't appear because he scheduled a doctor's appointment. With stunts like that, Bert's made enemies of half the trial lawyers in town. In fact, that's why I started working on 397 in the first place, because Jake can't be bothered with 150 plaintiff's attorneys, and most of those guys want to

turn on a tape recorder before they're willing to say so
much as good morning to Bert.

Out in the hallway I heard my name being repeated on
the paging system, asked to dial Lucinda's extension. That
meant it was time to go to Toots's hearing. I was about to
turn off the p.c. when I saw a name in Bert's letter directory
that struck sparks off my heart: Litiplex.

I fiddled with the buttons to call up the file. I was
nervous, sure that I'd hit the wrong key and obliterate the
whole thing, but I didn't, although there was not much to
see, just a short little cover memo.

CAGE & GRISWELL
Office Memorandum
ATTORNEY WORK-PRODUCT
PRIVILEGED AND CONFIDENTIAL

20 November

TO: Glyndora Gaines, Supervisor
    Accounting Section
FROM: Robert A. Kamin
RE: 397 Check Requisition—Liti-
    plex, Ltd.

Per the attached, re agreement with
Peter Neucriss, please draw for my
signature separate checks to Litiplex, Ltd. in invoice amounts as indicated.

I read this over four or five times. Finally, when I'd made as much sense of it as I could, I printed it.

"Hey."

I started. I hadn't heard the door open over the printer's whine. It was Brushy. She was standing with my coat and hers and the file on Toots's case all bundled in her arms.

"It's ten to. We're just going to make it." I guess I had some telltale look, because she came straight up to Bert's desk chair where I sat. I had a thought of fending her off so she couldn't read Bert's little memo over my shoulder, but on the whole I was too pleased with myself and my skills of detection to make much of an effort at that.

"Holy smokes," she said. "What's 'the attached'?"

"Hell if I know. I searched—there's no other mention of Litiplex. I suppose I'll have to go ask Glyndora. I've been meaning to talk to her anyway."

"You said the Committee told you there wasn't any paperwork to cover the checks."

"They did."

"Maybe this memo is phony," she said. "You know, so Bert had something to show if anybody asked why he signed the checks."

That was possible. It even made sense. The odds against Bert reaching any kind of "agreement" with Peter Neucriss approached the level of mathematical certainty. Neucriss is Kindle's number-one personal-injury lawyer, a portly little demon whose commanding ways and courtroom successes have led him to be called "The Prince" to his face, with "of Darkness" added when he turns his back. He and Bert haven't exchanged a civil word since the *Λ.a.:den* case some years back, when Neucriss in closing referred to Bert as "the attorney from the fourth dimension" and got a laugh out of the jury. It would make sense, I supposed, to talk to Neucriss too, although that was never a welcome prospect.

"Will you tell me what happens," she asked, "when you talk to them?"

"Sure," I answered, "but no blabbing. You know: attorney-client. I don't want this getting around before I figure it out."

"Come on, Malloy," she said. "You know me. I always keep your secrets." She gave me her own special smile, whimsical, flirtatious, tickled with herself and her hidden adventures, before she rushed me out the door.

B. The Colonel

"State your name please and spell your last name for the record."

"My name is Angelo Nuccio, N, u, c, c, i, o, but since I'm a kid folks like to call me Toots." The Colonel, as he is generally known, displayed a grand showman's smile for the members of Bar Discipline Inquiry Panel D arrayed beside him at a long table. We were trying our case, such as it was, before them, a three-member jury of other attorneys, volunteers with a part-time yen to sit in judgment of others. In response to Toots, the chair, Mona Dalles, yielded something, but the two men at either side of her maintained expressions of utter self-imposed neutrality. Mona is at the Zahn firm, G&G's biggest competitor, and is known as amiable, level, bright—qualities that were not helpful on Toots's case if you looked at it from the perspective of the defense. What we needed was somebody certifiable. A large reel-to-reel tape recorder spun in front of Mona, preserving, for those who might care to listen in the future, the final stage of one of the county's most vivid public lives.

Colonel Toots is eighty-three years old and a physical wreck. His bowed little legs, one of which had been shot up at Anzio, are brittle with arthritis; his lungs are smoked out, curled up, as I imagine them, like dead leaves, so that he has developed a wheezy little breath that punctuates every word. He has diabetes which is imperiling his sight, and various circulatory ailments. But you have to give it to him, the guy is still full of it—Colonel Toots has been running on premium all his life. He is a man of the city who has been a bit of everything—a soldier in three wars, and a ludicrous chest-thumping patriot; a pol; an accomplished clarinetist who on two occasions has rented the entire Kindle County Symphony to back him when he did a not-bad run-through of a Mozart number for clarinet; a mobster; a lawyer; a friend of whores and gunmen and virtually anyone else in the tri-cities who common sense taught him might count. When I was a copper twenty years ago, he was still in his heyday, an elected city councilman from the South End who, when not politicking, was fixing judges, selling jobs, or, so it was claimed, killing a fellow or two. You could never tell for sure with Toots. He was an absolute stranger to the truth. But a storyteller such as might have beguiled Odysseus, charming even when he recounted matters that better sense told you were absolutely revolting—how he bought votes from "shines" for turkeys ("November is a good month for elections") or once shot the knees out of some dunce who refused to pay a poolroom debt.

At eighty-three, Colonel Toots has survived just about everything but BAD, which has fired at him an even half dozen times over his career and is still reloading. During a recent federal investigation, it developed that Colonel Toots for fourteen years running had paid the country club dues of Daniel Shea, the chief judge of the county Tax Division, a court where Toots' firm was especially prominent. Judge Shea had wisely died before the U.S. Attorney's Office could indict him on various income tax charges. The government couldn't prove that any matters in Shea's courtroom had been influenced, so there wasn't much of a case on Toots. But the payments violated a number of ethical provisions and the Justice Department had referred the matter to BAD, where my former colleagues, beetle-browed do-gooders, knew at once they had Toots's number, eighty-three years old or not.

So at 10:00 a.m. this Wednesday morning, Brushy and I and our client had arrived at the old school building where BAD is housed. Our presence in itself was a sign of defeat. At my client's urging, I'd employed various gambits to put this off for over two and a half years. Now the ax was certain to fall.

I stipulated to the Administrator's case, a collection of grand jury transcripts offered by Tom Woodhull, the Deputy Administrator, who years ago had been my boss. Standing up to rest his case, Woodhull appeared himself— unruffled, tall, handsome, and completely inflexible. I called Toots to the stand at once, hoping to appear eager to begin the defense.

"When did you become an attorney?" I asked my client, after he had given a gaudy review of his war record.

"Was admitted to the practice of law sixty-two years ago, nineteen days. But who's counting?" He supplied the same corny smile he used every time we went through this.

"Did you attend law school?"

"At Easton University where I was taught contracts by the late Mr. Leotis Griswell of your firm, who was my conscience throughout my professional life."

I turned away from the panel for fear I might smile. I had told Toots to drop the Jiminy Cricket routine, but he did not take easily to correction. He sat in his chair with his walking stick against his knee, a little trail of spittle on his lips from all the heavy mouth-breathing, a bulbous tuber of a man, all belly and cigar, with woolly eyebrows that meandered halfway up his forehead. He wore what he always wore—a shocking-green sport jacket, somewhere in color between your lighter watermelons and a lime. I would wager a considerable sum that neither of the men on the panel owned a tie that bright.

"What has been the nature of your law practice?" I asked next, a tricky question.

"I would say I had a very general practice. I would say," said Toots, "that I was a helper. People came to me who needed help and I helped."

This was about as good as we could do, since Toots in sixty-two years as a lawyer could not name a case he had tried, a will he'd drafted, a contract he'd written. Instead, folks came to him with certain problems and their problems were solved. It was a very Catholic concept, Toots's practice. Who, after all, can explain a miracle? Toots helped many public officials too. There was someone in almost every significant public agency with whom Toots maintained a special friendship. There was a debonair Assistant Attorney General for whom Toots bought suits; a particularly important State Senator who'd had three additions to his home built by a contractor friend of Toots for the remarkably low cost of fourteen grand. This generosity had made the Colonel quite an influential fellow, especially since his methods were always understood. He relied first on his rogue charm. After that, he had other friends, guys from the neighborhood who'd smash your windows, torch your store, or, as happened once to a club singer who got crosswise of Toots, perform a tonsillectomy without benefit of an anesthetic.

"Did you practice in the Tax Division courts?"

"Not at all. Never. If I was goin there today I'd need to ask directions."

I glanced down at Brushy to see how this was going. She was seated beside me, wearing a dark suit, trying to record every word on a yellow pad. She gave me a wee smile, but that was just being friends. She was too tough to hold out any more hope than I did.

"Now, did you know Judge Daniel Shea?" I asked.

"Oh yes, I known Judge Shea since we was both young attorneys. We was terrific friends. Like this."

"And did you, as the Administrator here alleges, pay the country club dues of Judge Shea?"

"Absolutely." Toots had not been quite as sure when the IRS asked him the same question a number of years ago, but he had cut the interview short; it would not prove too damaging when Woodhull began his cross-examination, which was guaranteed to be wooden in any event.

"Can you please explain how that occurred?"

"That would be no trouble at all." Toots grabbed hold of his walking stick and shifted, as it were, into forward gear. "In about 1978 I run across Dan Shea at a dinner for the Knights of Columbus and we started talking, as fellas do, about golf. He told me that he had always wanted to get into the Bavarian Mound Country Club, which was right in his neighborhood, but unfortunately for him, he did not know a soul who could sponsor him. I volunteered for that job with pleasure. Shortly thereafter that, the president of the club, Mr. Shawcross, called to my attention the fact that Dan Shea was having some trouble making his dues. Since I was his sponsor, I felt it was up to me to pay them, and that's what happened ever since."

"Now did you mention these payments to Judge Shea?"

"Never," he said. "I did not want him to feel embarrassed or uncomfortable. His wife, Bridget, was in very bad health then and the expense and trouble was weighing quite heavy on him. Knowing Dan Shea, I'm sure that he had meant to get to this and it slipped his mind."

"And did you ever discuss with him any of the business in his court that your firm had there?"

"Never," he said again. "How could I? The younger fellas in my office do any number of things. It never crossed my mind that they was in that court. There's so many courts these days, you know.'' Toots spread his arms wide and smiled, revealing the worn yellow stubs of what were left of his teeth.

Brushy handed me a note. ''The cash,'' it said.

''Oh yes.'' I touched my tie to revert to role. ''We've stipulated that when Mr. Shawcross was in the grand jury, he testified you made these payments in cash and asked him not to discuss them with anyone. Could you explain that, please?''

''That would be no trouble at all,'' said Toots. ''I did not want it to become known among the members of the club that Judge Shea was having a problem with his dues. I felt that would embarrass him. So I paid in cash, hoping that the bookkeeper and all of them would not see my name on a check, and I asked Mr. Shawcross to very kindly keep this to himself.'' With effort, he cranked himself about to face the panel. ''I was just trying to be a friend,'' he told them. I didn't notice anybody up there reaching for a hanky.

Woodhull spent about fifteen minutes stumbling around on cross-examination. Toots, who hadn't missed a word on direct, was suddenly virtually deaf. Woodhull repeated every question three or four times and Toots often responded simply with a vague, addled stare. About noon Mona called a recess. That was enough for today. Seven lawyers, we all got out our diaries to see when we could resume. We went through the mornings and afternoons clear from today to next Tuesday before everybody was free.

''How'd I do?'' Toots asked on the way out.

''Great,'' I said.

He lit up childishly and laughed. He thought so too.

"Why does a guy who's eighty-three want to be disbarred?" asked Brushy after we'd put him in a taxi. "Why doesn't he just resign from practice?"

Toots's forty-year career as councilman for the South End had come to a conclusion in the early 1980s, when it turned out that the city's Parks and Playgrounds Commission, which Toots controlled by appointments, had voted for a decade straight to award its refuse-hauling contract to Eastern Salvage, a company owned through various intermediaries by one of Toots's sons. Since then, Toots's life had been confined to his role as the man for desperate occasions. He needed his law license to lend his activities some air of legitimacy. I explained all this to Brushy as we walked back toward the Needle through the noontime crowds. There had been a light snowfall last night which had been ground to gray mush and crept over the toes of our shoes.

"There's no listing in the Yellow Pages for Fixers. Besides, it would stain his honor. This is a man who wanted to wear his medals to the hearing. He can't accept the public disgrace."

"His honor?" she asked. "He's had people killed. Those guys in the South End? He eats lunch with them. Dinner."

"That's an honor too."

Brushy shook her head. We entered the Needle and rose by elevator to G&G's reception area, where oaken bookcases had been erected and filled with dozens of antique books, bought by the gross, to lend the proper air. Our offices had been redecorated at Martin's direction a couple of years ago in the manner of an English hunting lodge. This main reception area was refurbished with planked pine and tufted leather chairs of royal maroon and little landscapes and hunting scenes on the walls, pictures in brass frames with broad green mats, second-rate decorative crap, but who was asking me? That kind of stage setting, though, made it easier to fall into some kind of fugue state—new faces every day, young people striding about with urgent anguished looks, all this important stuff going on that didn't have a damn thing to do with me. Bonds issuing. Deals closing. You could see it all from a considerable distance: Men with phallic symbols around their necks. Women with half their legs exposed. What on God's green planet were they up to? Why was it that they cared and I didn't?

"I've told him we can't win," I said of Toots. "He kept asking me to get continuances."

"I see that." She thumped the file. "Two years four months. For what?" She was backing down the corridor. She had a meeting with Martin but reminded me about racquetball at six.

"Time."

"What's he going to do with time?" asked Brushy.

"Die," I said, before turning away.

IX. TOUGH CUSTOMERS

A. Slave Queen of Accounting

Like the engine room of an oceangoing vessel, where soot-spotted hands shovel coal into great fires, the firm's Accounting Department burns on belowdecks. On 32, between an investment banking operation and a travel service, the location has a sub-basement feel, because it is cut off from the three other floors we occupy. Yet in many ways this is the heart of G&G: to Accounting our billable hours are reported on a daily basis; from Accounting our statements for services go out every month. Here the great profitmaking motor of the law firm whines away at high r.p.m.'s.

One of the most peculiar things about going from BAD to G&G was getting used to a world where money—which as a cop and then a public lawyer I regarded as inherently evil—is, instead, the point of axis of an entire universe.

Money's why the clients hire us—to help them make more or keep what they have. God knows, it's what we want from them. It is what we all have in common. At this point in the calendar, when our fiscal year concludes, the firm takes on the air of a campus before the Big Game. We have partnership meetings about collecting that can't be easily distinguished from pep rallies, where Martin, and especially Carl, make speeches designed to give us the stomach to demand our clients actually pay our bills. It was one of Carl's many clever innovations to move the close of our fiscal year back a month to January 31, in order to give clients the chance to book our fees in either calendar year. On February 2, Groundhog Day, after the receipts are totaled, the partnership meets in tuxedos, while the Committee announces each partner's "points"—our percentile share of firm income.

Accounting is housed in a couple of rooms, garish with fluorescence, nine women in an environment of white Formica. Their figures are reported daily to the Committee and various CPAs. The staff supervisor, the resident person in charge, is Glyndora Gaines. When I came in she was on her feet, studying a clipping torn from the newspaper. The paper itself was spread on her desk, the only thing there besides a framed photo of her son. As soon as she saw me, she walked away.

I was in my overcoat, on my way out to see Peter Neucriss. I'd called Glyndora three or four times now without response, and I asked if she'd gotten my messages.

"Busy," she said, the gal who'd just been reading the *Tribune*. I followed her around Accounting while she slammed through cabinets.

"This is important," I added.

I got a look that could have smelted lead.

"So's what I'm doing, man. We're 10 percent below budget and looking for ways to reallocate every expense we got. Don't you want to make *money*?"

Boy, this is a lady with an attitude—capital A—one of those powerhouse African-American women whose chief regret seems to be that she has but one life to fume over the indignities of the last few centuries. No one gets along with her. Not the attorneys, the paralegals, the staff. During her years as a secretary Glyndora worked with half the lawyers in the firm. She couldn't cut it with another woman and lasted only a week with Brushy. She'd been far too intimidating for Wash—and many others. In all the ensuing scrapes Glyndora's been protected by—guess who?— Martin Gold, patron saint of the local eccentrics. He seems to find her amusing and, as I knew well, is inclined to forgive every sin except sloth for the sake of ability. Able Glyndora is. That's the problem. She resents the way she's been enslaved by circumstance. She had a kid at fifteen, whom she raised on her own, with no chance after that really to make her way.

Recognizing that Glyndora could not resist the chance to prove how capable she is, Martin had ultimately teamed her with Bert, the lawyer for whom she'd worked longest. Glyndora filed his motions, kept his schedule, wrote the routine correspondence, filled in the blanks on the standard interrogatories, made excuses when he took a powder, even went to court for him in a couple of emergencies. (And had an income about 10 percent of his, if you'll excuse the son of a union man.) The only problem was that about a year ago they began to fight. Here I am not being euphemistic. I do not mean occasional cross looks or even one or two sharp words. I mean standing in the hallway bellowing. I mean papers flying, clients in the doorways of the conference rooms staring down the halls. I mean Scenes. Finally, someone who must have been in the army or on a police force got the right idea: promote her. Glyndora was less a tyrant as a boss than she had been as an employee and she clearly enjoyed having a universe of her own. Bert, naturally, carried on like a baby when they took her away. And Glyndora undoubtedly enjoyed that too.

"Glyndora, it's this Litiplex thing. The money." That stopped her. We were in front of a row of bone-colored cabinets. Her face was narrowed by her customary suspicion. "When you searched for the paperwork, I think you could have missed a memo. From Bert. Maybe attaching some kind of agreement with Peter Neucriss?"

She shook her head immediately, a copse of long hair, dulled by straighteners. I nodded firmly in response.

"Hey, man." She swept her hand wide. "I got 80,000 files here and I had my nose in each one. You think you can do a better job, Mack, help yourself. We lock up at five."

The phone rang then and she picked it up, long sinister sculpted nails painted bright red. Glyndora is past forty and showing little wear. This is one good-looking woman and she knows it—built like the brick shithouse you've always heard about, five foot ten in her stocking feet and female every inch of it, a phenomenal set of headlights, a big black fanny, and a proud imperial face, with a majestic look and an aquiline schnozzola that reports on Semitic adventures in West Africa centuries ago. Like every fine-looking human I have ever met, she can be charming when there's something she wants, and with me, in certain moods, she's even something of a tease, picking up, I guess, on a certain susceptibility. I've lived most of my life with women like this, who were suffering from the peculiarly female frustration of feeling there had never been any way out to start—and besides, a body can't ignore how she looks. I've heard men speak of Glyndora with admiration for years—but only from a distance. As Al Lagodis, an old pal from the Force, told me one day when he came by for lunch, you'd need a dick like a crowbar.

She had no use for me now. "I told you, Mack," she said when she was done on the phone, "I don't have time for this."

"I'll see you at five. You can show me what you went through."

She laughed. Glyndora and non-essential overtime were mutually exclusive.

"When?" I asked.

She picked up her purse, dropping something into it, and gave me a little tight smile that said, Go jump. She was on her way down the hall, where I couldn't follow. I said her name to no avail. She left me by her desk. The newspaper from which she'd ripped that item was still open. It looked like it had been an article, an eighth of a page. A little portion of the headline remained. WES, maybe part of a T. West? I looked up. Sharon, one of Glyndora's underlings, was watching me, a little brown woman in a pink outfit that was half a size too tight. Twenty feet away, she eyed me from her desk with suspicion—worker against boss, woman versus man, all of the workplace's silent little competitions. Whatever I was looking for, she figured, I shouldn't know.

I tried a silly smile and stepped away from the forbidden zone of what was Glyndora's.

"Tell her to call me," I said.

Sharon just looked. We both knew I had no chance.

B. Prince of Darkness

TransNational Air Flight 397 went down in a horrible fireball at the Kindle County Municipal Airfield in July 1985. A TV crew was coincidentally at the airport to cover the arrival of the Peking Circus at a nearby gate and so the footage played again and again across the country, you've probably seen it, 397 bouncing on its front wheel and taking air again, looking a bit like a kiddie's book where the hippopotamuses dance ballet, all quite slo-mo and graceful until the thing canted forward, hit square on its nose, and fire ignited, flashing through the cockpit first and then rolling back through the plane, lighting the windows as it went, until the engines and underbelly blew off in a memorable eruption of orange and yellow flame. No survivors—247 fried.

At this point, the plaintiffs' lawyers took the field, the guys and gals who prate to juries about the misery of the widows and orphans and then take a full third of what is forked over in sympathy. As someone who works the other side of the street, I'll spare the high and mighty—let me just note that Peter Neucriss, Barracuda-in-Chief of the local plaintiffs' bar, had filed three lawsuits in behalf of the families of crash victims not only before the remains were buried but in one instance before, quite literally, they had cooled. Within six months, there were more than 137 cases on file, including four class actions in which some enterprising lawyer claimed to represent everyone. All of these cases were consolidated before Judge Ethan Bromwich of the Kindle County Superior Court, a former law professor at Easton whose brilliance is exceeded only by his regard for his own abilities. And in every single suit, TransNational Air, our client, was the lead defendant.

Being the airline in an air crash case is sort of like driving a bumper car at the carnival. There are more drivers than you can count; no one knows or cares about rules of the road; everyone's headed in his or her own direction; and every single one of them seems to get his jollies out of ramming you in the behind. It's not just that there are 247 individual victims, each one with relatives and lawyers looking for money to assuage their misery, but you also have ten or twelve co-defendants, ruthlessly pissed off to be involved. Everybody gets sued, not just the airline and the pilot's estate, but any poor son of a bitch who left so much as a fingerprint on the plane: the folks who made the body, the engine manufacturers, the flight controllers, even the company that distilled the gas—anybody with deep pockets who might conceivably be blamed or forced by the prospect of a decade of expensive litigation to throw a few million bucks in the pot. And every one of those folks has a stop-loss insurer who steps to the plate looking for a way to deny coverage to the company that pays their premiums, or, if that won't work, to blame somebody else and get them to pay. There are weathervanes that do not point in as many directions. We blame the people in the flight tower; they in turn say the ailerons weren't working; the manufacturer speaks of pilot error. The plaintiffs all stand on the side and gloat.

About a year after 397 went down, Martin Gold began an effort that seemed to me as romantic and ill-considered as the Crusades: settling 397. Martin has a mind like a cloud chamber, that device where nuclear physicists trace the course of complex atomic reactions; he is probably the only lawyer I know who could even have embarked, let alone succeeded, on a negotiating process which, at one point, had him taking calls from 163 different attorneys.

Under what Martin is always careful to refer to, even sometimes in the office, as "The Bromwich Plan" the defendants, meaning for the most part their insurance companies, put together a fund of $288.3 million. In return the plaintiffs, led by Neucriss, agreed that the damages in all the cases together could not exceed that sum. Over the last five years, every individual case has been either tried before a Special Master, or more often settled, with Captain Bert heading the TN litigation team and supervising administration of the settlement fund which G&G has held in an interest-bearing escrow.

Recently, as the last of the damage trials have been resolved, we've had an unforeseen development: there's going to be millions left over which, accordingly, will remain the property of little ol' TransNational Air. Indeed, the only problem for TN has been keeping this news to ourselves, since it would be a public-relations nightmare to explain how, when everything is added and subtracted—legal fees, interest, the surplus, and TN's initial contribution to the fund—the company netted close to $20 million by killing 247 people. More pertinently, the plaintiffs' lawyers, who have never seen a dollar they didn't think was rightfully theirs, would use that vulnerability to weasel themselves a bigger share, and the co-defendants of course would wail piteously. We have been on a self-conscious campaign to make sure that every plaintiff has been paid out and signed a release before we submit our final accounting on the settlement fund to Judge Bromwich. Nonetheless, if you put liquor into Tad Krzysinski, TN's CEO, in an intimate setting, you can get him to laugh pretty hard at the inevitable jokes about crashing more planes.

When I was finally allowed to see Neucriss about 4:30, he had a tuna steak on a plate before him. Just out of court, he was enjoying a light supper, preparing for an evening's toil. He had a full kitchen and a chef in the office. The immediate air was savored with ginger, but there was still the frantic feel of trial. Peter's $100 foulard was dragged down; the sleeves were rolled on his white-on-white silk shirt; he stood as he ate, rumbling out every free-associated thought as a command. Four or five associates came charging in and out with questions about exhibits that they would need tomorrow. It was a bad-baby case, worth in Peter's hands at least $10 million. The mother was going on in the morning.

Meanwhile, I sat there in the mendicant pose in which Peter prefers to see everyone around him. I was hoping to get a quick answer and go. I had brought over drafts of the payout documents on 397, and had casually mentioned Litiplex, using the routine Wash said had been employed with others—correspondence we couldn't place, maybe Peter had an idea?

"Litiplex." Peter touched his forehead. He stared, unseeing, toward the middle distance. "I did talk to somebody about that."

"You did? Was it Bert?"

"*Bert?*"

"He's been out of town, I haven't been able to ask him."

"Right. Visiting his family on Mars." Neucriss rolled his eyes. "No. Who?" He drummed his fingers, he yelled for one of the secretaries, then stopped her with an explosive clap of his hands. "I know who asked me about Litiplex. Jesus Christ, what a squirrelly bunch you are. Don't you guys even talk to each other? Gold. Gold brought it up. Is he out of town too, or just out to lunch?"

My heart went flat, I wasn't even sure why, except I knew something was wrong. There were plaintiff's guys Martin could talk to with confidence, whereas even hello on the street with Peter required full body armor for Martin and an Alka-Seltzer afterwards.

"Martin?" I asked.

"No, good as. Yeah, Gold called three or four weeks ago. Doing the same soft-shoe as you, talking to me about something else, then trying to slide this Litiplex name in so I wouldn't notice. What the hell are you guys up to now?"

Nothing, I said. Lying to Peter is not even a venial sin: speaking to a Frenchman in French. Wash had said Martin phoned a couple of plaintiffs' lawyers with discreet inquiries about Litiplex, but it had never crossed my mind they might include Neucriss. In the meantime, I tried to smooth over the concerns all this Q and A about Litiplex seemed to have raised. Just getting ready for distribution, trying to cover all details, who more likely to know all than Peter?

With Neucriss, flattery is always the best way. Perhaps because it is the social world's realm of ultimate restraint, the law seems to attract more of these types, the utterly self-impressed who regard the bar as the pathway to a frontier where will and ego can go virtually unbounded. The sole partner in a seventeen-lawyer firm, Neucriss is the only lawyer I know who earns more every year than a good left-handed pitcher makes in the National League. Between $4 and $6 million are the printed estimates, and this year, with some $30 million worth of settlements in the 397 litigation about to pay out, his income will, as he puts it in his own unctuous way, "reach the eight figures."

This success has not been achieved by adherence to scruple. Peter's political contributions are vast—he hits every limit and gives in the name of his sixteen associates, his wife, and his children. Even so, he leaves nothing to chance. His witnesses are skillfully tutored; documents disappear; and in the bad old days, perhaps not entirely gone, when cash on the barrelhead bought judicial favor, Neucriss was figured to do this as well. Worst of all, his very prominence is a sort of revolting advertisement of the fallibility of the jury system. Ten minutes with this guy and you know the story: ego run wild, some form of character disorder. But somehow, from juries, Peter's schmaltzy performance, his self-congratulatory baritone and silvery mane, have drawn nothing but rave reviews for forty years. He goes on, with all of us knowing that no matter what his triumphs, his wealth, the national accolades, all the purchased adoration, the only motive force in nature surer than gravity is Peter's desire for more.

He continued talking about Martin, always a raw nerve with him.

"Oh yeah. What was Gold's line? Something like yours. A letter to be forwarded. I asked him, 'What game is this? Post Office? I thought that was adolescent foreplay.' " Neucriss roared at himself, his mouth still full. Being profane, he kept Martin on edge.

"But what about it, Peter? Litiplex? What is it?"

"Listen to this. How the hell do I know? For crying out loud. Call information. Ask them about Litiplex. Jesus Christ," he went on, "how do you stand stuff like this, Malloy? One hundred forty lawyers running around bumping into each other. Two senior partners sorting the mail. And now you'll bill Jake Eiger five hundred bucks for looking at an envelope and tell him it's the plaintiffs' lawyers who make legal expenses so high."

Jake and Neucriss were sort of on speaking terms, since Jake's dad was one of those pols to whom Neucriss had barnacled himself decades ago. Peter, in the meantime, was off and running, going on about big law firms, the Gog and Magog of his universe. In his own oleaginous way, he was even attempting to appeal for my support. He knew where I stood at G&G—the entire legal world, local and national, was mapped in his head. Hanging on there by my fingernails, I might be brought to side with him against my partners. Instead, I fended him off lamely with wit.

"If I didn't know better, Peter, I'd think you were offering me a job." As soon as I said it, I heard that the tone was all wrong. Neucriss's quick eyes registered something, the possibility of corruption, which around here is always in the air, like carbon dioxide. He held on just a second before rejecting that thought.

"Not you, Malloy. You're an old plowhorse." That's all he said. Dead or dying went unspecified, but either way, my bones in his view would soon be tromped upon, ground down by some other dray treading my row. He went back to work and I went on my way, fighting him off, trying not to be diminished by his estimate, but of course feeling absolutely flattened. I wasn't even worth buying off.

I was on the street, my overcoat open for the short walk to the Needle, buffeted by the thick pedestrian traffic on all sides, workers departing in the sullen dwindling light of winter. Overhead, the sky was dimming to the color of a burnt pot. The morning snow was now nothing but a dampness on the walks, freezing over amid the little hummocks of salt that rimed the concrete and would stain my shoes.

In the interval, I tried to figure what was doing. I wouldn't say I believed Peter. It was safer to bet on the Easter Bunny. But I couldn't figure why he had anything to hide. I was feeling surly, in a formerly familiar cop-mood in which everyone was a suspect. Bert. Maybe Glyndora. Even, possibly, God's emissary on earth, Martin Gold. The vague unpredictability of Martin's behavior bothered me especially: the way he'd been with Jake; the fact that Martin had called Neucriss, which he ordinarily did only when somebody was paying premium rates. I stopped on a corner where a little boy in a hooded sweatshirt was hawking papers, while a sudden wind snapped my muffler in my face. Here I stood in the city where I've lived my entire misbegotten life, the canyons I've been prowling for decades, feeling depressed and undermined, full of the convincing if momentary illusion that I didn't know where in the hell I was.

C. Somebody Else's Girl

For unexplained reasons, I always found it a shock seeing Brushy's pale meaty thighs in her athletic shorts. Her adolescent acne still flared on the parts of her body that were ordinarily concealed, high up on her arms and in the V-neck of her tennis shirt, but I found her appealingly girlish. She did not spend much time letting me look her over, though, and began to bat the ball around the racquetball court. We went through more or less the same routine each week. I moved well left and right, and had superior reach and better strokes. Brushy swung with an awkward roundhouse, elbow locked, but she scrambled all over the white-walled court like a squirrel and got to every shot; she'd run me over rather than call hinders. Each week we'd play the first two games even. I careered around, yelling oaths and curse words whenever I mishit the ball. Then Brushy, who had not hit drop shots out of deference to my knee, would dink one ball after another, until I was limping and so short of breath I could faint.

We were at the usual fateful pass between the second and third game in the little low corridor outside the court, toweling off. She wanted to know what had come of my visits with Glyndora and Neucriss.

"Zero," I said. "Nobody knows nothin. Maybe you were right. Bert was just trying to phony up something to cover his tracks." She started asking me questions and I told her a little about Archie and his betting scheme, and my misadventures yesterday, in which, in my version, I had stood up heroically to my old nemesis from the Force.

Brushy took in as much as I said and with her usual cool deliberation got fast to the bottom line.

"So whose credit card is it," she asked, "Bert's or Kam's?"

I had no idea.

"Where'd you find this card anyway?" she asked.

I was still keeping that part to myself. I didn't want anybody to put me near Bert's refrigerator. I invoked the magic words "Attorney-Client" and pushed Brushy back onto the court, where she shortly whipped my butt once more, 21–7, dropping shots to the corners and banging the ball off the ceiling like a storm of large blue hail.

"Would it kill you if I won just once?" I complained as we were leaving.

"I know you, Mack. You have a weak character. You'd want to win every week."

I denied it, but she didn't believe me. She was heading

off to the ladies' locker room, and I asked about dinner, which we did now and then when we were both in the office late.

"I can't. Maybe later this week."

"Who's the lucky fella?"

Brushy frowned. "Tad, if you must. I'm meeting him for a drink." Brushy's occasional rendezvous for lunch or cocktails or dinner with Krzysinski had been going on for some time, and nobody at G&G knew what to make of them. Tad had been on the job at TN no more than a month when he was personally named in a securities fraud case which Brushy had handled and won, filing a successful motion to dismiss. Purportedly, Krzysinski was just staying in touch, but everybody at the firm alternately suspected or hoped that he was getting the usual from Brushy, since any direct line to the top was valued, given the precariousness of our relationship with TN. The part that didn't fit was that Krzysinski had the rep of a serious family man, nine kids, and had been known to fly back from Fiji so he could be around for family Mass late afternoon on Saturday. On the other hand, as my mother would say, the devil finds a way into the safest home.

I greeted Brushy's news with a lascivious wag of my brow.

"Ooo la la," I said. Between us, Brushy generally took this kind of joshing pretty well, but today she called the foul.

"I resent that," she answered, and her eyes heated up. Brushy wanted to be thought of as a counselor to titans, a hotshot who'd be a logical drinking partner for a Fortune

500 King. Instead, here was her ace partner and pal assuming that she'd have one hand on her martini and the other on Tad's privates. I stood there in the hallway, a foot taller, sweating, and felt myself vulnerable for the lack of any smart remark.

"You happen to be wrong," she went on, "and you're getting to be worse than anybody else. Why do you suddenly think *my* sex life is *your* business?"

"Because I don't have one of my own?"

She remained in a huff.

"Maybe you should work on that," she told me, and marched off down the narrow white hall that led to the locker rooms. The door was too heavy to slam but she gave it a try.

It was rare, but there were instants like this when between Brushy and me there was the throb of something, maybe lost opportunity. Especially in her early days, Brushy let a guy know she was available not long after you said how do you do, and for ten years or so we'd had this running thing about the great fun I was missing. I smiled but kept my distance. Not, by the way, that I was a man of perfect virtue. But it was bad enough being known around the office as a lush, and something about Brushy seemed to make her a daunting proposition, maybe just the well-worn story of a college student who worked in the mailroom and let it be known after one magic summer night that Brushy had so inspired him that they'd had, count them, nine separate encounters between 7:30 p.m. and the following dawn, an achievement that led the young man to be known thereafter solely as *Nueve* and cast such a pall over every man in the place that there was a palpable atmosphere of celebration the day the kid finally left to go back to school.

Anyway, during that period when my life seemed to be demonstrating some law of thermodynamics or entropy, all to the effect that if things could fuck up they would, with my sister dying and Nora wandering and Lyle in his teenaged funk and me sworn off the bottle, I finally spent an afternoon with her at the Dulcimer House, a class place around the corner. Sex with Brushy was, well, brief. I did not completely fail, but various thoughts of home and spouse, a staid life, and even social disease had suddenly crowded within me, leaving me weak as water and quick as mercury.

'So what?' Brushy had said, and I welcomed her kindness. For Brushy it was all conquest anyway. No doubt she felt better finding that she hadn't missed much.

As for me, I probably expected it. The only good sex I've had was when I was drunk, which must tell you something about me, I wish I knew what. Still, something was easier when I could blame each mishap on the bottle. I was so gassed, et cetera—that's why I spent two saw-bucks on the hooker who sucked me off in the back of that taxi; that's why I plugged that girl, even after she puked. A lot of guys lose the capacity that far along, but now and then after half a bottle of Seagram's 7, I lit up like a firecracker.

Without it, there is not a lot left to be said. Every now and then some fancy still strikes me, the oddest things—some gal in a cosmetics ad or some ordinary-looking female whose skirt hikes up in a provocative way as she is crossing the street—and I find myself engaged in Man's Oldest Amusement. I know this is revolting to imagine, a grown man, a big one, with a hand on his own throttle, but we're not really talking about much. Afterwards I am full of Catholic shame, but also curiosity. What's wrong with me? I wonder. Am I just half-dead in that region, or is it that no woman can be as good as what I dream up myself? And what is it I dream? you ask. People. Couples, frankly. I admit it, I like to look. X-rated movies, but in my own theater. The man is never me.

So that's what I was thinking as I came out of the locker room into the reception area of Dr. Goodbody's Health Club. There were a couple of chairs with a little table between them where most of the papers for the week were piled up, as well as the usual health and fitness magazines, and feeling somewhat morose anyway, I plopped myself down there, having half a mind to look for something in the newspaper, although at the moment I could not quite recollect what. The sports page was full of hype about the Super Bowl on Sunday and the high point of local interest, Friday night's Hands game with UW–Milwaukee. The season records of the Hands and the Meisters were in a box on the inside pages, and I noted, in passing, that Bert or Kam, whoever, had won the $5,000 wager he'd called Kam's Special on Infomode, the U. over Cleveland State. I diddled around with that thought. The card statement had a $9,000 credit for December. He'd been winning, Kam or Bert, which meant nobody had a reason to steal to pay Archie.

I remembered then, suddenly, why I'd wanted to see the paper—to check what Glyndora'd torn out. I went through the day's *Tribune* twice with no luck, and was ready to quit when I found it at last in the late edition, an item from the City section: WEST BANK EXEC MISSING. The wife of prominent insurance industry executive Vernon "Archie" Koechell confirmed that her husband had not appeared at home or work for the last two weeks. Koechell's disappearance had been reported to the Kindle Unified Police, who were investigating a possible connection to an undisclosed financial crime. On the jump page, there was a picture of Archie, a noble-looking business type with a round mug and a widow's peak. The photo was old, twenty years, but I recognized him, no doubt of that. We'd met face to face, so to speak, and I'd be a long time anyway forgetting the man I'd seen in Bert's refrigerator.

X. YOUR INVESTIGATOR RESUMES SOME OLD BAD HABITS

A. Your Investigator Is Misled

Glyndora lives in a triplex in one of these resurrected areas in the shadow of the projects. I swear to God, when I come back from the dead I want to be a real estate developer. Sell people a three-room apartment for two hundred grand and when they go out in the morning their car has no hubcaps. Two blocks away you could see the kids, in tattered coats in this season, playing basketball and looking through the chain-link with their devastated dead expressions. But here the construction was reminiscent of a Hollywood set, perfection in every visible detail, and the feel that you could put your hand right through it. The effect was Williamsburg. Little wooden doodads at the roofline and wrought-iron rails; starving saplings, bare sticks in January, were planted in little squares removed from the pavement. One could not help thinking of a theme park.

"Glyndora, it's Mack." I had found her address in the firm personnel directory, and I wasn't expected. I made my apologies for bothering her at home through the buzzer intercom. "I need to talk to you and I don't have a lot of time."

"Okay." Silence. "Talk, man."

"Come on, Glyndora. You don't need to be so entertaining. Let me in."

Nothing.

"Glyndora, cut the crap."

"Call you tomorrow."

"Like you did today? Listen, I'm gonna stand down here freezing my chestnuts and pressing on this buzzer and shouting your name. I'm gonna make a big goddamn scene, so that your neighbors wonder about the company you keep. And in the morning, I'm going straight to the Committee to tell them how you've been horsing me around." Something here might pass for a credible threat. Especially the Committee. I stomped around on the stoop another minute in the dark, breathing smoke beneath the brass colonial lamp, with my chin nuzzled into my muffler. Finally I heard the buzz.

She waited for me at the top of the stairs, backlit by her own home and barring the way to her door. She was wearing a simple housedress and no makeup, and her stiff hair had been released from barrettes and looked somewhat shapeless. I more or less moved her across her own threshold, waving my hands to show I wouldn't take no for an answer. Inside, I seated myself at once on her sofa and opened my overcoat. I did my best to look heavyset and immobile.

"Aren't you going to offer me coffee? It's cold out there."

Standing near the door, she showed no sign of moving.

"Look, Glyndora, there are a couple of things. One, maybe you can think again about whether you ever saw a little memo from Bert about the Litiplex checks. Two, the name Archie Koechell mean anything to you?"

She was going to stare me down, the way sideshow performers overcome certain fearsome creatures, cobras or bears. She put her hands to her waist and slowly shook her head.

"Glyndora, you answered Bert's phone for years and this guy Archie is a big pal of his. Think again. He's an actuary. And he's missing. Just like Bert. There was an article in the paper today. Maybe you saw it?"

Nothing. The same fiercely baleful expression. I blew on my fingertips to warm them and again asked for coffee.

She went this time, but not before she cussed me, tossing her head about in disbelief. I wandered around the apartment. Very nice. The sort of discreet middle-class taste I would have preferred in my own home. Light carpeting of a Berber weave and patterned fabrics with big flowers on the cushions of the rattan-sided furnishings. There was a kind of decorator painting, a lot of innocuous wave motion, over the sofa. Otherwise the walls were bare. Glyndora was not a person attached to images.

She was gone awhile. I looked into the kitchen, a little galley affair hinged to the cramped space the architect had probably called the "eating area," but she was not in there. No coffee brewing either. I could hear her movements through another door or two and thought I detected her voice. Maybe in the john, or putting on her battle regalia. It would not be unlike Glyndora to be holding an animated conversation with herself, but I also had some thought of picking up the phone to see if she had reached out for somebody else. I held my breath, but I could not make out a word.

Across from me, in a corner of the dining room, was a little round étagère, a multilevel thing of chrome and glass. There were various glass animals—Steuben, if you asked Nora Goggins's ex-husband—and pictures of Glyndora's kid, a high-school graduation photo, complete with mortarboard, and a smaller snapshot, more recent, in a frame. An okay-looking guy, lean and muscular, the mother's strong build and good looks gender-translated, but with an impish unfocused expression that had never emanated from Glyndora since the day of her birth.

"You still here?" Over my shoulder, she looked remotely amused, probably with herself.

"Still warming up."

She had combed her hair a little and reddened her lips, but her manner remained unyielding.

"Look, Glyndora," I said, "you're a smart guy and so am I, so let's skip the horseplay."

"Mack, you ain been no po-lice for twenty years, and I ain never been no mope. So just take it somewhere else, man. I'm tired." Glyndora is often at her blackest around white people, especially when she's on the offensive. In the office today, she'd spoken the same English as me.

"Come on, Glyndora. I already told you how it is. I'm the Question Man and you're the Answer Lady. Otherwise we can all sit down and discuss this tomorrow—you and me and the Committee." I hoped the renewed threat, which had been enough to get me through the doorway, would make her relent. But the notion seemed to perk her up with a kind of tough amusement.

"I gotta do what you say, huh?"

"Sort of."

"That figures, man. You like that, right?"

I shrugged.

"Yeah, you like that. Just you and me and I ain't got no choice."

"Come on, Glyndora."

"Yeah, that's why you got to come round after dark to my house. Cause I ain't got no choice."

Glyndora has what you might call issues. For her it always comes down to this, master and slave. She was moving in my direction now, sashaying slightly, a hip-rolling walk that was both deliberately provocative and defiant; I got back to my feet to greet her, but she still came a little bit closer than she was supposed to. She knew what she was up to and so did I, we'd both been to the movies. She was just going to back me down with her boldness. She'd cinched the waist on her dress and projected herself and her formidable anatomy at me, rocking a little on her toes, hands on her hips. She might as well have said, I dare you.

"So tell me, Mr. Mack. What-all is it I *gotta* do for you?" Up close, her dark skin was a complex of colors, pointillistic. She was giving me a taunting smile, revealing a gap in her teeth which I'd never noticed over the fifteen years I've known her.

I said again, quietly, "Come on."

She stayed right there, head high, eye mighty. As a grown-up I have believed that priests, schoolteachers, and criminal investigators should have no carnal knowledge of the people over whom they exert authority. Temptations, naturally, abound. What it is with some gals there's no telling, but it sometimes seems they'd stand in line to screw a copper. You can take a guy built like a Franklin stove, half bald and dirty looking, a fella who'd sit at the end of the bar all night and attract no company, and once you put a uniform on him and a pistol on his hip, the guy's a freakin ladykiller. It's just a thing. Some fellas on the Force, it was a dream come true, they'd work for free, and others, so what.

For me, this was one of the few areas in my life where I had actually exhibited self-control. Naturally I was not perfect. There was a party girl from Minnesota one time who made me dizzy, witness in a white-slavery case in which we were making our usual effort to catch some of The Boys by hiding behind a tree. Twenty or twenty-one years old, beautiful blond thing who looked so innocent you'd have thought she'd sailed in off some fjord. Terrible life. Ran from home because her old man was cornholing her each night, fell in with the wrong crowd in the city, and Jesus, forgive me for sounding as if I had a Catholic education, but then did everything in the world to degrade herself. There was some big TV star, a comedian whose name you'd know, who paid her two g's each time he was in town for her to come to his hotel and let him take a dump on her and then—prepare yourself—watch her eat it. This I am not making up. Anyway, Big Bad Mack thinks she's pretty neat. And Christ, this is her life, she catches on like that, the way a plant will turn to face the sunbeams. And so one day it comes to pass, I'm supposed to take her from the stationhouse to her apartment, pick up some address book where she has the name or two of some big-time gumbas, and we both know what's cooking, nature is about to take its course, and she opens the door to this rummy place—I remember the door was like a pockmarked face; somebody had taken an ax or crowbar to it—and inside is this little Chihuahua, this pygmy animal, spotted with black sores from the mange or some similar doggy disease, charging our feet. She tells it once to scoot and then chases this poor mutt around, kicking and cursing it with a look of such fixed and intense hatred that it sort of let the air out of my heart. It woke me up, I admit it, seeing the ugly mark all that cruelty had made on her, beaten up, assailed, like her door.

And I was awake now with Glyndora. Chugging right up to fifty and potbellied, I was not, I knew, the image rousing Glyndora in a parched erotic heat at night. But something wild and screwy was turned on in me, especially to see how far this was going to go, and feeling the daring that is always leaping up in me, else I die of fear, I took each index finger and with a thrilling directness settled them one at a time on the point of each breast, then, gently as somebody reading Braille, let my fingertips come to rest on the thin fabric of her dress. I could feel underneath the lace pattern of her brassiere.

The moment that then passed between us was what we used to call on the street p.f.s.—pretty fucking strange. Nobody was supposed to mean it. I wasn't supposed to squeeze her tits and Glyndora wasn't supposed to like it.

We were playing chicken or the Dozens. It was as if we were both on camera. I could see it in my mind's eye— the bodies here and the spirits hovering fifteen feet above, wrestling like angels over someone's soul. In theory, we were merely disputing power and terrain. But with all these faces, the secret self was set free and was frisking about. Those rich brown eyes of hers remained dead set on mine, thoroughly amused, determinedly defiant: I see you. So what? I see *you*. But, folks, we were both pretty goddamned excited.

This contact, encounter, call it what you like, lasted only seconds. Glyndora pushed her arms up and slowly parted my hands. Her eyes never left mine. She spoke distinctly.

"You couldn't handle it, man," she said and turned for the kitchen.

"Are we taking bets?"

She didn't answer. I heard her say instead that she needed a drink.

I was ringing—the body after 4,000 volts. It was the whole idea of it, me playing with her playing with me. Mr. Stiffy downstairs was definitely awake too. I heard her banging around in a cabinet and swearing.

"What?" I asked. She had no whiskey, and I offered to go out to get her a pint. I wanted her to relax. This could be a long conversation, a longer evening. "You make coffee." I pointed at her but didn't linger as I leaned into the little kitchen; I was afraid to see what showed. Something in me was already clinging to the weird intimacy of that instant between us. With any invitation, I might have kissed her goodbye.

So I went charging out toward the Brown Wall's, a local chain I'd seen on the way in, a grown man running down the street in the dead of winter, with his flag half unfurled. The store was in the neutral zone, between the projects and the upscale, its bricks spray-painted with gang signs, its windows holding gay displays but guarded by fold-back grates. I grabbed a bottle of Seagram's off the shelf, feeling I'd seen something pornographic when I looked at all those glass soldiers arrayed side by side. As an afterthought, I detoured to pharmaceuticals for a three-pack of Trojans, just in case, I told myself, because a Scout is always prepared. Then I barreled back down the block oblivious to the three gangbangers who stood on the corner in their colors checking me out. I took all the front steps in one bound and hit the buzzer, waiting to be restored to paradise.

I rang intermittently for I'd say maybe a minute and a half before I began to wonder why she was not answering. My first thought? That I'm a big dumbbell? That I'd let the little head think for the big one? No, I actually worried about her. Had she fallen ill? Had one of the neighborhood muggers come through the window and done her while I was gone? Then I recalled the little fatal click behind me that I'd made nothing of as I flew down the staircase. Suddenly, as I stood on the stoop, shriveled by the cold, I realized that was the sound of the dead bolt being set, of a lady locking up for the night.

I will say this for myself—I did not go gently. I punched that buzzer like it was her fucking nose. After about five minutes, her voice came up clearly, just once, and not long enough to allow any reply.

"Go way," she said, alive and well and not waiting for me.

Let me be honest: it was not a good moment. I had beaten Lyle to the car tonight, my shitbox Chevy; Nora got the good car, a jade-green Beemer which I always drove with a pleasure that made me feel as if I had taken a pill. I retired to this worn-out wreck, where I was always ill at ease with the stains Lyle and his friends left on the seats, and tried to assess the situation. Okay, I told myself, some gal won't let you in, then puts the make on you, then locks the door. The point is . . . ? Fill in the blank. Pictures? Maybe some dope was in the closet with a camera.

I had to give her credit, though. Glyndora knew where the belly was on this porcupine. Let him strike out with the ladies once again, then put liquor in his hand. In my palm, the bottle had a strange magical heft. I always had drunk rye, same as my old man. God, I loved it. I felt a little thrill when my thumb passed across the tax labels on the bottle's neck. I was a civil drunk who did not get started until nightfall, but by two in the afternoon I could feel a certain dry pucker back in the salivary glands and the first shot was always enough to make me swoon. I used to think all the time about Dom Perignon, the monk who'd first distilled Champagne. He fell down a flight of stairs and announced to the brethren who rushed to his rescue, 'I am drinking stars.'

It all seems so goddamned sad, I thought suddenly, looking out in the bleak night toward Glyndora's apartment. My breath was fogging the windows and I turned the engine over for heat. The whole appeal of this venture had been to take some sudden startling control over my existence. But I felt again some faraway master puppeteer whose strings were sewn into my sleeves. The fundamental facts were plain again: I was just a lowdown bum.

I wondered what I always do—how'd I end up this way? Was it just nature? In my neighborhood, if your old man was a copper or a fireman, you took it for granted he was a hero, these mystical men of courage donning their helmets and heavy coats to brave one of nature's most inscrutable events, how substance turns to heat and color, how the brilliant protean flames dance as they destroy. When I was three or four, I'd heard so much of this stuff, sliding down the pole and whatnot, that I was sure that when he wore his boots and fire slicker my old man could fly. He couldn't. I learned that over time. My father was no hero. He was a thief. ''T'eef,'' as he used to pronounce the word, never in application to himself. But like Jason or Marco Polo, he brought back treasure from each adventure.

I often heard my father explain his logic when he engaged my mother in bouts of drunken self-defense. If a house is burning to the ground, woman, why not take the jewelry before it melts, for heaven's sake, you're there risking life and limb—you think you went outside and asked the residents, as they stood there with the flames shooting through their lives, that they'd say no? When I studied economics in college, I had no trouble understanding what they meant by a user's fee.

But I was not inclined to forgive him. I used to wonder as a kid if everybody knew the fireman stole. Everyone in my neighborhood seemed to understand—they'd come nosing around, looking to buy cheap the little items that were nicked and fit well in the rubber coats. 'Why'd you think they made them pockets in the coats so big?' my father used to say, never to me but to whoever had sidled by to examine the table silver, the clocks, the jewels, the tools, the thousand little things that entered our household. He'd laugh as he made these subverted displays. 'Where'd it come from?' the visitor would ask, and my father would chuckle and say that bit about the coat. Kind of dumb, of course, but he wanted people to think that he was bold— all frightened people do, they want to be just like the people who scare them. I had a cousin, Marie Clare, who came by once and asked my father to keep an eye out for a christening dress for her baby and he got her a beauty— why'd you think they made them pockets in the coats so big?

For me, as a kid, the shame of it sometimes seemed to blister my heart. When I started confession, I confessed for him. 'My father steals.' The priests were never uninterested. 'Oh yes?' I wanted to leave my name and address in the hope they'd make him stop. A boy's father is his fate. But this kind of stealing was a matter of society, forgivable and common. They told me to respect my father and pray for his soul, and better mind my own conduct.

'So much of life is will.' I had spun the golden cap off the pint before I knew what I'd done, and repeated that old phrase to myself. I had heard it from Leotis Griswell, not long before he died. I looked into the open bottle as if it were a blind eye, and was reminded for whatever reason of looking down at something else, another seat of pleasure. The sharp perfume of the alcohol filled me with a pang, as acute and painful as the distant sighting of a lovely woman whose name I'll never know.

So much of life is will. Leotis was speaking to me about Toots, his old student. Leotis had the skill I'd noted in many of the best lawyers, ardent advocates who at the same time held their clients at a distance. When he talked about them he could often be cold-blooded and he did not want me to be beguiled by Toots. 'He'll make excuses to you about his harsh life, but I've never cared much for sociology. It's so negative. I don't need to know what holds down the masses. Any fellow with an eye in his head can see that: it's life. But where does that rare one come from, what is the difference? I still spend hours wondering. Where the strength comes from *not* to surrender. The will. So much of life is will.' A certain subtle incandescence refracted through the old man as he said this, the feeble body still enfolding his large spirit, and the memory of it and the standard he set as a person punished me now.

Still, Leotis had it right, about life and will. It's an appropriate belief for a man born in the last years of the nineteenth century, yet it's out of phase for anybody else. Now we believe that a nation is entitled to self-determination but a soul is a slave to material fate: I steal because I'm poor; I feel up my daughter cause my ma did that to me; I drink because my ma was sometimes cruel and called me names and because my father left that trait, like some unhappy lodestar, in my genes. On the whole, I still prefer Leotis's outlook, the same one they taught me in church. I'd rather believe in will than fate. I drink or don't drink. I'll try to find Bert or I won't. I'll take the money and run or else return it. Better to find options than that bondage of cause and effect. It all goes back to Augustine. We choose the Good. Or the Evil. And pay the price.

And this, this may be the serpent's sweetest apple. I did not even seem to swallow.

I am drinking stars.

Thursday, January 26

B. Your Investigator Loses Something Besides His Self-respect

I have awakened so many mornings vowing never to do this again that there was almost pleasure in the pain. I felt like something fished out of the trash. I held absolutely still. The sunlight was going to be like a bullet to the brain. Along the internal line from head to gut there was a bilious feeling, some regurgitive impulse already stirring. "Slow," I told myself, and when I did I sensed for the first time that I wasn't alone.

When I opened my eyes, a kid was looking square at me, Latin he seemed to be, crouched about an arm's length away on the driver's side beneath the dash. He had one hand on the car's tape player, which he'd lifted half out, revealing the bleak innards of the auto, colored cables and dark spaces. Cutting the wires would be the next step. The door was cracked behind him and the dome light was on. There was a little sniffle of cold air riffling across my nose.

"Just cool," he told me.

I didn't see a gun, a knife. A kid, too. Thirteen, fourteen. Still with pimples all over the side of his face. One of your sweet little urban vampires, out in the early-morning hours rolling drunks. Fifty coming, I could still pound this little fuck. Hurt him anyway. We both knew it. I checked his eyes again. It would have been such a frigging triumph if there was just a dash, a comma, an apostrophe of fear, some minute sign of hesitation.

"Get out," I said. I hadn't moved. I was sort of folded up like a discarded shopping bag, piled sideways onto the passenger's seat. With the adrenaline I was waking fast and turning dizzy, whirly city. My tummy was on the move.

"Don't fuck around, men." He turned the screwdriver to face me.

"I'll fuck with you, shorty-pants. I'll fuck with you plenty. And after I do, you won't be fuckin anybody." I gave my head a sort of decisive nod. Which was a bad mistake. It was like tipping back in a chair too far. I rolled my eyes a bit. I picked myself up on my elbow. With that, it happened.

I puked all over him.

I mean everywhere. It was dripping from his eyelashes. His nappy head had got little bits of awful stuff all over. His clothes were soaked. He was drowning in it, spluttering and shaking, cursing me, an incoherent rap. "Oh men," he said. "Oh men." His hands danced around and I knew he was afraid to touch himself. And he was out of there fast. I was so busy waiting for him to kill me I actually didn't see him go until he was running down the street.

Well, Malloy, I thought, you are going to like this one.
I patted my back all over a few times, before I straightened
myself up, then realized that this story, like the tale of
what really happened between Pigeyes and me, was going
to go untold. After all, I had been bad. Weak. I'd had a
drink. A bottle. I had fucked around with fate.

My guy at AA, my angel, guardian, hand in the dark,
was a fella named Giandomenico, LNU, as we said on the
Force, last name unknown, none used. Even though I
haven't shown at a meeting in sixteen months, I knew he
would talk to me and tell me that I still had what it took
to do it. Today was no different than the day before yesterday. It was a day I wasn't gonna drink. I was going to get
through today and work on tomorrow then. I knew the rap.
I'd memorized all twelve steps. Somehow over the long
haul I found AA sadder than being a drunk, listening to
these folks, 'My name is Sheila and I'm an alcoholic.'
Then would come the story, how she stole and whored and
beat her kids. Jesus, sometimes I wondered if people were
making things up just so the rest of us wouldn't feel so
bad about our own lives. It was a little too much of a cult
for me, the Church of Self-denunciation, I used to call it,
this business of saying I'm a shit and I turn myself over to
a higher power, LNU, who'll keep me safe from John
Barleycorn, the divil. I welcomed the support and got all
warm and runny about a number of the people who showed
up each week and held my hand, and I hope that they're
still going and still safe. But I'm too goddamned eccentric,
and reluctant to contemplate the mystery of why, with my
sister's death, I no longer felt the uncontrollable need to
drink. Had I finally filled even my own bottomless cup of

pain? Or was this, as I often feared in my grimmest moments, some form of celebration?

Glyndora's little complex was across the street, gray on gray, the colors almost indecipherable in the subdued elements of winter, still looking like a stage set except for the sign in front, announcing that units were available, from 179 grand. What was her point last night? Was that whole thing, that interlude, just for laughs? I didn't think Glyndora enjoyed that kind of subtlety. She told you off face-to-face. But for some reason she had wanted me out of there. Was she afraid I would catch on to something? A boyfriend, maybe? Somebody's clothes were in the closet, shoes by the door. Archie's? Or Bert's?

I straightened myself up. I had a pretty good yuk thinking about Lyle getting in here with his buddies south of midnight and taking a whiff. I'd bet a lot of money he wouldn't know who to blame. He'd sit here trying to recall who'd hurled night before last. The little bastard had left worse for me. Still, I opened all the windows and threw the floor mat on the street. I shoved the radio back into the fragile plastic membrane of the dashboard. I thought about that little thief running all over the North End in the cold, searching for a hose. He'd smell like something when he got to school. Yep, I was feeling mean and humorous. I gathered myself together and slid across the seat behind the wheel, and only then noticed the absence against my hip. I began to swear.

The goddamn kid had got my wallet.

XI. EVERYTHING IS JAKE

A. Your Investigator Gets Interrupted

If Bert Kamin was dead, then who had the money?

This question struck me suddenly as I stood before a mirror at Dr. Goodbody's, where I'd come to clean up before heading on to the office. A shower and shave had not done much for my condition. I still had the shadowy look of some creep on a wanted poster and my headache made me recollect those cavemen who used to open vents in their skulls. I phoned Lucinda to say where I was, asking her to make the calls to cancel and replace my credit cards. Then I found a lonesome corner in the locker room to figure things out. Who had the money? Martin had said that the banker he talked to in Pico had hinted that the account where the checks went was Bert's. But that was hardly authoritative.

A refuge, even a phony one, is where you find it, and

I was irritated when the attendant told me I had a call. One of the things I hate worst about the world of business at the end of the century is this instant-access crap: faxes and mobile phones and all those eager-beaver, happy delivery people from fucking Federal Excess. Competition in the big-bucks world has made privacy a thing of the past. I expected Martin, Mr. Impatience, who likes to call you with his latest brilliant idea on a case from some airplane at eleven o'clock at night as he's bounding off to Bangladesh. But it wasn't him.

"Mack?" Jake Eiger spoke. "I'd like to see you ASAP."

"Sure. Let me get hold of Martin or Wash."

"Better the two of us," said Jake. "Why don't you come up here? I want to give you heads-up on something. About our situation." He cleared his throat in a vaguely meaningful way, so I suspected at once what was coming. The powers-that-be at TN had reviewed this fiasco—Bert and the money—and concluded there was a certain large law firm they could do without. Cancel the search party and pack your bags. I was going to get to give my partners the news as a "leak."

It had been some time since Jake and I had sat down man-to-man. They became uncomfortable meetings after my divorce from his cousin—and Jake's decision to stop directing TN cases to me. We never speak about either subject. The unmentionable, in fact, is more or less the bedrock of our relationship.

As usual, a long story. Jake was not an especially good student; I've always suspected he got into law school on his father's pull. He's bright enough—downright wily at times—but he has trouble putting thoughts on paper. A whiz at multiple choice but gridlock when he was writing essays. His own term was "cryptophobic," but I think in today's lingo we'd say learning-disabled.

I had been at BAD about a year when Jake invited me to lunch. I thought it was some kind of family obligation—one of Nora's aunts hopping his keester about buy Mack a meal and give him some advice, maybe he'll amount to something. But I could tell he was uneasy. We were at some snazzy rooftop place and Jake squinted in the sun. The wind flapped the fringe of the umbrella overhead.

'Nice view,' he said.

We both were drinking. He was unhappy too. Jake's handsomeness has always had room only for boyish easiness. The worry was like a painted sign.

'So,' I asked, 'what?' There had to be something. We did not have a real social relationship.

'Bar exam,' he said.

I didn't understand at first. I thought it was one of those clever, stylish remarks he made that was beyond me, richkid talk. He was just starting his third year at G&G, Wash's favorite flunky, three years out of law school, with one year spent clerking for a judge, and the bar ordinarily would have been long behind him. I ordered lunch. You could see Trappers Park from there and we talked awhile about the team.

'I should get out there,' Jake said. 'Haven't had much chance.'

'Busy? Lots of deals.'

'Bar exam,' he said again. 'I just took it for the third time.' And he looked from the distance to me, the level sincere agonized way he probably took in the ladies he wanted to lay. I did not need a guidebook to know I was being compromised.

'Three strikes and you're out,' he said. Three failures and you had to wait five years to take the test again. I knew the rules. I was one of the guys who made them. 'The firm has to fire me,' he said. 'My old man'll die. Die.' His career as a lawyer would, practically speaking, be over, but no doubt for Jake his father would be the worst part.

While I was growing up, Jake's dad was a colleague of Toots's in the City Council and a considerable figure. Invested with the medieval powers typically exerted by a councilman in DuSable, Eiger *père* lived in our close-knit Catholic village like a prince among the folk. June 18, 1964, the day I turned twenty-one, my father took me to Councilman Eiger to ask him to find me a place on the police force. I'd had a couple of years of college by then and was sort of supporting myself selling vacuum cleaners door-to-door; I had bombed out around the art department and was a kind of bookstore beatnik, your average troubled youth, an Irish lad still at home with his ma, absolutely mystified about which way to go in life. The Force at least would get me off ground zero and keep me out of the service too, not something I said out loud to anybody, and no left-wing politics involved either, just a pit stop on the life track I didn't want to make, never one to enjoy taking orders from anybody. Three years later I wrecked my knee and had a free shot at law school, no draft, no Nam to trouble me, and went, mostly to be in school again, another of those funny accidental ways things just happen in a life.

Sitting there in the ward office, which looked like a basement rec room decorated with maps and political posters from past campaigns and four of those clunky old-style telephones, big and black and heavy enough to be murder weapons, absorbing most of the space on his desk, Councilman Eiger assured me that my police application would get every consideration. You had to love him, a man so richly endowed with power and so generous about its use. He was the kind of pol you could understand, whose lines of loyalty were long inscribed and well known: first himself, then his family, then his friends. He was not against law or principle. They were just not operative elements. I was a cadet in a previously selected entering class at the Academy within three weeks. Now his son was sitting in front of me, and even though Jake denied his father was aware of anything, the message was the same. I owed. I owed the family. You knew his old man would see it just that way.

I made my one and only stab at rectitude.

'Jake, I think we ought to talk about something else.'

'Sure.' He looked into his drink. 'I took the test last week. There was a question—I fouled up so badly—a civil-procedure question, you know, revising a divorce decree, and I wrote this ream about matrimonial law.' He shook his head. Poor old handsome Jake was about to cry. And then he did. A grown man almost, sobbing like a kid into his gin and tonic. 'Hey, you know, I'm sorry.' He straightened himself up. We ate in absolute silence for about ten minutes, then he said he was sorry again and walked away from the table.

One of the peculiar things you learn in life is that what makes Great Institutions great is the stuff people attach to them, not their actual operation, which is often purely prosaic. The scoring of the bar exam was like that. We sent the bluebooks out to ten graders around the state, one for each question. The booklets came back UPS, thousands of stacks, piled up no more ceremoniously than rubbish. The secretaries sorted them for days, then added each individual's totals, and the staff attorneys checked the arithmetic. Those were the results. Seventy passed, 69 failed. Jake was at 66 when I found his stack on another assistant administrator's desk the night I decided to go hunting for it. The guy who graded Jake's civil-procedure answer had given Jake three out of a possible ten. A 3 and an 8 of course can look a lot alike, even if you don't have a gift for forgery. I wasn't taking any risk; no one would ever know. Not counting me, of course.

Still, you wonder, why'd I do it? Not because of Jake, God knows, not even because my old man and my ma'd have been ashamed to think I wouldn't look after a friend. No, I suppose I was thinking of Woodhull and his minion, who confused ethics with ego, those judgmental prigs, my colleagues, one more team I didn't want to play on, one more group I would not allow to claim my soul. Same reason I did it to Pigeyes, then lied, unwilling to play for either side.

Jake took me out to lunch the week after the results were mailed. He was pleased as a puppy. He slobbered all over me and I wouldn't say a thing. I congratulated him when he told me that he passed. I shook his hand.

'You think I'm going to forget this, but I won't,' he said.

'*No comprendo*. Thank yourself. You took the test.'

'Don't give me that bull.'

'Hey, Jake. Practice makes perfect. You passed. Okay?
Give us both a break.'

'You're all right. You know, after my performance last
time—I got sick. I thought to myself, A cop, for Chrissake. You talk like that to a guy who was a *cop*.'

His look said everything. Us pals. Us guys. That smug
fraternity thing Jake over the years has never lost. His life
now is country-club golf courses and screwing around
behind the back of his third wife, but there, twenty-one
years before, I could see I'd restored the central faith of
his life: we were special people who could outwit harm if
we stuck with each other. I wanted to spit in his eye.

'Forget it, Jake,' I said. 'Everything.'

'Never,' he answered.

And I knew it was a curse.

B. Your Investigator Visits
Herbert Hoover's America

Waiting for Jake, I sat in reception on 44, TN's Executive
Level, feeling inferior. There is a jazzed-up air of self-
importance here that routinely deflates me. Someday someone will explain to me why this system of ours that is
supposed to glorify diversity and individual choice becomes instead the vehicle by which everybody ends up
choosing the same thing. With its airlines, banks, and
hotels, TN did business last year with two out of every
three Americans who make more than 50 g's. Many of
those folks think of TN as nothing better than a kind of
flying bus, but in a mass society it turns out that even a

trivial connection to twenty-five million lives, especially prominent ones, imbues an institution with an extraordinary aura of grandiosity and power.

Jake's secretary steered me back and His Handsomeness rose to make me welcome. The office is so vast that when I walked in he actually waved. Once we were alone, Jake sat on the corner of his desk, one foot on the rich carpet. You could not help thinking it was a pose he'd seen in some ad in a magazine. He had his jacket on. His hair was perfectly combed. To fill air time, Jake usually likes to talk to me about the old neighborhood, guys from high school, our place among the generations. But today he came to the point directly. As I'd feared, he had Bert on his mind.

"Look, old chum, I have to admit I'm playing catch-up. What in God's name is going on down there?"

"I wish I could tell you, Jake."

"And you," he went on. "You're not helping much. I understand you went to see Neucriss."

Word travels fast.

"He was on the phone to me before your elevator had reached the ground floor," said Jake, "wanting to know what was wrong. Can I ask what in the world you were doing?"

"Hey," I said amiably. I never offend Jake. I had all those years watching my old man kiss the fire captain's ring. "You know, I'm playing hunches. We can't figure what the hell Litiplex is. Maybe the plaintiffs know. I didn't realize that Martin had already tried the same thing with Peter."

Jake took that in levelly. He was assessing me.

"Yes, but he had. And when you showed up, you really

began ringing bells. We can't have this kind of fumbling."
Neucriss, on the phone, had obviously had a great time:
These klutzes you employ at three hundred an hour. Get a
load of this. Two of them busy forwarding the mail. Ho,
ho, ho. Jake had felt the needle and I was paying the price.

"Look, Mack, my friend, let's review the bidding."
Jake is a master of these phrases, the corporate idiom, one
more style he is on top of. It softens the edges, but he's
still as ham-fisted as his father and I knew him well enough
to see that no matter how fashionably, he was about to be
coarse. "He"—Jake pointed to the door of the chairman's
adjoining suite; he had lowered his voice—"the Polish
gentleman next door. He likes me, he doesn't like me.
Who knows day to day? Let's assume he's not president
of the fan club. All right? Let's say he thinks I use the
wrong lawyers and I pay too much to the ones I choose.
All assumed. But he's going to put up with me. Do you
know why?"

"The board?"

"The board, that's right, the board. Because there is a
faction there, a number of members who believe I fly
without wings. And do you know why that is?"

"Why?"

"Because I—and the lawyers I chose—handled a $300
million disaster for this company, a litigation mess where
we'd reserved $100 million to pay for our share and we—
I, your firm, Martin—we handled that and actually *made
money* for this company. Almost $20 million. Every dollar
left in that trust account is a badge of pride. For all of us.
And a point on the scoreboard. All right?"

I nodded. "Sure," I said. I had to sit still for this, tutored like a child, simpering and pretending he was inventing cold fusion.

"Now let's look at this supposed business with Bert. Very disturbing. Frankly, personally, I don't even believe it. If I did, I'd be more alarmed. But in the end, if we're patient about getting to the bottom of it, perhaps review the accounting, I think it may develop that something else is going on. But it appears as it appears— Fine, investigate. Look into it. That's the responsible thing to do. But, old man, let's keep our eye on the ball. If you go out and rile up the plaintiffs' lawyers so that they want a bean counting before we distribute next month—if you do that and fellows like Neucriss catch wind of the fact that we're running a surplus, they're going to do their utmost to lay hands on every dime. Not to mention our co-defendants. So no matter what you think has happened with Bert, all that would be far, far worse for us all. Okay? So let's move ahead carefully. I told you the other day. *Be discreet*."

More or less on cue, Tad Krzysinski, Board Chairman and CEO, poked his head through the side door. In a perfect world, this guy would be somebody you could comfortably hate, a prig like Pagnucci, a wild fucking success drunk on ego. He is nothing like that. No more than five foot four, he is a sunny little fellow, and in every room he enters it feels as if somebody has suddenly installed a compact nuclear reactor, a force so vital you half expect to be blown back through the walls.

"Hack," he greeted me, and advanced to pump my hand. He is a musclebound former gymnast with an engaging eye. I took a moment to wonder, as usual, about what gave between Brushy and him, but he always seems so goddamn cheerful there is no way to tell.

"Tad," I said. The guy holds no brief for proprieties, never anything but who he's first to tell you he is, the son of a plumber, one of eight kids, now with nine of his own, a three-hours-of-sleep guy who by his own admission cares only about his family, his God, and increasing the wealth of the people who've put their faith in him by plunking down their dough to buy TN's common shares. You could see that just nodding and shaking hands he scared Jake to death. They were the two sides of ethnicity, the Americans, once excluded, who since the sixties have found their way in corporation land—Jake, a deracinated wimp who aspired to everything vain the upwardly mobile envisioned, and Krzysinski, who accepted like Holy Writ all that stuff the immigrants believed about hard work, fortitude, and the capacity to alter the face of the world. I stood there uneasily between them, with a sudden recognition that this was an impossible match. Jake had powerful boosters on TN's board, but Krzysinski had to hate him. Which was what Jake meant about the 397 surplus being his lifeline.

"Well, I see you here, Hack, we must be in trouble again." Tad pounded my shoulder good-naturedly and laughed at his own joke and then talked to Jake about a problem they had in Fiji. TN of course owns hotels everywhere. Tokyo. Paris. But they got to the Far East ahead of everybody else, which in these lean times means those operations have become particularly important. Many days Tad is far more concerned about Prime Minister Miyazawa than Bill Clinton. Somebody ought to sit down and think about this, because your corporate types are soon going to be a stateless superclass, people who live for deals and golf dates and care a lot more about where you got your MBA than the country you were raised in. It's the Middle Ages all over again, these little unaffiliated duchies and fiefdoms, flying their own flags and ready to take in any vassal who will pledge his life to the manor. Everybody busy patting himself on the back because the Reds went in the dumper is going to be wondering who won when Coca-Cola applies for a seat in the UN.

As Tad at last disappeared, Jake darted a nettled look at his back.

"Let's take a walk." Jake headed down the hallway and I followed, acknowledging the people I knew. For me, a visit up here called for a lot of glad-handing, trying to remind folks on the counsel's staff I was neither drunk nor dead. When we reached the elevator, a messenger, one of the members of that minimum-wage cavalry that slams through the Center City traffic on bikes, came charging out, wearing an optic-orange vest over his worn parka. Jake and I stepped in, now alone.

"I want to be sure we're singing from the same hymnal," said Jake. He jammed the button labeled "Doors Close" and turned to face me when they had.

"Bert?" I asked.

"That matter," he replied.

The elevator began to move and Jake pumped the button for the floor below.

"You know what I want—make this tidy," Jake said. "And if Kamin really doesn't turn up?"

"Yes?"

He took a step so that he was no more than a foot from me, his finger still anchored on the door-close button as the car slowed.

"No one up here has to hear any more." He looked at me solemnly before the doors peeled back slowly and he stepped again into the brighter light.

XII. TELLING SECRETS

A. Boys and Girls Together

"SOS," I said as I poked my head into Martin's office. His secretary was gone and I'd given a quick knock and leaned in from the hall. Glyndora was standing there with him.

"Oh shit," I said. It just sort of popped out and they both stared. It was an odd little moment. Glyndora shot me a look that might have contemplated my death, and my first thought was that she was here complaining about my investigative technique. That was one of Martin's many roles, Mr. Fix-It, in charge of the disgruntled, the waylaid, the weak. Our first year can't cut in practice, a partner flips out or has a problem with substance abuse, Martin takes care of you. You'd say compassion, but there's no there-but-for-the-grace; it's more his Olympian thing. I'm here, the mountain.

But Martin seemed unconcerned when he saw me. He actually smiled and casually waved me into his office with all its funny overstated objects. He said something about Glyndora showing him yesterday's numbers on cash received, the Managing Partner and the head of Accounting measuring our progress at year end. Somehow, though, I remained struck by the pose in which I'd initially found them. Nothing untoward: she was at a distance from him, a few feet from his chair. But she was on his side of the desk, and Martin was facing her and the milky light coming from the broad windows behind her, sitting with his legs outstretched, hands on his tummy, relaxed, open to her in an uncharacteristic way, less our Martin, ever on alert. Maybe, though, it was just the shock of seeing Glyndora, who was still charged up for me like a magnet.

Martin, at any rate, said they were about done, and with that hint she arranged herself and strode past me in the door without so much as turning my way. I admit I was disappointed.

"I just had a conversation with Jake," I told Martin when she was gone.

"Troubling?"

He could see it in my face, I imagined. My heart was still skittering around like a squirrel. Jake in his own way had given off quite a sinister air. I began to describe my encounter with Jake, and Martin listened, absorbed. When you actually study him, Martin has distinct ethnic looks; he's one of those hairy darklings you'd expect to see loading a truck, with a dense beard that lends his face a bluish cast. His father was a tailor who cut the clothes of various gangsters and Martin refers now and then to his upbringing when it is availing to charm a client of humble roots or to worry an opponent; he has a number of racy stories about delivering tuxedos to the famous Dover Street brothel in the South End. But unlike me, Martin takes no refuge in the past and allows it to make no claim upon him. He evinces the airy noblesse of a fellow who grew up summering in Newport. He is married to a graceful, tall British woman by the name of Nila, whom you sort of picture in a garden with a Pimm's Cup the minute you see her. Large hats and shirtwaist dresses, with petticoats. He is thoroughly the man he decided on being, and that fellow showed little reaction to what I related, except that something abruptly caused him to interrupt.

"Better save this," he said. "My colleagues and I should probably hear it together." He meant the Committee. "Carl is in town again today."

Martin proposed a meeting at four and left me to arrange it. I went back to Lucinda to ask her to make the calls, though I tried to reach Pagnucci, since I wanted a word with him myself. Then I stood over my secretary's desk for a moment, examining the list of my credit card issuers she'd reached. It struck me for the first time that the Kam Roberts card had been in my wallet too. I had no idea what to do about that.

Brushy came ambling by in her sturdy fashion and did a double-take when she saw me.

"Jesus, Mack, you look horrible." No doubt that was true. Jake had stirred my adrenaline but it still felt like my heart was pumping motor sludge. "You sick?" she asked.

"Maybe a touch of the flu." I turned away, but she followed me into my office out of concern. "Could be I'm depressed."

"Depressed?"

"From our conversation yesterday."

"Hey," she said, "you know me, spirited Mediterranean type. I say things."

"No," I said, "I thought you had a point."

She looked herself, little chopped-down hairdo, big pearl earrings, honest face, solid and peppy like she could step out of her heels and give you a good block.

"Maybe I did." She sort of smiled.

"Yeah," I said, "I even went out and had a minute last night where I thought I might practice my hokey-pokey."

I could have filled in her dental chart.

"And?" she demanded.

" 'And' what?"

"And?" she said once more, Ms. Mind Your Own Personal Business.

"And I ended up getting rolled."

She actually laughed out loud. She asked if I was okay, then sang, far off-key, a few bars of "Looking for Love in All the Wrong Places."

"You don't have to gloat."

"Why should I gloat?" she asked and laughed again.

I turned my back on her to look through the mail. More memos from the Committee about the lagging pace of collections; the Blue Sheet. I heard her close the door, and the click of the bolt gave me a weird little amorous thrill, some vagrant inspiration from our conversation and the last twenty-four hours, an idling recall of what happened when men and women were alone. Brushy, however, did not have anything like that on her mind.

"Did you see the paper?" she asked. Apparently there'd been another small piece this morning about Archie, basically just saying he still hadn't been found. She described it and asked, "Do you think that's the guy? The one they talked about at the steam bath?" She never missed a detail.

"I think," I said, and then, not quite understanding myself, added, as I thumbed through the mail, "he's dead, by the way."

"Who's dead?"

"Him. Archie. Vernon. Dead-dead."

"No," she said. "How do you know?"

So I told her. "Bert has a problem in his refrigerator that baking soda will not help." She took a seat on my worn-out sofa, threshing her fingers through her short hair as I described the corpse.

"How could you not tell me this?" she asked.

"Hey, get real. The better question is why I tell you anything at all. This one's attorney-client, no kidding. The coppers'll sweat me if they find out I was anywhere near that body."

"Did Bert kill him?"

"Maybe so."

"*Bert?*"

"Your idea," I said.

"Never."

"Probably not."

"So who?"

"Somebody else. Probably the heavy-cuff-link crowd."

"Those guys don't do that anymore, do they?"

"Don't ask me," I said, "you're Italian."

"Come on," she said. "I mean to regular people."

"This guy wasn't regular people, Brush. If you make book you've got to be connected."

"Why?" she asked.

" 'Why'? Because this is *their* business. Coast-to-coast. And these guys don't believe in competition. You keep a book, fine and dandy, but you give them a share—they call it paying the street tax. Otherwise you suffer physical harm or they snitch you out to their favorite law enforcement type. Besides, they provide many valuable services. You got a customer who's slow-pay, these guys can hurry em up, believe you me. You can't do business without them."

She stared. She still didn't see why.

"Here," I said, "it's like your insurance client. What's the name?"

She reminded me, a fair-sized outfit that sent her their coverage litigation in the Midwest. A significant piece of business, and even saying the name she had a hard time managing her pride.

"Let's say they have four billion in property and casualty coverage in California," I told her. "How do they make sure that they don't go under when the hills burn?"

"They reinsure."

"Exactly. They find a few large, reliable companies and literally insure their insurance. And bookies do the same thing. A good bookie isn't a gambler. Any more than your insurance client is. Bookie makes 10 percent vig on your bet, if you lose. You bet 100, you owe him 110 when your team comes up short. That's where his money is. On any given game, he wants you to bet the loser and me to bet the winner. He gets $110 from you, keeps $10 vig, and gives 100 to me."

Brushy interrupted.

"No chance, Malloy. He'd use *your* money to pay *me*."

"Very amusing." I faked a little pop to her biceps and went on. "Anytime his book puts him at risk, when he has a lot more win money than lose money or vice versa, he'll do like the insurance company. Lay off. Reinsure. Call it whatever. And in this business, you want to lay off, you better be part of the network. Otherwise no one's going near you. Besides, if you need Mr. Large and Reliable, the outfit who can always handle your action, it's them."

"So what did he do wrong? Archie?"

"Maybe he was screwing around with the street tax." Guys had gotten fixed for less than that. With his gimmick with the credit cards, Archie might have thought he didn't need them. But even an actuary using the Vegas line was going to have to lay off. What I could use was a little heart-to-heart with somebody connected. At that moment Toots crossed my mind.

Having run out of answers, I asked Brushy about lunch.

"I can't," she said. "Pagnucci's in town. I said I'd have lunch with him."

"Pagnucci?" This was not one of Brushy's known allies or liaisons, but remembering yesterday I bit my tongue. "What's doing?" I asked. "Groundhog Day?"

That was her guess. In our firm, a partner is guaranteed to make 75 percent of what he earned the twelve months before, drawing it out after each of the first three quarters of our fiscal year. Then on January 31 the Committee divvies up the remainder and announces the results on Groundhog Day. Everybody puts on a tuxedo and goes to the Club Belvedere for dinner. We are served in elegance and joke with each other. On the way out, we each receive an envelope listing our share of firm income. Nobody carpools to this event. Each partner returns home alone, full of the elevating light of success or in fitful depression. The carping begins the next day and often goes on most of the remaining year until the next Groundhog Day. Some people campaign with the Committee, listing all their good deeds and achievements, the many new clients, the great rate of collections. To minimize discord, Pagnucci, who does the first draft of the point distribution, makes the rounds of influential partners to be sure they can accept the Committee's view of their worth. At least, that's what I hear. Pagnucci has never made luncheon reservations with me. The only info I get generally is by gossip, before or after the event, since your share, like your private parts, is supposed to be known only to you. When I got my first cut three years ago, I was in enough of a snit that late one evening I took a peek in the drawer in Martin's credenza, where he stashes the point-distribution record. I just about opened a vein after seeing all the layabouts and losers making more money than me.

"How about if we do lunch tomorrow?" Brushy asked. "I'll get some place with tablecloths. I want to talk to you." She touched my knee. Her round face was warm with feeling. Emilia Bruccia is probably the only person I know who feels any concern for my spirit.

B. Police Secrets

After Brush left, I got on the phone and called McGrath Hall, headquarters of the Kindle County Unified Police Force. Twenty-two years, but I knew the number by heart. I reached Al Lagodis, who was now up in Records, and told him I was gonna swing by. I didn't give him a chance to say no, and even so, I could hear he was about as enthusiastic as if I'd told him I was selling raffle tickets for some charity.

The Hall is a big graystone heap the size of a castle on the south rim of Center City, just where the big buildings stop and the neighborhood turns littered and bleak, full of taverns with garish signs sporting mention of dancing girls, places where lushes and perverts, released from the big buildings at lunchtime, drink beside the hustlers. I was at the Hall in ten minutes. I had to check in at the front desk and they called Al to fetch me.

"How are you?" Al gave me both eyes, a look of dead sincerity, as he was walking me back.

"You know."

"That good?" He laughed. Al and I go back to the time when I was in Financial Crimes and he thought I did the right thing on Pigeyes. Not that Al did anything himself, except, I always suspected, a little confidential muttering to the FBI— deep background stuff, a cup of coffee and some hard information that he'd refer to as "rumors." I always figured it was Al who put the Feebies onto me. He was one of the few folks here who would still talk to me afterwards—although he preferred to do it when nobody was around. Two decades and old Al was still going all shifty-eyed, hoping nobody saw him with Mack Malloy, legendary no-good guy. Around here not much changes. There were gals now, stepping through the dim old halls, wearing guns and ties and shirts that to my eye were not really designed for folks with tits, but even they have got that cop-roll, do-me-something stride.

"Nice digs," I said. He had a cubicle, steel partitions painted police blue, that rippled plastic stuff for windows, and a door. No ceiling. Life where you keep your voice down and can literally touch each wall when you stretch. Al worked Financial fourteen years. When Pigeyes was transferred in, he transferred out—discretion and valor, you know how that is—and went to the Records Division, which anyway is a better end to the road. He is now one of those coppers whose hard-charging days are behind them, who've found their cul-de-sac on the police life map and can hide here till it's retirement time, pretty soon now for Al, come age fifty-five. The Hall is full of these types, guts like saddlebags and smoked-out voices. He works 8:00 to 4:30. He supervises the clerks and fills out forms. Nobody shoots at him, nobody kicks him in the ass. He has his memories to keep him warm and a wife to set him straight whenever he's had a brewski too many and begins that lamebrained talk about how nice it would be to get back on the street. A good sod, with features blown out by alcohol.

"Need you to check me out on a couple things," I told him.

"Shoot." I was seated right beside his little desk and he could reach out from there to shut the door, which he did.

"You worked Financial a lot longer than me. I've gotta get information from Pico Luan—i.d. on who controls a bank account."

Al shook his head. "No," he said, "forget it," then asked, trying to be casual, "Whatta we got here?"

I was dodgy. "I'm not completely sure. I'm real confused. Here, let me try this one on you. Guy tells me he had a conversation with the General Manager of a bank in Pico Luan, long-distance telephone, and the G.M. sort of gives him between the lines whose account it is. How's that sound to you?"

"Not like any of them I ever talked to. Not on the telephone. Those guys got a patter. Go over to the Embassy. See your diplomat with the palm oil. Fill out a form. Wait an eon. Then another one. They'll send you a beautiful document back, honest to Christ, you never saw so many seals and ribbons, you'd think it was the fuckin VFW on parade, but it's spit, they won't tell you momma's first name when it comes to whose money's really in the bank. You been down there. You know how it is."

I knew, but I hadn't thought twice on day one, when Martin told us about calling the bank, because, after all, it was Martin. Now suddenly I was wondering how I sat still for that. 'Like trying to grab hold of smoke.' Jesus, I thought.

"Once or twice," said Lagodis, "we were desperate, we hired some sickening creep called himself a lawyer who claimed he had inside connections at the banks. What a snake charmer this character was. Ninety-nine and forty-four one-hundredths percent stinko, if you ask me. You could give him a try. Me, I believe more in the guys who get up and walk at the tent meetings." Al shook his head again, but I told him I'd take the name.

Scraping his chair across the floor, he walked out into the clamor of the central Records area, computer terminals and files, a number of empty desks at the lunch hour. From where I sat, I saw a sole uniformed type eating a burger out of the wrapper and glancing over the *Tribune*. The Hall, the h.q., units like Records especially, remain a sort of central backwater where it's like everyone took Valium, you'd swear every thirty seconds took a real-world minute, but I felt sort of cheerful to breathe again this gloomy bureaucratic air, this stolid, police thing of being utterly invulnerable.

The sad truth is that being a copper won't ever quite leave me. I never was in a flatter moral landscape. Or happier, as a result. Cops see it all—the Scout leader who scouts out the little boys, the business guy who makes 300K and gets caught stealing more, the mother who's beat her baby black and blue and wails in agony when you come with Child Welfare to take the kid away. You see her reach out, kneel and plead, tears a river, you see the utter knotted-up violence of her own agony, you see that you are taking her whole universe, cockeyed or not, that everything was in this child, not only her wild pain but some squalid hope, if maybe she could just get the suffering out of herself into some realm where it was more tangible, it might be easier to control. You see it and wonder how can you understand if some of that's not in you? It's just that today you're on the right side, you're wearing blue.

" 'Joaquin Pindling.' " I was reading the card Al handed me. "Jesus, what kind of name is that?"

"He'll cost you a buck or two, I promise that. Course, maybe a guy like you," offered Lagodis, "lots of personality, you could go down there yourself and make new friends, get information on your own."

"Kind of friends who'll leave me lighter in the pockets?"

"Anything's possible. Then of course could be somebody don't feel as friendly as you do. Then you become a sort of firsthand big-time expert on Due Process in Pico Luan."

"Now that's a subject, I'll bet."

"Oh yes indeedy. I talked with a couple visiting scholars

once. Prison conditions in Pico Luán, friend, not like the Regency on the Beach. They let you crap in this big hole in the middle of the cell, deep, deep, goes down who-knows-where-the-fuck. Nighttime the guards like to play hide-and-seek with the white guys. Watch where you step, mon. You lose, you find out where who-knows-where-the-fuck is."

"Got it."

Al waited a bit, seeing how it was. He was still on his feet. He was wearing a tie and, here in the dead of winter, a short-sleeve shirt a little snug over the beer gut. I told him I'd run into Pigeyes, but he'd already heard. This was the Force. That was yesterday's news.

"He let me go too," I said.

"Better be no next time. He'll tear off your head and shit down your neck. From what I hear, he skins his knees he still mentions you. I think what it is is his feelings got hurt."

"That must be it." I had some idea to ask if Al knew what Gino was investigating, in hopes of getting a little more info on Kam, but all in all, I'd probably pressed my luck already.

"Yeah," said Al, just filling in, hitching up his trousers, which dropped six inches every time he rocked on the balls of his feet. "You got a lot to watch out for," he told me.

That part wasn't news.

XIII. WHO SAYS LAWYERS
AREN'T TOUGH?

A. Toots's Walls

I was received in Toots's law offices with the air of ceremonial grandeur undoubtedly lavished on every guest. Stumbling along on his cane, his cigar extinguished but comfortably couched inside his jaw, he introduced me to each secretary and half his partners, the greatly renowned Mack Malloy, who was helping out the Colonel on that ethics thing. Then he showed me into his office and propounded a lengthy commentary on each memento on the walls.

Toots's office should have been moved intact to a museum somewhere, if not as a monument to twentieth-century political life then to one individual's capacity for self-appreciation. It was a virtual Colonel Toots Nuccio shrine. There were of course signed photos of the Colonel with every Democratic President from FDR forward, and two with Eisenhower, Toots in uniform in both. There were plaques from B'nai B'rith (Man of the Year), Little Sisters of the Poor, and the Kindle County Art Museum. There was a special award from the symphony, a clarinet cast in bronze; religious relics received from grateful clerics; and a lengthy salutatory letter from the Urban League, perhaps the only compliment Toots had received from people of color in the last thirty years, but which nonetheless had been framed. There was a gavel he'd been given from the City Council upon his retirement, his years of service engraved on the brass hand that circled the mallet head, and scores of photos of Toots with sports stars and political luminaries, some so long gone that their names had vanished from memory. At the absolute focus of attention, mounted immediately above his ponderous old desk, were his medals, aligned in a glass-doored case with a separate little high-intensity lamp that trained on Toots's silver star, which was pinned to black velvet. I spent the required instant marveling at it, wondering as I always would if it had been awarded for real bravery or as part of one of Toots's inevitable deals. Within these walls, one tended to realize that self-congratulation, the collection of banners and ribbons, was far more real to Toots, far more important than the events they were intended to commemorate.

"So," he said, finally seated, "I didn't figure you made house calls."

"Occasionally. There's something I want to talk to you about."

"This here hearing?"

I told him it was something else and hiked my chair a little closer.

"Toots. Can a fella ask a question? Between friends?"

He gave me the usual fulsome stuff, for me anything. I replied in kind, saying he was the only person in the tri-counties I knew who might be able to answer this. He smiled, deeply pleased by any compliment, without regard to its sincerity.

"I wondered if you might have heard something around town. There's an insurance guy, an actuary, who the papers say is missing. Vernon Koechell. They call him Archie. What I have to find out is if you know any reason for somebody to pop him."

Toots laughed quite merrily, as if I had made a saucy remark just within the borders of good taste. The shrunken old face showed not a sign of even vague offense, but I noticed that he had drawn back on his walking stick and within the milky elderly eyes was perhaps lodged a trace of something lethal.

"Mack, my friend, can I make a little suggestion?"

"Sure."

"Ask another question."

I stopped on that.

"See, Mack, I got a rule for life. Always followed it since I didn't even have hair on my chin. I known you a long time now. You're a smart fella. But let me share my thinking with you: Don't talk about other people's business. It's their business and it's for them to worry about."

I received this advice solemnly. Looking at me, Toots winked.

"I hear you, Colonel, but I've got a real problem."

"Whatsa matter? He rate you on your policy or what?"

"Here's how it is, Colonel. I have a partner missing, a guy named Kamin. Bert Kamin. Where he's gone, I haven't the foggiest. But this guy Archie, he's got a white shirt on and a nice tie, but he's keeping a book. And my guy Kamin's laying bets with him. At least that's the way it looks." I peeked up at Toots. I had his attention.

"Anyway, Archie, he's quite dead. That's a fact. Something I know. And pretty soon, any minute now, the coppers are going to show up to talk to me about that. And I'm frankly not interested in getting myself in Dutch with the wrong folks. So that's why I ask. I gotta know what's doing here, because I may have to do some fancy steppin'." I tried to look hangdog and sincere, reverencing one of the many powers that dominated Toots's life. He wasn't really buying it.

"You a straight shooter, Mack?"

"As much as the next guy."

Toots laughed. He liked that. He removed the cigar and in the gloomy light of the room considered the mangled end. It looked like a hunk of seaweed pulled up on a line.

"You understand with bookies," he said.

"Not everything."

"See this here— Guy makes a book, you know, he's got to lay off, right?"

"Like insurance companies. He doesn't absorb all the risk. I understand that much."

"This guy, he had some very good luck. Somehow he always had laid off his losing action."

I waited.

"How could he lay off only losing bets? Doesn't he lay off beforehand? I mean, before the event. The race, the game, whatever?"

"That he does," said Toots.

I was on very delicate ground. Toots worked lovingly on his cigar.

"You mean he knew how these events were going to come out? Is that what you're saying? He knew these games were fixed?"

"You see," said Toots, "you share risks, you share no-risks. *Capisc'*? A fella's gotta look out for his friends. Otherwise he don't got friends, he got enemies. Right? That's how life is, right?"

"That's how it seems to be, Toots. There are no victims."

Toots liked that one. No need to explain it to him.

"So you see," he said, "you asked a question, you asked another question, you told me some things, I told you some things, we had a talk. Okay? Somebody asks, some things you know, some things you don't know. Right?"

"Right."

"Sure," said Toots. He gave a quick, smug, frightening little laugh. "So. We gonna win this hearing?"

"I wish I could tell you yes, Colonel. The hill's pretty steep."

He shrugged, here in his element capable of seeming worldly-wise, ripened by life.

"Give it your best. I ain't gonna get the death penalty, right?"

We agreed on that.

"And who's there, you or the skirt?"

"The skirt's good," I told him.

"They say," said Toots. "So they say. Bit of a punch-board, I hear." I'd known he would check her out.

"Woman of the world," I answered.

"A big world," he said.

"I'll try to be there, Colonel. I have to worry about this too. Archie. Bert."

He understood. Sometimes a fella got himself into a spot. He walked me to the door.

"Remember my rule." He pointed with the cigar. Don't talk about other people's business. I had it firmly in mind.

B. Accounting Secrets

On the way back into the Needle, the elevator stopped at 32. No one got on, but I felt destiny beckoning and I jumped off and trod the hall to Accounting. When I came through the door, the unit manager, Ms. Glyndora Gaines, was sitting right there.

I took a seat beside her. Her desk was completely clean, windswept but for one file she was examining, a state of order which added to the usual impression of a dominant, unremitting soul. Glyndora continued to look over the file, determined not even to acknowledge me. Maybe there was a trace, a vapor, of a smile being willed to oblivion.

"Glyndora," I said quietly, "just as a matter of curiosity, not saying I'm gonna do it, but you know, what if.

What if I go tell the Committee the way you've been screwing me around? What if I act like I'm one of your bosses, instead of a chump?''

I was trying to sound sort of reasonable, maybe not pleasant, but calm. In the big room out the door, a dozen people were whizzing around, overwhelmed by the year-end rush, adding machines chugging out tape and phones giving their little electronic chirp. Checks were at a number of desks in colorful stacks.

"You gone talk to the Committee? Then tell them this.'' She rose up in her chair as she took a surveying glance toward the doorway. "Tell them you come to my apartment, you pounded on the buzzer causing all kind of commotion, talking all kinds of jive about Bert, and when I let you in, man, there wasn't barely one little word about Bert. The next thing, dude's got one hand on my titty and the other on my ass, and the only way I got rid of his rasty old self is cause this boy talkin all that AA shit went out to buy something to drink. Tell that to the Committee.''

She smiled in her way, tight like she was fastening down a bolt or a screw, and sized up the effect all this had. With Glyndora everything is a contest and she knew she had me beat. My side of the story was going to sound weak. Worse than that, ridiculous. Nobody would believe I was just posing with my hand on her breast. And if they knew I had been drinking again, my time as Deadeye Dick, Private Detective, would probably be over, not to mention my employment.

"Glyndora, you know exactly what's going on here.''

She leaned forward against her arms, making her frontal

equipment prominent in a blouse of orange flourishes. A layer of purple shadow lay thickly on her lids like pollen.

"Here's what I know, Mack. You are weak, sucker." She was leering again, amused by the thought that she knew my secrets. But I'd been there too and learned some of hers. I pointed.

"And you like white guys." I let that out and nodded myself, maybe imitating her. Even so, I regretted it. She stiffened; she reared back. We were headed where we always headed—me beats you, hah hah. One more contest. The Dozens, some kind of phony signifying. It was nothing I wanted, and I did what seemed under the circumstances somewhat daring and reached out to grab one of her hands. The touch, my big pink hand on her brown one, was shocking to us both. And that was the point.

"Hey," I said, "you know, I'm like you, I work here. I'm not trying to be your lord and master. Have I ever done that? Call me callous, I'm crude, et cetera, et cetera. But have I ever gone out of my way to do some kind of job on you? These guys tell me 'Find Bert' and I wanna find him. I'll tell you the truth—it's something I *need* to do. So just give me a break, okay? Be a person." In the bleakness of the tone I'd assumed, I suddenly heard a confession to myself. All along, I'd talked about this whole escapade, tracking down Bert, as a boondoggling effort at life reform. But that was kidding around, teasing myself with fantasies of running away with the money or earning my partners' esteem. Yet somehow I'd staked a lot more on this venture than I had admitted. Maybe my life was on its last legs. Maybe my chances were few. But I saw now that I'd promised myself that I was not coming out of this funhouse the way I'd gone in. Somebody within me believed that and was connected to what even in this meager, glimmering form you'd have to call hope.

And in admitting that, I was doing to Glyndora the one thing she tried to warn everyone against—being vulnerable, hanging it out for her to tromp on. She stared, disbelieving, insulted, and not altogether happy with the physical approach. She withdrew her hand from mine and slid her chair back so she could view me from a more distant perspective as we continued sizing each other up. Glyndora has her routine, the Hey-I'm-a-tough-black-bitch number, and she does it on autopilot, a piece of racial rhetoric that's as much mask and cipher as Steppin Fetchit onstage. Oh, I know she means it. I know she's tough. Like Groucho, who would not want to be a member of any club he could join, Glyndora wants to be the first one to reject you. Mission accomplished. But swimming through her eyes on occasion is some misgiving, a recognition that she's someone else. I don't know if she gets caught up in crackpot fantasies about how she is being poisoned by aluminum pots or whether she is a secret reader of the Koran. But there is more to her than she lets on. And that's the final insult she hurls at most of us. That she'll never let us in. Yet Glyndora has her secret place. He says with confidence, a denizen of his own secret places. Somebody who'd been there briefly with her the evening before and was knocking on the door again now.

"I *need* to find Bert," I repeated.

Finally she leaned toward me and spoke in a softer tone, maybe an appeal of its own.

"No, you don't, Mack. You just gotta tell them you looked." That was a message. Glyndora was playing the role of medium, of oracle, but even so, I wasn't sure if I was being beseeched or warned.

"You have to give me more, Glyn. I'm clueless. Who are you fronting for? I mean, at least tell me about the memo."

Her posture became rigid again, her face hard. It was like watching a book slam closed.

"You're asking too much, man." It wasn't clear if the excess was on her end or mine, if I wanted information I wasn't entitled to or if it came at a cost she wasn't willing to pay. But the answer, whatever, was no. She stood up and walked past me. She was running for cover. I thought about what I ought to do. I could demand her keys and toss her office. I could hire a service and get thirty temps to tear through the files. But I'd just made a deal. Without turning, I spoke before Glyndora could get far.

"One thing," I said. Her heels stopped clacking, so I knew she was hanging there by the threshold. "I never put my hand, not once, on your behind."

When I looked back, she was smiling a little, something like that. I'd gotten that much. But she wouldn't give any actual ground.

"Says you," she told me.

C. The Devil Himself

"It's a pact with the devil." Thus spake Pagnucci as Carl, Wash, Martin, and I sat in the same paneled conference

room where we had encountered each other at the start of
the week. There was a moment of rare winter sun, a part
of the circle escaped from the clouds like something hanging out of a pocket. The heavy drapes had been permanently sashed by the decorator and the long walnut table
was bright with the glimmer of the late light, thick as
caramel. I had found the three of them waiting for me and
quickly reviewed my conversation with Jake Eiger that
morning. I skipped Bert's memo and my trip to Neucriss.
Glyndora had made me shy of both subjects, and I wasn't
eager to take on Martin, whose motives remained per-
plexing to me. He and Carl gravely received the message
I'd brought, but Wash was slower on the uptake.

"He's telling us that if we can't put this crime right, it
will go unreported," Martin said to him. "Jake is concerned about Jake. He can't go to his Chairman, to
Krzysinski, with this without endangering his own position. After all, who put Bert in charge of the 397 escrow
in the first place? He wants us to keep our mouths shut."

"Ah," said Wash, who did a poor job of hiding the fact
that he was quite pleased. "And where do we end up with
Jake?"

"In bed, I would say," said Martin. "Holding dirty
hands. He can't very well cut us off, can he? He's our
hostage."

"And we're his," said Pagnucci, invoking by his remark a pointed silence.

"But," said Wash, continuing to muddle it through,
"we've reported the matter to the client. We've done our
duty. If he chooses not to do his—" The back of his
elegant white hand traveled off to the land of moral obliv-

ion. Wash was already sold. A tidy solution. Five million gone and a secret forever.

"Jake says he doesn't believe it, actually," I offered. "He says that he's hoping that an accounting will prove it's not true."

"That's horseshit," said Pagnucci. "He's posturing. We know the client isn't really informed. If we go along with this, it's the same thing as having said nothing at all."

With the only difference of course that there was a far lower risk of detection. Auditing of the escrow account from which the money had disappeared was under Jake's direction and control. He'd cover us in order to cover himself. That was the meaning, I realized now, of that remark he'd made to me this morning about an accounting.

We were silent again, all four of us. Throughout this session, my attention remained on Martin. Wash had already set his course down the path of least resistance, and for Carl the problem-solving method was equally apparent, a question of benefits and costs. In his head, the pluses and minuses were already totaling. But Martin's calculations, in line with his character, figured to be more complex. Like an Aristotelian figure, his eyes were raised to heaven in the course of higher contemplation. Martin is your veritable Person of Values, a lawyer who does not see the law as just business or sport. He's on one million do-good committees. He's against the Bomb, the death penalty, and damage to the environment, for abortion, literacy, and better housing for the poor. He's been the chairman for years of the Riverside Commission, which is devoted to making the river clean enough to drink or swim

in, goals that frankly will not be achieved until long after
we have colonized Mars, but he'll still take you for a walk
along the tangled, littered banks, soft with prairie grasses,
and describe out loud the bike paths and boat piers he sees
in his head.

Like any Person of Values who is a lawyer, Martin is
not in it for goodness alone. These activities make him
prominent, help him attract clients. Most of all, they invest
him with the same thing that knowledge of the law imparts
to us all: a sense of power. Martin gets off with his hand
on the throttle. When he talks about the $400 million public
offering we did for TN two years ago, his eyes glow like
a cat's in the dark. When he says, 'Public company,' he
says it the way the priest passing out wafers says, 'The
body of Christ.' Martin has a grasp of the way business
runs America and he wants to help be in charge.

Yet it's not just the sense of being important by attachment that excites him. It's also what his clients want to
know: right or wrong, allowable or no. He's the navigator,
the person with the compass, the man who tells the high
and mighty, if not about morals, then at least about principles and rules. His clients can go out in the vineyard and
get their boots covered in muck. He's back in the office,
charting their course by the stars. When Martin goes to
sleep at night and asks God's blessing, he tells the Lord
that he helped his clients move with grace and speed
through the difficult and ambiguous world He has made
for us. Though perhaps not even Martin can tease out the
logic, he believes that he is engaged in an enterprise that
is fundamentally good.

Listening to this, I'm sure you're humming ''The Battle

Hymn of the Republic'' and marching in place. All right. I'm just trying to tell you how it is. But don't sneer. It's easy to be a poet sitting behind the gates of a university or a monk in a monastery and feel there is a life of the spirit to which you are dedicated. But come into the teeming city, with so many souls screaming, I want, I need, where most social planning amounts to figuring out how to keep them all at bay—come and try to imagine the ways that vast unruly community can be kept in touch with the deeper aspirations of humankind for the overall improvement of the species, the good of the many and the rights of the few. That I always figured was the task of the law, and it makes high-energy physics look like a game show.

Wash finally interrupted this extended silence by posing the question that no one had been willing to ask: ''How would anybody ever find out?''

Martin actually smiled and without saying more looked to each of us, ducking his chin in a brief, suggestive way. The gesture by itself, his mere acknowledgment of what was held within the room, was vaguely shocking. The next step would be to dip a pen in blood.

''Where would you say Bert went?'' I asked. ''There are three hundred people here asking already.''

''Say that, so far as we know, he's in Pico Luan,'' answered Pagnucci. ''Retired from the practice. That'll pass the red-face test. Forward his mail to the bank there. None of that is what bothers me.''

''Retired?'' I asked. ''Just like that? He's forty-one years old.''

''There is not a soul who knows Bert Kamin well who wouldn't believe him capable of something só impulsive,'' said Wash, waving his pipe around. He had a point. Bert had done stranger things half a dozen times in the last five years. "This is doable," said Wash, "quite feasible. And as to your concerns, Carl, about Jake ignoring our report—" Wash filled the pipe bowl with fire from his lighter. "I personally do not believe Jake Eiger would lie." It was something of a non sequitur but we all saw what Wash was up to. If it ever proved that the secret had not held, we could say that we had placed our faith in Jake—to be honest, reverent, and true, to protect the best interests of TN, to tell what-all must be told. The silence upstairs we took to reflect TN's desire to save face and to protect the settlement fund from raiding by the plaintiffs' lawyers. We would express shock about Jake. In the face of calamity, Wash, who had placed Jake at TN like a spore years ago, would trot out his protégé for drowning.

But Martin saw through Wash instantly.

"If we go that route," said Martin, the man I love, a fellow who could make Keats think twice about whether beauty is truth and vice versa, "and the day comes that we have to explain, we'll all lie. You'll hear four different versions of what went on in this room." His look panned each of us and settled on me.

"Lest I repeat myself," he said now, "I hope you find Bert."

D. The Head of Finance

Pagnucci said, "That was troubling," as we headed toward my office after the meeting, strolling down the book-lined corridor. Martin and the decorators have decided that it is the right touch to fill the halls with the gold-spined federal and state reporters, though it's hell on the associates, who never know where to find the volumes they need.

Carl was in town from D.C. for the second time this week. Eager to please TN, and to minimize their dealings with other large firms, we had opened the Washington office fifteen years ago to handle matters before the FAA and CAB. When airline regulation went the way of white tennis balls, we had about thirty lawyers with nothing to do. Enter Pagnucci, a former Supreme Court law clerk to Justice Rehnquist, with six million dollars in annual billings, thanks to Ronald Reagan, who in 1982 made Carl the youngest member ever of the Securities and Exchange Commission.

The saying about law firms is that there are finders, minders, and grinders, referring first to people like Carl and Martin and Brushy who find big-time, big-money clients to employ them, then the service partners, guys like me, who make sure that skilled work is carried out by supervising the third group, the young toilers laboring in the library amid the ghosts of dead trees. The sad fact is that there are far fewer finders than minders and the finders increasingly demand more of the pie. Carl left his former firm because they were not contemporary enough, meaning they did not pay him what he thought he was worth, and his very presence among us on those terms means we have to make sure the same thing does not happen here. There are only so many ways to do it. Maybe you can get the associates to stay another quarter hour past midnight, or pile on charges for ludicrous extras—fifty cents a page for running sensitive documents through our shredder—but in the end the best way for the top guys to stay ahead is if they have fewer people to share with, fire a few minders and give Carl their points. Lots of people around G&G claimed we'd never do it, but the pressure's there, and Carl, who heads the subcommittee on firm finances, has never expressed the same resolve. No doubt he thought that's what I wanted now—to lobby him about next year's pay—and as soon as my door was closed he raised another subject.

"So what's the latest from the Missing Persons Unit?"

"Gaining a little ground," I said. "Still no sight of our man."

"Hmm," said Pagnucci. He allowed himself a bit of a frown.

"I had a request to make to you as head of finance."

He nodded. No words. He was steeling himself. Unconsciously he raised a hand to his head. There's a bald spot the size of an orange at the back of his head and you can tell from the way he's always fussing that it drives him nuts—the imperfection, the lack of control, the fact that he is as subject as anyone else to the whims of fate.

"Suppose I told you I want to take a trip to Pico Luan?"

Carl deliberated. Even crossed up, he was disinclined to quickly agree.

"You didn't think that was such a clever idea earlier this week."

"It's the only lead I have left."

Carl nodded. He'd been right from the start; he could accept that. For my own part, I felt too much vestigial loyalty to tell him there was something squirrelly about

Martin's account of his phone call to the International Bank of Finance.

"There's a lawyer down there I'd like to retain. Subject to your approval." I handed him the card I'd gotten from Lagodis. "The guy's supposed to do black magic getting stuff out of the banks."

Pagnucci made a sound but otherwise failed to react. Off-camera, Pagnucci has quite a life, this trim little guy with a stiff little mustache cuts some figure. He's on wife number four—each of them blondes, drop-dead gorgeous, who are getting progressively taller as his marriages wear on—and he runs himself to work in one modified Formula One car or another, Shelbys and Lotuses, all kinds of hot stuff. At some point, maybe all day, his fantasy life must be running wild, John Wayne movies probably, banal stuff like that. But in the office, none of it shows. Not a muscle twitches. He did not seem to have any more to say now. He touched the corner of his mustache with a lacquered fingernail.

"I was going to charge the trip to the recruiting budget, frankly," I said. "I'll probably take someone with me to witness any interviews. But I wanted you to know so there's no squawk when the bills come through."

"Have you talked to Martin or Wash about this?"

"I'd rather not." I was telling Carl a good deal now and he absorbed it like all else in silence. I was taking a chance. But Carl by his nature liked keeping things to himself. And I couldn't see him vetoing his own idea.

"You're turning out to be a much more complicated fellow than I imagined," said Pagnucci. I tipped my head slightly. I thought it might be a compliment. Before he opened my door, Carl said, "Keep me in the loop," then drifted off, smug and unruffled, leaving behind his usual aura: every soul for itself.

Rational self-interest is Carl's creed. He worships at the altar of the free market. The same way Freud thought everything was sex, Pagnucci believes all social interaction, no matter how complex, can be adjusted by finding a way to put a price on it. Urban housing. Education. We need competition and profit motive to make it all work. It is, I know, quite a theory. Let everybody struggle to get their bucket in the stream and then do what they like with the water they fish out. Some will make steam, some will take a drink, a few fellows or ladies will decide to take a bath. Entrepreneurship will flourish; people will be happy; we'll get all this nifty indispensable stuff like balsamic vinegar and menthol cigarettes. But what kind of ethical social system takes as its fundamental precepts the words "I" "me" and "mine"? Our two-year-olds start like that and we spend the next twenty years trying to teach them there's more than that to life.

I stayed down for the evening, cleaning up what I'd ignored while running all over town the last couple of days. Memos and letters. I returned all my calls. I hadn't eaten much. I was tired, my eyes and bones felt acid-etched from the hangover. Now and then I closed my eyes and thought I could still catch far back in my throat the fierce taste of rye, which I savored.

Eventually I picked up the Dictaphone. The city out the window at this hour has a sort of painted stillness, all black forms and random lights: a woodcut pattern—gray on indigo and jet. A lone car races up the ridges of the superhighway. I am one more life in hiding amid the occasional heaving and cranking of a big building in the darkness, talking to myself. A single coast guard icebreaker's mast light bucks along the river.

It seems increasingly obvious, even to me, that I'll never show a word of this to anyone on the Committee. Ignoring the insults, which I could cross out, I've lied to or hidden things from each of them half a dozen times. And for you, sweet Elaine, a Dictaphone or some typing won't really make our communication improve. So we all wonder: who am I talking to?

In my mind's eye, there are faces. Don't ask me whose. But I see some reasoning and sensate being who will get hold of this thing, some someone of largely indecipherable characteristics who I nonetheless find myself addressing now and then. You. The universal You. U You, in my mind. Gender, age, and disposition unknown. Experience unimagined. A somebody floating like dust in the outer reaches of the cosmos. But still—I think, bud, this is for you.

Of course, I try to imagine reactions. You could be a copper, or a Bureau agent, with a soul rough as sandpaper, who locks this up at night to make sure your wife does not get ruffled by the bad words, while you, when you're alone, rifle the pages looking for another passage about my hand on my crank. Maybe you're some fifty-year-old Irishman who thinks I don't sound a bit like you do. Or a kid who says this is boring. Or a professor who concludes it is generally vile.

Whoever, I want something from You. Not admiration, God knows, I don't feel much for myself. What more can

I call it but connection? Comprehend. Let that mighty
magic lightning flow across the gaps of space and time.
From me. To you. And back. The way the bolts explode
from sky to earth and then bounce again into the heavens
and the universe beyond. Going on forever, to the regions
where the physicists tell us matter equals time. While in
one spot on this single humble planet, a tree is split, a
rooftop smokes, a human being sits awake and startled by
the miracle of energy and light.

TAPE 4

Dictated January 30, 1:00 a.m.

Friday, January 27

XIV. YOU GUYS

A. The Murder Suspect

Friday a.m. I was heading in through the revolving doors of the Needle when a young guy stopped me, pockmarked skin and a slick-backed do and a fancy jacket made from the skin of some creature with a two-chambered heart. Familiar from someplace, like an actor you've seen on TV.

"Mr. Malloy?" He flipped his tin at me, and naturally I recognized him then, Pigeyes's wormy companion, Dewey.

"You guys," I said.

"Gino'd like a word with you." I looked in all directions. I didn't believe I could get within one hundred yards of Pigeyes without picking up some sensation of him, like a missile detector homing on infrared. Dewey was indicating the curb where I saw only a rusted conversion van.

I asked what would happen if I said no.

"Hey, fella, you do what you wanna do. Me, I wouldn't fuck with him. You're in a lotta deep doo-doo." Pigeyes was in a mood, Dewey was saying. There was a vaguely plaintive quality to his address. Life forges all kinds of fraternities and Dewey and I were in one of its strangest: partners of Pigeyes. There were only so many people on earth who could understand his plight, and dogmeat or not, I was still one of them. We looked at each other a moment as the Center City crowd scurried past, and then I followed him to the curb and the van, which looked like a weary delivery truck bearing sclerotic rust marks on its rocker panels and six of those grayed-over bubble-type portholes, two in the back and two on each side.

When Dewey opened the rear doors, Pigeyes was inside, along with a black guy, another copper. It was a surveillance van. No way to be sure how long they'd been watching me; long enough to know I wasn't upstairs. They could have followed me from home or, more likely, called Lucinda and learned that I hadn't arrived. There were video cams mounted on swivels over each of the portholes and two rows of recording equipment in small wooden consoles behind the driver's seat. The entire interior had been carpeted in a mangy gray shag, which had matted and worn away on the floor and was marked here and there with cigarette burns. Guys spent long nights in here, begging each other not to fart, watching whoever they watched, dopers or Mafia dons or nuts who'd said they wanted to kill a senator. There were cup holders fixed to the walls and carpeted benches over the wheel wells. Pigeyes was sitting next to the electronics, wearing one of those short-billed county caps. I suppose this was his getup when he was undercover. I nodded rather than use his name and Dewey took my elbow to help me up. Inside, the van smelled of fried food.

I was impressed by Pigeyes's access to this equipment. Surveillance was a separate department unit. When I was on the Force, they would have shitcanned a request for assistance from Financial Crimes faster than junkmail. But Pigeyes sort of had his own police department, his own affiliations and rules. His cousins were coppers and so were two of his brothers, and he had one of "his guys," as he put it, in every nook and cranny of the Hall. He could fix up any little problem—leave or sick days, expense money to take care of a snitch. Naturally he'd return favors—outside the Force, too, for that matter. The guys he grew up with, fellas who these days were importing tunas stuffed with brown heroin or gambling for a living, were all the time giving him a holler when they got in a jam and Gino'd always help out. No questions asked. The Pigeyes National Bank of Favors Owing and Owed. The only thing I found disconcerting was that he was spending his markers to watch over me.

As soon as I took a seat on the wheel well, Pigeyes was on his feet. Make no mistake, he was unhappy.

"I know one fucking douche bag, Malloy, who isn't as fucking smart as you think you are." He waited for me to buy the straight line but I wouldn't bite. "You knew I was sitting on the goddamn credit card, didn't you?"

I looked at the black copper, tall, wearing a tweed jacket

and a wool vest but no tie. He was lurking around near the equipment. The van, I would bet, was assigned to him.

"He's having those visions again," I said.

"Don't smart around." Pigeyes pointed. "That's some story he's tellin, this kid. How much did you pay him?"

"I don't know what you're talking about," but of course I did now. Pigeyes had been tracking Kam Roberts the same way I had—with the Kam Roberts credit card. Being a police officer, and one in Financial Crimes, he had clear advantages. The bank card people needed pals in Financial, guys who'd maybe visit some deadbeat who was twenty grand over his limit to suggest that a payment was due soon, otherwise this could go down as a criminal fraud. Now it was payback. Every time a transaction was posted to Kam Roberts's account, the computer center down in Alabama would call Pigeyes. He could track Kam all over the planet, and when Kam showed up in the tri-counties, Gino could skedaddle over to wherever, collar Kam if he was lucky, or at least ask where Kam had been and what he looked like and tell the store owner, the hotel manager, if this guy or anyone asking for him popped up again, to pronto give Pigeyes a jingle. That, I now realized, was how he'd set up on me at U Inn.

All well and good, but apparently Gino and Dewey had spent the last day chasing all over the North End, exploring a rash of purchases of CD players, high-top sneakers, Starter jackets and video games, receiving consistent descriptions of a thirteen-year-old Latino who was not a twenty-seven-year-old black man with receding hair.

Dewey was using a fingernail to pick at his teeth as the three of them watched me.

"I didn't pay him," I said.

"Sure you didn't," said Dewey. "He says he took your wallet off you while you're passed out in some Chevy near the projects."

"Sounds right to me."

"Not to me," piped in Pigeyes. "What I hear, you're on the Life Plan down there at AA. They take attendance?"

I looked pretty clever from Pigeyes's perspective. On the street, everyone knows you use a juvenile to do dirty business, because practically speaking, there's no such thing as jail for a kid that age. The gangbangers employ twelve-year-olds to make dope runs, even as triggermen. Pigeyes figured I gave the kid the Kam Roberts card and told him it was Shop-Till-You-Drop or the coppers come round, in which case here's your story.

"You're buying him time to run, Malloy." I wasn't sure if Gino meant Bert or Kam Roberts, or if they were actually one. "What's this guy to you?"

"Who?" I asked.

"Who am I looking for, fuckface?"

"Kam Roberts?" I really was guessing.

He mimicked me, a long face, a bit of Brando. " 'Kam Roberts?' " He repeated the name half a dozen times, his voice capering up the scale. Then he turned vicious. There was a rheumy turn to his eyes and something inflamed near the bridge of his nose; I could see why people were talking about Pigeyes and dope. On the other hand, he'd always been fast to anger.

"You fuckin tell me right now where he is. Now."

"You holding paper on him?" I still wanted to know what it was for, what Kam, whoever he was, was supposed to have done.

"Uh-uh, no way, Malloy. You give, you get. No one-way streets."

"You have the wrong address, Pigeyes. I don't know a thing about this guy beyond what I told you last time." I raised two fingers. "Scout's honor."

"You know what I think, Malloy. I'm thinkin, you're dirty here." Pigeyes's instincts were highly reliable and his inclination to view me with suspicion did not need to be explained. "I think it's adding up. We been looking for your friend Mr. Kamin." Pigeyes placed his hands on his knees. He put his face right in mine. His breath was heavy; his flesh was laden with a dense, cruel light. "You wouldn't happen to have been in his apartment in the last couple days?"

I'd known for seventy-two hours this was coming, but the papers were already writing about Archie, and the homicide dicks have all got deals with the reporters—dinner and drinks and spell the name right before the sixth graph—and I thought for sure we'd be hearing an item on News Radio 98, with one of the secretaries scooting down the hall going, Oh my God, did you hear about Bert's place? So this one caught me by surprise.

You probably know it already, U You, but I really am crazy. Saying that, I mean what people usually do, not that I act without reason, but that my reasons, lined up with each other, don't make too much sense. Contradictory, you'd say. In conflict. I'm such a smart-guy who has all the answers, then I whistle in the dark with all these fears racing inside me and, worse yet, pull stunts like breaking into hotel rooms and apartments that would give the heebie-jeebies to the daring young man on the flying trapeze. But now and then even a knucklehead like me gets a wake-up call from reality and without warning I felt, in the radiance of Pigeyes's usual aura of menace, that I was in danger. Somehow with all my preoccupations, my good-time visions about what I'd do when I caught Bert, I hadn't recognized the opportunity I'd handed Gino. I'd known he'd vet me, give me a proctoscope, the third degree. But I had touched a lot of things in Bert's apartment. Doorknobs inside and out. The mail. Homicide was there now, taking lifts off every surface. My sworn enemy, Detective Gino Dimonte, finds a dead body, my prints, and evidence of a lot of peculiar behavior on my part. Guess what comes next? The panic arrived with the same sudden welling power as tears.

"I told you, the guy's my partner. I go to his place all the time." Gino knew just what I was up to. If I admitted I was in the apartment recently, I'd give him the break-and-enter cold, a forcible felony, and a leg up on the murder, since I put myself close to the body. If I denied it, I'd have no way to explain my prints.

"Bull," Pigeyes said. "You're such a pal of his, you know his friends? You know a bookie named Vernon Koechell?"

"No."

"Never heard of him?"

"Don't know him."

"That's not what I asked, Malloy."

I'd been down at the Russian Bath talking about Archie,
and it would not take too much bullying to turn somebody's
memory around about who'd brought up the name. Pigeyes
could monkey with a lot of things, in fact, the evidence
techs and the path reports. The people who owed him and
played his way were all over the department, and I'd broken their code. A lift off the doorknob could be identified
as coming from the refrigerator or the vegetable crisper.
My hairs found in the kitchen might eventually appear on
Mr. Koechell's lapel. I suddenly knew why there'd been
no news flash about Archie's body. It would be easy to
mum this in the papers, for a few hours anyway, if the
coppers needed time to lay hands on the killer. In the folds
beneath my chin, I could feel a slick of telltale dampness
beginning to gather.

"This bird Koechell—I been looking for him. Did you
know that?"

"No." I was relieved to give one honest answer.

"Some questions I need to ask him about his buddy
Kam Roberts."

In the midst of all this sensation, mixed up and intense,
I suddenly knew what Pigeyes was investigating—at least
what it had been to start. It came into clear view like a
birdie flapping through a cold sky as I recalled my conversation with Toots. Fixing games. Kam Roberts and Archie.
That's why it was being looked at out of Financial Crimes
instead of Vice. 'Kam's Special—U five.' Bert maybe had
been in on this too.

"I got lucky, sort of. One of those good news, bad news
things. Run into some rummy asshole I used to know, sort
of sweat him a second, and bingo, this guy gives me the

name of Robert Kamin, tells me go look for this dude, seems he knows Kam Roberts. And I do. I even take a look round Robert Kamin's place.''

"With a warrant?" I asked. It was a question, an obstacle. The fear was still all over me now, like a brick on my heart.

Pigeyes sneered. "Listen, jagbag, a warrant for his apartment don't make any difference for you." We both knew he was right. "Here. Show him the warrant."

Dewey reached for a briefcase next to the passenger's seat. I closed my eyes briefly, in spite of myself.

"Now I'm asking you again, Malloy, you didn't happen to be in that apartment, did you?"

I was a copper during those years when it was starting that the police had to give somebody arrested Miranda. I never saw the point. It was a nice idea, I recognized that, put everybody on the same footing, rich guy and poor, they'd all know the same rules. But the problem was human nature, not social class. Because a man in a corner is never going to shut up. If he shuts up, if he says what I knew I should say, call my lawyer, then he's going to the station, he's going to get booked, he's going to court. For a guy in a jam, there's only one way out, to keep explaining, hoping that somehow bullshit buys liberty.

"Pigeyes, what do you think I did?"

"I asked if you were in that apartment." He pointed at Dewey to make a note. "That's twice he's not answering."

"Gino, I'm the guy who gave you Bert's name and told you to go shag him. Write *that* down," I said. Dewey, of course, didn't move. "What kind of sense does that make, if I'm hiding something?" He knew where I was going—

if I killed Archie, why would I suggest they go looking for Bert? But I knew the cop answer: If everybody didn't do dumb things, nobody'd get caught.

"Malloy, nothing with you makes sense. You're not a sensible guy. You tell me why you send some punk with pimples on his ass to run all over the city with that fucking credit card? You tell me why the guy I'm looking for and the guy you're looking for got the same names inside out? You tell me why you're looking for this Robert Kamin in the first place? Or how come you don't know nothing about his asshole pal Vernon Koechell? You tell me why you're fronting for this fucking homo?"

Homo. I wasn't making the reference. I didn't know if he meant Archie or Kam or Bert.

"Now maybe," said Pigeyes, "third time's the charm. We'll try it again, and listen up. Yes or no. Last few days, were you in that apartment?"

I felt like he'd shoved his whole fist into my throat.

"Pigeyes, do I need a lawyer?"

"Hey, I thought you were a lawyer." All three of them laughed. The black guy covered his face with his hand. My, my, my. He was wearing a square diamond ring that was bright on his fingers. "See, here's why I ask. Cause I looked all over that place, Kamin's. Checked the dust on the window ledges, postmarks on the mail. I opened the fridge to see any food spoiled, pull date on the milk carton and orange juice. Know what I found?"

"No," I said. Without looking away from me he pointed at Dewey to make another note. I tried to be resolute but he was drilling holes in my peepers, reading every thought in my head. He knew he had me. He'd seen me frightened before. He knew the look and he savored it. And I knew him too. I'd watched him drag these poor kids into the station for questioning and go put on a stained butcher's apron he kept in his locker, knowing there was nothing these young bloods wouldn't believe about the Kindle police. He had the same expression. He was going to deliver the rabbit punch now, the body, and how the path report, the hair samples, the digestive track enzymes, somehow spelled Malloy. He bent close, he put his harsh face right back in mine. Mr. Stranger Danger in person.

"Not a fuckin thing," he said. "That's what I found: not a goddamn fuckin thing. This guy's gone two weeks at least. And if you ain't been in that apartment, you tell me how you come up with a credit card that the bank says they only mailed twelve days ago?" He took a real bite on the words and smiled a little bit as he did it.

And so did I.

B. He Looks Like Kam Roberts

I felt mostly cold in the wake of my panic. I might have belched or sung a song. I felt a little like I could fly. Gino had said, distinctly, that there was nothing in the refrigerator, and so far as I could see, he was having too much fun intimidating me to bother to lie. Who had moved the body and why were questions for later.

Satisfied he had nailed me, Pigeyes stumbled back through the divide between the front seats and sat to have a chuckle; he laughed so hard he held on to his hat. He'd had a great time. His buddies here, Dewey and the black guy, they were smiling right along. Nobody was feeling sorry for Malloy.

Pigeyes finally wiped his eyes. "Let's be straight guys, okay? I don't give a flying foreign fuck what you're up to, Malloy. Robert Kamin? I don't care if he diddled the senior partner's wife—or the senior partner, for that matter. All I want is this guy Kam Roberts, whoever he is. You gimme that, he gimmes that— Go have your fucking little life. Sincerely." Gino touched his chest. I thought he was wearing the same shirt he had on the other day.

"You gonna tell me why you need him?"

"You gonna tell where I find him?"

"Gino, I don't know." He weighed that, the doubt hinged in his eyes. "I never met the guy in my life. The card gets billed at Kamin's place. Don't ask me why. That's all I know." That, and Infomode, one or two little things. But they were my business. Besides, who knew better than Pigeyes that sometimes I lie? "That's it. Okay? You did a great job breaking my balls."

Pigeyes motioned to Dewey. "Show him."

Dewey went for the briefcase. They had a sketch. It was on mat board, done with pencil and stored in a little plastic sleeve. Surveillance van. Police artist. Pigeyes had a lot of support. Dewey handed the drawing to me.

A black guy, late twenties, nice-looking, receding hair.

"Ever see him?" Dewey asked.

And this was the strangest goddamn part. I had.

"I'm not sure," I said.

"Maybe?"

Where? I would never remember. Not now anyway. If it was coming, it would hit me when I was half asleep, or scratching my fanny, or trying to recollect some clever gambit I had meant to include in a losing brief. Maybe he was the guy at the cleaner or a fella on my bus. But I had seen him.

I kept shaking my head. "This is him? Kam?"

Pigeyes rolled his tongue over his teeth. "Who is he?" he asked.

"Gino, I swear to God, it beats me. I see him on the street, I'll make a citizen's arrest. You're the first guys I call."

"Would Robert Kamin know?"

"I'll have to ask Robert Kamin next time I see him."

"When would that be?"

"No telling. He seems to be somewhat indisposed."

"Yeah, he seems to be." He shared looks, a smile, with the two other coppers. Finding Bert, I suspected, had recently occupied a lot of their time. "What about Koechell?"

"Honest to God, I never met him." I raised a hand. "Honest. And I have no idea where he is now." That was true too.

Pigeyes contemplated all of this.

"Which one's the homo, by the way?" I asked. "Koechell?"

Pigeyes put his hands on his knees again, so he could get up in my face.

"Why ain't I surprised that's of interest to you?"

"If you're trying to disparage me, Pigeyes, I'm going to have to call the Human Rights Commission." We were heading back to where we had been. Fun and games. Gino's bladder had run dry on the hot piss of vengeance for only a moment. The reservoir was filling and he was ready again to lower his fly. It came back to him as the lodestar of his universe: he really did not like me.

"Suppose I tell you," he said, "that you could fit a Saturn rocket up Archie Koechell's hind end, you gonna tell me how come you're so curious?"   •

"I'm just looking for clues to Bert's social life. That's all. Guy's out of pocket. You know that. My partners are worried and asked me to find him." I gave an innocent little shrug.

"You find him, I wanna know. He talks to me about Kam, he can go home. But you screw around, Malloy, it's the whole load: break and enter, credit card fraud, false personation. I'll fuck you up bad, big guy. And don't think I won't enjoy it."

I knew better than that. Dewey opened the van door from inside and I stepped down to the street, enjoying the daylight and the cold, the greatness of all outdoors. Twice now, I thought, two miracles. I spoke words of thanks to Elaine. Pigeyes had let me go.

XV. BRUSHY TELLS ME WHAT SHE WANTS AND I GET WHAT I DESERVE

A. Brushy Tells Me What's on the Menu

For our luncheon on Friday, Brushy had chosen The Matchbook, a quiet old-line place that tried to preserve some atmosphere of leisured sanctuary for the business class. You walked down from street level into a feeling of soft enclosure. The ceiling was low; the lack of windows had been obscured by little puddles of light projected onto the faux marble wallpaper from the top of the plaster columns dividing the room. The waiters in black waistcoats and bow ties did not tell you their first names or get so chummy that you started hoping the meal might be on them.

Following my adventure with Pigeyes, I'd had an uneventful morning, ruminating periodically about the body vanished from Bert's fridge. I wanted to believe that its

disappearance had nothing to do with my visit to the apartment, but I was having a hard time convincing myself.

Eventually I tracked down Lena in the library. She had
her feet up on her oak carrel and was absorbed in one of
the heavy gold-bound federal reporters as if it were a novel,
giving off the fetching aloof air of all brainy women. I
asked if she had a passport and a free weekend and still
wanted to work on that gambling case, the one where
she'd cracked the bookmaking code on Infomode. She
was enthusiastic. I did the usual law firm delegating, shit
always rolling downhill, and told her to call TN's executive
travel service, pull strings if need be to get us on a plane
to Pico Luan Sunday and a decent hotel, the beach if they
could. She took notes.

"So," I said, when Brush and I were seated side by
side in a booth at the back. The maître d' had greeted
Brushy by name and took us to a rear corner on a raised
terrace of the room, with a column and a plant buying a
little more privacy. The table was adorned with big linen
napkins and a splendid anthurium, looking like a priapic
valentine, and a huge cloth, stiff and white as a priest's
collar, that ran to the floor. I looked about and marveled.
For Center City, The Matchbook was a great place. A few
years ago I would have pleasantly surrendered to temptation and had a drink at lunchtime, which would have been
the end of my day. I asked Brushy when she was here last.

"Yesterday," she said. "With Pagnucci."

I'd forgotten. "How was that?"

"Strange," she said.

"What did he want? Groundhog stuff?"

"Just a little. Basically I think he was trying to figure out why I keep having lunch with Krzysinski."

"Jeez, I hope you slapped his face."

She squeezed my knee with a grip strong enough to cause pain.

"He wasn't being like that. It was business."

"Pagnucci? What a surprise. What did he want to know?"

"Well, he said it's a turbulent period for the firm. He wondered how I viewed things, my practice. He made it sound like a management review."

"Sort of checking you out for a mid-life crisis?"

"Sort of. I thought he was trying to set a context. You know, for Groundhog Day. Points. But the way he ended up putting it was, did I think that my personal relationship with Tad was strong enough that TN would remain a client of mine, come what may?"

" 'Come what may'?"

"His words."

I took a moment. Brushy and Pagnucci would make a great team, a litigator and a securities guy, two up-and-coming Italians.

"Did he actually say it? That he was thinking of leaving the firm and taking you with him?"

"Mack, we're talking Pagnucci here. He barely gets a word out. He made it sound, you know, like some remote curiosity."

"Like a dinner party game. Who Would You Be If You Weren't You?"

"Exactly. And I cut him off. I told him I was fond of

my partners and proud of the work we do and that I didn't spend my time thinking about questions like that.''

"Good for you. Leotis couldn't have done better. Was he abashed?''

"He completely agreed. He fumpfered around. 'Of course, of course.' He tried to act as if it was nothing to him.''

"Carl obviously thinks I'm not finding Bert, the money's not coming back, TN's going bye-bye, and the firm is too. Right?''

"Maybe. He's probably just being cautious. Considering all the angles. You know Carl.''

"Maybe he *knows* I'm not going to find Bert.''

"How would he?''

I couldn't figure much that made sense. Especially after Carl had blessed my voyage to Pico.

The waiter came and we ordered iced teas, then Brushy on second thought asked for white wine. We looked over the menus, a foot and half if they were an inch, old-fashioned, with vellum pages and a tasseled binding. I remained puzzled by Pagnucci's game, but Brushy cut me short when I returned to the subject.

"Mack, do you really think I wanted to have lunch so we could talk about Pagnucci?''

I told her if I had, I probably wouldn't have come.

"I want you to try to be serious about something,'' she said. "You hurt my feelings yesterday.''

Within, I recoiled. Some ancient retractile mechanism set in. Another lecture from another woman about how I'd disappointed her. We were going to have feminist reconstruction of my spicy remarks about her wandering loins.

"Hey, Brush, I thought we went past that. It's me, us, you and me. Pals forever."

"That's the point." She faced me in a casual way, so that we were more or less knee to knee. Her back was to the adjoining wall and she propped an arm on the top of the banquette and leaned her full face and her soft hairdo against a hand in an appealing fashion. She looked frank and friendly, like a teenager in her rec room. "I thought the next time you danced the hokey-pokey, Malloy, it was going to be with me."

That one took me a sec.

"You did?" This was apparently one of those male-female understandings that so often eluded me.

"Yes, I did." She pouted. Cutely.

"I guess, Brush, I thought I'd missed my chance. I figured we'd just sort of finished that."

"I guess I figured we'd just sort of started." Her little eyes were luminous and very much alive, full of the quest. Like a great institution, say a university or the President of the United States, Brushy was seldom formally rejected. According to the know-alls with whom I served on recruiting, nosy fishwives who somehow always heard this stuff, Brushy over the years had mastered a perfect line: 'I'm wondering if I should let you make love to me.' The nonplussed or the sincerely uninterested could back off, with little harm to either party. I was touched that she'd actually gamble, but I was confused in the presence of real emotion. While I went blank, she, as usual, took the lead.

"Unless," she said, "there's no spark." I felt, with that, her fingers laid daintily on the meat of my thigh, and then as she held my eye, her palm touched down and her hand skated home. She gave my little business a squeeze which in the scheme of things might best be called affectionate. I had no doubt anymore why she'd wanted a place with tablecloths.

How to respond? The adrenaline, the shock inspired an elevated mood, a kind of lunacy which in retrospect I attribute to the dizziness of the rare feeling that something significant was at stake. She was, as I have always known, a hell of a gal. And I was vaguely amused by how close this was to what I'd imagined with Krzysinski. But Brushy had the talent of all seductive females, to recognize a guy's fantasies and play along with them, without feeling debased.

"I would say there's a spark," I told her, still caught up in that fixed look, her green eyes with their clever gleam. "I would say you'd make a hell of a Boy Scout."

"*Boy* Scout?"

"Yes, ma'am, cause you keep rubbing that stick, you're gonna get a lot more than a spark."

"I'm hoping for that."

We were eye to eye, nose to nose, but in the dignified air of The Matchbook there would be no embrace. Instead, I turned a bit on the bench, diddled my fingers a little on her knee, then, leaning close like I was about to impart a little joke, slid my hand up her hosiery toward the female zero point, thinly guarded by the layer of panty hose. I looked her square in the eye, gathered the fabric, and gave it a sharp yank so that Brushy actually flinched. But she kept watching me, highly amused, as I found the gap I'd rent and tenderly as I could nuzzled two fingertips against her labia.

"Is this what we call equal opportunity?" she asked.

"Maybe. But you see, Brush, I got further than you. It's still a man's world."

"Oh," said Brushy, and lay back a bit, grabbing the tablecloth and tenting it in a casual way over my hand, which was already beneath her napkin. She opened the menu and rested it between her waist and the edge of the table, making it more or less a roof, a privacy panel. Then her hips came forward and her knees parted. She lit a cigarette. And took hold of her wine. She faced me, taking her pleasure with a wild gimlet eye, a woman who loved life when it reduced itself to this basis.

She said, "I'm not sure I'd agree with that."

B. Would You Call This a Success?

In the room at Dulcimer House things were going pretty well until I took off my shorts. Then Brushy screamed. She covered her mouth with both hands.

"What's that?" She was pointing at me and it wasn't because she was so impressed.

"What's what?"

"That rash." She steered me to the mirror. There I was with half a boner and a livid band, shaped like a land mass, covering my hip. There was an island extension that broadened as it crossed my circumference and disappeared in the pubic overgrowth. I stared, feeling direly conspired against. Then it hit me.

"The fucking Russian Bath."

"Ah hah," she said.

She reared back when I moved toward her again.

"It's dermatitis," I said, "it's nothing. I didn't even know I had it."

"That's what they all say."

"Brushy."

"You better see your doctor, Malloy."

"Brushy, have a heart here."

"It's the nineties, Mack." She stalked naked through the room. She pushed through her clothes and I was afraid she was dressing, but it was only a cigarette she was after. She sat across from me on an overstuffed brocaded chair, smoking, naked as a jaybird with her heel on the fancy fabric, leaking female fluids on the nice furniture. The stick figures do well for clothes racks, but naked, a woman with Brushy's Rubensesque proportions was still a lovely sight. I remained rosy and pointed for action, but I could tell from her posture that I had reached my sexual high point at lunch.

I lay down on the bed and, feeling I had every right to, began to moan.

"Mack," she said, "don't be like that. You're making me feel bad."

"Jeez, I hope so."

"It'll just be a few days," she said. She gave me a doctor's name and said he might even prescribe over the phone. She sounded authoritative, but I stowed all those questions she didn't like me to ask.

I quieted eventually. Soon I was back to being myself, primarily sad, staring at the classy ceiling here at the Dulcimer House, where the plaster decorations around the light fixture radiated off in various whitish doodles. We had been here once before, of course—with similar success. I had felt it was a mistake to start, checking into the same hotel—the same amiable stroll over here, a little frozen up with anticipation and propriety, trying, within hailing distance of the office, to look like anything but two people going to fuck; the same kind of sycophantic desk clerk; the same sort of room with heavy furnishings, a bit too dated to be tasteful. One more failure to connect. I felt rather imprisoned by the cycles in my life.

"I got drunk two nights ago, Brush," I said suddenly. "What do you think of that?"

"Not much," she said. I didn't think she meant she had no opinion. When I cranked my head around to see her in the chair, still naked, still smoking, I could tell from her level expression that this hadn't been a thunderbolt. "You looked pretty awful yesterday," she said. She asked if I had enjoyed it.

"Not particularly," I answered. "But I can't seem to get the taste out of my mouth."

"Do you think you're going to do it again?"

"Nope," I told her, and then, feeling almost as tough as she is, added, "I might."

I lay there feeling all the weight of my big fat body, this belly like a medicine ball, these saddlebags of fat that ride my back above the hipbones.

"Oh, don't you get sick of it?" I asked. "Another Irish lawyer. Another Irish drunk. I'm so tired of being myself—of fucking things up the way I do. It's a tiredness not lost in sleep and only worse on waking. I can't help thinking how great it would be to start new. A really clean slate. It's the only thing left that excites me.''

''It makes me sad when you talk like that,'' she said. ''It doesn't become you. You're just asking for someone to tell you that you're really okay.''

''No, I'm not. I wouldn't believe it.''

''You're a good man, Malloy. And a good lawyer too.''

''No,'' I said, ''no. Wrong on both fronts. To tell you the truth, Brush, I don't really think I'm cut out for the law anymore. Books and bills and briefs. It's a black-and-white life and I'm a guy who loves color.''

''Come on, Mack. You're one of the best lawyers there. When you do it.''

I made a sound.

''In the old days, you were there all the time. You had to enjoy some of it.''

When I drank, I worked like a demon, billed twenty-two, twenty-four hundred hours a year. I was in the office until eight and in the bars until midnight—then back in the Needle at eight the next morning. Lucinda used to bring Bufferin with my coffee. When I set about changing my life at AA, that was another of the habits I broke. I went home at six—saw the wife, the kid. And was divorced inside a year. It doesn't take Joyce Brothers to figure out what that proves.

''The truth?'' I asked. ''I don't even remember. I don't remember what it was like to be busy. I don't remember where I stood at the firm before Jake decided I was a useless piece of dung.''

''What are you talking about? Are you grumping because he doesn't send you work right now? Believe me,

Mack, you have a great future with that client. Krzysinski respects you. Give that time. It'll work out.''

Krzysinski again. I mulled on that, then set her straight.

"Look, Brush, there is no future. Jake stopped sending me work because he knows it's his ass if anybody at G&G drops the ball and he figures I'm a guy who can't catch a pop fly.''

"That's not so.''

"Yes, it is,'' I said. "And he's probably right. I mean, I liked trying cases. Getting up in front of a jury. Waving my hands around. Seeing if I could make them love me. But nobody's sure I can handle the stress anymore and stay sober. Including me. Without that, I don't like it all. I'm just hooked on the money.''

I felt bruised, lying there, pounding myself with the truth. But I knew I was on the mark. Money was worse than booze or cocaine. God, it could just go in the sweet rush of spending. You start visiting the tailor, buy the Beemer, maybe pick up a little country house, find a club or two not picky enough to keep you out. Next thing you know, two sixty-eight before taxes, and you're looking in the button drawer for coins to pay your bridge tolls. Not to mention being a drunk who used to arrive home routinely, pulling my pockets inside out under the light of my front porch, wondering, sort of abstractly, where it was all those twenties went. (As well as my house keys, which on one occasion I eventually realized I'd thrown into the tin cup of some beggar.) Now I had an ex with a nice German car and a house in the country and God to thank that I paid alimony and had something to show for the money I made.

"We all are," she said. "Hooked. To some extent. It's part of the life."

"No," I said. "You meant what you told Pagnucci. You love it. You love G&G. You'd work there for free."

She made a face, but I had her nailed and she knew it.

"What is it?" I asked. "Seriously. I never got it. To me, you know, all these lawsuits, it's my robber baron's better than your robber baron. What do you get off on? The law?"

"The law. Sure." She nodded, mostly to herself. "I mean, all this right and wrong. It's nifty."

" 'Nifty'?"

She came over and lay beside me, belly down. She had those bandy legs and her bad skin, but she looked awfully good to me, a perky little derriere. I patted her rear and she smiled. The flag was unfurling again, but I knew it was no use. Besides, she had her mind on the law now, and that, as I'd told her, was really the love of her life.

"It's the whole thing," she said, "all of it. Money. The work. The *world*. You know how it is when you're a child, you want to live in a fairy tale, you want to play house with Snow White, and I mean, here I am, hanging out with all of these people I read about in the *Journal* and the business pages of the *Tribune*." Brushy, Wash, Martin, all of them, they kept track of the movements of big-time corporate America—financings, acquisitions, promotions—avid as soap opera fans, gobbling up the *Journal* and the local business press every morning with a hunger I felt only for the sports page.

"Like Krzysinski."

She darted a warning look at me but answered straight.

"Like Krzysinski. And they *like* me, these people. And I like them. I mean, I think about what a mess I was when I got here. I was the only female lawyer in Litigation and I was scared to death. Remember?"

"Couldn't forget." She had been on fire in the self-consuming fashion of the sun. Brushy knew she was a woman in a man's world—just ahead of the female gold rush to law school—and she confronted her prospects with a combustive emotional mix of hell-bent determination and ravaging anxiety. She was the only girl in a family of five, born plug in the middle, and her situation here matched something that had faced her at home, some yes-and-no game she was always playing with herself. She'd do something brilliant, then come to one of her confidants—me or somebody else—and explain, with utmost sincerity, how it had all been accidental and would never be repeated, how she felt doomed by the expectations created by her own success. It was exhausting—and painful—just to listen to her, but even then I felt drawn to her, the way certain free molecules always react. I shared, I suppose, all these alternate moods, the brashness, the fear, the inclination to first blame myself.

"And now. All these people—they *need* me. I did this piece of takeover litigation for Nautical Paper a couple of years ago. My father worked there for a while, you know decades ago, but after we'd won the case I got this note from Dwayne Gandolph, the CEO, thanking me for the great work I'd done. It made me dizzy. Like inhaling Benzedrine. I brought it to my folks' home and we all passed it around the dinner table and looked at it. The entire family was impressed with me—*I* was impressed with me."

I understood what she was saying, perhaps more than she did, that her membership in this world was too hard-won not to be valued, too much a symbol to her to be understood as anything else. But she was smiling at herself for the moment. Gosh, she was great. We both thought so. I admired her enormously, the distances she'd dragged herself and her baggage. I gave her a smooch and we lay there necking for maybe ten minutes, two grown-ups, both of them naked in the daylight in a goddamn hotel room, just kissing and touching hands. I held her awhile, then she told me we had to go. There was G&G, the office, work to do.

We both laughed when she poked her fist through the hole in her panty hose. She put them on anyway and asked how I was doing finding Bert.

"I'm not going to find him," I said. She went quizzical and I told her what I hadn't yet said to anyone else—that I thought Bert was dead.

"How could Bert be dead?" she asked. "Who has the money?" It required only an instant, I noted, for her to reach the question that had come to me after a week.

"It's an interesting window of opportunity, isn't it?"

She had sat down in the chair again, half-dressed and posed against the fancy brocade. I loved looking at her.

"You mean," she said, "if somebody knew Bert was dead, they could blame it on him?"

"That's what I mean." I was off the bed, stepping into my trousers. "But they'd have to *know*," I said. "They couldn't be guessing. If Bert shows up again, they'd look pretty bad."

"Well, how would they be sure?"

I looked at her.

"You mean someone killed him? From the firm? You don't believe that."

I didn't, in fact. There was logic to it, but little sense. I told her that.

"These are just theories, right? Bert being dead? All of it?" She wanted more than my reassurance. She was being her true self, relentless, beating the idea to death like a snake.

"Those are theories," I told her, "but listen to this." I told her then about my meetings yesterday, first with Jake, then with the Committee. This time I caught her off guard. She sat far forward, her mouth formed in a small perfect *o*. She was too distressed to feign valiance.

"Never," she said finally. "They'll never agree to something like that. That kind of cover-up. They have too much character."

"Wash?" I asked. "Pagnucci?"

"Martin?" she responded. Brushy's reverence for Martin was even greater than mine. "You'll see," she said. "They'll do the right thing."

I shrugged. She could be right, and even if she wasn't, she was improved by thinking the best of her partners. But she could see she hadn't really persuaded me.

"And Jake," she said, "my God, how sleazy. What's wrong with him?"

"You just don't know Jake. If you'd grown up with him, you'd see another side."

"Meaning?"

"I could tell you stories." I fumbled in her purse for a

cigarette. I was tempted to tell her about the bar exam, but realized on second thought that she'd think less of me than Jake.

"You don't trust him, right? That's what you're suggesting. He wasn't brought up to be trustworthy?"

"I know him. That's all."

In the green chair, she was stilled by disquiet.

"You don't like Jake, do you? I mean, all that palling around with him. That's bull, isn't it?"

"Who wouldn't like Jake? Rich, good-looking, charming. Everyone likes Jake."

"You've got a chip on your shoulder about Jake. It's obvious."

"All right. I have a chip on my shoulder about a lot of things."

"Don't wait for me to say you're wrong."

"I'm bitter and petty, right?" She could tell what I was thinking: I'd heard the tune before, someone else had sung the words, another chanteuse.

"I would never say petty. Look, Mack, he's lucky. In life, some people are lucky. You can't sit around despising good fortune."

"Jake is a coward. He's never had the balls to face what he should have. And I let him make me a coward with him. That's the part that frosts me."

"What are you talking about?"

"Jake." I looked at her hard. I could feel myself turning mean, Bess Malloy's son, and she saw it too. She stepped into her pumps and fixed the clasp on her purse. She'd been warned off.

"This is attorney-client, right?" she finally asked. "All

of this. About Jake saying not to tell?" She wasn't being humorous. She meant that the communication was privileged. That she was forbidden to repeat it, to TN or anyone else, and thus that BAD could never criticize her for failing to come forward, as, ethically, each of us was obliged to do.

"That's right, Brushy, you're covered. There's no shit on your shoes."

"That's not what I meant."

"Yes, it is," I said, and she did not bother to answer back. A certain familiar melancholy attacked me midline, spreading from the heart. Ain't life grand? Every man for himself. I sank down on the bed, on the heavy embroidered spread which we'd never removed, and couldn't quite look at her.

Eventually she sat beside me.

"I don't want you to tell me any more about this. It makes me feel weird. And confused. It's too close to home. And I don't know what to do. How to react." She touched my hand. "I'm not perfect either, you know."

"I know."

She waited.

"I think this thing is frightening and out of control," she said at last. "All of it. I'm worried about you."

"Don't worry. I may bitch a lot, Brush, but in the end I can take care of myself." I looked at her. "I'm like you."

I wasn't sure how that sat and neither was she. She went to the chair and picked up her purse, then on second thought stopped off to kiss me. She had decided to forgive me, that things, everything, could be worked through. I held her hand for a second, then she left me there, sitting on the bed, alone in the hotel room.

XVI. INVESTIGATION APPROACHES CLIMAX, INVESTIGATOR GOES FURTHER

My afternoon with Brushy left me in a state. Longing—real longing—took me as a walloping surprise. I reeled around in an adolescent fit, captured in transported recollections of the impressive qualities of Brushy's person, her pleasant scent of light perfume and body cream, and the pure transmission of some as yet unnamed form of human-emitted electromagnetic sensation which continued to grip my thorax and my loins. From my house that night I called her at home, reaching only her machine. I told myself that she was in the office, a number I did not have the bravery to dial.

I had called her doctor, who'd prescribed a salve, and I went to the john to give myself another treatment. In my sensuous thrall, I soon found myself otherwise engaged. Unspeakable activities. I sweated in my bathroom, imagining wild amours with a woman who'd been naked in my arms a few hours before, and wondered about my life.

I had just reholstered when I noticed the catarrh of an engine idling outside. I was stabbed at once by the kind of probing guilt my mother would have cheered, chilled by the thought that Lyle and his pals might have seen my filmy shape through the wobbled glass blocks of the bathroom window. I would have made quite a sight, backlit, bending and swaying as I squeezed the sound from my own sax. I heard the front door bang and gave some thought to remaining locked up there. But that was not my approach with Lyle. In any circumstance, I felt committed to staring him down.

I encountered him as he galloped up the stairs. In his various rangy parts, he looked a little more organized than usual; I suspected he was with a girl. His spume of hair was combed and he had on a Kindle County Unified Police Force leather jacket, not mine but one he'd purchased from the cop supply house on Murphy Street and which he wore in unspoken comment on the time when I had what he judged a more authentic life. He stomped past me, muttering something I did not catch at first.

"Mom's downstairs," he repeated.

"Mom?"

"Remember her? Nora? It's boys' night out." I wondered if it meant anything positive that he was treating his parents' foibles with humor rather than undiluted contempt. We were in the dim interior hallway between the upstairs bedrooms, and after a few steps he turned back to me with a smirk. "Hey, man, what the hell were you doing just now? In the john? We were like taking bets."

"You and your mother?" I asked. I summoned all my courtroom dignity and told him I was blowing my nose.

Frankly, he could not have cared less, but when he walked off down the dark corridor, I felt so hollowed by shame I thought I might stumble. Often humiliated and seldom saved. Is it just a Catholic thought that sex will always get you in trouble? God, I thought. God. What a moment that must have been. A boy and his mother laying odds on whether the old goat's actually up there having a wank. I headed down in an appropriate mood to see my former wife.

Nora was standing in the bright lights of the front entry, framed by the white molding and the storm door, holding on to her purse and not venturing any farther inside. I kissed her cheek, a gesture she received stoically.

"How are you?" she asked.

"Jolly," I said. "You?"

"Jolly."

Serve and volley. Here we were, a total standoff after twenty-one years. After flips and swirls and curly dos, Nora had let her hair go straight, so that it hung lank and fine and almost black, looking as it does on those Japanese gals who seem to have surrounded their faces with a lacquer frame. She had given up makeup too. I saw Nora infrequently enough that she was starting to look different to me. The work of time was no longer undetectable for being observed day by day. Her chin was getting full and her eyes were sinking into shadow. She looked okay, though, except for her manifest agitation at being here.

Nora had a different life now, one that she thought of as better and truer than the decades she'd spent with me. New friends. New interests. A big-city life. Female circles principally, no doubt, with meetings, lectures, parties. I'm sure that days went by before she woke to any recollection of me—or Lyle. One foot inside this house and something fearsome gripped her, I suspected, not nostalgia, but the terror that she would be confined again, imprisoned, held hostage once more from her real self.

"You can sit." I swung a hand beyond the black slate of the foyer to the worn meal-colored carpet of the living room.

"It's just a minute. He wanted to stop for money. He's going to take me out."

"Money?" With that, I heard footsteps overhead. He was in my room, rooting for cash. Nora heard the same thing, and gave me the wrinkle of some happy, suburbanized expression she'd seen on TV.

"He's no better," I told her. "Not a bit."

The plainness of this observation seemed to catch us both; somehow a sense of tragedy reared up between us so large that I thought we'd both go down like bowling pins. You could never get around the future with Lyle, the way he was now and the suspicion that it foretold something grim, that he was worse than an unhappy kid, but was one of those people—everybody knows several—who turns out to be lame, crippled, not even up to the dismal functions, like holding a job or hanging in with someone else, which allow us our meager share of daily satisfactions. In the moment of recognition nobody—not Nora, not me— could run from the unhappy evidence that our lives were once one thing, not merely a failure of spirit but an institution of cause and effect of which neither law nor will could annul the unfortunate consequences. Those would roll on through another generation or two.

"And whose fault is that, Mack?" she asked. The answer, if we were going to be honest—which we weren't—was probably elaborate. We could start with Grandma and Grandpa and go on from there. But I knew Nora. We were starting a game of Matrimonial Geography, in which Nora would point out how all roads on the map of blame led only to me.

"Desist," I said, "cease. Let's fight about something less predictable. A new subject. Just skip Lyle, money, or me."

"Look at your life, Mack. You're Mr. Entropy. What can you expect from him?" Her observations through the bathroom window seemed to have emboldened her, though ordinarily she did not need much excuse.

Mr. Entropy, I thought. There were entire universes saved from self-reproach by that remark. Jesus, this was one person who didn't take long to get under my skin.

"He's thirty years younger than me and doesn't have the same well-worn excuses." I smiled tightly and she made various faces, implying it was all right, she could take being stiff-armed. We confronted one another in simmering silence until Lyle returned and blew past me, taking his mother in tow.

In the aftermath, I settled by the TV in the living room. The Hands were playing UW–Milwaukee the usual tough first half—both their bench and self-confidence would give out in the last twenty minutes, when they would resume their role as this decade's Mid-Ten doormat. Within, I continued prolonged fomenting. Nora fucking Goggins. Entropy! How long had she been storing up that one? There was always a hundred-megaton warhead in her silo.

When I stopped drinking, Nora used to tell me I was really no fun anymore, a line that served the great principle of relationship transitivity by which she could both put me down and make excuses for herself. If I was no fun, she should have fun on her own. We reached a seven-week period where she went off for weekend conventions three times and then finally a midweek night when my bride of nineteen years simply did not come home.

When I marched through the door the next evening, the house was clean, I could smell a hot meal, a relative rarity, and I immediately made out the plan: life as normal. The idea was that I should ask nothing. Neither of us had enough fingers and toes to count the occasions when I'd pulled more or less the same stunt in those nineteen years, nights when I was so drunk that I sometimes felt I had to hang on to the grass to keep from falling off the earth, though usually the barkeep knew enough to give her a call. Nonetheless, about 9:30 I finally glued together my courage.

'I was with Jill,' she answered. Jill Horwich, her erstwhile manager and bartime buddy.

'I know you started out with Jill. I want to know who else you were with.'

'Nobody else.'

'Nora, don't bullshit me.'

'I'm not bullshitting.' When I fixed her with one of those looks she might have given me, she said, 'I don't believe this is happening.' She was on her feet, twisting the wedding ring around on her finger, posed in a corner of the living room where a lovely brass vase with gladioli was arranged. I was, I admitted, struck at that moment by the enduring phenomenon of beauty. 'Mack, leave it be. I know I don't have the right to ask that. But I am.'

'Motion denied,' I said. 'Let's go. The sticky truth.'

'You don't want to know.'

'You're right, I don't. But I'm asking anyway.'

'Why?' She looked at me bleakly.

'I suppose I sort of think it's important.'

Silence.

'So who's the guy?'

'There is no guy, Mack.'

'Nora, who were you with?'

'I told you, Mack, I was with Jill.'

Press your buzzer when you have the correct answer. It was the next afternoon before I got it, sitting in my office, being, as usual, no use to anyone, talking as I recall to Hans Ottobee, an interior decorator hired to do something about my furnishings. Nineteen years, you think you've seen everything from a person and then some guy mentions a modular wall unit and somehow you see something else. I always loved cubism. What a wonderful illusion that you can see all sides at once.

At home that night, I didn't wait long. She'd cooked again. I took my plate of pot roast from the oven and started right in.

'So how long have you been like this?'

'What do you mean "like this"?'

'Spare me. When did you start?' I finally got the heart to look at her straight on, which was more or less the end of the game.

'Always.' She blinked. 'As far as I know.'

' "Always"?'

'Do you remember Sue Ellen Tomkins?'

'From the sorority?'

She just nodded.

'I don't think women are like men,' she said. 'I don't expect you to understand.'

'Jesus,' I said.

'Mack, this is taking incredible courage for me.'

She apparently did not consider that it wasn't particularly easy for me. People who stay married, who hold on for the long pull, put up with a lot from each other: personal oddities, bad habits, ill health. For some it's tolerance, others commitment, many, like me, fear the unknown. For a while I tested myself with the notion that I should put up with this too. People stay married without sex. I'd known plenty. After all, I grew up a Catholic. And who even said it had to be like that? But it just sort of cut to the heart of things. I never saw this issue in normative terms. I wasn't worried that it was a perversion, or something that would have made my sainted ma faint, and I gave Nora no points just because it was the latest in style. It just seemed like an awful lot not to know. For her not to tell. For me not to recognize.

So what was it like for her, those many years with drunken old Mack, whose sails on rare occasion would blow full of lust and fall upon her, riding her waves, mast in her harbor? What did she think? How much was she faking? Inquiring minds want to know. I sat there tonight with the wretched dark broken by the flickering of the sporting event and the announcer's occasionally hysterical pitch, trying to fathom it all, and found myself, for me, admirably charitable. I doubt she knew what to think. She must have felt uncertain, not really herself. Not resentful. Not engaged. How could she not know? you ask. The law governs acts, not evil intent alone, and we seem to take that lesson to heart. In this life—Catholic theology notwithstanding—we are what we do. She must have thought about her college friend from time to time and been surprised to find herself stimulated by the memory. She must have put it off to voyaging youth, the same untamed daring that let her give fellas blow jobs on the second date, and dismissed her continuing reflections as part of the universe of unruly and unsavory things rattling around in the average human mind. At times she must have confronted herself starkly with the question—*Am I?*—and at other instants comforted herself with the facts: husband, boys in the past, her roots in the present, her child. It must have taken her by surprise to have been so pleased the first time Jill Horwich laid a hand on her shoulder and then, feigning inadvertence, brushed against her breasts. That's what I think. I didn't know, whatever the disbelief with which that state of knowledge—or grace—is greeted. We see a person, hear a voice, are drawn most intimately to them, and yet so much remains unknown. No matter how earnestly we search, the mysteries abide. As Nora would tell you, we do not even know for certain when we look in the mirror.

Practicing man's original sin, I have found my own unruly mind passing over the image of the two of them, with Jill's face buried up to the brows in Nora's female region and my wife lolled back in an ecstasy she only aspired to with me. I see this, I admit, with an unseemly exactness of detail, imagining it from Nora's eyes, another of those figures I can't manage to paint. Afterwards, I am morose, immobilized by grief. But often in the instant of sensation and heat, in that image of Nora finally free, relishing her own sensations like the finest music, I have a certain flight myself, as if something similar were even possible for me.

So that's what I thought, staring frozenly at the TV, suddenly recollecting how much I loved to drink and hating my surroundings. I swear, aren't the Irish the tackiest decorators in the world, dark and cheap, with so many fucking little knickknacks collared in dust that I never can find an inch of space on a tabletop to put down a glass, and too much lace and all the required family pictures? My ma's place looked just like this too, kind of a savage irony, since Nora hated Bess, both her tightfisted, pursed-lipped, judgmental ways and her flipside moods where she was worshipfully reverent of her men. More's the marvel, since as time passes and I close my eyes, it feels as if they both filled the same space inside.

The TV screen was full of a big close-up of the referee. As I watched the picture, some extraordinary sensation of discovery took hold of me: I was at once suddenly focused, rescued, finally free.

"That guy!" I shouted in the empty house. I knew him, I'd seen his face.

In Pigeyes's drawing.

That was Kam Roberts.

XVII. I COULDN'T HAVE BEEN
MORE SURPRISED IF THE HANDS
HAD WON

A. Phantom of the Fieldhouse

Among the many noble institutions that, years ago, had first sought Leotis Griswell's counsel was the U. For his partners, this connection was priceless, inasmuch as it allowed us to obtain prime seats for football and basketball games and private tours of important university facilities like the bevatron or the fieldhouse, where the Hands played their games. I'd been down on the lacquered playing floor, with the huge-knuckled hands drawn at the center line amid a collar of vermilion, had capered down the tunnels and visited the locker rooms. Most important now, I'd also been to the ugly little changing room, where the refs dressed before games and sat out halftime and, after the final buzzer, immediately showered and put on their street clothes and dark glasses and escaped by mixing into the throng, rather than waiting for any lurking villain who wanted to engage in his own instant replay of various calls.

Flying out of the house, I grabbed only a tweed sport jacket and drove recklessly over the river back into the city, wary of black-and-whites as I spun the dial to find the game on the radio. I had to lower the windows to clear the odor from yesterday morning and the Chevy was frigid. I blew on my fingers when I stopped at each light. It turned to halftime, the Hands down by only a bucket. I was desperate to get there while the refs were off the floor so that I'd have some chance to get hold of this Kam.

Approaching this guy, whatever his name was, was going to be dicey. As far as I was concerned, the bookies and he could fix what they liked, but I didn't expect him to be carefree about that, and almost everything I might mention was likely to spook him. I was curious, naturally, although it didn't take much imagination to see how having a ref in your pocket could be, as they say in the law, outcome-determinative: a foul here and there, an out-of-bounds, a jump ball, a goal tend, a travel, all called or not. You could probably swing twenty to thirty points a game without being too obvious, given the usual grousing about officiating and the fact that in a sport like basketball, where everybody's always pushing and moving, a ref can only be expected to see so much. Archie had a great thing with this Kam, no question, but I had retired as a policeman. All I needed was to know about Bert—alive or dead, and if the former, how to make contact. For my sake, aside from my usual snoopy impulses, I didn't even need to know where Bert fit in their scam.

The fieldhouse, "The House of the Hands," as it was

known, was the usual old university structure, a formidable mass of the same red-clay bricks from which most of the U.'s buildings were constructed. The House was relieved of utter grimness by roofline adornments of turrets and battlements and gunsight notches blocked out of stone. Someone will have to explain to me someday why the architectural plans for so many of the land-grant universities seem to have been borrowed from Clausewitz. What was the idea, that if the South rose again these buildings could be converted to armories?

At the moment I could have used my own militia, since without it I could not find any place to park. The attendant at the lot across the street stoutly refused the two twenties I tried to force on him to get the Chevy inside, and I tore off around the block, sweating, swearing, itchy and bitchy, running out of time. Outside the fieldhouse the hawkers with the pennants and cups, buttons and banners, were milling with nothing to do, putting up with the little black kids in hooded sweatshirts and tatty coats who hung out just to get a scent of the game and the players. A dribble of early departees emerged through the gates two or three at a time. There were no more than five minutes left of halftime by now. The teams would be out there warming up, trying to look loose and jovial while they strutted their stuff without opposition, jamming and blocking, doing drills; the refs would soon follow them back out. I finally left the car on the street in a red zone. With luck, if I found this guy, I could be back out in ten minutes.

I did not have a ticket. This didn't occur to me until I saw the gate attendant. They guarded the entrances throughout the game due to the little kids outside, who employed considerable craft figuring out how to get in. I ran back to the ticket windows in front, which were closed when I got there. I had to get a glum kid to go fetch some old biddy, who raised the shade halfway, eyed me serenely, and said, "I'm sorry, we're totally sold out."

"I'll take standing room."

"Fire marshal doesn't allow that here in the House." The shade dropped. I heard her walking away while I pounded on the glass.

Back in front, I found some guy with three young kids, leaving to put them to sleep; he did not mind parting with his ticket stub for ten bucks, and I ran back to a different gate. The two student ushers, a boy and a girl in their red sport coats, were both overweight and obviously amorous, still overcome by that first thrill of love, the amazing news that in the flight of life, solo thus far, there might be a co-pilot. Watching them, I had an abrupt thought of Brushy, pleasing and then somehow muddled and pained. I bulled through the stiles between them, shaking my head and smiling and telling anyone who could hear how glad I was that I'd remembered the car lights. As I rushed on, I heard the boom of the horn and the crowd suddenly rousing itself: the second half was starting. I was in the dark rampway by then and I stood beneath the enormous welling crowd noise muttering, "Fuck." I could be one of those jerks who run out on the court, but the best that would come of that would be a trip to District 19, maybe even a clubbing.

Instead, I slowly paced through the warren of brick corridors, trying to remember where the refs' changing room was. The old interior bricks of the place were all painted in a heavy enamel, a garish Hands' vermilion that refracted the spectral light. The air had a sort of salty smell, not so much sweat as excitement, the way lightning leaves the pungency of ozone in its wake. Already there was a lull in the clamor, which meant that the Hands were fading. Passing by a ramp up, I caught a look at the big four-sided scoreboard suspended on taut cables between the rafters and the blue ribbons of smoke floated in from the hallways. Milwaukee had put up six points in the first forty seconds out of the locker room. Maybe the Hands weren't even on the court.

Finally I found what I was looking for, a simple wooden door painted the same red as the bricks and labeled "Authorized Personnel Only." I caught my only break of the night. The security guard in his ill-fitting red jacket was down the concrete corridor a good fifty yards, his radio clutched to his ear as he meandered, probably on his way for a leak now that halftime was over. I grabbed the knob and went through like I knew what I was doing. There were steel stairs, then a long low passage lit by bare incandescent bulbs, a janitor's gangway running downward beside the boiler pipes and plumbing into the fieldhouse basement, where the refs changed.

To be under there while the game roared above was strange. Overhead there was glamour. The ash floor gleamed under the phenomenal brightness of the stadium lights. The cheerleaders, heartbreaking emblems of youth, simple in their grace, like flowers, flounced their skirts and jumped up and down. In the stands that timeless thing that goes back to when we ran in packs was strumming like the current in a high voltage wire in 18,000 sober citizens who were now nothing but one mass of screaming freaks.

People with troubles, with a disabled kid or a mortgage they couldn't meet, were shouting so loud that tomorrow they wouldn't be able to speak at work, but now they were thinking of nothing but whether some long-bodied kid in shorts could throw a leather ball through a hole.

And the refs would be out there, dressed in black and white amid the colors and brightness, the very figures of reason, the law, the rules, the arbiters, the force that kept it a game, not a fistfight. Down here was where they got ready, where they steadied themselves and came to grips with reality, and believe me, it stank. Literally. I remembered from visiting before. The changing room would be gamy with sweat, a little closet with a seven-foot ceiling, an architectural afterthought carved out of the service channel that runs for the sewer pipes. The walls were wood, painted some miserable yellowish eggshell lacquer that glimmered cheaply under the unshaded bulbs. There were two little partitioned changing cubicles and a shower and a crapper, each behind a blue canvas drape, a setup that offered about the same level of privacy that inmates get in a holding cell.

At the bottom, the gangway joined a tunnel that ran up at an angle, leading to the court. Noise and light were funneled down, and as I got close to the door of the changing room, looking up the concrete channel to courtside, I could see the legs and red coat hems of two security guys stationed there to guard this area. The crowd above and the fury of the game, the pounding sounds of the court, the whistles, the yells, reached down here like exotic music.

The door to the changing room was like the one I'd come through above, an old wood thing painted red, with three raised panels. If the security guys up there were smart, they'd have locked it. If not, I'd hide inside, waiting. When I rattled the knob, it didn't give; I shook it twice and swore. I'd have no choice but to lurk about ten feet down the gangway, hoping for a chance as the refs came rushing down the tunnel right after the game. I was likely to get grabbed by security guys. They'd drag me away as I was screaming something dumb like "Kam! Kam Roberts!"

I was still holding the doorknob when I felt it move. The bolt shot back inside, and as my heart seized up, the door opened toward me.

Bert Kamin looked me up and down.

"Hey, Mack," he said. "Jesus, am I glad to see you." He waved me inside and threw the bolt at once when I was beside him. Then he told me something I already knew.

He said, "I'm in a lot of trouble."

B. Troubled Heart

Bert has never really mastered the gestures of amiability. In my unworthy suspicions about him, I imagined he was reluctant to put a hand on your shoulder for fear of what he might reveal. But the fact is that Bert is just strange. His usual manner is of some hey-man hipster. He chews his gum and gives forth with cynical carping from the side of his mouth. I'm never sure exactly who he thinks he is— he comes on like somebody who didn't quite get the sixties, who wanted to be in on what was happening but was too tough or unsentimental to take part. He reminds me at times of the first guy I ever busted, an engaging little rat named Stewie Spivak who was a student at the U. and seemed to enjoy peddling dope much more than taking it.

Bert stood there now bucking his head, telling me I looked good, man, I looked good, while I appraised him too. His dense black hair had grown to an unbarbered length and his hands kept moving to shove it in place; he was unshaved and that weird out-of-kilter light in his eye was brighter than ever. Otherwise, he was neatly turned out in a black leather jacket and a fashionable casual ensemble: Italian sweater with a snazzy pattern, pleated trousers, fancy shoes and socks. Was this the attire of a man on the run? He didn't look quite right, but then he never did.

"So who sent you?" he asked me.

"Who sent *me*?" I reeled around on that line. "Come on, Bert. Who the hell are you kidding? Where've you been? What are you doing here?"

He hung back, squinting a bit, trying to comprehend my agitation in the forgiving way of a child. He remained happy for familiar company.

"I'm waiting for Orleans," he finally said.

"Orleans? Who in God's name is Orleans?" At that Bert's eyes glazed—an aura of galactic mystery took hold. I might as well have asked the secret of the universe, of life. The level of misunderstanding between us was immense—different dimensions. In the silence I noticed that a radio was on. Locked away here in this dungeon, he was still listening to the game. The ceiling was low enough that he was hunched over a bit out of caution, which furthered the impression of something more yielding in his character. He hadn't replied yet when I figured out the answer to my own question.

"The referee," I said.

"Right." He nodded, quite pleased. "Yeah. I'm not supposed to be in here. You either."

Kam Roberts was Orleans. I was piecing it out in my head. Archie owned Orleans, and Orleans, the referee, was Bert's friend. Archie was dead and was once in Bert's refrigerator and Bert was alive and hiding from somebody, maybe just the conference officials of the Mid-Ten. It was not adding. I tried it again, hoping to settle him down and get better information.

"Bert, what's going on here? The cops are looking high and low for you and, especially, for Orleans."

He jumped then. There was an old teacher's desk, probably requisitioned from a classroom, on which the radio sat. Bert had rested against it until I mentioned the police.

"Whoa, whoa, whoa," he said. "For Orleans? The police are looking for Orleans? Why? You know why?" I realized then what was different about him—his emotions were unmasked. Grim and adolescent before, he now seemed almost childish. He was jumpier than I recalled, but also pleasingly sincere. I felt like I was dealing with a younger brother.

"Bert, it's not like the traffic reports, they don't explain. I've been putting little bits together here and there. My guess is that they think your buddy Orleans there has been shading games. For bookies."

He took this badly. He brought his long fingers to his mouth to ponder. The refs' room, as I'd remembered it, was strictly low-rent. On the other side of the court, where the Hands changed, the boosters had provided carpet and whirlpools, weight rooms, a country-club air. But there was nothing similar here. In the center of the room, there was an old backless bench of varnished oak splintered at a corner, and against the wall facing the door three crummy-looking lockers listed. They were rusted in places and one of them was pretty much staved in from a foot or fist hurled by some ref who'd heard those remarks from the crowd about his mother, his eyesight, the size of his penis a little more clearly than he'd allowed out on the floor.

"Bert, there's a lot of screwy stuff going on. There's a body in the refrigerator in your apartment. At least, there was. I think it's another pal of yours. Did you know that?"

He glanced up barely, grimly preoccupied, and nodded a bit.

"That's jail, right?" he asked.

He couldn't have meant murder.

"Fixing basketball games? I'd say that one's pen time, yeah."

He swore. He took a step to the door and then stopped.

"I gotta get him out of here."

"Bert, wait a minute. Why was this guy in your refrigerator?"

"How'd they find out, you think? The cops? About Orleans?"

Talking to Bert is always the same thing, his subject is more important than yours. You have to follow him around like a puppy or a three-year-old child.

"I have no idea, Bert. Frankly, they seemed to have known about Orleans before they knew about you. Actually, they're looking for somebody named Kam Roberts. Is that him?''

He answered me this time. ''It's complicated.'' Then he pounded a fist on his thigh. ''Shit,'' he said. ''I don't understand. How'd they find Archie? Nobody knew he was in there.''

Nobody knew Archie was in there and Bert liked it that way. A brief qualm of something, a feathery spooky feeling like being touched by a moth, passed over me. I scrutinized Bert's vacant manner for signs as I explained to him how it was that I, not the cops, had seen the body.

''By the time they got there, somebody'd adiosed the corpse. Maybe you know who.''

He had the nerve to draw back and look at me as if I'd lost it, then he reverted to his calculations. If the cops hadn't seen Archie, he asked, what brought them to Orleans?

''Bert, how am I supposed to know? They were down at the Russian Bath asking questions. Would they have heard about Kam Roberts there?''

''Oh right,'' said Bert. ''Right, right, right.'' He snapped his fingers a number of times and did a few paces. ''God, me and my mouth, man. My fucking mouth.'' He held still, in considerable pain. When he opened his eyes, he looked right at me.

''If anything happens to me, Mack, can you make sure he gets a lawyer? Will you promise me, man?''

''I promise you, Bert, but give me a hint here. What's gonna happen to you? What are you afraid of?''

With that, there was the first sign of the old Bert, the

sometime madman, always on the brink of falling into his own volcano. Red fury mobilized his expression.

"Come on, Mack! You said you saw what they did to Archie."

"Who we talking here? Outfit?"

I got that much from him, a nod.

"And they want what? Money?" That was my first thought, that they were demanding to be made whole for the losses Archie had palmed off on them.

He looked at me.

"Orleans," Bert said.

"Come again."

"They want Orleans. You know, man. How to find him. Who he is. I mean, that's what they wanted from Archie."

"Did he tell them?"

"How could he? He didn't have any idea where I was getting this stuff. I had a guy I called Kam. That's all he knew." Bert was bouncing around pretty good now, twitchy, scrambling all over the little refs' room like a hamster in a cage. But I thought I was following him. Bert was giving Archie advance word on game outcomes. "Kam's Special." Archie knew only that.

"Did Archie tell them about you?"

"He said he wouldn't. At first. And then the last time I talked to him, he told me— You know, he was pretty emotional. He said they'd kill him if he didn't let them know where it was coming from. They wanted Kam. They gave him like twenty-four hours to bring them Kam. You know, he was beggin'." Bert dared a little look my way, just to see how I handled that thought, some guy pleading with you for a secret to save his life. Which Bert didn't reveal. That's why he was only peeking at me.

"I knew he'd give me up. I already figured I'd have to run. I was edge-city, I kind of snuck home, and I like open the fridge, and I'm so fucking freaked out, I'm like out of my mind, for Godsake what they did to him—" His voice cracked, it broke, big bad Bert Kamin. He squeezed his hands to his eyes. The sight was so strangely out of keeping with what I knew and expected of Bert that a little inky blot of suspicion again darkened my heart. This might all be showtime. Bert after all was a trial lawyer, which meant he was part hambone. But Bert's long dark face appeared earnestly tortured and weak. "What they fucking did to him. And I'm next. I knew that. They're not kidding around, these guys."

My days as a copper sort of deprived me of any respect for the mob. Mind you, there are policemen who fall in with them, who gamble, particularly, and end up on the vig, with their asses owned in a city minute. And there is even an Italian son or two who I always was told had come on the Force because the uncle was some big something who wanted a toehold in the department. But as guys, who are they? Just a bunch of dark Mediterraneans who didn't finish high school really. If you've seen a guy selling fruit down at the market you've seen your basic mobster—some dese dems and dosers with a lot of jewelry who couldn't find something better to do. Accepting the fact that human beings are pretty mean, who but some guy who feels like a pygmy gets his jollies out of making everybody crap in their boots? And they are also the most overpublicized group in history. A city this size has maybe fifty, seventy-five guys max who are really inside, and a bunch of little rats running beside them hoping to gobble up crumbs. That's the mob. They live out in these bungalows on the South End because they don't want the IRS asking where they got the dollars for anything else; they drink coffee and Amaretto and tell each other that they're tough and worry over which of them's wearing electronic underwear, FBI issue. Bad dudes, no doubt about that, not folks you want to get crosswise of or even have to dinner, but their business these days is shrinking. The gangs control drugs. Hooking, that's mostly for oddball stuff now, golden showers, Greek, not straight sex; pornography's the same. The only place they can really still turn a buck is gambling.

"And what do they want to do with Orleans? Kill him?"

"Maybe. I mean, who knows. Do you know? They say not. That's what Archie said, they won't hurt him."

"So what do they want?" I asked, but I caught up at that moment. Orleans was a golden goose and golden geese are not slain. They would want him to give them what he'd given Archie. Points. Fixes. Games. I said that to Bert. "They want him to perform, right?"

"He'll never do it. It's not him. Even if he wanted to, he'd mess it up somehow. They'll kill him. Sooner or later."

"And that's why *you're* running? Here's what I don't get, Bert. What's that to you? In the end."

He didn't answer, but it was there for a second, just a sudden stricken look, his dark face riven by feeling. And I'm slow, Elaine, lumbering, like the coach said in high school, but I get there eventually. Bert was in love with him. With Orleans. There's no real etiquette for this. It's still not the thing to do, to tell your gay friend that you knew all along. So we said nothing.

"Anyway," I said eventually. "You're protecting him."

"Right. I've got to."

"Sure," I said.

He was back by the desk, haunted, caught up in the vastness of all these troubles. He said it aloud a couple of times—"God, what am I going to do?"—and then without any real warning or connection he focused on me.

"And what's with you?" he asked. "I don't get why you're here, man. Who sent you?"

"Our partners, basically, Bert."

He drew back again. He closed one eye. "For what?"

"They want the money back, Bert. No questions asked."

I'd caught him, surprised him. He hung there, mouth vaguely parted as he sought the right words. Taking a step closer to him, I was startled by my own impulse. I was actually halfway to some sly remark, some ingenious quip about splitting the dough. It was as if I'd stuck a hand inside myself, trying to find out what was there. But it was just the same awful mess and I said nothing.

There was a tremendous commotion outside about then. Footsteps, pounding, lots of voices. My first thought was that the ball had rolled down the tunnel and they were playing the game right there. Someone began hammering on the door so that it seemed ready to jump out of the frame. But that happened only after Bert had looked me square in the eye, blinked, and swallowed so his large Adam's apple wobbled in his long throat where the hair grew coarse and unshaven. His face was utterly empty of guile.

He asked me, "What money?"

XVIII. RUNNING MAN

"Okay, pissface, open up." I recognized Pigeyes's voice. "Come on, Malloy. Give it up. Come on," he kept saying. He'd had me again. The guy gets a surveillance van to watch me gambol down the avenues and I don't wonder. I was a dangerous fool. I had been followed.

Bert started to speak and I lifted a finger in warning. When I mouthed the word "Police," Bert circled his jaw and did a brief swoon.

Pigeyes was still pounding, while I waited. The tail could not have been that good because I'd have heard somebody behind me in the gangway. So they were guessing. It was a good guess, but there was always the chance they'd go away.

I found my datebook in my pocket and wrote Bert a note: "If I can get rid of these guys, grab your pal as soon as the game is over and scram." We both started hopping around, trying to figure out where he should hide, while

Pigeyes went on walloping the door and calling me names. Finally we noticed the shower and I helped Bert chimney up so that his back was braced against one tile wall and his feet were parallel. I drew the blue curtain slowly; none of the rusty hooks gave even the slightest tinkle. It looked okay.

By now somebody was working on the door hinges. I heard the tapping of a hammer and a screwdriver.

"Who is it?" I called sweetly.

"It's Wilt Chamberlain. Open up so we can play one on one."

Pigeyes was dressed the same as yesterday. With him, he had his reptile-skin sidekick, Dewey, who was holding the screwdriver and hammer, and the two security guys I'd seen at the top of the runway up to the court, who were along for the ride.

"*Voi*-fucking-*là*," Gino said. He pointed a finger at me and said, "Back." He was awfully pleased. He'd got the drop on me twice now, counting U Inn. You'd never take this out of Pigeyes. He loved hunting some scumbag down, the whole pure adventure. Plenty of squirts come on the Force like that, adventure their watchword, it's all in their head, car chases, street scenes, kicking doors in, girls in the cop bars who can't wait to see them get hard. But the biggest adventure most of the time turns out to be department politics, seeing who gets back-stabbed in the latest downtown deal. Oh, plenty of excitement in the abstract. Every day you go to work and know in some fraction of your heart you might not come home. But usually, everyone does. Instead, there are hours of paperwork; there are nights of lame jokes and burning your tongue on bad coffee; the same old same-old on the street. Lots of folks, and I'm one, they get their fill and move on, knowing that life's life and can only be so much of an adventure. The guys who want adventure and stay—Pigeyes—they're the ones who seem to go wrong. Being a smartass, a wise guy, a rogue on your own—that's an adventure too. That's how they figure. That's one of the reasons he is like he is.

The two security types followed Pigeyes in, both of them looking around, deeply chagrined. As Bert said, no one was supposed to be in here. Dewey stayed at the door. I talked to the security men, one white guy, one black, with matching potbellies, and the same vermilion sport jackets with the university crest on the breast pocket, both with polyester trousers and cheap shoes. This was too good a gig, getting paid to watch basketball games, for me even to have to guess what these fellas did for a day job. Coppers off duty, or my ma wasn't named Bess.

"You didn't let him get away with that old thing that he was looking for someone, did you?" I asked. "I've seen him badge his way into Sinatra. He'll say anything to get in for free."

Pigeyes cast me a dirty look as he wandered around. He flipped the doors on the three banged-up lockers against the far wall, not really expecting to see anything inside.

"What gives, Malloy?"

"I'm hiding."

"Funny place."

I told him about representing the U., getting the tour, learning about all the out-of-the-way places in here. "Billy Birken from Alumni Relations took me around." The name, I could tell, bought me a little something with Security.

Sensing this, Pigeyes said, "He's full of shit" and, as if to prove it, pointed one of his thick fingers at me. "Who you hiding from?"

I went to the door and grabbed the doorknob, which was so old and so often handled that the brass had worn off. I leaned past Dewey, who laid a hand lightly on my chest as I scouted the hall. Both the gangway and the tunnel runway up to the court were clear. I looked back at Pigeyes.

"You," I said and with that gave Dewey a little shove so he wouldn't be hit as I slammed the door between me and them and took off. I turned back once to make sure they were all right behind me.

I got a hell of a lot farther than you would think. Four hardass cops shagging my fanny, but all of them heavier smokers than me, and they were lagging after the first twenty feet. Mack the Moose with one bum wheel made a hairpin when I got courtside and bolted up the aisle beside the first-tier seats, taking the stairs three at a time. As I came up from beneath, the smell and color of the enormous crowd in all its great clamoring power seemed startling, like falling into the hot breath of some beast. Pigeyes was shouting prosaic things like "Stop him!" but nobody seemed inclined. People watched us—those who didn't crane around so they could keep up with the game— with the same amused curiosity they'd take in a parade. It was nothing to them, part of the spectacle. Though it slowed me down, I could not keep myself from laughing, especially with the thought of Bert sneaking out of the room. One guy in a Milwaukee sweatshirt yelled, "Sit down, you clowns."

When I reached the mezzanine level, my knee hurt like a bastard from my gallivanting, but I was holding my lead. Huffing and puffing, I went down the exit passageway, ran past a big refreshment stand, with its Coca-Cola sign clock and long stainless-steel counter, and took a quick right up the old concrete stairs for the upper tiers. I could hear their voices ringing up the stairwell behind me. On the top level, I popped into the men's room and hustled into one of the stalls and waited. In about five minutes the game would be over and I'd have a chance to get out with the crowd. But that meant entertaining Pigeyes at my house. Besides, if they lost me completely, they might go back to the changing room, near which Bert would be lingering, waiting for Orleans. So I hid out another minute or two, then adjusted my sport jacket and found a seat in the second balcony.

There were about forty seconds left on the big game clock when Pigeyes sat down beside me. The Hands were losing now by eighteen and were taking bad shots for treys, with the Meisters picking up the long rebounds. Gino was winded. His forehead was bright with sweat.

"You're fucking," he said, "under arrest."

"For what? There a law against running in a public place?"

"Resisting."

"Resisting? I'm sitting here talking to you almost like we were friends." Dewey came up then. He put his hands on his knees for a minute to catch his breath, then he sat down in the seat on the other side of me. The place was emptying, but there were enough people left to keep me safe. "I wanted to see the end of the game."

Pigeyes told me to fuck myself.

"Did you tell me I was under arrest, Gino? Did you have a warrant?"

Pigeyes looked at me levelly. "Yes," he said.

"Fine," I said. "Show me the warrant. Hey, miss," I called to a fat college girl two seats down, and reached for her sleeve. "Would you please witness something?"

The girl just stared.

"Don't be a smartass, Malloy."

"Battery of a police officer," said Dewey.

"The way I remember, you put your hand on me first."

They exchanged a primitive look. I could remember how much I hated lawyers when I was a cop. The game horn went off then. Various people swirled out on the floor, the cheerleaders, photographers, TV crews, more security guys and kid ushers, the players from both benches. Bert Kamin was right at the edge of the court, among a hundred gawking fans. I saw him from three levels above, a distance of two hundred feet. He motioned to Orleans and went running down the tunnel behind him.

"I think they could play in this conference," I said, "if they had a big man inside."

"Listen, pencil-dick. You're way past being humorous."

"Have I forgotten something, Gino? Did I take a shower with you?"

"Keep it up, Malloy." He sighted me down the line of a finger. "We been on your ass since six tonight. You tear out of your house, you run around here like some fuckin mutt smelling heat, I say you're here for a meet. You got a call and you showed, lickety-split."

"And who would I be meeting?"

"Stop playin, Malloy. Who am I looking for?"

He still didn't have the remotest idea who Kam Roberts was. He was suspicious of course, because this was a basketball game and that was what Archie was fixing. But he didn't know how. Eventually, of course, the significance of my presence in the refs' room would come to him. But he'd been too busy running after me for that glimmer to strike home yet.

"I'm going to tell you this again, Pigeyes, and so help me, if I'm lying then put me in the paddy wagon. I've never met this Kam Roberts. Never said boo to him."

"Then it's the other guy. What's-it. Bert."

"I'm a basketball fan."

"I've had it a lot with you, Malloy. Not a fucking little. A lot. I want to know what gives."

"Forget it, Gino." I puckered my lips and made that little motion, the lock and the key.

He wasn't kidding about having had it. He was all gone. Looking into Gino's eyes, no one would be surprised to find that humans are carnivores.

"Stand up." I didn't at first, but when he repeated it, I figured I'd about run out the string. He tossed my pockets then. He pulled them out viciously so they were hanging from my trousers. He threw my keys and folding money down on the floor. He jammed his hands in my sport coat and found my datebook there, which he went through page by page until he got to the note I wrote Bert. He passed Dewey the book and was so overheated that his lips were sort of rumbling around on their own. Finally, for lack of anything else to do, he spat a big wad on the floor.

"Illegal search," I told him. "With only two, three hundred witnesses. And all of them holding season tickets. I don't even have to take names."

He snatched the datebook from Dewey and threw it as hard as he could toward the scoreboard over the court. It flipped around in the air over the seats, then opened along its main seam and looked like a swallow in flight, diving at last and disappearing between the lights. Pigeyes got up close and lowered his voice.

"I'm coming back with a subpoena."

"Do what you like. You start subpoenaing a lawyer, Pigeyes, with all those privileges and stuff, you'll have some poor assistant prosecuting attorney still dragging to court after you've got your thirty."

"Malloy, I cut you too much slack, twice now. I could have jacked you up good with that credit card, and I'm feeling what I always felt about you. That you're an ass-wipe. That you don't know dick about how to say thank you."

"Thank you, Pigeyes."

It was as close as I'd come yet to getting cracked. He was about ready to handle the beef. Public place. Lots of witnesses. He didn't care. He'd make up some outrageous insult I'd uttered, one that took in his manhood, his mother, the Force, in one breath. I didn't flinch either. A scaredy-cat like me, but I was ready to take what was coming. Go figure. Something with me and this guy. I couldn't back off or give him a break. We were an always thing, me and Pigeyes. With the death rattle I'd have one hand groping to yank on his chain.

And he, in the meanwhile, had to hold back. He didn't have the room he wanted. It was the past, I suppose. I had more liberty with him than just any stray dog on the street. An instant passed before Gino got his impulses under control. Then he did what he liked to do. He threatened me.

"I'm still making you as dirty on this thing. You were stinkin with sweat yesterday when I was puttin you in it. And I'll find out why. I'm going to be as close behind you as a fart. You better mind your fuckin manners. Cause when I tag you, Malloy"—he touched me on the lapel, just his fingertips—"you'll be It."

He and Dewey walked away. They were about half a row down when Gino turned back.

"And by the way. We got an amazing videotape of your bathroom window. Strictly fucking amazing. I'm gonna show it in the Squad Room tomorrow night in case you want to come by." He had that slug smile, oily, evil, enjoying the contemplation of pain.

I picked up my things eventually, after they were gone, figuring all in all it probably wasn't going the way I would have liked. A guy from the cleaning crew appeared, filling a huge trash bag and advancing me little dark looks in the hopes I would beat it, but I stayed put. I was wondering about Bert. Did he have the money or not, and if he didn't, who did? In the big empty stadium, I felt the perpetual nature of doubt, the way it's always with us. In life, we just never know.

It struck me eventually that I was going to have to find some way to get home. I walked out, hope against hope, but I knew it. My car had been towed.

XIX. SATURDAY

A. Possible Connections

On Saturday morning I went to the office. I had little to do but attend a lunch of the Recruiting Subcommittee and answer my junk mail, but I came in as a matter of habit on Saturdays. It kept me from fighting with Lyle and impressed those of my partners who saw the sign-in sheet. I liked the day, in fact, wandering down the uncrowded streets of Center City where other attorneys headed to work, moving at leisure with their briefcases and overcoats and blue jeans. The whole day had the off-center, underwater slowness of a dream. No flipping telephone. No secretaries sneaking looks at the clock. No hubbub, no filing dates. No stressed-out aura from all those striving young people running around. I got in early and checked my voice messages and E-mail, thinking I might have heard from Bert, but the only word was from Lena, asking me to call when I arrived.

279

She came up from the library, wearing a button-down shirt of broad green stripes. She'd gotten the plane tickets and a beachfront hotel booking for Pico.

"What are we going to do there?" she asked.

"Investigate. Meet with a lawyer named Pindling. Find out what we can about an account at the International Bank of Finance."

"Great." She seemed pleased by the prospects, by me.

When she was gone, I took out the file on Toots's case, reviewing some of the records we would be offering to complete the defense, once Woodhull finished mauling Toots on cross-examination. My mind though remained on Bert and his problems, which would soon be getting worse. By now, Gino would have done the arithmetic: he'd seen the note in my datebook; he'd found me in the refs' room. Pigeyes would figure one of last night's refs was involved and would start hunting. I wanted to warn Bert—and finish our conversation about the money.

I tracked down a copy of the morning's *Tribune* in a stall in the john, but the refs' names weren't listed in the box score. After some reflection, I called Media Relations at the U. I figured they might not answer on Saturday, but I got hold of an obliging young woman. Introducing myself as Detective Dimonte, Kindle Unified Police, I awaited a telltale response, something like 'You again?' but she seemed unsuspecting.

"Brierly, Gleason, and Pole." She was reading to me from last night's press handout. Those were the refs' names.

"How about their first names and addresses?"

"Care of the Mid-Ten. Detroit."

"You're not gonna make me send a subpoena?"

She laughed. "You can send what you want. We don't have that information. The conference doesn't even like giving out the last names. There was a lawyer a couple of years ago who wanted to sue one of these guys for smashing somebody's car in the parking lot and he had to get a court order. I mean it. As far as I know, you will need a subpoena. You can call Detroit Monday, but they're incredibly tight with this stuff."

That made sense. No off-color fan mail. No fixes. When I put down the phone, I got out the local phone book. I found an Orlando Gleason, but nothing else close. Bert must have made Orleans's acquaintance out of town. All in all, Pigeyes had more hurdles ahead than I'd figured.

Not long afterwards, Brushy came in, full weekend regalia, blue jeans and running shoes. She looked pretty cute, wearing a big tan hat and carrying her briefcase, big as a saddlebag, and a bundle from the laundry wrapped in bright blue paper. She took just a step or two inside my door.

"That was nice yesterday," she said.

"I'll say."

"You mad? About your rash?"

"Hey," I said amiably. I told her I'd called her doctor.

"How is it?"

"Wanna check?"

"I'll remember you offered." She stood there, small, buttoned up, brimming with a great jolly glimmer. It made me a little sad to think how often Brush had been here before, walking into the office and feeling the thrill of knowing that she had this secret something going, a recollection of the senses in this quarter reserved for the grimly logical and perpetually banal. Everybody else arrived thinking of contract clauses and case names, and she rode up the elevators realizing she was going to share the sort of rosy smile we shared now, ripe with the anticipation of pleasure, of things that ought not be spoken of with the door open to the hall.

"I called you last night," I said.

"I was here late. I called you, too, when I got home, but you weren't around."

"Guess who I ran into?"

She actually dropped her laundry and clapped her hands when I mouthed Bert's name.

"He's alive?"

I motioned to close the door.

"Where is he?" she asked. "What's he been up to?"

I reminded her about what she said yesterday, about wanting to stay in the dark.

"Starting tomorrow," she responded.

I told her just a bit—Bert running from bad guys.

"But what did he say about the money?"

"Not clear," I said. "Our negotiations didn't get very far." I explained that we'd been interrupted by Detective Dimonte.

"It sounds like this guy's really after you," she said.

I just made a sound. Boy, was that true.

"So when will you hear again from Bert?"

"I'm sitting by the phone." I touched it, right next to me, the latest in technology, sleek and black, like something from Skylab. "In the meantime, I'm going to Pico Luan tomorrow to nose around."

"Tomorrow? Toots's hearing is on again Tuesday."

"The Committee only gave me two weeks. I'll do a two-day turnaround. Back Monday night. We're ready on Toots, right?" I lifted the brown expandable folder to show her I'd been minding the file. I added, "I'm taking Lena."

"Who's Lena?"

"First-year. From the U."

"The redhead? The cute one?"

"I'd say stylish."

Brushy frowned. "What do you need her for?"

"A prover." A witness—someone who could testify, if need be, in court. "This lawyer I want to see is supposed to be a little slippery."

Brushy wagged a finger and let forth in a self-mocking singsong, "Don't be forgetting who's your girl now, Malloy."

"Brush, you flatter me."

"Mmm-hmm," she answered. I was not sure whether Brushy was feeling wise to the ways of humans in general or just me, but somehow we'd blown past airy humor; her expression was wizened by mistrust. This mood of few illusions reverberated between us, with its bluesy wave forms, and I felt a momentary commission to get to the point.

"Think you're ready to be a one-man woman, Brush?" It was as close as I could come to mentioning Krzysinski.

"I've always gone one at a time, Mack. It's just now and then the time's been short." She smiled a bit, but I realized intuitively that she meant it. Every one-night stand was a piece of Cinderella inside her head, a part of her always hoping that this slipper was going to fit. People's

fantasies, even when they're morbid or trite, are somehow
touching; it's the vulnerability, I suppose, the fact that
lives, like cardboard cartons, fold so reliably along certain
lines.

"You know," I said, "if the gals break my heart again,
I don't think anyone'll find the pieces."

"Malloy, give me some credit, okay? I know you. I get
it." She looked to the door to be certain it was closed,
then walked to the desk and removed her hat before she
gave me a smooch. I was still not ready to be soothed.

"How old are you now, Brush?"

"Thirty-eight," she said, then thought twice of it and
looked at me fiercely. Jesus, this gal could be tough. She
asked what difference that made, as if she didn't know.
The riff of the independent person is, I don't need nobody.
I used to hear the same thing from certain old coppers. But
God never made a soul for whom that was completely true.
I sort of felt sorry for Brushy. She didn't really take me
as the hottest thing on the market and she couldn't misap-
prehend my reliability or my nature. She just thought I was
the best she could get or, maybe, that she deserved. But
we both knew I had certain virtues. I'd do what she told
me; I needed her guidance. She was smarter than me. And
she thrilled me through and through.

"I was just thinking about you," I said.

"Thinking what?"

"How it is," I answered. "You know. The bright fires
of youth burning down. A body gets lonely."

"Very literary."

"The Irish." I touched the inside of my wrist. "Verse
is in the blood."

"You have a dislikable side, Mack.'

"So I've been told."

"It doesn't give you the right to hold someone in contempt, just because you get their number. You're not such a mystery yourself, you know."

"I see."

"You're a miserable wretch, in case you think anybody else hasn't noticed."

I told her to ease up and got to my feet. I took her firmly by her full shoulders and gripped her to my chest, where she willingly lingered, a foot shorter.

"Lunch?" she asked.

"Recruiters," I said.

She groaned sympathetically at the prospect of committee work.

"Tonight?" I asked.

"It's my parents' anniversary." She brightened. "You could come. Warm Italian family."

"Uh-oh."

"I suppose you're right."

We looked at each other.

"Tuesday," I said. "Toots."

"Toots." From the door, she cast a gloomy eye as I stood by my desk. Maybe there is never really a chance to fully combine after adolescence. Maybe all those tribal types, the Indians and the Hebrews, had it right, marrying everyone off by the age of thirteen. After that it's hit-or-miss, the spirit singing out but forced to surmount the channels, the borders dug deep of what has become recognized, if not cherished, as the self.

"Open or closed?" she asked from the door.

I flicked my hand.

"I'm here," I told her, "either way."

B. Checking My Points

In a bow to democracy and to help with the work, the
Committee over the years has created more subcommittees
than either House of Congress, each one empowered with
dominance over some minor region of law firm life. We
have subs on ethical questions, on staff employment, on
computer usage, pro bono work, and paper recycling. In
this regime, recruiting is regarded as a mixed bag. It wields
genuine authority, hiring both summer clerks and the first-
year lawyers who join G&G every fall following the bar
exams, but the workload is substantial and can never be
fully managed in the rush of the week. By long-standing
agreement, we meet when we have to for Saturday lunch.
At this time of year, when our activities lull, it's only once
a month, and after reviewing a final list of summer hirings
and calendared interviews for next fall, the five of us—
Stephanie Plotzky, Henry Sommers, Madge Dorf, Blake
Whitson, me—fell, as we generally do, into gossip.

"So what do you hear?" asked Stephanie. "I saw Martin this morning. He just said, 'Bloodier than ever.' He
looked beat and it was nine o'clock." We were two blocks
down from the Needle at Max Heimer's, a deli character-
ized by second-rate food and Third World hygiene. Stephanie had ventured this goody, leaning over the table, her
round face, highly made up even on Saturday, close to the
container of pickles, whose side was spattered with grime.

"The corporate guys are getting hit," said Henry. "The eighties are over." He was a bankruptcy lawyer himself, on boom times. Madge, a deal person, didn't really agree, and we debated a little among ourselves, as if it made any difference.

The Committee members were over at Club Belvedere today, in one of the elegant conference rooms, licking their pencils and passing out points. Groundhog Day was Thursday. My partners reacted with the same anxieties all the good boys in grade school exhibited on Marking Day, when the nuns sent us home so they could fill in our report cards. I never worried. I knew what was coming—A's and boxes of corrective checkmarks in the sections reserved for deportment.

But I was not as sure where I was headed this year at the firm. I thought my deal with the Committee when I agreed to go looking for Bert was no more pay cuts, but nobody'd actually said that. My four partners on Recruiting were up-and-comers and it was clear that Pagnucci had given each one the treatment—some soothing, some encouragement. They were all going to make more money next year. As for me, I could tell from the sidelong glances that each of them sensed, supposedly privately, that my share was going to be reduced again. It was never ax murder. Just a 5 percent cut every year. Still, I walked back to the building after lunch alone and brooding.

All right, I admit it—these decreases each year hurt my feelings. Money's the big scorecard in this kind of life; there's no winning percentage, no runs batted in. It's always struck me as meaningful how we refer to the percentage of firm income we each are awarded as "points."

Your partners tell you each year what they think you are worth. By now I can live without everything the marginal dollar buys, except self-esteem.

I sat in my office. The cold winter sun could be seen through the screen of clouds; its light played on the river, tossing Christmas spangles across the greenish reflections of the big buildings on the banks. I tried to set aside my feelings of deprivation to think about Bert, but I got nowhere with that. How much? I kept thinking. How much were they taking away this year? What an effing load of nerve. I'm running from coppers and they're cutting my pay. I kept this up until I was seething. I was in one of my states, angry and mean, Bess Malloy's boy reeling from what he was missing. I drifted upstairs, not really telling myself where I was going, then looked both ways down the book-lined hall and slipped into Martin's office, figuring he'd have retained a draft of the proposed point scheme somewhere in his drawer where I'd peeked at it three years before. I wasn't worried at that moment about being caught. Let somebody catch me. Fucking let them. I had a few things to say. Eighteen years, for Chrissake. And they're paying Pagnucci on my back.

The most important papers in Martin's office were locked in his credenza behind the thousand-year oak. I'd seen him open the drawer a hundred times before, lifting the rubber belly on his hula dancer clock to reveal the battery and the little gold key. I had the usual drilling sense of isolation when I was alone in the firm and screwing around. The big corner office with its reliquary of goofball objects—the paintings, the sculptures, the weird furniture—was dim and I hesitated to turn on the light. What the hell would I accomplish? I wondered. Would I shit in the drawer, like some badass burglar expressing himself? Could I complain? I might. There were a lot of people around here who lay on the floor and moaned as GH Day approached, or went office to office sniping. It didn't matter, though, really. I was being bad. I felt just like a kid, but I'd felt like that before and there was some peculiar purification in acting on impulse.

Martin's private drawer is a mess. I was shocked to discover that the last time I did this. I would have expected exacting order. Martin is one of those persons, so large and voluble, so much a presence, that it is always disquieting to realize how much of his soul he conceals. I suppose Martin did the filing himself, given the utter sensitivity of the documents, and chaos reigned without a secretary's assistance. There were hanging folders in the drawer but many of the papers had been slopped unstacked on the unfinished slats of the bottom. A lot of the most intimate secrets of the firm were in here. Letters from a shrink saying that one of our first-years would slit his throat if we fired him. (We hadn't.) Financial projections for the end of the year, which looked pretty bad. There was also a file with written evaluations of the performance of each partner. I was tempted to read through the disdainful comments about me, but decided to pass on the chance for more self-laceration. Finally I found a folder marked "Points."

Inside was a photocopy of an early draft, handwritten by Carl Pagnucci, of this year's point distribution plan. I didn't look at it closely, because in the same file I found a memo. It had been folded in four, but the handwritten initialing at the top could not be mistaken. J.A.K.E. John

Andrew Kenneth Eiger. Jake loved his initials. They were
on everything, his shirt cuff, his beer mugs, his golf bag.
Like anything else in his hand, I could imitate the initials
so well that I didn't even need a subscript to show I was
signing with his authority, but nobody else around here
was quite as skillful. I had no doubt this was authentic.

PRIVILEGED AND CONFIDENTIAL

18 November

TO: Robert Kamin, Gage & Griswell
FROM: John A.K. Eiger, General Coun-
sel,
TransNational Air
RE: First Wave 397 Settlements

I wanted to advise you of a flap concerning the 397 settlement payments
which arose while you were trying
the Grainger claim. As usual, the
plaintiffs' lawyers are fighting
with each other about litigation expenses. It seems that Peter Neucriss engaged a firm in Cambridge,
Mass., called Litiplex for litigation support—apparently they provided crash reconstruction,
computer modeling, consulting engineers, expert testimony, analysis
of the NTSB proceedings, and rec-

ords management. Litiplex has a series of invoices outstanding
totaling about $5.6 million. Neu-
criss says he hired them with the
consent of all lead counsel for the
class and says I agreed at the time
of the settlement that Litiplex
would be paid from the 397 fund. The
class lawyers say there was no such
agreement——not too surprising,
since paying Litiplex off the top,
as Neucriss is demanding, will reduce the class lawyers' fee by about
half a million dollars. Both sides
are threatening to take up the issue
with Judge Bromwich. I am very much
afraid that Bromwich will ask for an
accounting, which will lead to discovery of the fund surplus. Rather
than take that risk, and accepting
that I may have made a commitment to
Neucriss, I'll authorize payment of
Litiplex's invoices as a below-the-
line charge against the surplus.
Please deliver the following checks
to me.

Attached was a listing of Litiplex invoice numbers and
the amounts supposedly due.

I no longer had to look for what Bert had transmitted
to Glyndora. *'Per the attached, re agreement with Peter*

Neucriss . . .' This, clearly, was it. But I read the memo three or four more times as I sat there in Martin's empty office, feeling as if somebody had put a cold hand on my heart. I kept asking myself the same thing, the voice within speaking in the forlorn tones of a child. What was I going to do now?

XX. MEMBERS OF THE CLUB

The Club Belvedere is Kindle County's oldest social club, erected in the Gilded Age. Here the true elite of the county, men of commerce and standing, have dined and played squash with each other for more than a century. Not your usual grubby politicians whose power is transient and, worse yet, borrowed, but people with fortunes, the owners of banks and industrial concerns, families whose names you see on old buildings, who will still be prominent here in three generations and whose children are apt to marry one another. These are folks who, generally speaking, like the world as it is, and virtually every achievement in social progress which I can recall has involved a celebrated fracas among the club membership, some of whom have inalterably opposed the admission of first Catholics, then Jews, blacks, women, and even a single Armenian. You would think that a sensible human would find this atmosphere repulsive, but the cachet the Belvedere confers seems to

overwhelm almost every scruple, and Martin Gold, for
instance, in relaxed conversation spoke of nothing but "the
club" for a solid month—how good the food was, how
handsome the locker rooms—when he was elected to
membership over a decade ago.

The club is an eight-story structure in Revival style that
occupies half a block in Center City, not far from the
Needle. I dashed over there, Jake's memo in my pocket,
and swept in past the doorman. The facility is splendid.
The entire first floor is paneled in American walnut, hand-
somely burnished to a deep tone which seems to embed
the glow of low lights and reminds me inevitably of the
brown-skinned men who chopped these trees, and their
descendants in livery who've kept the wood polished to a
sheen like somebody's shoes. An imposing dual staircase
of white marble rises at the far end of the lobby, adorned
with the club crest and winged cherubs, emblems of the
period when Americans felt their surviving republic was
destined again to achieve the greatness of Greece.

Naturally, I was not even in the lobby long enough to
check my topcoat when here, goddamn it, was Wash. He
was carrying, of all things, a golf club, a wood, gripping
it like a dead goose by the neck, right below its lustrous
persimmon head. I could not imagine what he was doing.
It was in the twenties outside and the ground was frozen
hard. He was equally surprised to see me, and met my
appearance with a member's vaguely scornful air for a
known outsider. He was wearing a smashing houndstooth
sport jacket, checks of black and autumnal gold, and
gleaming tasseled loafers. Squashed down below the neck
of his open button-down shirt so that it was partly con-

cealed, as if even Wash recognized that this was a ludicrous affectation, an ascot peeked out, spotted with itsy-bitsy paisleys. I had no idea what I was going to say when he greeted me, but I was saved by instinct.

"Meeting over?" I asked. Wash is far too cowardly to want to discuss with me the Committee's decisions about points, especially mine. That job fell every year to Martin, who, after the formalities of Groundhog Day, would honor me by a visit to my office and clap me on the back, creating the impression that he, at least, maintained firm opinions about my value. Instead, Wash's face weakened at once into a sappy ingratiating expression. Up close you can see a certain studied nature to Wash's amiable mannerisms. Pressed, he has no instincts of his own. He is a collection of everybody else's gestures, the ones he sees as appealing, winning, sure not to offend.

"Not quite," he answered. "Martin and Carl needed a break for the phone. We'll resume at four. Thought I'd take the opportunity to clear my head." Wash hefted the golf club; only the fear that I might actually detain him kept me from saying that I was glad to finally know what it was for. Wash, meanwhile, escaped gladly from my company and headed for the gilded doors of the elevators.

I did not leave the lobby. With my topcoat checked, I took a straight-backed chair in a small paneled alcove near the cloakroom and the telephones. I still didn't know what I was doing here. I had rushed over to confront Martin, but now I was moving as if my weight had tripled, and thinking at the same pace. What would that exercise accomplish? Plan, I told myself, think. Beneath my hand, my knee, to my considerable surprise, had started to tremble.

A few years ago Martin's pal Buck Buchan, who was running First Kindle, got in Dutch in the S&L crunch and Buck made a few calls so that Martin was hired as special counsel to the board. Buck and Martin go back to a time when the mind of man runneth not to the contrary, Korea and the U. when they were both trying to get in the girdles of the same sorority girls. There's a picture someplace of both of them in white socks and bow ties. I was with Martin the morning he had to go tell Buck they were taking his job. It was the end of the line for Buck, the conclusion of an upper-class life of achievement, a daily existence of hopping along the highwire, with the eyes of the world upon him and his body full of the erotic pleasure of power. The tent was coming down for Buck; he would have to tend his wounded soul in the festering dark of scandal and shame. Buck had dropped the ball and Martin was going to tell him, eye to eye, man to man, and remind Buck of what he undoubtedly always knew, that for all the hours he and Martin had spent together matching lively minds and senses of destiny, no one could expect Martin Gold to take a dive, to abandon the noble traditions of his professional life. Martin went off to this meeting with a graven face, shadowed and grieved. Everybody here admired his grit—and so did the board at First Kindle, which has hired Martin since then with increasing frequency. But how good are all those principles when you and your law firm come out on the short end of the stick? The answer—the memo Martin had stashed—was folded in my shirt pocket.

I should have known better of course than to go after Wash. He's a weak person, never any help at all in a crisis. But when push came to shove, I wasn't ready to take on

Martin—I lived with my father until I was twenty-seven and never once told him that I knew he was a thief. Nor did I want to confront Pagnucci's icy calculations. That would require more forethought and surer resolve. Instead, I went to an attendant, the kind of good-looking retainer you expect in this sort of place, a guy in a navy blazer and white gloves, retired military probably, and asked if he had any idea where Mr. Thale could have gone with a golf club.

He directed me to the second sub-basement, a cavernous service area that had probably doubled as a fieldhouse decades ago, before a sturdy running track had been put down under a dome on the roof. Now a flooring of green plastic turf had been laid over the concrete and a line of folks stood whacking golf balls. Many of these people were in sweats. Down this low, it was chilly, maybe 65 degrees. The green rug of the tee area extended twenty feet or so to a curtain of netting that was suspended from the ceiling and draped in layers like a veil. Beyond was a region of complete blackness, darker than doom. Somewhere out there must have been some kind of wiring, because mounted from the concrete abutments, directly over each golfer, was what looked like a green electric scoreboard. I watched as the guy nearest me hit and then studied the screen overhead, where a progression of white dots appeared, meant, I eventually realized, to show the predicted flight of the ball. After the last dot lit up, a digital readout popped up, announcing the supposed distance of the shot.

I finally spotted Wash down the line, flailing away. He had a bucket of balls and had laid his fine jacket out neatly

behind it. He swung awkwardly. He'd probably been playing his whole life, without ever quite getting the game.

Seeing me approach, Wash's look hardened. I knew at
once he thought I'd come to beseech him about my points
and he was already drawing himself up to a high-minded
stance in which he could remind me, with his usual perfect
cordiality with underlings, that I was way out of line.
Instead, to disarm him, I took the memo from my pocket
and watched him unfold it. He read it standing on the
driving mat. His eyes had a sort of hyperthyroid extension
from his face anyway and they were quick, with little
throbbing veins jumping about. The air around us raced
with the steady rhythmic click of balls struck and rising.
When Wash finished, he looked utterly uncomprehending.

"It's Jake," I said.

He recoiled somewhat. He checked over his shoulder
on the other golfers, then pushed me back toward the steel
door I'd come through to enter this area, where the light
trailed off and the full subterranean dark began to reach
toward you, along with the spooky underground sounds of
the building.

"You're making assumptions," Wash said. "Tell me
where this came from."

I told him. I didn't know how to explain and I didn't.
But even Wash recognized that my bona fides were a side
issue. It was obvious from the results that I had good
reason to search.

"The memo's a phony, Wash. There's no Litiplex,
remember? There are no records at TN. Jake faked this.
Maybe Bert's in on it too. There are a million questions.
But it's Jake for sure."

Wash scowled again and took a gander over his shoulder. His look was reproving, but he was too well brought up to tell me to keep my voice down.

"I say again you're making assumptions."

"Like hell. You explain this."

The whole notion of a challenge clearly vexed him. I was putting him on the spot. Then I saw Wash's pale, soft face become firm as he fixed on an idea.

"Perhaps it's Neucriss," said Wash. "Some game of his. Maybe he made all this up." Peter, God knows, was capable of anything. But I had realized still sitting in Martin's office why he had contacted Peter. Martin had the memo. He wanted to know what was going on. He wanted to know if the document was real or a fraud, if Neucriss, by some improbable circumstance, could explain. But it wasn't Neucriss jacking us around. It was Jake.

"Sure," I said to Wash, "sure. So we get Jake in Martin's office and tell him there's no Litiplex, and does Jake say, 'Oh my God, Neucriss told me there was'? Hell no. He acts like this whole thing's a shock to him. 'How dare Bert,' he says. 'And by the way, if you don't find him, let's never hear about this again.' This only adds one way. Jake wrote this frigging memo to Bert. Bert gave him the money. And Jake's got it now. He's covering himself, Wash. And Martin's helping him."

"Don't be absurd," he said immediately. He was reacting to the idea of Martin as corrupt. His mouth worked around, as if he could actually absorb the bad taste.

"Absurd? You think about this, Wash. Who was it who said he'd called the bank down in Pico? Who told you that the General Manager, whatever his name is, Smoky, that he indicated between the lines it was Bert's account? Who'd you hear that b.s. from?''

Wash is a good deal shorter than me, and my height seemed at the moment, as it is now and then, an odd advantage, as if I was out of reach of refutation.

"Think about Martin's performance the other day," I said, "dragging Jake in and spilling the beans after you and Carl had decided otherwise. What did you make of that?''

"I was put out," Wash said. "I told Martin so afterwards. But that's hardly the sign of some dark conspiracy, that he felt he had to speak up.''

"Come on, Wash. You want to know why Martin whistled Jake in? He *wanted* Jake to know. He wanted it, Wash. He wanted Jake to know that Martin had the goods on him and was keeping his mouth shut.''

A certain blankness set in as Wash pondered all of this. He was very slow.

"You're putting this the wrong way. I'm sure Martin found this document somehow and realized, I suppose, that for the time being it was best not coming to light. You're making it sound sinister.''

"It is sinister, Wash.''

He frowned and torqued away. He took one more look in the direction of the other golfers. I could see that my brusqueness and bad manners had finally stimulated Wash to a sense of offense.

"Look, man," he said, using that term, "man," in an old-fashioned high-born way, "he was following the logical imperatives here. Don't be so quick to scorn. Or condemn. Think this through. This firm cannot go on without Jake. Not in the short run. Tell me, Mack, you're such a clever fellow—tell me. If you run and do something half-cocked, you tell me what your plans are.'' His aged light eyes, pocketed by all that used flesh, glimmered with rare directness. The plans he was asking me to specify were not an investigative scheme. He meant what plans did I have to make a living without Jake. I actually took an instant to let the little logical steps descend. Nobody was going to reward my virtue if I put a knife in Jake's heart. I knew that. I'd been hugging his hind end for years with that realization. Nothing had changed really. It's just that the cost would be a little bit higher, in terms of my own self-respect.

"So that's it? I'm supposed to say dandy? That's Martin's answer. Let Jake steal. Just so long as he sends business. 'Hey, Jake, you know that I know. So cut the crap with the firm in Columbus. Let's resume the gold rush.' Come on, Wash. This is making me sick.''

There was a sudden thunderous rumble above and we both jolted. One of the golfers had bounced a shot off the heating ducts on the ceiling. They were padded in foam but still let forth a tremendous sound on impact. The instant of brief fright seemed to prompt Wash to an effort at candor.

"Look, Mack, I can't read Gold's mind. Obviously he prefers to keep his plan, whatever it is, to himself. But you've known this man for years. Years. Are you telling me you can't trust Martin Gold?'' Wash and I, in this basement, snapping in whispers, posed close as lovers, both stood struck by that question. Wash was doing what he always did—what he did the other day when the Com-

mittee talked over Jake's proposal that we stay silent if
Bert didn't return. Wash was posturing, shooting air-balls,
taking the easy way out. He knew just what was happening.
Not every detail; neither did I. I still found it impossible
to calculate how Bert fit in, how Martin had been able to
blame him confident that he would not reappear. But Wash
nevertheless had the lowdown on this scene: it was grubby
and evil. He knew that instinctively because it was exactly
what Wash, with no reflection, would have done—swap
Jake the money for the survival of the firm. And he was
keeping himself from speaking that sooty truth by pretending that Martin might have been up to something better.

"You're a fool, Wash," I said suddenly. In the midst
of everything else, the seething emotions, the basement
gloom, I walked away feeling great. Pure primitive pleasure. I had needed to say that for years.

I had wrested the memo from Wash without resistance.
I folded it into quarters again and jammed it in my pocket
as I strode up the gray steel stairs that had led me down.
It was all clear now. By the time I was back up in the
grand surroundings, amid the wooden walls and the cut-
crystal sconces, I felt motivated and strong, mean and
myself. I was done being little boy disappointed. I was
man among men. When I forged through the revolving
doors to the winter street, I was starting to plan.

XXI. THE INVESTIGATION BECOMES AN INTERNATIONAL AFFAIR

A. International Flight

The TN Executive Travelers Lounge, where I waited for Lena Sunday morning, afforded a rare vantage on a world askew. The place looked terrific. The interior designer produced the kind of tasteful space-age effect I'd have strived for in my office if I ever decorated, lots of curved woods and big windows, sleek leather chairs and granite end tables upon which were perched those special telephones operated by credit cards with two or three jacks for your portable modem and fax. The elegant-looking ladies guarding the door examined the entrants, who, every one of them, flashed their membership cards with the same air, Hey, look at me, I'm in the front of the boat, I really made it. Nipponese businessmen flying for thirty hours dozed on the fancy furniture; well-turned-out executives cracked away at their laptops; wealthy couples conferred, one of them always looking anxious with the prospect of flight. A waiter in a white jacket wandered around with a tray to see if anybody wanted a drink, while voices from the Sunday-morning TV news shows emerged from the bar.

Here met is the Flying Class, a group ever expanding, whose real workday is spent in the sky, whose true office is an aisle seat on a DC-10, folks who have so many million award miles they could fly to Jupiter free. These are the orphans of capital, the men and women who have given up their lives for the corporate version of manifest destiny, who are trying to fling far some company's empire in the name of economies of scale. I had an Uncle Michael who was a traveling salesman, a sad sack with an ugly brown valise, one of those lacquered boxes that seemed welded to his hand. His was regarded as the fate of a misfit. Now it's a badge of status to be away from home four nights a week. But on God's green planet is there anything more depressing than an empty hotel room at ten at night and the thought that work, privilege, economic need not only claim the daylight hours but have, however briefly, entitled you to these awesome lonesome instants in which you're remote from the people and the things, tiny, loved, and familiar, that sustain a life?

Listen to me. What was *I* missing but my easy chair and the TV set and bloviating moments interacting with Lyle? And I'd have Lena's youthful company. My briefcase and travel bag were between my knees. I'd packed light— underwear, a suit to do business, swimming trunks, and a few items I'd need: my passport, my Dictaphone, some TransNational Air stationery from the office, an old letter signed by Jake Eiger, and three copies of TN's annual report. Plus the memo I'd found in Martin's drawer, which was never going to leave my sight. Like Kam, I'd also taken a $2500 cash advance on my new golden credit card, which had been messengered to the office on Friday. I had been up most of the night scheming and I shut my eyes, imagining the wind on Pico, fragrant with sea salt and tanning oil as it rattled the palms.

"Yoo-hoo." The voice was sweetly familiar, but I still jumped a little when I opened my eyes.

"Brushy Bruccia, as I live and die."

"So," she said, seeming perky and young. She looked happy and pleased with herself. Her bag was slung over her shoulder and she carried her coat. She wore jeans.

"Where you going?" I asked.

"With you."

"Really and truly? What happened to Lena?"

"Emergency assignment. She'll be in the library all night."

I got it then. I told Brushy I didn't need to ask from who.

"That girl has a lean and hungry look."

"She's got a look," I said, "I'll give you that."

Brushy punched me solidly in the arm, but I was too embarrassed to carry on in front of all these men. We walked over to the leather chairs. Neither of us said anything.

"You're supposed to be pleased," she told me eventually.

"How could I not be?" I was feeling impinged upon. I had my plans for Pico, which depended on a traveling companion who was more credulous than Brushy.

"Let's try this again."

She walked away and came around a handsome rosewood divider that sported CRTs listing arriving and departing flights.

"Mack! Guess where I'm going."

"With me, I hope."

"Now you've got it."

I told her she was odd.

"By the way," she said, "what are we doing down there?"

" 'By the way' nothing," I said. "Forget 'we.' Remember our deal? No askee, no tellee. You're not on the team."

A gal with a radio voice announced our flight, while Brush absorbed my rebuff lightly. She hung her head sideways; she fluttered her eyes.

"Oh dear," asked she, "whatever will you do with me?"

B. That Old Dance Step

This, the high season, was not my favorite time in Pico Luan. I had last been here years ago during the summer, when the capital, Ciudad Luan, was almost a ghost town, but in this season the homebound travelers, grown-ups and kids in their bright clothes, were crowded in the airport like the huddled masses from a steerage vessel. Their tanned faces were as surprising as the sweet breath of heat that greeted us as we descended the TN airliner staircase.

Even in the long light, the tropical sun was compelling, so vital that winter at once was only a sad memory.

"God," said Brushy, shaking her hands free in the mild air.

There was a rental car waiting. TN, as usual, had coughed up great accommodations right on the Regent's Beach, a nine-mile stripe of sand, white and uncluttered, that polishes the toes of the Mayan Mountains. Enormous and green, the foothills loom above the coast. In this season, with all the high-flyers and snowbirds down here, the narrow roads were crowded, and I found a back way out of the airport. Brushy opened the windows and took off her hat and let her short dark hair rise in the breeze. We whizzed along past the little lean-to houses with their metal roofs, the hand-lettered signs of occasional stores and stands offering local foods. Huge plants with leaves the size of elephant's ears grew in clumps at the roadside. The eternal Luanders strolled unmolested in the middle of the narrow roads, yielding for the car and then returning, pacing along down the center stripe, frequently barefoot.

The Luanders are pleasant people. They know they have it made, having mastered the white man through his greed. They have been bankers since the Barataria Bay pirates began storing their gold in the caves above Ciudad Luan— C. Luan to the locals—and the Luanders today remain as casually indiscriminate about clientele. International narcotics magnates, tax cheats from many lands, and upper-crust bankers mingle congenially in this land of little restraint, sharing the tiny nation with its polyglot people in whose blood is mingled the DNA of Amerindians, African slaves, and a variety of runaway Europeans—Portuguese, English, Dutch, Spanish, and French. Pico has survived despots, Indian conquerors, and two centuries of Spanish rule, which ended in 1821, when Luan chose to become a British protectorate rather than be subsumed by the sovereignty claims of nearby Guatemala. In 1961, when Pico achieved independence, its parliament adopted the strict bank-secrecy laws of Switzerland and some of the B.W.I. islands.

With the acceleration of the offshore economy and the vast riches of today's pirates in neighboring Latin nations, who trade in powder rather than pieces of eight, Pico has gone through startling development in the last three decades. All the dough that's stashed here goes untaxed, and for that reason is not apt to leave. There's a $100 airport tax, a $10 tariff for every wire transfer, and a flat 10 percent VAT on everything that's bought or sold. Burgers for the family in a restaurant in C. Luan can cost one hundred bucks. But the combination of no income tax and financial privacy means there is steady commerce and plenty of jobs. The Luanders remain remote, cordial, even, as British discipline made them, correct, but confident about the native way of wanting less. Fast-paced and ham-fisted, white people are regarded with whatever good nature as freaks.

Our hotel, at the far end of the beach, three or four miles outside C. Luan, was terrific. We had two little thatch-roofed cabanas side by side, self-contained units, each with a kitchen, a bar, and a bedroom that looked out on the water. Brushy had to reach her secretary at home to rearrange tomorrow's appointments, and I stepped outside on the small terrace of my unit as her voice rose in occasional frustration over the difficulty of getting a U.S. connection.

The sun was heading down now, a great rosy ball burning away in the clear sky. We'd been traveling all day most companionably, doing crosswords on the plane, holding hands, gossiping about our partners and items in the Sunday *Times*. Out on the beach, various mothers, weary at the end of the day, called for their kids with fading humor. Pico, originally the haven either to guys who stepped off planes with wraparound shades and a firm grip on their valise, or a few archaeologists drawn by the enormous shrines the Mayas had built high in the mountains in sight of the ocean, is, after decades of promotion by TN, taking hold as a family vacation spot. By air, it's an hour farther than the islands, but it's less overrun and sports more notable sights. I watched kids scramble around between the legs of their parents, the little ones flirting with the waves and running screaming up the beach. One boy was lugging coconuts, still in their smooth brown husks, so that it looked a little like he was mounting a collection of heads. The sailboats were still out, but the water was losing its color. In the blazing sunlight it was a radiant blue, the result perhaps of copper deposits on the coral floor, a hue you thought existed solely in ads for color film.

"All done." Brush was off the phone. She'd put on a kind of sundress and we walked up to the hotel and had dinner on the veranda, watching the pink fingers take hold of the sky, the water licking down on the beach. With my blessing she had a couple of drinks while I knocked down iced teas. She was looking happy and loose. Halfway through dinner a native band started playing a few rooms away in the bar inside, and the music and laughter came through the open french windows. The rhythm and themes were haunting, that Central American sound, pipes and flutes, sweet melodies like an echo out of the mountains.

"What a place." Brushy looked with yearning at the sea.

"I kind of think this is charming," I said. "Your following me."

"Somebody had to do something," she told me.

I was as ever dishonorable, and pretended to have no idea what she might mean. She peered into her drink.

"I thought a lot about that conversation. In your office yesterday? People are entitled to change, you know." When she raised her eyes, she had that look again, all pluck and daring.

"Naturally."

"And you're right about me. But I don't have to apologize for that. It's a natural thing. The older you get, the more you wonder about things that are—" She faltered.

"What?"

"Enduring."

I flinched. She saw me.

She put a hand to her eyes.

"What am I doing?" she asked. Even with the candle guttering on the table, I could see she had flushed suddenly, maybe the liquor, maybe the heat adding to the effect of the strong emotion. "God, what do I see in you?"

"I'm honest," I told her.

"No, you're not. You're self-deprecating," she said. "There's a difference."

I gave her the point. "You deserve better," I told her.

"You're not kidding."

"I mean it." I was as resolute as I could be. It was not, I swear, easy for me. But I was having one of those lucid moments when I could tell just how it would go. Brushy would always blame me for not being better and herself for not wanting more.

"Don't tell me what's good for me, okay? I hate when you do that, like you're Lazarus, who crawled out of his cave just to do Ann Landers's column for a week."

"Jesus Christ," I said. "Ann Landers?"

"You try to make people dislike you, Mack," she told me. "You lure them in, then drive them away. If that's supposed to be some form of winning Irish melancholy, I want you to know I don't find it charming. It's sick," she said. "It's nuts." She threw her napkin in her plate and looked out to the sea to gather herself.

After some time she asked if it was too late to swim.

"Tide's out. It's shallow for a quarter of a mile. The water is 83 degrees year round." I tried smiling.

She made a sound, then asked if I'd brought a suit. She held out a hand as she stood.

The path to the beach was carved through the high ragged weeds and Bermuda grasses and lit by little fixtures on stanchions at the point of each stair. Sunday night, even in Pico, was quiet. There was action on the beach, but that was closer to C. Luan, where the big hotels were clustered. Down here, where it was mostly condos, there was a deserted, summery air, except for the band that struck up periodically a few hundred yards off in the hotel bar. We swam a little, kissed a bit, and sat there while the water washed around us. Middle years and acting like eighteen. Every time I thought about it, I wanted to groan.

"Swim with me," Brushy directed, and she splashed out a bit to a deeper point. Closer to shore the gathered shells were hard on the feet, but about fifty yards out the sand was soft and she stood lolling against me. The moon had been up for a while but was growing brighter, a blue neon glow spilling down like an apron beneath a few boats moored for the night. The hotel and its little outbuildings and the giraffe-like coconut palms hulked on shore, dark on darker.

"There are fish in these waters," I told her. "Gorgeous things. Stoplight parrot fish, and sergeant majors trimmed in yellow, and whole schools of indigo hamlets with colors more intense than you see in your dreams." The thought of this great beauty, below, unseen, moved me.

She kissed me once, then placed her face on my chest and swayed to the band that had struck up again. The small swells rose and fell about us.

"Wanna dance?" she asked. "I think they're playing our song."

"Oh yeah? What's that?"

"The hokey-pokey."

"No shit."

"Sure," she said, "don't you hear it?"

She left her bikini top on, but she removed the bottom and then wrestled off my trunks. She held our suits in one hand and with the other grabbed hold of the horn of plenty.

"Salve work?" she asked.

"Miracle drug," I said.

"And how do you do the hokey-pokey?" she asked. "I forget."

"You put your right foot in."

"Right."

"You put your right foot out."

"Good."

"You put your right foot in and you shake it all about."

"Great. What's next?" she asked and kissed me sweetly. "After the foot?" She boosted herself up on my shoulders and with the slow controlled grace of a gymnast parted herself in the dark water and settled upon me so that I was somehow reminded of a flower.

"I don't think this'll work."

"It'll work," said Brushy with all her familiar confidence in matters sexual.

So there we were, Brushy Bruccia and me, hokeying and pokeying, cruising through the tropical waters among the beautiful fish, with the silver of the moon spilled out like glory around us. In and out and shaking it all about.

Mon, it was something else.

T A P E 5

Dictated February 1, 1:00 a.m.

Monday, January 30

XXII. BANK SECRECY

A. Staying Alone

With a woman beside me, I suppose I should have slept well, but I was away from home and near the heart of darkness and I could not pass through the portal to my troubled dreams. A high-voltage anxiety coursed through me, like some grid from which the tortured lightning seems to leap. I sat on the edge of the bed with my face screwed up in the dark and begged myself not to do what I had a mind to, which was head to the bar, where the band was still tootling, to get one of those five-dollar shots of rye. It is not really an illusion that liquor makes you brave. It does, because it is so much harder to be hurt. I have a catalogue of significant injuries inflicted while I was crocked—second-degree burns from cigarettes and boiling liquids which went awry; twisted ankles; sprained knees; and some walloping insults from an angry wife that were

317

hurled with the force of a cannonball. I survived them all with only a little Mercurochrome or an occasional trip to the emergency room. I had a right to think that was what I'd need.

I got up and, for comfort, like a child who fixes on a blanket or a teddy bear, went back across the veranda to my cabana, and found my Dictaphone. I spent an hour telling my story to myself, my voice hushed but still seeming to travel on the sweet evening wind so that I worried that Brushy might hear.

It was my father I thought about, my father and mother both, actually. I tried to figure how it settled with her, his being a thief. Many of the little treasures he carried off in his pockets were offered to her first. Perhaps I flatter her memory to say that she never seemed at ease. 'We don't need this stuff, Tim.' Encouraging him, I would say, to be a better man. She wore a brooch once that especially pleased him, a large ruby-colored stone in the middle and a lot of antique filigree, but usually she ended up declining anything, which led naturally to many quarrels when he'd had something to drink.

I talked to my mother about what was happening on a single occasion. I was sixteen then and full of opinions.

'He's no worse than everybody else,' she told me.

'They're thieves.'

'Everybody's a bit of a thief, Mack. Everybody's got something they're wantin to steal. It just takes the rest of us watching to make most folks stop.'

She was not so much trying to defend him, I thought, as standing a parent's high ground. Either way, I didn't buy it. I was still at the age when I wanted to be a better man than my father. It was a thirst in me. Unquenchable. One of those many appetites I tried to sate thereafter with the fiery taste of liquor. I never wanted to see a woman regard me with the blighted disappointment he saw from my mother. But, you know, life is long, and I loved my old man too, all those moody Irish songs and his hapless affection for me. He never told me to be better than he was. He knew what life was like.

I fell asleep upright on the sofa, briefcase in my lap. Brushy's searching about woke me. Even groggy, I recognized from the fretful way she inspected me that this was a woman who had awakened before to discover herself disappointed and alone, and I was quick to comfort her, having had some lonely mornings of my own. We had a fine time together, in bed and on the terrace, where we eventually took breakfast squinting and sweating in the unremitting sun. Around 11:00, I stood.

"I'm going to meet that lawyer," I said.

Still in her robe, Brushy asked me to wait for her.

"You stay," I answered. "Get some snorkel gear from the beach attendants. Go look at the fishies. It'll make the trip."

"No, really," she said. "I knew there was work to do."

"Hey. You don't want to know. Remember?"

"I lied."

"Listen." I sat down beside her. "This whole thing's turning mean. Just stand clear."

"Mean in what way?" she asked. Her face became

absorbed in lawyerly precision. She wanted to ask more, but I held her off. I kissed her quickly and headed downtown with my briefcase.

B. Foreign Banking

The International Bank of Finance, whose block stamp appears on the back of each of the eighteen checks cut to Litiplex from the 397 escrow account, is a little tiny place, almost a storefront, except for the grand mahogany interiors. Since my days in Financial Crimes, it has been known as reliable. Ownership, as ever, is a mystery, but there are impressive correspondent relationships with some of England's and America's biggest banks, and rumor always had it that it was one of the American royal families, Rockefeller or Kennedy, somebody like that, with an ancient knowledge of the relationship between wealth and corruption, who was really behind it. I don't know.

I said I wanted to open an account, and in the cordial Luan way the manager presently appeared, an angular black man in a blue blazer, Mr. George, an elegant fellow with that peculiar Luan accent, an island lilt fugued with the patois still spoken by the coastal peoples. George's office was small but richly paneled, with wooden columns and bookcases. I told him I wanted to discuss a seven-figure deposit, U.S. funds. George didn't even twitch. For him stuff like this is every day of the week. I hadn't told him my name yet and neither one of us thought I was going to. This is an entire city where nobody's ever heard about I.D. I want to be Joe Blow or Marlon Brando, that's fine.

Bank passbooks down here all have your photo pasted inside the cover, no name.

"After deposit, if I want to transfer the funds while I'm Stateside," I asked, "what's the procedure?"

"Telephone," he said. "Fax." Mr. George wore round black glasses and a bit of mustache; he had long fingers which he raised in a steeple as he spoke. For phone transfers, he said, a customer was required to give an account number and a password; prior to the transaction the bank would telephone to confirm. I considered it unlikely that Jake was sitting in his office at the top of the TN Needle taking calls from bankers in Pico Luan. I asked about fax.

"We must have written instructions, including a handwritten signature or other withdrawal designation," he said. Very artful, I thought. Withdrawal designation. For all those who didn't like names.

"And how long before the transfer takes place?"

"We wire to Luan-chartered institutions within two hours. If we receive instructions before noon, we promise good funds in the U.S. by 3:00 p.m. Central Time."

I reviewed all of this thoughtfully and then asked him for whatever I would need to open an account and whether I could do it by mail. George replied with an enigmatic Luanite gesture: white man can do what he likes. He opened a drawer for the papers.

"The account holder should kindly supply two copies of a small photo. One for the passbook, one for our records. And here, in this space, we should have the account holder's handwriting, whatever designation will be used to authorize withdrawals." 'The account holder,' he said, surmising that I was a stand-in for somebody too important to be seen in C. Luan. And of course he never used the words "signature" or "name." It struck me then that Martin had to have spoken to this guy. His description was dead on. 'Like trying to grab hold of smoke.'

In the office there was a small window, discreetly shaded by jalousies, through which you could see the street traffic passing. There was no screen, since on this side of the mountains there is nothing as troublesome as a bug. At that moment a bird landed on the windowsill, a little wrenny-looking thing, no make I recognized. He, she, it hopped around and finally took an instant to look straight at me. It made me laugh, I must admit, this birdy scrutiny, the thought that you didn't even have to be a mammal to wonder what gives with Malloy. George whisked the back of his hand and told it to shoo.

With the papers, I returned to the street. The sun was high now, savagely bright and thrilling after the indoor weeks in the Middle West. Down here I always understood how people could worship the sun as a god. The business district is only a few blocks, close-set buildings, three and four stories each, stuccoed in Caribbean pastels with roofs of Spanish tile. The tourists roamed among the business folk. Good-looking gals in straw hats and beach coverups, their legs tanned and fully revealed, strode among the suits with their briefcases.

I looked around for more banks, the names of which were unobtrusively displayed on the building sides in English and Spanish, both of which are official languages. Many of the great names in world finance are present, with Luan affiliates housed in pocket-sized spaces like the International Bank's. In this modest fashion a $100 billion economy thrives, Luan-chartered corporations and trusts, funded with fugitive dollars, borrowing and buying and investing around the world, money without a country, as it were, and happy to stay that way.

I found the office of one of the big banks from Chicago, a name I knew—Fortune Trust—and told them I wanted to open a personal account. Same drill as across the street, except this time I wasn't just fishing and did it. I put down $1,000 American in bills and they took my picture twice with one of those machines. When the photos dried, they pasted one in my passbook and the other to their signature card. I elected to keep all deposits in dollars—I could choose from a menu of fourteen currencies—and said I wanted no statements, which saved me from the need to provide an address. Interest would be posted whenever I showed up to present my passbook. I checked a box on a form authorizing them to debit the account $20 U.S. any time money was wired.

"And what will be the designation for purposes of identification?" asked the smashing young woman assisting me. By her accent I took her for an Aussie, here to scuba and be free of something, parents or a guy or the throttling force of her own ambitions. The whole place was free, with the gorgeous fish that decorated the warm waters, the sun, the rum, the sense that many of the world's rules were disregarded. I eventually realized she wanted my code word.

"Tim's Boy," I answered. She asked if I cared to write it, and I did that as well. I was now free to transfer money in and out, to check my deposits by phone.

According to my prior calculations, I still needed one

more account. For that, I did not even have to leave the building. There was a Swiss bank on the second floor, Züricher Kreditbank, and I listened to the lecture on their procedures, which included access to funds out of either Swiss or Pico facilities and the full benefit of the secrecy laws of both nations. I deposited another thousand. I had two new passbooks now in my briefcase.

Outside, I stopped a guy on the street and asked if he knew of a secretarial service, somewhere I could have a letter faxed. I wandered down toward one of the big beachfront hotels where he directed me. I had my suit jacket off, tucked under my arm with my briefcase. I looked into the windows, as if I was shopping, but I was thinking solely about myself, wondering who I was, what I was going to be. A guy getting ready to cheat on his wife has to feel like this, examining the island curios and the fancy knits, the scuba gear in vivid colors, seeing but not seeing, senses focused mostly on his heart and pondering why this is necessary, what this hunger is that he just has to feed, how he'll feel forever after, with some fraction of him cringing whenever he hears words like "faithful" and "true."

U You, I know what you think: usual Catholic upbringing, the only sin not forgiven is sex. But I'm looking at a bigger picture than that. Okay, it's true, most people's secrets are sexual; that's still the realm where a soul is most often unknown. Just ask Nora. Or Bert. We tell ourselves that nobody's hurt when the wishes become real, it's consenting adults, so who cares, but you can't sell that story to Lyle—or to me. Hurting happens. But we still have our needs. That's the point. Whatever it might be, sex or dope or stealing things, everybody's got some weird not-oughta-be that lights them up when it crosses their brain. Nora, Bert, and, in a few minutes, me—we were all members of a teensy-weensy minority group, having fulfilled our sly, unspeakable yearnings. For most people it goes the other way, hanging on that fulcrum where the greatest despair is not really knowing if misery is larger in the realm of fulfillment or restraint. Me, I'd about had it with that balancing act.

I was down at the Regency on the Beach now, and I walked through the hotel, its lobby of fronds and air like dry ice. I sat on a cane chair to think, but I was frozen up, unable to feel much. I asked the concierge to direct me to the secretarial service, and he introduced me to the attendant of their Executive Center. His name was Raimondo, short, sun-coppered, perfectly groomed. I told him I needed a typewriter and a fax machine and gave him fifty Luan. He took me to an area in back, right next to the hotel offices. Raimondo set me up in a small booth that resembled one of the firm's library carrels; an old IBM reposed there like a roosting bird. He offered to arrange for a typist, but I declined, and he left me alone after pointing out two phones and the john around the corner.

I ducked into the head then and studied myself in the mirror one last time. I was still me, a big graying galumph in a suit rumpled up like some elephant's knees, with this gone-to-pot face. I knew I was going to do it.

"Well, well," I said, "Mr. Malloy." Then I looked around to make sure nobody was lurking in the stalls who could overhear me.

Back in the carrel, I withdrew a piece of TN stationery from my case. I typed:

TO: International Bank of Finance,
  Pico Luan
Please immediately wire—transfer
the balance of account number
476642 to Fortune Trust of Chicago,
Pico Luan facility, Final Credit Ac-
count Number, 896—908.
——————————
John A.K. Eiger

In my briefcase I found the letter from Jake I'd brought along. I didn't remove it, just spread the sides of the case to get a good look, eyes reminding the hand, then signed Jake's name, the way I customarily do, a perfect imitation. Examining my work, I felt an odd flare of pride. I really am world-class. What an eye! Someday, for amusement, I'd have to take a whack at G. Washington on the dollar, frame a copy for Wash. I smiled at the thought and then below the signature wrote "J.A.K.E." I was guessing, of course. As a code, Jake could have used his mother's maiden name, or whatever was written on his last mistress's shoulder tattoo, but I'd known him for thirty-five years now and this didn't feel much like gambling. If he needed a password, he was hard-wired to come up with only one thing: J.A.K.E.

I gave the letter to Raimondo and watched him feed the paper through the machine. My heart suddenly bolted.

"The origination line," I said.

He didn't understand. I tried smiling and discovered my mouth dry. On the fax, I explained, there was a line printed on the top to identify the sending machine. Some of the people I was dealing with were under the impression I was Stateside. I wondered if he'd be able to block that line out.

Raimondo went mutton-mouthed and hooded his eyes. This was C. Luan, nobody had names or a sure point of origin. He just shook his head in silent reassurance that no one around here would even consider setting that feature. At the other end, they wouldn't know if the fax had come from around the corner or from west Bombay.

After watching the letter buzz through the machine, I felt like a drink. I wandered out through the garden. I laid my jacket over my lap as I took a seat by the pool. The waitress came by in sort of a safari outfit, pith helmet and khaki shorts, and I ordered a rum punch, no rum. I wondered if I could stand this for the rest of my life, this nation of rock hounds, archaeologists, inland tribes, and sunning exiles.

Around the pool at this time of day there was pretty much nobody, a few scuba widows and a number of the babes who various big buckeroos stash down here and shtup whenever they pay a visit to their secret, hidden dough. These young ladies, each one generally better-looking than the next, naturally attracted my attention, but in a somewhat abstract way. They spend their days working on their tan, oiling down their perfect flesh, reading or plugged into headphones, and then when the heat is too great, they strut to the shower and cool down so that the nipples peak up in the tops of their skimpy little string suits. They excite the few guys around—the towel boys, the old goats like me—and, having made sure that they're still full of magic, lie down again for another couple of hours. I've never been in another place like C. Luan, where the cookies on the side all gather and are laid out together as if on a baking sheet, and it makes you wonder, What do these gals think, twenty-five or twenty-six years old, who are they and where do they come from? How does a person settle for life as a trinket? What do you tell yourself? This is great, this old guy's only here to paw me every other week, I'm living rich and free. Do they all need daddies? Or do they wish they'd had the luck and stuff to get through law school? Do they puzzle about where they'll be when they turn forty-three? Do they hope the guy is going to sack the wife, like he's always saying, that someday soon they'll have babies and a house in New Jersey? Do they figure they're just the same as an athlete, in great shape till the body goes? Or do they think, as I think, that life is neither sensible nor fair, that this, however objectively miserable it may be as an outcome, is the best that luck will allow and they'll enjoy the moment, since there will be time to suffer down the road?

I sat there about half an hour, as long as I could stand it, and then went back to the Executive Center to call the Fortune Trust office where I'd been today.

"Tim's Boy, checking a deposit by wire transfer to account 896–908." I thought the voice on the other end belonged to my girlfriend, the glamorous young Aussie. The image of her, long-haired and lean, deeply tanned with eyes so light they verged on yellow, lingered—but there was a coy absence of recognition and I was simply shifted to hold, that electrical nowhere, as empty as whatever is between the stars. Up until then I'd been in control. A day in the life. But at that point, where I was, hoping and having no real connection, my bloodstream froze over and I was sure I'd lost my mind. I knew this was never going to work. Please, please, *please*, I thought and the only thing I wanted was not to get caught. I realized, with the exactness of clairvoyance, that I'd done all this simply to give myself an instant of pure fright. The man awake at midnight offers solace to his tormentors: Don't bother torturing me, I'll do it myself.

Now I could see it had to unravel. Jake in all likelihood had adopted a different code word, or had long ago transferred the money somewhere else. Maybe I'd miscalculated and the money was not even Jake's. It was Bert's after all. Or Martin's. In any case, Mr. George, the General Manager at the International Bank, was probably out on the street, frantically waving to attract the police. This was not a casual infraction. They would ransack the nation. Bank secrecy was a national treasure, the key to an entire people's way of life. I remembered Lagodis's words with a painful clarity that felt like somebody was putting a brand to my heart: Watch where you step, mon.

I had escape plans, naturally. Sitting up late on Saturday night I'd thought of several and I comforted myself by remembering them now. I'd say I was investigating, trying to pierce bank secrecy only to confirm the commission of a crime and restore the funds to their rightful owner. I'd have Brushy phone the Embassy and her buddy, Tad the K. He'd think I was a hero when he heard how I was saving TN's money; he'd call his Governmental Relations folks and his lobbyists who knew half the pols in this country; they'd get me out in an hour. And who, anyway, was going to catch me? There was bank secrecy here, designed even to protect thieves, and no one knew my name. I didn't care what anyone said to lure me back on the premises at any of these banks. That there were problems with the wire. That the Aussie lass wanted to meet me for a drink. They'd never see me again. I'd thought it all through. It was a lark, a chance, a lottery ticket.

But standing here, I knew I was done joshing. The scheming, the fantasies—I'd had my fun. Now it turned out, I had never been kidding at all. It no longer seemed that Martin or Wash or anyone else had driven me to this. Instead, I was back with Leotis: So much of life is will. I'd made my choice. And I had no idea where it was leading. It was like some scary sci-fi story about a skywalking astronaut who gets cut loose and can't be retrieved and just drifts off forever into endless space. At that instant, if Raimondo'd walked by, I'd have given him another of those funny-looking Luanite fifties just to touch his hand.

"We confirm a deposit, Tim's Boy. Five million, six hundred sixteen thousand, ninety-two dollars, U.S." Just like that. Boom. She didn't even say hello when she got back on the line. From where I stood in the phone booth, I looked out a mullioned window to a stout palm and a bed of flowering shrubs with fronds like spears. A gal in a bathing suit was scolding her child. The doorman lugged somebody's case, and a little native bird, maybe against every improbable chance the one I'd seen in George's office, hopped down the walk, skittering a few steps, as if it was hoping no one was catching up from behind. All of this—these things, these people, this little dumb creature—appeared to me as if they'd been etched on time, distinct as the facets of a diamond. My life, whatever it was, was different.

I started to speak, then started again.

"Can I give you a further transfer of funds, confirmed by fax?"

That, she said, was fine. I read from my passbook. To Züricher Kreditbank, Filiale Pico Luan. I repeated the account number.

"How much?" she asked.

"Five million, U.S." I thought I was safer, leaving something in this account, enough that Fortune Trust would continue to feel I was a customer worth protecting from inevitable inquiries. Not that they would think twice about the whole thing. This happened all the time down here, money hopscotching across the planet. Nobody asked why. They already knew. It was being hidden from someone. Tax collectors, creditors, a weaseling spouse. But I wanted a second transfer to cut off the trail. Jake would raise hell at the International Bank. They'd show him they'd sent the money to Fortune Trust at his instruction. But secret is secret and Fortune wouldn't be saying where the money went from there, or whose account it landed in in the first place.

I waited more than an hour to call Züricher Kreditbank to confirm the second transfer. All was well. My money was safe in Swiss care. I was ready to go back to Brushy. I wished I could drink wine with her. I wanted to be in the grasp of her strong skillful hands. Checking my watch, I reassured myself there was time to make love again before our plane. She would ask where I'd been, what I'd done. She'd want to know every secret. But I wouldn't tell. She'd inquire about Pindling; her brain would be full of intrigue. She'd envision a character like Long John Silver, with a macaw on his shoulder and a hook for a hand. Let her imagine. Ask me no questions, I'll tell you no lies. I felt dangerous and elusive. Light-headed, light-fingered, amused. On the way out of the hotel I poked my head in the john again, just a quick little look-see, a peek in the mirror to find out who was there.

Tuesday, January 31

XXIII. BAD RESULTS

A. Toots Plays for Us

At two on Tuesday, when Toots's disciplinary hearing was scheduled to resume, only Brushy and I were present for the defense. The members of the inquiry panel looked on dispassionately but I surmised from their weary disciplined air that they'd already heard more than enough. After they recommended disbarment, we had a right of appeal to the Courts Commission. Still, in less than a year, Toots's law license would be a relic, one more memento he could tack to his walls.

The old school housing BAD is the kind of structure whose starkness you don't notice until you remove the color and randomness of children. We were in a grim old classroom, with wood floors and walls of that shiny functional tile that resisted abrasion and ink pens. There was a distinct resonance when anyone scraped a chair or cleared his throat.

By ten after, I knew there was a serious problem. Across the long conference table where we were arrayed, Tom Woodhull questioned us about our absent client. The distinguished governmental functionary, enforcer of rules, man with cool white skin, no dark spots or bug bites, Tom had never cared much for me—my drinking, my moods, my occasional assertions that commingling client funds was not a crime on the level of treason. I had long suspected that he had held on to this file for the sheer personal pleasure of kicking my ass.

Brushy rooted in her purse and handed me a quarter.

"Better find him."

Jesus Christ, I thought. Another one.

As I was on my way to the door, my client poked his head in. Toots was heaving for breath and he motioned me into the hallway.

"Got," he said and repeated it many times. "Got someone for you to meet."

By the dusty stairway, hanging on to the square steel newel post was a rotund little fellow in the same condition as Toots, red as Christmas from exertion, breathing hard and spotted with sweat. Brushy had followed.

"You won't believe this," Toots said. "Tell them." Toots motioned with the cane and again asked the man to tell us.

Taking a seat on a plain wooden bench in the hall, the man removed his topcoat. At that point I saw the Roman collar. He was a little guy, bald but for a white fringe and some fried-up strands growing straight out of his scalp.

He held out his hand. "Father Michael Shea."

Father Michael was Judge Dan Shea's younger brother, retired from a parish in Cleveland and attached to a friary there. He had come to town last week to visit relatives— Dan Shea's son, Brian, as a matter of fact, Father's nephew—and in conversation he had heard that Mr. Nuccio here was still having trouble over that old business.

"I give Mr. Nuccio a ring at once. I talked many a time to Daniel about this and he always told me he never knew a t'ing about any generosity from Mr. Nuccio. The dues over there by the country club had just completely slipped his mind. I was skeptical, I am the first to say. Daniel was no angel and he confessed some terrible things to me, as a priest and as a brother. But he swore on Bridget's memory that there'd never been any kind of funny business between him and the Colonel. Never." Father Shea absently touched the crucifix that he wore.

My partner and the love of my life, Ms. Bruccia, absorbed this intently. Our fine tropical romance was now past. There was sand in our shoes and sweet feelings between us which we had nurtured at her apartment all night. But we were again in the cold Middle West, in the land where the subdued winter light, dull as pewter, makes some people crazy and where troubles abounded. She had a million concerns. Us. And all the stuff I wouldn't tell her. Groundhog Day approaching at the firm. But Brushy was now a trial lawyer ready for trial. In her own theater all the seats were sold to Toots, even the standing room. Her powers of concentration were phenomenal; great performers of all kinds, athletes, entertainers, share this single-mindedness. And when I assessed her now, I saw nothing subdued. Rather, there was glee, the flame of celebration. She was looking from Toots to Father Shea to me, about to win the case that everyone told her she'd lose, ready to prove to the world at large what every trial lawyer secretly yearns to establish, that she was not merely an advocate or a mouthpiece but a palpable magician.

Toots had finally recovered his breath and, if possible, looked happier than she did. His old stoved-in face danced around the fire.

Hitching my shoulder, I strolled them both down the old school hall. There were still those little half-height metal lockers on either side on which various enterprising youngsters had scraped their initials, hearts, and an obscenity or two, all of these symbols now enlarging in rust.

"Can you believe this?" Brushy asked. "It's phenomenal."

"It certainly is," I answered. "Just phenomenal. Right at the last minute. *After* the last minute. So late nobody could even ask this guy boo."

Brushy looked at me strangely.

"Tell her, Toots," I said.

The old guy stared up at me dumbly. He wiped his mouth with the heel of his hand.

"It must have been a tough decision, Toots, to hire someone who looked more like Barry Fitzgerald or Bing Crosby."

"Mack," said Brushy.

Toots wouldn't even feign injury.

"Forget me. Forget you," I said to him. "*She* could get disbarred for a stunt like this. And *she* has a career."

He displayed the rumpled-up sour face that appeared

whenever I corrected him. He'd sunk onto another bench and was staring vacantly down the hall, rattling his cane and doing his best not to look at me. Somewhere a radiator spit a bit. I had not quite shaken the chill of winter since getting off the plane.

Brushy, now that it had come through, had lost color. "Is he a priest at least?"

"A priest? I'll bet you a bundle this guy's name is Markowitz. He's straight from central casting."

"I believed it," Brushy said. She touched her head with her short hands and bright fingernails and sat down next to Toots whom she fixed with a brief, baleful look. "I *believed* it."

"Sure you did," I said. "So would that dope Woodhull, probably. But somebody would figure it out eventually. Here or on the Court's Commission. If anybody ever asked for this guy's fingerprints, I'd book a seat on the next stagecoach."

The old guy still wasn't saying anything. He'd learned from the best. If you get caught, dummy up. No good ever came from confessing. I thought about his luminous expression when he had Brushy going. It must have been music to him every time he fixed something. The unraveling of society was his secret symphony. He was the hidden conductor, the only guy who knew the real score. In a way you had to hand it to him. This was the *coup de grâce*. Imagine corrupting your own ethics hearing. Now *that* would make a story. After all, they forced him. He'd just wanted a continuance.

Woodhull appeared down the hall, outside the door to the hearing room.

"What's going on?" he demanded. His straight thick hair, dirty blond, had fallen down over one eye. Hitler youth. "What are you up to now, Malloy? Who's that guy?" he asked as he came closer. He meant Father Markowitz, who was still on the bench down the way.

"Who's the guy?" Tom repeated. "Is he a witness?"

Brushy and I looked at each other, neither of us answering.

"You have a new witness? Now?" It didn't take much from me to set Tom off. He'd brought a yellow pad with him and he began worrying it in the air, while he let his temper mount. "Eleventh hour, we're going to get a surprise witness? Who we haven't heard word one about? Now? Who we haven't even had a chance to interview?"

"Talk to him," Brushy said abruptly. I reached for her arm, and that gesture of restraint was all the encouragement Tom needed.

"I will," he said and advanced past the three of us.

I whisked Brushy around a corner and asked, concisely, if she'd lost her mind.

"It's unethical to put him on to testify," she said. "I know that."

" 'Unethical' isn't the word, Brush. You do straight time for that stuff."

"Okay," she said. "But you said Woodhull would believe him."

"So what? You don't think he'll drop the case. Woodhull doesn't know how to change his mind. The testimony's hearsay, and even if it comes in, he'll argue that it's worth nothing, that the judge was just too ashamed to level with his brother. You know the pitch."

"But he'll believe him, right? That's what you said."

"Probably. He's probably having a shitfit right now."

"So he'll be afraid he's going to lose. Suddenly. A case everybody thought he was going to win." She was giving me the reverse of her own logic, which is what I mean about her being quick-witted and devious. "He'll be willing to settle. For something short of disbarment. That's what we want. Am I right?"

I finally saw her point. But there were still problems.

"Brush, think about this. You just introduced the Deputy Administrator of Bar Admissions and Discipline to a supposed witness who your client told you is an impostor."

"My client didn't tell me anything. I didn't take any fingerprints. I'm an advocate. And I made no representations. Or introductions. Tom was free-associating. Am I supposed to protect him from himself?" She stared at me. "*I* believed this guy. If somebody else doesn't, fine. The witness won't testify either way. I mean, Mack," she said quietly, "there's no downside."

Toots was gimping our way. He was having a great time. Father obviously was selling well. There was no point in warning the Colonel about consequences. He'd lived his life jumping chasms, scaling perilous heights. I heard Woodhull's voice rising around the corner.

The deal we cut was unique. Under the state law attorneys could be disbarred for five years. After that they were free to reapply, and the Court's Commission, with a frequency exasperating to BAD, tended to readmit them on the theory that for most of these men and women it was the only profession they knew, like shoemakers who could only make shoes. What we offered on Toots's behalf was something better: Toots would promise never to practice law again. Not much of a concession, since he didn't practice anyway, but he would take his name off the door of his firm, give up his office there, and not receive another penny from firm income. If he ever violated the agreement, he would consent to an order of disbarment. In exchange, the proceedings against him ended. No findings. No censure. No record. His name stayed on the rolls. He would never be publicly disgraced.

Toots, in the grand tradition of clients everywhere, refused to be grateful, becoming reticent as soon as the agreement was announced to the panel.

"How'm I gonna support myself?" he asked out in the hallway after we had put on our topcoats.

We both gave him the fisheye. Toots couldn't spend what was in his mattress if he lived to one hundred.

"Toots, it's what you want," I told him.

"I like the office," he said, and no doubt he did. The secretaries who called him Colonel, the phone calls, the pols coming to visit.

"So take an office down the hall. You've retired. That's all. You're eighty-three, Colonel. It's logical."

"All right." But he was downcast. He looked elderly and glum. His color was bad and his skin seemed ripply like the rind on an orange. It's always sad to see the high brought low.

"Toots," I said, "they have never done this for anybody else. It's a one-of-a-kind. We have to swear to God and the Governor that we'll never leak one word of this deal to anyone. They can't admit they backed off on a disbarment."

"Yeah?" He liked that better, being a category of one. "So what's so special about me?"

"You hired the right lawyers," I told him. That, finally, made him laugh.

B. Final Accounting

Back in the office, Brushy and I went for what is called a victory lap, moseying by the offices of various litigators and casually describing the result. The acclaim was universal, and by the time we reached the desk of our secretary, Lucinda, we were feeling roundly admired, a sensation I experienced with a surprising rush of sentiment, since it had been some time.

Brush and I stood there checking out our message slips and mail. The firm's fiscal year ended today, and all partners had received a solemn memo from Martin stating that even with good collections before midnight, income was likely to be down 10 percent. That meant the distribution of points two days hence on Groundhog Day was going to be a slaughterhouse for the lower-level partners like me, since Pagnucci would not allow the top tier to be stinted. As we'd moved cheerfully between offices, the air was already growing fraught. Brushy ran off with her phone messages—one triumph behind her, a world of possible triumphs ahead. I lingered by Lucinda's work station. There was, as usual, not much doing for me.

"Same guy's been calling," she told me. "Keeps asking when you'll be back in town." She had described these calls to me this morning, saying they had started yesterday.

"Any name?"

"Just hangs up."

Brushy and Lena and Carl were the only people who'd known I was leaving. I hadn't even told Lyle much more than the fact that I might not be home for a night or two. As near as she could recall, Lucinda said, it sounded like the same man who'd phoned the office on Friday morning before Pigeyes nabbed me out on the street. That fit. Gino or someone from his crew had probably been keeping an eye on the house, maybe even tailed me to the airport, and was trying to figure out where I was now. If Gino was good to his word, he was toting a subpoena for me.

Or, I thought, it could be Bert. If he'd spoken to Lyle first, he might have figured I was gone. But Lucinda surely would have recognized the voice. Maybe he had Orleans calling for him?

Lucinda watched me with her usual brimming expression. A stout, handsome, dark-skinned woman, Lucinda keeps her own counsel, but it bruises her heart to work up close to such a living mess. She is a great pro—my salvation, as loyal to me as to Brushy, even though everybody in the place understands that I am the underbill and Brush the big star. Lucinda keeps plugging. A picture of her husband, Lester, and their three kids was at the corner of her desk. They were all posed around the youngest, Reggie, at his high-school graduation.

"Oh my God!" I said then, when it hit me. "Oh my God, Orleans." I actually ran the first few steps before I looked back to tell Lucinda I was on my way to Accounting.

Down there, it was chaos. The place was like a cam-

paign headquarters on election night, with computer terminals clicking and adding machines spilling tape and a lot
of people running around full of purpose or desperation.
Because of the IRS, everything collected had to be booked
today. A number of secretaries and messengers were in
line to process the booty of fees finally bludgeoned out of
clients. Money—collecting it, counting it, making it—
thickened the atmosphere the same way gunpowder and
blood embitter the air of battle.

Behind her clear white desk, Glyndora started out of her
chair the instant she saw me, her intent manifest to avoid
any further intimate *tête-à-têtes*.

"Glyn," I said, blocking her way. "Whatever happened to the photo of your son? Didn't you keep it right
here?" The picture had been on her desk for years, and
on the credenza in her home, a fine-looking lad in his
mortarboard and graduation gown. "Remind me," I told
her. "What's his name? Orleans, right? Not Gaines,
though. Carries his dad's last name, doesn't he?" I'd remembered now where I'd seen Kam Roberts.

Junoesque, Glyndora confronted me in silence, a beautiful totem, her dark face tight in anger. But it was like a
closet where you couldn't quite squeeze the door shut
because of everything packed inside. There was an edge
of something unwanted, beseeching, that undermined her
expression and riled her, no doubt worse than anything
which I'd said.

"I don't want to hurt anybody," I said to her quietly,
and she allowed me to lead her out to the hall. It seemed
a bit of a haven, away from the urgent clamor.

"Have Orleans get a message to Bert," I told her. "I

need to see him. Face-to-face. In Kindle. ASAP. All Bert
has to do is name the time and place. Tell him I have
to sort things out with him. Ask him to call me here
tomorrow.''

She didn't answer. Man, those were eyes she had, black
and infernal, sizing me up, her mind flopping about furi-
ously behind them. It didn't take a lot of imagination to
figure out what caused all the legendary squabbling in the
hallways between Bert and Glyndora, throwing things and
calling names. Stay away from my boy. This wasn't a
scene that pleased her, her boss and her lad in the mode
of the ancient Greeks. She was probably glad Bert was on
the run.

"Glyndora, I know a lot now. About your son. And
I've got that memo you bootlegged to Martin, which, you
notice, I'm not even asking about. I'm going to try not to
hurt anyone. But you've got to get that message to Bert.
You're gonna have to trust me.''

I might as well have asked her for a pot of gold. She
despised the position she was in—the weakling, the
wanter, the one to say please. Worst of all, she felt something I knew like the back of my hand, as familiar to me
as darkness and light, which Glyndora as an act of will
had simply abolished from her existence: she was scared.
She gummed her lips into her mouth to control herself,
then turned to look down the hall where there was nothing
to see.

"Please.'' I said it. It was the least I could do. She
shook her head, the mass of dark hair, not so much in
answer as dismay, and, still without speaking a word, went
back to counting our money.

C. A Word for the Big Guy

Near five I phoned home, rousing Lyle from a sound sleep. He reported that he'd been getting the same strange calls as Lucinda: 'Mack there, when's he back?' He did not recognize the voice.

"Did you tell him?"

"Fuck no, Dad, I know better than that." His pride and his assumptions, the whole tone of his response, struck me in the desperate total way only Lyle could. It was so clear where he was frozen—the latchkey kid of thirteen whose mommy had warned him about strangers. My boy. Listening to him, I felt for a moment I might simply expire from the pain. It eased a bit as he carried on about the Chevy, which he'd retrieved from the pound with two flats. One hundred eighty-five bucks it cost, plus the ticket, and he wanted the money back. He made the point a number of times.

I've come home again with Brushy tonight. We had takeout Italian, fancy stuff, rigatoni with goat cheese and obscure antipasti, which we consumed between screws. I won't say how I ate my tiramisu. About an hour ago, as we were drowsing, her back to me, saved from drowning in my arms, Brushy said, "If I ask, you'll tell me, right?"

"Ask what?"

"You know. What's going on. With the money. Bert. The whole thing. Right? You know, attorney-client. But you'll tell me."

"I think you don't want to know. I think your life is better without this kind of news."

"And I accept that," she said. "I do. I know you're

right. I trust you. But if I decide, if I really have to know, for whatever reason, you'll tell me. Right?''

My eyes were wide in the dark. "Right."

So that's how it is. My warped little dreams, private so long, are now hurling themselves through my life with volcanic force. Perhaps the sheer peril made my lovemaking with Brushy vigorous and prolonged. She sleeps as she's slept the previous nights, in the comforted grip of her own improbable fantasies, immobile almost, but I am desolate and awake in the dark, chasing away goblins and spooks, out here in her living room now, whispering again into my Dictaphone.

So you ponder, U You: What is he up to, this guy, Mack Malloy? Believe me, I ask myself the same thing. The apartment is surrounded by the odd silences of winter— the windows closed tight, the heat whispering, the cold keeping idle souls from the street. Since I actually committed this stunt, robbing TN blind and preparing to blame it on somebody else, my ma's barking accusatory voice seems to be with me wherever I go. She regarded herself as devout, one of the Pope's own Catholics, her life whirling like a pinwheel where the Church was at the very center, but her religious thought seemed to dwell mostly on the devil, who was regularly invoked, particularly whenever she was remonstrating with me.

But it wasn't the devil that made me do it. All in all, I think I'm just sick of my life. It seemed like such a terrific idea. But it was *my* fancy, my folly, my fun-time escapade. There's no sharing. Hell, it turns out, is being stuck forever listening to your own jokes.

So who is this for? Why bother talking? Elaine always

had the same hope. 'Mack, you won't die without a priest at your side.' Probably right. I'm a short-odds player. But maybe this is the first act of contrition, part of the process that the Church these days calls reconciliation, where your heart, unburdened, rises to God. What do I know?

So here goes. Big Guy, Big Entity, Big Being, if you're up there listening, I suppose you will think what you like. But please forgive me. I need it tonight. I did what I wanted and now I am sorry as hell. We both know the truth: I have sinned, big-time. Tomorrow I'll have my stuff back. I'll be bitter and ready to stick it to everyone else. I'll be the apostate, agnostic, you won't cross my mind. But like me tonight, accept me one moment before I reject you, as I reject everyone else. If you can forgive infinitely, then forgive this, and have an instant of pity for your ragtag creation, sad Bess Malloy's boy.

TAPE 6

Dictated February 2, 9:00 p.m.

XXIV. YOUR INVESTIGATOR
HIDES OUT

A. Waiting for Bert

Brushy had an early meeting and went rushing off at seven, wrestling into her coat as she grabbed her briefcase, a jelly doughnut stuffed whole into her mouth. I was still in bed and lingered amid my lover's possessions. Brushy's apartment had an overcrowded urban air. She was on the first floor of a brownstone with nifty Victorian touches—raised moldings and patterned plaster, and those little breastlike caps in the ceiling where the gas fixtures had been removed. There were tall pine shutters on the street-side windows that ran floor to ceiling, and many plants, and walls of books, stacks of everything. No real art to speak of—a couple of tasteful posters, but strictly representational stuff, no more adventurous than a bowl of fruit. In the bedroom, where I would have expected maybe a mirror or a trapeze, there was little furnishing, except for a king-size bed and heaps of dirty clothing at the corners of her closet, laundry on one side, dry cleaning on the other. She looked, appropriately, like a person with a busy life.

About eight-forty, as I was getting ready to head out, the phone rang. Better not to answer, I figured. What if it was one of Brushy's pinup legion of male admirers? What if Tad Krzysinski was asking if he could slip her the big one at lunch? I let it go to the answering machine and heard Brush emphatically telling me to pick up.

"You better stay where you are," she said.

"You're coming home for an interlude?"

"I just met Detective Dimonte."

"Oh Christ."

"He was looking for you. I told him I was your attorney."

"He have a grand jury subpoena?"

"That's why he was here."

"Did you accept service?"

"Told him I wasn't authorized."

"Clever lady. What else did he want to know?"

"Where you were."

I asked what she'd said, then realized the inevitable response and repeated it with her: "Attorney-client."

"I'll bet he was in a mood," I added.

"You might say. I told him I'd have you get in touch."

"When I'm ready."

"He'll come looking for you, won't he?"

"He is already. He may even follow *you*. And I wouldn't talk too much more on this phone either."

"Could he get a wiretap order that fast?"

"Pigeyes doesn't know from court orders. He's got a

guy at the phone company he caught buying cocaine or with his thing in a glory hole who he makes throw switches for him when need be.''

"Oo," said Brush.

"Attractive guy, right?"

"Well, actually," said Brushy. "I mean, you'd say masculine."

"Don't do this to me, Brush. Tell me you're only saying that because he might be listening."

She laughed. I took a moment to think.

"Look, I better cut out—just in case he got enterprising. I'm supposed to hear from a certain tall missing partner of ours today. Make sure Lucinda forwards the call to you. Don't get into any extended conversations over this phone. Tell him to give you the information I wanted on 7384. Follow?" She. assured me she did. 7384 was G&G's fax line. I looked forward to Gino listening in on that screech, the mating call of two machines. He couldn't tap that.

I gathered my briefcase, still packed with everything from Pico Luan, and walked down about three blocks, where there was another location of Dr. Goodbody's. I knew I'd have to deal with Gino eventually. But only after I talked to Bert and figured out what I could say. I had plans—millions, in fact. Soon I'd have to choose.

I spent the day at the health club, hairy-eyeballing the gals in their leotards and playing with the machines. I've passed time like this before. After all those years in saloons, I just get this yen to be near people I don't know. With a towel around my shoulders, dressed in a pair of gray sweats, I hop on the stepper, punch in a bunch of numbers, and jump off shortly after the thing begins to move. I do some pulls at one of the weight stations. Eventually I find someone to talk to, one of those dumb little chats that a drunkard gets to like, where I can pretend to be someone who's never exactly like me.

Today I stuck pretty much to myself. Every now and then I'd try to think through all the alternate routes up ahead, if this, if that, but it was too much for me. Instead, I found myself oddly preoccupied with my mother, feeling as I did last night, punished and without too much hope. I'd made my big move, so why wasn't I happy? At times I sensed myself on the verge of laments I'd heard from her, all this stuff about life being hard, being bitter, barren choices, none of them good.

I called the office now and then. Brushy had heard nothing from Bert and instead ended up describing the intense local anxieties with Groundhog Day tomorrow and firm income down 12 percent from last year. When I called again at four, Lucinda answered Brushy's line. Brush was out at a meeting. There was still no word from Bert, but I had two other messages. Martin and Toots.

I phoned the old guy first. I knew just what was coming: he'd thought it out overnight and was going to back off the deal with BAD, he'd rather get clobbered, he was too old to change. The thought was excruciating.

"I love the deal," he said first thing.

"You do?"

"I wanted you to know, on account of yesterday I might not a looked too happy, but I love the deal. *Love* it. I told some guys, they tell me, you musta hired Houdini for your lawyer. Nobody's ever heard of nothing like this."

I mumbled something, just once, about how Brushy deserved credit too.

"You done me right, Mack."

"We tried."

"So listen, so you know: you need, you got. Call Toots."

The Colonel was not the kind of guy who was hot air when he said he owed a favor. It was, in fact, quite a privilege. Like having a fairy godmother and three magic wishes. I could have a leg broken or get certain performers to sing if Lyle ever had anything like a wedding. This was the part of the practice Brushy was addicted to, somebody saying thanks for the help, not everyone could have done it. I told Toots at length how great it had been to represent him and, at the moment, meant it.

"Where are you?" asked Martin when he came to the phone.

"Out and about."

"About where?" There was a new note here, a harsh tensile quality to his voice. I'd heard Martin talk like this to opponents, the man raised among tough guys.

"About where I am. What's up?"

"We need to talk."

"Okay."

"In person. I'd like you to come in."

It struck me just like that—Martin was doing me wrong. Pigeyes was sitting there, with his smug smile, loving it as my mentor delivered the sucker punch. Then, just as quickly, I rejected the thought. After all the sewage under the bridge, I still wanted to believe in the guy. There are no victims.

"What's our general subject?" I asked.

"Your investigation. There's a document you found, apparently." The memo. He'd talked to Glyndora. He was going to posture. He was going to be magical Martin, potent and charming. However slyly, he was going to ask me to give it back. I breathed in the phone.

"No can do." Sentiment was one thing, but I wasn't going anywhere near the Needle with Pigeyes and his posse posted nearby.

"Just maintain the status quo, will you?" said Martin. "Will you promise me that?"

Without answering, I put down the phone.

I called in again at five-thirty. Brushy picked up herself.

"He's ready to see you," she said.

"Don't say anything else."

"Okay. But how can I get this message to you?"

I thought a second. "Maybe you should come see me."

"What about being followed?"

"You and I had lunch last week."

"Right."

"And then we went somewhere else."

"Okay." The hotel. She got it.

"Before we went upstairs, you went somewhere on your own. Remember?"

She laughed a little when she caught my drift.

"That's where you'll be? Where I went?"

"Center pew. One hour."

"O-kay," she sang. If I said so.

B. Looking for Love in All the Wrong Places, Part 2

The bar at the Dulcimer House hotel has one of those great after-work scenes where the young gals, the secretaries and bank tellers and female functionaries who are not sure if they're looking for fun or a life, go to be ogled and throw back half-price drinks while various guys, bachelors and married fellas with undisciplined dicks, line up three deep at the bar, hoping for some quick drunken action to think of tomorrow at work. As I stood in the distinguished lobby, with its wedding-cake ceiling ribboned in gold, the emanations from the bar intruded, strange as radio signals from deep space: the booming dance music, the garlicky reek of various warm hors d'oeuvres, the carousing voices hoarse with thwarted emotion and ambient lust.

The restrooms were down a short carpeted corridor off the lobby. I waited outside the Ladies', which Brushy had visited as we were checking in last week. Pigeyes would never work with a female cop and he was too old-line and prudish to even think of following her in. He'd wait at the door like Lassie. I spent about five minutes in the hallway, circumspectly checking out the ingress and egress, then stopped a young lady ready to enter.

"Say, my wife's been in there awhile. Would you let me know if she's okay when you come out?"

She was back in a jiffy.

"There's nobody in there."

"No," I said. She was standing at the door, which was decorated with a buxom silhouette, and I held it with one hand and gradually slid into the vestibule, pushing shyly at the inner door. "Shirley?" I called, averting my face so I did not even peek. I turned a little more front and center, yelled in again, and heard my voice ringing off the pink tiles. The girl hunched her shoulders and went back to party.

As soon as she was gone, I stalked into the john and locked myself in the center stall. Resting my briefcase on the toilet paper dispenser, I stood up on the fixture so that no gal would see my wingtips and start yodeling. I squatted there hoping Brushy would be hasty. At 255, my thighs would burn out quickly.

I found myself eye level with two bolt holes originally meant to hold some coat hook or other apparatus. Unutilized, they could serve from this peculiar vantage as a kind of peephole. A gentleman never would, of course, but who said I was Sir Galahad? About a minute along, a great-looking gal in a black dress with tassels entered the stall next to me and I got, as usual, just what I deserved. She didn't touch her zipper or hike her skirt. Instead, she took a minute to remove her rings, then put the middle three fingers of her right hand as far down her throat as could fit. When they came out, she touched each hand to the metal sides of the stall, bucked her head deliriously a couple of times, and puked her guts out. Varoom. Breakfast, lunch, and dinner. The force of it all drove her down to her knees, and she shook her fine head of black curls a little bit, then cleared her throat with a crackling expulsion. A second later I peeped over the top of the stall and saw her by the sink freshening her breath with an atomizer. She tossed out her curls with her long red nails and shoved her boobs back into her push-up bra with a hand underneath each, then lingered to give herself a sizzling look in the mirror. Wednesday night and ready for fun.

I was still trying to figure out what to make of that one when I heard Brushy say my name. She rattled the door. After I closed us in together, she gave me a big smooch, right there next to the toilet bowl.

"I think this is all very exciting," she whispered. That was Brushy, part of what had led her on the world penis tour or ignited some of her interest in me: raw curiosity, the fact that she wanted to see life's every side, savor every far-flung experience. As I've said, I always find female bravery notable and attractive.

"So where is he?" I asked.

"Wait. Don't you want to hear how I shook the tail?" She loved the lingo, the cops and robbers. Brushy thought she was in a movie where I was going to do something smart and save us all, not run away with the money. She described a circuitous route through various buildings in Center City, a stop at a client's, and entry here through the back door of the bar. She would have eluded Joe Friday.

She was searching through her little black purse when we heard the restroom door open. I jumped back up on the bowl, so that I was basically rubbing my zipper on Brushy's nose. Being Brushy, she found this pretty amusing. I covered my lips with a straight finger, and just to let me know she cared, Brush gave my pecker a pat and took the opportunity to start unzipping my fly. I swatted her hand.

The water ran at the sink. Somebody was doing a make-over. Brushy tugged on the zipper. I scowled and mouthed various vituperations, but she loved the circumstance, me in this bondage of silence and place, and pretty soon she was down to business and getting a response. She had old J.P. out there, touch, kiss, prod, and consume, aided by some quick dancing work of the fingertips, and she might have finished if some gal hadn't pulled into the stall next door. The nearby audience diminished my interest, but the whispers and giggling and squirming around were apparently audible to our neighbor, who seemed to jump up. On her way out she put one eye to the breach between the stall door and the post and said, "Weird."

"You are," I said, when we were alone again. "Weird."

"To be continued," Brushy answered. I was in my rough tweed sport jacket, and when she saw my sour look she dug her fingers in. "Come on, Mack. This is wild. Be wild. Enjoy it."

I just shook my head and asked about Bert. She gave me the note he had faxed: "Behind 462 Salguro. 10 p.m." Recognizing the address, I laughed.

"It's the Russian Bath."

"Aren't they closed then?"

"I suppose that's the point."

"Will you come see me afterwards?"

"They're gonna sit on your house, Brush. They might."

She was funny and melodramatic. "Is this goodbye forever?"

I don't think she liked the uncompromising square-jawed expression she got in response. She wanted to be lovey-dovey and lighthearted here in the bathroom stall, giddy and teenaged, as if singing a chorus or two of "I Got You, Babe" would conquer all.

"I want to see you," she said. "I want to make sure you're all right."

"I'll call."

She gave me the eye. After all, she'd followed me to Central America. So we made a plan. She wouldn't go home, because Gino might pick her up there. Instead, she'd grab a taxi, have it circle the block twice to see if she was being followed. Maybe in the movies coppers can tail somebody for days unseen, but in real life it takes four cars at least, someone to go in every direction, and if the mark knows you're there, nine times out of ten you get lost or he's flipping you off in the rearview or sending you a round when you follow him into a tavern. If she came away without company, we agreed Brushy would go to a chain hotel three blocks down. Just check in for the night. Leave a key at the desk. And buy me a toothbrush.

I told her to take off first now. I waited in the vestibule between the doors and she rapped once to signal the hallway was clear. Then I gave her a few minutes to get a lead and take any trailing companions with her. Naturally some old biddy with flossed-up beauty-parlor hair came in then and did a triple-take and a haughty who-are-you look, and I had to pirouette around and play like I thought this all-pink enclosure was actually the men's room and then bow my way back out the door.

No Pigeyes in sight, none of his pals. I put on a winter hat and drew up my muffler and went out to see if I could talk a hack into taking a ride at night into the West End. I was thinking about Brushy. She had kissed me goodbye in the bathroom, a long, lingering embrace full of all her spunk and ardor, and issued fateful advice before disappearing: "Don't get another rash."

XXV. THE SECRET LIFE OF KAM ROBERTS, PART TWO

I got to the West End with more than an hour and a half to spare and I spent the time in a little Latin bar on the corner near the Bath where almost no English was spoken. I sat sipping soda pops, sure every second that I was going to break down and order a drink. I was thinking about Brushy and not enjoying it much, wondering what-all that was coming to, whether I wanted what she did or could give it, and as a result, I was in one of my most attractive moods, refusing to move my elbows and waiting for somebody to try to hoist my no-good Anglo ass.

But the fellas here were pretty good-natured. They were watching one of those taped boxing matches from Mexico City on the bar TV, commenting *en español*, and taking peeks now and then at yours truly, figuring all in all I was too big to mess with. Eventually I got into the mood, joshing with them, throwing around my four or five words of Spanish, and recalling my longtime conclusion that a

neighborhood joint like this might be the single best class
of places on earth. I was more or less raised at The Black
Rose, a terrible thing to admit maybe, considering the
rumpot I turned out to be, but in a neighborhood of tene-
ments and tiny homes, people longed for a place where
they could expand, lift an elbow without knocking down
the crockery. At the Rose, it was all right if your wife
came; there were kids running round the tables and jerking
on their mothers' sleeves; there was singing and those
jokes. Humans warmed by one another's company. And
me, as a kid, I couldn't ever wait to get out of there, to
blow the whole scene. I recollected this with chagrin, but
suspected for reasons I couldn't explain that I'd end up
feeling the same way if you put me back there today.

Ten o'clock even, I headed out and walked down the
alley. This was a big-city neighborhood where the cops
and the mayor long ago installed those orange sodium
lights with their garish candlepower that seemed to turn
the world black and white, but the alley was still all kinds
of menacing shadows—garbage cans and dumpsters, sinister alcoves and iron-barred doorways, a lot of lurking spots
for Mr. S/D, Stranger Danger, to smile and wield his knife.
Walking on, I had the usual dry rot in the mouth and
watery knees. I heard a grating clank and stopped dead.
Someone was out here waiting for me. I reminded myself
that was how it was supposed to be, I was meeting somebody.

When I got closer, I saw a figure beckoning. It was the
Mexican, Jorge, Mr. Third World Anger, who'd questioned me the day I was down here. He stood in the alley
in bathroom slippers and an iridescent blue silk robe. His

hands were shoved deep in his pockets and you could see the great puffs of his breath hazing above him in a blade of light angling from the doorway behind. He chucked his face in my direction and said, "Eh."

Bert was inside, out of sight of the door. We seemed to be in a supply area behind the locker room, and he greeted me as eagerly as he had the other night. Meanwhile, Jorge engaged the dead bolt on the door and padded off. Apparently he was going back to sleep. He paused to poke his head down the hall.

"When you leave, lock it. And, men, don't leave nobody see your ass. I don' want no fuckin shit here. I tole you a long time ago, *hombre*, you was fucked up, all fucked up." He said this to Bert, but he pointed at me. "I tole you, too."

Jorge, Bert said, had to get up at four, arrange the stones which had been in the oven firing all night, and make the place ready for the bathers who'd begin arriving as early as 5:30 a.m. I wondered where Jorge stood with the outfit guys. There were a lot of them that came around here to steam off the stink of corruption and ugly deeds. Jorge, I suspected, kept everyone's secrets. But if a guy with a tommy gun or a coat hanger knocked on the front door now, Jorge'd point out where we were and go back to sleep. It was a tough life.

I told Bert we had to talk.

"How about the Bath?" he asked. "You know, oven's on. It's blow-your-brains-out hot in there. It'll be great. Get all that oil and stuff right up to the skin. How about it?"

I had some thoughts, silly bigoted ones, about sitting

around naked with Bert, even wrapped in a bedsheet, and then I began to feel sheepish and stupid, sure that if I said no he'd read that as the motive. So we hung our clothes in the lockers and Bert found the way down, both of us in the ocher-colored bedsheets cinched at our bellies and worn much like skirts. Bert didn't dare burn a light near a window. The shower room outside the bath remained dark, and the bath itself was lit only by a single bulb that left a gloomy light the color of tea. The stones had all been shoveled back into the oven and the room was arid, the great fire roasting the air. Even so, the place still had a vaguely vernal scent. Bert cracked the door a bit on the oven and then sat himself down on the top bench in the stepped wooden room and made exultant noises in the withering heat.

You'd have thought he had no troubles, chatting away about the Super Bowl, until I asked him to tell me on the level how it had been. He looked down then between his knees and didn't answer. Scary times, I suppose. Here was a fella who'd flown wartime missions, who knew what it was like being throttled by fright. But time had passed; the imagination takes over; honest memories fade. The pain of fear had plainly surprised him.

"I been eating fried food. Drinking bad water, man. Can't tell what's gonna get me first. You know?" He smiled. Loopy old Bert. He thought he was funny. Lead from the tap or a gun barrel was lead either way.

"And where the hell have you been hiding out?" I asked.

He laughed at the question.

"Brother," he said and laughed again. "Here, there, and everywhere. Seeing the sights. Tried to keep moving."

"Well, let's take today, for instance. Where'd you start out?"

"Today? Detroit."

"Doing what?"

He fidgeted in the dense heat while words evaded him.

"Orleans had a game up there last night," he said finally. He was looking the other way as he said it and he didn't say any more. I got the picture: Bert was seeing all the best places, Detroit and La Salle–Peru, chasing Orleans, romancing on game nights in funky motels, places like the U Inn.

"And what about money? What've you been doing to live?"

"I had a credit card in another name."

"Kam Roberts?"

That startled him momentarily. He'd forgotten what I knew.

"Right. I thought it'd be better than using my own, they'd have a harder time tracking me down, but they did anyway."

"I thought Orleans used that card."

"I had one, he had one. We scissored them finally. The cards were about to expire anyway. But we piled up some cash. That's okay. What the hell do I need? A motel with cable, I'm cool. It's just those guys, man. They were right on us. They were checking at stores where Orleans used the card, stuff like that. Scared the hell out of us both. Man." He looked at me. "Those guys were cops, you're saying?"

"They're hot on the trail." I had remained on my feet. I figured if I kept the sheet clutched around me and my butt off the boards, I'd make Brushy happy and come home unblemished. "That's our problem, Bert. The coppers. They know I've been looking for you, so now they're looking for me, especially after that runaround at the House of the Hands on Friday. I haven't slept at home for four nights. You and I have to scope out what I tell them, Bert, cause 'I dunno' doesn't really seem to cut it. This whole thing with Orleans—I'd like to know how it happened, just so we can figure what kind of dance step I do."

I wasn't facing him then. There was no point in that. Even so, I could feel him sort of hanging, suspended in space as we sat here in this hot wooden box.

"I mean, you know," he said behind me.

"Right," I said. We were going forward easy. "You met him when he came to visit his mom at work. Something like that."

"Right."

So we stumbled around in conversation and Bert told me the tale of Orleans and him in his own half-ass way. We were there broiling, not looking at each other, just two voices in the tea-gloomy light and incredible heat. Bert wasn't much of a storyteller. He did a lot of shit-out-of-luck mumbling. "You know," he'd say, "you know." And I did, I guess. I got the point. Orleans changed Bert's life the way people's lives are ordinarily altered only by human violence and natural disasters—volcanoes, hurricanes, typhoons. You see the pictures all the time, some poor son of a bitch in his hip waders, looking with zoned-out disbelief at the roof of what used to be his house, now angled into the black waters of the flood. That was Bert after Orleans. I'd only seen the guy across the distance of a basketball court, so I couldn't tell you a thing about him, except that he was a fine-looking young fellow. But as I put the pieces together, my two bits, he was sort of high-strung and erratic. Apparently he'd been a high-school football star who tore up his knee and suffered a lot over that, getting cut out of athletics, then started refereeing various sports while he was still in college. These days he taught grade school p.e. as a sub and reffed, but his principal occupation apparently was fighting with his mother. He had a peculiar job history, moving in and out of town, always coming back, living at home half the time. I suppose Glyndora wanted him to be different and he was engaged in the usual parent-child struggle, always angry with her and wanting her to accept him, the way we all want with our folks at one level or another.

Somehow, though, they connected. For Bert, it was epochal. Orleans, I took it, was Bert's first actual real-life thing, and Bert was in love with him the way you'd love the genie if you'd found that magic lamp. Orleans to Bert was liberty. Destiny. In the midst of his longing, his attachment, Bert was also wild with gratitude. It's hard to believe that this could really happen in this day and age—people who live on the other side of earth from what they're really feeling—but the old copper in me says it occurs every day. Look at Nora. Look at me. Suddenly you're at an age when your own naughty thoughts exhaust you; no matter how much you try to ignore them, they remain. Whatever ugly stamp they place on your soul is impressed there indelibly. You might as well be whatever it is they say you are. You are anyway.

So they got their rumba going, Bert and Orleans, and Glyndora caught on and went wild. I got the feeling that was okay with Orleans, to be causing that kind of ruction.

Bert was walking back and forth now on the tier above me, roaming on his big feet with the long nails and the calluses from his loafers and athletic shoes. His black hair was heavy with perspiration and his unshaven cheeks looked darker in the heat.

"And how'd this betting thing happen? Whose idea?"

"Oh, you know, man," he said again, for the one hundredth time. "There was never any idea about it. We'd talk games. Players. Stuff like that. You know how it is, you hang with somebody, you kind of figure what they're thinking, I mean maybe he'd say— He'd say. You know, before the Michigan game, he'd say, 'I'm going to call Ayres tight, he's a street player, you got to call him tight.' Or Erickson at Indiana. All elbows."

"And you'd bet it. Right? If Ayres was going to be called tight, you'd bet against Michigan."

"Yeah," he said. He was slowed by shame. "It didn't seem like much. Just a little edge. I didn't really think twice."

"Did Orleans know?"

"To start?"

"Eventually?"

"Man, do you know I bet the games?"

"I do," I said. Orleans, he was saying, knew too. I thought for a sec about Bert as a gambler. What was it that compelled him? Did he lust to feel favored by chance, or did he want to dare punishment? What drew him? The men? Or the sport? The grace, the fact that it was all winners and losers with no compromise? Something. It was part of the game of hide-and-seek he was playing with himself.

"Did he ask if you bet his games?"

"Not like that. He'd just ask what I was down on. You know, I'd tell him. He wasn't even sure where he was going until 4:30 the day before." This was slow: "He never said I'm gonna fix this. It was nothing like that."

"But did you notice that he was taking care of it?"

I dared a look back at Bert, who was standing on the top tier, his head in the rafters, his black eyes still and stricken.

"You want a real fucking yuk? When I knew what he was doing—when I saw it, you know, I was happy. I was fucking pleased. God." Bert suddenly reached forward and hooked one hand on the beam and leaned out, muscles articulate in his long arm, wincing, holding on to his sheet with the other hand. What he'd thought was that Orleans was in love with him. That's why he liked it. Not the money. Not even bragging rights in this room. Because it was a token of love. Now he was in pain.

"What a sick stupid thing," he said.

I realized suddenly that I had been looking forward to having this out with Bert for my own reasons. Here we both were, two middle-aged men, big-deal successes, sort of at least, and both of us felons. There may be no honor among thieves, but there is a kind of community, knowing that you're no weaker than somebody else. And I guess I'd been thinking that cornering Bert, making him account

for himself, I'd have an answer or two to throw back at
that nagging voice of my ma's. But this was a letdown.
Bert's was a crime of passion. Not in the sense that the
object of the scam was secondary; maybe it was with me
too. But because for Bert and for Orleans there was really
no scam at all. It was simply a stepping-stone, a point of
access to the place they needed to go, Bert especially,
where "wrong" didn't even exist.

"And how did Archie find out?" I asked him.

"Well, Christ, he's taking the bets. All the sudden I'm
betting one game heavy three times a week and making a
bundle. I didn't want him to get hurt. I'd tell him, Watch
out for this one. Everybody down here had money in
Archie's book." Bert took an instant to explain Archie's
system with Infomode, everybody with a credit card and
a funny handle. One guy's Moochie. Hal Diamond got
called Slick. Bert was Kam.

"We sit here, we're talking games for hours. And, you
know, we keep track of each other. Real close. You know
how that is. We're all in each other's pockets."

So pretty soon everybody here knew. They'd kid Bert.
'What's Kam Roberts got today?' Bert realized it was a
mistake. Afterwards. At the time he couldn't resist. That
was his way: talk and swagger. I'm a fella. Who says we'll
ever change?

"Archie had no idea where you were getting the information?"

"I wasn't talking, I don't know what they thought.
Some connect to the players, I guess."

I paused to put it together in my head. "And Orleans
got the credit card?"

Wrong thing to say. Bert popped. He came down a tier, cat-quick, got right up in my face. My favorite madman.

"Hey, fuck yourself, Mack. It wasn't like that. Christ, it's part-time work. Refereeing. He's a teacher. You know, you have money, you give a friend money. Get real. I had this credit card, money to spend. That's all, man. But it wasn't like that. Don't give me that crap." Orleans wasn't really fixing games. Bert wasn't really sharing the proceeds. It wasn't corruption. Not in their minds. It was love. Which, of course, it was.

Behind me I heard a faucet loosen and water begin to run. He had turned on one of the spigots between the boards and was filling a bucket, getting ready to do that number with the icy aqua over the head.

I realized about then that I'd sat down. I jumped up and did some heavy-legged version of the hootchy-kootchy, swearing, swatting at my big broad Irish bottom as if that was going to do any good. Bert watched, but I didn't explain. I pushed him back to the story.

I said, "So play it out for me. Some dude with brass knuckles starts making an impression on Archie, telling him he's got to give up the fixer, and all he can give them is you. And you find Archie in your refrigerator and go for the world tour, right?"

"Sort of. I knew I was leaving. Martin had pretty much convinced me of that."

Bingo. I watched the sweat gathering among all my gray chest hairs, the rivulets running over the swell of my belly and dampening the sheet bundled there.

"Martin had?" I asked. "Fill in the blank, Bert. Where does Martin fit?"

Bert's reaction was amazing. He hooted.

"What a question!"

"Where he fits? Martin?"

"Hey, the answer's like, 'In Glyndora,' " said Bert and, smirking like an absolute juvenile, circled his index finger and thumb and poked a finger through the form a couple of times. The gesture was so silly but direct that we both laughed out loud. What a life! Here we were, me and Bert of all people, giggling about somebody's else's peccadilloes.

"*Mar*-tin?"

"Fuckin A," he answered.

"No way."

"It's ancient history. Years ago. Not now. Orleans was in grade school. But they're still like, what would you say—" Bert shifted a hand. "I mean, when things get heavy for her, that's who she goes to. Not just around the firm, man. You know. Life."

"Martin and Glyndora," I said. I was still marveling. I have made addled party-time chatter with Martin's wife, Nila, for years and know nothing more about her than what meets the eye: elegant looks and cultivated manners. I'd always assumed that Martin was happily wed to his own pretensions. The idea of him with a girlfriend was somehow at odds with his projected image of complete self-sufficiency.

"So what problem did Glyndora come to him with?" I asked. "I still don't understand why he got involved."

Bert didn't answer. By now I knew what that meant. Go gently. We were on that subject.

"She was upset about you getting to know Orleans?"

"Right," said Bert. He took his time. "He was in the middle at first. A mediator, I don't know what you'd say. She was just out of control. You know her. She's pretty nuts on this subject." He glanced up bleakly, a one-eyed peekaboo. In the meantime, with that remark, I got a load of the family dynamic. Orleans had grabbed Mom's attention big-time. Not just 'This is how I am,' but 'I am— with your boss. Your world.' I knew Bert would never recognize these intentions. He was like somebody with a perceptual disorder. His own emotions so dominated him that he had little perspective on anyone else.

"Then Martin found out about this, the betting. Man, it was Mount Saint Helens. He was more ticked than Glyndora. He told me straight up we were in way too deep. You know, he learned all about these guys growing up. He said the best thing was for me just to clear out. Disappear.

"And it started to actually sound okay, you know?" Bert said. "New life. That whole thing. Just drop out of sight. For a while anyway. Get out of the firm. You ever hear of Pigeon Point?"

"No."

"It's in California. North. On the coast. I found this ad. For an artichoke farm. I've been out there now. You know it's foggy. Amazing, man. The fog comes in over the artichokes twice a day. You barely have to water them. Great crops. And it's a phenomenal food." He started on the fucking vitamin count, more information in five seconds than a label on a can, and I let him go on, struck again by that notion. The new life. The new world. God, the mere thought still made my heart sing. Then, unexpectedly, I recalled that I had nearly six million dollars in my name in two foreign bank accounts and was gripped by an urgent question I could just as well have asked myself.

"So why aren't you gone?"

"He won't *leave*." Bert threw his big hands in my direction, the fingers crippled by desperation. "The dumb-fuck won't go. I've begged him. I beg him three times a week." He stared at me, unhinged by the thought, and then turned away rather than confront what he could tell I was seeing—that Bert had given up his life to protect Orleàns, and Orleans, when push came to shove, lacked the same dedication. Maybe Orleans couldn't honk off his mother sufficiently from two thousand miles away. Maybe, in the end, he didn't really have it for Bert. However it went, Bert's crusade was a one-way thing. I saw something else then, that this romance, Bert and Orleans, wasn't the high-flown love of the poets. There was something bad in it, it was tethered to pain; there was a reason Bert was so long telling himself the truth he did not want to know.

And even so, I envied him for a minute. Had I ever loved anybody like that? My feelings for Brushy seemed flimsy in the intense heat. But what about time? I thought. Maybe with time. Life has these two poles, it seems. You go one way or the other. We're always choosing: passion or despair.

"I've told him about the police," Bert said. "He doesn't believe it."

"They'll be pretty convincing if they catch him."

"Can you talk to them?" he asked finally. "The cops? Are they friends of yours?"

"Hardly," I said, but I sat there smiling. It was terrible

really, the joy I took at the notion of skunking Pigeyes. I already had a few ideas.

The heat and the hour were gradually making me faint. I turned on the water and poured a cold bucket for myself, but didn't have the stamina or the courage to dump it over my head. I stood there before Bert, dabbing the water on my face and my chest, while I tried a moment to figure out what all this meant for me. There was a whisper about of the oven and the rocks barely sizzling.

"You don't know a thing about what's been going on at the firm, do you? The money? That whole thing?"

The sweat ran into his eyes and Bert blinked. He had his impenetrable black look: he doesn't understand you and never will.

I asked if the name Litiplex rang any bells.

"Jake?" he asked.

I nodded.

"Didn't Jake send me some memo? And I wrote him a bunch of checks on the 397 account? Yeah." Bert let his long body bob. He was remembering. "Something was very touchy. It was a mix-up with the plaintiffs. Jake was afraid Krzysinski would roast his hind end when he heard Jake had to pay these expenses. Big, big goddamn secret. Jake was very uptight on this thing." Bert reflected. "Something's fucked-up, huh?" he asked.

"You might say."

"Yeah," he said, "you know, now that I'm thinking, maybe a month ago Martin asked me about this. This Litiplex. But he was like, no problem, no big deal."

That would have been when Martin saw the memo and

the checks. Glyndora, of course, would have come to him first when she noticed.

"So what's the story?" Bert asked.

I laid it out briefly: No Litiplex. The numbered account in Pico Luan. Bert seemed to regard it as remotely amusing until I got to the part where Martin and Glyndora manipulated appearances to make it look like the money was his.

"*Me?* Those *fuck-ers*! Me? I *don't* believe it." He'd jumped to his feet. I was abruptly reminded of trying cases with Bert, his sudden courtroom rages, objecting to a leading question like it was the landing of foreign troops on our soil. I waited for him to cool off.

"Just answer me straight, Bert. There's no deal between you and Martin for you to take the blame for this? The money?"

"Are you kidding? Fuck no, man."

"Nothing? No wink, no nod?"

"No. NFW. That's scumbag stuff." This was Bert, who had deceived millions of Americans about the outcome of sporting events, who had thought with his dick and made a profit besides, but he was on his high horse. He had the same lunatic look as when he talked about the secret poisons some faceless "they" put in his foods. He got back up on one of the moisture-blackened benches and poured the bucket over his head, and came out of the flood glaring. I had an odd thought at that moment of how much he reminded me of Glyndora.

We went upstairs to dress then, both turned pretty sulky and without much to say. Bert had a bag in his locker with deodorant and whatnot and let me use his stuff.

"Who is it?" he asked me suddenly. "With the money?"

"Doesn't matter."

"Yeah, but—" He shrugged.

I'd spent the last few days delving into the depths of the mind of Martin Gold. It was like walking downward in some endless cave. From the start Martin must have figured that if he hung this on Bert no one would ever contradict him. Not Jake, of course. Not Bert, who was on permanent leave, hiding from hit men among the artichokes. Not clueless old me. Not even the TN board, which, if informed of the loss, had nothing to gain by making a public fuss that would only attract attention to what was left of the 397 surplus. By blaming Bert, Martin would keep everything tidy.

And I could have gone along with that, Martin's scheme to save the world as I knew it. Unless Pigeyes caught him, Bert wasn't going to surface. Any day now Jake would discover that he'd developed a hole in his pocket down in Pico Luan, but so what? Self-preservation would prevent Jake from making an international scene. He couldn't start hollering, Where's all that money I stole? Trumped and taken, Jake would probably blame Bert too. It could work out for me Martin's way. In a couple months I could retire from the firm, vacationing when need be in Pico Luan.

But when I'd steamed out the shellacked doors of the Club Belvedere on Saturday and sat up all night hatching plans, I was gripped by ornery impulses. I'd developed the fixed intention to smite Martin and the whole smarmy scheme. Since then I'd hoped against hope at moments. I came here wanting Bert to tell me there was a galaxy of good intentions involved, some aspect that was wholesome, or at least excusable, which I hadn't seen. But he couldn't. Because that wasn't the case. And recognizing that, I found myself under the same internal momentum. Maybe I was still a cop on the street, committed to my own kind of rough justice. God knows, I never have played well for the team. But I was going to do it my way. Brushy hung there somehow in the balance, an indeterminate weight. Yet there was no reason, really, I couldn't make that work out. I kept telling myself that.

"Jake," I answered at last. "Jake's got the money." That's where this was going. I was gonna be mean. Even so, the details were daunting.

"Jake! Whoa." Bert brought his long hand to his jaw and rubbed it as if he had taken a blow. He was sitting there on the bench in the dim locker room, holding his socks, the only light borrowed from a single bulb burning in the john.

"Martin's covering for him, protecting the firm."

"Jake," Bert said again.

It struck me with an exactness that had completely eluded me before that if I was going to carry through with this, undermine Martin and pass out just deserts, I'd have to figure some way for Bert to return. Without that, it might come down to finger pointing. Martin and Jake could still call Bert the bad guy somehow. Why else was he running? Mystery Thief on the Loose. To make my version fully convincing, Bert had to be here to tell his story: he got the memo from Jake, gave the checks to Jake, listened when Jake told him it was all hush-hush. I couldn't imagine, though, how that could be engineered. Amid the dank atmosphere of the locker room, we sat in silence. One of the steam pipes eventually emitted a distinct clank.

"Look, Bert, I'm going to try to help you. I want to see you get out of all this, but I really have to put my thinking cap on. Just stay in touch. Make sure you call every day."

The guy saw right through me. Not what was wrong. But something. That I had some stake. And he couldn't have cared less.

"Please," he said quietly. He watched me there, his face buried in shadow but still rimmed by some eager hope.

When we were dressed, he took me to the back door and unlocked the bolt, the grate.

"Where you going?" I asked.

"Oh, you know." His eyes floated away from me. "Orleans is in town."

God, he was lost. Even in the dark you could see him, swarthy and lean, in the grip of his sad hopeless love. He was being tortured and teased. Moth and flame. I thought to myself again, What is this? A character like Bert, you figure his gyroscope's wacky. But the head, the heart— who am I kidding? One man's rationality is another fella's madness. Nothing ever really adds up. Either the premises are faulty or the reasoning sucks. We're all of us pincushions, lanced by feelings, full of wounds and pains. Reason is the lie, the balm we apply, pretending that if we were just smart enough we'd make some sense of what hurts.

I'd already stuck my nose into the cold when I realized one question remained. I barred the door with the arm of my overcoat.

"So who moved the body, Bert? Who took Archie? Did Orleans?"

"Fuck, never," said Bert. "He'd freak." Bert shook his head violently at the thought and repeated that Orleans wasn't up to something like that.

"So who?"

We stood on the threshold, eyeing each other, surrounded by the deep alley darkness and the harsh touch of winter, hovering with the unspoken improbabilities of our futures, everything that was simply unknown.

Thursday, February 2

XXVI. MACK MALLOY'S FIFTEENTH
CONTINGENCY PLAN

A. Step One

So. It was midnight. I was the only white man for a mile, a guy in an overcoat with a briefcase and a prominent urge to begin making plans. I stalked through the tough old neighborhood, headed in the direction of Center City, an exercise in fifty-year-old daring, striding from the rescuing glow of one streetlight to the next. A bus came along presently and I boarded gratefully and bucketed down the avenues with the winos and the workers returning from late-night stints. A few blocks from the Needle, I jumped off. Kindle County at night is not lively. The lights are on but the streets are empty; it has its own spectral air, like a deserted building, a place even the ghosts have fled.

I entered the lobby of the Travel Tepee, where Brush and I had agreed to meet. The big lobby was quiet; even the Muzak had been turned off for the night. I sat in an

ugly easy chair with a horrible bold print and considered
the future. Finally the lone registration clerk asked from
behind the front counter if he could help me. From his
tone, I thought he was pretty sure I was just a better-
dressed derelict whom security would have to give the
heave-ho. I went over to make peace, told him he had a
Ms. Bruccia registered, and picked up my key, then I sat
down again, counting out the steps in my plan. I thought
of waiting until morning to begin putting this together, but
I was feeling edgy, compulsive, call it what you want. I
was wide-awake anyway and a little reluctant to be with
Brushy, now that I actually knew what I was going to do.

About two blocks down there was an all-night phar-
macy, another Brown Wall's, built near the exit ramp of
the Interstate, a place with a bus station air, a lot of downtown creeps hanging around near the doors, and a cop car
parked right at the curb. I bought two pens—one ballpoint,
one felt tip—and some glue and a pair of scissors. I asked
at the counter if they had a coin-operated copying machine,
but the answer was no, so I walked back to the hotel,
waved to the desk clerk, and found a little phone alcove
which had a laminate surface I could use for a desk.

I already had the rest of what I needed in my briefcase—
the signature form I'd received at International Bank of
Finance, the letter of Jake's I'd used as a model to forge
his signature to the fax I sent from the Regency, and the
copies of TN's annual report that I'd toted down to Pico.
The report contains pictures of all the corporate officers,
including Jake Eiger, and I'd brought copies along thinking
Jake's photo might come in handy if I had to do any of a
number of things I was then considering to get at the

money, such as phonying up a passbook or some form of
U.S. I.D.

The signature form was printed on onionskin with a
schmaltzy heading in script: "International Bank of Finance, Pico Luan, N.A." There were only four or five
lines of information required, the descriptions written in
all of the major Western European tongues. Using the felt
tip, I filled in the account number that appeared on the
back of the Litiplex checks, 476642. I named the account
owner as Litiplex, Ltd., Jake Eiger as president. Then just
to remind myself of the look of his hand, I took Jake's old
letter from the briefcase and signed his name to the form
with the ballpoint, dead on again, so close you'd think it
was traced. After that, I cut Jake's grinning puss out of
the TN annual report and pasted it down where Mr. George
had shown me it would go in the upper-right-hand corner
of the form. Finally, in the little block labeled "Designation," meaning code word, I wrote out, perfectly,
"J.A.K.E."

Then I went back to the clerk at the counter. He was
starting to get used to me. I gave him a weary sigh, dragging my hands down my raddled kisser.

"I have a presentation in the morning and I forgot to
copy one thing. Just two pictures of it, one page. You must
have a machine in the office." I had a twenty between two
of my fingers, but this guy, young, maybe a graduate
student, somebody still starting out in his life, wouldn't
take it. He was still feeling bad for thinking I was a bum.
He brought back the copies of the signature form and we
talked about the weather, how quiet the city could be at
night.

I returned to the phone booth. I took the original of the
signature form and tore it into pieces, throwing them in
the opening in the long sand-topped trash canister by my
feet. The two photocopies the desk clerk had made me
went into my case. Then I called information for D.C.
The latest Mrs. Pagnucci, a six-foot blonde, answered the
phone. She said nothing to me when I explained who I
was. Instead, in a voice I'd heard now and then in my own
home, the soul of tedium, she remarked, "One of your
partners."

B. Step Two

Brushy was asleep when I let myself into the room. It was
about 3:00 a.m. She still slept like a child, in a small fetal
ball, and her hand was close enough to her mouth that I
wouldn't have been surprised if she suckled a digit or two.
Vulnerable, with her sly wits turned off for the night, she
looked dear to me, maybe precious is the word, and I felt
really bad, my heart twisted around like a cloth being
wrung. I threw my clothes down and crept into bed. As
my night eyes came on, I could see this was not exactly
the bridal suite. The headboard had been nicked in many
places, revealing the mealy composition of the underlying
particle board, and directly over the bed the old textured
wallpaper had peeled from its butt joints and hung down
from the plaster like an extruded tongue. I drifted a hand
against Brushy's solid flank to comfort myself.

"How's Bert?" She still hadn't moved.

"Okay," I said, "safe at least." I apologized for waking her.

"I was waiting for you." She snapped on the light and covered her eyes like a child with the backs of her hands. While she was blinded, I touched her, just kidding around, pulled the sheet down and nuzzled my cold cheek to her breasts, but she held me there and we heated up fast. Every time we had screwed so far it was different. There was horseplay sometimes, as in the hotel ladies' room, and she also had a lot of daring and skill, a bold way of laying her hands on that cut to the basics, that said this was for pleasure so let's not kid ourselves. Now suddenly, in the cheap hotel room, as beaten down as Center City around us, we were quick and desperate, wanting to overcome everything else. Real fire, and afterwards, spooned to her from behind, I could tell she thought that was great. We were quiet, with the empty sounds of the hotel and the street reaching us—sirens at a distance and the shouts of drunks and kids like my son who should have been at home for the night. I asked if she had brought cigarettes, then sat beside her on the bed, trading one back and forth with her in the dark.

"Does he have the money?" she asked.

"Come on, Brush."

"Just that. Does Bert have the money?"

"Brush, aren't we too old for Twenty Questions?"

"Attorney-client," she said. "Does he have it? Yes or no?"

"No."

"Really? Did he ever?"

"He doesn't have the money. Go to sleep." I went to the john, found the toothbrush she'd bought me, and lingered there hoping she'd fall off.

When I snuck in beside her, I slept dreamlessly, a velvet pit. Near seven, I snapped awake with a tiny outcry, quickly muted, the sound of inspiration. I dressed quietly and left Brushy a note that said I'd be back.

I had a walk of about six blocks and I jogged a step or two now and then as I penetrated Center City from its grotty outskirts, getting closed in by the morning hubbub, the trucks double-parked and wreaking havoc with the traffic, the silent army of workers marching the streets. It was pretty cold, less than 15 degrees, and I threw myself down into my coat.

Toots ate breakfast every morning with the same guys, old pols, ward types, and lawyers, at a corner table of a Greek joint called Paddywacks right across from his office. This was a legendary event. Toots greeted half the folks in the restaurant and waved to them all with his cane. In the corner booth Toots and his friends gossiped about dirty business in any number of venues—the courthouse, the council building, the mob. A few years ago the feds had put a microphone in one of the saltshakers, but Toots and his pals had got word somehow. One of them, it was said, complained loudly about the taste of his eggs, then slammed the shaker on the tabletop and blew the listening agent's eardrum out.

Paddywacks was slightly overdecorated—brass fixtures and tufted benches and floors that were mopped once a week. I was beginning to be afraid I'd missed Toots, when he came in about 8:15 on his stick, two paisans on either side. One of them, Sally Polizzo, had been a federal guest up until six months ago. Toots greeted me like a visiting king. I shook hands with each of his companions, then strolled him down to a booth where he took a seat alone. I stayed on my feet.

"Did you mean what you said about a favor?" I asked him. Sitting on the little velveteen bench, the Colonel looked tiny, a little guy shrinking worse with age, but when I asked if he'd meant what he said, he just drew back with a look tough enough to make you believe he'd been a killer. I corrected myself.

"This may be too much. If it is, you say so. You remember we talked about my partner?" I went over it quickly, but I told Toots the truth. How his pals were looking for my guy and his friend and how my guy was hiding. Somebody else was going to end up dead, and for nothing. The bookie had paid the big price, and these other guys were scared straight. Justice of the kind Toots practiced had been served. I asked him to get his friends to lay off Bert and Orleans. Favor for favor.

Toots sat there silent, the rubbery old mouth pursed, his eyes still. He was working it out in his head. If he called that guy and reminded him of this thing, then that guy could get to someone else. It was all geometry to him, and power. He wanted to justify my faith.

"Maybe," he said. "Depends. I think so. I'll let you know this afternoon. This fella got any money?"

"Some," I said, then thought of Pico and added, "yeah, he's got money. Why?"

"This here's a business. Somebody's got a point to make. He gets paid, that's his point. Right?"

"I suppose."

Toots said he'd leave word for me at the office. Then I helped him to his feet so he could totter down to the corner booth and his courtiers. There were already two old guys with rubbery faces waiting to say hi.

C. Watch That Step

"I went to see Toots," I told Brushy when I got back to the room.

"Toots?" Sitting by the window at a little cane table arrayed with a light room-service breakfast she'd ordered—coffee and rolls, half a cantaloupe—she considered me intently. The heavy-lined night curtain had been pulled back, admitting the light and revealing a sheer that nestled about her. She was wearing her overcoat as a robe and she'd made up her face. When I came in, she'd been reading the paper.

"Mack," she said, "I want to know."

I didn't say anything and threw my coat on the bed. I was hungry and she watched me eat, measuring the meaning of my lack of response.

"I called the office," she said, "to say we'd be late. Detective Dimonte's been there already."

I made a sound. No surprise.

"And Lucinda said Martin's looking for you. He's left two messages." She looked at the phone as if to guide me, but I didn't move.

"Look, Mack," she said, "I can handle it. I'm a grown-up. Whatever it is. It's just—"

"I thought you were going to take my advice."

"It's my life too."

I hated this moment. But I'd always known it was coming. One of the problems about settling for Mr. Not-Quite-Good-Enough is a sense of peril about accepting his guidance. With my eyes closed I ruminated, then I grabbed my briefcase and looked into its dark, disordered depths. Balled deposit slips rested in the bottom, along with fragments of papers, and paper clips; stick-on notes adhered to the sides. I pulled out one of the photocopies of the signature form I'd made up last night. I laid it down on the rattan table. Litiplex, Ltd. Jake Eiger, line 1.

"Don't ask how Pindling got it. We don't want to know."

She studied the document with a hand on her forehead as the weight of the tangible evidence bore down on her visibly. I got her cigarettes and we shared one, the odor of the smoke filling up the little room. I cracked the sliding window a bit and the curtains flowed around her like spirits.

"Jake?" she asked.

"That's what it says."

"You've known about this all along, haven't you? That's why you were so peeved with Jake." I think I winced when she said that. Even with alarm bells clanging, she was listening for good news about me.

"I've known a lot," I told her.

"Like what?"

I was just sailing here, no charted course. I didn't have the will to resist her and the lying made me feel childishly eager to cry. In my briefcase I found the memo I'd pulled from Martin's drawer. As she read, she picked a fleck of tobacco off her tongue. Her expression was flat, intense. She was being a lawyer.

"I don't understand," she said. "This isn't from Pindling. This memo."

"Martin."

"Martin!"

I told her the story, some of it anyway, about finding the memo, chugging over to the Club Belvedere. I was moved by her pain. As she often told me, Brushy liked these people. Martin. Wash. Her partners. The firm. These were her colleagues, who admired her abilities, who trusted her years ago with the things that mattered to them, who applauded her many triumphs and had received her assistance with a gratitude that was often intense. She knew she'd survive. She had clients, a growing reputation. That was not her worry. The point was commitment, allegiance, shared enterprise. She was devastated.

"They were setting up Bert? Right? To take the blame for Jake. Isn't that how this looks?"

"That's how it looks."

"God," she said, and raked a hand through her hair. I opened the sliding door for an instant to crush out my cigarette on the small cement balcony, and the cold briefly forced its way into the room. The sun was out but seemed to offer no heat, as if it were just posed in the clear sky for decoration. Brushy asked me how Bert fit in and I told her his story and why I'd gone to see Toots. Her mind, though, remained on the Committee.

"Oh, it's so stupid. Stu-pid," she said. "Is this all of them?"

"Couldn't say. Martin obviously. Pagnucci doesn't

seem to be in it. Wash—well, I told you what his attitude was."

"Martin," she said again. The Great Oz. She'd taken a seat on the bed, clutching her coat. I'd be willing to bet she wasn't wearing a stitch underneath—not that either of us would be pursuing that prospect in our present mood.

"What are you going to do with all of this, Mack?"

I shrugged. I'd lit another cigarette.

"I'll probably do the right thing."

She watched me, assessing, wondering what that might mean. Then she shook herself in a lonesome spasm of disbelief.

"Something," she said. "I mean Jake. Why? It doesn't make sense. He makes money. His father is rich. Why do this?"

I leaned over the bed. I peered in her eyes.

"Because that's how he is." The sheer viciousness gripped me and she looked on as if it were some kind of spectacle. She didn't care that I was saying I told you so. And she wasn't afraid. She held me at a distance, marveling.

"You're going to blackmail him, aren't you?"

It was the weirdest fucking thing. I felt like I'd been kicked. My mouth hung open and my heart felt hard as a fist and filled with intense physical pain. The humiliation ran like an acid to my eyes.

"Kidding," she said.

"Bullshit."

I walked around the bed and picked up my coat.

"Mack." She reached for me. "I don't care what you do."

"You don't mean that. Don't even ask me to believe it. I know who you are and so do you." Looking into my case, I realized I'd left the papers on the table. I waved them at her as I picked them up. I was hating myself for having said anything.

"Attorney-client," I remarked to remind her she was ears only, that I was the only one with options, the right to act. Then I went down the shabby hallway to the elevator. I punched at the button, calling the car, and leaned against the wall, hollowed out and hopeless, certain that I would never understand the first thing about myself.

Especially sensitive to hear from Carl. Ci... had no view of what he was and should be receive authorise...

XXVII. PLAN EXECUTION

A. Up to His Neck in Sand

"This is distressing," said Carl. Those were the first words from him in a number of minutes. He had read the memo, then looked over the photocopy of the International Bank signature form. When he asked me about Pindling, I used the same words as Lagodis.

"A real snake charmer," I said. "You call him, he won't even know my name. I had to pay him in cash." I'd show the charge on my golden credit card if I ever needed to prove that.

We were at the airport in the TN Executive Lounge, in a tiny conference room just big enough for a small table of black granite surrounded by four chairs. There was a telephone between us, as well as an insulated thermos of coffee which neither of us had touched.

Last night I had told Carl it was urgent. He didn't seem

especially surprised to hear from me. It fit both his view
of what he did and himself to receive emergency phone
calls after midnight. It probably happened a lot, some
young genius noticing a snafu in an offering circular three
hours before they were going into the market. There was
the usual deliberative pause when I asked Pagnucci to catch
an earlier plane, leave himself time before Groundhog
night. I promised to meet him at the gate. It was almost
one now.

Carl looked at the papers a second and then a third time.
His mind was moving at a phenomenal pace, trying to
absorb everything, but I could tell from his deliberation
that he was having trouble figuring it all out, especially
the next move. He compared Jake's handwriting, first on
the signature card, then on the old letter I'd given him as
an example, and minutely shook his head.

"And what is it you propose?" he asked me at last.

"We'll call one of the nice ladies outside in the service
center to make copies of all this. The originals I hold."

"Yes?" He watched me alertly.

"You phone Krzysinski right now. Tell him you have
to see him at once. Highest priority. Then you take these
documents to him. Say you're proceeding on behalf of
G&G. You express appropriate emotions. Horror. Regret.
Disclosure of course is the only avenue."

"And I do so without advising Martin or Wash?"

"Right."

Pagnucci was sallow, his eyes small and intent. He
nibbled a bit at his little mustache.

"Are they in league?"

I didn't follow.

"Wash, Martin, Eiger," he said. "Are they in this together?"

I shook off the question. "That's beside the point. I've been around G&G a long time. A lot of people have been good to me."

That was not the sort of feeling I'd expect him to share. One thing about Pagnucci I was banking on was that he was as tough as he made out, the kind of guy who, if he was up to his neck in quicksand, would have the brass to tell you to walk on. I knew cops like that, guys who felt they could prove something essential by refusing—ever—to yield to sentiment. They believed what they believed, absolutely. He sat there quite erect in his perfect blue suit.

"Yes, but let's play this out," said Pagnucci, unconsciously patting the bald spot behind his head. "My partners told me that this memo couldn't be found."

"It turned up. It was a surprise."

"And what about that meeting the other day, where you outlined Eiger's proposal to keep all of this mum? What's to be said about that?"

"Tell Tad. It's part of the evidence. Jake wanted the whole matter forgotten. But we continued to investigate and now you're here on behalf of the Committee, the firm, to bring everything out. Look, no one's ever accused you of saying too much, Carl. You can handle it. But it's your obligation to go forward." Talking to Pagnucci about his obligations felt as vain and mindless as saying, Have a nice day. In the stuttering movements of his dark eyes, you could see him calculating, his mind on the roam.

"But who had the memo?" he asked. "Wash?"

I didn't answer. Pagnucci may have had questions, but

he'd like what he saw. Carl Pagnucci—man of grit and integrity. Forthcoming with the truth, even when it was devastating to his firm. Pagnucci had already been making contingency plans with Brushy, and this would fit. He understood how his candor was likely to be recalled and rewarded by Tad in the future, now that TN would be floating free as a client. Moving on, he would take some of TN's work with him, even as G&G sank. There was an irresistible cocktail here for somebody like Carl, looped already on the ethers of self-importance.

"And you wouldn't advise sharing this with Martin or Wash before we act?" The fact that his caution exceeded his greed startled me a bit.

"Afterwards you can tell them what you've done, what you've said. They can only follow. If you tell them in advance, they'll try to derail you. They have to. You know that."

Carl continued his silent reflection. The thing that bothered him most, I suspected, was that he was depending on me.

"Carl," I said, "there's no choice. We have a duty to the client. Someone from the Committee has to go to Krzysinski, someone who speaks on behalf of the firm."

He considered me soberly. We both knew I was manipulating him shamelessly. But I'd given him what he needed—a good excuse. It had all the right appearances. Highly principled. Above criticism. And very good for Pagnucci. He could salute the flag and steal the client. Beyond that, it did not matter much what I was up to.

I pulled the phone close and dialed TN. It took some

time to get to Krzysinski, but he said he had a few minutes for Carl before two.

B. Some People Want Me and Some People Don't

I waited until three to leave the airport, then took a cab home. Right about now, big powwows were going on at TN: Carl and Tad and TN's head of security, Mike Mathigoris. They were figuring what to do with Jake— question him, crucify him, or just throw his ass out. In another hour or so, they'd be calling the FBI.

When I got home, I stood on the low concrete stoop before my front door and the vines. The rare sunshine had continued, but the air remained cold, with an astringent wind. I looked around for the surveillance vehicles and waved. I raised my hands the way Nixon used to, fingers in V's, and pivoted about for a full minute. Nobody appeared. Inside, I changed into my tuxedo for Groundhog Night and drove downtown. Lyle had even cleaned up the car.

I walked the entire block outside the TN Needle three times, looking for the tail and waiting for them to pick me up, but there was still nobody there. Finally I headed up. Lucinda handed me three messages. All from Martin. He wanted to see me at once. In my office, I went to the phone.

"Financial Crimes," I told the operator at the Hall.

Pigeyes picked up himself. I was relieved to hear his voice. I thought he might have called off his forces because he'd grabbed Bert, but his voice was full of bovine indifference for the paperbound life in Financials.

"You drop your investigation? I thought you were looking for me?"

"Who the hell is this?" he asked, and then, figuring it out, added, "You think you're all I got to worry about?"

"I'm at the office. I'm ready to tell you whatever you want to know."

He was thinking. Something, God knows what, had him buffaloed.

"Ten minutes," he told me. "And don't go running again to the fuckin dark side of the moon."

I found a cigarette in my drawer. Lucinda stuck her head in. Toots was on hold.

"All done," he told me. "All square. Your fellas are in the clear. Had to remind one or two guys a some things."

"Toots, you're a miracle worker."

Over the phone, the old guy basked in the praise. You could hear it.

"Only one thing," he said, "is the money. We gotta talk about that. I think, you know," said Toots, "I think it's gotta be 275."

The number was a blow. I hadn't been thinking of bankrolling Bert like that, but I began to reason it through. Bert was useful to me, essential really. Besides, I was happy to prove to myself that I wasn't quite the lowdown bum Brushy had implied.

Toots was explaining. "This here was big stuff, that's what I'm hearing. So it's gotta be that, you know, 275." This was not so much a negotiation as Toots setting a price. And it came to me—maybe something I was supposed to know from the start—that the Colonel would be getting his share. This was Toots's skill, his profession, fixing things up, making big problems go way. We didn't defend him for free either.

I explained how I wanted to do it. I needed an account number at a local bank. Sometime in the next seven days a wire transfer would hit there from Fortune Trust, Pico Luan.

"What are the ground rules?" I asked. "Is my guy in danger until the money arrives?"

"I got your word, they get my word. It's all done, this here. Never happened. But tell your partner: there can't be no next time."

Next door Brushy was on the phone. She mugged up and made kissy-face when she saw me, sweeping a hand in admiration of my gallant look in my tux. I tried to smile. She put her caller on hold.

"Can I say I'm sorry?" she asked.

"Sure." I closed my eyes. What was I supposed to be angry about anyway? That she suspected me of bad intentions toward Jake? "Anything from Bert?"

He had phoned an hour ago, she said, and promised to call back soon.

"What about Toots?" she asked. "Did he work it out? Really?" I got a great smile. I was some kind of fella. The door was open to the hall, so she just took my hand. We did an instant of that stuff, gazing fondly. We'd found a sick little cycle, swords and wounds and soft rapprochement. I saw her eyes shift to the threshold. Lucinda was there. The policemen had arrived. And Mr. Gold wanted me upstairs in ten minutes.

"He sounds angry," she added.

"Tell him I'm with the police." I turned to Brushy, who had finished her call. "That'll get his attention," I said.

C. I Try to Satisfy Pigeyes

"Okay, Gino, let's see if I've followed the bouncing ball. After talking to Mrs. Archie, Missing Persons made a trip to the Bath, where somebody with a weak bladder snitched out this little game-fixing thing, and Missing did what they always do, lateraled to someone else, Financial Crimes in this case, telling you what a great investigation you had, and by the way, should you run into an actuary or a corpse, assuming you can tell the difference, give Missing a call. Am I guessing good so far?"

He didn't say a thing. We made an odd little group— me, Brushy, Pigeyes and Dewey, scattered around Brushy's high-tech office, each of us visibly wary. Brushy was behind her glass desk, which was sided by the potted jungle plants. I was the only one standing, walking around, waving my hands, having a great time. I was in full dashing formal array, tuxedo and cummerbund and a boiled shirt I'd owned for twenty years and never replaced; it sported silly button-on frills that reminded me of the comb on a cockatoo. Gino'd looked up and down at my getup when he walked in and asked for a T-bone, medium well.

"So that's why you're looking for these guys, Kam Roberts especially, and Archie and Bert along the way, and you're pretty sure you have a hot one and you get half the Force helping out cause here's what you see: A, a bunch of characters from the Russian Bath say they were winning money with Bert, who was getting information from someone he called Kam Roberts. B, Bert has got a credit card in the name of said Kam Roberts. C, we have sightings here and there of said Said. And D, the bookie, Archie, is among the disappeared. But there are a few questions: One, who the screw is Kam Roberts? Two, how does a partner in a big law firm fix basketball games? Three, why is he playing hide-and-seek all over North America? And four, by the way, where's Archie? Am I on the right track?''

Pigeyes gave me something, a shrug, a tip of the hand. He still wasn't talking. You never explain what you're investigating, not until you tell them the charges when they're under arrest. Still in their overcoats, Pigeyes and Dewey were seated side by side on Brushy's chrome-trimmed sofa. I could tell Gino was uneasy because I was having such a good time.

"Okay, so let's explain some of this. Hypothetically, of course, since if one is a big-goddamn-deal lawyer he has to watch out for BAD and his shingle, which is why you're hearing from me. But let's get one thing straight to start: Nobody was fixing games. Nobody here and nobody anybody here is friends with.''

That got a rise. "No?'' Pigeyes asked. Skeptical, you might say.

"No. Here's how it ran. Archie is a tout, but he's an actuary to start. Clever with computers. Does his number runs. Let's say there are some gentlemen, we'll call them Valpolicella and Bardolino, V&B, who just always seem to get certain Mid-Ten games right. Let's say Archie notices. The nature of the world is that Archie is supposed to keep such thoughts to himself. V&B are making suckers out of the suckers, and Archie's getting a break on his street tax.

"But let's imagine Archie's got a buddy—a real good-type close intimate friend." I hit Pigeyes's peepers to make sure he got it. "Archie clues him on this info. The friend, a certain hotshot partner in a certain big law firm, starts betting what V&B do, winning big. So far so good?"

Pigeyes somewhere had acquired a photo of Bert and he withdrew it now from the many layers of his coats.

"Good-lookin here? We sayin he's that way?"

"How you talk, Gino. Let's not get too personal, okay? Just remember, you're the one who told me about Archie. Pecker tracks in the porthole, didn't you say?"

He and Dewey liked that one. Brushy covered her eyes.

"Anyway, Bert, which is what I'll call this lawyer hypothetically, he tries to be discreet, but these guys at the Russian Bath are always in each other's pockets and heads, they've got to know everyone's action. One thing leads to another. And pretty soon everybody there realizes that Bert, or Kam Roberts as he's called when he's putting down money, is hitting big on certain games. Now he's not about to explain why. Everybody sweating there is in Archie's book. It's bad business to favor one customer. And the reasons for doing so are highly personal. So Archie and Bert start this little thing like it's Kam Roberts who's got inside stuff. But it isn't. It's Archie all along.

"Sooner than Archie hoped, V&B hear about what's going down at the Russian Bath and they know sure as shooting the info ain't from any Kam flippin Roberts. It's their proprietary confidential trade-secret business-time information and Archie's peddled it, denting their odds, and they let it be known that Archie is about to literally have his private parts fed to some mutt. Archie scoots and V&B start hunting, which brings them pretty quickly to Bert's door. They give Bert the choice—twenty-four hours to dig up Archie or he's the one who's dog food. So Bert scrams too. Until one of his intrepid partners who knows a guy who knows a guy who knows another guy arranges what we might call an amnesty. High-priced. Could be, hypothetically, that Bert is repaying his profits at interest rates that exceed the ceiling on usury."

Brush, when I glanced her way, was sunk back in her desk chair regarding me with an uneasy eye. It troubled her, I suspect, to see me lying with such élan.

"And?" Pigeyes asked me.

"And what?"

"And where's this crumb Archie? Today?"

"I'd look in the sanitary canal. Watch what comes out of the treatment plant. That's the way I hear it. V&B found him. He's got something around his neck besides his tie. And if your people on the street are half as good as they used to be, Gino, you've heard the same thing."

Whacking a guy, making him dead, is not something anybody owns up to, but word spreads. It has to. It's the way those guys keep everybody in line.

Lucinda knocked. "Mr. Gold," she said.

"Tell him five minutes."

"He wants to talk to you right now."

"Five minutes," I repeated.

Lucinda stepped to the phone and pressed a button. She held out the extension. It's been this poor woman's lot for years to protect me from myself.

"We are not amused," Martin said when I put the handset to my ear.

"I'm busy."

"So I hear. What, pray tell, are you and the nice policemen discussing?"

"Detective Dimonte had some questions about Bert." I smiled at Gino when I mentioned his name.

"We're not talking high finance?"

"Bert," I said.

"Did Bert do something else that was naughty?"

"Never kid a kidder, Martin. I'll be up in one minute. We're just about done." I put the phone down without allowing further comment.

Gino was waiting. "So this Kam Roberts thing was strictly an act?" he asked.

"Exactly."

"Except there's a Kam Roberts." Pigeyes sneered.

"No. There's a certain young man who's·used Bert's bank card a few times. That doesn't make him Kam Roberts."

"No? Who is he?"

"Friend of Bert's."

"Another one? Good-lookin's real frisky, isn't he? He's two-timing the other guy?"

"Hey, Gino, call it what you like. But remember, I used to ride with you. I've seen you stop off with three different gals on the same *shift*."

He was flattered, of course, by the memory. He stole a

glance toward Brushy, hoping she was impressed. Someday I'd have to tell Pigeyes about *Nueve*.

"Anyway, there's this young man," I said. "Bert's piling up a lot of credit on the card, so he's got plenty to share. Now it could be, hypothetically, this young man, he's got a connection to the U. Maybe he's the one who let a certain middle-aged lawyer into the refs' room the other night so Bert and the middle-aged lawyer could confer outside the watchful eye of the law in the hopes of straightening some of this out."

"That so?" Gino asked.

"Could be," I said and rested on a chair arm to see how it had gone down. Better, it seemed, than I might have thought. I was trying like hell for Bert's sake and my own, vamping like crazy, and when it came to Gino, there was no end to my daring. But I still thought I'd gone over the top. The whole thing was too much, too curious, way too lame. I didn't know what I'd do if, for instance, they wanted to quiz the young man from the U. And there wouldn't be any smart answers if Gino ever started matching the games the guys at the Bath called Kam's Specials with the ones officiated by Friday night's referees.

But the great thing with people is that you never know. After two weeks of riding my fanny, chasing me everywhere, and spooking my dreams, Gino seemed to have run out of gas. Not that he believed me particularly. He knew better than that. But he was clearly afraid the prosecutor's office would toss him out on his keester because he was nowhere near beyond a reasonable doubt. Bogus or not, I'd touched all the bases; it was a comprehensive defense. And my history with Gino was enough to make a conscientious deputy P.A. think twice anyway. Pigeyes didn't come to these conclusions peaceably. When he looked at me, his eyes were stilled by a hatred entirely void of goodwill, like black being the absence of color, but I could see he knew I had him beat.

He turned to Dewey, who shrugged. Go figure. They both got to their feet.

"Great to see you again, Gino."

"Yeah, really," he offered.

Lucinda peeked in, beckoning, and I followed her out, departing with a cheerful wave as Brushy started with Gino and Dewey toward the door. Lucinda had a note: "Bert's on the phone." I picked up in my office.

"Listen," I said. "I've settled your problems. Those guys won't be looking for you anymore."

The line gathered static. I could hear from the gray roar behind him that Bert was on a pay phone somewhere near a highway.

"Humor, right?" he asked.

"Don't ask me how. You're done. D, o, n, e. I've got it squared with the coppers too. What you oughta do is get down here. You'll probably need to answer some questions about Jake." Mathigoris from TN security would want to go over the whole thing many times. The memo, the checks. Jake telling Bert to keep it strictly hush-hush.

"And what about—"

"I covered both of you. Go rent a tux and get over here. It's GH Night."

"God," he said softly. I could tell that in the instant of relief the terror suddenly had hold of him. He'd been flying combat again. Now he was on the ground, torn up by what he'd been through, the great concussions of noise and the light that had rattled the plane and trailed him through the sky. "God," he said again. "Mack, man, what can I say?"

"Just come back," I repeated.

This was getting exciting, everything falling in place. My phone rang again.

"I'm waiting," Martin told me.

XXVIII. HOW MARTIN SOLVED
THE CRIME

Martin was dressing. He had on his tuxedo pants, striped in satin along the seam, and his wing-collared tuxedo shirt, into which he was nimbly inserting the studs, little diamond jobs that glimmered in the pearly light of the late-winter afternoon. In an hour or so my partners, all similarly dressed, would stroll down the avenue to the Club Belvedere, share a drink or two and some canapés, and then over dinner get a report on financial results and the size of their share. It promised to be an excruciating evening in every regard.

Martin did not speak at first. Standing, he worked over the shirt for some time. Every now and then he stopped to examine a small blue note card on his desk, reading it to himself. It was, I suspected, his GH Night speech. Rah-rah from the managing partner. Picking up his pen, he made a few corrections. I said nothing either. The large corner office, fully lit from the long windows, was quiet enough that you could hear the whirring of the gyroscope device that powered one of his clocks. I was tempted to play with some of his toys, the shaman stick or the coffee-table games, but I took a seat instead in a wooden side-chair painted up in Southwestern shades. I'd brought along my briefcase.

"I've been too fucking good to you," Martin said at last. He didn't talk dirty and this was meant to be shocking. He wanted me to know he was pissed, that our partnership agreement didn't include a search warrant for his drawer. He continued fooling with the shirt.

"How much trouble is Bert in?" he asked in a moment.

"Now that I've had a little chat with the police, probably none."

He glanced my way briefly to be sure I was serious.

"How'd you arrange that? This policeman an old friend?"

"You could say."

"Very impressive." He nodded. I was sorry, frankly, he hadn't been there to see it. In a law firm it took all types, and I was one of the best bullshitters in town. It was like having a guy in the bullpen who could get away with throwing spitballs. Witnessing that performance would have rewarded Martin's faith in me, all the time he'd spent telling our partners I might come back yet.

"I've been doing a lot of impressive stuff," I said. "I was in Pico Luan over the weekend."

Martin's eyes stayed with me for the first time. Standing there, his figure was framed by the black iron circle of the enormous arc lamp that cut the space over the desk.

"Are we forestalling one another with humor?"

"No, I'm demonstrating my investigatory powers," I told him. "I'm telling you politely to cut the crap."

I took one of the dupes of the International Bank signature form from my briefcase and threw it on the desktop, where Martin studied it at length. Finally, he sat down in his tall leather chair.

"What are you going to do?"

"I'm done doing. Mr. Krzysinski has been informed."

The last stud, which Martin still had within his thick fingers, caught his attention somehow. He considered it briefly, then let it fly at the windows. I heard it bounce but couldn't see where it went.

"Carl's up there with that document and the memo you were hiding, and Tad and he and everyone else are trying to figure out why Jake Eiger would do something like this."

Momentarily Martin covered his whole face with his broad hand, blackly pelted on its back. From the hall I could hear through the closed door the phones, the voices of the workday.

"Well, that's not going to take very long, is it?" Martin asked finally. "The motive is hardly elusive. Jake's planning for his future. He knows that Tad doesn't like him and that sooner or later, when Tad's alliances on the board are firm, Krzysinski is going to be opening the bays and dropping Jake without a parachute, golden or otherwise. So Jake provided one for himself. That's the explanation, isn't it?"

"Seems right," I said.

Martin looked at me through one eye as he canted back in his chair.

"What else is Carl saying?"

"I covered your butt, if that's what you're asking. Which is more than you deserve. You were fucking around with me, Martin."

He made some move to deny it and I challenged him.

"I can give you a hundred examples. I don't have to ask who Glyndora called for advice on how to get me out of her apartment last week, do I?"

"No." He laughed suddenly, and I did as well. I was being a good sport, but a mood of disclosure was also beginning to lighten the air. I suppose it made a great story, the way I went running down the stairs like a little elf, trying not to stumble on my you-know-what.

"Didn't want anybody messing with your girl, huh?"

Martin rolled his jaw. He looked again through one eye. I wasn't sure how he'd take this assault on his secrets, whether it would make him frantic or if he would get up and try to throw me out of the room. But I guess he knew himself well enough, because he seemed to accept this with a faint resignation.

"Don't let me stop you," I said. "You were about to explain."

"My personal life? That's before the flood." It wasn't quite a rebuff. He was looking out the broad windows toward his city and its life, and his tone suggested worlds, universes of emotion suppressed. God, I thought, to have been a fly on the wall for that romance, to have observed these two characters surmounting the many barriers to get into each other's pants. Glyndora must have stuck out all her prominent parts and dared him to touch them—a way to put him in his place. I'd seen that routine: You think you're tough? I'm tough. I'm the best-looking woman in four city blocks. I'd wear you out. I'd get you up four times a night, I'd screw you dry and tell you I needed more, I'd be so much you'd want to unhitch it and put it in my trophy case. You didn't have wet dreams as a puppy 10 percent as good as me. And you won't dare touch it. Cause I ain't gonna have it.

She probably laid it on thick. And he accepted the World Championship Challenge of treating her kindly. Glyndora'd stomp and sulk and he must have signaled in a hundred ways that he thought she was valuable and would never change his mind. He must have worn her down until she had to succumb to the fantasy that everything she rejected before it refused her might, instead, fold her in its embrace. And Martin visited that shadow zone where not much matters, where pretense and power, every one of his bets which was always on the future, had to surrender to the pure sensation of the present. I'll bet until ten minutes before they were screwing it was no more than daily titillation for each one of them, a dirty movie that was always shuttered in their minds.

"But what happened?" I said. "You know. With you and her. Can I ask?"

"It didn't work out," he said. His hand skirted the air. "We were kidding ourselves." The remark hung there, with all its potent sadness—the American predicament. Martin had these kids, this wife—and there was the Club Belvedere, clients who'd snigger that he'd taken up with a colored girl. But the result probably suited Glyndora. It would have been a lot to ask of her, to be herself in his world.

"I am very fond of Glyndora," he said then, impaled on whatever the remark conjured and concealed. He looked at me. "Do you believe in reincarnation?"

"No," I said.

"No," he said. "Neither do I." He was quiet then. Martin Gold, the most successful lawyer I knew, wanted to be somebody else too. It was touching, though. Loyalty always is.

We were silent some time. Eventually Martin started talking about what had happened in a depleted, reflective tone. He had not been fooling with me, he said. Not intentionally. I gave him far too much credit. Circumstances had mounted. Combined. His honesty as he spoke was beguiling. You so rarely got Martin to talk straight from the heart.

"Glyndora came to me with the memo and the checks as soon as they'd cleared. Early December, I think. Around then. It looked odd to both of us, of course, business checks negotiated offshore, but I didn't feel any great concern until I started doing the research—talking to Bert, Neucriss, the banker down there in Pico. No Litiplex registered anywhere. No records upstairs. I was shocked when I saw where it pointed. I never perceived this in Jake. He'd lie to the Pope for the sake of his vanity, but I was stunned to learn he was a thief. And it was gruesome, of course, imagining the consequences."

Martin, like any man with an empire, was accustomed to problems—big ones, situations that could bring him and everyone who depended upon him to doom. Like TN walking out as a client, or Pagnucci making a move. He got used to it, accustomed. He learned to walk the highwire, sailing along with gumption and a parasol. This thing with Eiger was a problem too. He left Glyndora on alert for more checks and took some time to ponder the common good.

"At which point," he said, "Glyndora's life began coming apart."

"Bert and Orleans?"

He emitted a sound, the old wrestler's grunt, a little eruption of surprise, self-consciously controlled, when he was snatched for the takedown. He peered, his squat face immobile, engraved by shadow in the dwindling light.

"You know, Malloy, if you'd done half as good a job around here in the last few years as you did looking into this, you would have made my life a great deal easier."

"I'll take that as a compliment."

"Please," Martin answered.

"What's he like?" I asked. "This son of hers?"

"Orleans? Complicated fellow."

"He's her heartbreak, I take it."

Martin made various ruminative gestures. It seemed he had tried to be good to Orleans as a boy.

"Very bright individual. Mother's son, that way. Very capable. But not steady. Temperamentally. Nothing you could do about that. She thought she was going to prohibit him from being the way he clearly was. And he wasn't willing to be prohibited."

"She found Bert an upsetting development?"

"Not Bert as Bert. It's a situation she's never wanted to confront squarely." He made a sad face.

"Yeah," I offered. I got it. But I felt for Bert. In all

likelihood, he'd been largely beside the point with Orleans from the start.

"Did you warn Bert?"

"No one here has accepted my warnings. No one." He remained momentarily forlorn, even as his agitation visibly mounted. "Jesus, what a mess. What a mess! This one may have been the single stupidest thing—" Martin waved. "This ludicrous, insane novelty with these basketball games— And worse, both of them, neither had given a moment's thought, not a bare instant, to the costs of this behavior— Imprisonment, bodily harm, my God, the prospects, and the two of them are *surprised* by this, shocked, absolutely, positively disbelieving, like tiny children, the two most immature grown men I have ever known, neither with the remotest—" Martin stopped himself; he was losing the thread.

"You were explaining how you decided to cover for Jake."

"This is part of it," he said. "I told you. It's happenstance. Circumstances conspire. This is part. This is what led Glyndora to it."

"Blaming Bert? You're saying that's Glyndora's idea? For what? To get even with him?"

He waited. He smiled.

"What kind of mother do you imagine Glyndora is, Mack?"

You could take your choice of adjectives. Intense. Protective. She'd have sheltered Orleans through the ravages of war, scavenged food, or sold her body. For all I knew, that's what she was doing with me that night. But I still wasn't following. Martin saved his partners, his professional life, by covering Jake. I didn't see much gain to the chief clerk in Accounting.

"Look, Mack, Bert's decision to drop out of sight was well-intentioned as far as it went. He thought he was being heroic. But it was hardly a solution for Orleans. Not as far as Glyndora was concerned. She wasn't going to have him running for the rest of his life. She wanted him safe to stay here, and he wasn't."

I still didn't get it.

"You're the one who asked the question, Mack. Last week. 'Where did Bert go?' Where do *we* say Bert went? This is a lawyer. With sixty-seven partners. And clients. Never mind his family. There's not much. His friends, so-called, were all implicated in the same thing and surely willing to keep their peace. But what the hell do we say around here? How do we keep somebody from notifying the police who, in investigating Bert's absence, will promptly discover that whole basketball mess? The only way to insulate Orleans—to completely protect him—was if there was another credible explanation for why Bert disappeared—even if that explanation was understood only by a few people who'd make excuses to everyone else."

I rolled my head around, this way and that. I sort of liked it. Until I saw the next part.

"That's why you needed some hapless stumblebum to go look for him." Someone, I realized, who wasn't supposed to really catch Bert or even figure out what he'd actually been up to—just state convincingly that he was gone. That was what Glyndora had meant in the one sincere moment we'd had. Absorbing my observation about their estimate of me, Martin, I noted, made no effort to differ.

"And that's why you hid the body," I said. It came to me, just like that. "Once I started looking for Bert."

"We *what*?" Martin's entire weight was suddenly planted on one hand fiercely gripping the arm of his chair. This aspect of alarm, of incomprehension, could have been posed, I realized. But Martin didn't look like he was fooling. Instead, I recalculated: Orleans and Bert, already shamed and scolded, yelled at, told they were irresponsible fools, hadn't confessed the worst. Martin and Glyndora thought Bert was running only from threats. Archie's disappearance, when it hit the papers, must have terrified them.

"Figure of speech," I said. "The memo. You hid the memo."

"Oh," said Martin. He relaxed. "Right. We hid the body." He made a brief effort to smile. For an instant, I wondered again about who'd moved the body. The only thing certain was that Archie couldn't have walked.

In the meantime, Martin had resumed his explanation, telling me how they had come to blame Bert for stealing the Litiplex money. The first few times Glyndora and he had discussed it, he said, the whole plan, it was in the vein of magnificent fantasy, a perfect future where all problems came to an end. He worked it out with her dozens of times, calculated how the dominoes would fall, saw at once how advantageous it would be to the firm not to have to sacrifice Jake. It was fun to discuss, lots of laughs, like a couple saying they'll rob a bank to pay the mortgage. Eventually he recognized that she was urging him to pursue what he'd regarded as jest.

"I told her this was lunacy. Worse than that, impermissible. A fraud. But you see. Really." He sat up. He faced me squarely. "It's me. It's mine. It's my precious values. My law. My rules. Take that out of the equation— My right," he said, "my wrong. My precious abstractions." He halted in the midst of the litany he must have heard from her for years and lingered like some bug in the breeze, manifestly pained. Watching him, my heart spurted with sudden hope that Brushy and I might resolve what divided us the same way, until I recollected, as quickly, that we were both supposed to believe in the same thing.

"Here are these people," he said. "Glyndora and Orleans. My partners. Jake. Bert. Even you, Mack. Even you. This is an institution. It's the product of lives. Hundreds of lives. All right. I sound like Wash. Forgive the sanctimony. But do I lay that all on the altar? I've made worse compromises."

Both hands were thrown wide. He had a touch of priestly majesty. He thought he was revealed.

I said, "It doesn't hurt you either, Martin. We all know who gets the biggest share." I was enjoying this—being the man of greater rectitude, even if we both knew it was situational and I knew it was an act. Fact is, I've enjoyed my acts, every one of them—copper, hard guy, smartass, lawyer. I can be a good anything, if it's only part time.

Martin had absorbed my remark with a lingering, rueful grin.

"Not me," he said. He backhanded the little note card

he'd had on his desk so it spiraled through space; I picked it up off the rug. Martin's handwriting is atrocious—slashes and squiggles indiscernible to me, even after all these years. But certain words were clear enough. "Resigning." "Mayor." "Riverside Commission." "Long-held passion." In tonight's speech to the partnership assembled, Martin Gold was going to quit.

"Think the public sector can handle me?" he asked.

"You've got to be kidding." I couldn't believe it. The circus without Barnum.

He muled around. Stubborn. Set. It was time, he said. The deal was done. Martin Gold, head of the Riverside Commission. Starting April 1. He talked about thirty years in private practice, giving things back, but I understood the imperatives. If he took a dive for Jake, if he didn't march stalwartly to Krzysinski's office and let his law firm pass into the great beyond, then Martin would punish himself instead. His people might survive, but he wouldn't get to the promised land. It was an old idea, and its mixture of shrewd practicality and highfalutin principles was quintessentially Gold. Lawyerly, you'd say. But still nuts.

"You should have been born a Catholic," I told him. "You really missed your chance. There are all these obscure fast days and penitential rites. We've been working for centuries on strategies for self-denial." He thought I was funny of course. He always did. He laughed out loud.

All these years I've figured that if I somehow eluded Martin's defenses and peered into his core it would be a vision of glory: I'd see a lionheart, beating at mach speed and enlarged by passion. Instead, what was within was some little gremlin that made him believe that his greatest nobility came from cutting himself off from what he liked best. Glyndora. Or the law firm. He was cheap with himself, with his own pleasure. It was crushing to recognize: he was more productive than me, but no happier. I didn't want his life either.

He was still disagreeing.

"As of today"— And he nodded toward me—"I'm not giving up much. Not once the dust settles upstairs. Whether Tad instructs his new General Counsel to cut us off or just cut us back, this place won't hold together. A fellow like Carl—" Martin stopped himself; he never spoke ill of his partners. "Not everyone will settle for less. In the end, frankly, there will be those who paint me as an opportunist. First man to the lifeboat."

There was, of course, a subtle accusatory element to these observations. Martin had removed a limb or two for the team. I'd destroyed it. The Catholic boy, ever guilty as charged, still reared up to defend himself. It was comic, of course. I'd stolen nearly six million bucks and wasn't beset by thoughts of giving it back. But in that goofy way we have of thinking we are what we're seen to be, I cared about Martin's impressions.

"Am I supposed to apologize?" I asked. "It's an ugly deal, Martin, the one you were trying to cut with Jake— five and a half mil of the client's money so he continues throwing slops to G&G."

Martin went still—just the way he had when I mentioned the body. He gave his head a distinct shake.

"Is *that* what you think?" He smiled suddenly. Luminously. He used the chair arms to boost himself. What I'd said actually pleased him. I knew why too. I'd made some error that allowed him to resume his familiar supremacy.

"Oh, I see," he said, "I see. I was bartering with Jake. TN's business for the money. Is that it? That's it?" It was a contest now, a stalking. I just kept my mouth shut as he kept moving in. "I plead guilty, Mack. I was trying to preserve the firm. I was even trying to save Jake from himself. And God knows I was hoping to shelter Orleans. I trimmed some corners off my conscience in the process— I admit that too. Maybe more than corners. But do you honestly think the object of this was that—that crass?"

I didn't answer.

"I can't imagine how you viewed this. Why would I confront Jake with Wash and you last week? Why not just whisper in his ear that I knew he was a thief and demand he send all business now and hereafter?"

He was safer, of course, not confronting Jake openly, but I knew he would ridicule that suggestion.

"Don't you see?" he asked. "Look at this, for God's sake, from Jake's perspective. We tell him the money's missing, we believe Bert's got it, we can't locate any records related to the disbursement to Litiplex. But we also say we're looking high and low for Bert, and when we find him, we'll beg him to give the money back and come home. We even tell Jake we want his blessing for that arrangement. You were sitting right here. You heard that. Now how does Jake know that you're not going to find Bert? How can he be sure?"

This was like law school. The Grand Inquisitor. I swallowed and admitted he couldn't.

"He can't," said Martin, "that's right. He can't. He can't be certain. And when Bert is found, when he returns from whatever exotic detour he's taken, Jake knows where Bert is going to be pointing. Straight at Jake. There's no safety for Jake in the fact we blame Bert. He *knows* it's a misimpression.

"But now let's consider an alternative. You're out searching up Bert, trying to get him the message that all is well if he just gives back the money, and lo and behold, lo and behold, Jake Eiger, Glyndora, someone is able to report that mysteriously, wonderfully, a wire transfer has come in from Pico Luan. God bless Bert. God bless us. Case closed. As promised, not another word will be spoken on the subject. My God, Mack! Could you really have missed this? Don't you understand that the point was to offer Jake a discreet way, a last opportunity to give the goddamned bloody money *back*?"

It settled in then, like the mystical presence of some nearby angel. Martin, of course, was speaking the truth. It had all the delicate signs of his typical engineering. Nothing so direct as a confrontation with Jake. That would have been shabby and extortionate—and risky as well, if Jake ever told tales. This way the world could go on, with all its false faces. Oddly, it would be exactly as the Committee had told me from the start. Except for the identity of the thief, the plan was precisely the same: Get the money back, sweep it under the rug, kiss and make up.

"He could have run," I said to Martin.

"He could have. But he hasn't run yet. Jake obviously

wants to hold on to this life. He just craves some security to which he's not entitled. I was letting him know it was time to make a more realistic choice.''

''And what happens when he doesn't give the money back? You're not telling me you were actually thinking of turning him in?''

He looked at me like I was nuts.

''What other choice is there? That was the one limit I set with Glyndora to start.'' He could see I was astonished. ''Look, Mack, if I was determined to say nothing, no matter what Jake did, I would have burned that memo, not kept it in a drawer.''

''But you *didn't* say anything.''

''Why should I? You're the one who brought us Jake's message last week: Be patient, Bert's not to blame, it's not what it appears, future accountings will show that there's been a mistake. That was clearly the prelude. Jake was planning to get the money back.''

A strange qualm passed between us then, some recognition of the differing planes where we'd stood which was transmitted in a stark look. Martin got to his feet.

''My *God*,'' he said. It was just coming home to him, not the dimension of our misunderstanding—he'd seen that before—but rather, its consequences. He'd assumed I'd sent Carl to Krzysinski out of disdain for the grubby arrangement Martin was orchestrating—protecting Jake and the firm, breaching our duty to TN to fully inform them of what we knew about the General Counsel. Martin saw only now that I'd been propelled by imagining malefactions far grander. He spotted his stud on the floor and pitched it at the windows again—full force, so the jewel flew off in a kind of musical ricochet. He pointed at me. He called me names.

"You goddamned dumb bastard! You wouldn't even talk to me on the phone."

He stood there huffing and puffing. And how did I feel? Pretty strange. Confused. In a peculiar way, I was actually relieved. When I recovered some sense of myself, I realized I was smiling. I'd misjudged Martin and his complexities. You wouldn't call his conduct saintly, but he'd done better than I thought—and, God knows, a hell of a lot better than me.

There was a knock on the door. Brushy. She had put on her formal, a sleeveless black floor-length job with sequins. She wore long white gloves. A rhinestone tiara was perched in her hair like a sparkling bird. Her eyes went to the desk where the copy of the form from the International Bank still lay and she tolled that, as usual, at the speed of a Univac. I whistled at her and she diverted herself for a fraction of a second to smile.

"Is Wash here yet?" she asked. "He just called and asked me to come down. He sounded upset."

Wash arrived presently. In the condition she'd discerned.

"I'm just off the phone with Krzysinski. All hell's broken loose up there." He was in his tux, with a jazzy red bow tie, but his face was pale and he had broken a sweat. "Tad asked for everyone TN works with—'my dependables' was how he put it." Wash closed his eyes. "He wants all of us upstairs. You. Me. Brushy. Mack. Bert as well. What do we say about that? About Bert?"

Martin waved his hand to pass off the question; Wash, as usual, was missing the point. Martin asked what precisely Tad wanted and Wash at first seemed unable to bring himself to answer. The old age descending on him, where he would be bewildered and addled, seemed at hand. He stood there with his mouth vaguely moving and his eyes never quite fixed. He answered at last.

"Tad said he wants to figure out what to do about Jake."

XXIX. AND THIS TIME IT'S THE TRUTH

A. Office of the Chair

In Tad Krzysinski's huge office we found the disjointed air of a large, unhappy family. Tad's assistant, Ilene, met us and said that Pagnucci had stepped out to put on the tuxedo his secretary had brought up. Mike Mathigoris, the head of security, was also elsewhere for the moment, while Tad's four o'clock meeting was going on in his adjoining conference room. Only Tad and Jake remained here, paying no attention to each other. Krzysinski was taking a phone call and Jake was abjectly hulked on the edge of his chair, staring without much comprehension at the many portraits of Krzysinski's children that were the principal decoration on the far wall, between the three doors that led to Jake's office, the office of TN's CFO, and the conference room. You could tell from the empty way that Jake first looked at us, the wan smile, that he couldn't explain what was wrong with this picture, why Brush in her floor-length gown and the three men in tuxes appeared out of place. Martin's bow tie was still hanging loose through his collar, and his shirt was held closed over his stomach principally by his cummerbund, since he'd never managed to insert the last stud.

"I wanted you to hear this." Krzysinski had gotten up to shake each of our hands, the usual crushing grip. In college, I'd heard, Tad's nickname had been "Atom" and that about said it all—size, structure, the barely contained power. Tad, of course, had a vast corner office. The parquet was covered by an enormous Oriental rug—fifty grand at least—and his view ran all the way to the airport on a clear day. When the weather was good, Tad liked to stand at the long windows and watch TN's planes rise, giving you the flight numbers and the names of the pilots.

Now, once he'd greeted us, he jiggled a commanding finger at Jake, instructing him to proceed. Jake recounted the story somewhat methodically, drained of emotion. You could tell that he'd repeated it about six times already and it was beginning to get routine. He was, as usual, perfectly groomed, hair stiffly parted, his gray herringbone suit buttoned at the waist to add to the impression of his ordered form. But his face was out of focus. Jake, for once in his life, was under the crush of sensible pain and it threatened his sanity. I felt only a twinge of regret. Asked to speak, I might well have said, "Goody."

In November, Jake said, as we were thinking about making the final disbursements on 397, Peter Neucriss and Jake had a talk. Actually, Peter took Jake out for the evening, a characteristic manipulation, wooing the enemy.

Royal treatment. Dinner at Batik. Many drinks. Hockey game. Afterwards, as Jake and Peter were having a nightcap down at Sergio's, Peter got to what he had been leading up to all night. He had a business proposition for Jake. For TN, really. Neucriss had three different settlements on 397. Huge cases, naturally. A mother and child one of them. The total was nearly thirty million. Peter was working on the usual third. He had almost ten million in fees coming.

"He told me this long farfetched tale, how a fortune was owed to this litigation support group, Litiplex. He said their work had benefitted all the plaintiffs, but the class lawyers were acting as if they'd never heard of them and Peter was in a spot because he was the one who'd retained the company and made some cozy deal with them, these Litiplex people, something a little unsavory. You know Neucriss when he gets like this. You'd expect him to leave a spot on the wall. At any rate, he felt it was his obligation to pay Litiplex even though I—me supposedly—I'd said at one point it would come off the settlement fund. I objected. A number of times. I mean, I'd had a few drinks, but I knew I'd never said anything like that.

"I couldn't imagine what was going on, until suddenly he made this proposal: If we'd pay Litiplex offshore—$5.6 million was the number he'd come up with—set up an offshore account in their name, disposition subject to Peter's later direction, then Neucriss would let us reduce our remaining payment to Peter's clients to $22.4 million. That way, TN would be two million dollars ahead. He assured me his clients would net the same amounts. You know how it goes—we pay him, he deducts his share and remits to the clients. He'd just cook his books so it looked like he was working on a 10 percent contingency instead of a third. Why should I care? It's two million to us. That's the bottom line."

"I'm not following," said Wash. "What does Peter get out of it?"

"It's a tax dodge." It was Brushy who spoke. As usual, she didn't need a book of instructions. "There's no Litiplex. Not really. It's a sham for Neucriss, who gets his fee offshore and never pays income taxes on it, not this year, and not on whatever it earns in the future. That's why he was willing to take two million less. He'd save two or three times that in the long run."

Jake was nodding eagerly as she ran it down. Eagerly. Even Jake had understood this much.

"Neucriss denies all of this, by the way, the entire conversation." It was Pagnucci, in the doorway. Carl was dressed in a double-breasted dinner jacket, blue sharkskin no less, smoking a cigarette and looking somewhat haggard. Considering the assembly, he said dryly that he'd already listened to this story several times.

"Mathigoris and I were just on the phone with Mr. Neucriss," Carl said. "He states, most emphatically, that the only time he's heard of Litiplex was when Mack and Martin spoke with him recently."

"Naturally," said Jake, "naturally he denies it. I told you he would. He's engaging in tax evasion. I don't expect him to put up a billboard. But I'm telling you, that was the deal. I set up the account with that understanding. When he presented me with signed releases on our cases, I'd give him the balance of the settlements and a letter of direction entitling whoever he designated to the account. Don't you see? I wasn't stealing anything. This was for the company. For TN.''

He looked at Krzysinski, but Tad's attention was on Ilene, the assistant, who stood at the door signaling obscurely. Tad stepped into his conference room to attend to whatever fire was burning there.

''And what were you thinking the IRS would say about the company and you, Jake?'' Brushy asked this. Wash in the meantime was peeking up hopefully. He didn't understand everything, but Jake's last lines had buoyed him. He could see it coming. Undeserved salvation. Story of his life.

''Me? We haven't lied to them. We haven't filed any false documents. I haven't even seen Peter's return. God knows, I've got suspicions, but who can fathom the mind of Peter Neucriss? If the Service ever asked, I'd tell them the absolute truth. And I'm certainly not hiding any income. We *want* to declare it. It'll be on every return and financial statement. That's the point. Let's not pretend. We all know the story. Tad has been *very* concerned about the level of legal expenses. And quite pleased with the way 397 has turned out. This is two million, straight to the bottom line. We need that. All of us. The company and everyone here.''

''I still don't think you'd get a good-conduct medal from the Service,'' said Martin to Jake.

''Or the SEC,'' said Pagnucci.

''Or Tad,'' Brushy said.

''Admittedly,'' said Jake, ''admittedly. True on all counts. Krzysinski hates it. *Hates* it. Look at him. It's not his style." Glancing darkly at the conference room door, Jake lowered his voice. "But he'd *love* the result. So would the board. Friends, really. A tree falls in the forest. Is there sound if nobody hears? If I'm discreet, what does anyone know? Neucriss won't say a word. The IRS has no reason to audit an escrow account. We're showing a *surplus*, for crying out loud. That's why I told no one. I sent the memo to Bert, explaining that it was very sensitive. I left no records here. And I made my own hell by doing it that way. I'm the first to admit it. The very first. There was not a thing I could say when all of you began looking into the matter, except what I told Mack last week: If we just wait, it's going to turn out all right. When the disbursements were made, there would be *no* money missing. There'd be two million more than expected. Who would complain? Don't you see? I'm not a thief." He looked around the room at each of us. He was being achingly sincere, wounded and vulnerable, that Jake-thing I'd probably last seen when he talked to me about the bar exam.

Krzysinski had returned for the latter stages of this performance, but he did not allow it to hinder him as he walked back to his desk. He addressed Jake without rancor. Tad was just himself—completely in charge. His job was deciding things. He was better at that than most people, the way certain guys can jump a foot over the rim. He roamed an empyrean landscape where he figured out what would happen with the perfect instantaneous reflex of a machine. He asked Jake where he wanted to go while we spoke.

"Home," said Jake, and Tad nodded. That was a good

idea, he said. Go home. Stay by the phone in case there were more questions. Jake departed, clearly at a loss for the right gesture of farewell. He reverted to his friendly little wave, a politician's touch that he'd absorbed from his father. It was, in the circumstances, sadly wrong. His departure, disappearance, seemed fateful and left a silent, troubled wake.

"So what do you think?" Tad asked after a moment. "I wanted your opinions. You've all known him much longer than me." He swiveled about in his big chair. This might well have been Tad's ultimate test—would G&G's lawyers shoot straight when the target was Jake? Maybe, in order to decide about us, he was matching our estimate against one he'd derived already. But I thought he was merely making smart use of the available resources.

"I believe him," Wash said instantly. He had summoned himself to sound stalwart. He brought all that upper-crust nobility back into his face.

Krzysinski pursed up his mouth. "Mathigoris thinks it's a cover story. Carefully planned. Carl shares that opinion."

Carl nodded. As usual he wasn't saying much. But his ego would suffer no blows and he preferred the sinister to admitting he had failed in divining the situation. Now and then he had looked darkly at me, suspecting, I imagine, that I'd set him up. But I'd hung in there, meeting his eye meaningfully, and now he was not backing down.

Martin, when Tad addressed him, wasn't there, lost instead at mystical depths within himself. He'd still not fit the last stud into his shirt and he was tossing it up and down in one hand, in a mindless way, the jewel glinting as it turned in the air. He caught me eyeing him and gave me a wry look.

Tad asked the question again to gain his attention. What did he think?

"Oh," Martin said. "Do I think it would tickle Neucriss to see your General Counsel doing tricks for him like a streetwalker? Naturally. Neucriss's favorite pastime is proving that all human nature is as base as his. On the other hand, do I think Jake is capable of this deception on his own?" Martin smiled fleetingly at me, with his usual deep appreciation of irony. "Quite," he said. "Quite. Frankly, Tad, I don't know what the hell is going on."

Martin stood up in his half-secured formal wear and hoisted his striped trousers; he threw his stud in the air one more time. He was enormously cheerful. You wouldn't quite say he didn't give a damn. But you could tell he felt free of this life. Martin was on the road to being somebody else. He smiled again when he looked at Krzysinski.

"To me it sounds typically Jake." That was Brushy. "I hate to say it, but we all know Jake's consuming interests are corporate politics and what makes him look good. Frankly, Tad, I'm not even sure he realized he was breaking the law. I believe him."

I wasn't certain I'd ever seen Brush in the same room with Krzysinski and I watched them for signs. But all that showed was Tad's native intensity. His searching look lingered with her even after she'd spoken.

"I think I do too," Tad stated finally. "You see," he said to Wash, picking up on some dispute from the boardroom, "this is what I never liked. Always the easy way out. Well, he's gone today. That's given. Given. And

I have to advise the board. But I need to know what to recommend. Everyone will prefer to avoid the scandal. I'd hate to turn him over to the authorities if I didn't have to. I guess you go on your gut. I just wish I had some experience. What's your view, Mack? You're the one who's done this for a living. What do you say? Does Jake look to you like a crook?''

We were back to where we had been last week. I had their attention. Everyone's. The fly ball once more was coming my way. I knew I could save Jake. I could tell one of my wonderful wild-ass stories. There were already six of them in my head. Say, for example, that Jake must have forgotten that long ago he had vaguely mentioned some shady deal with Neucriss which I'd told him to avoid. That would do it. Give me five minutes with a fax machine to rip off messages to Pico Luan to the Züricher Kreditbank and Fortune Trust and I could even replenish Litiplex's secret account. I could do it all.

But I wasn't going that way. It's happened to all of us, especially as kids. The screen goes dark; the music fades and the speakers hiss; the sudden lights sting the eyes. How can it be over, the heart cries, when the film's still running inside me?

It turned out that it no longer mattered what had actually happened. I was set on my way—another direction. I felt that. Somewhere new. Somewhere else. Me and Martin. I'd made the decision. Brave new world. No turning around. If I wasn't headed for a better life, at least I was going toward something unexpressed in the life I presently had.

Looking back, I suppose it's sort of funny that we'd all

been so willing to believe Jake was a thief. That slippery side of him must be out there for everybody to see—which was why we were still hanging in doubt. Isn't that life? Seeing it, hearing it—how much is there we don't really understand? Caught in our own foxholes, we never see the battlefield scene. I had wanted to believe they were no better than me. All of them. But we think what we do for a reason. Call me a fool or the victim of my own expectations. The one guy I wasn't wrong about was me.

"I believe him," I said. And I did. Not because Jake was too honest to steal. God knows, he wasn't. It was the story he'd told. About Neucriss. It wouldn't come to Jake in one thousand years. Not in REM sleep. Tad had it right. Jake always took the easy way out. If Jake was going to need phony cover, he'd find some fall guy, some flunky. Somebody like me.

"I believe him," I said again, then added, "assuming there's no problem getting the money back."

"No, no," said Krzysinski. "He and Mathigoris ran off an hour ago to send a fax to the bank. Mathigoris has been standing by the machine waiting for a confirmation. Wait, here he is now."

There he was, Mike Mathigoris, security chief, nice-looking, right-in-the-middle kind of guy, former vice-commander of the State Police, out after twenty and in a great job here, fending off future skyjackings, ticket frauds, travel agents with commission schemes. I'd worked with him a lot before Jake let my well run dry. He handed the papers he was carrying to Tad without any ceremony. Tad read them and started to fume.

"Son of a bitch," he said. "Son of a bitch."

Brushy, in her vaguely familiar manner with Krzysinski, stood to read over his shoulder. Soon the documents were passing among the rest of us. The first page was a fax cover sheet from the International Bank of Finance N.A., Pico Luan, with the following message at its foot:

```
Account closed, January 30, per
attached letter of direction.
Best wishes,
Salem George
```

The letter I'd faxed over on Monday from the Regency was attached. When I looked at the signature, I admit I smiled. Handwriting analysts can't work with a copy. And I'd fool them anyway. Brushy, it turned out, was watching me, something solid, maybe even fatal, in her eye. She mouthed: "Why are you having such a good time?"

"It's ironic," I said aloud and turned away.

Pagnucci was reading now, looking quite smug. He made little pontifical sounds but might just as well have said, Told you so.

"What in the hell is Jake up to?" asked Tad. He had said this already a couple of times and nobody had replied.

"He's running," I answered. "He put together this story about Neucriss to buy himself time. Now he's headed for the hills. And the money."

"Oh Christ," said Krzysinski. "And I let him out of here. Oh Christ! Let's go. Let's get the police." Krzysinski was waving at Mathigoris.

Wash had turned to wood right in front of me. He was dead as a stump.

"Who do we call?" Tad asked.

"Mack has friends on the police force," Martin volunteered at once from across the room. "He just had one in the office before."

"Wrong guy," I said immediately. "Not for this case."

"Who's that?" Mike asked me.

"A dick named Dimonte."

"Gino?" asked Mike. "Tough cop. He's working Financials now. He'd be fine."

In desperation I looked to Brushy, but she'd turned away.

"Don't you think the Bureau would be better with an international case?" I asked Mathigoris. He was indifferent. "This guy's idea of investigative technique is to scare you to death," I told Tad.

"That sounds like just what Jake deserves. Call him. Go," Tad said to me. "Quickly, please. Jake can't get away. We'll move from bad to worse."

Because the conference room was in use, I ended up in a little phone closet off the TN reception area, where there was a colonial print of a woman in a Dutch collar, a poor cousin of Rembrandt. This was a kind of in-house phone booth, designed for visitors, a place they could take a call from their office in privacy. There was a small bowl of potpourri that sweetened the tight air. I considered the alternatives. I had none. 'I couldn't get through' is not a credible excuse on a call to the police. 'I called him' wouldn't work, because when he didn't show up, somebody would just call him again.

"Gino," I said. I tried to be upbeat and bright. "When you hear this one, you're gonna love me."

"In another life," he answered at once.

I told him the story. If he ran quick, he could get Jake at home. I gave him the address. Jake of course would be sitting there. Like some beaten hound. Right by the phone, as he promised. Maybe he'd called a lawyer. Or his dad. But he'd be there. I'd have paid some money to see the look on his face when Pigeyes grabbed him. God, I thought. God, I hated Jake.

"You won't need another collar before you retire," I told Pigeyes.

"I just want you to know," Gino said when I finished, "I didn't buy one word of that."

I had no idea what to say.

"Not one fucking word. I don't want you going home and laughing in your beer tonight, or whatever you drink now. Postum. I knew that whole routine was a crock. About these three guys all doing the bunny hop." He was talking about what I'd said when he'd come to the office, the tale I told about Bert and Archie and the could-be-Kam from the U. This was *mano a mano*, him to me. He wanted me to know I hadn't gotten the best of him after all.

"It's all wrong," Pigeyes told me.

"How?"

"Archie ain't bent, for one thing."

"You're the one who told me, Pigeyes. About Archie. Rocket up his ass? Remember?"

"No. You told me. I said, What if. I said, Give, and you said, Has this guy got an elastic asshole? and I said, What if. This mutt Archie, I know the story of his life and his mother's life. He's straight. He don't got nothing but dingleberries back there, same as you and me. So it's a crock. That whole routine. Just so you know."

Just so I knew. The other one, his young bootlicker, Dewey, he was taken in. Not Gino.

"I'm not following."

"What else is new?"

"Are we done here or what?" I asked.

"Are we done, you and me done, is that what we're asking?"

"I mean Bert."

"Fuck 'em."

Nothing but fuzz on my screen. I did not understand. Which was just what he wanted.

"So what is this? Favor done, favor owed?" I thought maybe with the big collar on Jake, he was calling the score even.

He laughed, he roared. There was a phenomenal clanking wallop in my ear when he banged the phone on something hard.

"You done me enough favors. When you're miserable in hell, suffering your sins and thinking it can't get no worse, you look behind you and I'll be there. Payback time with me and you ain't gonna end, Malloy. Just so you know. I'm telling you, you're dirty somewhere. I said that from the git-go and I still say so. You're covering your ass, same as you were doing with Good-lookin. So stay tuned. Same time. Same fuckin station." He slammed the phone again and this time it went dead. Maybe he'd hung up. Maybe he'd broken it.

But he'd done what he wanted. I sat in that tight little space and broke a sweat. This time I was really scared.

B. Closing the Circle

In the elevator, on the way down, Martin announced his resignation. I suppose he was forewarning Wash and Pagnucci. He seemed to regard his statement as dramatic, but it fell flat. This group had already been through too much, and as Martin had acknowledged before, there was not much left now to resign from. Brushy, a good kid to the last, started to talk to him anyway about changing his mind.

When the elevator doors parted, back on 37, Bert was standing there. He was dressed in supposed formal wear—a leather coat as a dinner jacket and four days' growth. He looked like a rock star. I guess Orleans was picking his clothes. He remained in the elevator doorway confronting us all in an auspicious posture, sneaking a glance to see who was inside. A lot had gone on since we'd last seen him here, and there was an instant so still it could have been suspended animation.

Martin, in particular, seemed undone by the sight of Bert, finally bereft of all his survivor's aplomb, that intense belief in his own powers which ordinarily sustains him. He stared a bit, then shook his head. Finally, he took note of the last diamond stud, still in his fingers. He seemed to weigh it. I think he had some impulse to throw it again, but in the end he simply paused to insert it in his shirt.

"Well," he said presently, "some of us have an appointment at the Club Belvedere." It was time to worry about the future. For the person of importance, the moment never waits. Martin was going to read the firm its epitaph. He was good at that kind of thing. When we'd buried

Leotis Griswell last year, Martin had made the eulogy, the usual funeral folderol, stuff he did not fully believe about how Leotis was a lawyer's lawyer who knew that the law in the end is not a business but is about values, about the kinds of judgments that were not meant to be bought and sold. The law, as Leotis saw it, said Martin, is a reflection of our common will, meant to regulate society and commerce, and not vice versa. God knows what Martin would tell the partners tonight. Maybe just goodbye.

Wash, Carl, Brushy all followed him, going off to get their coats. I tarried with Bert but gave Brushy a palsy little wink as she departed. She responded with a blistering look over her bare shoulder, the motive for which eluded me entirely. Here we go again. Fuck did I do? She said, coolly, that she had a call to make and would wait in her office to walk over with me.

Standing with Bert, I could tell he was shook up to be back. He was near the windows behind the receptionist's desk, facing the glass where his reflection loomed, vague and incomplete, like an image on water. He looked bleak.

"I wish I'd done it," he said to me, out of nowhere.

"Done what?"

"Stolen the money."

I recoiled a bit and gripped his arm to quiet him. But I could see his problem. He had a future again suddenly. His high times and adventures were over. He'd been out there on the edge, mad with love, crazy from danger. Now, if he liked, he could go right down to his office and answer interrogatories. He had lived for a while with all those neat shows playing in his head. Gangsters and athletes—his honey and him doing weird stuff in the moonlit artichoke fields, being covered and chilled by fog in the perfect still nights. Never mind that it was mad. It was his. Poor him. Poor us. Dragged to sea in our little boats by the tide of these irresistible private scenes and crashing come daylight on the rocks. But who can turn back?

"Somebody beat you to it," I told him. He laughed at that. Eventually, he asked if I was coming to the Belvedere, but I sent him along on his own.

XXX. THE END AND WHO'S HAPPY?

A. Brushy Isn't

I went home. A man in a tuxedo boarding a plane would grab too much attention. And although I distrusted the sentiment, I wanted a word with my boy. It was time for the get-tough speech: Hey, I know you think your life is grim. But so is everyone else's. We're all grinning in spite of the pain. Some do better than others. And most do better than I have. I hope in time you grow up to join that majority.

For Lyle, this talk figured to be largely beside the point, but I could feel I'd made a final effort. Upstairs at home, I found him asleep, knocked cold by some intoxicant.

"Hey, Lyle." I touched his shoulder, sharp-boned and bitten by ugly acne marks. I shook him some time before he seemed to come to.

"Dad?" He couldn't see straight.

"Yes, son," I said quietly, "it's me."

He froze there on his back, trying to focus something, his eyes or his mind or his spirit. He gave up quickly.

"Shit," he said distinctly and rolled back so that his face went down into the pillow with the lost despairing weight of a felled tree. I understood Lyle's problems. As he saw it, his parents owed him apologies. His old man was a souse. His mother pretended all his young life to be something she only later told him she wasn't. Having found no adults to admire, he'd decided not to become a grown-up at all. In strict privacy, I couldn't even quarrel with his logic. But what's the further agenda? Granted, all of it, guilty as accused, but you tell me how to repay the debts of history. I touched the tangles of his long dirty hair but quickly thought better of that and went off to pack.

I had been at it about twenty minutes when the front door chimes jingled. I was feeling cautious and glanced down through the bedroom window that overlooked the stoop. Brushy was there in her sequins, no coat, stomping one patent-leather pump on the concrete and casting occasional foggy breaths behind her as she looked to the taxi which waited in the street. Once I hadn't shown in her office, she must have checked at the Belvedere, then called a hasty search party of one.

I opened the various locks and bolts I've mounted on the front door to shield me from the Bogey Man and his captain in arms, Mr. S/D. We stood with the glass of the storm door between us. Brushy's long white gloves were wrapped about her, and the flesh of her upper arms, where the daily workouts had never quite slackened the softness, was mottled and goose-bumped from the cold.

"We need to talk," she said.

"Attorney-client, right?" I'm afraid I was smirking.

She turned to wave off the taxi, then snatched the door open in her own decided way and, as she stepped up on the threshold, smacked my face. She struck me open-palmed, but she's a strong little person and very nearly put me on my seat. We stood in the doorway in the midst of a nasty silence, with the rugged breath of winter flowing around us and invading the household.

"I just predicted to our partners that all the money was going to be returned by tomorrow at 5:00 p.m.," Brushy said.

"Did anyone ever tell you that you're too smart for your own fucking good, Brushy?"

"Lots of people," she answered, "but they've only been men."

Brushy smiled then, but the look in her quick eyes would have fit well on Hercules. She was not taking any crap. Not that she'd never forgive me. But she wouldn't back off. Those were her terms. I rolled my jaw to make sure I was all right, and she stepped in beside me.

"You've misjudged your man," I said.

"No, I haven't." When I didn't respond she approached me. She put her sly little hands on my hips, then slipped her chilly fingertips into the expandable waistband of the tuxedo pants I was still wearing. She shook her wind-draggled hair out of her face so she could see me squarely. "I don't think so. My man is attractively nuts. Impulsive. A practical joker. But he's in touch. Really. In the end."

"Wrong guy," I said. I touched my cheek one more time. "What's going to happen to you when the money doesn't come back? Huh?"

She kept watching me with the same intent light, but I could see her beginning to melt down inside. Her bravery was fading.

"Answer me," I said.

"I'm in big trouble. Everybody will ask what I knew. And when."

I put my arms around her. "Brushy, how could you have been such a chump?"

"Don't talk to me like that," she said. She laid her head on the silly frills of my shirt. "It makes me sad when you pretend you're mean."

I was going to tell her again she had the wrong guy, but went instead to the front closet and groped in the gummy pocket of Lyle's leather police jacket where he hid his cigarettes. I brought the pack back for us both. I asked her what she had in mind.

"What about the truth?" she asked. "Isn't that an alternative? Telling the truth?"

"Sure, I'll just give Gino a jingle: 'Pardon me, Pigeyes, you got the wrong guy behind bars. I'd like to swap places with Jake.' Gino's already hoping for that."

"But doesn't somebody have to file a complaint? I mean, what if it's all right with TN? I can explain this to Tad. Mack, I *know* Tad. Give me twenty minutes with him. He'll *love* you for scaring Jake this way. He'll think it was just what Jake deserved, having someone turn the tables on him for a while."

"Twenty minutes, huh?"

Her face fell. "Go to hell," she said. She sat on Nora's old rose-printed sofa and scrutinized the spotted meal-colored rug, caught between anger and some scandalized sense of her life.

"What's your deal with this guy?"

"Not what you think."

"So what is it? Pals? Sodality meetings?"

She went through a retinue of reluctant gestures—evasive looks, nervous fretting with her cigarette—always committed to protecting her secrets. Finally, she sighed.

"Tad's asked me to be the new General Counsel at TN. I've been thinking about it for months."

"You replace Jake?"

"Right. He wants somebody whose independence he trusts. And who'll spread TN's business around a lot more over time."

Tad of course had not arrived at the top by accident. He knew corporate politics, too, and this move was slick. Wash and his coterie on the TN board wouldn't have stood in his way if Jake's replacement came from G&G.

"Martin doesn't think the firm can survive without a big share of TN's work," I told her.

"Neither do I. Not in the long run. That's why I was reluctant."

Jake was gone now, though. Tad would make the change anyway. Brushy's course was clear. I saw the future.

"And what happens to Mack under the Brushy plan for the world, with Emilia as General Counsel of TN and G&G a wreck at sea?"

"You're a lawyer. A good one. You'll find work. Or"—she smiled somewhat, the shy-sly routine—"you can be kept." She got up and put her arms around me again.

I still had my cigarette in my mouth and I drew back with the smoke in my eyes.

"Wrong guy," I told her. I broke away and headed upstairs. She followed to the bedroom eventually. She considered my canvas, the Vermeer mounted on the easel, before turning to watch me pack.

"Where are you going?"

"To the train. Which will take me to the plane. Which will take me far away."

"Mack."

"Look, Brushy, I told you. My pig-eyed former colleague, Detective Dimonte, already smells bullshit in the air. He said so when I called him."

"You can handle him. You've handled him for weeks now. Years."

"Not now. He's flat-out said he thinks I'm dirty. He's thick-witted but he's like a cow. He always ends up in the right place." I went to the easel. I thumbed through my sketchbook and threw it in the bag.

"Why, Mack?"

"Because I'd rather live rich and free than in the penitentiary."

"No, I mean, why? The whole thing. How could you do this? How could you think you wouldn't get caught?"

"You think everybody's as smart as you are? The only reason you figured it out is because screw-loose here ran his mouth. You really believe you'd have seen it if I hadn't told you from the jump about how much I'd love to steal the money myself or how much I hate Jake?"

"But don't you feel bad?"

"At moments. But you know, once it's done, it's done."

"Look." She started again. She put her hands together. She lifted her pert rough-skinned face. She tried to sound even and rational, to look persuasive. "You wanted to make a point. You wanted to get Jake, all of us, you wanted to hit us where we live. And you did it. You felt ignored, undervalued, wounded. Deservingly. And—"

"Oh, stop."

"—you want to get caught."

"Spare me the psychoanalysis. What I wanted was to do it. There's such a thing as infantile pleasure, Dr. Freud. And I got mine. And now I'm doing the adult and responsible thing and saving my ass. Just like you're going to do very shortly when they ask you to account for five and half million dollars which you said would be repatriated tomorrow." I pointed at her. "Remember the privilege," I said. "Attorney-client."

"I don't understand," she said and bounced herself off the bed in sheer frustration. "You have to hate everyone. You do, don't you? Everyone. All of us."

"Don't manipulate."

"Come on. Don't you see how angry you are? My God. You're Samson pulling down the temple."

"Please don't tell me about my own moods!" I'm sure for a moment I looked violent. "Why would I be angry, Brush? Because I had such great choices? Should I have whored around like Martin to cover Jake's hind end? Just so Jake could ignore me while Pagnucci pushed me toward an ice floe, after I've surrendered my adult years to this place? I mean, how does Pagnucci put it when he bothers to justify himself? 'The marketplace speaking'? I forget the part of the theory, Brushy, which explains why the people the market fucks over are supposed to let the tea party continue for everyone else. So I showed some initiative, entrepreneurship, self-reliance. I helped myself. Those are free market concepts too.''

She didn't say anything for a while. I took off my pants and my shirt and hopped around in my underwear, putting on clean slacks and a pullover. I wore my athletic shoes. Ready to run.

"What about your son?"

"What about him? He'll fend for himself. Or live off his mother. It's high time, frankly, for either one.''

"You're twisted.''

"Sick," I said.

"Hostile.''

"Granted.''

"Cruel," she said. "You made *love* to me.''

"And meant it.'' I looked at her. "Each time. Not something every fella could say to you.''

"Oh.'' She closed her eyes and suffered. She wrapped her long white gloves around herself. "Romance," she said.

"Look, Brush, I've seen ahead of the curve from the start. I told you this was a bad idea. I think you're a great human being. Honest Injun. I'd share your bed and your company for the foreseeable future. But Pigeyes is now on the scene. So that leaves only one alternative: You have a passport, you're welcome to come. As I've always said, there's enough for two. The more the merrier. Wanna start a new life? My impression is that you're pretty attached to the one you have here.''

I held out both hands. She just looked at me. The idea, I could tell, had never crossed her mind.

''No sweat,'' I told her. ''You're doing the right thing. Take it from your old buddy Mack. Cause I'll tell you the real problem, what I keep coming back to: Honey, you ain't gonna respect me in the morning, not when you think this whole thing through.''

She eventually said, ''I could visit.''

''Sure. Tell Mr. K. He'll love hearing that from his new General Counsel: I'm going to visit that crackpot who destroyed my law firm and looted your company. Face it, Brush, your life is here. But hey, prove me wrong. I think you've got ties. And''——I closed the case——''I've got to go.''

I grabbed her by the shoulders and kissed her quickly, hubby speeding off to work. She sat on the bed and put her head in her hands. I knew she was too tough to cry, but I said something anyway.

''Let's not be mushy, Brushy.'' I whined it. I made it rhyme. I winked at her from the doorway and told her goodbye. I saw Lyle down the hall, dressed only in the jeans in which he'd fallen asleep, groping to make something of the voices. Maybe he'd been roused to check out his dream that it was Mom and Dad, home again and happy, one of those dream things that never really happened. I stood on the threshold considering them both, enduring one of those moments. Up to now I'd been beset by great emotional constipation. Pour me a couple of drinks and I could bawl my eyes out, but in the present I'd felt smug and stuck on myself. Only with the actual instant of departure at hand was the pain beginning to mount.

"God, Mack," said Brushy, "please, *please* don't do this. Think about what you're doing to yourself. I'll help you. You know I will. You know how hard I've tried. I mean, at least, Mack, think about me."

Oh, what about her? She imagined, no doubt, I was running from her. And I'd succored myself with disarming comparisons to the devotion of others—Bert to Orleans, Martin to Glyndora. But who was I kidding? My heart was suddenly sore and afflicted, full of a hurt that seemed to double its weight.

"Brush, there's no choice."

"You keep saying that."

"Because it's the truth. This is life, Brushy, not heaven. I'm out of alternatives."

"You're only saying that. You're doing what you want."

"Fine," I said, though I knew in a way she was right. Standing with her now, I was abruptly some kind of suffering blob, ectoplasm without boundaries in which the only point of form was a hurting heart. But even in that condition there was a sense of direction. It wasn't hope, I saw now, that drove me. Perhaps I was at one of those passes again, doing what I most fear, because otherwise I'm paralyzed, worse off than some slave in chains. But the compulsion was strong. I was like that figure of myth, flying with his wings of wax toward the sun.

"Mack, you talk about my life? What am I going to say? How am I going to explain why I let you run, why I didn't just call the police?"

"You'll think of something. Look." I took one step back into the room. "Here. Go to your pal Krzysinski. Right now. Today. Tell him the *whole* thing. Everything. Tell him how you couldn't stand by and let me ax Jake. Tell him how noble you are. And smart. You were going to sucker-punch me. Get me to give the money back. *Then* turn me over to the police."

She was sitting on the bed, holding on to herself, contracted with pain, and she recoiled a bit. The words seemed to strike her with the reverberating force of an arrow. I thought at first she was again overwhelmed by shuddering wonder at my facility when it came time to lie. Then, at once, I saw something else.

I held absolutely still.

"Or did I just get it right?" I asked her softly. "Was I finally reading your mind?"

"Oh, Mack." She closed her eyes.

"Grab me and love me and let them haul me away? The Brushy-first plan?"

"You're lost," she said. "Do you even know the truth? When you're seeing it? When you're telling it?"

She thought she had me with that one, but you could nail most folks like that from time to time. I refused to back off anyway. Brushy, as I well knew, was a four-wall player. She had all the angles in her head, and I'd found something, some notion, some line of reflection she couldn't keep herself from seeing, any more than I could help being myself at that moment, full of a liberating spite, an anger so generalized but intense I didn't really know what was making me mad—her or me or some unnameable it.

"Was that the idea?" I put on my coat. I picked up my bag. "Well, you haven't been listening." I said it again and I suspected by now she believed it.

"You've got the wrong guy."

B. Pigeyes Isn't

The little light-rail system that ties Center City and the airport was one of those genius planning notions for which Martin Gold occasionally takes some credit. He was counsel to the Plan Commission and our bond folks worked out the financing. The thing doesn't always run on time, but in rush hour it beats the traffic, which you can see stalled on either side as the train rambles down the divider strip. The LR, as it is known around town, terminates in an underground station, a big cantilevered space with the rising ceiling of a cathedral and various-colored block-glass windows lit from the rear to simulate daylight.

I arrived there lugging my case and still yelling at Brush in my head, purging my guilt and explaining again how she ought to be blaming herself, there are no victims. I was a few steps from the train when I saw Pigeyes at the end of the platform. I'd had a few intense and unsettling visions of Gino nabbing Jake, booking him, printing him, putting him in the police station cell where the gangbangers would grab Jake's Rolex right off him without even saying thanks, and I briefly hoped I was seeing things. But it was Gino. He was leaning on a pillar in his scruffy sport coat and cowboy boots, picking his teeth with a fingernail and eyeballing the passengers as they alighted from the cars. No doubt about who he was looking for, but I didn't have too many places to go. He'd caught sight of me already and the return trip to the city wouldn't begin for another five minutes. So I kept walking. It was daytime, but I was dead in my dreams, headed for that mean dangerous stranger. He had me now and my blood was suddenly pumping at 30 degrees.

As he watched me approach, Gino's little black eyes were still and the rest of his big face harsh with purpose. He was ready to chase me, maybe to shoot. I took a quick peek for Dewey but it looked like Pigeyes was flying solo tonight.

"What a delightful coincidence," I told him.

"Yeah," he said, "what. Your girlfriend gimme a call. Said I ought to track you down." Pigeyes faked a smile without showing his teeth. "I think she likes me."

"That so?"

"Yeah." He was not near my height. But he got good and close. His face was in mine, all his heavy breath and body odors. He was chewing gum. I was taking in a lot at that moment. I'd been soft about Brushy. I thought she believed all that stuff, attorney and client, my secret to keep and hers not to tell. She could give me one hundred reasons the privilege didn't apply; I could probably give you fifty of them on my own. But I hadn't thought she'd sell me out. She was always tougher and quicker than I figured.

"What'd she say?" I asked.

"Nothing much. I told you. We talked about you."

"How good I am in bed?"

"I don't recall that being mentioned." Pigeyes smiled the same way. "Where you off to?"

"Miami."

"For?"

"Business."

"Oh yeah? Okay I look in your little case there?"

"I don't think so." He had one hand on it and I tightened my hold.

"I think maybe there's a bankbook in there. I think you got a connecting plane for Pico-whatever. I think maybe you're about to take flight."

He took a step closer, which didn't seem physically possible.

"Careful, Pigeyes. You may catch something."

"You," he said. He opened his mouth and tried to belch. He was standing on my toes now, so that if I moved I'd fall over. If I pushed him, God knows what he'd do. "I knew I'd catch a piece of you. Guy asked me to do this thing, this whole caper, and I said to myself, Maybe you'll meet up with your old pal Mack."

I believed that. Pigeyes was always looking for me, and I was always watching for him. Immovable object. Irresistible force. In that moment that is worse than dying, the flaming terror that wrests me from sleep, Pigeyes will always be there. How do we explain that? I turned this over in my mind, that same old thought, that there are no accidents, there are no victims. And then, God only knows why, I had one last revelation. I was okay now. I knew it at once.

"I think," said Pigeyes, noting the intensity of my

expression, "you just wet your socks. I think when you walk, your shoes'll go squish."

"I don't think so."

"I do."

"No, I've got this too well figured."

"That's what you thought."

"That's what I know. You always talked too much, Gino. Especially to me. Couldn't live with me thinking I'd skunked you one more time, could you? You couldn't resist straightening me out when I called to tell you about Jake this afternoon."

His belt buckle was still under my belly, his nose was one inch from mine. But a certain caution had set in. Once badly bitten, Pigeyes was an unusual creature in the depth of his respect for me.

"All of these things I should have seen," I said, "I couldn't explain. Why you never arrested me. Or served me. You must have thought I was deaf, dumb, and blind. You say you knew I was spreading manure this afternoon with that myth about Archie and Bert, but you left Bert alone even so. Why? Why didn't I see it? You'd been called off. Whoever hired you in the first place unhired you. The capo, or whoever. What are they holding your marker for, Pigeyes? Gambling? Dope? G-Nose take one sniff too many? Or are you doing it for one of the old buds from the neighborhood? You're the guy, though, right? You're the one who was supposed to get Archie to give up his connect. You're the one who was going to make the connect grateful for staying alive so he could throw basketball games for some ungrateful types. It's you."

I had his attention now.

"How could I not catch on? I should have known as soon as you said you were following Kam with the credit card. Christ, where the hell do *you* come by that card? I know where I found mine. And the envelope was open. There were footprints on the mail. You were in there before me, Gino. At Bert's. And that wasn't the first time.

"The first time, Pigeyes, was when you guys put Archie in the icebox. You were gonna scare Bert into telling what you wanted to know. Big-time lawyer? I don't care whose windpipe is severed. Bert couldn't call the police, because he can't answer their questions. He's not gonna throw away the money, the shingle, by admitting to the coppers how he's been fixing national sporting events. He'd be meat when he saw that body. He'd be yours. Bert would cry on the telephone. Beg for his life. He'd tell you just where to find this Kam fucking Roberts who Archie kept mentioning. Bert would even have to take care of dumping Archie himself. It never figured he'd run—not when all he had to give you was a name. But he wasn't there when you called."

Pigeyes's dark eyes were caving in. He was not as smart as me. He'd always known that.

"So that was trip number two to Bert's, right? Looking to find where he'd gone. That's when you picked up the credit card. And decided you better lujack Missing Persons' case. That way you'd be the only cops looking for Archie. You got Missing to send the case to Financial— those guys are always happy to lose one—then you went sniffing around the Bath to see if you could get a hot lead on Kam.

"And if guys didn't do dumb things, Gino, they'd never get caught. Why didn't you get the body out of Bert's when you had the chance? What was the problem? Upstairs neighbor at home that week? Not enough help? But when you nabbed me with the bank card down at U Inn you knew where I'd been. And what I'd seen. I mean, Gino, who's the guy who taught me to look first thing in the refrigerator? But dim-bulb Malloy, he gives you the perfect excuse to go back in. With a warrant, no less. That's why the body disappeared then, right? Before I could tip Homicide. That's why we had our scene in the surveillance van. So you and Dewey could get me on paper in front of a prover, saying I never saw anything of interest in Bert's apartment. I mean, Christ, was I dumb or what? Why would *you* wanna make me say that? And that's why you didn't want to run me in on any of the chickenshit that you could have. It wasn't worth it. I'd be out in an hour, so why take the chance that I'd have second thoughts and start free-associating to some stray Homicide dick about this body I'd seen?"

Somewhere along there he had gotten off my toes. If we had been having this discussion out on a dark road, he'd have shot me. But we were standing in the subway stop underneath the airport, and various passengers burdened with heavy cases and garment bags were coming and going on the platform, glancing back to get a load of what looked like it might turn into a fistfight. Pigeyes was not a happy dude.

"Tell me you didn't start out to murder poor Archie, Pigeyes. Tell me you just got carried away when Archie wasn't coming up with Kam's real name. Tell me you felt sorry.'' I pulled away the briefcase from where he had continued resting his hand.

"What do they pay for a job like that? Fifty? Seventy-five? You getting ready for retirement, is that it? I'll make that in interest in a couple of weeks." For emphasis, I tapped him right over the heart, grazing my fingertips on the same dirty knit shirt he'd been wearing for days. We both knew I had him.

"So turn me in," I said. "Think I can swing a deal for immunity if I give them a hit man who walks around with a star?" He didn't answer. He'd been to Toots's school. "The guy I hung with," I said, "my old partner, he wasn't that bad. He cut some corners, he did some things. But he didn't torture people for money. Or dope.'' I picked up my suitcase and nodded to him.

With that, I had a serendipitous recognition. If you gave Pigeyes truth serum he'd explain to you how this was partly my fault. Years ago I'd taken his good name. And cheated to do it. The neighbors, his ma, the people in church—they now knew what he was. He couldn't pretend. He looked to them suddenly the way he looked to himself. I put it to him out loud, here in the public way.

"You're a bad guy," I said.

You know how he responded: *Fan-gul! Fan-gul!* "I gotta take that from you?"

"Have it your way, Gino. We're both bad guys." I didn't mean it. I wasn't as low as him, not in my mind. We were two different types, two different traditions. Pigeyes was like Pagnucci—really tough, really mean, capable of courage and cruelty. One of those men for whom it's always wartime, where you do what you have to. I was the second in a line of thieves—deceivers. But we'd both touched bottom, Gino and I, and I saw then that was the point of all the bad dreams: I am him and he is me, and in the dark feelings of night there is no discernible difference between wishing and fear.

So that's where I left him, on the train platform. I looked back once, just to make sure he was absorbing the full effect of letting me go. I made my plane to Miami, and now the connection to C. Luan. I'm sitting here, in first class, telling the end of my story to Mr. Dictaphone, whispering so that my voice is lost below the engine's great hum.

When I get off, these tapes, every one of them, are going to Martin. I'll send them Federal Excess. I will be wildly pie-eyed by then. At the moment, on the fold-down table in front of me, four little soldiers, hot off the attendant's drink cart, are dancing with the vibration of the plane, the sweet amber liquid bobbing in the throat of each bottle so that I can almost feel it in mine. I will be drunk, I promise, for the rest of my life. I'll travel; I'll sun. I'll engage in prolonged dissipation. I'll think about how ecstatic I was sure this gig would make me and how, in that frame of mind, I couldn't tell the right guys from the wrong ones, the merely plain from the plain ugly.

Now that I'm done, I'm thinking that telling this whole thing was for me. Not for Martin, Wash, or Carl. Or U You. Or Elaine up above. Maybe it's me I meant to entertain. A higher, better me, such as Plato described, a kinder, gentler Mack, capable of greater reflection and deeper understanding. Maybe I wanted to make another of those failing efforts to figure out myself or my life. Or to tell it all in a way that is less ambiguous or boring, remembering it with my wit sharper and my motives more defined. I know what happened—as much as memory serves. But there are always blank spots. How I got from there to here. Why I did whatever at a particular moment. I'm a guy who's spent so many mornings wondering just what happened the night before. The past recedes so quickly. It's just a few instants under the spotlight. A couple of frames of film. Maybe I recount it all because I know this is the only new life I will get, that the telling is the only place where I can really reinvent myself. And here, I am the man who controls not just the words but with them the events they record. The higher, better Mack, sovereign over history and time, a fellow more earnest, honest, more fully known than the mysterious guy who has always recovered from one disaster just in time to rush on to another, that incomprehensible being who blinks at me in the reflections on windowpanes and mirrors, who treated most of the settled items in his life with scorn.

Nonetheless, I've had the final word. Taking blame where it is due and otherwise assessing it. I don't make the mistake of confusing that with an excuse. I have regrets, I admit, but who doesn't? Still, I had it wrong. Completely.

There are only victims.

ACKNOWLEDGMENTS

A number of friends allowed me to prevail on them
with an early draft of this book. To all of them—
Barry Berk, Colleen Berk, David Bookhout,
Richard Marcus, Vivian Marcus, Art Morganstein,
Howard Rigsby, Teri Talan—and to the
sustaining lights,
Annette Turow and the world's
greatest literary agent,
Gail B. Hochman,
special thanks.

PRAISE FOR CH   S

"The queen of paranormal romance . . . I love everything she does."
— J. R. Ward

"A new cast of characters as heartwarmingly interesting as those in her Drake Sisters novels and as steamy as those in her Dark novels."
— Fresh Fiction

"Ms. Feehan is at the top of her game with this magical romance."
— The Romance Readers Connection

"Suspenseful, engaging—fraught with magic, action and romance . . . I HAVE to read the next one in the series."
— Smexy Books

"An action-packed and romantic tale. Awesome as always!"
— *RT Book Reviews*

"Avid readers of Ms. Feehan's work should dive in."
— Fiction Vixen

"Once again, Christine Feehan brings a sizzling story of seduction and sorcery to her readers. Fans of previous Feehan novels, particularly the Drake Sisters series, will be enchanted by her new series."
— Examiner.com

"Stunning, vivid, lushly visual . . . It's the perfect way to escape."
— Romance Books Forum

"A wonderful love story . . . Truly original."
— Penelope's Romance Reviews

"Gives the reader a thrilling and heartwarming story . . . I can't wait to read the next one."
— ParanormalHaven.com

Titles by Christine Feehan

JUDGMENT
ROAD

CHRISTINE FEEHAN

JOVE
New York

A JOVE BOOK
Published by Berkley
An imprint of Penguin Random House LLC
375 Hudson Street, New York, New York 10014

Copyright © 2018 by Christine Feehan
Excerpt from *Covert Game* copyright © 2018 by Christine Feehan
Penguin Random House supports copyright. Copyright fuels creativity, encourages
diverse voices, promotes free speech, and creates a vibrant culture. Thank you for
buying an authorized edition of this book and for complying with copyright laws by not
reproducing, scanning, or distributing any part of it in any form without permission.
You are supporting writers and allowing Penguin Random House to continue to publish
books for every reader.

A JOVE BOOK and BERKLEY are registered trademarks and the B colophon is a
trademark of Penguin Random House LLC.

ISBN: 9780451488510

First Edition: January 2018

Printed in the United States of America
1 3 5 7 9 10 8 6 4 2

Cover art © Cliff Nielsen / Shannon Associates
Cover design by Judith Lagerman
Torpedo Ink logo design by Patrick J. Mears
Book design by Kelly Lipovich

For my beloved grandson and wild child,
Mason Stottsberry. I'm certain you're riding a Harley
across the sky, surfing the longest comet and teaching
the angels to dance. You'll always be in our hearts.
As promised, this one is for you!

FOR MY READERS

Be sure to go to christinefeehan.com/members/ to sign up for my private book announcement list and download the free ebook of *Dark Desserts*. Join my community and get firsthand news, enter the book discussions, ask your questions and chat with me. Please feel free to email me at Christine@christinefeehan.com. I would love to hear from you.

ACKNOWLEDGMENTS

As with any book, there are so many people to thank. First, Nancy Rich, who was gracious enough to talk to me at length about clubs. Ed, my go-to man, who answers my questions when needed. A huge shout-out to Patrick J. Mears from Spread Eagle Tattoo for working so closely with me to create my vision and concept of the Torpedo Ink graphics. Brian and Sheila, for competing with me during power hours for top word count when I wanted to move fast on this one. And Domini, for always editing, no matter how many times I ask her to go over the same book before we send it for additional editing.

TORPEDO INK MEMBERS

Viktor Prakenskii aka *Czar*—President

Lyov Russak aka *Steele*—Vice President

Savva Pajari aka *Reaper*—Sergeant at Arms

Savin Pajari aka *Savage*—Sergeant at Arms

Isaak Koval aka *Ice*—Secretary

Dmitry Koval aka *Storm*

Alena Koval aka *Torch*

Luca Litvin aka *Code*—Treasurer

Maksimos Korsak aka *Ink*

Kasimir Popov aka *Preacher*

Lana Popov aka *Widow*

Nikolaos Bolotan aka *Mechanic*

Pytor Bolotan aka *Transporter*

Andrii Federoff aka *Maestro*

Gedeon Lazaroff aka *Player*

Kir Vasiliev aka *Master*

Lazar Alexeev aka *Keys*

Aleksei Solokov aka *Absinthe*

NEWER PATCHED MEMBERS

Gavriil Prakenskii

Casimir Prakenskii

PROSPECTS

Fatei

Glitch

Hyde

ONE

The wind blew off the sea as the three Harleys made their way through the last series of snaking turns and hit the straight stretch on Highway 1 running parallel to the ocean. The night was well under way, a fact that Savva "Reaper" Pajari was well aware of. He had to report to the president of his club, Czar, the moment they arrived back in Caspar, but time didn't matter for that. Even if Czar was at his home in Sea Haven, tucked in close to his wife, Reaper'd just hit the roof and climb in through the bedroom window. He'd done it more than once.

He lived for two things: riding free and fighting. He needed to feel solid muscle under his knuckles. He needed to feel fists hitting his body, tapping into that well of ice that covered every emotion. That swift explosion of violence and sweet pain as fists connected was his life, and had been his life since he was five. Now, he needed to stay sharp somehow, in this new bullshit direction the club had taken.

He rode along the highway, aware of the others on either side of him. Brothers, some for over thirty years. Men he counted on. Men he called family. Still, he was apart from them and he knew it, even if they didn't. He turned his head toward the ocean. Waves sprayed up into the air, rushing over rocks and battering at the cliffs. Sometimes he felt those battered rocks were him, time wearing him away, little by little.

His soul had been gone so long ago that he couldn't remember having one. Now, his heart was slowly disappearing. There wasn't a place on his body without a scar. He had another to add from this last trip. He also would have to have Ink tat his back, three more skulls to add to the collection of those resting in the roots of the tree on his back.

Viktor Prakenskii, the man known as Czar, was the best man he knew. Reaper's job was to stand in front of Czar, his self-appointed task from the time he was a little boy. He'd been doing it for so long now, he didn't know any other way of life. He stood in front of all his brothers and sisters—in Torpedo Ink, his club. He was proud to wear the club colors. He'd die for those colors and still detested any mission he ran if he had to take them off.

They turned off the main highway onto Caspar Road leading to the town of Caspar, where they'd set up home. They'd designed their compound around the old paymaster's building for the Caspar logging company. They had spent the first few months working on the building, turning it into their clubhouse. It housed multiple bedrooms, a bar, their meeting room—known as the chapel—and a kitchen. They shared bathrooms, whichever was closest to their assigned sleeping room. Czar had insisted each of them purchase a home nearby. He wanted those roots put down deep.

Reaper didn't give a damn where they all slept. As long as he could defend his club and their president, he was fine. The compound had a bed and right now, he needed one. He was forty-eight hours without sleep. He'd stitched up the wound in his side himself, making a piss-poor job of it too, but all he'd had was a little whiskey to disinfect it, and that had burned like hell. It still did.

They rode up to the compound, and Storm and Keys parked their bikes while he scanned the lot. Either Czar was home or at the bar. Reaper was fairly certain he'd be at the bar waiting for a report. He didn't like to disturb his wife, Blythe, or their four adopted children. Reaper didn't shut his bike down and waited for the others to turn to him.

"Goin' to find Czar," he said, unnecessarily, but they were looking at him like he should say something. He didn't like stupid shit, like the formalities that seemed so important to others. He didn't care if people liked him; in fact, he preferred they stay the hell away, except for his brothers, who understood him and made it clear they expected him to at least talk once in a while.

"I can report in," Keys offered. "You could use the downtime."

Reaper shook his head. "Won't be able to sleep right away. I have to check on him anyway. You know how I am."

"Want company?" Storm asked.

He shook his head. "Not necessary. Savage will be with him, probably a few others. Get some sleep. We all earned it." Savin "Savage" Pajari was his birth brother. Like Reaper, he acted as sergeant at arms, protecting Czar at all times. Between the two men, they had their president covered whether he liked it or not around the clock. "I already texted Czar we were comin' in when we were an hour out."

He was certain if he did that, Czar would go to the bar rather than have Reaper come to his home—exactly what Reaper wanted. It was the new bartender. Reaper didn't like anything out of the ordinary. He didn't trust it. The woman was definitely something out of the ordinary. Code could find dirt on anyone, but he hadn't found a single trace of her anywhere. She worked for cash, under the table. She wore designer jeans, but she drove a beat-up car on its last leg, rust breaking through the paint. The fucking thing smoked every time she turned the engine over.

Torpedo Ink had a garage up and running. Did she take her car there to get it fixed? Hell no. She drove off every night thinking no one knew where she was going. That was the hell of it. She drove back toward Fort Bragg, took Highway 20 and turned off at the Egg Taking Station, a campground in the Jackson Demonstration Forest. Why the fuck would a classy woman be bartending in a biker bar, drive a beat-up Honda Civic older than she was and be camping? It made no sense. He didn't like puzzles, and Anya Rafferty was not only a puzzle, but one big headache.

Reaper had watched her for over a month. Five weeks and three days to be precise. He'd learned she was a hard worker. She listened to people, remembered their names and what they liked to drink. She flirted just enough to get good tips, but not enough to cause fights. She was generous with the waitresses, sharing tips she didn't have to share. She was careful and guarded yet gave the illusion she was open. She was kind to those less fortunate.

He'd watched her give a homeless man a blanket she carried in her car, and twice she'd brought him coffee and a meal. Twice she'd spent money he was certain she didn't have to get food or shoes for someone living on the streets. She seemed to have an affinity for the homeless, and he was certain she knew all of them by name. She volunteered in the soup kitchen Saturday mornings even though she couldn't have had more than a couple of hours of sleep.

She didn't flinch around the bikers, but it was obvious she wasn't from their world and didn't have a clue how to fit in. She took her cues from Czar and sometimes asked him questions. She'd never asked Reaper a single question, but she sent him a few shy smiles, which he didn't return. He'd spent more time in the bar in the five weeks she'd been there than he'd ever spent in a bar in his life.

Reaper glanced away from the compound, up toward the

bar. He could see the lights shining through the dark from the banks of windows. His heart accelerated. His cock jerked hard in his jeans. That was unacceptable and that was why the woman had to go.

Every one of those in his club had been taught to be in complete control of their bodies at all times. They'd been beaten, starved, tortured and had unspeakable things done to them in order to shape them into disciplined killing machines. He felt very little emotion and certainly not physical attractions. The bitches partying hard, getting it on with anyone and everyone, did nothing for him. Not one thing. He often walked through a room full of half naked or naked women and his body didn't so much as stir.

One look at Anya Rafferty. Listening to the sound of her voice. Her fucking laugh. The way all that hair fell around her face like a dark cloud. A waterfall. She had more hair than two women put together, and he found he thought a lot about that hair when he should be thinking about keeping his president alive. Or himself. He refused to allow his cock to drive him. That part of his anatomy would never drive him. He didn't trust anyone, especially not a woman who made his body ache until his teeth hurt.

He sighed and turned his Harley, heading for the bar. He'd told Czar Anya had to go. She was a problem. Nothing about her added up. Nothing. Protecting Czar was his number one priority, and if she wasn't forthcoming, she had to go. He told himself that shit, but he knew it wasn't the truth. He hated bullshit. *Detested* it. Especially when he was trying to bullshit himself. He could make all the excuses in the world, but the truth was, the bartender upset him. She got under his skin without trying.

Once in the parking area, Reaper swung his leg over his motorcycle and forced himself to stand upright, his two feet planted on solid ground. He'd been on his bike so long he wasn't certain he had the legs for earth any longer. Placing his dome on the bike he did a casual sweep of the parking

lot. In that one moment, he took in every detail of the cars and lines of motorcycles parked there. He recognized several of the bikes. Two prospects were lounging close, keeping an eye on the bikes. He didn't acknowledge them, but he saw every detail. He removed the small leather bag from one of the compartments hidden in his bike and made his way across the parking area toward the bar, still looking around to every conceivable parking spot.

What he didn't see was the bartender's old rust bucket. He paused for a moment at the bottom of the stairs, breathing deeply, not knowing if that made him happy or if his mind went somewhere he refused to acknowledge. She was gone. Czar had done what he'd asked, and her presence was removed. That should make him happy. Well, he was never happy. He didn't know how to be. He'd forgotten. Relief maybe—except now he had to go to the campground and make certain she was okay. Damn it. He swore under his breath and climbed the steps leading up to the bar. His gut burned like hell with every step, but it wasn't nearly as bad as the ache in his chest.

Music poured out of the building, a loud, drubbing beat. That only added to the pounding in his head. He ignored it and yanked open the door. Raised voices and laughter mixed with the clink of glasses. Funny, now that it was an established biker bar, the place was hopping almost every night.

He stepped to the side of the door and took a long look around, noting every jacket or vest with colors. Mostly small-time clubs, or weekenders. A couple of legitimate road warriors. Three wannabe hard-asses, drinking, looking for women and most likely a fight. Five, sitting in the corner, badasses wearing Demon patches. They noticed him the moment he walked in. All five were packing and they weren't drinking, at least not enough to say they were there for a good time. He did a quick inventory of his body. He could move fast if needed. He never minded a good fight and most likely, any minute, he'd be welcoming one. He let the Demons see his gaze linger on them before he allowed himself to scan along the bar.

He had a gun tucked in his waistband at the small of his back. Another was down in his boot along with a knife. A third gun was inside his jacket, easy access, just a cross-body pull and he was in business. The truth was, he rarely used a gun or a knife when he killed. He preferred silence, but weapons came in handy occasionally and he was proficient in the use of all of them.

He knew he was looking for the bartender. Anya. He fucking loved that name. It suited her face. Her voice. It was possible her piece of junk car had broken down and she had hitched a ride with someone. He didn't see her anywhere and it pissed him off that he'd even looked. Worse, the pressure in his chest grew.

Tonight's bartender, Preacher, looked harassed. He glanced up from the sea of customers and shot Reaper a welcoming grin, his eyes scanning for wounds, dwelling for a moment on the blood on Reaper's shirt and then jumping back to his face. Reaper gave him a nod, indicating he was fine, and Preacher nodded back. He jerked his chin toward the hall behind the bar. There was a doorway to the left of the bar, but Reaper stalked across the room and flipped up the jointed wooden slab that allowed him to walk through the opening to get behind the bar. He moved down the long hallway straight to the office.

The door to the back office was closed, signifying a meeting of some kind. If the door was closed, any waitress or non–club member stayed out. Unzipping his jacket, Reaper went right on in, hoping Savage didn't put a bullet in him as he waltzed through the door. Savage was unpredictable at times. His brother gave a quick scan of his body, much the way Preacher had. Czar stood up to face him, doing the same. He frowned when he saw the blood. Shit, he'd forgotten his shirt was a mess. It wasn't all his, either. Savage's gaze jumped back to his face.

"I'm fine," he said, to stop the questions.

Code had been poring over books with Czar, which was laughable. Czar hated number crunching and only pretended to listen to Code half the time. With Czar and Code at the table were two other club members, Absinthe and Ice, Storm's twin brother. All had their eyes on him and the blood on his shirt. Something was up to have so many gathered this late at night.

"What happened?" Czar snapped before anyone else could say anything.

Reaper tossed the leather carrier bag onto the table. "Assholes called us in a little late. Who the fuck goes off to hide, leaving their wife and kid to face certain death because they don't want to pay a gambling debt? He's supposed to be the big-assed president of a club and he's hiding in a dark hole surrounded by his brothers, leaving his woman and child exposed." He poured a wealth of disgust into his voice, because, really? Who did that? Who could live with themselves? How could his brothers look up to him? "I wanted to cut his throat." He glared at Czar. "Don't send me on a mission like that one again. Next time, I won't have such restraint."

Czar studied his face. Reaper kept his expression blank. Czar shook his head. "First, tell me how you got blood all over your shirt. Is that yours? Or someone else's? Please tell me it isn't the client's."

Reaper shrugged because, hell yeah, some of it was that douchebag client's. He'd gotten exactly what he deserved. The club was called Mayhem. Laughable. Truly laughable. In Reaper's opinion the bullshit president had deserved to die so, yeah, he'd shown restraint. "Maybe I didn't make myself clear. The weasel ran up a gambling debt and then, rather than pay it, when the goons showed up to collect, had his boys get him to safety. He went across two states and only then remembered he had a wife and daughter."

"And he contacted us to get them to safety," Czar reminded, his tone mild.

"*After* he made sure his ass was in the clear. Two days later, Czar. Two fuckin' days. He didn't even warn her. By the time we got there, so had the idiots sent to collect. Bodies or money." He touched his side. The burn of that blade going in was still fresh. "They decided to have a little fun with the two of them before they cut them up. Girl is fourteen."

"You stepped between the girl and the knife," Czar said.

Reaper didn't answer. What was there to say? Was he really going to let a pathetic excuse of a human being kill a fourteen-year-old girl and her mother? Not happening.

"How many stitches?" Code asked.

"What the hell difference does it make?"

"Someone's in a bad mood," Code observed. "Five? More?"

"Six. I don't need the doc. I took care of it myself."

A small hoot of derisive laughter went up. Reaper flipped them off.

"I gotta see this," Ice said. "If it's anything like the last one you stitched up yourself, you'll be looking like Frankenstein in no time."

"Already does," Code said. "Just a little."

Reaper glanced at Savage. He hadn't cracked a smile and there was a slight hint of worry in his eyes, but he didn't say anything.

"You taking antibiotics?" Czar asked.

"I will. I'll get them from the doc."

"Tell me what really happened, because otherwise, I'm going to think you're slowing down. You could have killed these idiots in seconds, Reaper. What the hell were you doing to take a hit that cost you six stitches?"

"We're done talkin' about this," Reaper declared.

"We're done when I say we're done." Czar's voice dropped an octave, low enough that the room went silent. Low enough to caution Reaper that his president wasn't asking.

Reaper shook his head. When Czar talked like that, he

expected answers. "Didn't want the kid to see me kill him. I directed the hit where I knew it wouldn't do much damage. She had Down syndrome and she was terrified. Her father left them hanging out there like that. Pissed me off. I didn't want the kid to suffer any more than she already had."

Czar sighed. "Reaper, she's the daughter of the president of a motorcycle club. The Mayhem club may not be as big as the Diamondbacks, but they're violent. She's bound to have seen things."

"She was terrified," Reaper repeated. "It was my call. I had her close her eyes, turn her head away, and then I killed the bastard. Before she could look, I covered her eyes and took her the hell out of there."

"You don't get to take chances with your life," Czar hissed, slamming his palm on the table.

Reaper leaned toward him. Looked him in the eye. "I've been takin' chances with my life since I was five years old. I been killin' that long. I know how to take a blade when I need to."

"The point is, you didn't need to," Czar snapped.

"My call. I'm there, I have to make the decision. You'll be happy to know, I didn't kill her father when we delivered them safe to him, although it took restraint. He was willing to pay us the fee we asked for, but not pay his gambling debt? He put his wife and daughter in jeopardy, Czar. What kind of man does that?"

"The club paid for the fee to have us retrieve them and bring them safely to him. The gambling debt is personal."

"You know, if they catch up with him, he'll give us up in a heartbeat. He was already plannin' to do that. I killed the two hit men. Whoever sent them out will want revenge."

"All of you wore a mask and gloves," Czar said. "He never saw your faces."

"No, but Mr. Mayhem President put a tracker in with the money," Reaper said. "He was plannin' on selling us out to get out from under his debt. He'll give up the link online, that's all he's got." He smirked. "Killed the club member followin' us and put the tracker in his fuckin' mouth."

"Code said you texted him to shut down our online operation and he did. We'll set up again later."

"Just so you know, full disclosure and all, I beat the livin' hell out of that pissant president, Czar. Don't know if he lived or not, but if he did, he's not going to be the same man. He was going to give us up, and that tracker was the last straw. Already wanted to shove a knife down his throat."

Czar shook his head and pushed the bag of money across the table to Code. "Add that to everything else. We're in good shape. We've got most of the businesses up and running. Still working on some of the houses. Reaper, are you going to actually move into yours?"

Reaper shrugged. He had no idea what the hell he'd do with a house. Czar had insisted all of them have an actual home. His was on the edge of the cliffs with a stairway leading down to the cove and two roads winding around Caspar so he had access to old logging roads. He liked to know he could escape anything easily.

"Soon." He just required a bed. He had one at the compound. He didn't need a house to go to every night. Empty. Echoing every time he walked through it because he'd put the minimum amount of furniture in it. A bed. That was pretty much it. Maybe, if he was lucky, the entire structure would fall into the ocean and he'd be done with it.

He changed the subject. "Got a few badasses sitting at a table. Waiting, Czar. They request a meeting with you?"

Czar nodded slowly. "Waited until you got here. Code found out a few things about them. They're from up north. Demons, smaller club, but already have a reputation. They want to talk about extending their reach, using us to do it."

"Probably drugs." Ice spoke. "We don't do that shit anymore. We're rehabilitated."

The others laughed. "Yeah. We don't spread drugs around, but we kill people when it's needed," Absinthe said.

"A few hard-asses out there as well, think they're real tough from the way they're actin'," Reaper continued. "Look like trouble and they're drinking heavy. Talkin' loud. Didn't even notice when I walked through the door, but the others did. The Demons. We aren't a well-known club. Barely established. We aren't even the big club in this area. Why come to us?"

Czar shrugged. "Don't know until they talk to us."

"Did they indicate they found us online through the website Code has?"

Czar shook his head. "Don't think so. Think they chose us because we're here, on the coast." He studied Reaper's face. "I wouldn't meet like this with someone wanting us to do a hit." He made it an assurance.

Reaper moved away from the door toward the back of the room where the overhead light didn't quite reach. He was tired. Exhausted. Even if he went to bed, he knew he wouldn't sleep, or if he did, he'd have a nightmare. He had them often now, something he was careful not to share with the others—not even Savage.

"You up for this?" Czar asked. "We could tell them to come back."

"Told you, Czar, someone else should handle inquiries, make certain they're legit. We all have a lot of enemies, but you most of all. Don't like you out in front like this," Reaper said. He put his back to the wall, making certain he had a clear shot to the door. Savage was on the other side of the room. They'd have the five Demons boxed in.

"If you could, you'd build a wall around me," Czar pointed out.

"You've got Blythe and the kids," Reaper said. "Aside from the fact that you're the brains for all of us, you've got them."

Czar's face softened. "I've got all of you. I don't worry because I have my brothers." Still looking at Reaper, he continued. "Ice, go get them and bring them back. They come through the door one by one. You stay behind them. Box them in. Absinthe, you search them. Tell them they want to give up their weapons."

Reaper was happy Czar wasn't taking any chances. Absinthe could influence with his voice. He was smooth and charming and the moment he put the suggestion in the minds of the Demons, they'd hand over their weapons without hesitation. If there was going to be a firefight, it wasn't going to happen on Torpedo Ink's chosen home turf.

"Stay to the left of the room at all times," Reaper said, all business. "Savage and I will have them in a crossfire. None of you want to get caught in that. We'll mark the ones between us we'll take. The rest of you look comfortable and friendly." He was good at planning death. He'd done it hundreds of times. Czar was equally as skilled, probably his teacher, since Czar was older. He'd been the one to get them all out of that hellhole alive.

Czar nodded his head and Ice was gone, leaving the door open. Reaper leaned against the wall, relaxed. This was his world, one he knew intimately, and a woman like Anya Rafferty with her long dark hair and her bleeding heart didn't belong anywhere near it. He sighed, realizing she'd crept right back into his thoughts.

He should have followed her all the way into the campgrounds. They were a good distance from the entry, if he remembered correctly. His club had had a shootout there. A massacre. It was a place outlaws could hide, and that meant Anya wasn't as safe as he'd like her to be. He shut down that line of thinking. He wouldn't want *any* woman camping alone out there.

He straightened suddenly. What if she wasn't camping alone? There could be a man out there. She could be supporting some shiftless loser who didn't want to work or take care of his woman. He should have gone all the way in. Damn it. Now his head wanted to explode and wasn't in the game where it should be, just as he knew would happen.

The woman was wreaking havoc, and it was a damned good thing Czar had sent her on her way. Still, he had to check on her, just to be certain she was safe—just the way he would with any woman.

His bullshit meter was screaming at him but he ignored it as the first man stepped through the door. This would be their top enforcer. Sergeant at arms. The badass of the five. He studied the man's face as Absinthe took his weapons. Yeah, he was the real deal. What was he doing in a small-time club? There had to be more to the Demons than they had ferreted out. The enforcer passed over his weapons without a murmur, his eyes sweeping the room, taking in the setup, realizing he couldn't see either Reaper or Savage clearly.

Both men had a way of blurring their image. It was useful when hunting others. They'd developed the skill over the years, starting when they were toddlers and Czar had them practicing. Most of it was learning to choose the right place to stand. The shadows covering them. The stillness one needed so the human eye wasn't drawn in that direction.

The Demons came in one by one, just as Czar directed. Ice tailed them, closing the door behind them. Reaper made certain to watch each of them as they came through, noting which one would be the likeliest to start trouble—that would be Tether, the youngest, the one eager to prove himself. The first one, the one they called Razor, was the one Reaper determined was the most lethal. He marked him as the one to take down first.

"I'm Hammer," one said. "President of the Demons." His patch confirmed that.

"Czar." Their president extended his hand and shook. He indicated the chairs surrounding the oval table.

Only Razor hesitated. He realized sitting put them in a vulnerable position, especially without weapons. Absinthe had conducted a search of each man even after they'd obeyed his soft, whispered command to hand over their guns and knives. He was thorough about his search, knowing Czar

was in the room. They all protected their president. Czar
didn't always like it, but it didn't matter. He was their
number one priority at all times. In this instance, if things
went to hell, it would be Code's job to take Czar down and
protect him with his own body, while Reaper, Savage, Ice
and Absinthe killed every one of the Demons.

Soft feminine laughter drifted down the hall and Reaper
almost stiffened. Almost. He cursed under his breath but
managed somehow to stay disciplined enough not to move.
That sounded a lot like the bartender. He had to keep his head
in the game, not worry about some woman who'd probably
been sent to kill Czar. Well, okay, he didn't believe that for a
moment. He'd think about her later and the fact that those
three hard-asses were looking for women. Right now, the only
thing in his world was replaying step-by-step in his mind how
he would kill the Demons and protect his president.

Razor had to go first; Reaper would draw and shoot him
in the head. Two bullets to make certain, although he didn't
miss. The president second, even though Code and Absinthe
would go for him as well. Savage would take the two sitting
to either side of their president, the ones assigned to protect
him, just as Code was assigned to Czar. The two were named
Weed and Shaft. Their cuts had their road names as well as
their offices. It was unusual for a president, enforcer, secretary and road captain to all come to a meet at once. Something big was up.

"How can I help you?" Czar asked.

There was a small silence while Hammer sized him up.
Razor was clearly uncomfortable with the setup, but he kept
his mouth shut. His gaze moved restlessly around the room,
always looking for anything that might threaten his boss.

"I'll get right to the point," Hammer said. "Heard good
things about your club. You're small, but you get things done.
We've got a situation. We're small too. Three chapters. Good
territory. We keep it as clean as possible. Don't have trouble
with the locals. Hear you're in pretty good here as well."

Czar shrugged, but didn't respond, his eyes steady on the Demons president's face.

Reaper had seen him give that look a thousand times. He'd learned it in the school where hardened criminals ruled and if you wanted to stay alive, you didn't make mistakes, like flinching at the wrong time.

"We have a route that goes from our territory to here. Stops dead and then picks up on this side of Santa Barbara."

Czar shook his head. "This is Diamondback territory. You want something to go through their territory, you contact them, pay the fee and they'll take it through."

Hammer hastily shook his head. "They swallow any pipeline, use it for their own purposes and use a club like ours as pawns. They'd want a cut of what we're doing, and that cut would be more than we could afford right now."

"You get caught, they'll declare war and wipe you out. They have more chapters than just about any other club in the world. They're loyal to their brothers, and out of respect we're careful not to do anything that would step on their toes, like creating a pipeline without giving them a cut."

Hammer and his secretary, Shaft, exchanged looks. To Reaper they seemed a little desperate.

"What exactly is the product?" Czar asked.

"Counterfeit money."

Just the fact that Hammer told them straight up was another indication that they were desperate.

Czar leaned toward him. "I don't like bullshit. I'm two seconds from putting a gun to your head and pulling the fucking trigger. What are you doing here? My old lady is waiting for me and I don't like keeping her waiting. Not. Ever. So, don't waste my time."

Instead of looking worried, or even scared at Czar's words, Hammer looked as if he was relieved. He took a deep breath and told the truth. "This is going to make my club look weak, and we're not. We got in bed with a club that runs a gambling operation. We help launder the money. Recently they found out about the counterfeit operation we've been running. We keep it slow. Nothing big, feeding a few bills here and there along an eastern route we've got. They want to take it big-time."

"How'd they find out about your operation?" Czar asked, always going for the most pertinent fact immediately.

"One of our prospects decided to try his hand at gambling and got in over his head. Instead of coming to the club, he traded his debt for information." Hammer's tone was strictly neutral.

"Where is he now?" Czar's voice dropped an octave.

Just that tone put the room on edge. Reaper had seen him do it so many times, but each time it happened, he was always impressed.

"He didn't survive," Hammer said.

"Anyone else talkative in your club?" Czar asked.

"The men in this room are men I trust implicitly. The ones in my chapter, same thing. The other chapters wear our colors and I'll fight for them and with them, but I don't know them as well as I do my own brothers."

That was an honest answer. No one could know every man in every chapter of a club.

"They all in on the counterfeiting?"

He nodded. "Distribution. We have the plates. They're good plates. I've got a good man who knows what he's doing. We play it safe and don't get greedy, we can make it work, make it untraceable back to us. This other club wants to get greedy."

"How big are they?" Czar asked.

"That's the thing. They're ghosts. They call themselves Ghosts."

Reaper stirred then, something he never did. That called attention to him and the Demons enforcer nearly came out of his seat. Reaper ignored him. "A word, Czar."

That was never done either, especially by one of Czar's men. They always allowed Czar to make his play. They talked it over after.

Czar didn't give anything away as he rose and jerked his chin toward the only other door in the room. Reaper let him come across the room and then stepped so his body was between his president's and the Demons.

Czar closed the door and turned to him, his eyebrow raised, concern on his face.

"The bastards going after the Mayhem president's wife and child, the one we saved, it was the Ghosts after them. They weren't wearing colors, but they referred to themselves as 'ghosts,' as in I'd never see it coming because his friends are ghosts. Last words out of his fuckin' mouth."

"You think the Demons are setting us up?" Czar asked.

Reaper loved his brother. Czar believed in him, in his ability to protect not only him, but his family, and the others. He believed in Reaper's instincts, his gut. Right now his gut was telling him the Demons were in trouble with this new "ghost" club.

Reaper shook his head. "Got a bad feelin' in there. They don't want to be, but they're scared. Something more is going on than they're telling us."

Czar clapped him on the shoulder. "Never think for one minute that I don't need you, Reaper. It's always been you and me. We lived in hell. Now we're not, we're calling our own shots. Don't let the newness, the difference, fuck with your head."

Reaper knew he'd been taking chances with his life. Czar knew it too. Now, with his brother looking him in the eye, he nodded curtly, not wanting to talk about it. It was the damn woman. The bartender. That hair. That laughter. Her fuckin' skin. It looked so soft he'd been tempted to actually touch her. He didn't touch anyone unless he planned to kill them—then they were dead. No one touched him unless they planned to get dead—then they were. Not unless they were one of his brothers—he'd had to learn to tolerate that.

"Let me go in first, Czar," he cautioned. "Stay behind me. I'll get you to your seat and then slide back into position. Question him after I'm where I need to be."

Czar didn't argue as he often was prone to when it came to matters of his safety. He detested the others putting their lives on the line for him, but as far as Reaper was concerned, it was the one thing Czar had no say in.

Reaper led him back in and over to the table without seeming to. He was casual about approaching the table, leaning in to snag some peanuts that were sitting in a can toward the middle. If they'd been at Czar's home, his old lady, Blythe, would have put those peanuts in a bowl. He sauntered back to the wall.

Czar waited until he was nothing more than a blur, just as he'd asked him to. "This club you call the 'Ghosts,' are they an actual club? They ride? They have colors?"

The Demons president nodded. "They came to us with respect. We have no idea of their numbers. They're up by the Oregon border. We don't have much intel on them." He rubbed his jaw. "My fault. I should have looked into them more, but at the time my old lady was . . ." He shook his head. "No excuses. We did what we did. I need to be able to run my product through this territory. I need you to do it."

"You haven't said why. How did they get you to come to us? Did they specify us?"

Hammer shook his head again. "No, don't know if you're even on their radar. I think they're looking to get their hooks into the Diamondback club. A club that big must have gamblers. You and I both know if they start a war with them, the Diamondbacks will swallow us."

"Even so, why not tell them to go fuck themselves? You don't know their size. They have no reputation. Why not just kill them?" Czar's voice was mild.

"They have my wife." Hammer dropped the truth right into the middle of the room and the tension went up a thousand percent. Suddenly there was no air.

Czar looked up to meet Reaper's eyes. Who the hell made war on women and children? Who had the balls to kidnap the wife of the president of the Demons and hold her until the club did what they were told?

"How long have they had her?" Czar asked, suddenly all business. He went from mildly interested to total concentration.

Reaper loved the man, the way his brain kicked into high gear and he was aware of every detail, absorbing it, coming up with ideas and sorting through them for pros and cons until he knew exactly what to do.

"They took her two nights ago. Gave me a week to get it done. Came to you first. Her health . . ." He shook his head. "She had cancer. Just finished her last treatment. Immune system is down. She's only twenty-six. Young. Damn it, I don't know where she is, but she's a good old lady. She'll keep her shit together and she'll know I'm coming for her. I just need to buy some time to find her."

"These people don't play nice," Czar said. "This isn't the first time they've used a man's family against him. In that case, they were there to kill the wife and daughter. I don't think you have a whole hell of a lot of time."

"You willing to help?"

TWO

Czar glanced around the room. Ice was first, tapping out a soft rhythm on the table. Savage was next, tapping on the wall, short one-two beat. The others followed until it was only Reaper. Czar was patient. Reaper weighed the consequences. No matter what, he'd go after the Ghosts, find them, take back the woman, and kill them, but if they did this, partnering with the Demons, it exposed the club and Czar even more. Their reputation was growing in the outlaw world. They didn't need that.

Reaper took his time weighing the pros and cons just as he had in every other situation. Finally, with some reluctance, he tapped his agreement, a short, one-two-three tap. Czar nodded.

"Don't give a damn about your pipeline," he said, "but your wife is a different matter. No one fucks with our families. I need all the information you have on the Ghosts. Our man will start tonight finding out about them as well. If they're an official club, we'll know immediately and then we'll have all the information we need for recon. As far as stalling them, so they think you're working on it, tell them, if they ask, that you've got an appointment to see the president to pitch the idea of a partnership with the counterfeit money. He'll believe it's the president of the Diamondbacks. I'll handle the Diamondbacks if there's a problem. They owe me a favor or two."

Considering that Reaper had taken out two of their worst enemies to buy peace between the two clubs, Reaper felt that favor or two was a little more. The reputation of Torpedo Ink had grown faster than they'd wanted it to grow, bringing a few visits from the Diamondbacks. Things had been tense, but as always, Czar had worked it out. They didn't do anything to compete with the Diamondbacks, which, unbeknownst to that club, was perfectly okay with Torpedo Ink.

Soft laughter drifted into the room through the vents. Under the door. The sound surrounded him. He looked around the room, but no one else seemed to notice. Czar asked dozens of questions. He shook hands with Hammer and, at the door, Absinthe gave back every weapon, remembering exactly who had had what.

"We'll get her back," Czar assured.

Hammer nodded, his face bleak. "These guys play for keeps."

Czar smiled. There was no humor in that smile. He looked like the predator he was, all the easy charm gone. "So do we," he said.

The minute the Demons were gone and out of the bar, Czar turned back to his brothers. "Code, get on this tonight. I know everyone's tired, but we're going to run out of time fast. Reaper, get some sleep, even if you have to drug yourself. You look like hell, and I'm going to need you on this. Possibly you and Savage."

Reaper shook his head. "One of us stays on you."

"Every member of this club was trained as an assassin, Reaper. They know how to protect me."

"What happens if these Ghosts get wind of you and your

family? Blythe? The girls? They've already been through hell. Kenny? He has too. I'm not willing to take the risk. Your family is ours. Under our protection. We don't . . ."

"Fine. Just get some sleep. Get out of here."

Reaper was more than happy to get out of there. He had things to do, like go to the camp and see if Anya was still there. He told himself all that laughter was some other woman and they just sounded alike. Still, as he went down the hall, his gaze was already looking for her. He stood in the middle of the hall behind the bar.

His heart jumped. She was there. What the fuck? He'd been out getting himself nearly killed for the club. He'd asked one thing. *One thing.* She turned her head to look over her shoulder, flashing him a smile. His heart tripped. Went crazy. He ignored her. Wouldn't let himself notice how much fuckin' hair she had. Or that even swept back and tied in a long ponytail it nearly reached the curve of her ass.

He refused to see that her tits were perfection. Under that tight tee, the generous swells were outlined, lush, soft. That tucked-in waist only emphasized she'd been gifted with breasts and hips, a biker's dream. He wasn't about to notice the way her worn blue jeans cupped her ass so lovingly. Or the way that ass swayed when she walked. Or the fact that he had so many dirty fantasies about her ass and tits and hair. If any other man he knew had those same thoughts about her, he'd kill them.

He turned and stalked back down the hallway to jerk open the door of the meeting room. "What. The. Fuck." He spat the words at Czar. "What the *fuck* is she still doing here?" Reaper demanded. "I told you to get rid of that bitch. She doesn't belong, and you know it. She's probably a cop looking to take us down. That or she's a rich bitch slumming, wanting to fuck a biker. Either way, she's trouble."

He was desperate not to feel. Not to have his cock as hard as a fucking rock or his mind in chaos, or his heart stuttering like it might stop any minute. That didn't happen to him.

Not. Ever. He'd lost all that when he was a teenager and he'd had more women than he could ever want. He'd continued to lose that throughout his twenties when he'd had to run errands for the man who'd kept him locked up and then sent him after targets, men and women he'd had to kill in order that his brothers and sisters survive. So much sex. None of it good. He'd trained to have control of his body. He had no heart. No soul. He didn't need a woman to find her way under his skin. He was near panic and Reaper in a panic wasn't good. People around him would die.

Czar's gaze shot past him, and the president of Torpedo Ink stood up slowly. It was a measure of the chaos the woman created that Reaper hadn't known she was right behind him. He always knew. Czar's life depended on him knowing. He swung around to face her.

Her beauty took his breath away. Not just beauty. She was a fucking sex kitten, with all that dark, wavy hair. So much of it. A man would kill to feel all that hair sliding over his body, to see it on his pillow and brushing over his cock and thighs right before she wrapped her mouth around him.

Her eyes were large and a deep, emerald green. He'd fantasized far too much about those eyes staring up at him when she came apart in his arms. Right now, they blazed at him, twin gems sparkling with pure anger. He didn't speak. He rarely spoke to those outside the club, certainly not women. Her, in particular. She was everything he wasn't. Classy. Sex kitten classy, but still, she looked like she belonged in some penthouse, not in a biker bar.

"I haven't done one single thing to you," she hissed. "Not one. I've worked hard, and I need this job." When he didn't reply, the fury in her eyes increased and she stepped close, driven by pure desperation. That was in her eyes as well. "Answer me. You sit there staring at me night after night, like I'm some hideous insect you want to step on, and now you're trying to lose me my job."

He didn't answer. Czar knew what the fuck he wanted.
He'd said his piece and he'd meant it.

She shoved him. Put both hands on his chest and shoved
hard. He didn't move, but his fingers closed over her wrists
like vises, holding her palms against his chest. Every one
of his brothers stood, knowing no one put their hands on
him and lived. No one. He'd let her. He could have stopped
her. He was that fast. His brothers knew that as well.

Tears shimmered in her eyes, and something inside his
chest broke. He thought letting her touch him would end it,
the insane obsession he had with her. There was no other
word for what he was feeling, sitting in a bar for over a
month, not saying a word, just looking at her. Just trying to
keep his wayward cock under control. He'd failed miserably.

Letting her put her hands on him was a terrible mistake.
Now he had the sensation of her palms, the heat she generated. It felt like she seared her way right through his shirt
to his skin. Then through his skin to his bones. That deep.
Just melted right through. He could smell her scent. It was
light, grapefruit and tangerine? Whatever it was, it enveloped him and seeped right through his pores. It was an
aphrodisiac and his body responded to it, making him so
damn hard it went from an ache to sheer pain. She had to
be a witch or a woman trained as he was trained, to ensnare
the opposite sex and then deliver the kill.

He should have shoved her away. He shouldn't be holding
her tight up against his body so she could feel the steel shaft
in his jeans. He stared down into her eyes. Those glittering
green gems. The fury slowly receded until she looked afraid.
She should have been. He had no idea what he was going to
do with her. He knew no one would stop him if he dragged
her into the next room and shoved his cock into her. Claiming her. What the hell was wrong with him to even think
that? They might stop him if he killed her. *Might*.

His brothers knew no one touched him. They also knew
he could have stopped her long before her hands ever

reached his chest. He hadn't, and they were all right there, watching him, wondering what the hell he was doing. He was wondering that himself.

"You don't put your hands on a man's bike, Anya," he said softly. "And you sure as hell never want to put them on a man like me without an invitation, you got that?"

The tip of her tongue touched her upper lip and then her teeth bit down on her lush lower one. She nodded. He had to bite back a groan of need. Looking down into her face, all soft skin, large eyes, the kind a man could stare into for the rest of his life, he knew he shouldn't have ever spoken to her. He should never have said her name, not in front of the others. They knew him too well and everything he'd done so far was completely out of character for him.

He didn't want to let her go, but holding her close was putting his brain into a kill-or-be-killed frenzy. It wasn't safe. She wasn't safe with him. He let her go abruptly, noting as he did that he shouldn't have held her wrists so tightly. She'd have bruises. He didn't put bruises on women. He was so fucked. He had to stay away from Anya Rafferty.

She swallowed hard and, still looking into his eyes, directed her question to his president. "Do I still have a job, Czar?"

He could tell she was holding her breath. He was. He didn't know which way he wanted the answer to go.

Czar looked to Reaper. "It's up to you, brother. You want her gone, she's gone."

Shit. Shit. Fuck. She just stood there looking at him, her eyes wet, lashes dripping. He took a breath. There was no saving her. None. "I couldn't give a shit," he lied.

"Get back to work, Anya," Czar ordered. He was looking at Reaper, not at the bartender.

Relief flooded her eyes. Her face. Her body. For a moment she hung her head, just breathing deeply, and then she straightened her shoulders, lifted her chin and gave Reaper a snippy look. "Thanks, Czar, and I came back here to remind you we're still short on that order. Nothing came in today. I checked everywhere. Either someone took it, or they lied and didn't send it."

"Who signed for it?"

"I think it was Preacher. He was on yesterday as well as tonight. When he checked the order, we were short. I rechecked like he asked me to, and he was right."

"We'll take care of it," Czar said and glanced over his shoulder at Ice. Ice nodded his understanding. No one stiffed them. No one. If the company wouldn't make good, they were going to be very sorry.

Anya turned and walked back down the hall toward the bar. Reaper watched her go the entire way. His gaze was glued to her ass. She had a sway that made his mouth water.

Czar nudged him. "Go home."

"You didn't fire her." He didn't stop looking at her. That long thick ponytail called to him. He'd wrap all that silk around his fist, and use it to guide her head wherever he wanted it to go. He was so damned hard he couldn't take a step.

"More reason to keep her around than let her go."

"Never asked you for a fuckin' thing, Czar. Not one. Never. You didn't give me this. Why?" Because he needed to know.

"You had your chance to get rid of her. You didn't take it."

"You know fuckin' well I wanted her gone. Why is she still here?"

"You sat in that bar every night for over a month, Reaper. You followed her home every night. You want her gone. You tell me why she bothers you so much."

"That's not the point." She was at the bar now, leaning toward a customer. Laughing that laugh. Giving that to one of the wannabe hard-asses. He was looking down the front of her shirt. Leering. The lean had her bending over slightly. Just enough to make Reaper's head want to explode. "She isn't what she wants us to believe. That could be a threat to you." Even as he said it, he knew it was bullshit. He knew it wasn't the truth.

"I think she's more of a threat to you," Czar said.

Reaper tore his gaze from Anya and looked to the man he'd respected since he was not quite five years old. Czar wore a smirk. Reaper shook his head. "Has it ever occurred to you that I'm a threat to her? You know me. You know what I do. Hell, you were the one who sent me out for that first kill. I kill people."

"People who hurt others, Reaper. There's a difference. You don't kill indiscriminately. We're not assassins anymore. That was what we were trained for. It was our job. We did what we had to do to survive. We all survived because of you. Eighteen children out of nearly three hundred. Those eighteen live because of what you did for us. You aren't what you think."

"I am. You're the one who doesn't see it because you feel you owe me."

"Is that what you think? I feel I owe you? I would have let her go if that was the only reason. Figure it out, Reaper. Now get some sleep. And have Lana or Alena look at that mess on your ribs before you go to bed. Then tomorrow, I want you to see the doc."

Reaper stalked down the hall without acknowledging him. No way in hell was he going to bed now. There were three idiots leering at the bartender, and he wasn't going to allow them to hurt her in any way. She sure as hell wasn't going home with one of them—not that she'd ever done that. The two waitresses often did, but never Anya. But she closed. That meant she was alone in the bar and anyone could wait in the dark for her.

He found a table to the rear of the bar. It was dark and the music was loud, annoying the hell out of him. He sat down with his back to the wall where he had a good view of the bar. She was beautiful. He leaned his head against the wall and stared at her, not caring if anyone noticed. He was too damned tired to care. He was mesmerized by her. The way she moved. The way she talked to her customers. So easy. He didn't have that gift and he never would.

Betina, one of the waitresses, appeared in front of him. "Reaper, you're back. It's so good to see you." She bent forward until her breasts nearly tumbled from her tank top. She wore it two sizes too small, and her red lace bra showed against its black fabric.

"Coffee." One word. He hated even giving her that. He kept his eyes on the bartender. On Anya. She noticed the waitress at his table and was already pouring his coffee for him. Still, for some reason, there was a little frown on her face as she watched Betina practically shove her tits in his face. He wanted to push the woman away, but that would require touching her.

"Anything I can do for you tonight? Just say the word and I'll be happy to oblige." She smiled again. All predatory.

Anya was suddenly there. She put the mug of steaming hot coffee on his table. "Betina, we're packed tonight. You know what Reaper's order is, so get moving."

Betina looked shocked. She straightened immediately, glared at Anya and then flounced away. Anya turned away as well. Not looking at him. Not saying one word to him. He had no idea what his body was going to do before his brain kicked in. He caught her wrist, preventing her escape.

She stood facing away from him, taking a deep breath. He waited. She finally turned toward him, biting her lip, looking apprehensive. He turned her wrist over very gently, the pad of his thumb sliding over her delicate skin. There were marks already coming up. Smudges. His fingerprints. On her skin. A part of him. That should make him feel like a fucking dick, ashamed of using such force. He was strong. He prepared his body every single day for war. He knew better than to man-handle a woman.

He loved those fingerprints on her wrists. He took both hands, using his thumbs to slide over them, wishing his prints were tattooed on her. "You have trouble with those idiots at the bar, you look my way. Understand me?" It was an order. He didn't ask. The three were getting drunker, and they wanted trouble. They also wanted Anya. She nodded, and he allowed her to pull her hands away. She walked back to the bar.

Betina leaned into the bar, getting drinks for one of the tables. Deliberately she'd chosen to slide in between the three troublemakers. One palmed her butt, squeezing and making obscene noises, his tongue out of his mouth, simulating what he might do to her. She threw her head back and laughed, pushing back into him with her ass. When she turned with the tray, she made certain her breasts brushed his arm.

The bar had a bouncer they employed, Fatei, one of the newer prospects. He'd been in one of the schools in Russia with Czar's brother, Gavriil. He seemed to be a good man. He never interfered unless a waitress gave him a signal. He didn't now. Reaper picked up the mug and took a sip of coffee. It was fresh and hot. He needed that. He stretched his legs out in front of him to ease the wound in his side. To ease the ache in his jeans.

He shouldn't have spoken to Anya. He shouldn't have allowed her to put her hands on him. He could still feel her palms, just as if they'd melted through his shirt, right beneath his colors, and branded him to the bone. To the fucking bone. That's what she'd done. He touched his chest. He shouldn't have unzipped his jacket before going into the bar, but the blast of heat always got him when he came in from a ride, so he'd done what he always did. Now he wore her brand.

He wanted her. He considered that. Let it settle in his mind. It wasn't an order to seduce a woman, it wasn't the school run by pedophiles and sick, twisted criminals forcing him to perform every sex act imaginable. This wasn't something contrived. For the first time in his life, his body chose. He chose. His choice was her. Anya Rafferty.

She should have left while she could. Czar should have gotten her out of harm's way. He'd tried to save her. Sort of. Now it was far too late because he'd become obsessed with her. He wished it was Betina. He could use Betina and throw her away. She wanted that kind of lifestyle, but Anya held herself aloof. She was that elusive one. There, but not really. Unattainable. She didn't encourage or want her customers to put their hands on her.

He took another swig of coffee. The good thing was, he'd come in so late, the bar would close soon. He was tired and he wanted to get some sleep. He'd make certain Anya was safe and then hit the sack and sleep as long as his body would let him.

He drifted, letting his mind wander, but like always, when he did, he didn't go to a good place. He hadn't seen many good places. When he was four, his parents had been murdered and he'd been taken from his home along with his younger brother and two older sisters to a "school" to rehabilitate them and make them into useful tools for their government. It turned out that Sorbacov, the man behind the murders, was using the students in their particular school for his own twisted pleasure.

He jerked awake, refusing to go there. Russia was a long way away. Sorbacov was dead and could no longer force them to kill for him. The survivors had banded together, forming their club, coming to the United States, to the little town of Caspar where they made a permanent home. It was Czar's idea. His woman lived on the coast and he'd come to claim her. Her and every kid needing help for miles. Where Czar went, the rest of them followed.

"Honey, need another drink. Come over here. I'm feelin' neglected."

Reaper narrowed his eyes when one of the three men called out to Anya loudly. She was serving another customer down toward the end of the bar. Preacher had hung it up for the night, leaving the closing to her. Most of the bikers were gone, just a few hanging on until the bitter end. Reaper didn't like it that the three hard-asses were still there. They were waiting for the bar to close so they could go home with the waitresses, or they were waiting for Anya to be alone.

She sent a sweet smile to the biker. "One minute."

She turned back to her customer, smiling at him. White teeth. A soft pink lipstick showing off that pretty bow of a mouth. He couldn't decide whether he liked her upper lip or lower lip better, but suffice it to say, he loved her mouth. He didn't love it when she gave that biker her smile.

Very slowly he drew his legs back from the long sprawling stretch, pulling them from under the table so he could move fast if the man got out of hand. He glanced at Fatei. The prospect was alert, already having marked the three as trouble. The call for last drinks had just gone out so it was legitimate enough to ask for a drink. Just about everyone left in the bar was calling out, not that there were very many.

An old man sat on the stool at the far end. His name was Bannister and he was often in. He had long gray hair and a grizzled beard. He wore an old vest that had seen better days, but the man was obviously an independent and he'd been in their world a long time. He rarely talked, he was polite, but he gave off the vibe that he wanted to be left alone. He finished off the last of his drink, but didn't leave. He turned toward the three hard-asses and just waited.

Anya smiled at them, both hands on the bar, no leaning this time. "What can I get you? We're closing in ten minutes and I'm shutting it down, so last call."

"We're waiting for you, baby," one said. "I'm Deke. This is Trident and Skid."

She flashed another smile. "Drinks."

"Another round of shots."

She nodded and turned away. One of them reached across the bar, making a grab for her hair. She was gone before he touched it, and his hand dropped away. Fatei closed in on one side, and to Reaper's surprise, the older man did so on the other. All Anya had to do, if she felt unsafe, was raise her voice and call for help or press the little panic button behind the bar. Either way, Torpedo Ink members would pour out of the meeting room and annihilate anyone threatening her. She worked for them. She was under their protection from anyone but him. He was the only one she'd need that kind of protection from because he was right there, waiting to take anyone out who even looked as if they might harm her.

Deke looked to his left at the older man and laughed, straightening up. He was a big man and knew it. Most likely he hadn't been challenged very often. "Got a problem with me, old man?" His tone was belligerent.

Anya swung around, put the glasses on the bar unnecessarily loud and poured out the shots. "There you are. We don't tolerate trouble in here, Deke. Bannister is a regular."

She reached across the bar and put her hand on the older man's shoulder. Reaper hated that. More than hated that. She was touchy-feely. What the hell was that about? He'd never understood. Watching her, he knew it was a part of her makeup and she'd need that. When she was with him, there wouldn't be touching other men. Not. Ever. He'd have to learn to touch her often. To give her that.

What the *hell* was he thinking? With him? He was out of his fucking mind. She did that. She twisted him up until he couldn't think straight. He wasn't looking for a woman, an old lady. He wasn't looking to be tied up in knots. Things like this didn't last. Certainly not with a man like him. He was no prize. He was hard as nails. A killer. A scarred, weary man needing to inflict pain on others and have it inflicted on him. What place was there for a woman with a man like him?

"You want coffee, Bannister?" Anya laughed softly at the old man's expression. "Don't look at me like that. It won't poison you."

Deke, looking annoyed, tossed his shot back. "Let's go,"

he snapped to the others, looking around the bar. He spat at Fatei's feet and then stepped off his stool, hitting Bannister hard with his shoulder.

"Trash," Bannister said. "They'll never be more than that. Men like that find one another. You got anyone waiting around to make certain you'll be safe tonight? I don't like the way they were looking at you."

Reaper moved just enough to creak the floorboards. Bannister spun around and then settled when he recognized Reaper and the Torpedo Ink colors. He nodded, relief on his face. "Good. You've got someone."

He started across the room toward the door. Reaper signaled to Fatei to go with him. It wasn't only Anya the three hard-asses might go after. They were mad and drunk enough to pick a fight with the older man.

"You got this tonight?" Fatei asked. "I saw the others leave out the back door."

Anya nodded, mistaking the prospect, thinking he was talking to her. "I'm good, Fatei. Thanks for your help tonight." She glanced at Reaper from under her long lashes. "You don't have to stay. I'll lock up. Czar and the others go out the back door and lock that one."

For his answer, the same answer he'd given her every night he'd been there for over a month, Reaper went back to his table. He was out of coffee and lifted the cup. He needed the caffeine to stay awake. Anya brought the pot to him, crossing the floor and pouring him another cup. He'd had three now, more than he normally ever drank.

Betina and Heidi, the other waitress, collected all the empties and put them in the dishwasher and then wiped down all the tables but the one Reaper sat at and then called it a night. No one approached his table other than to bring him coffee or ask him if he wanted a drink again. They sure as shit didn't bother him to wipe the table down.

He watched Anya walk back to the bar. It was a thing of beauty, the way the woman walked. Her blue jeans were tight, cupping her ass. His palms itched. His chest burned. Yeah, she'd marked him, branded him, the little witch.

She was tall, with legs that went on forever. Legs that would easily wrap around his waist when he picked her up and drove his cock into her. Her hair was gleaming under the lights, and her eyes were large and heavily lashed. He liked the end of the night when they were alone in the bar and the night was all around them. She worked and he fantasized, which wasn't exactly fair, but if he offered to help she would have said no. He knew, because a few times, he'd gotten up and put the chairs on the table for her. She hadn't liked it. He still did it and supposed he would tonight, although it would hurt like hell when he raised his arm on his left side.

"What is it about me you don't like?"

Her voice startled him. Shocked him. She didn't speak to him, he didn't speak to her—that was the unspoken rule between them. She was breaking some law between them. She wasn't looking at him. She was working behind the bar. Cleaning up. Counting the money in the till. She never took a dime or siphoned money off; he knew because he made Code check carefully. Nothing with numbers ever got past Code.

"Reaper, you started this by trying to get me fired. I need the job. I would very much like to know what I've done to make you try to get me fired. I can't afford to lose this job."

She did pause then, tilting her head, looking him straight in the eye.

"You have the job." That much was obvious. Czar, for some bizarre reason, backed Anya, not him. That kind of thing never happened. He didn't want to think too much about what Czar was trying to tell him by letting Anya stay on with him. It didn't matter that Czar had thrown it on his shoulders and he'd ducked giving an answer, Czar knew Reaper wanted her gone.

She blew out a breath in exasperation. "That's not what I'm asking."

"Leave it alone." It wasn't a suggestion.

She looked hurt. God. He fuckin' hated it when she looked like that and he knew he was the one to put that expression on her face. She turned away from him and got back to work, closing the bar. She didn't even throw her usual attitude at him when he put the chairs upside down on the tables to allow the mop to be run over the floor. He was going to have a word with Czar about the waitresses leaving before all the cleaning was done. Anya—or anyone else closing—shouldn't have to do all the cleaning.

Anya was finished by three. She normally was. She was very thorough, making certain everything was done for the next shift before she turned off the lights, caught up her coat and keys and started out of the bar. Reaper did what he always did. He went through the back entrance and around the side of the building to wait for her in the shadows.

Anya thought he'd left. That he'd gotten on his bike and ridden away, leaving her when she got into her car, like he appeared to do every evening. He looked carefully around the parking lot. She had no car. He stood in the shadows, arms crossed over his chest waiting to see what she did.

Anya glanced at his bike. The other Torpedo Ink bikes were gone. Reaper's was still in the parking lot. She'd seen it enough times to recognize it as his. More to the point, there were three others down the street. Reaper had seen them when he did a sweep of the road just below the parking lot. He remained in the shadows, watching her.

She pulled on her coat, giving a little shiver, glanced again at his bike and then looked carefully around. When she didn't spot him, she started walking toward the highway, not on the road, but using the narrow trails in the grass winding through lots to take her where she wanted to go.

"Hey, wait a minute, sweet tits," Deke's voice called out. "Where you going?"

Anya swung around, still on the narrow path, but she looked as if she might run back toward the bar. She'd never make it. Deke and the others had spread out and she could never get through them.

"I'm going home."

"Party with us tonight," Deke invited, moving closer.

The other man with him, Skid, began to circle around behind her. Trident came at her from the left. Deke was closest. Feet from her now.

Reaper stepped out of the shadows. "You ready, baby?" he called. He kept his eye on the main threat, Deke. The man wouldn't like to be thwarted. The other two would follow the biker code and back their brother up. "Hurry up. We don't have all night." That was more of a growl.

To her credit, Anya didn't hesitate. She started back to him. Deke stepped directly into her path and grabbed her arm in a vicious hold. "She's not going anywhere with you," he snapped. "I've been watching this little cocktease all night. She gets a man hard and then she just—" He broke off, screaming as the knife cut through his upper shoulder. It was thrown so hard it went all the way in so the hilt was resting against flesh.

"Get the fuck over here, Anya," Reaper said.

She ran around Deke, didn't look at either of his two friends as they converged on him and, just as he'd ordered, got behind him.

"You're dead! You're a dead man!" Deke screamed.

"Call Czar. Tell him there's three dead bodies he needs to get rid of. He'll send someone to do cleanup. Deke's being a whiny little bitch. I could have put the blade right through his throat, but that was me being nice. For you, Anya. Remember, I was being nice." He was careful to keep his voice low. Conversational. Sneering with contempt in the appropriate places.

"No need to call Czar." Savage, his birth brother, slid out of the deeper shadows. "I'll handle this. You take Anya out of here. No need for her to see this."

"Go, Reaper." Ice stepped out from behind the building.

His brother Storm was there as well. "Preacher's lying up on the roof with a sniper rifle. He said Anya would have trouble with these pricks."

Deke had stopped screaming and cursing. Now, he and his two buddies edged toward their bikes. When they turned away from Reaper, they practically bumped into two more club members, Master and Keys.

Master shook his head almost sadly. "Our bartender is under our protection. Did you think we'd let you put your filthy hands on her?"

"She was coming on to me all night," Deke defended.

"That true, Reaper?" Ice asked. "You sat in that bar and let your woman flirt with pretty boy Deke here?"

"If she had," Reaper said, not denying Anya belonged to him, although what he'd do with a woman was anyone's guess, "I would have fuckin' killed him right then." He kept his voice soft, but he heard her swift intake of breath. He had to remember she didn't know the rules of their world. She didn't understand the violence they'd grown up with or the jobs they'd had as assassins for their government.

"Get her out of here," Savage said again.

Anya shook her head when Reaper turned to her. He didn't like the others doing his dirty work, but then she couldn't be a witness. "Let's go." He was gruff. He didn't mean to be, but he had no idea how to talk to a woman, let alone a woman like Anya, so far out of his league he didn't know how to breach the gap.

She shook her head again. "What are they going to do to them? What's going to happen?"

"Let's go," he repeated, and this time he caught her upper arm in an unbreakable grip. "What happens next depends on them. We're not in it anymore."

"I don't want them dead because of me, Reaper," she whispered, even as she let him drag her to his bike. "Seriously. Not because of me."

"If that happened, it would be because of what their

intentions were, not anything you did." He handed her his "dome," the small helmet he wore because it was the law, not because it mattered to him that his head might be saved if he crashed. "Put it on." It was the first time in his life he wished he owned a full helmet. He wanted her head intact if they crashed. He straddled the bike and looked at her expectantly.

"I can hitchhike."

That pissed him off. He let her see the anger building behind his eyes. "Get the fuck on." He waited again, staring her down.

She bit her lip. "My car broke down." She glanced over her shoulder. The murmur of voices was low, but his brothers had surrounded the three men.

Savage's voice drifted back to them. "Get my brother's knife, Ice."

Yeah. That was his brothers. Taking care of business. Watching out for him, even when he was the one who was supposed to watch out for them. Satisfaction gripped him for a moment. Affection. He sometimes knew what that feeling was, but most of the time he couldn't feel, or couldn't identify the emotion when he had it.

"Anya, look at me, not at them. That's over for you. You didn't see those three fuckers after they left. You understand me? No matter who asks, you didn't see them. They left the bar and they were gone. You chose to stay when you had your way out. That means you live by our rules. Get on the bike."

He backed it out and waited. Reluctantly she threw her leg over and straddled the bike right behind him. Close. God. He could feel her body heat. He reached around, caught her hands in his and yanked her even closer so she was welded to him. She locked her hands at his waist, and then they were flying down the road.

He'd never had a woman on the back of his bike. Not even Lana or Alena, the two female club members. He couldn't believe what it felt like, her body fused to his, the two of them connected to the bike so they all three moved as one. Man. Woman. Machine. Anya might be afraid of him, but on the bike, she trusted him implicitly, leaning with him, moving with him, her tits pressed against his back, her hands at his waist, so close to his cock he could feel it burn. The vibration of the powerful machine had never been so erotic as it was with her clinging to him.

THREE

"Egg Taking Station," Anya said against his ear, trying to shout loud enough that Reaper could hear her. The wind tore through her hair and whipped at her face. It felt cleansing. It was exhilarating. She felt more alive than she ever had as they hurtled down the road. She'd never been on a motorcycle, but she felt like she'd been born for one.

She closed her eyes and pressed her cheek against Reaper's back. Against his colors. She never thought, in a million years, she would be flying down the road on the back of his Harley. From the first moment he'd come into the bar after Czar had hired her, he'd taken her breath away. The attraction to him had been so intense, she had hardly been able to work. He'd settled into a chair at the back of the room, and he'd stayed there all night. He'd drunk coffee, not liquor, and he'd watched her.

After a while she thought of herself as a mouse, cornered by a large cat. His gaze hadn't been friendly. There was nothing friendly about Reaper. Nothing at all. His eyes were dead. When he looked at her, she felt he could gut her and not even blink twice. His eyes were dark holes, surrounded by dark, thick lashes. Why had she noticed his lashes when he looked so remote, his face carved from stone, all angles and planes?

He had scars on his face, dissecting the dark stubble on his left side from the corner of his eye all the way to his jaw, as if someone had taken a knife and carved a curving line down his face. Another line followed his angular jaw. Strangely, on his right side was carved a tic-tac-toe board with three *X*s in a diagonal in the squares. It wasn't a tattoo, the lines were scars.

She was tall, not quite the same height as he was, but close. His shoulders were very wide and his chest was extremely broad. His arms were defined with muscle, along with his narrowing rib cage and waist. His hips were narrow, his thighs strong. She'd looked a little too much because she was fairly certain she could map out his muscles on paper. Okay, truthfully, she had. She loved to draw, and she had a sketchbook filled with renditions of Reaper.

There were bikers in the bar every single night. She wasn't attracted to bikers. Not at all. Their world didn't appeal to her. She had promised herself she would move up in the world. She'd been doing that steadily. She'd done it all herself, carving a place for herself by her fingernails. For a shelter kid, she hadn't done half bad. No school, but she'd managed to get her GED. She'd worked hard and saved money to go to bartending school. She figured she'd be the best bartender in the world, and she was well on her way. She hadn't shown Czar, but she could do just about any trick done by the best. As she moved up to better and better bars, the tips had flowed.

She took a deep breath and looked around her as the ocean sped by so fast it was almost a blur. She was tired and had a long way to walk to get to her car. Truthfully, she was terrified of that walk. She knew wild animals were out at night, including mountain lions and bears. She thought maybe coyotes. She wasn't looking forward to it, but she'd done it a couple of times before.

They turned off at Highway 20 and as they roared down the road, he dropped one gloved hand and covered both of hers, pressing them closer to his waist. She'd never been so aware of another human being. She'd never been so aware of her own body, the bike vibrating between her thighs, her mound pushed against his butt, her breasts aching, nipples on fire, pressed so tightly against him, rubbing with every lean of the bike.

She loved riding on the motorcycle with him. It was masochistic being attracted to him. Insane even. Most of the other club members were nice to her—distant but nice. She supposed all the other members could be considered handsome, but Reaper was sexy. He was raw power. Scary dangerous. Whatever he did for the club, and she didn't want to know, it was hazardous work.

When she first pushed at Reaper's chest, every member of the club in the back room had come to their feet and they'd looked worried—for her. She knew immediately she shouldn't have touched him. Then he wouldn't let her go, and she'd been terrified. Right before Czar told her she still had a job, she saw a strange look pass between the club members behind Reaper's back. They'd gone from anxious to knowing. Amused maybe. Something she couldn't quite interpret.

The bike slowed, and Reaper turned onto the dirt road leading to the campground. She gripped his jacket and lifted her face so her mouth was against his ear. "I can walk in from here." How did he know where her car was? She hadn't told anyone she lived out here. It was utterly humiliating.

He hadn't asked her how to get to her car. He hadn't asked a single question. She stiffened, suddenly aware she was alone with the scariest member of Torpedo Ink. She didn't know a thing about him, other than he drank coffee and didn't like her. Her heart stuttered and then accelerated.

She'd been so stupid. She'd been so worried they were going to kill Deke and his friends that she really hadn't thought about her own safety. That was so stupid and so unlike her.

She was a planner. She'd planned out her entire life. When things had blown up in her face, she'd planned her getaway meticulously, even if it had been on the run. It was Reaper. There was no reason to be attracted to him, but she'd never had such physical desire for anyone in her life. She dreamt about him at night. Sometimes she fantasized about him during the day.

The biker life wasn't for her and she knew Reaper wasn't either, but just once, she wished she could have a night of blazing hot sex with him. The kind of sex women read and dreamt about but never really had. Reaper was that raw. That wild. That primitive. She knew he'd be raw, wild and primitive in bed. Just once, she wanted to experience that kind of hot, carnal, erotic sex. The urge wasn't strong enough to risk her life though. She had no idea what he'd do when he found her car. Best-case scenario, he'd give her a lecture and leave her there.

Reaper wasn't given to lectures. In the month she'd known him, he hadn't said a single word other than *coffee*. In one night, he'd shattered his record, and most of it wasn't good. He really, really didn't like her, but the fingers covering her hand drove her nuts. He kept stroking the back of her hand with a gloved finger. She didn't know what it meant, but it sent little tingles of awareness, little electrical charges slithering through her body until she was coiled tight.

She pointed to the right, and he veered from the main road to the campsite where her car sat looking dilapidated, rusted and sad under the trees where she'd been forced to leave it that morning. As soon as she knew it had given up, she'd set about hiking out to the main highway and then hitchhiking into town. Still, she'd been late for work. Really late. Preacher had raised an eyebrow at her—he'd been swamped when she came in—but he hadn't said a word. Not a single word.

She had to put her hand on Reaper's shoulder to get off the bike, and he couldn't have failed to notice that she was shaking. She hoped he put it down to the cold night. She stepped away, removing the helmet as he turned off the bike and silence settled in the forest. Still straddling the bike, he looked around slowly. She hoped that meant he was going to leave immediately.

"Thanks for the ride. My car gave me trouble this morning. It does that sometimes. I'll get to work on time though," she hastened to assure him.

"Why didn't you call? We would have sent a tow truck."

She bit her lip. She couldn't afford a tow truck. He wasn't going to like her answer so she remained silent.

"Anya. Let's get one thing straight between us." He swung one leg over his bike and remained sitting there, looking lazy. Looking scary. There was nothing lazy or casual about Reaper, so that casual pose scared the crap out of her.

She was still afraid to speak, so she nodded to indicate she was listening. She knew when someone said "get something straight," that usually meant she wasn't going to like what they had to say. There was a throbbing between her legs that shouldn't have been there. Reaper did that to her, even when he was being as scary as all get-out. She was very aware she was alone with him out in the middle of a forest, with no one around them.

"When I ask you a question, I want an answer. You got that?"

She felt the familiar rise of heat. Her temper. She had one. She shoved it down, even though she wanted to tell him to go to hell. She'd gotten ahead, following her plan, and she'd done that by keeping her temper in check. She nodded, because she didn't trust her voice.

"The tow truck."

He was looking into her eyes, noting her flushed face. He

knew she was angry, knew she didn't like him dictating to her. He didn't like her anyway, so screw him if he looked down on her for not having a home or money. She lifted her chin. "I can't afford it. If I could, do you think I'd be living in my car out here? It's freezing at night." Why she added that bit of information, she had no idea. Probably because she was so angry at him sitting there all lazy and superior on his bike.

God. He was the hottest thing she'd ever seen. Why would she want the one man who had more issues than she did? And she did want him. Desperately. Just one night of sheer bliss. Those hands. He was so strong. He knew what he was doing. Every time his gaze brushed anywhere on her body, it felt like a physical touch. Hot as hell. Lingering. He was *such* a bastard. He had to know how he was affecting her.

"You're living in that rust bucket?"

She nodded. "I'm tired. Thank you for the ride and thank you for saving me from Deke, although I'm not certain that throwing a knife at him was warranted."

"That was me showing restraint, just for you. Now, get whatever you need out of your car and get on my bike. I'm not arguing, I'm taking your ass to the clubhouse."

A shower. Somewhere warm. That would be heaven. She'd been washing up in the bathroom at work. There was no shower at the campgrounds, and no real bathroom. For one second she was tempted, but she knew not to let herself rely on anyone else. She had to get herself out of every situation on her own.

Anya forced a smile. "Really, thank you. I appreciate the offer, but I can't go with you. I swear, I won't be late for work tomorrow . . ."

He was up and off the bike. He was a big man. Huge. Coming at her, a solid wall of sheer muscle, and he was coming fast. She backpedaled, stumbled, barely caught herself, no air in her lungs and a frisson of fear creeping down her spine. She threw up one hand to fend him off, as if that would work.

"Fuck it," he muttered, going right past her hand. "I'll send Lana or Alena out to get your clothes." He caught her outstretched hand, yanked her to him and then she was upside down over his shoulder.

She let out a girly scream that she quickly shut down, and then she punched him. Hard. Right in his ribs. His breath hissed out and he flinched. His hand came down hard on her bottom. Very hard. Outraged, she hit him again. He repeated the swat in exactly the same place and fire rushed through her. Spread. She didn't know if it was painful or if her temper had kicked in, or if he was so sexy anything he did sent heat rushing through her veins and throbbing between her legs.

He set her down next to the bike, swearing under his breath. His color was off. Almost gray. She glanced at his ribs. She'd hit him, but this man was the enforcer of the club. She didn't know a lot, but she knew sergeant at arms meant protector of the club. He should be able to take a hit in the ribs without flinching.

"Get on the fucking bike."

"Stop swearing at me."

"It's a word. Doesn't mean a damn thing."

"Then it should be easy enough to stop using it."

"Anya." He said her name between clenched teeth. "I'm out of patience. I'm forty-eight hours without sleep and I've had enough of being polite. It's not my thing. Now get on the bike."

"Open your jacket."

His eyes were beautiful. So intense. Hooded. Shockingly blue. Cold as ice. Right now, those eyes bored into her and she couldn't help the shiver running through her body. She wasn't backing down no matter how afraid she was. He was hurt. She knew he was. It wasn't a small thing either. He looked like he might kill her if she continued to defy him. That didn't matter either. She sighed.

"I'll go with you if you open your jacket and let me see."

"You'll go with me because I fucking tell you to," he snapped.

She ignored the macho bullshit. "Willingly."

He studied her face for what seemed like an eternity. His gaze drifted down, over her body, touching on her breasts, the junction between her legs, dwelt there for a moment so she had to hold herself very still so she wouldn't squirm with need. So she didn't give away the fact that she was damp and her clit throbbed for no reason other than he was the sexiest man alive. No, he was a beast. Still, every time he opened his mouth, he brought the hot factor down a notch, at least that was what she told herself, but then she could be prone to bullshit when it came to him.

His gaze came back to her face. One hand went to the zipper of his jacket, and triumph burst through her. She'd out-stubborned him. Well, okay, he'd conceded. She knew it wasn't in his nature and he certainly wasn't a man that allowed a woman to tell him what to do, so what did it mean?

She saw the blood and her breath left her lungs. There was old blood, nearly dry, and new blood slowly seeping into his shirt. "Oh my God. I'm so sorry. I wouldn't have hit you if I'd known." She'd hit him *twice*. In the same spot. Hard.

He zipped his jacket up, his features pure stone. "Get on the bike." He slung one leg over and backed it up. "Right fucking now."

So much for concessions. She slipped her leg over, forgetting everything she might need the next day, only concerned with the wound she hadn't seen beneath his shirt. Settling behind him, she wrapped her arms loosely around him, afraid of hurting him. He caught her wrists and jerked her close, mashing her breasts against his back.

He pressed her hands into his waist tightly. She was forced to shift her body closer so that throbbing between her legs was pressed against him. Could he feel that? It was powerful. Intense. Insistent. The moment he started up the bike and it roared, sending vibrations between her legs, she was afraid she was going to get off right there.

Riding with Reaper was an amazing experience. She pressed her face against his back and gave in to her fantasies about this man. He was a *man*. Hard as nails. Protective as hell with the members of his club, especially Czar. Anyone with powers of observation could see that. She'd never had a home. Never had protection. She'd never had anyone she could count on. The club members definitely were apart from everyone else, but with each other, they often joked or ribbed, and all of them watched over the two women, Alena and Lana.

To think of being under Reaper's protection just for a night. To feel his body moving in hers. To have glorious sex, the earth-shattering kind, no matter how bossy he was, would be worth it—for a night. She wasn't the kind of woman to be in that world. She reminded herself often, every night, when she looked at him across the bar. Every single night.

Czar and the other members of the club treated her fine, but most of the bikers coming into the bar tried touching her inappropriately. Called her names she *really* didn't like. Sweet tits—the name Deke had called her—was the least offensive. Betina'd had sex with one biker right outside on the picnic table. Another time she'd let a man put his hand up her very short skirt, and if Anya wasn't mistaken, he'd gotten her off right there in the bar. Later, she'd given the biker a blow job right outside around the corner of the building. Anya had gone out to get some fresh air and had seen them.

The other waitress, Heidi, was just as bad. Both women wore either tube tops or halter tops with very short skirts to work. They got tons of tips and definitely knew how to handle the men coming in. Anya didn't understand why, when both women were so readily available, most of the bikers flirted with her and gave her equally good tips or sometimes, even better. She got along with both waitresses, unless . . . She squirmed, forcing herself to be honest. She'd detested it when Betina had gotten it into her head to flirt with Reaper tonight. She'd never done that before. She would want to kill either waitress if they went somewhere alone with him.

He didn't like her. She had to keep telling herself that. He wanted her fired. He'd almost *gotten* her fired. She had no idea why Czar spared her and let her keep her job even though she'd been very late coming in. She knew it was a big thing for Czar to go against Reaper's desire to fire her.

She closed her eyes and let the road take her, the sensation of moving with Reaper and the bike. It was perfect. She loved the way they took a curve, their bodies in perfect sync. Riding with Reaper, it never occurred to her that he could lose control of the bike. She couldn't imagine him ever losing control, but she'd want to try to . . .

She broke off that thought and forced herself to think about how tired and achy she was. Her feet hurt. She hadn't slept much the last few nights. She probably shouldn't have given her extra blankets away, but she had an old sleeping bag she'd gotten from a thrift store, so she wasn't as cold as some of the men and women sleeping in the streets. Still, she felt as if she would never be warm again.

The ride was over far too soon, and she found herself in the parking lot of the Torpedo Ink compound. It had been turned into a fortress. A high chain-link fence surrounded the property. The building was intact but modernized, according to all the gossip she'd heard—and there was plenty, particularly at the grocery store in Sea Haven. Sometimes she drove there just to listen to the locals talk about the club.

She got off the bike feeling a little unsteady. He backed the bike next to a row of other motorcycles and shut it down. She looked at him uncertainly. She didn't know what to expect. She could see he was exhausted. And he had all that blood on him. He wasn't going to throw her on the bed and have his wicked way with her. In spite of the exhaustion, he still looked like sin and sex, *carnal* sin. Animalistic. Primitive. Heat rushed through her to settle uncomfortably between her legs. That persistent throbbing stayed there.

What was wrong with her? She wanted that. Dirty. Wild. Uninhibited. She wanted whatever he would give her. It would be something she would have for the rest of her life. One glorious night with a man who knew what he was doing. She couldn't stay here forever. She didn't fit in and never would. She wasn't looking for forever. Just one night.

Her tongue touched her lower lip in a slow, sensual slide. Thinking about tasting him. What would he feel like? She bet he was beautiful. Thick. She bet he tasted like heaven. Her breasts ached. The tips were on fire. Thank God for her jacket.

"I'd like to take a look at that wound in your side."

"You a nurse?"

Why did he have to open his mouth? A woman should be able to have fantasies about the hot gorgeous body she was perving on without him ruining it by speaking. She sighed. "Nope. Not a nurse. Just thought I'd help you out seeing as how you took the time to give me a ride and all." So, screw him. She didn't need or want his shit.

She stayed silent. Two could play at that game. She just waited while he fiddled around with something on his bike, and then he gestured toward the building. She took a deep breath. He didn't like her. He wasn't going to jump her. Even if he did, it would only be what she wanted, a glorious night of sex and sin. She hoped they were really, really bad sins that would last forever. She knew her luck wasn't that good.

The door opened into a large room with a curving bar, tables and chairs, a couple of couches and more comfortable-looking chairs. She didn't get a good look at the series of doors because he led her down a hallway. "Bathroom is right there. No one is using that one right now. A few of the brothers are sleeping here tonight. They might wander around naked. No big deal. Just know they do." He pushed open a door. "You can sleep in here. Bed's clean."

She'd heard about the wild parties. She knew a few of the women who had partied here. A woman would come into the bar pretending to want to see Betina and Heidi, but Anya knew it was to try to get one of the men to claim her as their old lady. She studied the bed. Was it clean? She didn't want to be sleeping on sheets used for something else.

Reaper didn't move as she slowly slipped past him. He filled most of the doorway so her body brushed against his as she entered the room. Her heart accelerated the way it always did when her body got close to his. It was on overload, so stimulated, she wished she'd thought to pack her vibrator when she'd run. She hadn't had time to think of things like that.

"Reaper," she said softly as he turned to go.

He turned back and just stood there waiting.

"Thank you. It was really cold in the car. I appreciate you helping me. I won't be a bother."

"Give me your car keys." He held out his hand.

She frowned, but found herself digging through her pocket for them. She didn't obey anyone. It wasn't her style, but his voice was gruff. Mesmerizing. Somehow it seemed a little rusty, as if he rarely spoke. Going by the nights he'd spent in the bar, she was sure she was right. Just his talking to her made her feel special to him, even though she knew she wasn't. She knew he disliked her. She handed the keys to him.

He turned away from her and shut the door. He didn't do it hard, but he did it firmly. She had the feeling that if he was on her side of it, he would have turned the lock. "Good night to you too," she said loudly, just to piss him off.

There was no answer. She didn't even hear him going down the hall. Looking around, she took in the room. It was small: a tiny closet, a built-in dresser. Nightstand with a lamp. The bed was a double and looked inviting. She wasn't going there yet. She wasn't even sitting on it. She was too tired and would have fallen asleep. She wanted a shower. A real shower. She didn't care if she had clean clothes or not. If the men in the clubhouse could wander around naked, she could cover herself up with a towel—assuming they had towels.

She was shocked when she walked into the bathroom and found a tub. Why would the club members think of putting in a bathtub? She found bath salts under the sink. They weren't the standard Epsom salts one would expect; they were actual good-smelling salts. She turned on the hot water tap experimentally. Light was already creeping through the window, the first few rays of dawn. It lit up the room, hitting on the full-length mirror attached to the door.

This was a woman's bathroom. Reaper had said no one was using it. Did that mean, when they had their parties, this room was occupied by the women who came? The club members had sex with them in her bedroom and then used this bathroom? She inspected every inch of it. The towels were thick and fluffy, colored a soft apricot. They matched the apricot swirling through the shower curtain.

The two female club members. This had to be one of their rooms. Their bathroom. She sighed with relief and stripped. She stepped into the shower first, letting the hot water spray over her. She found really good quality shampoo and used it unashamedly twice. If she needed to replace it, she would do so gladly.

She conditioned her hair. When she rinsed, her hair felt nice for the first time in weeks. She'd washed it in the sink, but she had so much hair, she never felt as if she'd really cleaned it thoroughly. Sponge baths sucked. This was heaven. Pure heaven.

Wringing out her hair, she looked through the various drawers and found several hair ties and clamps. She put her hair on top of her head, secured it and sank down into the water. Pure bliss. She could stay there forever. She closed her eyes and put her head back and just drifted.

The water was cooling when she jerked awake. Reaper

was bent over the tub, one hand in the water, pulling the plug. She nearly did the girly shriek again, but managed to stop herself just in time.

"Get out of there. Water's too cold." He sounded abrupt. Annoyed.

"I'm naked. You shouldn't be in here." Hadn't she locked the door? She couldn't remember.

"Nothin' I haven't seen before," he said and stepped back, holding out a towel.

That killed any hope he was attracted, although he was a man. His gaze lingered on her breasts. So screw him, she'd give him a show if that's what he was looking for, although she didn't think so, judging by his stony features. She stood up, forcing herself not to blush when her entire body wanted to go red.

She knew she had good breasts. High. Rounded. Generous. Her rib cage was narrow, her waist small, in proportion with her generous hips, which made finding jeans that fit difficult. And she certainly had hips. No lie. And he was looking at them. She resisted the urge to turn her back on him because then he'd see her equally generous butt.

She took the towel just as the door opened. Reaper glided between her and the door.

"What the fuck, Savage? You don't just walk in when a woman's taking a bath. I thought Blythe went over the rules with you."

Savage shrugged. He was a younger version of Reaper, just as hard, just as scarred, his blue eyes just as dead. "You don't care about those shit rules any more than I do."

"Maybe not, but this is Anya's first night here."

"It's morning," Savage corrected. He glanced at her and then his gaze jumped back to his brother's face. "Want to take a look at those stitches. Doc gave me the antibiotics to give to you."

Anya remained frozen, the towel pressed to her breasts. She didn't dare move or Savage would see her in all her glory. It was one thing for the man of her dreams, who clearly thought of her as a burden he had to bear, to see her, but an altogether different one for his brother to walk in on her when she was naked.

Stitches? Had she broken open his stitches when she'd punched him? Good God. He'd just thrown her over his shoulder. Why did she have to punch him for it? Remorse hit hard. He might be gruff. He might not like her, but he'd rescued her.

"Stitches? Reaper, I'm so sorry . . ."

"Forget it." His tone told her to shut the hell up. "Wait outside for me," he ordered his brother.

Savage nodded and without a word to her, sauntered out. She closed her eyes and shook her head. She'd lived in shelters, places where there was little privacy, but men just coming into a bathroom . . . She *had* locked the door. She wouldn't forget something like that. She narrowed her eyes at Reaper. "That door was locked."

"Shit lock, babe. I put a couple of bottles of water on the nightstand by your bed. Waited for you to get out of here but when you didn't, knew you'd fallen asleep. Too quiet."

"It was unnecessary to come in."

He looked thoroughly unimpressed and as bored as hell. "Depends on which one of us you're talking to. Get to bed. I pulled the privacy screen for you. It will keep the room dark. Alena and Lana are going shopping for clothes." He turned and stalked out, leaving her standing there, the towel clutched to her chest, a little breathless and her eyes wide with shock.

He'd walked in, right through the locked door, unplugged her bathtub, handed her a towel and then stood in front of her when his brother had walked in. He'd gotten her water and pulled the privacy screen. She knew he was even more tired than she was, but he'd come to check on her. She wrapped the towel around herself and started back to her designated room.

A man came walking down the hall, totally naked. He glanced up, saw her, made no move to cover up and nodded before pushing open a door. Holy cow. That had been Ice. He was . . . impressive. She was *never* going to look at him the same way. Sheesh. He was built. She couldn't think about that, not when Reaper had her tied in knots and she didn't have anything or anyone to help with the frustration.

She found two extra blankets folded at the bottom of the bed, proving that Reaper had actually listened to her. She threw herself on the bed, facedown, grateful for the bath, the room, the comfortable bed, even the new toothbrush she'd found in the drawer, still in the packaging. She didn't care if Reaper walked in on her or she saw men with hot bodies walking naked through the halls, it was the best place *ever*. So much better than her car.

She dragged a blanket over her and drifted off to the murmur of voices.

⌒

"What are you doing with that woman?" Savage demanded.

Reaper didn't know what he was doing with her. He'd walked into that bathroom, knowing she'd fallen asleep, knowing she would be naked, but the idea of her lying in cold water had been more than he could take. He pressed his fingers to his eyes.

"She's living out of her car. The car wouldn't run. That simple. Woman shouldn't be out there by herself. Sooner or later her luck is going to run out."

"You let her put her hands on you, Reaper. Since she's been here, you haven't been acting like you."

What was he supposed to say to that? It was true. There was nothing he could say, because he couldn't even explain it to himself. "You get rid of those assholes, the ones that tried to jump her?"

Savage shrugged. "You put a knife in one of them. Sooner or later he was going to talk. Sad ending for them. Drove their bikes over the cliff about fifteen miles from here. Bodies won't be found."

"You tell Czar yet?"

Savage nodded. "Stopped by his house. Caught him and Blythe going at it." He smirked a little. Blythe was so much a part of their family now, none of them could imagine life without her. "Talked to him through the window. She told me she was going to shoot me if I didn't go away. I told her to stay busy while I gave Czar the minimum. Used our code so Blythe can sleep good at night. Not sure he got it all because Blythe did what I said, and he was a little distracted."

Reaper shrugged out of his shirt. "Hurts like hell," he admitted to his brother.

"Woman's turning you into a whiner," Savage commented, but his fingers were gentle as he examined the wound. "You need those antibiotics, bro. Some of your stitches have popped. I'll have to redo them."

"Woman packs a punch." For the first time in a long while, Reaper's mouth softened. It wasn't a smile, but it might have been a ghost of one. "She's got a hell of a temper, but keeps it covered."

"Why'd she hit you?" Savage kept his eyes glued on the laceration. He'd already laid out the needle and thread and antibiotic cream. He had topical lidocaine just in case as well.

"Smacked her ass twice. She retaliated. Had her over my shoulder."

"She know you were hurt?" Savage's voice was mild.

Reaper frowned. "No, she didn't. Don't go getting predatory on me. I recognize that tone. She's under my protection."

"You're under mine."

"Damn it, Savage, I mean it. I forced her to come here . . ."

"She doesn't put her hands on you."

"I let her. You know I let her." This was why he didn't let anything out of the ordinary into his life, and Anya was so far out of the ordinary he didn't know what to do. He could barely breathe when he looked at her. All he wanted to do was throw her over his shoulder like a caveman and fuck her until she couldn't walk. Until neither of them could stand. There were so many things he wanted to do to her, but getting her hurt wasn't one of them. "She's under my protection," he said again. "That means she's under yours."

It was a challenge and both knew it. A warning. Maybe even a plea. This scenario was out of both of their depths. Savage nodded and continued working. "We'll play it your way, Reaper. Maybe you should take her to Blythe."

Czar's old lady could do anything, fix anything, advise them on anything. As far as the club was concerned, she walked on water. She never minded if they all showed up for breakfast, lunch or dinner. She let them watch the four kids while Czar took her off for alone time—as alone as one could get with bodyguards. She was a screamer, so more than once, during the throes of sex, the bodyguards had run up on them, guns drawn, to find them going at it hard. She didn't look down on them, or act like she was embarrassed to be seen with them.

The members of the club had been raised, most from the time they were toddlers, without clothes or food in a particularly violent school in Russia. Their parents had been considered enemies of the State, so once they'd been taken, no one ever came to rescue them. They had lived in a small windowless basement a good deal of the time. Nudity didn't bother them. It sometimes was difficult to stay indoors. Every kind of sex was commonplace, their teachers forcing them to perform in front of the others. It became so usual, they didn't think anything of it. Now, trying to integrate into society, at least as far as they could, it was difficult to know and understand the rules. Some of the things they were used to, people on the outside frowned upon.

"Anya isn't going to change a thing for me," Reaper said, wanting to believe it. She already had, and now the nightmares had come back. He was afraid to go to bed. Afraid to sleep. Afraid to touch her. She made him want things he knew he couldn't have. It was far too dangerous. He looked at his brother. "It isn't safe. You know that."

Savage shrugged. "I get away with it."

"You're a man whore."

"Takes the edge off. You ought to try it." Savage squeezed antibiotic cream all around the wound. "Take those pills."

"I will." He swallowed two in front of his brother just to keep the peace. "I'm going to lie down for a while." What he really wanted to do was go into that room and lie next to her. Touch her skin. Put his fingers inside of her. His tongue. He wanted to taste her. Leave his brand on her. And that was just for starters. He had so many things he wanted to do to Anya Rafferty, he knew he couldn't fit them all into one night.

"Think about it, Reaper. You fuck her hard, it all stops for a few minutes. Sometimes an hour. If you're really lucky and you wear yourself out, you get longer."

Reaper walked away from him, concentrating on every step because his jeans were too tight and his cock hurt like a bastard. He'd put her in Lana's old room. Lana rarely stayed there anymore. He'd texted her first and asked. Of course she'd said yes. That was Lana. Tough as nails when she had to be, but so soft inside she stole your heart—if you had one.

He stood for a moment at the door of Anya's room, his hand on the wood, just about where her head would be. He liked that she was tall with long legs. He liked that he was even taller and she had to look up at him with those green eyes of hers. His gut clenched hard. His cock jerked. Needed attention. He should go take a cold shower, or at least take care of the problem, but he didn't. He dropped his hand to the doorknob. It was locked again.

The woman just wouldn't learn. They didn't use locks. Not ever. Having been locked up for years, it was something they all detested. He picked the lock easily and stepped inside. She lay on the bed, the blanket haphazardly pulled over her body. He'd seen so many naked women, women who deliberately tried to arouse his body while he was forced to be disciplined enough to resist. Roles were often reversed and he was forced to arouse a woman while she was supposed to resist. By the time he was a teenager, the women didn't win that battle. His body stayed under his control—until now—until Anya.

Just the sight of her, naked with the blanket revealing part of her buttocks, round and firm, her back, her left breast and nipple made his cock hard and dripping small, pearly beads. He swore under his breath and opened his jeans. Dropping his hand to his cock, he fisted it, watching her. He wanted to paint her back and ass with his seed, but now wasn't the time. Let her think she was safe. He had plans. Just not yet. His side hurt, and he was so tired he thought he might just go to sleep on his feet.

He reached down, snagged her clothes and went back out, holding them with one hand to his chest, pumping his cock with the other, every step painful.

FOUR

Anya woke with a small groan, rolling over to look up at the ceiling, one arm flung over her eyes to keep out the light. The light. She'd gone to bed with the privacy screens down, which meant the room should have been dark. Not good. Someone had been in her room. Catching hold of the blanket, she pulled it up over her breasts and forced herself to stop being a baby. She opened her eyes.

"Finally," a cheerful feminine voice said. "We didn't think you'd ever wake up."

She wasn't certain who "we" were. She sat up slowly and looked around the room. She had an audience of five. Two women and three men. She recognized the three men immediately. They were club members who came and went from the bar. Storm and Ice came in often, and Preacher worked as a bartender with her on heavy nights. She had just flashed her breasts at them.

She hadn't met the two women yet, though she knew who they were. She knew one had to be Lana Popov, Preacher's birth sister. He talked about her as though she walked on water. She was beautiful. Her hair was a true black, very shiny, tumbling around her face as if she was windblown. She was tall, a little taller than Anya, and very curvy. Reaper may have had an inch on her, but no more than that.

Alena was Ice and Storm's sister. She was shorter, but not short. Anya guessed her at five-five or five-six. Her hair was wild, a platinum glossy mass, and her eyes were the same stunning blue as her two brothers'. Anya felt dowdy next to the vibrant women. Both had long nails, perfectly manicured. Both were dressed in fitted jeans and Harley tanks that made them look elegant as well as biker babe. She wouldn't be able to pull off that look in a million years.

"Blythe wants to meet you," Alena announced. Where Lana had smiled, Alena didn't. She clearly was sizing Anya up.

Anya looked around for her clothes. She felt a little desperate without them. She was certain she'd left them on the chair by the bed, but there were no clothes there. "Good morning." She didn't know what else to say. She looked around a little helplessly, wishing for Reaper. At least she understood him, knew he wanted to get rid of her but was too chivalrous to leave her alone in a campground with a car that wouldn't run. She had no idea what these people wanted.

"We brought you some clothes," Lana said. She patted her lap, drawing attention to the pile of jeans, shirts and lacy underwear. She made no move to pass them to Anya.

"I locked the door. How did you get in?"

"It wasn't locked," Ice said. He had three tattooed teardrops dripping down his face just to the side and under his left eye. His eyes were so incredibly blue she thought they had to be contacts, but his twin and sister had the same eyes.

She believed him. That meant Reaper had been at his lock picking again. She was going to *kill* him. "What can I do for all of you?"

"We were just wondering what was going on between you and Reaper," Alena said.

Anya pushed at the unruly fall of heavy hair. She hadn't dried it the night before, and it fell in waves all around her to pool on the bed. Clutching the blanket even tighter around her, she took a deep breath. They were all staring at her, completely serious. She couldn't read their expressions, but she was terrified if she didn't give them the right answer, they might murder her and bury her body somewhere.

What had she been thinking hiding out bartending in a biker bar? It was the last place anyone would look for her, that's what she'd been thinking. "Nothing. Nothing's going on between us. Ice, you heard him. He wants me gone."

"He wanted you gone, honey, you'd be gone," Storm said. "So, what the hell is between you two?"

Hadn't he even been listening when Reaper demanded Czar get rid of her? It was a horrible moment. She *needed* this job. She was homeless—again. Living out of her car, not a shelter, terrified every minute of her existence that she wasn't safe. Not in the bar and certainly not camping alone out at the Egg Taking Station. Reaper's *I don't give a shit* meant he did, he wanted her gone and had expected Czar to fire her.

She took another deep breath, knowing they saw her hands tremble. "I'm telling you there's nothing between us. He took me to my car, which incidentally isn't running and . . ."

"Which he incidentally had towed to the garage for Transporter and Mechanic to fix," Storm persisted.

What could she say to that? Reaper was nice? "He didn't like me out there at the campground where I was staying, and he insisted I come here for the night. It was a nice thing to do. He was just being nice." Even to her ears that sounded lame, but what else could she say?

"Bullshit," Alena snapped. "Reaper's not nice."

"You might want to start tellin' us the truth," Storm insisted.

"He'll fuckin' cut your nuts off"—Savage's wide shoulders filled the doorway—"you talk to her like that again. There's no need for that tone. Just give her the clothes and leave her the hell alone."

The world had gone crazy. Everyone in the club was nuts. Savage coming to her rescue? He hadn't spoken a single word to her, in fact, he'd given her the death stare. Now, all of a sudden, he was going to stick up for her? That made no sense.

"It's all right," Anya murmured. What else could she do? She didn't want these men and women for enemies. "They just misunderstood Reaper's kindness."

"Or maybe you did," Alena pointed out. She stood up. "I hope you like the clothes. We did the best we could with Reaper's weird measurement system. We had to guess at your sizes." She sauntered out of the room, looking regal. Biker regal.

Anya watched her closely; the woman had a small limp, one she covered well. Her brothers followed her, giving her a little salute.

"I'm sorry we intruded," Lana said. "I could lie and say we didn't mean to, but I'm certain you'd know it was a lie, so why bother. We wanted to meet the mystery girl who has Reaper tied up in knots. You go, girl. But don't hurt him. You hurt that man and someone's going to cut your throat."

Anya stroked her throat with her fingers. "You don't have to worry. Your little warning is enough for me to keep my distance. I'm fond of my throat." Screw Reaper. Screw Lana. Screw the biker club. She was *so* getting out of there. She needed to know if her car was fixable. The moment it was, she was out of there. Out. Of. There. For good. Done with biker bars. Done with biker bullshit rules she didn't understand. Done with being scared.

She didn't belong. Not anywhere. Not with anyone. She couldn't even fit into the biker world. What did that say about her? She pressed the blanket to her mouth to keep it from trembling. "I'd like to get dressed now." The words were muffled. They made her feel vulnerable and inconsequential. She'd had enough of that growing up living at the shelter. They weren't going to reduce everything she'd worked so hard for to *nothing*. She wasn't going to feel like trash someone had thrown out onto the curb. So yeah, screw them.

Lana stood up gracefully, flowing, fluid like a cat, and carefully put the clothes in a neat stack on the end of the bed. Savage stepped back to allow Lana and Preacher to leave the room. He stood a minute studying Anya's face. "You all right?"

"Yes. Fine, thank you. No worries." She prayed her voice wouldn't tremble. Just let him leave, she'd put on the clothes, run to the bathroom and make her escape. She could walk to the garage. It wasn't very far. Visit her car. She had money stashed in it. She'd saved nearly every penny she made just in case she had to run again. There was a used car lot in Fort Bragg. She could make a deal with them. Maybe.

"You're full of shit," Savage said. "Reaper won't let anything happen to you." He waited. She didn't say anything. She wanted him to leave, and he got the hint.

The second the door closed, she pulled on the stretch lace underwear and matching bra. Neither did much in the way of covering her up. The jeans fit like a glove. Perfection. She'd never had a pair of jeans that fit so well, not with her smaller waist. The jeans fit, but the shirt was a disaster. It was small. It barely fit over her breasts, so that the material clung to her curves and showed not only the tops of her breasts and the valley in between, but also the lace edging on her bra—similar to Betina's tank. Had Alena and Lana done it on purpose? Probably. They were making a statement. She knew the difference between the women they respected and the ones they didn't.

She went to the closet in the hopes of finding something that would fit. It was empty. She sank down on the end of the bed and dropped her head into her hands. She didn't want to cry. She'd cried enough when she was a kid, trying to figure out where her next meal was coming from.

"Anya?" The voice was soft. The way Reaper said her name was almost haunting. "Baby, are you crying?"

She shook her head, not looking up.

"Savage said the girls were in here not being very nice to you. What did they say?"

"I just want to leave. I'd like to get to my car." She forced herself to stop being a coward and look up at him. The moment she did, her heart clenched hard in her chest. He hadn't deteriorated overnight. He was still hot as hell. Still scary looking. Still scarred and tattooed.

"Come on, let's go." He stepped back.

"I have to go to the bathroom first." She didn't want him to see her tearstained face. She hated crying. Hated that weakness. Mostly she didn't like that Lana and Alena had been the ones to make her cry. There should be a sisterhood that prevented women from making another feel left out. Ugly. Unwanted.

He nodded and stayed where he was. She could feel his eyes on her butt as she hurried down the hall to the bathroom. She had the mad desire to peel off the top and throw it. Maybe going around in her bra would be better than trying to outdo Betina. If Betina wore a top like this one to the bar, every man who came in would be all over her.

She stayed for a while, long enough to wash her face and try to tame her wild hair into some semblance of order. When she came out, she padded back to the room to find her shoes. "I'll need to go somewhere to find a different top. This one is a little small."

"It is?" Reaper leaned his hip against the doorjamb, looking lazy and tempting. "I think you look beautiful. I might have to fight half the male population off you though."

A compliment? He sounded sincere. She glanced up from where she was tying her shoe. There was no trace of humor on his face or in his eyes. She swallowed hard. "I can't wear this. I need a different shirt. One that covers me. I look too much like Betina."

"You don't look anything like Betina."

"Do you have an old shirt I can wear?" She was desperate. She wasn't going to cry again, but she had to change and get to the garage to her car. She kept her head down, hair tumbling around her face so she didn't have to look at him.

"Anya."

That was it. That was all he said. Her name. Nothing else. Her name sounded like a caress, a soft swipe of velvet over her skin. Fingers touching her face where the teardrops had been. She should have known he wouldn't let her get away with it. The silence stretched out. She couldn't stare at her shoes all day. Taking a breath, breathing him in, she slowly straightened and forced herself to look up at him.

"You don't want to wear that top, I'll get you a flannel to cover you up, although nothing as beautiful as you should ever be covered."

Her heart clenched hard. Her sex spasmed. He casually threw out compliments that she could tell weren't meant to be compliments. He meant them. To him they were facts.

She nodded. "Thanks. And then I'm just going to the garage to see about my car. I can walk there from here. It isn't far."

His piercing stare was unnerving. It was all she could do not to squirm under his gaze. Finally, he sighed, shook his head and turned, walking out of the room. When she didn't follow he paused and looked over his shoulder. "Coming?"

She wanted the shirt, so yeah, she was going to go with him, although being with Reaper even for a few minutes was a bad idea. She couldn't help checking him out as she followed him down the hall to his room. She peeked in the open door, but didn't go in. The room was much like the one she was staying in, but messier. It had the look of a room where the resident lived out of a suitcase, or in this case, a duffel bag. He rifled through it, came up with a shirt and tossed it to her.

Her heart did that weird stuttering thing it sometimes did when she was around him. She found herself just staring at him. He was sending so many mixed messages her head was spinning, or she could have been really hungry. It wasn't like she'd had a lot to eat lately.

Reaper stalked across the room to her, took the shirt from her hands and held it out so she could slip her arms in the sleeves. He stood close to her. Too close. She inhaled him with every breath she drew. Twice she tried to speak, but nothing came out. She couldn't look up at his face so she stared straight ahead. The view was good. A tight tee stretched across all those delicious muscles. She itched to trace them with her tongue.

His hands came up to the buttons on the shirt, and he began to slip them through the buttonholes. One by one. Slowly. His knuckles slid over her breasts, sending scorching heat rushing through her veins. A gentle brush. Damp heat moistened her panties. Another brush and the air was gone from her lungs. The third brush coiled need so deep and strong in her she thought she might spontaneously combust. She breathed shallowly in an effort to maintain.

His fingers caught her chin and he tilted her head up. She quickly veiled her eyes with her lashes.

"You wanted to stay. You're not runnin' because it gets a little rough."

"I'm not." That was *exactly* what she planned to do.

"Don't lie. I'm takin' you to a late breakfast or early lunch, not to your car."

"Reaper."

"This conversation is over." He caught her hand and pulled as he walked down the hall toward the common room.

"Just because you say it's over doesn't mean it is," she protested, telling herself she was going with him because he was bigger and stronger, not because he was hot as hell and she wanted him with every breath she took.

He sent her a look that ordinarily would have made her run. She was in the lion's den. There was no running, so she followed him. Lana and Alena sat on stools at the bar. Both turned as they entered. Their smiles faded when they saw Reaper's face.

"Not happy with either of you," he said as he stalked past them.

"Reaper," Lana started, but he dragged Anya right out the door, not saying another word to either woman.

At least she wasn't the only one. She knew Lana and Alena were important to every club member. She heard the way the men talked about them. Every mention of their names was said with respect and affection.

Reaper took her directly to his bike and handed her the dome. He straddled the big machine and backed it out.

"Are you going to at least tell me how that wound is this morning?" Anya asked. He was walking with his normal loose-limbed stride. Well, he didn't walk exactly. He prowled. Stalked. There wasn't really walking. God, she found him hot. Nothing had changed overnight.

"Nope. Get on the bike."

She sighed and climbed behind him. Glancing over her shoulder, she saw that both Lana and Alena had come to the door of the clubhouse. Behind them crowded several of the members. All watching. All staring. She shivered and involuntarily pressed closer to Reaper. He did what he always seemed to do—reached around and caught her hands, pulled her arms around him and pressed her hands to his waist. She ignored those watching and snuggled close, wiggling until she was right next to Reaper, so she could feel every inch of him. The bike roared to life and then they were riding with the wind. She freakin' loved being on his motorcycle with him.

Once on Highway 1, they headed south toward Sea Haven. The wind tore at her face and hair. She had shoved most of the thick mass into the helmet. It wasn't long before he turned off the main highway to a road leading east. She suddenly had a bad feeling. She thought he was taking her to a restaurant, but as far as she knew, this was private property.

He rode between two gates and continued along a narrow lane that led through the property. A house loomed up. He drove right to it and stopped. She stayed right where she was. He killed the motor, and she still didn't move.

"Where are we?" She couldn't keep the suspicion out of her voice.

Before he could answer, a little girl burst out the door. She was no more than five or six. "Uncle Reaper! I didn't know you were coming." She ran right down the steps, hopped around the motorcycle like a bunny and then seemed to notice Anya. The hopping stopped and curiosity crept onto her delicate features. "Who are you?" The child had the reddest hair she'd ever seen. Freckles spread across her nose, just a dusting, but Anya found it adorable.

"Emily, this is my friend Anya. I want you to be very nice to her and show her around. She's been having a little bit of a tough time lately. Can I count on you?"

Anya's mouth dropped open. His entire demeanor changed when he spoke to the child. His harsh features softened. He didn't smile, but his mouth didn't seem so hard. His voice was gentle. Sweet even.

Emily studied Anya's face for a long time even while she nodded solemnly. "She's really pretty."

"Great skin," Reaper conceded.

Anya's mouth refused to close. She was a little afraid bugs would fly into it. He shocked her. She didn't think Reaper could be so easy or soft. She couldn't believe he was talking about *her* skin. *Great?* He thought she had great skin? He held out his arm to steady her as she climbed off. She felt strange curling her fingers around his biceps to swing off the bike. When she looked up, a woman stood on the porch with Czar, his arm wrapped possessively around her waist.

"Reaper. Anya." Czar smirked at his friend.

Reaper flipped him off. "Lookin' for breakfast or early lunch, Blythe. Are we too late?"

Blythe flashed him a bright smile, her gaze sliding to Anya. "You're never too late for food around here, Reaper, you know that. Come on in."

Emily reached up and took Anya's hand a little shyly. That sprinkling of freckles across her nose endeared her even more to Anya, as did the gesture.

"Blythe's a good cook," Emily confided in a loud whisper. "Everyone likes to eat here. Specially Ice and Storm. They never stop eating."

Czar laughed. Blythe joined him. Anya couldn't help but notice Reaper still hadn't cracked a smile.

"Should we expect everyone this afternoon?" Blythe asked Reaper.

He shrugged. "Probably. They're all being asses. Even Alena and Lana. I thought I could count on them." He stepped back to allow Emily to escort Anya up the steps.

Blythe shot Anya a quick, sympathetic glance. It made Anya breathe a little easier. Czar's wife seemed normal. The house was beautiful, with wide-open spaces. She noticed that Reaper hesitated at the door before he stepped inside. She didn't know why that tugged at her heartstrings, but it did.

"Unusual circumstances, Reaper," Czar said. "They'll figure it out."

Anya had no idea what they were talking about. Half the time, the club members seemed to talk in code.

"Maybe you'd better fire up the barbecue, honey," Blythe suggested to Czar. "We can do something simple like hamburgers and veggie burgers. It will be easier to feed a large group."

"Large group?" Anya echoed faintly.

Reaper glanced over his shoulder at her. "Emily is right there. She'll show you around and keep anyone from saying anything mean."

"Was someone mean?" Blythe asked, sending an anxious glance toward Czar.

Instantly he wrapped his arm around her and kissed her. It wasn't a little peck on the cheek by any means. It was a full-on kiss to end all kisses. Anya had to look away. It wasn't hard to see that the president of Torpedo Ink was madly in love with the woman who wore his ring on her finger.

"I really shouldn't stay," Anya said, deciding if she didn't speak up for herself, she was going to be entangled deeper and deeper in a world she didn't understand, didn't want—that didn't want her in it.

Reaper stopped in his tracks. He turned, his motorcycle boots surprisingly noiseless as he stalked across the room straight to her. Both hands went to her waist. He didn't break stride, but kept walking, taking her to the wall so she was trapped there, his body holding her prisoner. She looked around him, expecting Blythe to say something, but Czar had already swept Emily and his wife into the next room, leaving them alone.

She stared up at Reaper's implacable face. He could have been stone for all the expression she got. He had that scary vibe again, the one he'd lost when little Emily had skipped down the steps outside and rushed him.

"You aren't leavin'. We had this discussion, and we're done with it."

Her breath hissed out as she struggled to hold her temper. "It isn't a discussion if one person lays down a decree and the other doesn't get to talk."

"That's all the discussin' we're going to have over this. Keep an open mind and let yourself have a good time. Blythe and her kids are . . . special. Give them a chance."

Great. Now if she didn't stay she'd look judgey. Well, she kind of was, if she were being honest. After first meeting Betina and Heidi, and then Lana and Alena, she had no more interest in meeting the women in the club. There wasn't anything to say without looking like she was giving in to him, and she had the feeling the slightest inch with him and he'd take that proverbial mile.

His hand came up to her hair. He sank his fingers deep, pulling gently on the strands. "They hurt you, didn't they?"

She pressed her lips together tightly. She wasn't a tattle-tale, running to her daddy to fix it because someone hurt her. She'd never had that option. No one had protected her. No one had fixed things for her. No one had ever given a damn whether she was hurt or not.

His body was so warm. Too big. Too close. He'd taken a shower and she could smell that faint scent she associated with him. Man. Motorcycle. Outdoors. She took a breath and her breasts brushed his chest.

"Stay, Anya. You have a job. I've got a place for you to stay. The fuckin' thing is an albatross around my neck. Big house right on the cliff. It's empty right now. You could stay there and help me get the fuckin' thing fixed up. I don't know what I'm supposed to do with it."

She frowned up at him, not understanding. "Are you saying you have a house? Your own house?"

He fiddled with her hair, nodding.

"You *own* a house but you don't live in it."

"Got nothing in it. Bed in the bedroom is all. Never slept in it. Halfway through the night I have to get out of there so I can breathe. Four walls close in on me sometimes. Czar insisted we all have a home, so there it sits, like a crouching monster, waiting to eat me alive."

Wow. Okay. What did one say to that? She had the strange desire to put her arms around him and hold him close. There was a lot he was saying in that strange description of his home. Her body was going up in flames, but it was her heart that had her worried. Reaper was such a strange man, violent, impenetrable, abrupt, alone, sexy as hell, suddenly sweet and then this . . . vulnerable. She could maybe hold out against his sexy, his sweet, but never this. Never such a strong man giving her something she knew he didn't give others—especially not his club brothers.

"I'm not the best interior designer," she said, lying her ass off. She rocked at it. She'd always wanted a home. *Always*. She'd dreamt her entire life about having her own home. Her own family. A man she could spoil. She'd learned to cook, although there was only her to cook for. She baked amazing desserts. She made bread. Every apartment she'd ever had she'd worked to keep clean and make as nice as possible because it mattered to her. She even read books on gardening, because someday, she was going to do that too.

"You've got to be better than me." He stepped back, allowing her to breathe air that wasn't all about Reaper. He took most of the heat with him.

"Stick close to Blythe when the others get here," Reaper advised.

She frowned at him. "Do you think the others are coming?" By *others*, did he mean Lana and Alena? She hoped not. She'd rather Betina and Heidi show up. At least they didn't pretend to be anything but what they were. She liked them both. She didn't want their life, but at least she liked them. She could understand wanting to be a part of something, and both women were determined to be part of the club in any capacity they could. Anya wanted to tell them they were doubtless going about it the wrong way, but what did she know?

She probably had put Lana and Alena on a pedestal. The two of them were almost revered by the male members of the club. She knew how rare something like that was. Every club member she'd met talked about them as if the two women were the backbone of the club. She'd been there long enough to realize the backbone was Czar. But the two women were definitely loved by the men in Torpedo Ink.

Reaper reached for her wrist, his long fingers closing around it like a bracelet. He was gentle this time as he led her into the kitchen where Czar leaned against the counter, his gaze fixed on Blythe's face as she deftly sliced tomatoes. She was laughing, her head back, her eyes shining. On the counter was Emily, her father's arm around her waist. It was a normal scene, a casual one, but it choked her up. Czar had a family he loved. She'd never seen this side of him, and it was beautiful.

Czar turned his head as they entered the room, his gaze dropping to Reaper's fingers circling her wrist. "You ready to give me a hand? I thought we'd fire up the big grill."

Reaper nodded. "I heard the hogs arriving."

He had? Anya hadn't heard anything. Did he mean the motorcycles or the men because they ate too much? She didn't know, nor did she care. She was going to do exactly what he said and stick close to Blythe. Hopefully, that would get her through the lunch. In the afternoon, she'd get to her car, pick up her clothes and some money and find out how much the repairs were going to cost her.

Ice and Storm sauntered in. She kept her eyes on the floor, trying not to think about Ice naked. He had a good body. A gorgeous body. Not that she'd looked, but how could one unsee something like that? He gave her a small salute and then leaned in to kiss Blythe on the temple. "Got coffee, babe? I need caffeine." He plucked Emily off the counter and swung her around. "Hey beautiful. Where's my kisses?" She squirmed until he put her down, and she ran a few feet from him.

"You don't get any, Uncle Ice," Emily screeched, her brown eyes dancing in merriment. "I'm giving them all to Uncle Storm." She raced across the kitchen straight into Storm's open arms.

Storm braced himself and then pretended to stumble

back against Savage, who leaned down and kissed Emily's forehead. "That's called stealing," he said. "Just pointin' it out, Em."

"You're taking up space in my kitchen," Blythe said. "Pick up a knife and get busy, or head out to Czar and Reaper." She pointed with the blade of her knife to the door leading to the backyard.

The twins held up their hands in surrender. Anya could see she was losing Emily to the good-looking bikers, but she couldn't blame the little girl. She caught Savage watching her as she stepped to the counter and picked up a knife and pulled a tomato to her.

"How bad is he hurt?" She kept her head down. It was stupid to ask when she was certain Savage wouldn't answer.

"It's under control. Not the first time, won't be the last."

She was pretty sure she got that. She nodded, pretending great concentration on her tomato. "Thanks, Savage."

It felt strange talking to him. Savage, like Reaper, rarely spoke. Certainly not to her. She wasn't part of the club and never would be. There was no role for her, other than bartender. Still, they'd protected her.

"Reaper was hurt?" Blythe asked, pausing in her slicing.

Savage shot her a glance. "No big deal, babe, he's fine. You makin' your potato salad?"

"I thought pasta," Blythe said. "It's faster."

"Potato," Savage said decisively. "Or both."

Blythe laughed and pointed with the tip of her blade. "Out." As soon as he was out of the kitchen, she pulled out a bag of potatoes. "They love to eat. I can never keep enough food in the house."

Anya took over slicing the tomatoes, pickles and onions for the burgers. "I can't imagine how much food you go through if they all eat here. Do you always cook for them?"

Blythe washed the potatoes. "A lot of the time, but everyone pitches in. This is impromptu in your honor."

Anya's heart jumped. "What?" She turned just as two more of the club members came in. Absinthe and Preacher gave her a wave, looked at each other, grinned and hurried to kiss Blythe. "Anything you need? Store run? You name it."

"We're good. The others are in the back." Blythe waited until they were out. "It isn't every day Reaper puts a woman under his protection formally. As in never."

"I don't understand." She didn't. She often didn't get the terms they used or understand the logic of their choices.

"That's all right, Anya. Just know, once Reaper says you're protected, the entire club will protect you. They have Lana and Alena they claim as their own. Me. My three girls and Kenny. Now you."

Anya ducked her head, shaking it as she deftly sliced pickles. "You misunderstand. He doesn't even like me. He wanted me fired. I think he felt bad over asking Czar to fire me when later he discovered I was . . ." She bit her lip. God. Was she really going to admit to Blythe that she was homeless, living out of her car? Did she want the woman to look down on her the way Lana and Alena so obviously had? Screw it. "Living in my car. Camping at the Egg Taking Station."

Blythe drew in her breath. "That wasn't safe."

Keys, Master, Transporter and Mechanic came in. With them was Fatei, the prospect. He trailed after them. The four club members kissed Blythe, nodded at Anya, really looking her over, taking their time until Blythe laughed and threw a wooden spoon at them. They went out, and Fatei looked around the kitchen.

"Be glad to help. What can I do?"

"You know where the paper plates and napkins are, Fatei," Blythe said. "Would you get them and take them out to the tables outside? Maybe the others can help you move the tables into the sunshine."

He nodded and was gone, leaving Anya and Blythe alone again. Anya wished she had Blythe's easy manner with the men. With the bar between them, Anya was in her element, but right now, she felt under scrutiny. "Why are they all acting weird toward me? They're staring."

"You have on Reaper's shirt."

The way Blythe said it, Anya knew immediately she had the wrong impression. Most of his club brothers probably did as well. "No, you don't understand. It isn't what you're thinking. Lana and Alena brought me some clothes because I didn't have time to get mine out of my car. The top was . . ." Now she was being a tattletale. "It just didn't fit, so I asked him for a shirt to put over it." She knew she was blushing. She couldn't help it, couldn't help remembering the feel of Reaper's knuckles brushing over her breasts as he'd buttoned the shirt.

Blythe turned away from the stove where she'd put the potatoes on to boil. "Let me see."

"It's pretty awful." She opened the shirt to show Blythe the tank with the lacy bra showing and her breasts bulging out everywhere.

Blythe looked at her and then turned her gaze to the doorway. Lana and Alena were frozen there, Steele, the vice president, just behind them. Both women looked at Blythe, shame on their faces. Steele put them gently aside and came across the room. Anya, horrified, her face bright red, buttoned up Reaper's shirt and wished the floor would open so she could fall through.

"We haven't formally met," Steele said, holding out his hand to Anya. "You're Anya."

She nodded. "Bartender," she reminded. She wanted that formal title now, to disassociate herself from Reaper. Everyone was getting the wrong idea. She didn't want them to get that idea about her. It would be too difficult later on when they all remembered Reaper had wanted her fired. Gone. He was being nice because of her circumstances, but that didn't change the fact that he didn't like her.

She held on to that. Held it close to her like armor. Her

only protection against what she was feeling for him. One night of wild, soul-destroying sex was one thing; anything to do with her heart was off-limits. She had to keep Reaper at arm's length. She couldn't see how vulnerable he could be. She couldn't recognize that he was traumatized by something that had happened in his past. She didn't want to see that the brothers in his club were worried about him and maybe wanted his kindness to her to mean something else just a little too much.

She shook Steele's hand, smiled at him and went back to her slicing while Blythe pulled eggs out of the refrigerator for the potato salad.

"Anya." Alena spoke first. "It was a shit thing to do, bringing a top that small. I'm sorry. We brought you a few that will fit better. Please try them on."

She glanced at them. There seemed to be genuine remorse on their faces. "What did I do wrong?" She put down the knife. "You have to be aware I don't know the first thing about this lifestyle. I needed a job. I'm a good bartender. Actually, I'm a great bartender. The club needed one so it was a good fit for both of us. I'm trying to learn, but I seem to get on everyone's nerves. Yours. Reaper's. Just straight up tell me what I'm doing wrong."

The two women exchanged a long look, mostly puzzled. "Why would you think you're getting on Reaper's nerves?" Lana asked, coming around the island to take the bunch of broccoli Blythe was holding out.

"He wanted me fired. He called me a bitch and asked Czar to fire me. I've never been a bitch to anyone. I don't even make Betina and Heidi clean the bar after hours, especially if they had a hookup." Anya was genuinely confused. "Then, today, it was made rather plain that no one wanted me around, I go to leave and Reaper won't let me. He won't even discuss it with me."

They were all crazy as far as Anya was concerned. She didn't mind confronting Lana and Alena. Her temper was close just seeing them. She might be a shelter child but she had enough pride to tell them both to go to hell rather than accept charity from them.

"What the fuck is going on in here?" Reaper demanded, making all of them jump. His voice was low. He hadn't raised it, but he sounded as scary as hell.

FIVE

"Reaper, language," Blythe reminded gently.

"Nothing's going on," Lana assured quickly. "Just girl talk."

Reaper stalked across the room, stealing Anya's breath and sending a little frisson of fear creeping down her spine. He just looked lethal. Dangerous. His blue eyes moved over her face. He didn't look at anyone else, or even acknowledge their presence. He caught the front of the shirt he'd loaned her and tugged until she was right in front of him. One hand slid under the mass of her hair, curling around the nape of her neck. It felt like possession. Ownership.

"Anya?" His thumb slid along her cheek.

That felt . . . sweet. Caring. She couldn't look at anyone, certain they would see her nipples pushing hard into the nearly nonexistent bra. They'd know her panties were damp and her clit throbbed with need. How did he do that? How was his voice like gravelly velvet, sliding over her skin like the touch of fingers? Rough. Soft. At the same freaking time.

Her eyelashes fluttered because her voice didn't work. She just stared into his blue eyes and was lost.

"We can go."

There was no way she was going anywhere with him, as tempting as it was. No way. She might lose her mind and jump him. She managed to shake her head, but she was unable to look away from the intensity of his blue eyes. She wanted to tell him he wasn't safe and he'd better get on his bike and run away as fast as he could go, but she couldn't do that with the other women looking on.

"You sure?"

She nodded. What an idiot. She couldn't actually talk? She was a bartender, for God's sake. A damned good one. She relied on her ability to talk bullshit with anyone, but around Reaper, she found herself completely gone. No brain. He reduced her to pure need and her brain just checked out. They said it was true of men; well, she was there to testify it happened to women too.

"All right. You need me, come and get me."

Anya nodded again. His fingers tightened for a moment and then he was gone, just as quickly and silently as he'd entered the room. She stood there like an idiot staring after him, wondering what was going on. A month of silence and now this. She would never understand him, not in a million years. Biker behavior was a far cry from what she'd thought it was.

Blythe cleared her throat. "So. Anya. You were just telling us that Reaper doesn't like you. That he tried to get you fired. You might want to continue the story for us. Because between the trying to get you fired and now, there seems to be a huge gap."

Anya looked from Blythe to Lana and Alena. All three were staring at her with the same shocked look on their faces. "He's just acting weird," she said. "It started last night when he took me to the campground where I was staying. My car was dead. It was cold, and he felt bad. Really bad."

Lana poked Alena. "Because Reaper is known for feeling bad."

Anya picked up the knife she'd abandoned when Reaper had come in. "I just don't understand any of this, so I can't explain it to you. He brought me back to the clubhouse and let me sleep there." When Blythe raised her eyebrows, she clarified. "Alone. We're not . . ." Her hands fluttered helplessly. There was no explaining Reaper's behavior. "He went from sitting in the bar every single night for over a month and not speaking a word to me, to wanting me fired, to bringing me here."

"He sat in the bar every single night for over a month?" Alena echoed. "Did Preacher tell you that, Lana?"

Lana shook her head. "He wouldn't rat on his brother."

Anya put her hand over her mouth. "I shouldn't have told you that? Why not? I really, really don't belong here. I don't understand anything." She'd never been so frustrated in her life. It wasn't like she normally went around desperately needing sex. Since meeting Reaper, she'd been on edge, moody and totally frustrated. Lately, it had been a thousand times worse. Coupled with not knowing the rules, she found herself ready to scream.

"Pasta salad," Blythe told the two club members. "You know how to make it. Get busy. I'm working on the potato salad, and Anya's getting everything ready for burgers."

"There's nothing wrong with telling us that Reaper sat in the bar, Anya," Alena assured. "Preacher wouldn't do it because there's this entire brotherhood code that's pretty ridiculous and makes the two of us crazy. We grew up with them. We're in the brotherhood, but because we have vaginas they treat us different."

"They're protective of you," Blythe pointed out.

"Which is rather silly, don't you think?" Lana asked.

"I think it's sweet," Blythe said.

"Where are you from, Anya?" Alena asked.

Anya should have been expecting the question. She

weighed her answer. She had to be careful. "San Francisco was the last place. I move around a bit."

"Where were you born?" Lana persisted. "We were born in Russia. All of us were. Every member of the club. We were all in a school together there."

None of them had much of an accent, but Anya didn't question what Lana told her. There was no reason to lie. "I was born in LA. I don't think I was actually born in a shelter but I don't remember anything else—my mother went from shelter to shelter. I can't remember anything other than the streets." She forced herself to be matter-of-fact. If they were going to judge her, the hell with them. There wasn't an ounce of shame in her voice, nor was she looking for pity. She didn't need it.

"Is your mother still alive?" Blythe asked.

"Nope." Keeping her voice casual was harder. "She died when I was a teenager. Drug overdose. I was surprised she lasted that long." But she'd loved her mother, and when her mother remembered her, life was good for the two of them. Even in the shelter.

"How'd you end up a bartender?" Alena asked.

"I saw a program on television. It was a bartender famous for his tricks," Anya admitted. "He was mesmerizing. He could toss bottles around like you wouldn't believe. I thought it was the coolest thing I'd ever seen. I knew if I could get to be that good, I could make money. Bartending school wasn't as pricey as college, and a bartender can get a job almost anywhere. The payout is much sooner as well, so for me, it made sense. It also helped that I have an amazing memory."

"Can you do some of those tricks?" Lana asked.

Anya nodded. "Absolutely. That's the fun part. I give my customers flair and they love it. I get better tips and it works great all around. It's not easy and I have to practice regularly, but I learned less is better."

"Preacher didn't tell me you can do tricks," Lana complained.

"He doesn't know. They're showy, only done in certain kinds of bars. They wouldn't be welcome here. I'd just look like I was showing off."

"Can you teach me?" Lana asked.

"And me," Alena added.

"Sure, if I'm around long enough. The garage has my car right now. They're hopefully fixing it."

"Wait," Blythe said, frowning. "You aren't sticking around?"

"Like I said, despite what you saw from Mr. Conflicted, I'm not his favorite person. I can't afford to have my job yanked out from under me when next he decides he wants me gone. I have to plan things. That's my personality. If I don't have a plan, I get overwhelmed."

The three women exchanged a long look again that Anya pretended not to see. Two men stuck their heads in the door. One was covered in tattoos and Anya recognized him as Ink. He rarely came in the bar. The other was named Maestro and she knew he played a multitude of instruments because occasionally, he and a couple of other club members jammed together in the bar. He was really, really good.

"Everyone out back?"

"No, Ink," Lana said in a snippy voice. "*Everyone* clearly is *not* out back because we're right here. Four of us. Women. You know, *females*."

Ink grinned at her. "That time of the month, huh, babe? Feelin' your pain."

He ducked when she threw a bag of pasta at him. They could hear his laughter as he joined the other men outside. Maestro put his hands in the air in surrender and followed him.

"Idiot," Lana huffed under her breath. "I'm going to run off to another state for a while. On my own. I need to get out from under them."

"I'll go with you," Alena volunteered.

"Oh, no you don't. You're not leaving me with all of

them," Blythe said. "They barely have manners. At least you two have them semitamed. Without you around to keep them in line they'd go rogue on us. You can just stick it out and help me."

Lana and Alena exchanged a long look and then burst into laughter. "You're hard up if you think we're the answer to helping you teach them manners. We don't know any better than the boys."

Anya could listen to them talk all day. The camaraderie was something she'd never experienced. The shared laughter. They had a past together. They had a future. Just from the way they spoke to one another, she could tell the three women would always be friends. She wanted that. She craved being a part of something. She wanted friends, a home, a family most of all. Getting those things seemed to be so much harder than she'd ever imagined.

She'd never considered that a biker club could be about family. She'd lived on the streets and run into all kinds of people, most just trying, like her, to survive. Many had run from their families, couldn't find their way back to them, but wished they could. She watched parents dropping their children off at school, hugging them, purchasing clothing and food for them and longed for that in her own life. She'd never considered a man like Czar, so remote and distant, would do those same things for his children—and when he couldn't one of his brothers was doing it for him.

She looked out the window, watching the twins chase little Emily around the yard and then lift her up to their shoulders. They brought her right into the circle of men and each one greeted her, teased her, talked to her like she mattered. "Preacher mentioned you had four children," she said, still watching the child. She envied her. She wanted that for her children as well. No shelters. She couldn't imagine these men turning their backs on that child if something happened to Czar and Blythe.

"We do. We have three girls and one boy," Blythe said.

"The three girls are sisters. Darby is the oldest, and she's amazing with her sisters, although she and Kenny argue a lot. I think they both want the other to concede they're the top dog." She laughed softly as if their arguing was funny rather than annoying.

"We brought Kenny home to Blythe," Alena confessed. "He was in a bad way, but she took him in immediately. It's a wonder what she's accomplished with him."

Anya had no idea what they were talking about, but she wanted to hear more. Clearly Blythe hadn't given birth to the four children, but watching Czar with them and hearing the love in Blythe's voice, she knew those children were theirs. They loved them as much as any birth parent could.

"Darby doesn't think so. She's after him all the time to study. They're at Airiana's house right now. It's just down the road. They go to school there. Zoe's with them." She frowned. "Our Zoe is still having nightmares. We've got her in counseling, but so far . . ." She broke off, shaking her head. "I think it's good for her to be with Airiana's children. They talk about what happened to them among each other at times. Darby says she thinks that's helping Zoe a little bit." She looked straight at Anya. "They were all victims of human trafficking. Airiana's children, other than her new baby, and other than Emily." There were tears in her eyes.

"Blythe." Alena's voice was soft. Gentle. Caring. It was the first time Anya had ever heard those notes in her voice. "I see them now, and I saw them then. You've done wonders for them. They love it here, and most importantly, they feel safe."

Anya's heart clenched hard. Safe. Safety. She would never have equated that with a motorcycle club either. Maybe it wasn't in all clubs, but certainly in this one, they cared about family and children.

Blythe looked out the window, her gaze on Czar. "Thank you, Alena. Sometimes, because we're so close to it, we hear them at night, or find them hiding in a closet, scared out of their minds, it feels like we're swimming against a terrible current." Her hand fluttered against her throat. "Czar is amazing. So strong. Always steady with them. I tend to be the baby and cry with them."

Alena put down the spoon she was stirring the spiral noodles with and went to Blythe, wrapping an arm around her. "You took care of me when I needed it, Blythe, that's why I can tell you without reservation, you're the heart of us. Of all of us. Of those kids."

Anya blinked back the tears shimmering in her eyes. She'd never, not in a million years, have thought Alena could be so caring. Hearing about the children broke her heart. She'd seen children come into the shelters, traumatized. Here, there were people who cared. A *lot* of them, clearly.

Czar, beer in hand, suddenly turned toward the house, looking at Blythe through the window. He saw Alena with her arm around her waist and immediately started jogging across the lawn. Anya watched him come toward them. He had eyes only for Blythe, although Anya had the feeling he saw everything. The minute he was on the move, the entire group went electric, on alert. Both Reaper and Savage flanked him, spreading out, as if watching his back.

A little shiver of awareness went down her spine as she looked at their faces. Hard as steel, eyes cold as ice, deep lines carved through their already tough features. She was looking at the other side of them. An image of the knife penetrating Deke's flesh, driving deep, all the way to the hilt, Reaper so casual. Savage saying he would take care of it. What was she thinking? She stepped back as Czar entered.

He went straight to his wife and pulled her into his arms. She heard him murmur something, and Blythe laughed, although Anya could tell she was crying. Reaper came in behind him, Savage was nowhere in sight. Reaper's gaze swept the room, a thorough inspection, and then he glanced at the couple before his gaze landed on Anya.

She detested that her body felt that penetrating look all

the way to her core. Heat coiled, moved through her veins, a slow burn that was like a hot fire spreading lazily through her entire body. She pressed her hand to her stomach where knots gathered. He was so disturbing with his rough edge, one minute shoving her away, the next bringing her close.

He didn't speak, only looked at her, and she had the feeling he knew she was trying to back away again, trying to talk herself into getting out while she could. She knew there would never be a relationship with Reaper. He wasn't that kind of man and he never would be. Even if he let himself care, he would want to control every aspect of their liaison. He would insist on ruling her. She wasn't that kind of woman, even if they could find a way to be together.

Czar spent a few minutes kissing Blythe and teasing her openly until she was laughing and smiling. Anya couldn't help noticing that his hands moved over Blythe's body, under her tank, over her butt, and no one seemed to pay the least bit of attention. Anya squirmed because the entire time, Reaper watched her, not them, and her body grew hotter, so hot she was afraid she might spontaneously combust. She ached. Really, really ached. Everywhere.

Czar finally lifted his head, grinning, appearing so much younger than Anya had ever seen him look. "Should I send Fatei in to help make the burgers?"

"That's your job," Blythe said.

"Babe."

Lana put her hand on her hip. "Tell Ink, *he* can make the burgers. He isn't doing anything but standing around trying to look hot."

"Are you still carrying a grudge against that poor man?" Czar asked.

"Poor man, my ass. If he ever tries to boss me again, I'm going to slit his throat," Lana declared, and Anya believed her.

She took a step back from the counter. This wasn't the place for her. She wasn't a violent person. She had a temper, but she didn't ordinarily strike out at anyone physically, as she had with Reaper. She'd put her hands on him more than once, and that wasn't acceptable behavior in her mind. These people thought nothing of slitting throats and throwing knives.

"Anya's going to help me put my house together," Reaper announced unexpectedly. Shocking her.

Her gaze jumped to his. His eyes were bluer than ever. A penetrating, piercing blue that took her breath and saw right into her. Every thought. She knew he'd done it on purpose, telling the others so she wouldn't back out. He knew she'd been thinking of running again. Clearly, she didn't have a poker face.

The room had gone so silent she wanted to scream just to fill it. Her tongue touched her lower lip and then she turned her attention to slicing the last of the pickles. She still had the onions to go. Maybe she could drive everyone out of the room if she started them.

"You going to be living there?" Czar asked Reaper.

Her gaze jumped back to Reaper's. He nodded his head slowly. "Anya needs a place to stay and I need the place fixed up. She agreed to help me."

Had she? She couldn't think straight with him looking at her like that. She just wanted to fall right into all that blue. At the same time, she wanted to run away, as fast and as far as possible. She was willing to have sex with him. Sex without strings. She couldn't live his lifestyle and no way was he changing it, not for any woman.

She knew in motorcycle clubs, women were second to the club. She'd been second her entire life. That would never happen with the man she loved. She intended that he would always be first, but she wanted—even needed—to be first in his life. Reaper would put all these men and women before he would ever put a woman—if he even kept one.

"Nice," Alena said. "If you need any help, Anya, let me know, I'd be more than happy to help. If you're into that kind of thing, I'm working on my restaurant right now, trying to come up with some interior designs. It's not really my thing and I wouldn't mind advice. Lana and I are hitting our heads on the wall half the time."

"You're starting a restaurant?" Anya asked. She'd seen the large building that had finally been completed. It had banks of windows, but inside, when she'd stopped to look, there was nothing on the walls or floors.

"I love to cook. I thought it would be fun to have a place to actually cook and have someone eat what I make besides my monster brothers who would eat anything and call it good."

Alena's voice was carefully casual. Anya could see the restaurant meant a lot to her.

"We've come to a standstill, because the interior is mine to figure out and I have no idea what I want. Ice and Storm told me to just hire someone, but then it's really not mine. I thought just talking it out would give me ideas, but so far, nothing. The building just sits there, after costing the club so much money."

"Babe." Czar's voice was gentle. "Stop that. That money is all of ours. We're golden right now, so no worries on how long it takes. You want it to be yours, do it your way."

"Thanks, Czar." Alena sent him a small smile.

"Won't hurt if Anya takes a look," Reaper said, volunteering her.

She would have volunteered herself a minute earlier because she felt Alena's genuine distress, but now that Reaper had done it she wanted to throw something at him. She was *leaving*. She'd made up her mind. She didn't belong in this world no matter how much certain aspects of it appealed to her.

"Would you mind, Anya?" Alena asked.

Anya wasn't certain whether Alena was trying to make up for the two-sizes-too-small tank, or really wanted her opinion, but she didn't have much choice. "Of course I'd

love to look at it. I've stopped a few times and peered
through the window because the building is so cool."

The foundation was cut out of the hillside, high enough to
give a view of the ocean, and behind it the hillside was ter-
raced. Already the plants were beginning to grow up, taking
the shape of a wild garden one could see through the banks
of glass. It wasn't huge, but gave a more intimate vibe, as if
it was a secret place one might stumble on and enjoy with
friends, someone special or family.

The club bought and employed locally if they could. They
had a good relationship with Inez at the grocery store in Sea
Haven and were in talks with her to open a smaller version
in Caspar for the locals. The small town already had the
new garage and tattoo shop. Both were building a reputation
for good service and excellent work. The bar was doing
extremely well, and on Friday and Saturday nights, there
was live music. Maestro, Keys, Player and Master played.
They were looking for a vocalist, but wanted the right one.
Now, if Alena had her way, they'd have a restaurant.

Reaper and Czar left, and the women immediately began
to prepare the food in earnest. While the potatoes and boiled
eggs were cooling in the refrigerator, Blythe chopped up
dill pickle and black olives to add into the salad. Lana and
Alena quickly put the rest of the ingredients for the pasta
salad together while the spiral noodles were cooling. Anya
sliced the onions.

"I can shape the burgers," she offered. "I don't mind."

"Let the men do it," Blythe said. "Czar knows there's
only a few of us and we can't cook for all of them without
help all the time. It won't hurt for them to learn to help out
in the kitchen. Czar's always helped me. Sooner or later,
those men are going to find women that they want to spend
their lives with. When that happens, I want them to be at
least partially civilized. Otherwise, I'm going to have a few
complaints on my doorstep."

Anya looked up, puzzled. "I keep missing parts of the

conversation. Why would you get complaints if the men aren't acting civilized?"

Lana laughed. "She's Wendy. You know, Wendy from *Peter Pan*. Alena read this article about how some men are Peter Pan and never want to grow up and every Peter Pan needs a Wendy willing to surround herself with lost boys. She's our Wendy. Czar isn't Peter Pan because he's definitely grown-up . . ."

"I might argue if he was in the room," Blythe objected with a smile.

"But the rest of us are her lost boys. Alena and I included. She's the one we all go to. She collects lost children too."

"Um. No. You bring them to me," Blythe corrected.

"But you take them in," Alena pointed out. She blew Blythe a kiss. "I was a total bitch, Anya, when I had to move in with Blythe and Czar. I was hurt pretty bad. Didn't think I'd live, didn't know if I wanted to. Blythe worked her magic. I can recommend her highly."

Blythe blinked back tears. "I love you, idiot. Stop making me feel all mushy. Let's get this food done or we'll have a rebellion on our hands."

Anya had felt safe in the kitchen with the women, but now she hesitated. She didn't want to go outside with *all* the club members. She knew most by sight, but they didn't really talk to her. Reaper was being nice for the moment, but that didn't mean he'd keep being that way. She wasn't certain what she was going to do with him.

Maybe he didn't know what to do with her, but it was clear, the club took in strays. That was most likely how he saw her. That, and he wanted her. She could see that in the way his eyes moved over her body. The way his cock was thick and long, unashamedly bulging in his jeans. He never attempted to cover up or hide it from her. She wished she could be like that. Like Czar and Blythe, who made no attempt to hide the way they felt about each other.

"Anya." Alena held out a bag. "Try one of these tops. I

think they'll fit better. All three are for you. There are limited choices here, but these are our favorite brands."

Anya took the bag, murmuring her thanks. Blythe indicated a door off the kitchen. The bathroom was spacious and smelled fresh with a hint of lavender. Anya found she was reluctant to unbutton Reaper's shirt. It enveloped her body in his warmth. It even smelled faintly of him. She had to give it back to him, because the longer she had it on, the more she felt she belonged to him. Pulling off the tiny tank, she examined the other three shirts. The two tanks were Harleys, and the other one was a brand she didn't know.

She chewed her lip as she pulled that one over her head. It was black, tight; although it fit perfectly, it was daring. Cut-out shoulder and sleeves with three more cutouts down the front. The largest right above her breasts, a smaller strip over the top curves, and a much smaller one showing a hint between the two mounds. She'd definitely fit in. There was a black bra that would go with it, support, but not show. It was sexy enough to get Reaper's attention one way or the other, but not so slutty that she would feel like her breasts were spilling out in front of everyone.

She pulled it on and examined herself in front of the mirror. Definitely sexy. What was she thinking? Entice Reaper? She was already out of her league here. She caught the hem to pull it over her head when the door opened and he walked right in. She whirled around, shocked, her mouth open. She didn't know why she was shocked, but she was. He'd done it before. Lana and Alena had done it. The club members thought nothing of locks.

"Um, Reaper. I was changing."

"Thought you might be hiding." He stared at her, took another step into the room and shut the door behind him.

Her heart went crazy. God. She couldn't breathe. He took up the entire room, and she'd thought it was a fairly large bathroom. She took a step back and bumped up against the sink. "I'm not hiding." Her voice came out a whisper.

He stepped closer. Very close. His eyes dropped to the front of her top. "This one." He said it softly, but it was an order. His finger slid over her bare skin, tracing the tops of her breasts.

"It's a little racy."

He didn't say anything, but his gaze jumped to hers. As he stared into her eyes, the pad of his finger went to the second open strip, spreading heat. Flames danced over her skin. Air was trapped in her lungs. He was touching her with one finger. *One.* That was all, and he owned her. He terrified her with his intensity. At the same time, the temptation of dancing with the devil was so strong, there was no resisting.

His finger left the second strip and slid to the third one. He never once took his gaze from hers, yet he was accurate, as if he had memorized exactly where he could touch bare skin. This time his finger stroked down her breast, tracing the swell, first on one side and then on the other. Her heart beat out of control. She had no choice but to let out her breath and then her breathing turned ragged. Labored.

Her sex throbbed. Clenched. Went more than damp. Went slick. Heat flared through her body. One finger. It was terrifying what he could do. She licked her lips, tried to think beyond the brutal pulsing in her body.

"This one," he repeated, making it a decree.

God. *God.* No one was going to save her from damnation; that was for certain. She nodded, although she didn't know if she could walk out there in front of all the club members dressed in such a sexy top. Lana and Alena wore them with ease, but she was no Lana or Alena.

The moment she nodded, his palm curved around the nape of her neck and he bent his head. She felt his breath. Warm. She closed her eyes, and his mouth was on hers. Her heart stuttered. She tasted beer. She tasted man. Then she was addicted, just like that, because *he* was there. Reaper. All commanding mouth. Hot as hell. Scorching. No hesitation. Not rough, like she expected, gentle, but totally in control of her. Leading her where he wanted to go, and he wanted to own her. To brand her. To make sure no one else would ever satisfy her. He accomplished all of it with his mouth moving over hers, his tongue sliding along hers.

One hand was at the nape of her neck, the other at her throat, his thumb sliding caresses over her soft skin while her heart pounded into his palm. His body wasn't touching hers, but she felt it, felt his heat like that of a furnace. She couldn't have moved if she wanted to because she was his prisoner, held there by his mouth, by his kiss. She had no idea anyone could kiss like that, or that a woman could be lost in a man, give herself to him, just with a kiss.

When he lifted his head, the terror was still there, maybe more so, her heart beating out of control. She knew she was lost, that he could take her over, that he *would* take her over. She had to remind herself that she didn't belong in his world and men like Reaper didn't stay. That her personality would never mesh with his. Sex was acceptable, but falling wasn't.

"Come on out of here." His voice was gruff.

It was difficult to find her voice. His hand was still on her nape, although the other reached to fiddle with her hair. The blue eyes remained on her face. "Um. Reaper. You just walked in again. This is a bathroom. I could have been on the toilet." That embarrassed her, but really, it had to be said. Even after the hottest kiss in the world. That should take the hotness factor down a peg or two for both of them.

He shrugged. "Everyone uses a toilet, Anya. No big deal." He turned and yanked the door open.

She caught up his shirt, the flannel, a security blanket just in case everyone stared at her and she couldn't take it. He took the shirt out of her hand and tossed it on the counter as they passed through the kitchen.

"I might need that. It turns cold fast here."

Reaper looked at her, took her hand and tugged until she followed him out the door. Heads turned. She should have known. She kept her chin up, but she didn't look at any of them. She kept her eyes on Blythe. If Blythe could function in this crowd of bikers, she could.

"Lana tells me you know how to do some fancy flair," Preacher said, handing her a beer as they approached the group.

She took the cold bottle from him, nodding. "It's just a fun little craft I used to work my way up through the bars to the big money." The moment the words left her mouth, she knew she'd disclosed too much. Far too much. What was wrong with her? They might be criminals. Okay, she was certain they were, but she couldn't tell them what she was running from. She didn't know them that well. Any of them. Not even Reaper. She'd come this far by keeping her own counsel.

"What are you doing slumming in a biker bar?" Czar asked, leaning his elbows on the back of Blythe's lawn chair.

She took a step away from Reaper and he caught her around her ribs, with one thick arm, just under her breasts and pulled her back to lock her tightly against his body. A claiming hold. She almost dropped her bottle of beer. Around her, the others gave one another looks she couldn't interpret. What the hell? Just because she hadn't seen him with anyone for the last month didn't mean he wasn't the resident hound dog. She'd seen the others, especially his brother, with women, so why hadn't she thought he was all over them?

A month of watching him didn't mean anything at all. He was too smooth. Too good at seduction. A touch. His mouth pure fire. Why did she ever imagine that she was special? What had given her that idea? The night before, he'd made it clear he didn't even like her. He'd called her a bitch and tried to get her fired. Now, suddenly, he was hot for her? It was sex. Pure sex. She had to keep her head in the game and her heart locked up tightly.

"You don't have to answer," Czar assured her. "You don't owe me an explanation."

Had she looked panicked? No, she'd just taken too long to answer him. She tried to shrug, to be just as casual as all of them. "I needed a change. Cities got old. I needed to breathe." That sounded good. It didn't explain her beat-up Honda or the campground, but he just said he didn't care if she didn't want to explain.

Reaper put his mouth next to hers as Czar straightened to go flip the burgers. "Better to stick to the truth, or just plain don't answer, than to lie."

She stiffened, tried to pull away, but his arm locked tight. He took another swig of beer, ignoring the tension in her.

"There's a chair right here," Blythe said, patting the one beside her.

"She's fine where she is," Reaper said.

Anya turned her head, one arm curving up and around, so she could put her hand behind his neck, looking affectionate. She put her lips against his ear. "She can answer for herself," she hissed, and bit his earlobe.

He didn't so much as flinch. He kept his arm around her body, caught her hair with his free hand, yanked her head back and took her mouth. This kiss was different. There was no gentle. This was rough. Hard. Wet. Fire poured down her throat. Not just fire. Magma. It felt like a volcano erupted and burst through her, spreading through her body, engulfing every nerve ending she had.

She felt him shift her in his arms, but her body burned for his and there was thunder in her ears. Blood pounded in her clit. His hands were on her bare skin, and she badly wanted to get to his bare skin. The roaring in her head was desperation. Need was intense. Brutal. So sharp and terrible she couldn't think straight.

Reaper walked her backward and voices faded. She found herself up against the side of the house, his hands cupping her breast, his thumb sliding over her nipple, brushing her with flames. His mouth devoured her. She heard herself give a little sob of need and then his mouth was on her, and the world felt like it exploded. Fireworks. Colors burst behind her eyes. His tongue and teeth never stopped, and then his hand was opening her jeans and sliding down.

Through the loud drumming of her heart in her ears, that booming thunder, she heard the faint sound of a child's laughter. Instantly she caught his wrist and dragged air into her lungs so she could speak.

"We have to stop."

He lifted his head, looking into her eyes. "Not happening unless you don't want me." His hand slid farther into her jeans, one finger curling into her. "You're hot and slick, Anya. Tell me you don't want me."

She looked around. They were on the side of the house away from the others. Foliage shrouded them, but she still didn't want to take the chance that Emily might walk up on them. She was a little ashamed that she would have gone for it even if the others were around, taking the chance, but not with a child.

"Emily."

Immediately he jerked his hand out of her jeans and licked his finger. "We're getting out of here."

God. Yes. She'd go anywhere with him.

SIX

Anya ducked into the kitchen to retrieve Reaper's shirt on the pretense that she needed it to stay warm on the back of his bike. It kept her from having to face anyone. Neither spoke as they hurried out, but right before she climbed on behind him, he caught the front of her shirt and kissed her again. Another blinding, fiery kiss that melted her stomach and had her kissing him back with everything she was. Giving herself to him completely. She hadn't known she could kiss like that. She hadn't known *anyone* could kiss like that.

She slipped behind him, her arms tight, and they were on the road, the big bike vibrating like a monster between her legs. One of his hands dropped to cover both of hers, pressing them tightly into his waist, the moment they were back on Highway 1. She couldn't have said how long it took to get back to the compound. The ride was a haze of need. Of dark, carnal desire. It pulsed between her legs, blood pounded in her clit and roared in her ears.

He had her off the bike and was dragging the flannel over her head as he pulled her toward the building, bunching it in his hand. He had the new top off by the time they hit the common room. She barely noticed that the two newer prospects were sitting at one of the tables, but Reaper did. He grunted something to them, reached down and caught her, tossing her over his shoulder and striding to the room he'd allowed her to stay in.

She caught at the hem of his colors, holding tight, her heart pounding. He kicked the door shut and tossed her on the bed and threw the flannel into the corner. Putting one knee on the bed, he reached for her shoes. She couldn't breathe, the need was so strong. His face was dark, cut with harsh lines of pure carnal lust. That took any breath she had left in her lungs away. She'd never seen him any way but in complete control.

His hands were strong as they peeled away her jeans and panties in one swift motion, leaving her sprawled out on the bed, naked except for her bra. Dropping to his knees at the end of the bed, he dragged her body to him, using her ankles. She had no chance to do anything to prepare. He jerked her thighs wide, tossed her legs over his shoulders, and his mouth was there. Right where she needed it the most.

She bucked, the world exploding, fragmenting as the orgasm rushed over her that fast. He didn't stop. He didn't even seem to notice. He devoured her. Ate her. Took complete control of her body so that she felt helpless against the onslaught of his mouth and teeth and tongue. He knew exactly what he was doing and he gave it all to her, so much that her mind turned to mush, so that there was no thinking person, only a wild, out of control woman, head thrashing back and forth on the sheets and her hips riding his mouth.

The third orgasm had her entire body shuddering with pleasure, but her hands fisting in his hair, trying to pull his head away. "You have to stop." He *had* to or she was going to go insane. She'd lost the ability to think properly or reason, she could only feel, and her body couldn't keep up with his wild tongue.

His head came up as if scenting something trying to deprive him of his prize. She looked into those blue eyes, so dark now, so wild, and he looked terrifying in his intensity. His face was slick with her, and that just added to the sensual, wanton lust stamped so deep in the lines there. "Belongs to me. All of this body. All of you. You take what I give you."

She couldn't. She *couldn't*. Anya shook her head, and then his mouth was back and he was once again taking control of her body and mind. Every word reverberated through her mind, bouncing off the walls until she was wailing again, his teeth raking her clit, sending her flying.

He stood, still wedged between her thighs, his eyes holding hers as he leaned down, caught her bra in one hand and ripped the stretchy lace right off her, exposing her breasts. Keeping his eyes on hers, he began to slowly pull his colors off, folding them neatly and setting them aside.

"Understand what's happening here. You're in *my* world. That means you live by our rules. This is done, you don't whine or cry or give me grief. When I say it's over, it is. You got that? I need you to say you understand."

She did. She *so* did. He was on board with the one night of pure, blazing sex, although it was daytime, but what difference did it make? This was so perfect. She needed this desperately. All those nights of looking at him, wondering what it would be like, and it was so much better than she'd imagined. Better, and yet, terrifying. She couldn't possibly keep up with Reaper's sexual needs. He was truly beyond her imagination.

"I understand. No whining. I promise."

She couldn't look away as he stripped. She felt exposed, vulnerable, her body throbbing with aftershocks, shuddering with anticipation. His body was rock hard, but covered in scars. So many. Tattoos slithered up his chest and curved over his arms. They were beautiful. Exquisite work. She wanted to explore every one of them, taste his skin, trace his muscles with her tongue. His cock was amazing. Beautiful. She wanted that too.

He didn't remove his boots or jeans, just pushed them down, caught her ankles and rolled her over, yanked her hips up so she was on her hands and knees, and then drove into her. Hard. Pushing through tight folds, so her body was forced to accept his invasion. The feeling of fullness was shocking. Stretching, burning, streaks of fire, it all was the most amazing sensation she'd ever felt. Her heart pounded. Her breasts jolted with every hard thrust.

He wasn't gentle. Not his hands, fingers digging into her hips, controlling every movement, forcing her body back into him, pushing her away and then slamming deep. Over and over. Her arms couldn't hold her and she dropped to her elbows, but he held her hips mercilessly, his cock a ruthless piston.

The fire was scorching hot. Every stroke hit a spot deep inside that sent waves of pleasure rolling through her. There was no air to breathe, but it didn't matter. Nothing mattered but the way his cock ruled her, the way it sent fire storming through every cell, building, building. He was so hot. His heartbeat thundered through her, felt through her tight muscles as his body raged in hers.

There was no holding back when the tsunami came, roaring through her, sweeping him along, his cock swelling, pushing at the sensitive tissue, striking like a hot iron, branding his name deep as she cried out, nearly sobbing as he emptied himself, as her orgasm drained him, milking every drop.

She lay there, her head on the sheet, eyes closed, fists tight, while her heart pounded out a wild rhythm. It had been the most insane, perfect storm of pleasure, and she couldn't move. She'd heard of that. Sex so great one couldn't move, but it had never happened to her. No one had ever taken control of her body like that.

Reaper lay over top of her for long moments, recovering

his breath, his hands still tight on her hips, his cock pulsing as the little aftershocks shook her. Then he withdrew and she collapsed forward. He let her, standing there, pulling up his jeans. She heard the zipper. She opened her eyes and saw his back. The tattoo that covered it, that same scary tree with so many branches, crows and skulls that was on his jacket. He caught up his jacket and without a word, left the room.

Anya lay there on the bed. Alone. He hadn't even looked at her. Not one glance. She reached for the pillow and pulled it to her, holding it tightly. She knew what she was getting into. He'd told her. She'd seen enough of club life. The women vying for their attention. She'd just become one of them. He'd spelled it out for her too. It wasn't like he hadn't. He'd said not to whine or cry. She'd wanted this.

She rolled over, wrapping her arms around her middle, staring up at the ceiling. She'd *wanted* this. So, would she do it all over again? Hell, yes. It had been that good. She'd wanted her one night of perfection, of wild, primitive, *savage* sex, and she'd gotten it with whistles and bells, and a million thundering orgasms. It wasn't like he hadn't been generous. She was a big girl and refused to cry over the abrupt way he'd left.

Reaper wasn't a nice man. She'd known that too. He wasn't a hearts and flowers man. He'd made that very clear. She'd said she understood. She had to be okay with the fact that it was a one-time deal. It didn't matter how great the sex had been, probably for him it was like that every single time. For her . . . She put the pillow over her head. For her, it was the best sex of her life. So worth it. No talking, no bossing her with his attitude. She scored. Hot. Hot, hot sex with no strings. Hell no, she wasn't going to whine.

She wasn't certain she would ever walk again. Every step would remind her of him. She felt like his name was burned deep inside her. Her breath caught in her throat. Had he used a condom? He had to have used a condom.

Oh. My. God. "Tell me he used a condom," she whispered to the universe, trying to remember if she'd heard him tear the wrapper off one. Her blood had been pounding in her ears, roaring so loud she hadn't heard much of anything.

No. She'd felt him. Every thick inch of him stretching her. Hot. Scorching hot. Burning her raw. Scraping her raw. She groaned and threw the pillow against the wall. She knew by the way his seed seeped out of her and coated her thighs that she'd been so irresponsible.

"Damn it!" she yelled and rolled over, burying her face in the sheets. There was no getting away from that shame. She'd been too crazy, too needy. Too desperate for his cock to think about protection. To think about modesty. She'd acted just like the women who hung around the club, eager to be used.

He'd carried her through the common room in just a bra and her jeans. He'd said something to someone, which meant she'd been seen. Did that mean, when she went to work tomorrow night, they'd all feel as if she were a fair target? Before, she'd been off-limits and no one in the club hit on her. She wasn't all that modest. She'd lived in shelters where there was very limited privacy, but she didn't want anyone to think she was going to be available to any other member of the club.

She sat up, groaning as her body protested. What if he went back to the barbecue and everyone was talking about her right this minute? She couldn't blame them if they did, but she wasn't sticking around and waiting for one of the others to walk in and expect her to have sex with them.

Anya reached for her bra and saw it was ripped to shreds, into two pieces, the scraps lying near the top of the bed. Sighing, she looked around for her top. He'd thrown it off of her. Where? She couldn't remember. She groaned again and buried her face in her hands.

"You're a big girl, Anya. You knew exactly what you were getting into before he even spelled it out for you, so no whining. No regrets. You want every minute of this time to be burned in your memory." It was burned deep inside of her for all time. She would probably have a spontaneous orgasm just thinking about it. "Okay, think." She whispered it aloud because she had to keep her brain working when her body was still in meltdown. He'd kept hold of his flannel, and she spotted it scrunched up in the corner. Very slowly, she climbed out of bed.

She'd keep this memory, not because Reaper had made her feel special, just the opposite, but because she knew she'd never have sex like that again. Never. She pulled on his shirt. It was long enough to cover her and she didn't want to put on her jeans until she washed up. Washed him off her. Out of her. For a moment she stood there, pressing her thighs together. Squeezing her inner muscles as if she could keep him.

"What are you thinking?" That was dangerous. That would lead to whining, and she'd promised. She'd meant that promise. She might want only one night for different reasons than Reaper had, but they both wanted the same thing.

She washed, brushed her teeth and dressed in her jeans, shoes and his shirt. She'd need to get to her car, get money and purchase a decent bra somewhere. She had a couple of T-shirts that were clean, folded and stacked with another pair of jeans on her backseat right next to the two sketch pads that had Reaper's image drawn in a hundred ways. She left the bed smelling of sex and them. Reaper and Anya. Let his club deal with the sheets; however they did that sort of thing, they had far more experience than she did.

She walked through the common room and thankfully it was empty. She spotted her shirt on the bar, where someone had picked it up off the floor and placed it in full view for everyone to see. She left it there. Everyone knew anyway. If they could be casual about sex and whatever else they did, so could she.

Anya walked out into the bright sunlight, blinking a little. The two prospects who had been in the common room earlier straightened as she came out, but she just sent them a vague smile and kept walking. Hopefully, the next time she saw either of them, she'd be behind the bar working. She was safe there. She knew how to deal with anyone from behind the bar.

She walked fast toward the garage. It was early in the day still. She could collect her money, hopefully the car, and get out to the Egg Taking Station. Thankfully, she had the night off. That was part of the reason she'd allowed herself to kiss Reaper the first time. She thought they'd have all night for his kind of glorious sex. Well, okay, if she was strictly honest with herself, she'd have to admit that once he put his mouth on hers she hadn't thought about anything but getting to a bedroom. Well, and getting into his jeans. Fast. Anywhere they were. She hadn't thought at all. She'd just felt, and that feeling had been spectacular.

She had to get to a clinic. Fast. What the hell had been wrong with her that she'd been the world's stupidest woman and had unprotected sex with a biker? He was clearly *very* experienced. You didn't get that kind of experience by being careful. When she'd run, she'd left behind everything, including her birth control pills. She never had unprotected sex. Never. Pills against pregnancy and a condom to be doubly sure as well as protection against STDs.

She pushed at her hair, reached into her jeans pocket and took out a scrunchie. He'd pulled her hair free the moment they were off the bike and she'd put down the helmet. He liked her hair. He seemed to like her body—until he was done with it. She pushed those thoughts away. She hadn't wanted a relationship any more than he did, and she wasn't going to blame him for something they had sort of mutually agreed on.

The garage had a sign on it that said "Back in a few." That was the other thing she'd learned about the club. They would show up when they wanted, no apologies. They lived their lives free of society's rules, yet they seemed to have quite a few rules of their own. Her car was sitting inside, looking miserable. She reached under the tire well and pulled out the spare key she'd hidden there. Nope. Didn't start. Sighing, she took enough money for food and water and hopefully a used sleeping bag. She knew where there were a couple of secondhand stores in Fort Bragg.

It only took a few minutes to hike up to Highway 1 and then she stood, thumb out. She got lucky. *Really* lucky. The huge black truck rumbled to a stop and she recognized the driver. Leslee worked at one of the local inns as a spa director. They'd met at the Egg Taking Station when Leslee was walking her dogs. The woman had been there several times and was very friendly, although she'd warned Anya repeatedly that it wasn't safe.

Anya didn't know her well, but Leslee was the only person she could halfway call a friend. She'd come over to talk to her while Anya sat alone on a picnic table drinking water. Leslee had immediately asked if she needed anything and offered to pick up things in town when she found Anya was staying there. She smiled at the woman, thankful her ride was someone she knew.

"Hey, lovey, where's your car?" Leslee greeted, steering the huge truck back on the highway. "I was surprised to see you."

"It's old and gets cranky on me," Anya admitted. "Had to have her towed to the garage for hopefully a very little amount of work."

Leslee studied her face. "Are you all right?"

Anya opened her mouth to answer, but closed it again, giving the question some thought. Was she? She didn't know. She had quite a bit of money saved, enough to get her to another small town. If she didn't leave and continued to work at the bar, provided Reaper didn't get her fired now that he'd gotten what he wanted—what they'd *mutually* wanted, she reminded herself—she would have enough for a room or a studio, if she could find a rental.

"Yes," she decided. She was all right. She landed on her feet because she took the time to plan. "My car is important so waiting to find out if it's fixable is difficult. I need a few things, like a bra." She tried not to blush. "And a sleeping bag. It's going to be cold without one."

"You're going to camp out without your car?" Leslee glanced sideways at her. "Anya, you're a woman alone. I go out there with my husband and four dogs—two are big mastiffs. You've been lucky not to run into any drug deals going on, or someone really losing it."

Leslee wasn't telling her anything she didn't already know. She tried to be as hidden as possible, discreetly using the outhouse and eating cold food so she didn't call attention to herself.

"I don't quite have enough money saved to get into an apartment or room somewhere. I'm close." She'd saved all her wages so she had "go" money. Renting an apartment was out because of the paperwork. A room in someone's home, that might work, but she had to make certain she had enough to leave on a moment's notice.

"Seriously, I don't like you going out there alone. I have a tiny house, but you could sleep on the couch, or we could make you a place on the porch that would be more private."

Anya's heart clenched. Few people would have made the offer, especially since, when they were talking at the camp, Leslee had laughed about how small her house was. She shook her head. "Thanks, Leslee. Really, but I don't mind sleeping at the camp. I've been taking care of myself for a very long time. I just need some supplies."

"I've got a little bit of time," Leslee said. "I'll take you to the thrift stores and then out to the Station."

⁓

Reaper backed away from the bed, yanking up his pants, his gaze glued to Anya's body. What the fuck had just happened? Everything he was, everything he believed in was gone in one second. She'd done that to him. He couldn't think. Couldn't breathe. He could only stare down at her, his mind so chaotic he didn't even know who the hell he was. He slammed the leather through his belt buckle, desperate to touch her, his body refusing his command to step away, to obey him. That brought him crashing down to reality. He hadn't been under control. At. All. Anything could have happened to her. *Anything.* What the *fuck* was wrong with him?

He kept backing up, a strange roaring in his ears. He couldn't catch his breath. His vision blurred. What had just happened? He never lost control. *Never.* A man like him couldn't afford to. His body had reacted of its own accord. Completely of its own accord. He hadn't told his cock what to do. He hadn't planned out a seduction step-by-step based on the woman and what he knew of her. This had been all natural. All real. What the fuck?

He turned on his heel and stalked out of the room, his heart pounding out of control. The pressure in his chest was enormous, pressing down on him, squeezing his heart hard. He lifted his hand to his jaw and rubbed it as he entered the common room. Both prospects turned to face him. Out of the corner of his eye he spotted Anya's shirt on the floor. He bent and picked it up, sliding the material through his fingers in a little caress, wishing he was back in the room, holding her.

"Watch her, but stay out of her way. Don't let her see you. Anything happens to her, you're both dead." He folded the shirt, placed it on the bar and strode out.

He meant it. They knew it. At least he'd protected her. The prospects knew he wasn't a man to fuck with. They weren't slouches, either of them, both had attended one of the schools in Russia. He considered those schools for pussies. He could have done that standing on his head. Still, they were both lethal, and that meant while he got his head together she would be safe.

He hadn't taken precautions. He hadn't even thought about taking them. He hadn't expected to burn until he couldn't think, until his body belonged to her, not him. What if he had killed her? *Fuck. Fuck. Fuck.* He could have killed her. He hadn't given her a gun or a knife. He hadn't cautioned Czar or Savage. He'd just taken her like a crazed bull, his mind a red haze, so far gone he could only feel.

He had no idea how many women he'd had, but never once had that happened to him. Never. He straddled his bike and hit the road. Fast. He needed the wind in his face and the devil at his back. He could have killed her because he'd been so damned selfish he hadn't considered the consequences. It never occurred to him that he would be so out of control. That his body would have a mind of its own. She'd been so hot. Scorching, so tight, surrounding him with a silken sheath that had been so pleasurable it skated close to pain. He hadn't wanted it to end. Everything about Anya appealed to him.

Her laugh. Her smile. That face. Those eyes. Her tits, so perfect, and he hadn't had time to explore what he could do with those. The way she kissed. Like fire. Like his. She hadn't even protested when he'd been rougher than hell, taking her like an animal, a savage beast gone mad. It had felt fucking great. Perfection.

She was so fuckin' beautiful. He loved the way she looked on her knees, elbows to the bed, head pressed against the sheets, all that long, gorgeous hair everywhere. Her breasts were perfect and . . . He shut down that way of thinking. It could only lead to disaster.

He lifted his face to the wind, letting it blow over him, trying to stop shaking, trying to see through the shimmering wetness. *Anya.* She'd given herself to him, done exactly as he'd instructed. That was the key. She needed to do exactly what he said and she'd be safe.

"Fuck!" He shouted it, hating himself. Hating what he was. He could just ride over the cliff, be done with it. If he

did, she'd be safe. She'd be safe and free to be with someone good. Someone decent.

He looked ahead. The curve was a long one and on the other side was the long expanse of blue. It glittered in the sun like glass. It was time. He'd always known he'd have to do it. He'd stayed alive for Savage. For Czar. Czar had them in a good place now. He wasn't needed so much by the club. By his brothers. And Anya. She needed saving, because there would be no saving her if he were alive. He'd known that from the moment he'd laid eyes on her.

Just as he entered that sweet, long curve, the one he intended to straighten out, two Harleys came up on either side of him. Ice. Storm. They moved in unison with him, in formation, just as they often did, leaning into the curve, riding the wind. They didn't say anything. They didn't look at him. They just kept his bike on the road. There would be no flying today. No soaring out over the ocean. No disappearing into all that blue.

He led the way. He knew where he had to go. Marc Centerfield ran the underground fights. They were moved from place to place, but once Savage and Reaper had competed—and won—Centerfield wanted them to compete and texted locations. He went straight to the nearest one, just on the outskirts of San Francisco.

The long drive should have cleared his head, but it didn't. Nothing could. He'd fucked up so badly, he couldn't even comprehend what had happened. He hadn't even used a condom. Never once had that happened. He'd been so out of control he hadn't even protected her that way.

It wasn't difficult to get a match immediately, and he was willing to fight one after another until he was defeated. Ice and Storm didn't try to stop him. They held his colors and kept them safe as he stepped into the ring.

The sweet pain of fists hitting flesh burst through him, clearing his mind, so there was only one thing for him. Survival. His brothers dragged him off each fallen fighter, time and again. He couldn't hear the shouts, the roars. He couldn't hear anything. He couldn't feel anymore, not the fists hitting him. Not the pain bursting through his body. He didn't react. He controlled it. Like he controlled everything. Like he'd been taught.

Ice dragged him off the fifth man and shoved him back toward Storm. "We're out of here," he informed Centerfield. "Give Storm the winnings."

"Not done," Reaper protested.

"Shut the fuck up," Ice snapped. "You're done." He shoved Reaper away from the ring, toward the hall.

Reaper went because Ice was his brother and Ice rarely got that tone. He didn't answer Centerfield when the man demanded to know when he'd be back. He just let Ice clean him up. His body had taken far more punishment than these fighters could ever inflict on him. It had been easy mopping up the floor with them. The hard part was not killing them, pulling his punches, so he didn't smash their brains, punish them for not smashing his brain the way he needed.

"You look like hell. I've texted Czar. Told him we'd be meeting him in three hours at his house. To clear the kids out or have them in bed."

Ice was back to his bossy ways. Reaper just nodded, because what was there to say? Yeah, he wanted his opponents to pound him into the ground? To take away what he was, to kill it, to kill him to keep Anya safe? It all came back to her.

Another three hours of hard riding did nothing to stop the chaos of his mind. One minute he was determined to never see her again, to send her away, keep her safe, and then the thought of never hearing her laughter, never seeing her face light up, never touching her, never having what he'd had for the first time in his life was too much to bear. That explosion. That pleasure he hadn't known existed. The absolute reality of his body making a choice. Making Anya *his* choice.

Czar stood in the yard, waiting. Smoking one of his rare cigarettes. That alone told Reaper he wasn't happy that he'd gone to Centerfield and participated in the fights again. Reaper walked right up to him. Just stood there, not knowing what to say. Ice and Storm had backed off to give him privacy, but Savage was there, looking him over, assessing the damage, just as Czar was. He had a black eye. His jaw hurt like hell and had to be swollen. There weren't many places on his body that had gone untouched. His knuckles had been iced down before they left, but they were a mess.

"Need you to make certain Anya's all right for me," Reaper said to Savage. "I put two prospects on her. Need *you* to check she's all right."

Savage nodded, hesitated, and then touched his shoulder before walking off, leaving him with Czar. It had been Czar since Reaper was that four-year-old, terrified toddler, beaten, starved, used by sick, perverted deviants and thrown into the dark. Czar had been the one to help him. To give him hope in all the madness. To make certain there was a shred of humanity left in him.

"Tell me."

Reaper wished he could hit something again. Smash it. Smash his body onto the rocks the way the waves did. "I was so out of control. My brain just shut off. Completely. I didn't think to protect her. Not in any way, Czar. I knew, watching her in that bar, I knew she could turn me inside out, but I didn't think this would ever happen."

A vision of her rose up. Anya on her knees, elbows to the bed, head pressed against the sheets, all that long, gorgeous hair everywhere. Her breasts, two perfect mounds, twin soft temptations, jolting with every stroke of his body as he hammered into her. So fuckin' beautiful.

"What happened?"

Reaper walked away from him. Paced. His mind went there again. "If she's anywhere near me, Czar, I'm not going to be able to stop myself. I thought I had complete discipline. I had none. Zero. God. I could have hurt her. I could have killed her. She could be lying on that bed right now with her throat cut."

He counted his heartbeats waiting for Czar's condemnation. Waiting for his brother to tell him he was a psychopath and now was the time to put a bullet in his head. When Czar said nothing, when there was no expected conviction, he swung around and glared at him.

"For God's sake, Czar. You know what I did. You know I killed Helena. Cut her fuckin' throat when she had her mouth on me." He looked around for something to pound. When there was nothing, he crouched low to the ground and drove his fist as deep as he could.

"Helena was a sick, perverted woman who enjoyed torturing children."

"That's not the fuckin' point and you know it." Reaper sank all the way onto the grass and dropped his aching head into his hands. "I don't have sex. Never. I tell my body what to do and it does it. I control everything. It isn't safe for anyone if I'm out of control. Even tonight, in those fights, I let Ice and Storm pull me off those pussies. I could have killed them, but I controlled how hard I hit them. I stay in control."

"Anya's alive."

Reaper nodded. The moment Ice and Storm joined him on the road, they would have texted Czar his condition. He would know everything.

"But that isn't any thanks to me. I kissed her. I kissed her and something in me just . . ." He shook his head and pounded his leg with his fist, trying to marshal his thoughts. How did he explain to Czar what he didn't understand himself?

"I lost it. I lost my mind. I was feeling things I'd never felt before. She opened up something in me, and I was crazy for her. I had to have her. I would have taken her right there, against the wall at your house. I had to have her. There was no controlling my cock from the first time I ever heard that laugh of hers. Saw that smile. I watched her give a blanket to a homeless man, a blanket she needed. I couldn't stop thinking about her after that. When I thought about her, my fuckin' cock was hard as a rock. When I saw her, it was the same. At night, I'd lie on my bed and jerk off thinkin' about her. Didn't get any relief. In the shower, I'd do the same. No help. I walk around like that all the fuckin' time."

Czar sat down in the grass facing him. "That sounds about right, Reaper. It happens when you find the right woman."

"Not to me. It isn't safe. I'm built a certain way now. They shaped me into a killer. I fight it. I control it, but I still am that before anything else."

"We all are killers. That's what they made us, but we're moving away from that life."

"No, you're moving away from that life. I'm still in that life and you know it. I'll always be in that life. That's what she'd get in her bed. A fuckin' killer. And that's if she survived the next time I touch her. You have to protect her. Get her out of here and somewhere safe where I can't find her, because I swear, I'd look for her. I'm addicted, and sooner or later, I'd have to go after her. Either that, or put a gun to my head."

There were so many things he wanted to tell Czar, things he just couldn't face about himself, things he was ashamed of and didn't want the one person in the world that he looked up to knowing. He was too ashamed. He would never be able to live with knowing Anya was somewhere in the world. He'd find her. She'd never be safe as long as he was alive.

"Slow down, Reaper. You're getting ahead of yourself. Anya is safe. She's alive. The boys are watching over her while you get your head straight. You had sex with her." Czar made it a statement. "And she's still alive."

Sex? Reaper wasn't certain he would call it that. He'd

had sex with targets. With marks. He'd studied them, met them "accidentally," seduced them and killed them. He'd been an agent for Sorbacov and his government. Sometimes the women had been killers they couldn't take care of using normal means. Sometimes they'd been women targeting high-profile scientists or government officials. Always there'd been a good reason they had a target on their backs, but certainly not warranting the way Sorbacov had insisted the hits be carried out. That had been for his own pleasure. That had been because he loved to watch. It got him off. He was a sick, sick man. Czar knew he'd been forced to go after any woman Sorbacov wanted dead, but he didn't know how sick the kills had been.

What Reaper had given to Anya had been himself. Nothing to do with training. Nothing to do with a depraved man like Sorbacov. That had been all Reaper and Anya. So sex wasn't what he'd had with her. He just didn't know what to call it.

"It's natural to want the woman you fall for, Reaper. Hell, I still can't think about Blythe without wanting her. Four kids in the house and I'm pulling her around corners, into bathrooms and closets. We sneak outside onto the roof. I can't stop and I don't want to. That's the way it should be. What they did to us, what they taught us, that isn't natural. Wanting your woman, Reaper, that's a good thing."

Reaper just shook his head, despair gripping his heart. His chest hurt. His stomach was tied up in so many knots he wasn't certain he could have stood even if his legs would have held him up. He couldn't tell Czar the entire truth without losing the man's respect.

"Wasn't it good?"

His head jerked up. "Good? Fuck, Czar. Never felt anything like that in my life. Never. That's why she's not safe. I'd find that woman no matter where she hid, that's why you have to protect her. The club needs to protect her. I'm asking for that."

"Did you even one time have it in your head to kill her? Even once? Before, during or after?"

"Are you even listening to me?" Reaper hissed it, wanting to smash his brother right in the face, knowing it was really himself he wanted to hit. "I wasn't *thinking*. I wasn't thinking about anything. Not killing, not protecting. I didn't even use a fuckin' glove. All I could do was get inside her. Wanting to live there. There was no thinking, brother. None. Never in my life have I felt that."

"You're the one not listening to me, Reaper. You're so certain something terrible is going to happen that you won't take a look at what *did* happen. You had sex naturally with a woman of your choice. You didn't think about killing her. There was no fake seduction. The two of you lit the place on fire. You didn't pull out a knife and slit her throat. You didn't put a gun to her head. You didn't garrote her. You had a wild ride and both of you survived."

Reaper took a deep breath. The air was salty. He was beginning to feel the bruises now. His body was stiffening. It hurt, but it was a good hurt, one he was familiar with. The roaring in his ears was beginning to settle enough that he could hear Czar. It helped that he'd been listening to the man since he'd been a toddler.

Czar was plainspoken. He didn't sugarcoat things. If he thought Reaper was a danger to others, he'd most likely pull the trigger himself. Of course Czar didn't know the entire story, and Reaper couldn't bring himself to tell him. They'd lived through shame together, but some things were too terrible to share, even with Czar.

He spread his fingers wide and his knuckles protested. The pain grounded him. He could take pain. He could dish it out. That was something he understood. Fire like he'd shared with Anya, wild and out of control, that was something terrifying and new. He thought he understood sex. He was an expert at it. They all were. They'd been taught every type of sex known to man, forced to learn, to be good, forced to be disciplined to resist it if needed. They'd never been taught what it would be like if the body responded naturally.

"What now?"

"Now, you explore the relationship with her, Reaper. You figure it out. That's what I had to do. That's what all the brothers will have to do when the time comes."

Relationship? What the hell was Czar saying? Reaper wasn't thinking beyond getting inside her again without harming her. Not a relationship. What did that even mean? No, sex was where he was keeping it, that was all he could do. He was so damaged there was no fixing him, and a woman didn't stay with the kind of man he was. No woman could, let alone a woman like Anya.

"What if I . . ." He couldn't bring himself to say "kill her," because the thought of that was so abhorrent he didn't dare let himself say it aloud again. He could have. "I'm not a good man."

"Neither am I, yet I have Blythe and she's a good woman. I count myself lucky."

Blythe was a miracle, but Reaper wasn't going to say that aloud. He'd said enough about his sins. "Gotta go soak before I'm too stiff to even ride. Won't be of use to you when Code gives us the information on the Ghosts."

"Then get to it. I have a warm woman waiting for me." Czar stood up and reached down with a hand to help Reaper to his feet. "Take it slow. See where it goes."

Reaper nodded. He wasn't promising anything. He had to think.

SEVEN

Anya heard the sound of the Harley long before it reached her. She was curled up, wrapped in the sleeping bag to stay warm, hidden in a circle of boulders. Thanks to Leslee, she had a ground blanket, and she'd swept off most of the rocks, but she was still cold. She sat up, listening, her heart accelerating. She'd recognize the sound of Reaper's bike anywhere.

She had no idea how to interpret her feelings. The moment she heard the bike and knew he was coming for her, her treacherous body went crazy. It didn't matter that he'd treated her like a whore, using her and walking out without a word, she still remembered every single touch of his mouth, his hands and his cock. Best sex ever. More than that, when he'd kissed her, it had felt like he'd been staking his claim. Telling her she meant something to him. Clearly, she hadn't.

Anya had replayed those kisses in her mind over and over. Replayed him walking out over and over. She told herself she was a big girl. She'd known what she was getting into. She thought she'd come to grips with it and was prepared to face him when she went to work the following night. She would be professional. Behind the bar, she could do anything, even face him picking up another woman. Maybe. Either that or she'd quit and leave like he'd wanted.

Her hair was braided in a tight weave. She reached for her bra. She was sleeping in his flannel. Damn. He'd see that and probably think she was trying to be clingy. He didn't hesitate, or call out, he rode straight up the narrow trail leading to her little nest, as if he had a tracker on her. That was impossible. The Egg Taking Station was a huge place. Lots of camping sites. How could he possibly know exactly where she was? On top of everything else, it was dark. No lights, just the moon, and that was covered in clouds. Dark clouds. That should have given her a premonition.

She extracted herself from her bag and pulled on her shoes, sitting on top of the boulder, watching him as he parked the bike. He didn't get off, or turn it completely off, he just sat there waiting. She shoved the rest of her clothes inside the sleeping bag and rolled it tight.

"How did you know where I was?"

He didn't answer her; instead, he reached behind him and pulled a jacket out of a compartment. She shoved the bag in and put the jacket on, then the dome he held out to her. She slid behind him, felt him wince when her arms went tight. Immediately she loosened her hold, using her fingers to bunch his jacket so she wouldn't have to put her arms around him.

Like he always did, he grabbed her hands and brought them around him. She didn't know why she let him or why she got on his bike without a word. She did know he was going to tell her how he knew where to find her—that is, until the pickup truck that had been parked in the campsite just below her nest fell in behind them. He'd had someone watching her.

Anya pressed her face against his back. She didn't know whether to be happy or upset about that. Upset because it felt icky to know someone had been spying on her. Happy that he cared enough to have someone looking out for her. Did that mean there was a good explanation for him going off without a single word to her? Probably not. It wasn't that difficult to say good-bye, see you later. No, Reaper was being Reaper, looking after someone working for the club, but he really was that jerk that screwed a woman and then just left her.

They drove straight to the compound, the truck sliding into the parking lot a distance from them, closer to the garage. Two men got out and in the light spilling from inside the truck, she recognized the two prospects who had been in the common room that morning. Had it only been that morning?

When Reaper slid off the bike, he looked stiff. As if his body hurt. She frowned. "Are you okay? Were you in an accident?"

He gestured toward the building, removing his gloves as he did. "Inside."

She considered hitting him over the head with the helmet, but placed it carefully on the bike instead. Head up, she walked in front of him, feeling like a wayward child whose father had come and gotten her from the wild party. It didn't help that several of the club members were seated around the bar and some at the tables. They all looked up when she came in. Some smiled. Preacher greeted her. She nodded to him, but Reaper put his bare hand on the small of her back, *under the jacket and flannel*, and pushed her into the hall.

She was very aware of his hand, so hot it felt like he melted right through her skin to her bones. Sinking into her veins. Deeper. To her core. It felt too intimate, as if he had the right to put his bare hand on her bare skin. It shook her how much just his touch sent heat waves radiating through her body. She tried not to think too much about what was between them.

She wanted him again. She knew that. She just didn't

know if her heart could take it. She went to the room she'd had the night before, and he reached around her to open the door. Once inside she turned and faced him, mostly because his hand had burned a hole through her entire back, all the way to her heart and it was melting that as well. She couldn't afford for that to happen.

As she turned, he flicked on the overhead light and her breath caught in her throat. "Reaper. Oh my God. Sit down. What happened to you? Were you in an accident?"

"Nope. A fight. A few fights." Those blue eyes stayed on her face. "What the fuck were you doing out there again? You have some kind of a death wish?"

She backed up until the backs of her knees hit the bed. "You didn't say anything to me, so I thought we were done. It's not like I can live here just because we . . ." She gestured in the air, uncertain what they'd done. Wild sex? Best sex in the world? What? What did biker babes call it? They'd fucked. It was over. He'd made that clear.

"I told you it was done when I said it was done. You hear me say that?"

She shook her head because he hadn't said they were done and that just left her more confused than ever.

"You eat tonight?"

"Didn't your minions give you a full report?"

"Babe. Long fuckin' day. You hungry or what?"

She shook her head.

"Good. Strip."

"What?"

"Take your clothes off."

"Just like that? I'm not so certain you're up to this, and without any talking or anything, I'm not sure I am."

"Can't kiss you because my lips are cut to hell. Can't talk because my cock is gettin' in the way. Makes it hard to think when I hurt like a son of a bitch. You shouldn't be so damn beautiful if you don't want me hard as a fuckin' rock when I look at you."

She bent down to untie her shoes. He stood draped against the door, looking beat up, bruised and swollen, but he was right, she could see the outline of his cock pushed tight against the fabric of his jeans. Even beat up he looked good. He wasn't making a move to undress and that worried her a little. She kicked both shoes off and peeled off her socks, stood up and pulled off his shirt. Her new bra wasn't as pretty as the lacy one he'd shredded, or the beautiful black one that went under the tee she spotted on the nightstand, but it was cheap enough that she could afford it. She wasn't taking chances with him tearing it off her, so she took that off too.

She had generous breasts. There was no getting around it. Just like her hips—she had those as well. She hesitated before turning to face him after putting the bra on top of his flannel.

"Keep going."

When she turned back, he had his jeans open and his fist circled his cock. Her breath caught in her throat. He looked sexy as hell standing there, still in his colors, fully clothed, with his cock out, stroking it slowly, his gaze burning through her.

"God, you're so fuckin' beautiful it hurts."

He sounded like he meant it—that he was in awe of her or something. A fresh wave of hot liquid dampened her panties. She pushed jeans and panties off her hips and stepped out of them. She was totally naked, and he was fully dressed. It felt decadent. Sinful. She also felt vulnerable.

She fully expected him to ask her to kneel down and suck him off, but he didn't. He indicated the bed. "Bend over the bed."

She couldn't believe the way her heart began to pound so frantically, or the way her body had already started into melt-down. He hadn't kissed her. He hadn't touched her. Nothing. But she wanted him desperately. What was wrong with her?

"Sure you don't want to lie down? I could ride you," she offered.

"Body's too sore. Get your ass over that bed. Not going to tell you again."

She sent him a look over her shoulder, moving to obey, but deliberately slow about it. He caught the nape of her neck and pressed her face into the mattress, one hand sliding between her legs.

"Fuck yeah, Anya. You're ready for me." He pushed her legs farther apart with his boot. One finger curled into her. "Can't eat you tonight. Hungry for you, but my mouth is a mess."

She didn't care, although his mouth had given her multiple orgasms. Right now, she just needed him in her. Deep. She pushed back. "Hurry."

"You're always thinkin' you're going to tell me what to do. Not happening."

He leaned over her, his body blanketing her, his mouth at the nape of her neck. She felt his lips, whisper soft. Then the erotic scrape of his teeth. More liquid heat. Her heart stuttered. Her belly did a slow roll.

He kissed his way down her spine, his teeth gentle, his tongue touching her here and there, tiny dots that sent pulses to her clit. How did he do that? One hand swept down her back and over her butt, shaping her, as if he was memorizing her.

"Love your skin, Anya. Love the way it feels."

Abruptly he straightened, and in one move, entered her. Just like before. Hard. Fast. Pushing through her tight folds with no warning, just taking her, burying his cock in her sheath. Lightning seemed to streak through her. His fingers bit deep into her hips and he yanked her back every time he plunged deep. Over and over. The flames ate her from the inside out. She went over fast. Too fast. The orgasm caught her before she had time to catch a breath and she cried out, trying to muffle the sound, knowing they weren't alone in the big building.

He didn't stop or slow to give her a chance to recover. To

ease down. He just kept pounding into her, driving her high and tipping her over the edge again. She couldn't stop the shattered cry the second or third time. She didn't know if it was one continuous orgasm after that or if it was more, but she couldn't catch a breath, her voice a sobbing gasp, begging him. For what she didn't know. All that fire pouring into and over her was too much. She couldn't think, only feel. Then it was building into something uncontrollable and she tried to move away from it, tried to get out from under him, terrified this one would drive her insane.

He gripped her harder. "Let go. Let go for me, I've got you."

She would have done anything he asked her. He was there, right there, and she gave herself to him completely. It hit, the wave bursting over her, sweeping her away, taking him with her. He gave a hoarse shout that sounded like a gruff version of her name and then he lay over top of her, his heart pounding through his cock. She could feel him inside her.

She closed her eyes and pressed her forehead into the mattress. They hadn't used a condom again. She knew better. What was it about him that made her lose her mind like that? She was definitely going to get back on birth control immediately.

He pulled out of her, and she heard his zipper. She rolled over, sprawled half on and half off the bed. "You're sleeping here. Tomorrow I'll show you the house," he ordered.

She put her hands behind her head, forcing herself not to ask if he was going to sleep with her. Clearly, he wasn't. He'd actually stepped back across the room so he was against the door. Watching her. There was something in his eyes she couldn't read, but it terrified her. This man was too complicated for her. Too scary. Too sexy. Too everything.

"I need to know how much it's going to be to fix my car." That should be safe enough.

"You aren't going anywhere. I told you. You started this

with me. I gave you the chance to leave and you didn't take it. You stick it out until it's done."

She sighed and sat up, feeling more vulnerable than ever naked, with his seed dripping down her thighs. "I don't understand you."

"What's not to understand? I don't like you putting yourself in danger by going out to that campsite. You don't have a gun. You're a woman alone. You're just looking for trouble."

That was pretty much what Leslee had said, but when she'd said it, the warning had sounded a lot nicer. "I don't have money yet for an apartment."

"Made myself clear."

"If you'd made yourself clear, Reaper, I wouldn't have left. I won't go back out there, but I still need my car. I'm not on birth control. I'll have to get on it, and it takes a month before we're safe. Condoms would be good. Maybe you need to carry them with you or something. You never take your clothes off so fill up your pockets. We'll be golden."

"Your car is a shit car, Anya. It's held together with rubber bands, electrical and duct tape. There's no hope for that rusted pile of bolts."

She laughed. It was an apt way of describing her car. She reached for his flannel and pulled it on.

Those blue eyes burned over her. "Don't like you covering up."

"You're covered up."

"Not nearly as beautiful as you."

How did he do that? It was such an un-Reaper-like thing to say. "Maybe I disagree with that. I think you have a beautiful body." He was covered in scars and tattoos, but she loved every inch of him.

"Not right now, I don't. You need the bathroom?"

She nodded. He was pressed against the door, one hand on the knob as if he needed to run from her. He looked bruised. His knuckles were smashed, swollen and torn. One eye was already black. She stood up, clutching the sides of the shirt together and looking around for her panties. He opened the door. "What are you doing?"

"I need clothes to go down to the bathroom."

"What for?" He looked as puzzled as he sounded. Like he thought she'd lost her mind.

"Reaper, anyone could see me walking around half naked."

He shrugged. "It isn't anything they haven't already seen. It's common practice. No one thinks anything of it."

She glanced out the door. His shirt did cover her. She followed him out, holding the edges of the shirt together. "It really doesn't bother you, does it?"

"Nope."

"It wouldn't have bothered you if we had sex and any of them walked up, would it?"

"Nope."

"Why?"

"We were raised that way. Don't like locks. Don't like walls most of the time. You're my woman, they'll respect that. They'll protect you." He kept walking. "It bother you?"

Did it? It should, because modesty dictated it should. Because society said he didn't respect her if it didn't bother him that other men might see her body. She would have let him have her against the wall of Czar's house had a child not been close. What did that mean? Had it bothered her that much that she'd seen Ice naked? Not really. He hadn't leered at her, or made obscene gestures. He hadn't made it about sex.

"I don't know," she answered honestly. Anya stopped abruptly in the hall, her heart beating fast. "Do you share women?"

He stopped too, turning to face her, looking down into her upturned face. He was close, close enough she felt the heat of his body. "Any man touched you, even one of my brothers, *especially* one of my brothers, knowing how I feel about you, I'd kill them." He touched her face gently and stepped aside so she could go in alone.

Anya closed the door and leaned against it. God. He was wonderful and terrible at the same time. They were raised together? Raised to have sex in front of one another? To be that casual about it? Yet at the same time, he claimed he'd kill someone that dared to touch her? She was fairly certain he meant that as well.

And what did it mean, the way he felt about her? He was maddening. She didn't care that he was waiting, she took her time, brushing her teeth, washing her face, enjoying hot water. She washed between her legs, wincing a little. If he wasn't waiting, she'd take a bath. But then, anyone might walk in. When she was finished, she went out into the hall. He was gone. She sighed, tilted her head back and hit it gently against the wall. So much for their great night together. She was taking a bath.

~~~

He'd done it. Reaper walked down the hall to the common room. He'd had sex with Anya a second time. Fireworks had gone off, but not once had he had a compulsion to kill her. How fucked-up was it that he had to worry about that? That he had to be elated that he didn't want to kill the woman who mattered to him just because he had sex with her.

He'd been careful to keep her pressed against the bed, to not allow her to touch him, but he planned on experimenting a little. See what he could get away with. He wanted access to the front of her. Her tits were beautiful and his mouth watered every time he looked at them. He had fantasies about her mouth around his cock, although he knew that was what had started the nightmares again.

He'd heard her laughing in the bar. He rarely went into the actual bar. He always went in through the back door straight into the meeting room. That laugh had changed everything. He'd gone down the hall, curious to see the face that went with the laugh. Her back had been to him and he'd watched her ass as she worked. She had a great ass and suddenly, for the first time that he could remember, he was having fantasies about all the things a man could do with a woman's ass.

Then he saw the front of her. Those tits. They were perfect, definitely more than a handful, and nicely shaped. Then he'd looked at her mouth. She had the face of an angel. Soft skin. Those large eyes made a man think about bedrooms. That mouth was made for pure sin. He never let his mind go there, not in all those years, not after the things he'd done, but it had. All on its own. Once he started down that path, he couldn't get the image out of his head. That led to the nightmares. That led to his sitting in the bar for over a month watching her. Listening to her voice. Following her to the campground every night to make certain she was safe.

He joined the others as they filed into their "chapel." This was their private meeting room, the one where they held their votes and talked over any club business. Czar looked him over but didn't say anything. He could tell Savage was pissed at him. When he fought, Savage always had his back. When Savage fought, it was the other way around. This had been the first time he'd ever done it without his birth brother.

"I've been looking into these Ghosts the Demons told us about," Code began. "I've got a friend, a hacker, one that's like me. I contacted her to see if she's heard anything about them. She said there's been whispers about someone paying big money for information on the clubs, looking for weak links, anyone with a gambling propensity. Looking for anyone who can hack into various clubs' financials. They contacted her and tried to get her to work for them."

"Your friend take them up on it?" Czar asked.

Code shook his head. "Told them she doesn't ever take any work involving the clubs. Doesn't want that kind of heat. She did try to trace the source. It seems the Ghost Club originated in San Francisco. They weren't a motorcycle club, but an actual nightclub. A speakeasy originally and then over the years, the family that owned the building kept a small club open. The rest of the building is rented out for various other businesses, supposedly. They have ties in Nevada to gambling operations there."

"A crime family? Are we talking mafia?"

"Far removed cousins. I can't see that they're in any way affiliated. But, it looks as if two brothers got together with several friends and started a little operation of their own downstairs in the basement of the Ghost Club. They keep it small, very private, so the cops aren't tipped off. You have to have an 'in' to get in to gamble."

"Your best guess is these are the 'ghosts' that took Hammer's wife?" Czar asked.

"Right now, I'd put it at a good eighty percent. That's where we need to start looking," Code said. "And boss, they're going after the Diamondbacks aggressively. My friend, "Cat," hacked their firewall, well, between the two of us we did it, and they've got files on most of the presidents of the Diamondback chapters here on the Northern California coast and all the officers of each chapter. They're looking for a weak link and they seem to have found one, although I'm not that far into their files to be certain. They need the right member and they need the right president, someone in love with his wife."

"Can we prove that?"

Code nodded. "Oh yeah, easy. I've got it any time you want it, but it will take a little digging to get it all."

"Before we do anything, we need to get Hammer's wife back to him. Then, if any of the Ghosts are still alive, we'll turn the Diamondbacks on them. It never hurts to show a little respect to the big club in the neighborhood. Steele, you want to pick a team and poke around? You've got twenty-four hours. We're on a major timetable here. These men play for keeps. They want the rep that will do exactly what they say. I don't need to tell you to keep it low-key. No engagement.

They can't know anyone's looking at them. They might kill her."

"No problem, Czar," Steele agreed. "We'll find out how many and, hopefully, where they're holding her."

"Any more business?"

Everyone shook heads and then they broke up for the night. Reaper stalked out, Savage right behind him.

"Don't do it again, bro," Savage said softly.

Reaper nodded.

Savage nodded back. "I'm headed for bed. Been up twenty-four hours and I'm wiped."

"Thanks for covering my shift."

"Absinthe and Transporter have him tonight," Savage said. "I got this bad feeling about the Ghost Club, Reaper. Don't know why, but it's sitting in my gut all wrong."

Reaper didn't like that. Savage's premonitions often came true. "We'll keep watch over him."

Savage frowned. "Don't know if the trouble is pointing toward him."

"Blythe?" Reaper asked with some alarm.

Savage shrugged. "Don't know yet. You handling this thing with Anya?"

"Trying to. Don't have a clue what I'm doing. Trying not to get her killed, but fuckin' don't want to give her up."

"Then don't, Reaper. Hang on to her. The club has your back. I have your back."

Reaper nodded, but inside his gut knotted tighter. Anya deserved so much more than a man like him. If he had any decency in him, he'd get rid of her so fast her head would spin. Instead, he was trying to pull her in deeper. He made his way back down the hall. Under the door, he could see the light was out. He turned the knob, noting she hadn't locked it this time. She was learning.

He hadn't pulled the privacy screen and neither had she. Moonlight spilled through the window. Anya lay on her stomach, the beams hitting her back and the curve of her butt. He sank into the chair just across from the bed and tugged off his boots. His shirt came next, then he peeled off his jeans. Every muscle hurt like hell. He stretched out his legs and leaned back, his gaze on her body. She had a fantastic body.

"Stop staring at my butt."

Her voice was drowsy, a little amused. It washed over him like the breath of sin, a temptation he'd never be able to resist, not even now, when he was so tired he could barely hold his head up. His body didn't want to move, but it still managed to make his cock harder than titanium. He leaned his head back against the wall, his fist closing around his shaft. After so many years of total control, he was beginning to like the fact that his cock went rogue every time it was near her. Or he thought about her. It didn't seem to take much.

"Can't help it. Love your ass. Gives me all sorts of ideas."

She turned her head to the side so she could see him. He was in the shadows, but the moon was spilling enough light into the room that she could probably make out his fist pumping his cock.

"Are you always hard?"

"Apparently around you."

"Hmm. Well, come to bed."

His heart stuttered. Tripped. Raced. Not yet. He didn't dare take that step yet. He had to be careful. He hadn't let her put her hands on him. He'd tested his reaction that first time in the hallway, when she'd tried to shove him. It had been a miracle that he'd been able to let her keep her hands on him without triggering violence. He wasn't going to push it, not yet. One small step at a time.

"Go to sleep. I like sittin' here lookin' at you."

"You're jacking off."

"That I am."

"You're jacking off looking at my butt."

"I am."

She smiled, but didn't lift her head. "Kind of a waste."

"Not from my point of view. Enjoying the moment. When I'm ready, I'm putting my mark all over your back and that pretty little ass. Going to rub it in and let you wear me all day tomorrow. When you're working and I'm sitting there watching the men go crazy, I'll know you're wearing me on your skin."

She shifted just a little, folding both arms under her head. He could see the outline of her breast, the swell of the side. "I just took a bath."

"That's good. You won't need a shower. I'll be there all day. I'm going to write on your back and ass and that will stay there too."

"You're a little kinky."

"You're just figuring that out?"

That made her laugh. It was small but melodious, playing over his skin like the cool touch of fingers. "What will you write on me?"

"I've been thinking on that." Her gaze was on his hand, watching that tight fist slowly pumping up and down. Her eyes on him made it all the hotter. He could feel the burn starting in his balls, a slow buildup this time. "'Reaper's woman' right across that sweet little ass."

"I have no idea why you can make just about anything sound hot, but you manage."

"Spread your legs wide." He waited. Counted his heartbeats through his stroking fist. She complied slowly, and his cock jerked hard and leaked more fluid. He used his thumb to smear it. "Put a pillow under your belly." It took three lazy pumps before she pushed a pillow under her tummy. That lifted her just enough that with her legs spread, he had a good view. She was beautiful. And damp for him. "Slide a hand between your legs and get yourself off. I want to watch you."

His mouth went dry when her butt muscles bunched and her hand slid between her legs. Her fingers curled in, and he heard her gasp. His gaze was riveted between her legs, watching her fingers disappearing, working, sliding in circles around her clit and then disappearing again. His fist tightened, squeezing harder, jerking up and then down faster. She was so sexy. He'd never seen anyone sexier.

His breath left his lungs. Her breathing turned ragged. His hips thrust, adding to the pressure in his balls. Her hips bucked. He couldn't take his gaze from her, his fist tight, pumping until pleasure was bursting behind his eyes, and he knew he was close. So close. He got up slowly, careful not to jar his stiff body. Took the necessary steps to get to the side of the bed, the side her face was turned toward so she could see his every movement and he could see her expression.

Bliss. Pure bliss. That's what she looked like, a woman in the throes of passion. Flushed face, half-closed eyes, lips parted, her breath ragged.

"You close, baby?" He hoped she was. She looked like it. "I'm there."

She nodded, unable to get the words past the waves that were overtaking her. He felt his release like a volcano rising, long ropes of white-hot liquid splashing across the small of her back and over her buttocks. Whips of white, claiming her body. That wasn't good enough for him. He wanted to claim all of her. Not just her body, her heart. Not just her heart. He wanted her fucking soul, because he was damn sure she'd somehow captured his in that long month of watching her.

"Stay still," he ordered and reached for her hand. The one that had been inside her. He pulled it to his mouth, deliberately sucking on her fingers, one by one. Taking what belonged to him. Her taste was addicting. He loved that she just lay exactly as he'd asked, watching him, her eyes dark as he licked at her fingers.

With his palm, he spread those white ropes all over her buttocks and back, caressing her skin, rubbing it in as if it was lotion. Then, with one finger, he wrote what he wanted tattooed on her back. *Reaper's woman.* "Someday, I'm going to have Ink tattoo my fingerprints like bracelets around your wrists and this on your back where I can see it when I fuck you."

Her lashes fluttered. "You think you'll be doing a lot of that?"

He liked the tinge of amusement in her voice. He always listened for that note when she was bartending. She was brightness in a world that could be bleak and ugly. He always saw a light around her, spilling out from inside her.

"I *know* we'll be doing a lot of that." He rubbed his finger along her lips until she opened up and sucked deep. Her tongue slid along his finger, and his spent cock jerked again. Fuck, the woman would kill him eventually with her tempting ways.

She smiled around his fingers, those long lashes veiling her expression. "I'd say something about the condition of your body, all those bruises you have, but you wouldn't tell me how you got them even if I did."

"Told you. I got in a fight."

"There's more to it than that."

If her tone had been anything but mild, casual even, he would have abruptly walked out. He'd told her as much as he was going to and that ended the conversation, but he could tell she wasn't really pushing.

He slid his finger from her mouth, trailed it down her chin to her shoulder and then slid it under her arm so he could trace the side of that soft mound exposed by the way she was lying on the bed. "You're going to sleep just like this, aren't you? Let me soak into your skin so you're wearing me all day."

"You really meant it, didn't you?"

The smile was in her voice again. That did something to his insides. Turned him to mush, and he didn't like the sensation. She was crawling inside him too deep. Places he didn't want her to go. Places where she might see things better left alone.

"Yeah, I meant it." He realized he *had* meant it. Just like he meant the tattoos, just as he meant to keep her. The thought brought him up short. Abruptly he turned away from her and caught up his clothes. Just the act of bending over to pick up his jeans and shirt, to collect his carefully folded cut, hurt his body. He needed another long soak in the tub. He yanked the door open and turned back to her, picking up his boots.

"Aren't you coming to bed?"

He ignored her question. He thought it was rather obvious he wasn't. He wanted nothing more than to lie next to her all night. Holding her. Watching her sleep. But he wasn't taking chances with her life. He was already a selfish bastard just for what he was doing. "You going to give me what I want?" He knew the question was far more than asking her if she was going to let his seed remain on her. Or the tattoos or the writing. He wanted to know if she could handle him the way he was. If she would even try.

She eyed him as he stood there, holding his clothes in one hand, his boots in the other, but she didn't lift her head or turn over. She didn't get up and storm into the bathroom to remove every trace of him.

He found himself holding his breath. He didn't have much to give her. He didn't know how long he had or what mistakes he'd make—and there would be a million of them. He had to find ways to know what they could and couldn't do together. He was asking for a miracle and giving her very little in return. Still, he wanted that miracle. He *needed* it. He stood in the doorway, naked, uncaring if the world saw him that way. Knowing he was naked and vulnerable in other ways, stripped down where only she could see with her sparkling, jeweled eyes.

"What are we doing here, Reaper?" The question was a whisper.

His heart clenched. "Told you I say when we're done, not you. We're not done. We stay together until then."

He saw her pull in a breath. He knew she didn't like that, but he didn't have much more to give her. Empty promises? He was a fucking killer and she was an innocent caught in his trap. He wasn't going to lie to her if he could help it.

Her tongue touched her lip. "Another woman ends it, Reaper. I walk."

He couldn't imagine, after all this time, that suddenly other women would become attractive to him. "I'll ask it again. You going to give me what I want?"

Those green eyes moved over his face moodily. Brooding. She must have seen something she liked because she gave him a little half smile that turned him inside out. "We'll see, won't we?" Her lashes drifted down. "Good night, Reaper. Soak in Epsom salt, and really hot water. It will do you a world of good. Wherever you go to sleep, it had better be alone."

He stood there in the open doorway until her breathing turned slow and even. Only then did he turn and head for the bathroom and a long soak in the tub.

EIGHT

Reaper sat in the back of the bar, legs sprawled out in front of him, the neck of a beer bottle between his fingers. Absently, he rolled it back and forth. He'd been busy all day and hadn't checked in with Anya deliberately. She was already ruling his thoughts. His mind. His body. He couldn't have her knowing that shit. She hadn't texted or called. He knew because he looked at his phone a thousand times, so much so that the others were giving him hell and calling him pussy whipped. He was. He didn't want them to know— or her.

He'd spent a good part of the day getting a couple of chairs and kitchen shit for the house. Ice and Storm helped him, but he was certain Czar sent them to ensure he didn't do anything else out of line, like drive off cliffs or fight a dozen men. He was paying for that little indiscretion with a sore, stiff body.

Anya was driving him crazy. She smiled at him a few times, flashing that bright, jerk-a-man-to-his-knees smile that had his cock reacting, but she didn't give him more than that. He was beginning to think he was an idiot. He should have walked in, pulled her over the bar and kissed her right there in front of everyone, so any badass biker walking through the door would know just who that woman belonged to. He might still do it if the place got any more crowded.

"You're looking good tonight, Reaper," Betina greeted, coming to stand directly in his way, blocking his view of the bar. "I'm on a break in five. We could go outside."

He raised his gaze to her face. "Do I look like I want to go outside?"

"It's dark enough in here. I could take care of that for you." She indicated under the table.

His body froze and that demon inside him stirred. Darkness welled up. Threatened to swallow him. He raised one finger and moved it sideways, indicated for her to move over. Something in his face must have tipped her off that she was in danger, because she took one step to the side, and then he could see Anya. His light. She shone there. Bannister, the older biker, said something to her and she threw back her head and laughed. The sound was like a melody playing through his mind, the musical notes streaking through the black rage, the need to kill.

Anya looked up suddenly, met his eyes and sent him her little half smile. That enigmatic one that told him nothing and everything. His muscles relaxed one by one. He breathed the need for vengeance, for self-preservation away.

He knew his cock had to look like a monster. It felt that way. Anya did that to him without trying, and watching her half the night, wondering if she wore him on her skin, was driving him out of his mind. That little half smile didn't give a thing away, but it looked as if she had a secret. A smug little secret. That kept his cock at attention.

"Don't want your help, Betina." He was blunt, but blunt might actually get her to listen. Nothing else he'd done had. She wanted to brag she'd had him. She wanted to go through them all. Even Czar was on her list. She had been all over their president until he'd told her she'd be gone if she didn't leave him alone.

Betina paled, her eyes showing fear. Reaper knew he'd given off that vibe the others had warned him about. He couldn't help it. Sometimes the devil escaped, and then no one was safe. He reined his control back and brought the beer to his lips, took a pull, his eyes never leaving Anya's before he set it back on the table.

Anya popped the cap off another beer and came around the bar, threading her way to him. He didn't like her out in the open on the floor. More than one biker thought he could put his hands on her. She slipped through them with practiced ease, leaned down to set the bottle in front of him and put her lips to his ear. "You need me to kick Betina's ass for you? I can protect you if you need it, honey."

Her lips, petal soft, brushed against his earlobe. That soft little laugh accompanied her question, but he knew she meant it. She'd make Betina want to quit. He caught the front of her tank in his fist and pulled her close. His hand threaded through her hair and he took her mouth. He loved her mouth. The instant his tongue slid into that hot haven, fire erupted and they both ignited. He nearly pulled her down onto the table, but he managed to stay enough in control to just hold her still while he kissed her over and over.

When he allowed her to lift her head, she smiled at him. "I think that should just about do it, honey," she whispered. "I'm pretty certain everyone got your message loud and clear."

"You do it for me? You wearing me all over my property?" His hand slid down her back to cup her bottom. His thumb caressed her, brushing back and forth over the words that declared her his.

She lifted a shoulder. "Maybe."

She left him, walking back through the crowd of customers, head up, regal, like a queen. He adjusted his cock, uncaring how many witnesses there were to what she did to him. He really couldn't drink two beers tonight. He might

have to ride. Steele and the others were on their way back
and they'd be meeting as soon as they arrived.

Hammer's wife only had so much time, and God knew
what those men were doing to her. The "ghosts" Reaper had
killed had been sick fucks. He didn't like thinking about
any woman in their hands too long, let alone one who had
been sick with cancer. He pushed the beer across the table
even though his woman had brought it to him.

His woman. He liked thinking of her like that. He liked
that Anya was his. He was even beginning to like that his
body responded to her of its own accord. Either that or he
was getting used to being in a constant state of arousal. He
pulled his gaze from her and took stock of the room.

The bar was as packed as it was on weekends, because
a small motorcycle club had come into Sea Haven, headed
up to the redwoods, and quite a few other small clubs joined
them. They stopped to check out the bar and liked what they
saw. Maestro jammed sometimes on Thursday, and played
shows on Friday and Saturday when the urge hit him. Although it was rarely scheduled, quite a few of his local fol-
lowers liked to come in on Thursday to catch him playing.

Reaper took in each person, man or woman, in the bar.
He always did when he was there. He sized up each
individual and appraised the threat level to Czar, and now
Anya as well. Aside from the obvious bikers, there were three
strangers sitting at the corner table opposite him that didn't
seem to belong. They kept to themselves and stayed quiet,
drank very little, just enough to keep Betina going back to
flirt with them. They weren't quite in the shadows as he was,
but they'd chosen their table carefully.

He kept watch on them. They didn't seem to look at anyone too long. They mostly put their heads together and
talked in low voices, but he noticed they were very flirtatious
with Betina, and very generous with their tips. One slipped
his hand around her thigh and rubbed. She leaned into him
like a cat, putting a hand on his shoulder and allowing him

to move his hand a little higher. Twice she glanced back at Reaper, as if to see whether or not he was watching—or to talk about him.

He kept his legs sprawled lazily in front of him and his eyes hooded so they couldn't get a lock on whether or not he was watching them. Betina knew better than to talk about the club. She was a lot of things and she liked playing games, but she wasn't into betrayal, not at any price. Not that he could see.

He glanced up at the camera and then tapped on the table. Three, two, three. He did it twice, as if he was tapping to Maestro's music. He didn't like puzzles, and those men were a puzzle. Code had equipment and access to databases most government agencies would kill for. He was that good. They'd have the identities fast.

He eased his hips forward to keep pressure off his rib cage. He'd been an idiot to fight when they were trying to get Hammer's wife back. He needed his body in good shape. It wasn't. The fists had torn open the laceration in his side. He hadn't bothered trying to neatly put the edges back together, he'd just bandaged the wound. He was a fast healer and he had that going for him, that and his body knew how to take punishment. He'd been taking fists, bats, whips and knives since he was a boy. That didn't mean he wasn't sore and he shouldn't have indulged his need to inflict pain as well as take it.

Betina came to his table to collect the empties. This time she didn't make the mistake of putting her body between his and Anya's. "I didn't know about you and Anya, Reaper. I apologize, and I'll apologize to her. She's my friend." She kept her voice low and her eyes downcast. She placed a new napkin directly in front of him and walked away.

Reaper wasn't surprised to hear Betina call Anya her friend. Anya, he was finding out, was well liked by just about everyone. He glanced down at the napkin. *They're asking questions about the club. I gave them the standard "not my business,"* but they're persistent. *What do you want me to do?*

He didn't want her to do anything until he knew what they were dealing with. Betina liked to fuck bikers. She liked the parties and the life, but she also liked the protection they afforded her. She didn't mind men putting their hands on her. She loved the big tips, but she wasn't about to trade the club for any of those things.

She'd walked off, making the rounds of tables. He held up his hand to indicate to the bar he wanted coffee and jerked his head toward Betina. Anya got the message immediately. That was another thing he loved about his woman. She didn't know the first thing about their world, but she picked up on things. One time was all it took and she learned.

She called Betina over, pushed a mug of steaming coffee toward her and indicated Reaper. Betina hesitated and then said something soft to Anya. Anya nodded once solemnly and then flashed a smile at the waitress. It was her bright, radiant smile, the off-the-charts one that sent desire snaking through his body. She'd just forgiven Betina for trying to encroach on her man. Anya didn't hold grudges. That was one trait she'd need with him, because he was bound to fuck up a lot.

Betina set the mug in front of him. "Anything else, Reaper?"

He knew, without looking, the three men were watching them. "Not one thing. Coffee's all for now."

She nodded. She knew to stay as far away from the three men as possible. Not to give them anything, not to attempt to listen in on their conversation. He didn't want her taking chances. Pictures of the men had been taken and Code was already working to identify them. He wouldn't ever peg them as bikers, but that didn't mean anything. They didn't blend, but that could be on purpose.

He tapped to the music, another code. His brothers and

sisters had perfected those codes when they were just children. Code had been their numbers man from the time he'd been brought to the school. He'd been skinny and tiny, with his hair sticking almost straight up, but he was a genius, and Czar had recognized it in him early. Reaper told Code to have the others keep Czar tucked out of sight with guards around him at all times. Two would be sent to his home to keep Blythe and the children safe.

Alena came down the hall, just as he knew she would. Alena was a heartbreaker. She was beautiful and a siren with the same call of temptation to destruction as the mythical sirens'. She looked like pure sinful sex with every step she took, dressed in her pencil-thin skirt and her tight little camisole. Earrings dangled from her earlobes, and her lipstick was bright red, framing her beautiful mouth.

Every man in the bar turned and looked at her. It was impossible not to, especially when she was working her hips and her breasts moved subtly with every step. She had perfect posture and looked like the most confident, sexy woman on the face of the earth. Very few men could resist her when she turned on the charm. Her siren's voice assured her of their attention. Another gift was her ability to lift anything from pockets without detection. Wallets, pens, a piece of paper, money, IDs. She had never once been caught, not even as a child first learning.

"Alena." A man stood up from the table, blocking her path. He stuttered her name, smiling like a boy in a candy store. "I was hoping I'd see you again."

She stopped, her high heels nearly making her as tall as the man blocking her path. Although she was only average height, she seemed taller. She was nearly to the table closest to the one where the three men were sitting.

"I'm sorry?" Alena never forgot a face or name. She knew exactly who the man was, but she pushed a little haughtiness into her voice, as if he might be a bug she was about to squash.

"Bronson. We met at the State Park. I'm a park ranger. You were on your way to check out Caspar. It was about a year or so ago."

"Ah. Of course." She gave the impression she was pretending to remember. "How are you?"

"I was hoping to run into you. I've come here a lot, but didn't catch you. Can I buy you a drink?"

She reached out and touched his collar, one swipe of her bloodred nail. "So sweet, Bronson, *now* I remember you. You had that sexy uniform on, didn't you? Weren't you going to throw us out of the park?"

His mouth flew open to protest. At the same time, he shook his head over and over. She pressed her finger to his mouth. "Another time. I've got to wait for my brother." She stepped smoothly past him and walked straight to the empty table, leaving the ranger staring after her, his gaze glued to her swaying hips.

Reaper was always amazed at how smooth Alena was. She commanded an entire room with her presence, leaving the faintest scent of perfume behind her, so faint it was elusive, and men wanted to follow that trail. She had the attention of the three men instantly. They would have been deaf and blind not to notice her. Bannister, sitting on his stool at the end of the bar, swiveled in his seat to keep her in sight.

Deliberately Alena sank into the chair facing the three men and crossed her legs. The action hiked the tight skirt halfway up her thighs. She wore silk stockings and a hint of a black lace garter showed at the top, sexy as hell. She glanced at her watch, sighed and then sat back and fidgeted with her hair. She happened to glance up and catch the stranger opposite her staring and sent him a faint smile.

Reaper watched that lure to get the stranger on Alena's hook. The man's breath caught. He pushed at his short, spiky cut and then his hand went to his throat as if to straighten a tie. That was a tell if Reaper had ever seen one. This man was more at home in a suit than in his casual blue jeans and

T-shirt. No wonder the three men looked so out of place. It wouldn't take long for Alena to reel them in. She'd have them eating out of her hand.

Reaper sipped at his coffee, keeping an eye on the park ranger. He had eyes only for Alena. They couldn't afford the ranger interfering with their plan. He lifted his coffee cup to catch Betina's attention. She immediately abandoned the table near the stage where the band played where she'd been taking orders and hurried to him.

She poured the coffee. "Anything else?"

Reaper jerked his chin toward the ranger. "Nope, coffee's fine." He pushed a tip toward her fingers. She almost shook her head but then took it when he lifted an eyebrow and jerked his chin slightly toward the park ranger again.

Betina flashed a smile and went straight to Bronson. She stepped close. Very close. Leaned in, right over the table so he got a perfect view of her breasts. Her red push-up bra showed under the low, dipping neckline. Bronson glimpsed a partial nipple. She smiled at him. "Hi, handsome, I've seen you around, but you're never in my section. I'm Betina. What's your name?" She stroked a finger down his arm.

The ranger coughed. She pressed closer on the pretense of patting his back. Her leg wedged between his, her thigh tight against his cock. "Are you okay?" She practically crooned it. "Let me help you. I've got a little break coming. Would you like to go outside with me and find a place to . . . talk?" Her voice was very suggestive.

She caught his hand and pressed it to her hip, right where her tank rose just a little, so he was feeling skin. "Please?" She widened her eyes. "I never get to meet any decent men when I'm working. They all want just one thing." She glanced over her shoulder to give Heidi, the other waitress, a heads-up that she would be leaving for a few minutes.

Reaper wanted to shake his head when the ranger stood up with Betina and, like a puppy dog, followed her right out the door, leaving the way clear for Alena to keep the three strangers occupied solely with her. He heard her give a sigh as she uncrossed her legs and recrossed them. Then she tapped the table impatiently to the music, swaying a little in her chair.

"Don't tell me someone was stupid enough to stand you up." The spiky-haired man stood up and walked over to her. Alena's restless fingers continued to tap a rhythm on the table, this time a signal for Maestro to swing into a slow ballad.

"My brother is notoriously late," she answered and then looked up, and, as if just really seeing him, letting appreciation and interest show on her face. "Hi. I'm Alena."

"Tom. Tom Randal. Can I buy you a drink?"

"Do you dance?"

"Slow."

She stood up, very close to him. Reaper knew how heady men found her. She smiled, staring straight into his eyes. "Tom, I believe the music is just slow enough." She put her hand in his.

Tom walked her to the dance floor, and she turned immediately and put both arms around his neck and pressed her body tightly against his. He locked his arms around her waist, and they began to sway together. She'd made certain to lead him close to the edge of the low stage. It was no more than a step. The way their bodies were locked together, Reaper knew Alena could feel every bulge in Tom's pockets. She knew exactly where his wallet was.

Reaper kept his eyes on her. So did Master. He played bass and every now and then dropped to a slight crouch while he played one-handed to fiddle with his amp—the amplifier positioned right on the corner. Alena's hand swept down Tom's body in a little caress as she turned her face up to his and talked softly, intimately to him, creating a spell with her voice. Reeling him in. Her fingers found his wallet and she handed it off to Master easily. He beckoned to Mechanic, who crouched, came to the corner of the stage to fiddle with the amp, took the wallet with a sleight of hand and disappeared.

It was smooth. Practiced. They'd done it hundreds of times. The wallet went to Code, the ID copied, put back and returned to Master in minutes. Alena laughed at something Tom said, and Master slipped it back into her hand. She went up on her toes and whispered, her lips against Tom's ear, her fingers slipping in a caress down his back and over his hip, the wallet smoothly sliding back into his pocket.

Alena had indicated twice that Tom was asking about the club. Or at least the president of the club. She'd delivered the information via code, tapping that rhythm right on Tom's shoulder blatantly.

Tom looked like he'd been lovestruck. He couldn't take his eyes off Alena. He walked her back to the table when the band went into something energetic, keeping possession of her hand as they neared her table. "Come sit with us."

She nodded immediately. "Storm's always late."

"Storm?" Tom echoed.

"My brother. He's got a temper and can create quite the storm when's he angry." She gave a small laugh. "Introduce me to your friends." Her voice had dropped an octave, throwing the lure that often got her exactly what she wanted.

"Steve and Mike Burrows," Tom said. "Alena."

"Are you just passing through?" she asked as she slid gracefully into a chair.

"Staying for a few days," Steve answered. "We like sea fishing and come to Fort Bragg occasionally to fish. This is our first time in the bar. Someone told us to come on Thursday nights to hear the band."

"They're good, aren't they?" Alena said. She moved, a slow subtle undulation of her body that kept their eyes riveted to her. All the while she tapped her fingers to the beat of the music, giving the other two names to Code through the camera.

"I can't believe they play in a small bar like this. They

could be quite a draw if they had a little publicity," Mike pointed out.

"They don't play on a regular basis," Alena said, leaning her chin into the heel of her hand, staring into Tom's eyes. "How long do you think you'll be here?"

"A few more days," Tom said hastily.

"Who owns the bar?" Steve looked around carefully. "It's unexpected. I was told it was a biker bar. I thought fights and broken glass."

"Torpedo Ink club owns it. My brother's Torpedo Ink."

"Is he the president?" Mike asked.

She shook her head. Reaper saw her sign immediately. She didn't like the way the conversation was headed. She ran her fingers through her hair—Storm's sign to get out there. Her brother strode into the bar within minutes, coming in through the front. He was wearing his colors, just as Reaper and the band members were.

Alena stood up instantly with a smile. "I'd better go," she whispered, almost as if she was afraid of what her brother might do to her—or to them—if he caught her sitting with them. Before Tom or the others could protest, she hurried straight to Storm. He caught her arm and dragged her out the front door.

Reaper gave Fatei a thumbs-up to indicate that he should let Betina know the coast was clear and she could get back inside. They'd all done their jobs. They were skilled at working together, one smooth, oiled machine. He glanced up to see Anya's gaze touch the three men, speculation in her eyes. She looked away quickly.

He had a sudden feeling of unease. His woman was intelligent. She noticed things and had a great memory. She remembered the name of every single customer, family members and even friends. She remembered the drinks they liked. Any bit of overheard conversation and eventually she would be able to put pieces of puzzles together. He'd have to caution the others to be careful around her.

The last thing he wanted was for Anya to know about any of the work they did. She had to know he wasn't a good man, she'd seen the knife he'd thrown at Deke, but she didn't know that they'd been assassins for their government and that they hunted pedophiles, or took jobs as couriers to escort people safely through gauntlets.

He had kissed her in front of the three strangers, men asking questions about their club, about their president. He had kissed her to stake his claim in front of everyone, but it had been a selfish gesture. He would have done better to ignore her. She would have followed his cue. She was always professional at work, and she was still unsure of the status of their relationship.

He stood up slowly, for the first time drawing attention to himself. Even in the bar, with Betina bringing him coffee and Anya kissing him, he knew he went still after as he always did, and that allowed him to become somewhat invisible. He was noticed only when he wanted to be. Stalking across the bar, he went down the hall rather than going behind the bar to access the meeting room. Maestro, Player, Keys and Master put their instruments aside and used the hinged slab at the bar to retreat toward the back room.

In the mirror above his head, Reaper noticed the three strangers going on alert. He nodded to Fatei to watch them. Gavriil and Casimir Prakenskii, two of Czar's brothers, stepped into the hall to guard the door while the club members went inside. Gavriil, Reaper had come to know over the last year, and he was every bit the badass Czar had warned them he was.

Casimir had earned the club's respect because he had been the one, along with his wife, to free them all from Sorbacov and his murderous son. The couple had killed the two Sorbacovs, allowing those left alive from the four schools to live in the open. Both men had been patched in. As the newest members, they still pulled guard duty quite often.

Reaper moved to the back of the room while Savage took the front. The rest of the club members, Alena and Lana included, gathered around the large table. "First, before anything else, Code, what did you find out about the Ghost Club?" Czar asked.

"We stumbled into a nest of vipers, Czar. Pure and simple. They've targeted the clubs, all of them, large and small. They have quite the racket going. We got close enough to hear that they want the Diamondbacks and expect to get them soon. Some prick, and I haven't gotten his name yet, but I will, is selling out his club, setting up the president of the Mendocino chapter's wife in exchange for his debt. They think they've gotten big enough to take the Diamondbacks on starting with the Mendocino chapter."

Czar shook his head. "Are they crazy? The Diamondbacks will eat them alive."

"The Ghosts are bigger than I first thought. They've got members in various states and no one knows who they are."

"Someone has to know."

"Their computers are like a fortress. Better than the government's, Czar. It took both Cat and I to figure out how to break through their firewall. I'm searching the servers now and will have the data to you soon," Code said.

Reaper was always impressed with the things Code did with computers.

"I did get into their emails. They use a code that was easy to break, unlike their firewall. There was quite a buzz around the fact that three of their men were killed in a botched raid on the president of Mayhem's wife." He sent a quick appreciative grin to Reaper.

Steele nodded. "We heard the same thing. They think members of Mayhem saved the president's wife and daughter. As far as we could tell from the conversation, we're not on their radar. At least not as someone that interfered with their scheme."

"How'd you get so close?" Preacher asked.

"Master gave us some good audio surveillance equipment and we picked up conversations the Ghosts held in their basement offices. The casino's down there and below that are the offices. They also have an escape tunnel below the Ghost Club."

"Nice, Master." Preacher smirked at him. "Knew your gadgets would come in useful."

Master flipped him off. He loved anything electrical. Mechanic and Master spent hours working on new equipment, trying to make each device smaller and smaller.

"Hammer's woman?" Czar got to the point.

The smiles faded from Steele and the others. "She's there. They've got her underground, down near the tunnel. It didn't sound good, Czar. I think it's best we get her out of there as soon as possible."

"Can we get a hold of the blueprints for the club, casino and offices?" Czar asked.

"Absinthe went to the city planning office to take a look. Nothing but the club itself. Whatever original plans were there, aren't any longer," Steele said.

Czar sighed. "It's damned hard to go in blind."

"Another thing that's important to know," Absinthe said, "the Ghost Club only hires bartenders who know flair. They have to be good. Really good."

Reaper stiffened. Alena and Lana had told them all that Anya knew how to do tricks, that she'd used that knowledge to work her way up through the clubs to better pay. No one looked at him, but he felt the tension in the room mounting.

"Did anyone think to find out the wages a bartender gets at the Ghost Club?" Czar asked quietly.

"It's one of the highest paying in the city," Steele acknowledged. "We didn't ask if they were missing a bartender, but . . ."

"Don't." Reaper's fist hit the wall. "Don't go there."

Czar sighed. "We have to go there, Reaper. You know that. We can't discount any possibility. We look at everything no matter how remote. It's a big coincidence that Anya showed up here with no money but wearing designer jeans. She gets paid under the table, the perfect damsel in distress. She's also gorgeous, has tons of experience and is guaranteed to bring in more customers. Of course we'd hire her, we'd be fools not to. We have to look at the possibility that they're putting bartenders in biker bars to gather information on club members. It would be a brilliant move."

The pressure in Reaper's chest was suddenly enormous. His heart ached. Anya—a spy? She had a memory. She put things together fast. He'd just been thinking that.

Czar looked straight at him. "A bartender hears everyone's woes. If they're gamblers, she's going to know."

Reaper shook his head. "This is fucked-up."

"We're just talking about possibilities."

"No, you're not. You know damn well you think it's a reality."

"I didn't say that," Czar said, "but it warrants investigation."

"You fucking mean interrogation." Reaper straightened, turning his gaze on Absinthe. "You go near her and I'll kill you. Do you get that, brother? I'll fucking kill you."

"I'm not interrogating her," Absinthe said. "I won't do it, and not because you're threatening me, you dumb fuck. I like her. She's a good person. I don't believe she's part of this crap going on. She isn't the type of woman to let someone harm other women."

"Reaper"—Czar's voice was mild—"shut the fuck up and rein it in. *I* say what we do, not Absinthe. I tell him to question her, he does it." He didn't look at Absinthe. "That's the way we work. We're a team, and you both are part of that team. Reaper, you aren't even with her yet and you're ready to turn on your brothers? That's not happening. God. I don't need bullshit when we have a real problem."

Reaper took a deep breath. He detested that Czar was

right. Why had his first thought been to protect Anya and not his club? Not his brothers? That was unprecedented. He was losing his fucking mind over the woman. First his dick, now his brothers. He was losing control. Maybe she was a plant; if so, he'd kill her himself. His stomach lurched and his heart jerked hard. Painfully. "Consider it reined in."

Czar nodded. "No one in our club has a gambling problem," he said. "Even if she was here to spy, she wouldn't have much to tell them."

"She went to your home, Czar," Master pointed out. "She met Blythe and Emily. She saw the way you are with them. The way all of us are with them."

"Actually, Czar, she's never asked a single question about any of us," Preacher said. "I work with her all the time."

Reaper sighed. These were his brothers and sisters. "No, but she's highly intelligent. She puts things together fast." He felt he had to at least admit that.

"Maybe," Lana said. "But I watched her at Czar's house. She wasn't pumping for information. She wasn't looking for it. She was all about Reaper and very nervous around us. I believe she's running from something, but I don't think she's spying on us. If she were, why wouldn't she have asked to stay in the compound instead of camping out in her car? There are apartments over the bar. She didn't ask to stay in them either. Those would be opportunities for a spy."

Reaper shot her a grateful glance.

Czar sank back in his chair for a long moment weighing the consequences, the damage Anya could do if she were a spy and then he hit the table with his fist. "Damn it. Just damn it."

Reaper's heart sank. Either way he was going to lose Anya. If they didn't question her, there would always be club members, even him, looking at her as if she might be a spy. If they did, she wouldn't forgive him, and he wouldn't blame her. He knew they had to question her. It didn't make sense not to. There was too much at stake.

"When?"

"After her shift tonight. We may as well get it over with, Reaper." Czar sounded tired. He looked at his oldest friend, the man they all owed their lives to. He had sacrificed his soul, his sanity for them, and now they were repaying him by accusing his woman of being a spy.

The air was heavy in the room. They all felt it. Every last one of them. Reaper pushed away from the wall.

"I'll be back. No one touch her until I get here," he decreed.

"Reaper . . ." Czar began.

He shook his head. He didn't want to hear it. Maybe it hadn't been redemption that had been close, he knew there was no such thing for him, but Anya had felt like that. He'd sacrificed everything he was, everything he could have been to give his brothers and sisters a chance at a life. Anya had been his reward for that. *His* one chance. He would have nothing after this, and he wasn't the only one who knew it.

He didn't look at them. In that moment, he detested all of them. He detested the unbreakable bonds he had with them. Ties that had been forged in hell. He went out the back door so he wouldn't have to face her. He didn't want to see her, to have her look at him with those green eyes and that smile that took his breath and sanity. He'd go to hell for her, but he couldn't stop what was coming.

Reaper went straight for his bike. He needed the wind. It wouldn't cleanse him of his sins, and it wouldn't stop what was coming, but he had to get his mind right because if, when she was questioned, he thought she was innocent, he'd stop the interrogation immediately. If he didn't, and she was the enemy, her death was going to be quick and clean and she'd never see it coming.

His vision blurred and he stumbled. He caught himself and kept walking until he was at his bike. Ice closed in on one side. Storm on the other. He didn't look at them, but he shook his head. There was a lump in his throat so large he could barely draw breath, and it burned like hell behind his eyes.

"Need to be alone."

"Not happening, brother," Ice said softly. "We're going with you." He straddled his bike. Storm did the same.

Behind him, bike after bike started up. His brothers, surrounding him. He still couldn't look at them. He pulled on his gloves, his dome, sank onto the familiar leather and backed his bike out. They were all there in force, Czar included.

Reaper roared out of the parking lot, uncaring of speed limits, reckless when water shimmered in his eyes, making it difficult to see. He flew down the highway, taking the curves fast, trying to run from himself. His life. The betrayal he knew he was about to visit on Anya. He believed her innocent, but the fact was, there was damning evidence against her. The timing couldn't have been worse for her to show up at their bar.

Her laughter echoed through his mind and he turned up his speed another notch, trying to outrun that as well. She'd taken hold of him, gotten inside, and twice he'd fucked her hard, without any tenderness, and he'd left her alone. He'd written his name on her and asked her to wear it. He had the feeling she had done that for him. He'd taken from her over and over, giving her nothing back and now, fucking hell, he was about to destroy her.

Anya was more fragile than he wanted to admit. He saw it sometimes in her eyes, that vulnerability that told him she hadn't had it easy. Maybe her life hadn't been like his, or that of any of the members of the club, but she hadn't had it easy. He hadn't even asked her about her life. He'd been too busy feeling. Acting on those feelings.

He headed to the point above the ocean where he often went just to look at that wide expanse of water. He stopped, uncaring that bikes pulled in behind him at his back. He couldn't look at them without wanting to . . . He shut down that line of thinking. Fighting anyone was out of the question, and it wouldn't change the fact that he would have to be the one to betray Anya. Or kill her if necessary, because that was always on him. In the end, that was all he was.

NINE

Anya knew something was wrong the moment she locked the bar and turned, finding Reaper right behind her. She looked up and smiled at him, pleased that he actually was waiting for her after work, even though it had taken her until three to clean. Preacher had let both Heidi and Betina off two hours earlier and told them to make themselves scarce. She was used to working that last hour of cleanup alone, but not two. It didn't make sense and had left her uneasy.

Something was off from the moment Reaper had disappeared into the back room along with Preacher and the members of the band. No one had come back for hours, until Preacher returned, let the waitresses off and just grunted something about her closing on her own. At first, she thought he was testing her to see if she could do it, but that didn't make sense because she'd been closing that last hour alone, handling the till, mopping up, locking the doors.

In the end it was Reaper who confirmed something was drastically wrong. He'd always been expressionless and scary looking with his scars and the streaks of gray running through his long hair and peppering the scruff on his jaw. But it was his eyes that had changed. Before, when he'd looked at her, even earlier in the evening, there'd been warmth under all that ice just for her. Now, no warmth. No ice. He had the flat, cold eyes of a killer. Distance was there. Death. For the first time, she was really afraid of him.

She shivered and rubbed her arms. He stepped back and indicated she go down the stairs first. In the darkness of the parking lot, she spotted several Torpedo Ink members, all wearing their colors. They were spread out in a strange pattern, almost as if they were blocking every exit. She hesitated and Reaper crowded her back, but he didn't touch her.

"Reaper?" He didn't respond, and her anxiety grew. "What's going on?" She didn't like the icy fingers creeping down her spine, or the sudden goose bumps on her arms.

"Get moving. Let's just get home."

She moved down the stairs with reluctance, trying to suppress the feeling of doom growing in her. She had a very healthy dose of self-preservation. It came from living in shelters and on the street. Her warning systems were blaring at her.

Reaper swung his leg over his Harley, straddling it. She started to step up and then hesitated again, looking around at the silent men waiting. "Tell me what's going on."

"Get on."

She shook her head. "Reaper, you're freaking me out." She gestured toward the others. "They're freaking me out. I'm not just getting on your bike and riding somewhere without you telling me where."

"The clubhouse. I'm taking you there. Just get on, Anya."

"Will I be safe?"

"What the hell kind of question is that?" he demanded. "You got something to hide?"

"We all have something to hide."

"Something that would hurt the club?" he persisted.

She frowned at him. "Of course not."

"Then you're perfectly safe."

She studied his face. There was no warmth. Nothing but those dead eyes. She climbed on behind him and sat up straight, not leaning into him. She held on to his hips, digging her fingers in when the bike moved into the curves. It was telling to her that he didn't reach back and take her hands to pull her arms around him. Did she believe him that she was safe? The others fell into formation around them. She didn't look at them, her mind running through the possibilities of what could have happened.

She had nothing at all to do with the club. She stayed out of club business deliberately. She was in trouble, clearly, or she wouldn't have been living out of her car, but they knew that or they wouldn't have agreed to pay her under the table. She had nothing to worry about.

She was off the bike even before Reaper shut it down. Her knees threatened to give out when she saw the number of Harleys lined up. Everyone. Something big had to be going on.

Reaper's fingers curled around the nape of her neck and he escorted her into the common room. She expected him to take her down the hall to the bedrooms, but instead, he chose to lead her behind the bar to one of the two doors there. The door he chose led to a narrow stairway. She didn't like it at all.

"Reaper?" She needed reassurance. His palm was warm on her neck, his fingers digging into her skin.

"You're fine, Anya. The club has a few questions for you. Just answer them honestly and everything will be fine."

She stiffened, slowed her pace, but he pushed at her, making it impossible to stop. At the bottom of the stairs was another narrow hallway. He shoved open a door, and she went inside the large room because she didn't have a choice. Immediately he closed the door behind them. Inside, the club members sat around a table. All of them. Even Lana and Alena. They all looked at her with varying degrees of expression.

Lana looked upset. Alena looked bleak. Preacher wouldn't meet her eyes. She turned to Reaper, the one man she thought would stand for her. "What's going on?"

"We have a few questions," Czar said, his voice pleasant enough. "Would you mind sitting over there, Anya?" He pointed to a chair that was on a raised platform. It was only one step up, the surface wide enough to hold two chairs.

She shrugged, and looked up at Reaper again, needing reassurance. He caught the nape of her neck and looked into her eyes. "You answer every question truthfully, do you hear me? Don't try to bullshit him, just get this over and tell the truth. Everything will be fine if you do."

"What's going on? Just tell me what's going on."

Reaper didn't answer. He took her arm and led her to the seat. She was alone then. She'd been alone all her life. She could do this, whatever it was, and then she would be gone. Reaper stood with the rest of them, not with her, and he'd made that very clear.

She pulled her arm away and sank into the chair without a word. Absinthe took the chair beside hers.

"He'll need to hold your wrist, Anya," Czar said. "Just answer his questions."

She held out her wrist to Absinthe. She wanted it over. Her heart beat too fast, but she was scared and couldn't control that. She shut off the part of her that was hurt beyond measure by Reaper. What had she thought? He'd fucked her. Hard. Left her alone. That was what she was destined to always be. Alone.

"What's your real name, Anya?" Absinthe asked.

His voice slipped into her head and beat at her. Like fists pounding at her mind, demanding entrance. It wasn't that his voice was loud, just the opposite. It was soft. Gentle even. That was so deceptive. It hurt and she nearly pulled her wrist away, knowing he was taking her pulse. That wasn't all he was doing. He wanted truth.

"Anya . . ." She hesitated. "I changed my name because it isn't safe to use my real name." She told him the strict truth.

"I need to know your real name," Absinthe persisted.

Anya looked around the room. These people were the ones she had contemplated having as her family. They'd banded together against her. Reaper stood in the shadows, close, but so far away she knew he was lost to her forever. She couldn't see his face, but he stood with them. Against her.

Her head pounded. *Pounded.* It felt like those fists were punching through her brain. "Stop it. You're hurting me," she whispered. "You have to stop." She didn't know what he was doing, but she knew it was Absinthe. His voice.

"Answer the question." That tone never changed, but the pounding increased.

She yanked her hand away from him and stood. "Fuck you. I'm not going to stay here and let you do this to me."

Absinthe didn't move. It was Reaper who did. Reaper who gently put his hand on her belly and pushed her back into the chair. Reaper who secured her wrists and ankles to the chair. For the first time, she noticed that the chair was bolted into the floor. She didn't fight Reaper because she knew his strength. She knew there was no use. She hadn't known he'd go so far in his betrayal of her.

Absinthe spent the next ten minutes asking her name, and Anya held out just because she was so hurt. So angry. She didn't know why they needed her real name, but she imagined that they'd been offered a reward for her. By the time she knew she had no choice, her head hurt so bad she could barely speak.

"Anya Mulligan."

Absinthe's fingers were gentle on her wrist, taking her pulse. He nodded his head. "Why don't you want us to know your real name?"

"Because someone wants me dead and I'm not stupid enough to leave a trail for them." She nearly spat that at him. They had her name, nothing else mattered.

"How did you come to work at our bar? How did you hear about it?"

"I was hungry, stopped in Sea Haven and went into the grocery store. On the bulletin board, there was an advertisement for a bartender and when I talked to the owner of the store, a woman named Inez, she said you were all very nice boys. That's exactly what she said. Go ask her."

"Where did you work before you came here?"

"San Francisco."

"Where in San Francisco? Which bar?"

God. She *hated* this. Hated that every secret she had was being forced out of her. The pounding never let up. When she was silent, he asked again, and this time there was a subtle change in his voice. That changed the feeling in her head. Along with the battering of fists in her head, she felt the sensation of a knife slicing into her brain, cutting away the barriers so Absinthe could get to the information he wanted.

Her stomach lurched. She was going to be sick. She tried taking deep breaths. "There's a club called the Ghost Club. I worked the bar there." What did it matter if they knew where she'd worked? They had her name, they could sell her.

"Are you still working for them?"

Her head was killing her. She could barely see, white spots dancing in front of her vision. "You have to stop." Tears came no matter how hard she tried to prevent them. Her stomach cramped, protesting the pain. She turned to look at Reaper. "You're letting him do this to me. You're letting him torture me. I'll never forgive you. Any of you."

He moved then, going to his knees in front of her. "Anya." Her name. Soft. Were there tears on his face? She couldn't tell because her eyes were streaming. "Answer the questions, baby, just answer him."

Why had she thought he cared? He only cared about her answers. Someone sobbed. It sounded like Lena, but maybe it was her own voice. She was hurting so bad she couldn't focus. What had Absinthe asked her? She just had to get it over with. Even if they killed her, it would be better than this.

"What did you ask me?"

"Are you still working for the owners of the Ghost Club? Did they send you here to get information on us? On Czar?"

That voice sliced into her brain one more time and her stomach heaved. She vomited all over her lap, all over Reaper. His cut. His disgusting colors that meant so much more to him than any woman ever could.

Someone pressed a cold cloth to her mouth. To her face. They were a blur, and she didn't care who it was. As soon as she could speak, she answered. "No. Of course not. I ran from them. They're trying to kill me."

There was silence. "She's telling the truth," Absinthe said. "No one could lie through that. She's not working for them."

"I'm getting her out of there," Reaper said.

"Finish it," Czar said. "We've gone this far. We have to know."

"Why do they want you dead?" Absinthe asked.

She felt hands working on the bonds on her ankles. She was too far removed from them all to know who it was. "I found construction plans on the floor of the wine cellar, for tunnels below the club, and I was crouched down on the floor looking at them because they were so cool. Two men came in to get wine and they were laughing, talking about scoring big, taking some big shot's wife and how they had him by the balls. I didn't think they saw me, but then one came back as I was heading up to the bar. I got out of there. By the time I decided to leave for good and went back to my apartment, I found my roommate dead. They'd done horrible things to her. I knew they thought she was me, so I ran."

Her stomach lurched again. Her eyes felt like they were bleeding. Tears tracked down her face. "I thought I'd found a family. I thought I had a man. God, how could I have been so stupid? You aren't decent people, any of you. You're no better than they are."

"She's done." Reaper lifted her into his arms, cradling her against his chest.

She tried to push him away. "Get off me. God, you want the truth? How about how I was real and you were fake? You fucked me and left, you bastard, but then it wasn't real to you, not ever." She swung at him. Connected. There wasn't much room and she was weak, so it didn't do more than bounce off his chest. He didn't even flinch. He ignored her struggles and started out of the room.

"I'm sorry, Reaper, I tried to be as gentle as I could," Absinthe said. "It's hard controlling it when someone holds out. She was holding out to protect herself, not because she was spying on us." He sounded ravaged. Destroyed.

Anya *felt* destroyed. She wanted to push Reaper away, but she didn't have the strength. She couldn't even see, just blurred images. She was covered in vomit, but thankfully, so was he. She hoped his colors were ruined. She hated the sight of them.

Reaper carried her up the stairs and into the bathroom. "I'm just going to clean you up, Anya," he said.

She couldn't stand so he set her on the bathroom floor. Immediately he tugged off his jacket and shirt, tossing them into the corner. Her shirt followed. His boots and jeans were gone, then her shoes and jeans. She didn't even protest. She barely was aware of what he was doing and she didn't care. Her head pounded out of control. She kept her eyes closed, because it was disorienting to open them with her vision so blurred.

Water hit her, hot and cleansing, pouring over her as Reaper leaned her against the wall of the shower. Her legs wouldn't hold her and she started to slide down the wall. Hands reached out and caught her. The water kept pouring over her body, washing the scent of vomit from her skin.

She pushed at the hands, wanting to turn around. Wanting him off her skin.

"Get him off me," she whispered, desperate to have Reaper removed. "I don't want any part of him touching me." She wrapped her arms around herself and once more tried to collapse.

Reaper caught her in his arms and stepped out of the stall. Savage was there, wrapping a towel around him while Lena wrapped a towel around Anya. Reaper didn't miss a step, even with the towels draped over them; he stalked down the hall to the bedroom. All the kindness in the world wasn't going to fix this, and he couldn't blame her. She was right in her assessment of him—of the club. They protected their own. She hadn't been included in that, not even by him.

Anya didn't burrow close against his chest. She didn't turn her face into him. She turned away from him. She didn't fight him, she lay passive and broken in his arms. Her words echoed in his head. It was the only thing he'd heard after the interrogation. The *only* thing. *Get him off me. I don't want any part of him touching me.*

She would leave and he would lose the only woman capable of saving him. Of living with a damaged, broken man. He didn't know anything other than the club. His sole purpose had been protecting the club members. He had done what he always did and in doing so, had watched them torture an innocent woman. It wasn't like there would be permanent damage. She would have a migraine, possibly for a couple of days, but then she would be fine. Fine without him.

"Reaper? Get these down her." Steele thrust four round pills into his hand. He was their acknowledged doctor. He knew more about healing the human body than most doctors. He'd been given specialized training once it was recognized he had a rare gift for healing. He'd been taken every day to do his studies with four of the most brilliant surgeons in the country. He devoured books at an astonishing speed and retained what he read. He had become a doctor at the age of sixteen and apprenticed under the four men, each sending for him daily and returning him back to the school in the evenings.

Reaper accepted the pills and put them on the bedside table. He finished drying Anya off while Lana pulled the privacy screens to ensure the room stayed dark even in the morning. He sat on the bed, stretching his legs out, his back to the headboard and then pulled her to him so she was forced into a half-sitting position, her body between his legs.

"You have to take these." He pushed the pills against her lips.

She shoved at his hand. "Don't want anything from you. Just go away."

"That's not going to happen. Take the pills. They'll help." He kept her prisoner in his arms, caging her against his chest.

She took the path of least resistance and tossed back the pills, following them with the water from the bottle he forced to her lips. He let her slide down into the bed, but positioned her head on his lap, his hand stroking her dark cloud of hair. It was falling out of the roped crown she had chosen to wear to work. He pushed his fingers into the thick mass, finding pins and pulling them loose to ease the weave, hoping to help with the headache.

"I know you're upset with me, Anya, and you have every right to be. I should have just asked the questions myself."

She remained silent, eyes closed, but he knew by her breathing she wasn't asleep. Her face was pinched with pain, and she rocked her body back and forth as if that could ease the torment of the headache.

"Would you have told me the truth if I'd just asked?" It was important for him to know if they could have avoided Absinthe questioning her, using his gift against her. Absinthe wouldn't have used that razor technique had she answered him and told him her name. He would have just gently pushed as he normally did when the club needed something.

Anya didn't answer Reaper immediately. Her lashes fluttered and eventually she gave a little shake of her head, her fist knotting in the sheets and pulling the hem against her mouth.

"The owners of the Ghost Club are targeting the families of club presidents. They spy on the club members to get dirt on them. They use gambling debts against them."

"Don't talk to me."

"Anya, they take the wife or daughter. If they aren't paid, they kill the women by cutting them up into little pieces. I imagine that was done to your roommate."

She winced, but pulled the sheet over her eyes. "I don't want to hear this."

"That night I came back and wanted you fired, I'd rescued a woman and her daughter. The hit squad was already there, and I interfered. Took a knife to do it. Now, they have another woman. She just finished chemo. They have to be stopped."

"And you thought I was helping them. That's what all of you thought of me. That I'd help these horrible people cut up women. Please go away. I'll be out of here in the morning." Her voice was muffled and it sounded as if she was crying again. He felt her breath on his thighs. He felt the wet of her tears and it gutted him. He deserved the pain, she didn't.

"I'm not going anywhere, Anya. Get that through your head and don't bother putting energy into fighting me on it." He massaged her scalp slowly, gently, wishing it helped ease the pain slicing through her head.

He let the silence stretch out, hoping she'd fall asleep. She didn't. He didn't. He stared at the wall, his fingers moving in her hair. He might have needed that touch more than she did, he only knew he couldn't stop. He needed her to make it through the night. Through another day. She'd said they were as bad as those targeting innocent women. Were they? He was. He knew he was—he'd shaped himself into a cold-blooded killer so the others could have life. Maybe someday live free.

"When we were children in Russia, we were taken from our homes, our parents murdered because they opposed a man by the name of Sorbacov. He was smooth and charming with his wife and children in public, but in private, he had certain proclivities. His appetite ran to really young boys. Torture and even snuff films. He liked to see girls tortured. He enjoyed watching them killed during sex. He surrounded himself, in one of the four schools he started, with like-minded men and women. Sick bastards that enjoyed inflicting pain."

He fell silent again, staring at the wall, seeing nothing but Anya's face as she sat in that chair beside Absinthe. So pale. Chin up. Defiant. Alone. His heart had stuttered. Melted. His stomach had cramped and he'd wanted to vomit right along with her. He'd let her go through that alone. He should have held her in his arms. He should have sat with her, his hand on her, connecting them. He should have done something to make her understand that truth was necessary to them, because they couldn't afford a spy in their camp. It wouldn't be tolerated. More, they didn't know any other way than what they'd grown up with.

"I was four years old when I was taken there. Savage was two. We had two older sisters. We came from a family of privilege and to see our parents murdered in front of us, and then to be taken to a place with thick walls, few windows and a dungeon of sorts in the basement, was terrifying. There were nearly three hundred children brought into the school over the years. To be accurate, two hundred and eighty-seven children. Eighteen survived."

Her hand moved on his thigh. A small brush of her fingers, but she was listening to him. He didn't know why he was telling her, and he'd never repeat his story in the light of day. Demons ruled him, demons he'd found inside of himself and deliberately cultivated. He'd fed that darkness, needing it, without knowing, when he was so young, what the consequences would be.

Reaper picked up her fist, opening the fingers so he could press a kiss into her palm. "You wondered why we don't think about nudity. They didn't let us wear clothes. We didn't have a bathroom. Often we had to watch when they hurt others. They taught us control of our bodies by forcing us to have sex with older men and women and then with younger ones. If we failed in our control, we were savagely beaten. If our partner failed to arouse us, they were savagely beaten."

He pressed her fingers to his mouth, his teeth scraping gently against the pads. "My sisters were brutally murdered trying to stop Sorbacov and his friends from taking Savage and me up to the rooms where they film the torture and rape of children. They left their bodies on the dungeon floor for two days. We were returned bloody and traumatized. You can imagine what it was like to have our sisters lying dead on top of everything else. If Czar hadn't stepped in, we both would have lost our sanity."

He wasn't altogether certain he hadn't lost his sanity that day. He remembered the pain and humiliation. He remembered rage and guilt because he couldn't stop them from hurting his younger brother, and he'd been only four. He also knew that was the first time he became aware of the darkness in him, a place he could go to be able to do whatever was necessary to stop men like Sorbacov.

"I don't know why I'm telling you this. I've never told anyone else. It isn't so you'll understand what we did in order to protect ourselves, it's more the need to have you know me. I wanted you fired to protect you. I've never had a normal erection. Not one I didn't order up to get a job done. I've never been all over a woman the way I was with you. Out of my mind. Needing to be inside you more than I needed air. It's always been a planned, run-by-the-numbers seduction. When we were given our freedom, a few years

ago, I didn't want to bother ordering my body to want someone. Not even for release."

He paused to look down at her. Her eyes were open, the
long lashes fluttering. He felt the kiss of them brushing
against his thigh. Her gaze searched his face as if studying
him to see if he lied. He pushed the fall of dark hair from
behind her ear, his fingers gentle when that particular characteristic wasn't a part of him.

"I saw you working in the bar. I heard your laughter. I
couldn't take my eyes off you. So fucking beautiful, Anya.
Not just your body, but something else. I tried saving you.
I wanted you gone when I realized I couldn't stay away from
you. When I realized my cock was so hungry for you it
wouldn't stop raging no matter how much I commanded it
to. I wanted you. I never wanted anything for myself until I
saw you."

He broke off. He couldn't tell her the rest. How he loved
the club. How that was his life, the best part of him. The only
good part of him. Now, he didn't want to look at his colors,
the colors he'd taken such pride in. He didn't want to look at
his brothers and sisters. Everything he loved, every person
he loved, had lost him the one person he cared for. He
needed. He'd been willing to try to change enough to have
a relationship with her. He'd believed he would be better
because of her. He'd convinced himself he'd find a way to
grow, that she would stick around and be patient enough to
let him make mistakes.

"In the end, though, it wasn't their fuckup, it was mine,"
he murmured aloud. His club hadn't forced him to do anything. He'd chosen to stand with them. He could have chosen
to stand with her. He should have. But there was Czar. He'd
been Czar's shadow, his sword, since that first kill when he'd
been five years old. He didn't know how to be any different.
Czar's sword was who he was. "You're right, Anya. I should
have stood for you. I knew that light in you was real, but

they needed to know it and somehow, at the time, it was important that they saw you the way I do."

He stroked her hair, willing her to go to sleep. His fingers still tangled with hers, because he wasn't willing to let her go. He only had until she was on her feet to try to find something to make her want to stay. His brain wouldn't shut down. He didn't talk. He didn't share. Now, it was like a floodgate had opened, and he wanted to share who he was. He was desperate for her to see inside, to look past all the layers of darkness and find that part of him she'd touched. The part that needed her to save him. He wanted her to see something good in him, because he couldn't find it and it would be lost if she wasn't there to bring it out.

The door was open and Lana stood in the doorway, knocking softly to grab his attention. "Is she asleep?"

He shook his head. "Drifting. The pills are starting to kick in."

She came in and sank down on the bed, dropping one hand on the blanket, finding Anya's ankle beneath it, as if she wanted that connection as well. "I like her, Reaper. I like her a lot. When you brought her to my room, I was so upset. I thought she was like the other women and I didn't want any of them in my private room. And then I could see she meant something to you so I really looked at her, the way I did at Blythe, and I realized she was someone very special."

Reaper nodded. "Gotta agree with that, Lana."

"I should have stood up more, fought harder for her. I said something, but I didn't push it. I wanted to because I knew the moment I took the time to know her, she was incapable of betraying us like that. Now, I feel like I betrayed both of you. You fought for her, but you needed someone to back you and I didn't do it. I'm really, really sorry."

Reaper sighed. "In the end, Lana, it's about Czar and Blythe. The Ghosts are targeting the wives and daughters

of the presidents of the clubs. That means they would go
after Blythe. Above all, we have to protect them. As much
as I hated it and hated everyone because they were insistent,
I knew it had to be done. I should have at least asked her
myself first."

"She wouldn't have told you, she was too scared." Lana
sighed and rubbed Anya's ankle through the blanket. "I hate
us sometimes, Reaper. I hate that we can't ever be anything
but what Sorbacov made us."

He nodded. "I know what you mean."

"They taught us two things, Reaper. How to have sex
every way possible and how to kill every way possible. They
left out relationships. They left out love. They left out all
the things everyone else knows about. Blythe wouldn't have
let us make the decision to interrogate Anya that way. She
would have stopped us."

Reaper shook his head. "Czar wouldn't have allowed her
to know or weigh in." He looked past Lana to see Czar's
wide shoulders framed in the doorway. His gut clenched. A
surge of rage boiled deep. He suppressed it, threading his
fingers through Anya's fingers, reminding himself she didn't
need raised voices and anger.

Lana glanced over her shoulder and saw their president.
"I'm staying close tonight and tomorrow. Just in case she
needs me. Let me know if you think of anything I can do."
She stood and touched Anya gently. "Those things she said
about you weren't true, Reaper."

He didn't reply, he just watched her go. He wasn't the
only one hurting over what had happened, and somehow
that helped.

Czar came all the way in to stand beside the bed.

Reaper shook his head. "You're not my favorite person
right now, Czar," he said honestly. "Go home to your woman
and leave me with mine."

"Reaper, you know Absinthe was as gentle as possible

under the circumstances. If she hadn't fought him so hard . . ."

"Bullshit. She was protecting herself. My woman's broken, Czar, so you could know yours was safe. Go home. This isn't the time." Reaper leaned his head against the headboard and closed his eyes, not wanting to look at the man he'd protected for nearly all his life. He was angry, but mostly at himself. At the choices he'd made and never stopped making. The choices he knew he would continue to make.

"I'll talk to her."

"You heard her. You heard what she thinks of all of us, especially me. She wore me on her skin, just as I asked, and I repaid her by letting Absinthe rape her mind." He knew Czar wouldn't have a clue what he was talking about, but it didn't matter. He knew. He knew and he was ashamed.

"Reaper."

Reaper shook his head. "Go, Czar." He was suddenly weary. "There isn't anything to talk about tonight. Tomorrow, maybe, not tonight. Tonight I'm going to hold her and make sure the demons don't come for her. Nothing's going to hurt her again. You can give me that much, can't you? One fucking night with her before she walks out of my life for good."

"I'll give you your space now. And I'm sorry, brother. Take some time with her, but we're going to have to talk about those three in the bar tonight. I really am sorry for the way this turned out."

Reaper was sure they all were sorry. Especially him, but it didn't change what they'd done to Anya. He waited to talk to her again until Czar left the room, closing the door behind him, locking the two of them in the room alone together.

"You awake?" Because her breathing wasn't even.

She nodded her head. Her hair slid over his thighs. Tangled around his cock. It felt right to just sit on the bed with her head in his lap. It didn't feel as if she was trying to control him. Or seduce him. It felt comforting. Peaceful. He imagined this was something men and women did at the end of the day, just breathing each other in when they were both hurting like hell.

"Is the headache any better?"

"Strong pills." The soft murmur was said against his bare thigh. Her lips whispered over his skin like a caress. He closed his eyes to savor the feeling, letting it comfort him even more.

The pills were strong. Steele had made certain he'd given her ones that would block the pain as much as possible. It wouldn't take away betrayal or hurt, but hopefully her head would be better.

"I liked them. Preacher. Lana. I liked them."

His heart sank. There were tears in her voice. "Baby, they liked you too. No one wanted you hurt, least of all me."

"I thought they were becoming my friends. Maybe even family."

"They were. They are. Families fight, Anya. Families get past hard things." He wanted to hope. He wanted a fucking miracle. Was it too much to ask for her? Did the universe hate him so fucking much that it wouldn't even allow him to have one good thing that was all his in his life?

"I wouldn't know," she whispered. "I never had a family."

That just about killed him. He brushed her hair back from her face again. She was still, holding her head carefully in case moving it brought back the throbbing pain. He held himself just as still in case just shifting his legs caused her pain.

"Is he some kind of human lie detector?"

They never discussed one another's psychic talents with outsiders. Was she an outsider? Not to him, but it was ingrained to protect the others. "Something like that." He was deliberately vague. There was no explaining Absinthe's talent anyway. He'd practiced for hundreds of hours, working to be able to use his voice to reach into others' minds. He'd sat on the floor in the dungeon, bloody and bruised, tears running down his face, practicing, so maybe the next time he could stop what the pedophiles running the school did to him and the others.

"Is my car fixed?"

"It's a shit car, baby. I told you that already. The boys are good, but they aren't miracle workers." His heart accelerated. She wanted that car so she could disappear out of his life.

"Did they get it running?"

He was glad to tell the truth. "Not yet. They're trying. Roller skates are probably safer." He hoped for a brief smile, even a small one, but he didn't get it. The only sign he had that she wasn't completely pulling away was the hand he was still holding. Either she was too worn out to notice, or, like him, she couldn't quite give up what they'd started.

"I don't know how to skate."

"You never learned?"

"No. It wasn't something we had a lot of time for. We would leave the shelter in the morning and hit the street, looking for food." Her head stirred then, rubbing against him like a cat. It was small, that little subtle movement, but he took it as a caress, just like her lips whispering over him. "Well, Mom looked for drugs, and I looked for food," she corrected. "She was only sixteen when she had me. Her parents kicked her out, and she stayed on the streets. I stayed with her."

"God, baby," he whispered. His fingers tangled in her hair.

"I didn't have it bad, the way you did. My mom ran interference. I didn't understand that was what she was doing, but to keep them away from me, she went off with them." She whispered the confession to him there in the dark, just as he'd confessed to her. "I wish I'd known what she'd sacrificed for me when she was alive."

"She didn't want you to know." He hadn't wanted Savage to know the brutal things he'd endured to keep the worst of the offenders off his younger brother. The problem had been Savage had thought he'd been keeping those same offenders off Reaper.

"I didn't want it to be over," she whispered, and then his thigh was wet with her tears. He wasn't certain if she meant her mother's death, or the two of them.

"I don't want it to be over either," he answered, and there might have been tears in his eyes. He knew he meant the two of them.

TEN

Anya woke to screams, to pounding in her head, and visions of shadowy men and women surrounding little boys, reaching for them, and she couldn't stop them. She tried to fight them. She tried pleading. She did what her mother had done and offered her body in their place. Nothing stopped those monsters from seizing the terrified children.

"It's all right, beautiful. I'm right here. I'm not going anywhere. I've got you." That voice, so like velvet, stroking over her skin, soothed the pounding in her head. "That's it, Anya, come back to me. Open your eyes."

It took a moment to realize there were arms around her and someone was moving a cool cloth over her forehead. She'd had plenty of nightmares in her life. She'd never once remembered waking up in someone's arms with a voice telling her it was all going to be okay. Her mother hadn't been a woman to allow her to cuddle at night. She'd had other things to do.

She took a breath and breathed Reaper into her lungs. He was still with her, still holding her close. She shivered with awareness, with the last remnants of her nightmare clinging stubbornly, but his body heat surrounded her and his arms felt strong. His heartbeat was close and steady.

"Baby," he whispered softly, his mouth against her temple, his lips brushing back and forth with kisses. "Wake up for me. You're having another nightmare." His hand pushed back the hair tumbling around her face, his fingers removing the silky strands that felt like cobwebs. "I shouldn't have told you about that school. It's gone now. Closed. The teachers are dead."

It took effort to lift her lashes and look at the face of her fallen angel. God. He was beautiful. A beautiful, troubled man, forged by the fires of hell, ravaged by monsters. She touched one of the scars on his face. She'd wanted to do that since the first moment she'd seen him, but Reaper wasn't a man one touched. She expected him to stop her, but he didn't. His eyes blazed down into hers and where before, she'd seen remoteness, cold, now she saw something else. Something that terrified her because it was there too late.

"You can't know that."

"What can't I know, beautiful?" He turned his head and caught her finger in his mouth.

Her stomach did a slow, fluttering roll. His mouth was hot. Scorching. His tongue slid along her finger. She was weak to let him do this. Hold her. Whisper to her. Be close when she was so vulnerable. Still, she didn't pull away because he was everything she needed, and just like the sex, she'd take what she could get before she had to force herself to leave him.

"You can't know those horrible people are dead. You were just a little boy."

His eyes changed. Went dark. Flat. He let her finger slide away. "I killed them. One by one. I crawled through the vents of that school or I waited until they beat the hell out of me and let me out of the chains. Then I did it." He rubbed his wrist and up his forearm.

Her gaze dropped to the scars there, evidence that he was telling the truth. "You were a boy. How could you manage against grown men?"

"And women," he added. "Some of the women were the worst."

She felt the shudder that moved through his body. She wanted to hold him. Comfort him. Take away the very real nightmare he'd suffered.

His hand moved through her hair. "I killed them, Anya, the first one when I was five. He'd tortured Savage. He brought him back to the dungeon, bloody, barely recognizable, and Czar and I decided enough was enough. We had to find a way to fight back or they were going to kill us too. That's who you're with. That's the man I try so hard to get away from so you don't have to be in bed with him, but he's the biggest part of me."

He told her looking her straight in the eye. She saw that he was expecting condemnation. No wonder her angel had fallen from the skies. She couldn't imagine that little boy, what he'd gone through and what he'd had to do to get out of such a hellhole. He really had been forged in the fires of hell. What of the others? She didn't want to have sympathy for them, but what had been done to them? What had a prison, pretending to be a school, filled with pedophiles pretending to be instructors, done to all of them? It was obvious: they had survived by working together.

"The first time I saw you, Reaper, I thought you were the most beautiful man in the world. A fallen angel. I still think that. I think you're the most amazing man to do the things in your life you've had to do. To overcome being in hell enough just to function."

For the first time his entire face softened, all those tough, hard features, all those lines and scars. "I'm always going to be in hell, baby," he said. "There's no other place for me."

Tears burned behind her eyes because that angel hadn't seen her. He hadn't looked into her to see the woman who would have walked through hell with him. "I know." Why hadn't he talked to her like this before? She might have had the courage to stay and try to fight for a relationship with him. Why hadn't he held her after having sex with her? That might have made her strong enough to outweigh the betrayal.

"My head hurts. It really hurts and I can't think."

"You're thinking. Too much. It's just us right now, Anya. The world can keep moving all around us, but just for now, in here, in the dark, it's just the two of us."

"Are you trying to persuade me to stay?"

"Yes."

His answer was stark and raw. So was the look on his face. She shook her head, and the action punctuated the pain. "I can't. I need a man whose first loyalty is to me. I want him fierce with his protection of me and our children. With you, the club will always come first, and I understand. I do. I just can't live with that. I want a family, Reaper. You have one. You have brothers and sisters who love you and are loyal to you in a way they could never be loyal to me. I'm glad you have that, I really am, but I need it too."

"They would accept you and be just as loyal to you. Baby, you have to understand what we're like. Czar is the glue that held us together. He was the brains that got us out of there. He was the driving force to make us work harder, to practice our skills so we could each contribute in our fight to stay alive. We have absolute loyalty to one another, that's true, but they'll have that same loyalty to you once you're with us. They will."

He hadn't. Reaper had chosen the club over her. "I'm sure they'd be very loyal to me until they considered me a threat." She might be able to find a way to forgive him, but not them, not the others. She would never believe they would accept her, and after what they'd done, she wouldn't accept them. She needed to bide her time, stay sweet and keep her temper under control until she wasn't so vulnerable.

"Baby, I know we're hard to understand. All we've ever known is protecting one another. The way this was handled wasn't right, but it was the way we were trained. The way we survived."

"My head hurts. Really, Reaper. It's getting worse." She didn't want to hear that his family would accept her and be loyal to her. She knew better even if he didn't. They had a bond that was unbreakable and she understood it. She did. They'd grown up together, suffered together, knew one another's worst secrets, of course they would be loyal to one another. It was an exclusive club and no one else would ever be truly welcomed.

"I know your head aches, baby. I've texted Steele. He'll be here shortly with the pain pills. You can go back to sleep after you eat something. You can't take that shit on an empty stomach."

"What time is it?"

"Around ten in the morning. Alena texted she was making breakfast for us. Do you need to go to the bathroom?"

"Desperately." She wasn't certain she could face the light that would be outside in the hall. Her head felt as if someone had taken a baseball bat to her, but to her insides. Or sliced her up so there were pieces missing, protective covering that had been stripped away by a sharp blade.

Reaper shifted her immediately and slid out from under the sheet, reaching for her. She loved being in his arms. He was extremely strong and gave her the illusion of protection. She knew that was what it was—pure illusion.

"Do you remember Lana coming by last night? Or were you too sleepy?"

He pulled open the door and the light hit her. It pierced her skull like a missile. She cried out, turned her head to bury it against his chest, her eyes squeezed shut as tightly as possible.

"Do you?" he persisted.

She didn't want to remember Lana or her voice. That

sadness. The regret. She knew it was genuine. Lana saying she liked her. That she should have stood up for her more. She'd said Reaper had and she should have backed him. Anya knew she needed to hold on to the fact that those she'd thought were her friends had turned on her. Reaper hadn't helped her. He hadn't stood in front of her and protected her. He'd chosen Czar and Blythe, not her.

Light bounced off the pale-colored walls in the bathroom, putting spots before her eyes. He set her on her feet, and she clutched at the sink to keep from falling. "I have to be alone in here, Reaper. I can't do the things I have to do if you're in here with me."

"I'll be in here if you fall, Anya," he warned. "Don't lock the door."

She knew it was a waste of time, so why would she bother? He reluctantly went out and she was able to breathe deeply. She hadn't realized she'd been breathing shallowly trying to keep him out of her lungs, out of her bloodstream.

After taking caring of business, she stared at herself in the mirror. She looked worse than she'd first suspected. Far worse. There were dark circles under her eyes. Her hair was wild. She had thick hair and it tended to get bigger as the day progressed, which meant, going through the night, it had increased to gargantuan proportions. Her brush sat on the counter, but she couldn't find the necessary energy to use it.

She stood at the sink staring at herself in the mirror, wondering how she had fallen so hard so fast. How she was going to live through leaving her dream behind. She'd fought all her life to pull herself out of the gutters, but life kept knocking her down, trying to tell her she couldn't leave the streets, she belonged there. She was the trash others threw away.

"Anya?" Reaper pushed the door open. "What the hell?" He was across the room, sweeping her into his arms. "Baby. You're crying."

Was she? She hadn't known, only that her image looked blurry in the mirror, but she really couldn't see herself anymore. The reality of her had blurred and she thought that was the reason. She didn't answer him. She just turned her face against the heavy muscles of his chest and let herself cry.

"Reaper, get her in bed."

Steele's voice penetrated the echo of her sobs. She clutched Reaper's neck tighter. The way these people were about nudity drove her nuts. Reaper didn't break stride, but took her back into the darkness of her bedroom. Dropping one knee to the bed, he put her in it. She caught the sheet and drew it up quickly.

"Sit up, baby. Just for a minute. You need to take these pills. They'll help the pain in your head. Remember last night? They took the pain away."

She took them without protest, her eyes downcast, but she could still see Steele standing in the doorway and knew he was watching her. She wanted to put the covers over her head. She remembered looking at him the night before. Looking at each of them, hoping to find some sympathy. Their faces had been as blank as Reaper's, with maybe the exception of Lana's.

"Reaper. We've got a meeting in an hour."

"Meet without me. I'm staying with Anya."

That made her heart beat faster. Hope moved through her, and she squashed it ruthlessly down. Why did women accept men back when the men that hurt them tossed a bone to them? Men broke hearts, betrayed women, did horrible things, but one nice gesture and women were ready to forgive. To hope that one little statement meant Reaper cared for her—that she meant something to him after all. Maybe she did, but it hadn't been enough. There was no fighting his club for him.

"This is important."

"I'm aware we have to plan getting Hammer's woman

back. You and Czar do the planning. When I have to go, I will, but right now, my priority is Anya."

"So is ours, Reaper," Steele said. "We have a situation."

Anya's heart jumped in her chest. Steele was talking about her. *She* was the situation. The meeting was about her. Her fingers found the hem of the sheet and she pulled it inch by inch into her palm to make a tight fist. Terror swept through her. She couldn't go through that interrogation again. Now she wanted Reaper gone so she could make her escape.

"Am I a prisoner?" She had to know.

Reaper spun around. "Of course not." He looked genuinely shocked.

"Then I want to go. Right now. Where are my clothes?"

Reaper exchanged a look with Steele. "Baby, settle down. You're in no condition to leave and you have nowhere to go. Lana and Blythe are working over at the house so I can take you there as soon as your headache is gone."

Her gaze strayed to Steele. "I'm not stupid. Something's up involving me. I'm not going through that again. I won't let any of you put me through that." She sounded weak to her own ears, weak and shaky, but she hoped her determination came through. She would fight them every inch of the way. A part of her was screaming at her to shut up, to pretend everything was fine, go with the flow, and when she had lulled them into a false sense of security, make a break for it, but terror was mounting and she couldn't help blurting out her resolve.

"Anya. Look at me." Reaper went to her, one knee on the bed, bending close so she was forced to look into his eyes. "I stand in front of you. That's my solemn word. Ask anyone. I never go back on it. No one will touch you again. Not one of my brothers. Not one of my sisters, and no outsider. You're under my protection. That's my promise to you. You got me? You understand?"

She searched his eyes. His face. Those beautiful features that were cut by numerous scars. Such a gorgeous man. So broken and damaged. Could she believe him? Would he really give her what he was telling her he would? She saw sincerity. She heard it in his voice.

Did it make her weak to want to forgive something so unforgivable? What kind of woman had the capacity to do that? And what kind of life would she have if she truly were able to forgive him? One with the club? She wanted to believe Reaper, and maybe she was beginning to, but she knew she wouldn't fit in. She just had to bide her time. Get stronger. Get some clothes . . . Very slowly she nodded.

"Then settle. It's a meeting. I'll find out what the problem is and I'll come back and let you know how we intend to fix it, if that's what you want. But be careful of asking. Sometimes the truth isn't easy," he cautioned.

She found she could breathe again. She nodded and looked past him to Steele. The man was young to be the vice president of the club. He was younger than Reaper. She had the feeling she knew why Reaper was called Reaper, but Steele? What did that mean?

"Anya." Steele addressed her. "I hope you're feeling better."

She looked away from him. He'd been there. They'd all been there. Now he, like Reaper, wanted it to be over. Maybe the pain was easing, but the fact that it had been done and done collectively, they'd all stood by and watched, she'd never get over.

"I felt like an insect pinned to a board while all of you watched him torture me. I felt like it wouldn't have mattered if I'd died like that. You all would have just sat there watching the show. So, no, I'm not feeling better." She could be a bitch and she let that part of her loose out of self-preservation.

"I can imagine it felt that way to you," Steele said. "I'm sorry you're hurting. There was no one in that room who felt good about what happened. All of us wanted to stop it and all of us wish it had never happened. I know that doesn't go very far to make you feel any better, but it is the truth."

He disappeared out of the doorway, and Reaper sank down onto the bed next to her. "Did it really feel like that?"

"Yes." She wasn't letting him off the hook. She could tell by the scars he'd covered with multiple tattoos that he'd been tortured. Maybe to the club members, what Absinthe had put her through wasn't meant to torture, was just a means to an end, but it was enough to show her these people didn't include her in their circle.

"I want you to remember what I said, Reaper. I meant every word. You and the rest of them are never doing that to me again. I'll find some way to stop you."

"I hear you, Anya." He reached for her hair, ran his fingers through the strands as if fascinated by the dark mass. "You remember what I said and we'll be fine."

They weren't going to be fine, not ever again. Already the pills were easing the ache in her head and she wanted to run while she could, but Reaper was right when he said she had nowhere to go. Her car had seen better days and had finally decided to give up the ghost. Ghost. She shivered and rubbed her hands down her arms. Those men were scary in a different way than the club members were.

"Do the men from the Ghost Club really have a woman right now?"

His eyes went on alert. It was strange how fast his demeanor changed, going from sweet to all business. "Why do you ask?"

"I was thinking about my car and it reminded me of the club where I worked and what those men did to my roommate. They didn't kill her outright, Reaper. They hurt her as much as they could before they let her die. At some point, they had to know she wasn't me, but they still continued."

"If you worked for them, wouldn't they recognize you?"

She shook her head. "These men weren't ever in the club. I hadn't seen them before."

"Wait." Reaper rubbed his jaw. "I'm confused. You *saw* these men, but they were never in the bar where you worked."

She shook her head. "No, as far as I know they were never in the club, but I saw them as I was coming home. They were getting off the elevator in my apartment building. I knew they were affiliates of the club though. They wear cuff links. Little gold ghosts. When I first saw the manager of the club's cuffs, I thought they were cool. I remember I even said something about them to him."

Reaper shook his head, annoyed with himself. He'd missed that. The two men attempting to take apart the Mayhem president's wife and daughter had worn suits. He hadn't thought to check cuff links. It was a good observation. "You think they have a hit team?" It was not only possible but probable. They would be men not used to wearing jeans and tees in a bar. His heart began a slow acceleration. "Last night, those three men Alena sat with briefly. Had you ever seen them before?"

She sat up, her eyes going wide. That was his woman. Smart. Catching on fast. "Those men . . . The meeting Steele wants you to go to. They may have been here for me."

"Even if they have found you, they'll never get to you. You're safe. Every man will fight for you. Lena and Alena too. The entire club."

"And who will keep me safe from them?"

Her voice broke his heart. "I will. Always. You can trust that."

The sheet slid down her soft skin to pool around her waist. She had full breasts. He hadn't had the opportunity to touch them, to feast on them. He'd thrown those chances out the window. Sitting there, looking at her, there was no resisting that temptation, not even when his mind went to the ugly possibility that those men had come to find Anya, not Czar and Blythe. Especially not when that was a possibility.

He had to find a way to make her want to stay. He wasn't good with words. He didn't know how men were supposed to act in a relationship. But he knew her body wanted his. He could see the desire in her eyes, feel it in the fine tremor that went through her.

He cupped the soft weight of her breasts in his hands, his thumbs sliding over her nipples in a whisper. "Sometimes, Anya, I can't breathe when I see you." He gave her truth when he would normally have kept his mouth shut.

Her breath hitched. She should have stopped him, but she didn't. Her eyes went wide and she bit her lower lip, but she didn't protest.

Reaper wrapped one arm around her back and bent his head. Taking his time. Giving her every opportunity to say no, but she remained silent. His mouth moved over the top curve of her tit. So soft. He felt his heart beat in his cock. He was exposed. He didn't want her to put her hands on him, not yet, not until he knew she'd be safe, but he couldn't resist the temptation of tasting her.

He nipped her skin, felt her body tremble in his arms. His tongue flicked her nipple. Her breath shuddered out. His mouth closed over her breast and he suckled strongly. Flattened her nipple against the roof of his mouth. Danced, flicked, sucked, then brought his teeth into the play. Her arms went around his head, cradled him to her, fingers stroking his hair while her body arched, offering him what he wanted. A small little cry broke from her.

She was sensitive. Responsive. He loved that. Her body really did belong to him. He wasn't alone in suffering that. His was all hers. It always would be. He hadn't ever responded to a woman the way he did to her. His mouth left her breast and he kissed his way up her throat, his tongue swirling over the pulse there before he trailed fire up to her lips.

He kissed her with everything he was. Man. Beast. Killer. Biker. *Hers.* Every single cell in his body belonged to her. She'd branded him, and along with the colors he wore on his back, he wanted her brand right over his heart. Her name tattooed right across it. Fire ran down his spine. Flames settled in his belly, roaring there. Burning spears pierced his skin and a firestorm hit his cock and balls. She did that with her kisses. He had barely started and she'd ignited an inferno beyond anything he'd ever felt.

A knock had him lifting his head to glare at his brother. "A little busy right now," he snapped, his thumb sliding back and forth across her nipple. His mind was on her lush body, and her fantastic tits that rivaled a perfect ass. His head was roaring and his cock raging. He didn't have time to put up with a bunch of bullshit from his brother.

Savage nodded solemnly. "I see that. Nevertheless, Alena sent me ahead of her. She wanted to know if Anya wants coffee or tea. I'm just the messenger, don't kill me."

Reaper glared at him. Anya's fingers slipped slowly from his hair as if she was working to keep them from being seen. She caught the edge of the sheet and brought it up over her breasts. Reaper hated to see them covered and wished he had a knife handy to part his brother's hair. She was suddenly tense, and he glanced down at her. She was completely covered. He knew she wasn't the same way they were about nudity. The tension running through her had nothing to do with nudity and everything to do with Savage being in the room. She looked as if she found the hem on the sheet very interesting, refusing to look up at his brother.

"Bad timing." He said it gruffly.

Savage shrugged. "Don't think it much matters when you're around her. Tea or coffee, Anya?"

"Coffee. Black." She shifted her body just slightly to put Reaper squarely between them.

Reaper liked that. Liked that she used him for protection, but he didn't like that she thought she would need it just because Savage came into the room. Her voice was polite. Pleasant. A mere whisper of sound.

"Would you get me the flannel? I put it here somewhere."

He liked that she wanted his shirt, that something of him would be surrounding her. Obediently he found it and handed it to her. She dropped the sheet and slid into the arms of the shirt. He caught her hands. "Don't button it, baby. Just bring the edges together." He slid under the sheet with her. Close, his leg tangling with hers. Shoulders touching.

She hesitated and then dropped her hands. "Reaper. We aren't going to have a thing."

They were going to have a thing. He just had to figure out the best way to go about it. "Not sure what you mean by that, babe. We aren't going to fight, if that's what you mean. I plan to give you everything you've ever wanted, so there isn't going to be any need to fight."

He slipped his hand inside the open shirt and caressed her tit. "Can't make up my mind which I like best. Your tits or your ass. You're so fuckin' gorgeous there's no way to choose."

She shook her head, color sweeping up her neck into her face. She leaned into his hand, and he used his fingers and thumb to stroke her nipple. Gently. Barely there. His touch whispering. Lulling her. Watching her face. God, he wanted her. Not momentarily. Not just for her body—he wanted to wake up to her. To go to sleep with her. He wanted to hear that laugh of hers all day long.

"I mean, I'm going to tell Czar to take his job and shove it."

"That's okay, you don't want to work. I've got money. Enough for both of us. That house is going to take some work." Deliberately he misunderstood her. "Needs your touch."

His finger and thumb stroked and then tugged. She gasped, and he tugged a little harder. Pinched down. Her body shuddered with need. His fingers went back to stroking. "Want to put my mouth on you. Go to sleep like that. Wake you up eating you. Nothing tastes so good, Anya. Like candy."

"Reaper, I can't stay here. Not after what happened. I get that you all thought it was necessary, it isn't even that. It's the club. It's the fact that I'll always be second to everyone else. Don't you think I want to stay with you? I do. I want this as much as or more than you. But as much as you want my body, you don't feel the same way I do. Not about a relationship. I told myself one night would be enough and I'd walk. Maybe I could have then, but I was fooling myself. I'm halfway in love with you, and you're pulling me in deeper."

He'd never been so happy to hear anything in his life. "Why do you think I'm not committed? You know what happened last night, so aside from that . . ."

"Um, really?" She pushed his hand off her breast and turned slightly in the bed to glare at him.

She didn't realize the action parted the shirt more, exposing one breast. That, her hair wild and tumbling around her, her mouth so close and her green eyes sparkling at him, sent another surge of heat right through his cock. She could get him going without even trying.

"Enlighten me." Before he jumped her. Talking was not his forte. Action was, and he wanted action.

"You left, remember? Just walked out without a single word. Did you think that made me feel like you cared? And then you did it a second time. Walked me to the bathroom and you were gone. Then again you left after you jacked off all over me."

"There's an explanation."

"Enlighten me." She used his own words against him.

He looked away from her. "Anya, sometimes, a man has history. Things in his past he doesn't want the woman he cares about to know. This is one of those things. I'm working on it. And I'm working toward maybe telling you one day, but you'll have to be patient with me. I never thought I'd tell you the things I told you last night."

"Worse than what you told me last night?"

Her voice was soft. Melting into him. Soothing him. She didn't push. She didn't demand. She just dropped one hand on his bare thigh and rubbed gently, comforting him.

"Worse. For me, far worse."

"Okay, honey, we'll drop it for now."

"You going to tell me if you wore me all day on your skin?"

"No." She leaned her head back against the headboard.

"No?" He was going to get it out of her. Just not then. "Here's Alena." The aroma of the food heralded her arrival. "Best cook ever." Because he knew it mattered to her, he pulled the flannel closed over her breast, depriving him of the view but earning him a quick, grateful look from under her lashes.

Alena stepped into the room carrying a large tray. Savage followed her with two full coffee mugs. "Can your eyes take a dim light, Anya?" he asked while Alena set down the tray.

Anya nodded. "I think. The headache is much better this morning, and I just took some more pain pills."

The hurt was still in her voice, but the anger was gone. Reaper would have preferred it the other way around. More, she was averting her eyes again, not looking at either Savage or Alena. Her body was tense against his. Small tremors moved through her. He put one hand on her thigh to try to help ease the anxiety, but she moved slightly away from him.

Alena dished up her famous eggs Benedict and toast, handing each of them a smaller tray to make it easier. She took a seat opposite them, the one nearest the door.

"Anya, I should have stood with Reaper last night and protested. I know it was important, I'm not saying it wasn't. We can't lose Czar or Blythe. You have no idea what Czar has done for us, how many times he saved us and from what, but I still should have backed Reaper. Blythe is trying to teach us how to be better people." She hesitated. "We didn't learn like other people how to . . ." She broke off again, frustrated.

"Thank you," Anya said quietly. Very politely. "I appreciate what you're trying to say."

Reaper frowned. He didn't like that she still found a way not to look at Alena, but there was nothing he could do about it, not without calling attention to it.

"It's just that we don't want you to leave. None of us. Not one single person in the club. You're important to Reaper and that makes you family to us. I wanted to give you the heads-up that Blythe is on her way over. Reaper, you might want to eat fast, dress and go to the meeting. Blythe is going to stay with Anya."

"Blythe?" Reaper's heart did a little stutter of happiness. Blythe was magic. Blythe could maybe fix this when the rest of them didn't have a clue how. And it needed fixing. For all his attempts, Anya still, despite her politeness, wasn't looking at any of them.

"Yes," Alena said, relief sliding into her voice. "Blythe."

"These eggs are fuckin' good, Alena."

"My sentiments exactly," Anya echoed in that same polite voice. "And the coffee is excellent as well."

"Coffee isn't really my specialty. I was telling Czar we needed a little coffee shop or drive-through. Something really small. His oldest daughter, Darby, could work in it. She's been saying she wants a job. Blythe and Czar want her close. If she worked here, we could all keep an eye on her and she'd be safe," Alena said.

"I didn't have a chance to meet her," Anya said.

"She's a great kid," Alena told her.

"Wild as hell," Savage commented. "We're always pulling her out of the parties and taking her ass home."

"She's a kid," Alena protested, "she's supposed to party."

Savage didn't say anything because they all heard the sound of a woman's voice laughing. Reaper nearly threw the plate of mostly eaten eggs onto the bed and jumped up, grabbed his jeans and stepped into them. Anya took her cue from him and buttoned the flannel. When Reaper turned to face the door, he gave Anya a good view of the tattoo on his back. It was the same as the one on his jacket. The tree, crows and skulls. Someday he was going to tell her the significance. Now wasn't the time. He'd seen the way she avoided looking at Savage and the colors he wore.

Czar brought Blythe right into the room. "Brought my woman to see yours, Reaper," he said. "She's going to stay with Anya while we talk. It's important or I wouldn't pull him away, Anya." He stepped closer to the bed. "How are you feeling this morning?"

The moment Czar came close, Anya moved subtly away. Her entire body was stiff and vibrating with tension. Reaper reached for her hand, brought it to his thigh, positioning his body to the side of the bed and a little in front of her. He knew Czar would never hurt her, but he couldn't let go of his resentment toward the man. Anya's strong negative reaction fed his own bitterness. Czar meant everything to him. Father, brother, mentor, best friend, and this was the first time they'd fought over anything other than Czar's security. Czar still had his woman. He hadn't seen her torn apart by his brothers and sisters.

"I'm better, thank you," Anya said in her most polite tone. Her voice was tight. She avoided looking at Czar and the cut he wore.

Yeah, his woman really didn't like his club or their colors. The last time he saw his jacket—his colors meant everything to him—it had been in the bathroom on the floor covered in vomit. Shit. He brought Anya's hand to his mouth and kissed her knuckles. "I won't be long. Have fun with Blythe or rest. Don't open the screens yet, Blythe," he added as a caution and a way to tell both Czar and Blythe that Anya was still hurting.

Alena stood and collected the trays, leaving the mug of coffee. She smiled when Anya thanked her so politely, but her smile was strained. Anya wasn't rolling over for them, and Reaper knew Alena had made breakfast to try to break the ice.

To his astonishment, Savage handed him his jacket. Clean. Even smelling good. Savage didn't look at him, just kept walking. He would never say a word about cleaning his brother's jacket for him, but he'd done it and Reaper was grateful. All the club members were working to make up for their screwup. Blythe closed the door and moved deeper into the bedroom. She smiled at Anya. "How are you really feeling?"

Anya watched her warily. This was a setup if she ever saw one. "The pain is a lot less. I was under the impression you weren't . . ." She stopped, not knowing what to say. Hadn't Reaper said Czar would never tell Blythe? How much did she know?

"Czar came in upset last night. Very upset. We have a rule in our home. He tells me the strict truth if I ask. Most of the time I don't want to know club business, but if I ask, I have to know I can handle the truth. I love my husband very much, so I'm careful of the things I decide to ask about. It's also a protection for me. I can't testify against him if it came to that because I don't know anything. They can't compel me by threatening to take my children away."

"And you're okay with the things the club chooses to do."

"He promised me no drugs. That was a high priority for me. I know they wouldn't touch human trafficking because they go after those that do. They have to do things, sometimes to get information they need. I understand that. But if I ask, he tells me. That simple. Last night, I asked." She sighed and sank down on the edge of the bed. "He told me what he did caused a rift between you and Reaper. It also caused a rift between Reaper and him."

Anya had heard a little of what had transpired between Czar and Reaper the night before. She knew their relationship was strained.

"You have to understand, they don't fight. They're always in sync. They trust each other and have each other's back. Czar has worried about Reaper for a very long time. The entire club has worried about him. Czar knew immediately that Reaper was attracted to you. You don't know what a big deal that is. Reaper stays away from everyone."

He'd stayed far away from Anya as well. Then he started coming into the bar and she couldn't get her mind off him.

"The moment he wanted you fired, which was completely out of character for a man like Reaper, Czar knew it was you. He came home so excited. He kept asking me to make certain Reaper didn't mess up and lose you. Then last night happened and Czar was so afraid for me, he insisted Absinthe question you. Reaper protested. Was angry with him. He said some of the others were as well. Ice, Storm. Preacher. Savage, of course. Lana and Alena. But he knew they wouldn't speak against him because they don't."

Apparently, Lana had. More and more it looked as if Reaper had at least protested. That was something. Anya held that to her. The pills were making her sleepy, but she wanted to hear what Blythe had to say. In spite of everything, she was beginning to hope there was a slight chance. She just didn't know if she could forgive them all, and she didn't want to come in second to the club.

"What they did to you was wrong. They were brought up as children without parents or society to teach them. They had Czar. He was ten when he started trying to save them all. A little boy with toddlers being brutalized, just as he was. They made their rules and code and have lived by it ever since."

Anya was well aware of that. She'd been on the wrong side of that code.

"Reaper has made it clear that you're the one for him. Everyone in the club has accepted you. I want you to know, when Czar came back to me, and he'd been gone for five years without a word, I didn't want anything to do with him. I was pregnant when he left. He didn't know it, but then . . ." Blythe stumbled over the words and her eyes filled with tears. "I was beaten with a baseball bat when I was eight months along. She lived two days. I couldn't have any more children, and he wasn't there."

"Oh, Blythe." Anya sat up straight, wanting desperately to comfort the other woman.

"I didn't think I could ever forgive him. Eventually, he

convinced me to try, and I'm so glad I did. I'm happy. Really, really happy, Anya, and I think if you can find it in your heart to forgive Reaper and the others, you'll find you have a huge family, men and women who will love you and watch out for you. I'm not saying it will be easy, Reaper is a damaged man. They all are damaged. But he's worth it."

"I don't want to be second to the club, and if nothing else, what happened showed me I would be."

"What happened to you was awful. Czar was devastated over the whole thing, so more than anything, that told me it had to be terrible for you. I'm so sorry. I know they seem horrible, frightening people with no real emotions, but that isn't true."

Anya didn't react, but just sat shaking her head, tears shimmering in her eyes.

"I wish I could do something to help you feel better, but I can only try to reassure you that they are good people with their own code and once you're with them, they will extend every protection to you and your family." Blythe shook her head. "I thought that I would be second to the club as well, but it isn't the case. They've all accepted me into their family. I know I'm one of them. The children are family to them. You would have that too."

"And if you left Czar? If you broke up with him? Would you still have them?"

"I think so. I think they'd always watch over me and the children. Certainly, if something happened to him they would."

Anya was silent a moment and then she shook her head again. "Reaper and I didn't have a past. We're not exactly in a relationship. I don't know what he wants from me half the time and I don't know if he can give me the things I need, because I can't be second."

"Czar puts me first. He loves the club, but I know I'm first. Reaper's playing catch-up with learning how to be in a relationship. He makes a mistake and learns from it. I don't believe that you'll ever be second again, not with Reaper, not if you give him a chance."

Anya pushed at the dark hair falling around her face. "I don't know if I'm strong enough."

"You're strong. Give him time to show you. I promise you, Anya, you won't ever regret it. I'll be here to help you. So will Alena and Lana. The men will help you. All you have to do is ask for what you need."

Anya slid down deeper under the covers. "I'm sorry, I can't quite keep upright. They gave me some pretty heavy pain pills."

"Go to sleep, honey," Blythe said. "We'll talk more later. Just think about what I've said."

There was no way Anya could do anything else when she closed her eyes—all she saw was Reaper.

ELEVEN

"Two of these three men are hit men," Code said, pointing to the photographs of the three men who had been in the bar the night before. "This one, Tom Randal, the one Alena conned, is an investigator and is on retainer with the Ghost Club. Steve and Mike Burrows are hit men and work, also on retainer for the club, under the guise of being consultants. They are uptown hit men. They work out of private offices, I kid you not, in San Francisco. Randal works from an office in the same building."

Reaper's heart took the blow like a hard punch. He'd been expecting it, but he'd also been holding out for a miracle. There were just too many hits coming at Anya. They weren't out of the woods yet, he knew that. She was still trying to pull away from him. He had to get her away from the club for a little while, seal her to him somehow before reintroducing her into their world.

"Are they here for Anya or Czar?" Steele asked the question the others wanted to know.

Code glanced at Reaper as if expecting him to lose his

shit. He held himself still, already knowing the answer. "Czar isn't on their radar. They were sent to track Anya. Apparently, Randal was the one to track her, and then he was told to get information on the club and the club's president for future reference. They didn't believe our club was large enough to bother milking our bank accounts . . ."

Transporter snorted. "They clearly haven't managed to hack into your books, Code. They'd see we stole billions from the Swords and that we all had healthy bank accounts before we ever settled here."

"No one's going to ever find my real books," Code said. "But I put enough firewalls and other protections in to make it look like I thought I had something to protect in case anyone came looking. Mostly I thought the feds would look our way at some point."

"Our paperwork is impeccable and will hold up under any scrutiny," Steele said. "How did Randal find Anya?"

"She's memorable. A beautiful woman like Anya? People notice," Code said. "He started flashing her picture around and eventually found the man she bought that piece of shit car from. Then it was a matter of tracking gas stations she visited, again, just by showing her photograph to the attendants. Randal arrived a couple of days ago, saw her with his own eyes and confirmed with the Ghosts that he'd found her. They sent the Burrows brothers."

"Where are they now?" Reaper asked.

"All three are checked into rooms at a motel in Fort Bragg," Code replied.

Czar tapped his fingers on the table, an indication that his brain was already putting together the pieces of the problem and working through it. "They're probably waiting for tonight. They'll check to see if she's in the bar and will try to make their move if she goes outside alone."

Code cleared his throat and glanced again uneasily at Reaper. "I read through all the email exchanges. They're in code, but the encryption is pathetic. Easy to break. They aren't going to kill her clean. The Ghosts want an example made of her. They want the Burrows brothers to spend time with her and slice her up, keeping her alive as long as possible."

Reaper started to rise. He'd go now, kill both fuckers and leave their bodies in plain sight so the Ghosts knew he'd declared war.

Czar waved him to his seat. "This one is for your woman and we want to do it right. We want her protected even after we kill them, otherwise the Ghosts are going to just keep coming after her." He waited until Reaper slowly sank into the chair.

"Who do we have on Anya and Blythe now?" Steele asked. He knew, but it was important that Reaper remember both women were being guarded.

"Gavriil and Casimir in the house and Fatei and Glitch," Reaper replied, naming the two newest patched members as well as two of the prospects, all who had attended at least one of the four schools in Russia. He reached for the bottle of water sitting in front of him and downed half of it. All four were good men, but he wanted to be looking out for Anya himself.

Czar nodded. "The Burrowses won't make their move on Anya until they know she's alone and they have time to spend with her."

Reaper's fingers curled into two tight fists. "They aren't going to get the chance. If you're thinking of using her as bait . . ."

Czar lifted his head and their eyes met, piercing, angry, two bulls ready to charge each other. The room went dead silent.

"Get your fucking head out of your ass, Reaper," Czar hissed. "You think I don't know I totally fucked up? You think I don't know I'm responsible for hurting a woman? Not just any woman? Your woman? My *brother's* woman? I know you're fighting to keep her and that's on me. She couldn't even look at me. I don't blame her. I take what we did squarely on my shoulders. Coming at me isn't going to help."

"I'm not so sure," Reaper snapped, standing. "You went home to your woman. She's still in your bed, safe and secure. You have that. I don't. Mine's ready to walk and there's not a fucking thing I can do or say that, so far, is changing her mind."

Czar stood too. "You're not going to make me feel any worse than I already do. We can beat each other if that's what you want, but the truth is, you want someone to punch and you want someone to punch you. You like to inflict pain when you're pissed and you like to take it. We can do that and be two utterly selfish bastards or we can figure out how to keep your woman safe and get rid of these Ghosts so they don't keep coming at her."

Reaper knew every word was the truth. He didn't have to like having Czar call him on his shit, but he had to do the right thing for Anya. He sank down into the chair and reached for the water bottle, downing the rest to give the adrenaline time to recede.

"We have Hammer's wife to get out of there as well. We're going to have to make our move fast to pull her out, especially after we kill the hit men coming after Anya. I want Randal alive, if possible. We need as much information as we can get from him. Alena, you're on that. Once she leads him close, Storm, you and Ice secure him and put him in the chamber. He can yell his fucking head off and no one will hear him. That will give us time to get down to San Francisco and get Hammer's woman before we have to deal with him."

"We still don't know what we're looking at once we get down there," Transporter said. "Do we take the bikes or one of the vans? I'll need to know how to prep the vehicles. Weapons, tools, paper to cover everything in case we get stopped. I need information to have a place to start."

Mechanic nodded. "We'll be going in blind, and if I don't bring the right tools for the job, they'll kill her for certain."

There was silence. It was imperative they have information, but getting it was going to be a problem.

Absinthe rubbed at a spot on the table, glanced warily at Reaper and then sighed. Looking down at the tabletop, he spoke in a low voice. "Anya might be able to tell us how to get through those tunnels. She can tell us how at least. She said she was looking at blueprints of tunnels under the building."

"Absinthe," Czar said quietly. "You were acting under my orders."

"Doesn't make it any easier."

"If she hadn't fought you, and I didn't expect her to," Czar admitted, "she would have been fine. I thought she'd answer the questions and we'd walk out of there without incident. I misjudged the situation because I was so blind, wanting Blythe safe. What happened isn't on you. It was my call."

"No," Steele said. "It's on all of us. We could have insisted on a vote and stopped it. We could have spoken out and sided with Reaper. We had options. Reaper could have told us all to go to hell and walked out with her. No one can stop him if he doesn't want to be stopped."

Reaper took a breath. That reality was a hard punch in the gut. Harder still, because he knew Anya was well aware of it. He had chosen the club over her. He'd put Czar's protection above hers.

"He's right, Czar," Reaper had to admit. "But it won't happen again. If she takes me back, I'm going to fight for her. You all might as well know that up front."

"I think you've made that pretty clear," Czar said. "Absinthe, I have to admit, I was more focused on Anya's state of mind than what she was saying."

"I absorb and can recall verbatim," Absinthe said. "You, better than anyone, know it was necessary to know exactly what an adult said, what they were planning, the times, the routes, everything. You trained me to hone that ability. But I trained myself to listen and sort of record what was said."

Preacher nodded. "She did say she was looking at blueprints. I hate this. I hate this for her and for you, Reaper. For all of us. We took the easiest and fastest route available to us to get the information we needed. She was innocent."

"We didn't know that," Steele said. "We can beat ourselves up or make her safe and get this other woman safe. It isn't going to matter if you get her to stay with you if she ends up dead."

That was Steele, the voice of reason. That was why he was Czar's VP. When the rest of them were out of sync, he managed to bring them back together.

"We need to find out just how much of those tunnels Anya remembers. Will she help us, Reaper?" Czar asked, going straight to the point. If she wouldn't, he'd have to find another way to rescue Hammer's woman yet still keep his men as safe as possible.

"I'm not going to say she isn't hurt. And pissed. She'd holding it tight, but it's there. None of us are her favorite people right now, me included," Reaper said. "But she asked about the woman a couple of times. I can't imagine her leaving another woman in the hands of these Ghosts, especially after seeing their handiwork. She told me when they're wearing suits they always wear little gold cuff links in the shape of ghosts."

"Alena and I can head down to the club to try to get information," Lana offered. "If we establish ourselves, we can be in a position to back you up. If we go in first, two tourists just checking out the club, we'll be of more help."

"I could follow them up," Mechanic added. "I can get the place wired as fast as possible. We could get lucky and get something to help. In any case, I'd be there if they get in trouble."

Alena snorted. "Not likely."

Lana flashed a small smile. "Just yell if you need us to bail your ass out, we'll come running and save the day."

Mechanic flipped her off.

Czar ignored the byplay. "We'll need you, Alena, to pull in Randal for us before the two of you go. Take the BMW. It's fast. Transporter and Mechanic swear that thing is a rocket now. It has all the compartments needed for weapons. The two of you look like you were born for a convertible. It will cost enough to give you the clout to get in, but not so much as to put you under suspicion. If you take enough cash, you might even see their casino. Don't push. That's not necessary.

"Reaper, we need to do this as fast as possible. I don't think Hammer's woman has much time left, regardless that they gave him a week to get the money together. They want to make a statement to the Diamondbacks. They want them to know they're serious. If they can make the Diamondbacks worry about their women, they have a pipeline all over the country. Remember, the Ghosts think they're just that . . . ghosts. They have no idea we're on to them."

Reaper was aware the rest of the club members were looking at him. Expecting him to pull his woman in with them. His heart sank. They had no idea the extent of their betrayal. She wasn't like them. She wasn't like Blythe, who hadn't had a decent beginning, but had found a family with five other women. Sisters who loved her. Anya had no one.

"I think she'll tell us about the tunnels."

"But she isn't going to stay, is she?" Lana pressed.

Reaper shook his head. "I don't think so, no."

"Maybe Blythe was able to persuade her to give us another chance," Czar said.

"Maybe." Reaper was afraid to hope.

"If she'll talk to us, Reaper, bring her into the common room," Czar said. "We'll be less threatening to her there."

"I'll make certain to get her clothes to her," Alena said. "She probably feels vulnerable without them."

"She can't go anywhere if she doesn't have clothes," Ice pointed out.

Alena glared at him. "We can't keep her prisoner."

"Why not?" Ice asked. "He only needs a few weeks to convince her to stay. If nothing else, knock her up. We're supposed to have been trained to be the best at sex there is; if we can't use it to keep our women, then what good was it?"

"He's got a point," Storm said. "I could convince her to stay for you, Reaper, if you don't think you're up to the task."

"Fuck you, Storm. I'd stick a knife through your heart and pin you to the wall."

Storm shrugged. "Just trying to help a brother out."

Reaper felt a little better. His brothers were there, at his back, trying to come up with ideas for him to keep Anya, joking to bring them all back together behind him. Solid. He just knew better. He knew it wasn't going to be that easy with Anya. Still, he nodded and pushed himself away from the table. He made his way into the common room and then down the hall. Blythe was sitting in the dark and she looked up when he entered.

"She's been sleeping for a long time." She took a deep breath and shook her head. "She's holding herself together, but just barely. Be gentle with her, Reaper."

He nodded and watched her go. He didn't know how to be gentle. He'd never learned. He didn't even know what that meant. Alena stuck her head in, folded clothes in her hands. He took them and shut the door to keep everyone out. He needed to talk to Anya again. To feel her out. See if she would help and tell her she had to stay. He needed her to stay.

He stood over her, looking down at her face. She thought him a fallen angel; he thought maybe she was one that had fallen into hell accidentally.

"You're staring at me. I can feel it." Her voice was a drowsy murmur that got him right in the cock. Shit. It was so much worse than that. She'd gotten to his heart somehow, and it wasn't going away.

"So, you're awake."

"My radar goes off when you're around."

He didn't know if that was good or bad and he wasn't asking. He only knew he was contemplating just how wrong it would be to follow Ice's plan.

She opened her eyes and caught him. Very slowly she pushed herself into a sitting position, never taking her gaze from his. "What are you thinking? Because I can tell you think I won't like it, but you're going to do it anyway."

What the fuck? He was supposed to be the man no one could read. She was seeing too much of him, and that wasn't a good thing and never would be. He was the club's enforcer. That meant while they all had other, legitimate, jobs, he had just one—to keep the club safe in any way necessary. The others might be climbing out of their old life, but he never would. He knew it was too late for him anyway.

"Alena brought you some clothes. Do you feel up to getting dressed? We can try a light to see if your headache gets worse."

"No. No, really, it's so much better." She threw back the covers and reached for her clothes, almost hugging them to her.

He didn't like that either. His woman was up to something. Like running from him. More and more, Ice's idea seemed like a good one. Maybe the only one. He turned on the dimmest light first, watching her face to see if she flinched. Her lashes fluttered, but her expression didn't change. At least that was something. He didn't want her in pain.

"I'll get dressed in the bathroom and then you can tell me what this meeting was all about."

"Get dressed here." He moved subtly, shifting his body just enough to put him in front of the closed door. What the hell was wrong with him? Was he really thinking he could keep her there if she wanted to go? He knew better, but he didn't move.

She studied his face, shrugged, pulled on the lacy little

boy short panties and then her jeans. "They told you at the meeting that those three men were after me, right?" She looked around. "There's no bra here."

"Alena hurried to get your clothes. She must have forgotten." He crossed his arms over his chest and leaned back against the door. He could look at her all day. He watched her unbutton his flannel, his gaze glued to her bare skin.

She sighed and pulled the tank top over her head. The material settled lovingly over her curves. She looked down at the cleavage showing and then around the room as if there was something else she might be able to wear.

"You look beautiful."

"You would say I look beautiful if I was wearing a burlap sack."

"I would think it too."

Her gaze flicked to him, the faintest ghost of a smile in her eyes. He liked that. He needed it. Something. Anything to show she might want to stay with him.

Anya pulled on his flannel. "I think this shirt is going to grow on my skin soon. Where are my shoes?"

"Not sure, baby. Is it important right this minute? Got things to discuss with you."

She tipped her head up, eyes going to his. "Let's discuss."

"The others are waiting out in the common room. They have information . . ."

She shook her head. "Absolutely not. I don't need their information. You tell me what I need to know. Anything else, I don't want to know."

He shrugged, although his gut knotted tight. She wasn't going to stay. The vehemence in her voice convinced him of that. He'd need a plan to try to keep her close to him. He needed time with her, just like Ice had said. "One of the three men in the bar last night is a private investigator on retainer for the Ghost Club. He tracked you here. He found the man you bought the car from using your photograph. You're beautiful, and people remembered seeing you."

She shook her head and reached back to braid her hair while he talked. He could sit and watch that shit for hours. The action lifted her breasts beneath the open flannel. He could see the movement of both breasts. Her hands were quick and sure, as if she'd performed the task countless times and was on automatic pilot.

"Stop looking at me like that. It's distracting."

He fucking loved that. It was the first real sign of encouragement. "Can't help myself, baby, can't help what you do to me."

"Stay on track. The jerk followed me here and brought those other two."

"Hit men. They're working for the club. Code got into their exchange of emails. They were encrypted, but he's a genius with that sort of thing, which is why we call him Code."

She swallowed hard and moved around the bed to grab a tie off the nightstand and secured her braid with it. She looked scared. So much so that he crossed the room, stepped in close and curled his hand around the nape of her neck. Possessive. Claiming. Because Anya fucking belonged to him whether she knew it or not, and he was going to find a way to make certain she knew just whose woman she was. He'd had enough of being anxious.

Reaper had taken what he needed to survive his entire life. He looked down at her, his gaze drifting over her face. Her eyes. That mouth that belonged to him. He was through thinking she was getting away from him because she wasn't. He leaned down and took her mouth.

Fire exploded in his belly. Her lips were soft, her mouth sweet and addicting. The minute he demanded it, she opened for him and gave him what he needed. He wrapped his arm around her back and yanked her up against him, kissing her over and over until he couldn't see straight. Until he knew she would give him anything he asked for and his world was right again.

When he lifted his head, he stroked the pad of his thumb

down her face, slid it over her lips and pressed it there on that bottom curve. "No need to worry about the two of them. We're working on a plan. I need you to tell me if you have those blueprints you were lookin' at memorized. The ones that got you into so much trouble."

"The blueprints?" she echoed. "I thought they came after me because I overheard them talking about having someone by the balls."

"It was most likely both. We think they're holding that woman they kidnapped down there. We need to get her out of there, baby, or she's going to die."

Immediately her shoulders straightened and she nodded. "Of course, Reaper, I'll tell you whatever I can. I have a good memory."

"I'd like the others there. We work together, and each of us needs to know different things."

She was silent, staring up at him. He could see he was losing her and that just pissed him off. He refused to feel fear. He had to take control of the situation the way he always did. He refused to allow her freedom when she tried to pull away, to put distance between them.

"Woman, I know fucking well my taste is still in your mouth, yet you're going to act like it isn't. I gave you my word. My fucking *word* that you would be safe with them. I know you were listening. You lay right on that bed and you heard me promise I'd protect you from anyone, everyone, even the club. You kiss me like that and then act like I'm not your man?"

Her lashes blinked rapidly and there appeared to be droplets on them. She took a breath and then tried again to push him away. She wasn't nearly as strong as he was and he held her still. "This isn't easy for me, Reaper. I don't trust them. You're one man against how many?"

He let his eyes go flat and cold, calling up the dangerous demon inside of him, the one that kept Czar and the others alive and continued to do so. He gave her that because she needed it—needed to see that he would do the same for her. "They know better."

She shivered. Swallowed hard. Studied his face for a long time. He didn't flinch or look away. He wanted her to know what she was getting into with him. He was watching her as closely as she was watching him, so he saw the moment when she accepted who he was. What he was. Hopefully, she believed he would be that killer for her if needed.

"Fine. I'll go, but if they try anything with their questions, I swear, I'm getting a gun and shooting you."

"Think there should only be one bloodthirsty person in our family, babe, and you're not near mean enough."

"I wouldn't test that theory if I were you," she cautioned.

She tried to give him the evil eye. He thought she looked cute, but decided it might not be wise to say so. His woman was getting back to herself without the bitch of a headache. He bent his head and took her mouth again. When she sassed him, he figured it was the best way to mellow her out. Just like before, she ignited without reservation, her body melting into his, all soft against his hard.

His hand slipped down her back, tracing that curve to the sweet ass he thought way too much about when he should be thinking about business. He kissed his way down her chin, along her jaw to her ear. He caught the lobe between his teeth and tugged gently. "You still thinkin' about runnin' from me?" He whispered the question, his breath warm in her ear, his lips brushing against the little shell that sometimes drove him nuts.

"Yes." She answered without hesitation, breathless, her breasts rising and falling with her ragged breathing, nipples pushing hard against the tank she wore.

He swatted her hard enough to make her yelp. "Well, stop. Solutions, babe, not runnin'. That's what should be going on in that fucked-up head of yours." He figured he'd handled her with kid gloves, at least to the best of his ability. He'd tried gentle, just like Blythe said, but he didn't know what the fuck he was doing. She'd fallen for Reaper. He was back to the Reaper he knew best, and that man wasn't going to lose his woman. He'd find a way. If he couldn't think of a solution, his club would help him.

She glared at him. "My head isn't fucked-up. Your club is fucked-up. And stop saying *fuck* to me. It's annoying."

He shrugged. "Just a word, Anya."

"It isn't a nice word."

"It's just a word." He took her hand and tugged until she was under his shoulder.

"I'm barefoot."

"You're stalling. The floor's clean. Club girls keep it scrubbed."

"Club girls? Sheesh, Reaper. You certainly want me to accept a lot of bullshit. I'm not sure what I'm going to get out of it."

That brought him up short because it was the truth. He stepped in front of her. Close. Caught her chin with his thumb and finger, lifting so she was forced to look in his eyes. "I swear to you, on my life, on the lives of my brothers, you'll be happy. You'll be safe." He didn't know what else to say. He'd spend a lifetime making her happy, but he knew he was a poor bet for a lifetime. He knew jack about a real relationship and no matter how hard he tried, he was going to fuck it up big-time. She'd need patience and tolerance and she'd need to want to stay.

"I'm trying," she said softly.

He knew that was the best he was going to get. He pulled open the door and walked her out of the bedroom, into the hall. She tensed up immediately.

"Don't worry, Anya, they'll be cool with you."

"Worry about them, not me," she muttered under her breath.

He glanced down at the top of her head. Her hair was always glossy. Shiny. Gorgeous. "Just play nice." He knew that would get a rise out of her. She was back to herself.

His woman had courage. She wouldn't have been able to pull herself up out of the streets and carve a life for herself if she didn't have discipline, determination and sheer guts. He had those things, all his brothers and sisters did. That was how they'd survived—that and working together. She'd done it on her own, and he respected her for what she'd accomplished.

"Play nice," she hissed, glaring up at him. "*You* play nice. They do one thing, *say* one thing I don't like and all bets are off."

"Got to fuck you again hard, woman. Only thing that mellows you out."

Her breath hissed out of her lungs. "Well, maybe you should, but you lost that chance hanging with your nasty brothers and club girls, didn't you?"

He smiled. He couldn't help it. It wasn't the greatest smile in the world because he didn't have a lot of practice at it, and his mouth quirked more than smiled, but he felt it in his gut. Happiness bloomed, the way it had done almost from the moment he'd laid eyes on her. Certainly, from the moment he'd seen her give away her blanket to a homeless man.

Anya stopped dead just outside the open door to the common room. The club obviously heard them coming because all conversation ceased. She touched his lips with her fingertips, her eyes wide. "I've never seen you do that before."

She probably hadn't. He hadn't had much to smile about—until her. He'd actually sat in a bed naked, holding her, and hadn't had one ugly thought. Maybe it had been the fear of losing her that had prevented the triggers from his past from rearing up.

"Don't do it very often, baby, but can't help myself around you." And that was the fucking truth. He pulled her finger into his mouth and bit down gently and then let her go. She looked up at him wide-eyed. Soft. That look in her eyes he was waiting for, the one that turned him inside out and set a fire roaring in his belly.

He glanced over her head to the others, his family waiting for him, even more shocked than Anya that he had smiled, or given what passed for one. Lana was there, and she smiled back at him and gave him the thumbs-up. She and Alena had located the jacket for Anya as he'd requested, and added the necessary patches. He'd been planning for this moment long before he'd ever spoken to her at the bar. He'd warred with himself, trying to save her, but somewhere deep down, he knew he wasn't going to let her go, even back then.

He just had to get Anya to accept that final assurance. Today. Tonight. She had to commit before he took off to help rescue Hammer's old lady. He had to go. He didn't have a choice, and he needed that promise from her before he left with the others.

Reaper took her hand again, tucked it in close to his chest and walked right into the common room. No one else was there but the fully patched members. Gavriil and Casimir were to the back, standing by the door. On the outside would be the prospects, making certain no one came close enough to overhear. Ordinarily, they would never conduct an important meeting outside the chapel—their private meeting room—but Anya would have been far too uncomfortable. The common room was open and would give her a sense of ease—they hoped.

Anya went stiff the moment she faced them all. They'd spread out, taking seats at the smaller tables, some of them on the couches or in the more comfortable chairs in order to make her feel the meeting was informal and she was a part of it.

Reaper slid his arm around her waist. "Before we get started, I want everyone in this room to know, I'm claiming Anya for my old lady. Lana has her jacket."

To an outsider, that wouldn't mean anything; to the club, it meant everything. Anya, in their world, was his wife. The woman he chose to put on the back of his bike—in Reaper's case, he hadn't ever put a woman on his bike until Anya. He just said he would be responsible for her, and that every member of the club had the responsibility of protecting her just as they would any other club member.

Anya glanced up at him, frowning. She wasn't familiar with their world, and only Czar had an old lady. Blythe rarely was in the clubhouse. Mostly, they went to Czar's home for their barbecues. She came to the parties at the clubhouse, but left early with Czar. Sometimes she rode on his bike, but it was usually when they wanted to run off together. Anya couldn't know exactly what it meant, but she'd find out soon enough.

Czar stood up slowly. He walked toward them, looking in complete command, the way he normally did. The closer he got, the stiffer Anya got. Her chin was up, green eyes glittering like gems. She was royally pissed at Czar. At the club. Reaper had no idea why she had softened toward him, but she had and he was taking advantage while he could.

"Are you certain that's what you want, Anya? Do you even know what that means when he tells his club members that you're his old lady? It's a huge commitment."

Anya stepped closer to Reaper as if for protection. He felt her slide one hand into his back pocket, her fingers curling into a tight fist. "It isn't your business if Reaper makes me his old lady. You don't have a say in my life."

The room went electric. Wired. Silent as hell. Reaper's heart dropped. Czar was president of Torpedo Ink. He had a say in every club member's life. He saw the same knowledge on Czar's face that was on every member's face.

"Honey"—Czar's voice was very gentle and very patient—"saying that just goes to show you don't understand what you're getting yourself into. By accepting Reaper, you're accepting all of us. Including my leadership. You're good for Reaper. For all of us, but we have to be fair here. You have to understand exactly what being part of us means."

"I don't have to do anything with the people who took

me to their interrogation room and put me through hell in order to be with Reaper." Anya stated it firmly.

"Reaper . . ." Czar shook his head, regret in his voice.

Reaper's stomach clenched. He felt, rather than saw, Anya look up at him. She knew something was wrong from the way everyone in the room sat or stood frozen, expressions of pure alarm on their faces. He was certain his countenance had the same look.

Time tunneled. His brothers and sisters. His colors. His way of life. He was torn in half, wrenched apart. He didn't know how to live without them. More than thirty years. All the pain. Suffering. The kills. The shared food they'd cut so carefully into equal portions. Images of screaming children, of ugly, vile men and women coming at him when there was no defense. Czar, comforting him. Whispering there was hope. They would find a way. It all came down to this.

Czar had led them here to make them human again. To force them to be better people. Half animal, all killer, they had choices now. Reaper looked down at the woman holding so tightly to him. She'd brought him more than natural releases. She'd brought him something close to happiness.

"You once said to me, Czar, that if you had to make a choice, if we couldn't accept Blythe into our family, equally, with all the rest of us, that you would stay with her while we moved on. Not accepting Anya gives me no choice. I go with her."

Anya heard Reaper say the words, looked at his face and knew he meant it. Heart pounding, she felt triumph burst through her. Czar was an asshole, a complete bastard to subject her to his inquisition. Reaper had chosen her. His arm nearly crushed her. She looked up at his face a second time and everything in her stilled. He was choosing her, but he was being torn apart in doing so.

"It isn't the same, Reaper. We accept her. She refuses to see us. To get to know us. We're your fuckin' family and she's shutting us out because of one mistake. Think about that, what could happen, because you're going to make mistakes, brother. You'll make a million of them. Anya"—there was a note close to a plea—"we're his family. We want to be yours."

Czar's eyes met Anya's. She felt the impact right down to her toes. He wasn't angry. He was ravaged. Destroyed. In pain. She looked from him to the others. Savage had risen to his feet and moved subtly, coming to stand near his brother. Ice and Storm had done the same. Lana clutched a jacket in her hands, all but crushing the material, her face showing the same pain. The others echoed that same broken sorrow as well.

Anya looked up at Reaper. It was on his face. Her beautiful scarred, damaged man was in the same pain the others were in. They shared it. She felt it, as if that pain tore them apart, shredded them, leaving them raw, leaving them all with a huge gaping wound she knew would never be repaired.

He would go with her. She had that power. But if he went, he would never be whole. He would never be Reaper. She'd had glimpses into his past, the past he shared with every single one of these men and women. It was ugly, and it was brutal. But something beautiful had come out of it. They had created a tapestry together. Or rather, Czar had woven them together so they would be whole. So they could live. She saw that so clearly in their faces. More, she felt it.

Anya looked around the room. Most didn't meet her eyes, looking down when her gaze touched on them, ashamed, guilty. Absinthe shook his head and looked away, but she thought she caught the sheen of water in his eyes. Her breath caught in her lungs and stayed there. Without Reaper, they weren't whole. Without them, he would never be whole. Intact. The Reaper she'd fallen for.

She saw each one of them look to Czar. She found herself doing so as well. She didn't know how to resolve the situation. She only knew that these broken, damaged individuals weren't quite so broken or damaged when they were together. Her eyes met Czar's.

"You see?" he said quietly. "You're part of him now. That makes you part of us. You feel it too. You know we need one another. We need you now too."

"I don't want to be second."

"Does it feel that way to you? Really? Look around you." He gestured around the room. "None of them are second. Does it feel as if Lana or Alena are second?"

"They were with you. In that school. They were with you. I wasn't."

"We need light to keep us out of the dark. Blythe provides that. You do too."

She liked that he said that—that he thought it. That he put her in the same category as his beloved wife. Anya had to find a way to make it right. For Reaper. Because in the end, she wanted to be with him more than she wanted to hold on to her anger, justified as it was. She also wanted the family, as insane as they all were. She knew she was going to stay with them and it made her crazy to think she had fallen for him that far.

"He's bossy. You're bossy. *God.*"

She feigned exasperation with Czar, with Reaper, but felt it mostly with herself because she knew she couldn't take Reaper away from these people. He would go, but he would be a shadow of himself. She threw her hands into the air, pushed him aside and stalked across the room to Lana. She held out her hand for the jacket.

Lana looked up at her, searched her face carefully and then smiled. Huge. She handed the jacket to Anya. Anya shook it out. On the back, it had stitching, beautiful patches that said *Property of Torpedo Ink. Reaper.* They couldn't have just gotten the patches. They had to be made up and that took time. She whirled around to glare at Reaper. He had to have ordered the idiot thing.

"Property?" She nearly screeched it. "Are you kidding me?"

"Someone has to keep your sweet little ass in line,"

Reaper said. "You've got a hell of a temper, woman. Pretending to agree with everyone and plotting in your fucked-up little mind doesn't get past me."

"*Property* means you're protected by the club," Lana whispered. "It doesn't mean he can order you around. Well, unless we're on a run. Then it's best not to embarrass him in public because he's kind of mean."

"I can see this is a bad, bad idea," Anya said aloud, but there were some butterflies, wondering how long ago Reaper had sent away for the patches.

"Too late, babe, you already said yes."

The others were gathering around Reaper, clapping him on the back. She heard Czar mutter something about a hellion, and Ice said he was glad they didn't have to kidnap her. She glared at him, about to ask questions, but then she caught sight of Absinthe. He hadn't moved. She took a deep breath. This one was for Reaper. If she was committing, she had to do it all the way and wipe the slate clean. She went straight to him. Immediately a hush fell over the room. She didn't turn around because she didn't want to lose her courage.

"Absinthe?" She held out her hand. "Buy me a drink later and we'll call it good, okay? If you're going to be my brother, though, we're setting some ground rules."

His smile was slow. It didn't reach his eyes. She couldn't imagine what it would be like to be him—to be any of them. Whatever talents they had, they'd all honed them to perfection in order to survive. Absinthe hated what he did, what he had to do for the others, but he did it.

"No worries, it's strictly forbidden to use on one another. That means you now."

She smiled at him as he took her hand and shook it to seal the deal.

"Now we need to get down to business," Czar said. "We don't have a lot of time. Anya, can you reproduce the blueprints you saw?"

"Yes. I like to draw. I have an eye for detail, and I really thought the blueprints were cool. They were very old. I sketched various pieces on my sketch pad with the idea that I would paint it on canvas someday, or cover the walls of a room."

"Your sketch pad?"

She shrugged. "What did you think I did all those nights sleeping in my car? I draw. It relaxes me. The sketch pad is in the backseat along with my clothes." She didn't have many clothes, but she had two sketch pads.

Czar glanced at Transporter, who immediately left the room. "What else did you hear while you were down in that wine cellar? You didn't just hear them say they had someone by the balls, did you? Because that isn't worth killing over. Even for that and the blueprints."

"They were talking about the Diamondbacks, the motorcycle club. The MC's president's wife. They had information on her, where she worked, she runs out by the Mendocino dam. That sort of thing."

"I'll need to know every single word you can remember," Czar said, all business.

Anya nodded. She had a very good memory.

TWELVE

"Alena." Tom Randal waved and hurried toward her.

Alena turned and sent him a high-wattage smile. She wore tight, pencil-thin jeans, ruffled leather boots with spike heels and a formfitting red top that hugged her curves. Her platinum hair was a fall of waves around her face. Red lips matched the blouse she wore as well as the color on her long nails. "Tom, how lovely to see you."

The private investigator came right up to her, all smiles, clearly happy to see her. Alena reached out and touched his arm, ran her finger from shoulder to elbow, over his biceps. His head jerked up and he reached for her packages.

"I've been out shopping. I love to cook," Alena explained. "I don't know if you noticed, but that building on the main street just past the bar is going to be a small, intimate restaurant. All mine."

"That surprises me," Tom said. "A beautiful woman like you enjoys cooking?"

Alena hung on to her smile. It was rather insulting the way he said it, as if because she was beautiful, she might not have the brains to cook. Or worse, that women who enjoyed cooking probably weren't good-looking.

"I love it. I cook for my brothers and sometimes all the others. I'm used to handling a large group, so I think I'll be good cooking for strangers. Are you enjoying our little town?"

Tom nodded, setting a slow pace so he had more time to spend alone with her. "It surprised me how nice it is here. The ocean is different. Wild one minute, and smooth as glass the next."

"I thought you were staying in Fort Bragg, but here you are in our lovely Sea Haven." Alena waved at Inez as she passed the woman on the opposite side of the street. "That's my car."

"Do you have time for a cup of coffee?"

Alena hesitated. Looked conflicted as if no, she didn't have the time, but really wanted to be with him longer. "I have to get these groceries home. I'd love to have a cup of coffee and be able to talk awhile. Do you have time to follow me to Caspar? It isn't that far."

It was his turn to hesitate. She knew he wanted to talk, not just because she was an alluring woman, but because he wanted information on the club, specifically, on Czar and Blythe. With his private investigation business, he was good at extracting the data he wanted from people—probably women. He was good-looking and knew it.

Alena laid her hand on his arm and dropped her voice low. "No one is around today."

Tom nodded, making up his mind, flashing her a smile. "I'll follow you. My car's just across the street."

Her smile jerked his head up again, it was so bright and happy. He strode across the street, and she glanced up toward the roof where Storm lay watching, his eye to the scope of a high-powered rifle. She sent him a quick smirk and a thumbs-up. Thomas Randal wasn't going to be having nearly the pleasurable afternoon that he thought he was.

Sliding behind the wheel of her classy little BMW, she drove straight back to the compound, Randal following. She led him through the parking lot, around behind the club-house building. The back of the compound was covered with trees and shadowed. They had made certain no cameras were recording to catch glimpses of Randal's car turning into Caspar and making his way to the Torpedo Ink compound. There were two parking spots, both empty. Tom slid out of his car and went straight to her, taking the two bags of groceries.

"Nice entrance."

"Much more private. I don't disturb the club. I have a room and bathroom to myself just off the kitchen." She unlocked the door with her key and, making a show of shielding the keypad, turned off the alarm system.

"I wouldn't think a system like that would do much good with all the club members in and out of here," Tom observed.

She glanced at him over her shoulder. "This wing of the compound is entirely separate from the clubhouse. They can come and go and I have no idea who is here and who's not. They don't have a clue if I'm home."

"It looked like your brother kept close tabs on you," he pointed out, setting the groceries on the counter and looking around.

The kitchen was very large and all the appliances were commercial grade and stainless steel. She worked efficiently at putting the groceries away, including the ice cream, her reason for making certain she needed to go home immediately.

"My brothers like to think they can rule my life, but they don't. They're good guys, and in the end, they want me happy. You want coffee or espresso? I can make a few drinks, but I'm no barista. I do have killer cookies to go with the coffee."

"Coffee's good." He leaned over the counter watching her work. Mostly keeping his eyes glued to her ass cupped lovingly in the jeans.

"How'd your brothers get involved in the club? No one knows much about Torpedo Ink or its members."

She shrugged and sent him another sweet smile over her shoulder. "We decided to settle here, but it's right in the middle of Diamondback territory. Czar immediately contacted the president of the Mendocino chapter to pay his respects and get permission for the club to reside here. They said yes, with the usual provisions, and here we are."

"You've met the Diamondback president?" Tom sounded both intrigued and a little in awe. "You say *Diamondback* and everyone immediately thinks criminals. Are they as bad as the press makes them out to be?"

She shrugged. "I wouldn't know. I stay out of club business. We go on runs with them sometimes, but that's all. We don't mix with them much."

"You like the life?" Now he sounded genuinely interested.

Alena decided his expression and tone when he asked questions was what made him such a good private investigator. He could make casual conversation, and sound as if every answer was important to him.

"I was born into the club. I don't really know any other life." She put his coffee in front of him, picked up the plate of cookies and her own mug of coffee. "Come on, I'll show you a phenomenal view. We'll take the shortcut. There's so many cool things about this building. There's a stairway that leads right to the cliffs. The smugglers used to bring their boats in close and the owners of the building would go down the stairs straight to the cliffs above the cove. There are stairs carved into the cliffs leading down to the cove. Of course no one uses them anymore, although they're surprisingly kept up."

She chattered away, giving out information a man like Randal would need to give to a hit team or just convey to his bosses at the Ghost Club. He followed her, once more enjoying the view of her swaying hips as she led the way through a door to a narrow stairway. The stairs were old, just as she'd said.

"You've never gone down to the cove?" he asked.

"My brothers would kill me. I think they have, but they strictly forbid it. They said it was too dangerous."

It was a way into the compound, one a beautiful woman with no brain would never consider a danger to the club. There she was, chatting away, giving out the kinds of information Randal wanted without even batting her long lashes.

"But they've been down there?"

She nodded. "Yes, more than once, that's how I know you can still go down to the cove from up here. It doesn't seem like it because the first stair looks as if you're dropping off into space. It's crazy. And a little scary. I've never tried it because, honestly, it looks as dangerous as Storm said it was."

"Why is he called Storm?"

"Most road names are given over some incident, usually funny, or unusual." She paused at the end of the stairway to wait for him. "I forgot to tell you," she added, taking a sip of her coffee. "We have a thing about anyone prying into club business. You have to be careful."

He frowned. "Asking about his name is prying into club business?"

She turned and walked deeper into the hallway. "This leads back outside. Cool, right? I don't know how many years it's been here, but I do know it's really old." She kept chatting and then came to an abrupt stop again and turned and faced him. "Want a cookie? They're so good. I'll hold your coffee for you."

"I'm good."

"No, really. Take the cookie, Tom. You're going to wish you had."

He took a cookie and bit into it. He smiled at her. "These are good. Best I've eaten."

She handed him the plate and took the coffee cup right out of his hand. "Enjoy them." Her gaze left him and lifted to the man behind him. "Hey, Storm. Nice timing." The smile faded as Tom looked behind him to see the big biker blocking his way back. When the private investigator turned back, Alena wasn't smiling at all.

"Tom, women aren't gullible, you know. Men are. Especially men like you. I don't like someone playing me. I don't give out information on my club. Not. Ever. I'm certain Storm and Ice will answer any questions you have."

Tom lunged at her, knowing he couldn't get past the big man blocking the hall behind him. Alena kicked him hard in the stomach, doubling him over. She put a hand on the back of his head. "Honey, I grew up with sixteen brothers and a kick-ass sister. You don't have a chance against me." She turned and walked down the hall, not looking back once, not even when Tom shrieked. Loudly.

～

Anya smiled at Bannister as she put the beer in front of him. "You look tired tonight, Harry," she said, her voice gentle. She had gotten his given name out of him the second day she'd worked. No one else ever called the old biker by his given name. He was always Bannister. "When was the last time you ate?"

He smiled back and patted her hand. "Don't worry about an old coot like me. I always land on my feet. Got a son who can't seem to pull his life together. Sold just about everything I have to help him out, but it isn't enough. He wants me to sell my bike."

Anya gasped and shook her head. In the six weeks she'd been bartending, Bannister had come in every day and sat on the stool, nursing a few beers. The only time he became animated was when he spoke about his Harley. He once told her if a man treated his woman as good as he did his bike, there would never be a divorce. She had laughed, but she could see he'd meant it.

"You can't sell your bike, Bannister," she said adamantly. "He doesn't know you very well if he asked you to do that."

"He's paying off a gambling debt. Swears he quit gambling, but the principal is never actually paid, only the interest." He rubbed his beard. "I swore the last time, when he took everything, including the house, I wouldn't help him again, but he's my only son, and I don't want to lose him."

Anya patted his hand, served two other customers and filled Heidi's orders for three tables before returning to him. She kept her eye on the door, although Reaper had told her to act normal. He wasn't happy with her being the bait, but if Alena and Lana could go to the Ghost Club and try to get information, she felt the least she could do was bartend as she usually did.

Reaper sat in the darkest corner of the room. In the shadows. He seemed to disappear, until he was a mere blur, one almost impossible to notice unless you looked for him. Heidi had been told to stay away from his table.

There were a few tables ringing the dance floor. Because the floor wasn't in use, it wasn't lit, so it was fairly dark. Savage sat in one of the chairs, looking like a lazy tiger. He was a lot like his brother, in that he was big and had defined muscles, but the resemblance stopped there. Anya knew there was only a two-year difference, but still, he looked quite a few years younger. He didn't have the scars on his face that Reaper did, but she knew the scars were there. They ran deep inside him. Heidi didn't go near his table either.

"You ever think that no matter how often you bail your son out, he's just going to keep gambling?" Anya asked. "Gambling is just as addicting as drugs to some people. They can't stay away."

"What if they kill him because he can't pay off the debt?" Bannister ran a hand down his face as if wiping away his tears when there weren't any. "I'm an old, used-up man," he declared. "Not much to lose, but he's young yet. He could have a life."

Everyone had a story, she realized, some far worse than

others. She liked Bannister. She liked most of those coming into the bar. Most, like Bannister, were bikers. On the weekdays, more locals came in, mostly, she was sure, to check the place out.

"You have a life, Bannister," she objected. "You aren't so old that you can't find a lady who would be crazy about you and want to spend her time on the back of your bike and in your bed. Don't give up on life. You just aren't that old."

Out of the corner of her eye, she caught sight of the Burrows brothers entering. They slipped inside, didn't even glance her way, but went straight to the table directly across the room from the bar. They would be able to watch her every move. She wiped down the bar for the millionth time, made three more drinks and popped the caps off four beers before she went back to Bannister, leaning in close to him.

"Busier than normal for a Tuesday night," she observed. "Who knew the bar would take off like it did. Preacher was grumbling about having to work so much."

"Heard they were thinking about putting in pool tables."

She nodded. "Working with the planning commission over here on the coast is difficult, especially if the buildings are in any way considered historical. They don't want you changing a thing. Czar came up with some solution, adding a second building, a small one just for the pool hall. It's kind of crazy, but it would look exactly like this building, so it would blend. They'd put in a large archway so it looked as if it was all one room, when it really is a separate building. I don't know how they're going to pull it off, but when he and Absinthe went before the board, they came back with the permits."

Heidi was taking orders from the Burrows brothers. Anya wasn't surprised they ordered beer. She knew they wouldn't drink more than that. She tried not to let her gaze stray in their direction. It helped that her favorite customer was distressed. She kept trying to think of a solution for him other than selling his beloved Harley. She knew he kept it in excellent condition. It was a much older bike but ran like one of the newer ones.

The door opened again and two men walked through the door. She stiffened. She couldn't help it. One was in a sheriff's uniform, the other street clothes, but she knew immediately he was a cop as well. She stepped to the other side of the bar when they beckoned her.

The taller of the two gave her a smile. A shark. A really intelligent shark was her assessment. "What can I do for you?" she asked.

"I'm Jonas Harrington," the tall one said. He flashed his badge at her. "Czar around?"

"I'm sorry, he's not here right now. If you need him, I could maybe get through to him on the phone," she offered, hoping that was what bartenders usually said when a cop wanted to question the owner.

"It's not necessary. I'll catch him later," Jonas said.

Was that some kind of play on words? She didn't know. She never talked to cops. It was the code of the street. It wasn't done. Heidi came up to the bar, waving her over.

"Excuse me. I have to make a couple of drinks." She wanted to kiss Heidi for interrupting. She made the drinks Heidi asked for, mentally composing herself before turning back to face the cops.

"Can I help you with something?"

The one in the sheriff's uniform pushed three pictures across the bar at her. "Name's Deveau. Jackson Deveau."

"Nice to meet you."

"Have you seen these three men?"

She glanced down. Yeah, she'd seen them. The three assholes who'd confronted her in the bar and then waited outside. She picked up the pictures, pretending to study them. "I have a pretty good memory," she said, stalling for time. "They've definitely been in here. They caused some trouble, especially this one."

She tapped Deke's picture, and left her finger on it. "I'm

trying to remember the date though. The days all run together after a while." She felt like it was better to stick as
close to the truth as possible. To be honest, both men were
a little intimidating, which was strange. After Reaper, she
didn't think she'd find anyone unnerving again.

"What kind of trouble did they make?" asked Deveau.

Then Reaper was there, leaning over the bar, pointing to
a beer, all but snapping his fingers at her. Any other time
she might have thrown the bottle at his head, but she was
grateful. She hurried to get the beer.

"Jackson Deveau. Haven't seen you for a couple of
months. And Jonas. Think this is the first time you've been
in the bar. You boys slumming?" Reaper drawled the question, turning the lawmen's attention to him.

"Looking for these three." Jonas tapped the photographs.

Reaper glanced down at the three pictures. "What'd
they do?"

"Beat up a couple of men and took their wallets in Fort
Bragg," Jonas said smoothly. "Witnesses said they were on
bikes so I thought they might show up here."

"They did," Reaper said, shoving the pictures across the
bar at him with some disgust. "Tried throwing their weight
around, were ugly to the waitresses and our bartender, and
they got their asses kicked. Last I saw of them they were
heading toward their bikes to take off. They know better
than to show their faces here."

Anya set the beer in front of Reaper and moved down
the bar to Bannister again. For some reason the older man
gave her comfort. Cops. Hit men. Bikers. She'd gotten herself into a mess all because she couldn't resist one man. He
sat on a stool bullshitting the cops, weaving a mixture of
truth and lies so it sounded not only plausible but probable.

"Keep talking to me, darlin'," Bannister said softly.
"Don't pay attention to them."

Was it that obvious? She wasn't good at being a biker
babe, that was for sure. Lana and Alena could carry off

anything, and look like a million bucks doing it, but she couldn't even handle cops in the bar.

"I lived on the streets most of my life," she confided. "You know the kind of code."

He patted her hand. "Did Alena make her chicken wings?"

"You smelled them, didn't you?"

He nodded. "I smelled them all the way down the highway. Couldn't resist."

They had a commercial kitchen and a license to sell certain items. Chicken wings were on that list and most of the locals knew to come on Tuesdays and Thursdays. Alena's chicken wings were spectacular. She moved quickly to get Bannister some, grateful he hadn't asked earlier. Going down the hall to the tiny kitchen to get him a batch allowed her to take a much-needed breath.

Player and Keys sat on the stools under the stainless steel counter, both eating the chicken wings and drinking beer. They sent her guilty smirks. "Doin' good in there," Keys said.

"Aren't you supposed to be watching the monitors?" she asked. "Alena's going to kill you if you eat up all the chicken. You have chicken thighs at the clubhouse."

"Got hungry," Player said. "Watchin' monitors is hungry work."

"You two are crazy. Did you see the cops come in?"

Keys slid off the stool and grabbed a napkin, his gaze on her face. "Just cops, honey," he soothed. "Nothing to worry about. Reaper ran interference. He'll get rid of them. You were smart to admit they came in."

"It's easier to stick to the truth."

Both nodded their heads. "Don't pay attention to the Burrows brothers. Stay on Bannister. He'll look after you. Suggest he talk to Czar about his problem," Keys added.

She wasn't used to going to Czar for every little thing, but she really liked Blythe and Blythe seemed to think the man walked on water. For that matter, they all did. She was secretly afraid she wasn't going to be good at being Reaper's woman. She was definitely out of her element, although she was very glad she wasn't dealing with two hit men who liked to cut up women alone.

She scooped chicken into a basket. "Those men aren't the same ones who cut up my roommate. How could the Ghost Club have more than one hit team?"

"Don't worry about it, honey. We've got this. You'll be safe."

She went to the door and then turned back. "Does Lana know the answer to that question?"

The two exchanged an alarmed look. "Is that a trick question?" Keys asked.

She glared at them and stomped out, wondering if she really wanted to know the answer. Plopping the basket in front of Bannister, she added two napkins and opened another bottle of his favorite beer. "Men are absolute swine, Bannister. Present company excluded."

The two cops were leaving and the churning in her stomach subsided a bit. She thought that made her pretty fucked-up, to be more terrified of the law than the hit men sitting in her bar, calmly waiting until her shift ended so they could slice her into little pieces.

"I concur," Bannister said. "Men *are* absolute swine. Not me, of course. You don't want to leap on the back of my bike and ride off into the sunset with me, do you?"

Reaper joined them, his back never quite to the Burrows brothers. "Wouldn't want to have to kill you, Bannister, but you ride off with my woman and I'd hunt you to the ends of the earth. It wouldn't be pretty when I caught up with you."

Anya shivered, fingers of fear creeping down her spine. He had to be joking with the old biker. Reaper knew she would never actually ride off with him. He just looked so scary all the time. There was never a hint of a smile out in public. She noticed all members of the club joked with one another, but real smiles were rare and in public, nonexistent.

"Got it, man," Bannister said, not in the least offended. "Do the same myself if she were mine." He took a bite of chicken. "Might kill for this food," he added, licking his fingers in appreciation.

"That's all Alena," Anya assured. She glanced at the clock. "Preacher's late. I need a break." She left the two men to fill Heidi's orders again. This time, thanks to Bannister opening the floodgates on the chicken, several more orders were placed. She spent time rushing to put baskets together, mix drinks and open beer bottles. By the time Preacher came in she was more than ready for her break.

"I'm going outside for a few minutes to cool off," she told Preacher. "It gets hot in here. We really need to install a couple of overhead fans."

"I agree," Preacher said, looking up at the ceiling. "One right over the bar and one over the dance floor."

"Do it soon before I roast," Anya said. "And we need a third bartender. You work alone on my day off and I work alone on yours. It's getting so our slow days aren't so slow."

Preacher nodded. "I'll tell Czar to put the call out. I was late coming in and worried you'd be swamped. Another waitress would be good as well."

"Heidi and Betina kick ass waitressing, but they need help too," Anya agreed. "All good for business, but bad for us."

She took off the apron she wore and folded it, putting it behind the bar. "I'm out of here."

"Fifteen minutes, Anya," Preacher called as she started down the hall toward the back door.

"You were late, that buys me thirty."

"Twenty then," Preacher bargained.

She kept walking, disappearing around the corner. Immediately Lana tugged her into a small room, pushing her down into a comfortable chair. "Put your feet up. In exactly twenty minutes, whatever happens, you go back into the front and start work. It doesn't matter if Reaper shows again, you just work, got that?"

Anya kicked off her shoes and pulled her feet into the chair. "I got it."

"And don't ask questions, especially anything you don't want to know about."

Anya nodded. "I've got it."

Lana pushed a bottle of water into her hands. "Drink this and read or something." She touched her jeans where her phone vibrated. She pulled it out of her pocket to look at the screen. "Savage says they're on the move. I'm up. Stay put, Anya, and follow the plan no matter what or Reaper will never let you help with anything again."

Anya nodded. She wasn't doing that much. She had headed down a hallway and was now safe, curled up in a chair while Lana took over for her. Lana was taller than Anya, but they were dressed in the same clothing and Lana would make certain she was in the darkest part of the yard, sitting down so height didn't matter. The two hit men expected to see Anya, so they would believe and walk right up to her before becoming aware that it wasn't Anya sitting there.

Reaper waited until the Burrows brothers went out the front door before standing and leisurely making his way across the room. At the same time, Savage stood also, but he went to the front door, shadowing the brothers. Reaper flipped up the slab of wood on hinges, going through the bar to the hall. Instead of rounding the corner as Anya had, he went straight down the hall into the meeting room. On the other side was a door leading outside.

He went out and was in the night. In the dark. He inhaled the salt air. Fingers of fog crept in from the ocean, reaching toward the bar, curling around the trees and touching the cars in the parking lot. He moved unerringly in the darkness. The others were close. He didn't need to see them. He felt them. Keys and Player were inside, looking after Anya just in case the brothers doubled back. Savage trailed the two men. He was capable of killing them if they suddenly realized they were being set up and tried to escape.

They'd done this squeeze in the school, when they were barely teens. It was classic Czar, no way to lose. Czar didn't believe in fighting fair, not when the stakes were life or death. He played to win. Their lives had been on the line, and he'd made certain every single one of them knew they could die if they didn't follow the plan. He'd been right too. A few times, someone had deviated and they'd been killed, or another child had. They all learned to trust Czar's plans.

Lana sat on a small stone ledge that wrapped around a narrow strip that passed for a flower bed. She swung one foot back and forth and tilted her head to look up at the sky. The fog was thickening, just beginning to draw a veil over the stars.

"Hey there, Anya," Mike Burrows greeted from a few feet away as he rounded the corner. "Is it okay to smoke back here?"

Lana waved her hand toward the open air and nodded. Mike came straight at her while his brother took a more circuitous route, one that brought him dangerously close to where Reaper stood as still as a statue just between two large bushes. Lana didn't move from her easy pose, but turned her head toward Mike.

She looked delicate and even fragile in the blurred light the fog caused. Reaper had never considered Lana either of those things, but watching her, he realized she gave off that appearance. Mike evidently bought into it. Reaper stepped behind Steven Burrows just as Mike whipped out his butterfly knife.

"You're going with us," he hissed, whirling the knife, only too happy to scare her.

"Oh please," Lana said. "Melodramatic much?"

Reaper caught Steven's head between the crook of his elbow and his hand, rolled him over his shoulder and wrenched hard. The crack was audible in the night air. Reaper held the man dangling over his shoulder to be certain all fight had gone out of him and he was dead. Mike glanced their way, but it was difficult to make out anyone in the darkness with the fog thickening by the moment.

He brought the knife in, blade up. "You should have minded your own business, bitch. Little girls shouldn't be listening to men's conversations."

"Bartender right here," Lana lied. "My job description is to listen." She made no move to get away. She just sat there, swinging her foot, watching him come closer.

Mike stepped nearer, suddenly frowning. No matter how hard he tried, he couldn't make Lana look like Anya. "Who the hell are you?"

"Not the woman you want to cut into small pieces." She inspected her fingernails. "I just got a manicure. I have a little job I have to do later, or seriously, you'd be wearing that silly knife as a necktie."

"Fuck you, bitch." Mike glanced around quickly for his brother.

"Why do men always say that? I mean really, no education? You don't get your way so you cry like a little baby? You have to play big braggart to pump yourself up? What is it? Women all over the world would like the answer to this question."

He loomed over her. "I'm going to cut out your fucking eyeball."

Her long leg snapped out and up. Hard. Exceptionally hard. Lana could generate a tremendous amount of strength in her kicks. She drove the very pointed toe of her boot into Mike's crotch, right into his balls. She stood in one smooth motion as he fell back, driving into him a second time.

Savage was behind him, and he was forced to crouch low to catch Mike's head in a vise, pushing the neck forward and down, suddenly wrenching until the snap was loud in the night. "Seriously, woman? You drove his cock right through to his backbone."

"He doesn't have a backbone," Lana said with contempt. "Slicing up women for fun? What a nasty human being." She dusted her hands as if removing the feel of him.

The van pulled up and Mechanic and Transporter loaded both bodies into it. Savage handed Mechanic the knife, his hands gloved. "Don't forget to throw this thing in the ocean, somewhere deep," he cautioned.

"Consider it gone," Mechanic agreed. "Nice show, Lana."

"Thanks. It's always nice to be appreciated." She blew him a kiss.

"Savage is heading down to the compound to go through the weapons," Reaper said. "Czar is meeting him there. Lana, if you and Alena want anything special, you need to put your request in now. Go with Savage. I'll stay with Anya and Preacher until the bar closes and will be ready to go tomorrow. Anya reproduced the blueprints and gave them to Ink. He's making us all copies. We should have those within the hour."

Lana nodded and wiggled her fingers at him. "Go be with your woman, Reaper. Make sure she knows it's over. She's holding it together, better than I expected, but she isn't like us. Maybe that's a good thing. We don't need more like us. We need more like her. You'd better handle her with care."

Reaper didn't know if he could do what Lana was saying, but he knew she was right, and he wanted to be that man. Anya had committed to him, but now he had to keep her. He had to find a way to make certain she was always safe with him, no matter what they did together. He also had to find a way to make her happy when he was tough as nails and didn't know the first thing about talking to women, let alone one he cared about. He was determined. He wasn't about to lose her through stupidity.

"Will do," he said and went to the back door of the roadhouse.

Anya sat in the little room, her eyes glued to the door. Her eyes lit up when she saw him and she jumped up, flinging herself at him. "Lana? Is she okay?"

He caught her in his arms and held her tightly against him. "Of course Lana is okay. Why wouldn't she be?"

"Maybe because she was going to confront two psycho knife-wielding nut jobs."

He shrugged, tipped her face up to his and rubbed his nose along hers. "Lana could have handled them both in her sleep. She looks sweet, honey, but she's got another side to her." He loved that her first concern was for Lana. That had to mean she was moving toward being part of their family whether she knew it or not.

He took her mouth. Holy fucking God, he loved her mouth. He loved the way, when he kissed her, she just opened up to him, let him take everything. She ignited until the firestorm was so hot he wasn't certain he could live through it. He slid his hand under her shirt, up her back to her bra. Deft fingers undid the clasp easily. "How long is your break?"

"It took you all of four minutes to get whatever you did, done, so I've got about sixteen minutes." She caught the bottom of her shirt and pulled it over her head, letting the bra fall to the floor.

He loved how she sounded breathless. How she didn't even hesitate. He caught both breasts in his hands, massaging, squeezing, bringing them together so he could suck one nipple into his mouth and then the other. He lavished attention on the soft mounds, flicking with his tongue, using his teeth, suckling strong enough to leave marks all over her soft breasts. He fucking loved her breasts as much as her mouth. Just once he'd like to try filling her mouth with his cock, feeling the burn of that hot cavern, seeing her lips wrapped around him, but he knew that wasn't safe.

"Your jeans," he managed to hiss, biting down on her nipple.

She let out a soft cry and her hands went to the waistband of her jeans, tearing them open. She kicked off her shoes and tried to push down the denim, but he hadn't released her, his mouth working her hard. He didn't even try to be gentle with her. He couldn't. He was too far gone. She was his, and the threat to her was over. He'd fucking killed the man with his bare hands. Hands that stroked over her body, claiming every inch of her.

He yanked down her jeans, forcing her to step out of them. He tossed them over his shoulder and caught her hard by the shoulder, spinning her around to shove her over the back of the chair. She could barely reach the floor when he kicked her legs apart and held her down by the nape of her neck. He liked that she had to struggle a little to stay in position as he undid his jeans one-handed.

He was ready. He was always ready when he was with her. His hand went between her legs to test her slickness and then he slammed home. Fire engulfed his cock. Her tight folds barely gave way, only doing so reluctantly, gripping him as he surged deep, surrounding him with thousands of fingers, a fist of silk squeezing him so tight it bordered on pain. She was scorching hot, both paradise and hell, a place he never wanted to leave.

He plunged into her over and over, his finger flicking her clit, listening to the sobbing musical notes pulse around his head just the way her hot little channel did around his cock. She was close, so close. He didn't want to stop, but if she went over the edge, she'd take him with her, no doubt about it.

"Damn it, Reaper. I fuckin' need her out here." Her jeans came sailing over their heads. "Finish up and give me back my bartender," Preacher snapped from behind them.

Anya stiffened. Reaper didn't miss a beat, working her clit to distract her. Going harder, suddenly aware he was bareback again. He couldn't imagine being in her with any barrier, no matter how thin, between them.

"Now, baby, give it to me now," he whispered and caught her hair, yanking her head back as he plunged into her again. He felt it like lightning streaking down his back. The strikes sizzled through his balls until he was a fucking volcano, erupting like it had been dormant for years. He blew big. Hard.

She surrounded him with those magical tight muscles gripping and milking, looking for every drop, draining him dry. Her body rippled around his, just as hard, the after-shocks shaking both of them. He collapsed over the top of her, his arms around her, kissing a line up her back.

"Nothing more beautiful than being in you, babe," he said.

She was still fighting for breath. She turned her head. "Do you ever think we're going to do this face-to-face?"

He stiffened. Pulled out and zipped up his jeans. "You complainin'?"

"Of course not," she said and turned, leaning against the chair, still fighting to breathe. The action drew attention to her breasts. His marks were all over her. "It's just that some-times, I think we might try with the door closed and me looking at your face."

"Workin' on it, Anya." Reaper tossed her the bra and found the jeans and panties Preacher had thrown. He pock-eted the panties and handed her the jeans.

"Hand them over. I'm on to your games," she said, snap-ping her fingers.

"Gotta pay a price, babe," he said and sauntered out. Inside, his gut was churning. He was going to have to find a way to get past his problems, a way to keep her safe and to just plain keep her.

THIRTEEN

The house Reaper had purchased was larger than he remembered. He unlocked the door, surprised to find it was warm. He should have known Lena and Alena would help him out. He stepped back to let his woman walk through the door first. His heart pounded out of control. He didn't know if she was safe with him, but it sure as hell felt like he wasn't. He was in new territory and uneasiness was making him edgy.

He wanted her there. He wanted her to like the place, even though he'd only walked through it three times. Once when Czar insisted he buy a place. He chose it, not for the house, but for the location and escape routes. It was in a defensible position. He'd barely paid attention to the actual house. Now he wished he had. What if she didn't like it? He had to be able to give her something, because she wasn't getting much of a bargain in him.

"This is your house? You *own* this?"

"Yeah." He owned it. Bought with club money. Money Code siphoned off from the billionaire Greek shipping magnate who'd been the president of the Swords club and the top asshole running human trafficking. He was dead, thanks to Czar's persistence. Czar had put his life and his marriage on the line for five long years to get his shot at taking the man down, and he'd done it. They'd done it together with the help of some of the women from Sea Haven and Jackson Deveau.

"Reaper. A house like this has to be worth millions. Your view is incredible. I've never been in a house like this one." There was awe in Anya's voice.

He followed her as she went slowly from room to room, looking at her the entire time, not at the house. He didn't give a damn about the house, but he did about the woman. Her face was lit up. Soft. Beautiful. She ran her hand over the granite counter, touched the stainless steel refrigerator and then the stove. The kitchen cabinets were all oak. The floor was a swirl of oat with circles of three different colors, all faint splotches in the tile.

Anya went straight to the bank of windows overlooking the ocean. "This is the most incredible thing I've ever seen."

"Bedroom's upstairs," he said gruffly.

She was thinking *nice house*. He was thinking he wanted to set her on that kitchen counter and devour her until she was screaming for mercy.

She glanced at him over her shoulder. "Honey, why were you staying at the clubhouse when you have this?"

He couldn't see any of what the house had to offer until she was in it. It had been empty, echoing when he walked through it, after meeting the furniture delivery truck with a bed the girls had chosen for him and the chair and kitchen supplies he'd added later. He'd hated the emptiness of the house, feeling like every echo was just a reflection of his own emptiness. Now, there was Anya lighting up every room.

Anya went to the great room. He didn't understand the term *great room*. It was large, high ceilings, all glowing wood and gleaming floors. One entire side of the room was made up of windows, letting in the sun, the sea and the view. She stood at the window, just staring out without speaking.

He wanted to strip her right there, press her against that glass and have her screaming for his cock and mercy. That would make the great room truly great. He didn't move. He didn't touch her. He just watched her, an exotic creature he was totally obsessed with.

"You don't have any furniture." She turned to face him. Her hair tumbled around her face, falling out of the confines of the messy ponytail. The silken mass was far too wild to be tamed by the tie she used.

He wanted to sink his fingers into all that hair, but he still didn't move. He didn't know what he was waiting for, but it was something. His heart kept pounding and he heard his blood roaring like thunder in his ears. He wanted her with every breath he took. Wanted to fuck her face-to-face. Have her on her knees, mouth around his cock, have her touching his skin. He broke out in a sweat, his heart accelerating even more, running a race he was terrified he'd lose.

"There's a bed. Upstairs."

"You don't even have a chair, Reaper. Why not?"

"Kitchen has chairs," he said gruffly.

"Why didn't you want to live here?" She persisted.

Because she wasn't there. He damn well wasn't going to say that to her. She already had him wrapped around her little finger and that just pissed him off. He didn't know what to do with it.

"Alena and Lana put together the kitchen. Pots, pans, I think they have silverware and dishes as well. Some food in the fridge. Bought that myself." He couldn't take his eyes off her, afraid if he blinked she'd be gone and he'd have the emptiness of the house again.

The club members had lived together from the time they were toddlers, most of them anyway. Being alone was difficult. Being alone with himself was worse.

"Are we going to live here?" Anya put her hands on her hips.

That just called attention to her curves. She had them. He loved them. She could be sassy, his woman. "Yeah, we're going to live here." Unless she didn't like it. Then they'd move wherever the hell she wanted to be.

"There's no furniture, Reaper."

"We have a bed. What else do we need?"

She burst out laughing. He loved her laugh. It poured over him like music, the notes dancing in his brain, soothing him when nothing but fists ever had.

"I can't believe you own this house, it's amazing. Beautiful. I can help with the mortgage payment. If I'm living with you, I can share expenses."

He narrowed his eyes at her, gave her the death stare. "That's bullshit. One, there is no mortgage payment. I own it outright. Two, I take care of my woman, not the other way around. Don't give me grief over it because you won't win."

She glared at him. "It's one thing for you to go all macho on me when you're with your brothers in the club, but when we're alone . . ."

"It's me, Anya. Not macho. Me." Was she going to be able to live with him? With the way he was? He knew she wasn't getting a bargain. He was trying, but damn it all, he didn't know how to talk to her. How to be what women seemed to need.

She stood there for what seemed like an eternity. His heart nearly exploded and his gut was so tied up in knots it was a wonder his belly didn't hit his backbone. A slow smile finally lit her face, and the relief was tremendous.

"Let's go check out the bedroom."

He shook his head. "I don't think we're going to make it to the bedroom."

"We're not?"

He shook his head again. "No. Not right now."

"What are we going to do?"

"You're going to strip for me."

"I am?"

"If you don't want me to rip off those clothes, then yeah, you are." He took a step toward her. "I don't mind taking them off you, but I won't be gentle." He wasn't feeling gentle. The pressure in his chest nearly consumed him. He couldn't tell her what she meant to him. He couldn't get words like that out. He could show her. He needed to know she was his. That she'd give him whatever he needed when he needed it. He wanted her to feel the same way about him. To take whatever it was she needed.

She laughed softly, the sound sliding down his spine, curling around his cock like the touch of fingers. He shrugged out of his colors, folding them carefully and tossing them to the thick carpet. Catching the hem of his T-shirt, he dragged it off and sent it flying across the room. Motorcycle boots were next. He didn't take his eyes off her while he pulled them off.

"Get a move on, woman."

"I like looking at you. It's better than the view, and that's saying something, because the view is pretty darn spectacular."

He peeled off his jeans and stalked her. She laughed and turned to run. He was on her before she'd taken two steps. He caught her tee and yanked it hard, ripping it from neck to hem, throwing the scraps away. Her bra was next. "Hate this fuckin' thing. Stop wearing them." His hands went to her breasts, cupping the weight, while he pressed his body tightly against her back.

"I'm too big not to wear a bra."

"You're perfect. I love the way your skin is so soft." His fingers were at her nipples. He'd been as gentle as possible before, but the animal in him, that beast craving her, worried sick she couldn't accept him, was out now and he couldn't put it away. He pinched and tugged, rolled and kneaded. She moaned and he kept at it, pulling at her nipples, wanting to use his mouth. His tongue. His teeth. He needed to put his mark on every part of her.

His hands dropped to the waistband of her jeans. She'd already opened them, so all he had to do was strip them off her body. He had her panties, so there was nothing between him and her bare skin. He spun her around, one hand fisting in her hair, yanking her head back so he could take her mouth. Fire poured through him. Absolute fucking fire.

He took her to the floor. He wanted a hard surface. Her hands moved over his chest, his back, up to his neck. The touch of her fingers drove him wild. He kissed her over and over, his knee nudging her thighs apart. Her hands smoothed down his back and gripped his buttocks. He loved that. Loved the way she touched him with such possession.

He left her mouth to kiss his way down her throat, around to her neck. He bit down. Hard. Wanting his mark there. Wanting her to know he meant business. She cried out, but her hips bucked. His hand moved between her legs, testing. Making certain. He wanted everything he did to turn her on more. Even his bite, his claim, sent liquid fire coating his fingers.

Her hands slid down his hip toward his cock. His heart stuttered. Time stopped. Tunneled. He caught both her wrists and pulled them over her head. Stretched her body out for him like she was on a rack. Tied there. "Want Ink to tattoo my fingerprints on your wrists. Like bracelets. Show the world who you fuckin' belong to."

She kissed his chest, flicked his nipple with her tongue. "Could he do that?" She sounded breathless.

"Yeah, baby, he can do that. Gonna ask him tomorrow." He kissed her throat and then ran his tongue down the valley between her breasts.

"Okay."

"Leave your arms right where I've got them." He nipped at her breast, ran his tongue around her aureole and then sucked her nipple into his mouth, flattening it against the roof of his mouth before tugging on it with his teeth.

Her hips bucked harder. She writhed under him. A low, keening cry burst from her. He took his time, his mouth moving over her soft skin, marking her, teeth nipping, stinging, tongue easing that ache. He kept one hand between her legs, judging her reaction to his rough. This was the real Reaper, loving on his woman. He wanted her to feel him, to know she belonged to him. He worshiped the fucking ground she walked on. He wanted to do the same to her body.

He took his time. It was the first time in his life he had ever enjoyed a woman like this. Using his hands and mouth to claim every inch of her. To learn what she liked, what she didn't. What really turned her on. What she was a little afraid of. He was face-to-face with her. Her front to his front. There were no murderous thoughts in his head. Only pleasure. Pure pleasure.

He spent a great deal of time on her breasts, learning how sensitive she was, how much she liked her nipples tugged and pinched. Pulled. Sucked. She was covered in his marks by the time he moved on to her rib cage, to her belly, that sweet little belly button he spent a few minutes teasing while she squirmed and thrashed under him.

Twice she moved her hands over his back and down to his buttocks. He loved the feel of her palms gliding over him, claiming him. He loved her hands kneading his ass, fingers digging in when she arched her body into his as he kissed or bit at her skin. Both times her hands slid along his hips, searching for his cock, he gripped her wrists and put her back in the stretched-out position under him.

"Stay there," he growled the second time, deliberately punishing her with a bite to the upper curve of her breast. "I'm starving here, woman. Let me have you my way."

"Your way just might kill me," she hissed. "Reaper, I need you in me."

"We haven't even gotten started. You wanted us face-to-face. You got what you wanted. Quit bitchin' and let me have my fun. I'll take care of you."

"Fine. I'll just lie here like a lump or something," she groused.

He lifted his head to look at her. Her eyes were so green they were nearly glowing. Her mouth was swollen from his kisses. Her face was flushed. She looked so beautiful his heart did a weird stuttering he was becoming familiar with. He couldn't help giving her a rusty smile. It was slow, but it was there. He felt it first in his gut. It blossomed out, spreading warmth through him. Radiated upward until it reached his mouth and curved that bottom lip. Happiness. He barely recognized that emotion for what it was. All he knew was she made him feel, and the way she made him feel was better than good.

"You do that, baby. You lay there like a lump," he challenged and dipped his head again toward her belly button. Lower. Kissing his way to her mound. He loved the silky little dark curls hiding what was never going to be kept from him.

He pushed his shoulders between her thighs, keeping her legs spread wide apart. Turning his head, he kissed his way up from her knee, inside her thigh all the way to her entrance. He did the same on her left leg. "Thought you were going to lie there," he whispered against her slick, inviting sex. Amusement was shocking. He didn't play. He didn't tease. He didn't know one could feel that way during sex.

"I *am* lying here," she lied. "Not moving."

Her hips were bucking so hard he had to use strength to hold her down. He laughed softly, bit her thigh close to her entrance. He breathed warm air. Waited a heartbeat, two. She was dripping now in anticipation. He might have to buy a new fucking rug if they kept this up. He smiled again and put his mouth to her, claiming her little pussy, that sweet, sweet part of her that was made just for him.

She screamed and pushed up with her heels, driving her body into his mouth. He sucked on her clit, used his tongue ruthlessly, devouring liquid gold, an aphrodisiac that was all his. He took his time, savoring her taste. Savoring the fact that he could take his woman face-to-face, her body under his. His mouth on any part of her he wanted. She was his, and he could have her any way he wanted. He wanted everything. Every fucking thing.

The first orgasm took her hard. She screamed his name. The second was even harder, and she sobbed his name. The third time she just opened her mouth, her head thrashing back and forth, her hair wild. He wiped his face on her thighs and knelt up between her legs.

"Open your eyes," he ordered, cock in his hand. He felt ready to burst. His balls were thick with his seed. His back-bone hurt. His ass. His legs even, as if that volcano was somewhere deep and ready to blow any moment.

She obeyed him, those long lashes lifting so he was staring into all that green. He loved the way she looked right at that moment. He wanted that image burned into his brain for all time. "Keep looking at me, baby," he said. He was big, and she was tight. He wanted to see her face, watch her eyes, know she could take him like this. Not at his worst, but maybe close. He wasn't going to be able to hold back.

"I'm looking at you," she said softly.

He pressed into her tight slick entrance and wanted to throw back his head and roar. Watching her face, he pushed steadily, firmly, not thrusting, just a steady pressure, forcing her tight folds to give way for his invasion. Nothing could keep him out. There was nothing that hot. That perfect. Pleasure and pain collided together in one unadulterated mix.

Her sheath gripped him hard, squeezed and milked at him. Beads of sweat dotted his forehead as her scorching heat surrounded him in a tight fist. He withdrew, watching her eyes go wide. Slammed deep. He lifted her hips and repeated the motion. Her eyes went dark with lust, with desire. Her breath hissed out. Her breasts jolted, calling his attention to those marks of possession. Maybe he'd have Ink tatt his fingerprints all over her.

He took his time, staying in control for as long as he could, taking her harder than he ever had, needing the feel of his body buried deep in hers. Needing those flames licking all over his body, down his spine, over his ass, dancing down his thighs. Her body clamped down on his and she sobbed through the orgasm, but he didn't relent, not when she began to thrash again, twisting, her body so beautiful, the sheen of sweat making her glow.

He would have tried to stop had she moved her arms, but she didn't. Her eyes remained locked with his and her arms stayed over her head. He increased his speed, feeling the buildup, the fire leaping through his veins, threatening to destroy them both. Her eyes went dazed. Her mouth opened. No sound emerged. Then her body once more clamped down on his like a vise. The volcano was ripped from his body, molten seed blasting into the walls of her sheath, mixing with all that heat to turn into an inferno.

He collapsed over her, letting her take his full weight, his face buried in her neck, cock still jerking hard. He stretched his arms along hers, threading his fingers through hers, his heart pounding, gliding now, trying to come down from a rush like he'd never known. He'd done it. Fucked her face-to-face. She was safe. Hell, he might even be able to sleep in the same bed with her. The minute the thought came into his mind he shut it down. Maybe the floor would be better. Open spaces. He kissed her eyelids as he lifted himself, took his time at her mouth, letting her taste herself on his breath, on his tongue.

She didn't turn her face away, she kissed him back. He framed her face with both hands, looking down into her eyes. "You're so fuckin' sexy. You like the things I do to you, don't you?" All the heat. The storm. The pounding.

She nodded. "Yes."

"You were made for me."

She smiled at him. An angel's smile. He didn't see how that could be when he'd just pounded the hell out of her, but there it was. "I thought it was the other way around, Reaper. I thought you were made for me."

Her fingers were on his chest, moving. He was very aware of them slipping down toward his belly. His cock jerked. Wanting her touch. Needing it. Before her fingers could go any farther, he pulled out of her abruptly and rocked back, sitting on his ankles, out of reach.

"We're a mess," she observed, looking around her. "If you grab my shirt, I can wipe off so I don't get anything on the rug."

"Fuck the rug. We can buy ten of them. I don't want you to wipe off. I like knowing I'm inside you."

She laughed. That sound. That magic. Filling his house with her. With warmth. Pushing away the emptiness.

"You're so crazy. And maybe a little kinky."

He reached down and gripped her inner thigh. "You think that's kinky? We're only getting started, babe. I'm going to teach you things that will blow your little mind."

"It's late. Can you teach them to me later? If I don't get sleep soon, I'm going to be talking gibberish. Where's the bathroom?"

He hoped to hell there were towels and toilet paper. He never thought of those things. Lena and Alena always took care of everything, ordering what the club needed. He'd never thought to thank them and he needed to remember to do that. He stood and reached down for her hand.

She ignored his hand and reached instead for his cock. He was semihard, a state he was used to around her. The moment her fingers brushed him, that demon inside him exploded. He moved fast, knocking her hand away. Hard. He turned around and stalked across the room, cursing himself. Cursing her. Cursing everything he could think of. He heard her move, but he stormed to the door leading to the long, curved verandah that circled the living room. Once outside, he could breathe away the pressure in his chest. The need for violence. The terrible need to kill.

He lifted his face to the night and roared his pain. It was pain. His woman couldn't touch him without triggering his kill response. Years of training. Years of killing. Years of being a fucking monster. It was still there, waiting. Lurking. But he wouldn't let it win. Not her. Not Anya.

"You don't get her," he whispered to Sorbacov. To the night. "You don't get Anya." She was his. Reaper's. He wasn't going to let anything happen to her. "You don't get her," he repeated. It was a vow.

The great room was empty when he returned. He had no idea how long he'd stayed outside, but it was long enough to cool the heat of his body. He left his clothes lying on the floor and went up the stairs. The sound of water abruptly stopped. She'd taken a shower in the master bathroom. Not wanting to face her and any questions, he used the guest room shower. The hot water helped to soothe aching muscles, but it didn't do anything to alleviate the fear growing in him. He couldn't give her up. He had to find a way around this.

He wanted her touch. He even needed it. He wanted her mouth on him. He wanted everything with her—her body, every way he could have it. He wanted her to be able to touch him freely, to kiss him where she wanted when she wanted. The water blurred his vision, burned behind his eyes. Caught in his throat until he couldn't swallow. The pressure in his chest was enormous, threatening to crush him.

He slammed his fist into the wall, feeling the pain explode up his arm. That was good. What he needed. Striking out. Feeling the burn. The sweet promise of retaliation, of driving the demon off for a little while. He hit again and again, wishing he was hitting someone, needing them to be punching back so he could feel fists slamming into him.

"Stop it."

Her voice penetrated. He looked down at his hands. Blood was everywhere, even running down the broken tiles.

"I mean it, Reaper. Stop it right now or I swear, I'm walking out of here."

Fury burned through him. He spun around and gripped both her upper arms, giving her a little shake. "Don't you ever fuckin' threaten me with that. Not ever. You don't like something I do, you can yell at me, hit me over the head with a frying pan, but don't you threaten to walk out on me. Do you understand me?" If he could stay and figure this shit out, then she could too.

Her eyes searched his face. She took a breath. "I think you made it abundantly clear, Reaper. Let go."

He did, forcing his fingers off her warm skin, afraid he might have hurt her. "Damn it, Anya. I'm sorry. I didn't mean to hold you so tight."

"You didn't." She rubbed at the blood dripping down her arm. His blood. "I don't like you hurting yourself."

He frowned. "I'm not hurting myself."

She caught his hand, held it up under his nose, completely disregarding his no-touching rule. "What the hell is this, then? Looks like blood to me. Looks like that tile is all broken to shit. What is it, if it isn't you hurting yourself?"

"Woman, you have a mouth on you when you're angry."

"It seems to be the only thing you understand."

She dropped his arm and turned away. She was wearing a shirt. His shirt. The fucking flannel that seemed to follow them everywhere they went. Lana and Alena again. They must have moved clothes over to the house. Trust Anya to find them. He watched her storm away. It would have been a great show of temper, but her ass cheeks peeked out from under his shirt now and then as she walked fast, arms moving hard enough to lift the shirt.

He caught up a towel, buried his face in it and then swiped the dots of water from his skin, following her, mesmerized by the sway of her hips and the occasional glimpses of her ass. He thought his fingerprints tattooed there might be just the thing as well.

"Are you following me?" she snapped, spinning around at the door to the master bedroom.

"Woman, did you look at my knuckles? I could use a little TLC. What kind of woman leaves her man bleeding and hurt?"

"A woman who is going down to the kitchen to find herself the largest and thickest frying pan possible. That kind of woman." She backed up two steps. "And stop walking. Go away."

She shooed at him with her hand. He kept walking toward her.

"Reaper, you've got me wanting to throw things. It isn't safe for you to get near me. I mean it, go away."

"You need to take a punch at me?" He walked right up to her. She smelled like heaven. Her hair was piled on her head in some messy knot that just asked to be yanked out. He caught her hand, closed her fingers into a fist and pulled it to his heart. "Right here, baby. Hit me right here. You need to do it, I'm all for you taking the shot."

She stared up at his face for a long time. Very slowly her fingers uncurled until her palm lay flat and his heart beat into her hand. To his shock she leaned into him, pressing her body close to his. "Tell me what I did wrong. Tell me why you keep leaving me after you touch me like you do."

He wrapped his arms around her head and held her tight, held her so it was impossible for her to look up and see his face. Ordinarily he could keep a mask there, but he didn't know how to deal with such intense emotions. "You don't do anything wrong, Anya," he assured gruffly. "I'm not good at this. It's all new to me. I'm making it up as I go along."

She lay against him, her body soft. Pliant. Not at all stiff. If she was angry, it wasn't over him leaving her after they'd had sex. It was because his knuckles were bleeding. If that was the case, she was going to be angry a lot.

"Baby, let me work this out. Give me a little time. You wanted face-to-face, and I gave you that."

She nodded. "I know you did. I really loved face-to-face. I loved on my knees. I loved bent over a chair. I love being with you any way I can. I'll take whatever I can get, Reaper, but you have to tell me if I'm doing something wrong."

He took a deep breath. It had to be said if she was going to be safe. "Don't touch my cock unless I give you permission." He forced the words out. "Don't ask me for reasons, just give this to me. It's necessary or I wouldn't be saying it."

She stepped back and looked up at his face. "You don't want to be in my mouth? You don't want my lips wrapped around you? My fist holding you tight?" There was a little wicked temptress in her. Any other time he would appreciate it, but now wasn't that time.

Her words conjured up images. Her mouth was made for fucking. He wanted his cock there. He wanted to see her lips stretched around him. He wasn't small and he would stretch her limits. She would find it hard to take him down her throat, but she would. He was hard as a fucking rock all over again. Her gaze was glued to his cock, but she didn't make the mistake of reaching out to touch him. She put both hands behind her back and looked up at him innocently.

"Innocent my ass," he snapped, spun her around and pushed her into the wall.

He kicked her feet wide, yanked back her hips, shoved the flannel up and slammed his cock home. Lightning forked up his back and down his spine. Fire raced through his veins. He drove into her over and over. Hard. Punishing. Loving her. What the *fuck* was he thinking? He couldn't stop, not wanting to examine that thought or where it came from. He plunged into her over and over, while their breathing turned ragged and she sobbed his name and he heard the roar of his blood in his ears. She was an inferno, searing her name into his cock, branding him with her tight muscles and scorching hot silk that surrounded him like a fist.

"Reaper." His name came out as a whisper.

He loved hearing it like that. Soft. Meaning something. The rapid building of pressure increased tenfold. There was no holding back. He yanked her head back, using the messy knot on top of her head. Bending her back, pressing her tits into the wall, keeping her hips pulled into him while he took her deep and hard. He let the firestorm rush over him. Let it blow his fucking mind. Her body clamped down so hard around him he thought the top of his head would come off right along with his cock.

He locked his arm around her waist and held her up when her legs threatened to give out. He shoved his face into her neck and breathed her in. "I love fucking you."

She didn't say anything, but kept her forehead pressed tightly against the wall.

"Baby? Did I hurt you?" She had gone too still for his liking.

She shook her head. "I need to clean up again."

He stepped back and, keeping his arm around her waist, took her into the bedroom. He'd forgotten how large it was. Spacious. High ceilings. That long bank of windows just like those in the kitchen and great room. French doors led to a balcony that overlooked the ocean. The bed was made, two pillows. Blankets. Sheets. He let her slip away and stepped back.

"We're sleeping downstairs. In the great room. On the floor." He made it an order, walked past her, ripped the blankets off the bed and stalked out.

He was feeling the pain in his knuckles now. He needed to soak them. He was going to San Francisco tomorrow to rescue Hammer's old lady. He'd need his hands. He tried to keep his mind on the pain and not whether or not Anya was following him downstairs. He threw the blankets in front of the fireplace and went on through to the kitchen so he could run his hands under cold water.

He stayed there a long time, wishing he was different, knowing he probably never would be. When his knuckles were so numb he couldn't feel them, he jerked open the fridge door, found two bottles of water and pulled them out.

He really wanted whiskey. Maybe the whole fucking bottle. He went back into the great room expecting it to be empty.

The blankets were laid out in front of the fireplace. Flames danced along the fake logs. The remote was next to her. She sat in the middle of the blankets brushing out her hair. He sat down behind her and took the brush.

"I found a first aid kit in the upstairs bathroom. It had gauze in it and antibiotic cream. Your sisters know you, don't they?"

"Yep." He ran the brush through the long, thick mass. He was a little in love with her hair. Not only did he want her mouth wrapped around his cock, he wanted her hair wrapped around it too.

He kept brushing, ignoring the thoughts and images that filled his brain and let him know he could just be the biggest pervert on the planet when he was around her. Worse, he liked it. She reached back, took the brush and began to braid her hair. "I can't believe this is really your house. It isn't that far from the clubhouse. Or work."

"You want to keep working? You don't have to."

"Of course I'm going to work. I love bartending." She turned to look at him over her shoulder. "Reaper, Preacher or one of the others is always there. You know someone watches the monitor. I have a panic button. You don't have to be there every night because I am."

"You're there, I'm there if I can be."

She sighed. "If that's what you want to do. I'm just saying it isn't necessary." She tied off her hair, scooted back and turned to face him. The first aid kit was close. She opened it and brought one of his hands to her, inspecting his knuckles. The cold water had stopped the bleeding and controlled the swelling. He'd been fighting all his life and his knuckles showed that. They'd been smashed more than once.

She lowered her head, and his heart nearly stopped when he felt the light brush of her lips across his mangled flesh.

It took control and discipline not to jerk his hand away. It wasn't because she'd aroused the monster. It was because no one had ever done that before. No one had ever kissed a hurt on him. He didn't know what to do with it or how it made him feel. He wanted to move away from her, withdraw and protect himself from the overwhelming feelings he didn't understand or want. But he didn't. He gave her so little and he was going to give her this if it fucking killed him.

She spread antibiotic cream over the raw lacerations and then gently wrapped gauze around his hand. She took his left hand and did the same thing, brushing her lips gently over the wounds. Her lashes lifted and she looked up at him. Those green eyes did something to him. He couldn't look away, not even when she dropped her gaze to his hand and applied the ointment and wrapped his knuckles. He couldn't take his eyes off of her.

She hadn't asked him questions, or argued about sleeping downstairs. How could he explain he could sleep indoors surrounded by his brothers and the girls, but not in a bedroom upstairs where there was only the two of them? That it didn't feel safe? She hadn't gotten upset when he'd knocked her hand away when all she'd wanted to do was touch his body the way he touched hers. He couldn't explain his reasons for that either, but he had to give her something.

"Anya . . . I wouldn't be in this house if you weren't here. It's our house. I want you to make it a home for us."

She smiled at him. "That's good, because I have all kinds of ideas. I wasn't lying when I told you I was good at this. I'm excited to help Alena with the restaurant as well. She told me she'd teach me to ride. I had no idea Lana and Alena had been riding as long as all of you."

His gut knotted. "Ride?" he echoed.

She nodded. "I love being on the motorcycle. I had no idea how it could make me feel."

"Let's learn to walk before you try to run, baby. Stay on my bike with me for a while." Hell. If he was lucky, he'd knock her up, just like Ice suggested. That way she wouldn't leave him, and she would forget all about wanting a bike of her own. He was going to strangle Alena. He knew damn well she'd made the offer on purpose just so she could laugh at him when he lost his mind. He wasn't going to fall into Alena's trap and protest though. He was going to bide his time.

He wrapped his arm around Anya's shoulders and pulled her back into him. "Can you do that for me? Just for a little while?"

She smiled that beautiful smile, the one she reserved for him. "I can do that. Are you going to try to sleep? If you need me to, I'll go upstairs, honey."

His gut clenched at the offer. He knew she wanted to sleep with him. A thousand reasons why she couldn't ran through his mind. He was naked though. No weapons close. If he got his hands on her, he'd be able to pull back. "Stay here, this is good. I want to sleep next to you." He did want to sleep next to her, more than anything.

Her smile was worth all the anxiety he tucked away deep. She lay back and turned on her side, facing away from him. He knew she did it on purpose. He wrapped his body around hers, pulling her into him, his arm locking around her waist, his cock snug against her ass. He inhaled the scent of her hair. He fucking loved it. He had no idea it would feel like this to lie next to his woman, his arms around her, her hair in his face, feeling at peace. He'd never had that before either.

A couple of hours later, Reaper jerked awake, his heart pounding, his fist wrapping in silky hair, already yanking up before he could stop himself. He had turned over in the night, onto his back. She lay across him, her hair sliding over his cock and thighs, that thick braid an erotic snake bent on destroying him.

She gasped and he took her mouth, desperate to prevent her from seeing the demon and how close she'd come to innocently arousing him. He kissed her until neither of them could think. Then he took her on her hands and knees, her back to him, her hands occupied with keeping her body lifted off the blankets, although she went to her elbows, her breath coming out in singsong moans.

After he held her, his heart still beating too hard, his mind in chaos. The sweet peace hadn't lasted nearly as long as he needed it to.

FOURTEEN

Lana drove the BMW right up to the front of the Ghost Club. She looked the handsome valet up and down with cool eyes, letting her gaze drift over him from head to toe and then back up to his groin speculatively. When she lifted her lashes, she smiled at him. He rushed around to open the door for her. She shifted in the seat, turned sideways and put both elegant legs out. She wore stockings that ended at the tops of her thighs, held there by lacy black garters. Her skirt pulled up as she stepped out onto her two-thousand-dollar, very high heels.

He offered his hand, and she took it as if it was her due. She stood up gracefully, the skintight golden dress clinging to every curve. Her hair, black as a raven's wing, swung around her face, drawing attention to the perfect oval, high cheekbones, luscious red mouth and long black lashes. Diamonds dripped from her ears on golden chains. She dropped her keys into his hand and watched with amusement as he rushed around the car to open the door for Alena.

Alena complemented her, with her natural platinum hair

wild and glossy, impossible to tame. Her eyes were icy blue, made even more startling because her lashes were long and dark. She wore red. Crimson. The material seemed burned into her skin, a stretchy lace that could have been shocking, but was only erotic. She smiled at the attendant as well. When she moved her head and her hair shifted, red rubies sparkled in her ears.

Lana swept toward the door, Alena in perfect step with her. The parking valet watched them walk to the door of the club. He didn't take his eyes off them until the door closed behind them. He stood there, as if in a daze, before his head jerked up as if coming out of a dream and he ran around and slid into the driver's seat.

From his vantage point on the roof across the street from the club, Preacher watched the entire drama play out through the scope of his rifle. *Girls are in,* he reported. Once Lana and Alena were safely inside, he switched his attention to the valet. *He's definitely the spotter. He's chatting into his little radio no one is supposed to notice. Lana gave me the sign that he's wired. You've got this, Lana, he's marked you both.*

I made certain he noticed us, Lana returned, her voice filled with amusement. *A little bit of leg and a lot of attitude gets them every time. He bit hard.*

Don't overplay your hand. Make them come to you, Czar advised.

No worries. Alena found us a table and we're going to sit, drink, and talk. I'm using the cash. Flashing it. Gave valet boy a nice tip.

Preacher turned his attention to the street and alley. From his position, he could see partway down the alley, enough to cover Mechanic as he set up very powerful listening devices. He staggered around as if he'd been drinking, placing the tiny bugs along the very edge of the building and down along the stairway that led to the basement.

Audio in place, Mechanic reported. *Changing in the van and going in.*

Keys set up on the corner of the alley, pacing, looking at his watch, glancing at traffic as if waiting for a ride. *I'm in position,* he said. *Have eyes on the inside of the basement, but can't see anything but an empty room. Will change and follow Mechanic inside.*

Van's in position, Transporter said. He had signs around warning people of high voltage, the manhole open and a vest on, just to complete the scene. *I'll tell you when it's clear.*

Preacher used binoculars to sweep along the buildings, the rooftops, and then the street and alley. It was dark enough with several good places for his brothers to disappear. They were true phantoms in the night. The members of the Ghost Club were high-powered attorneys, corporate presidents, and CEOs of companies. These were men no one would ever guess were behind the Ghost Club, or that they might ride with colors into the territory of the Diamondbacks and demand a cut of everything they did.

They weren't taking the risks of running drugs or guns, counterfeiting, overseeing prostitution or human trafficking, they simply demanded a share or they would start slicing up the women the various clubs cared about. Code had meticulously worked to uncover identities, following the emails and chatter between various companies. It was all in their ridiculous encryption they thought no one would notice or break.

Code was an elite hacker. His friend Cat, a woman he'd never met, was as elite as he was. They often worked together to get through a particularly difficult firewall, and she'd helped him so the club could get the information fast. She followed one trail while he followed another, both working through the night and all the next day to find various members.

Those in the Ghost Club thought themselves invisible, impossible to find even if a club came after them. They used outside resources to do their dirty work, to ride Harleys, wear colors and approach the other clubs. They had others who enticed club members to gamble. Their tentacles reached not just to motorcycle clubs, but many businesses. Those men sat back in their corporate offices, certain of their own safety, getting richer, more powerful, and feeling very entitled.

You're clear, Preacher said. *Hurry though.*

Mechanic and Keys emerged from the van dressed in dark suits that easily cost several thousand dollars. They looked like wealthy Russians, in town for a few short days just to relax and have a little fun, maybe pick up women for a night or two. They were tall, good-looking, with a few facial scars, just enough to look interesting.

They talked to each other in their native language, pausing just outside the club to crush out a Russian cigarette, giving the valet a good look at them. They didn't deign to look at the kid in his uniform, they just pulled open the ornate door and sauntered in like they owned the place.

He took the bait, Preacher reported. *He's chatting into his radio.*

We're getting an audio feed. The casino is in full swing, Code reported. *I can hear a couple of employees talking about Lana and Alena. Girls, you've got a few of them excited.*

Shame on us. Alena purred her response, keeping in character. *We've had several drinks sent to our table already. Hard to flash money, but giving generous tips to the waitress. Let her catch a glimpse of the roll of cash. And no, Czar, we weren't obvious about it.*

The club was crowded, the light dim, the music loud. The dance floor was packed and nearly every table taken. Alena watched as the bartender slipped one man in a suit a thin card, much like the key to a hotel room. He did it when he handed the man a drink.

"Look alive, Alena," Lana said, leaning across the table to touch Alena's hand, laughing softly to give the illusion she was telling her friend something funny. "Looks like we've got a fish on the hook. Maybe a whale. Look at his cuff links." Her brothers could hear everything she said.

A man loomed over them, coming up to the table to stand between them. "Ladies." He was very good-looking and he knew it, giving them a smile that might have fluttered a few hearts. "Welcome to the Ghost Club. I'm Raul, the manager. If there's anything I can help you with, just let me know."

Lana gave him her beautiful smile. "It's our first time here. Alena came to visit, and I want to show her a good time in my hometown. This is a beautiful club. I thought we might dance, drink, find some friends. Maybe go to the Lucky Lady Casino just for added fun. I've been there a few times and want to show Alena a good time." She named a casino frequented by many San Franciscans and tourists.

Lana's voice was friendly and open, but throaty, husky, sounding like sin. She ran her finger up and down the table-top as if stroking it. Once she crossed her legs, allowing the slit in her clingy dress to show off her thigh and just a peek of her sexy garter. The manager's eyes strayed several times to her legs.

"I think our club can provide you with dance, drinks and maybe a friend or two," Raul answered.

Lana looked around, taking in all the suits and ties. "Looks that way. I think we've found our new favorite place to unwind."

"What do you do?" Raul asked.

Lana shrugged. "The two of us started a little company, one that makes apps for businesses such as this. Mobile apps. It's all the rage and very useful." Her fingers tapped on the tabletop. "Alena oversees our employees in San Diego, and I work out of San Francisco."

"Really?" Raul looked very interested. "What's the name of your company?"

Code had created a company for them overnight. He'd built the website, the facts, adding them to the *Forbes* entrepreneurs under thirty, putting their fake company and the stats there.

One hundred and thirty million. That should entice Raul. Two bored women with more money than they know what to do with. They've already casually mentioned a casino. He'll take the bait, Preacher said.

"Perhaps my club would benefit from such a thing."

"On the Move," Lana said, sounding bored. She wasn't there to work, she was there to play and she wanted that very clear. "We can send a rep if you're interested." She wanted to make it clear as well, she didn't sell her own product.

Raul glanced toward the bar. Immediately his phone beeped. He gave them a rueful smile. "I'll be back in a moment. Can I have Dirk send you drinks on the house?"

"We've got more than we can handle right here," Alena declined, her hand sweeping along the array of drinks in front of them. They couldn't take a chance on getting any new drinks from the bar just in case they were drugged.

"Good to meet you, ladies. Enjoy your evening." Raul turned away from them, looking at his phone.

He's checking on the company. Yeah, he fell for it. Mechanic and Keys are getting the same treatment from a female manager. Interesting, Czar said.

Are you getting anything from the tunnels?

Some chatter. It's pretty quiet. There's a woman down there for certain. She's crying, but very softly. I heard two men talking in low voices, Transporter said. *I'm trying to clean up the audio now. The walls are thick.*

The club members had learned from childhood to be patient. To be precise and meticulous about details. Lana and Alena ignored Raul. They danced several dances with different men. Keys asked Lana to dance, and Mechanic asked Alena. They chatted but stayed in their roles, knowing they were being watched. Keys made a move to join Lana and Alena, but they just shook their heads, declining the invitation. The two men shrugged and went on the hunt for other women. They had no trouble picking up partners.

Raul seemed to make his rounds and then came back to their table. "Are you having a good time?"

Lana nodded. "It's been fun." She picked up her small clutch and fiddled with the catch. "We'll definitely be back again. Nice club." She made it clear she was ready to go.

Raul had a thin card in his hand. It had a bar code on one end. "For some VIPs we have a little place that is far more fun, especially if you like to gamble."

"What kind of gambling?" Lana tipped her head up. Alena put her chin in her hand and looked up at the manager as if interested for the first time.

"Cards, craps, roulette. You name it, we have it." He kept his voice low.

"I don't know. I'm damn good at cards," Lana said. "I don't lose. It's a thing I've got with numbers. Someplace small, they get upset. I like this club and want to be able to come back, so I think I'll pass."

"You're that good?" Raul put a little sneer into his voice.

"She is," Alena assured. "I'm better at craps, but I've never won big the way she does at cards. I'm a sometimes-big winner."

Raul concentrated his attention on Lana. "I think you'll find we accommodate winners here as well. Would you like to try? It's exclusive and illegal."

The two women looked at each other and then broke into smiles. Lana brought her purse in close. "We're in."

"Follow me, ladies," he said.

Lana and Alena stood up, glanced casually around the room to see that several players had been selected. Keys and Mechanic were among them.

One diversion coming up. Give us a half hour to wreak havoc. I'm going to break their stupid bank. Take these assholes down.

Don't get cocky, Lana, Czar cautioned. *You stick to the*

plan. You're the diversion. Win big. If all four of you win at separate things, you'll cause a commotion. They'll pull off security in the basement to get to the casino. Don't do anything that will have them putting a gun to your head.

They do that, Alena said, *and I'll burn this club down around their ears.*

Innocent people are partying there, Czar reminded.

You're such a downer, Czar, Lana said. *You let the tigers out to play with the lambs and now you say don't hurt them.*

Damn it, the goal is to get Hammer's woman out, not have fun, Lana.

Lana made *tsking* noises and the sway of her hips became more exaggerated. The casino was far larger than she thought it could be. She took a good look around so the tiny camera in her necklace could pick up everything and feed it to Transporter and the others in the van. Alena, Keys and Mechanic did the same. They had separated, to wander through different areas so they could record every detail of the room. They also wanted to be in four separate sections so there was no way, when the owners reviewed the tapes, that they could look like they were working together.

Lana won immediately, the first three hands. She dropped out several times, lost a couple more hands, but losing only a few hundred, and then she won consistently, hand after hand. It was rare for her to drop out, but when she didn't, she was either bluffing or she had the winning cards. It wasn't long before others were watching.

Alena took her time, playing a few hands of blackjack. Going to one of the slot machines and then making her way to the craps table. Like Lana, she won a few and lost a few. She'd nearly lost all of her chips when she suddenly went on a winning streak. She was vocal about her wins, and soon quite a few people abandoned what they were doing and gathered around her at the craps table, placing their bets based on what she did. Very soon, she wasn't the only big winner.

Mechanic chose the slot machines, the ones with the biggest payouts. Any machine responded to his touch. Tumblers dropped, skipped, the big wins popping up so that chaos reigned. The noise blared loudly, declaring him a grand prize winner. It was five hundred thousand. He played it off when the manager hurried to his side, checking to make certain he'd really won. Others gathered around him, excited for him. He was given the money right there. It was an underground casino, no taxes reported because one couldn't report the income.

He went to the bar, ordered a drink and watched the bartender carefully as the man made it. Bottles were thrown in the air in a show, but Mechanic watched his hands, that quick flick, fingers sliding into his pocket. The alcohol was poured and in one move, as the bottles did a triple flip and everyone's eye went there, the bartender poured a clear liquid into his drink. He tipped the man big, picked up the drink and wandered back toward the slot machines.

Manager just nodded to a waitress. Watch yourself and watch your pockets, Transporter cautioned. *Lana, Alena and Keys, watch your drinks,* he added.

Lana won another big hand, and several people clapped. Alena was practically dancing and the crowd around her grew in direct proportion to the pile of chips in front of her. Keys sat down at the high-stakes blackjack table. He won so many times they changed dealers. And decks. Mechanic scored another large win, this one fifty thousand. He'd been watched carefully by the waitress flirting outrageously with him. Half the time he appeared as if he wasn't paying attention as he shoved in fives and tens and pulled the lever several times before it suddenly hit. Within ten minutes he had his own crowd. The four of them were taking the casino for a ride.

Soon they had three managers and several security guards watching them intently. The crowds grew around them, and as the four continued to win, others won at the craps table and the slot machines.

Now or never. Two men are running up the tunnel to assist in the casino. I've counted five left down there. Probably in the little rooms to the left of where they are holding their prisoner, Transporter said. *Just be aware, I don't have exact numbers. I've counted five individual voices coming from that side of the room. They're closest to the transmitters. It's possible I'm not picking up everything.*

Thanks, mother hen. Czar clapped him on the back as the van's doors opened and first Reaper, then Czar emerged, with Savage behind him and Steele and Player bringing up the rear. The five men walked quickly along the sidewalk, hands in their pockets, the shadows blurring their images, hoodies pulled over their faces. The cameras had been disabled as well as the ones along the street, in the surrounding buildings and the Ghost Club itself. That didn't mean some random camera wouldn't catch a glimpse of them, or someone with a cell phone wouldn't take it in their head to capture the five of them walking down the basement steps.

That was their entry point. It was easy enough for Steele to put his hands on the bars covering the entrance, warm them and remove them. He then found the lock and worked his magic there. He was good with any kind of alloy, manmade especially. He stepped back and once again, Reaper took lead.

The plans Anya had drawn for them showed the long hallway skirting around the walls of the casino that shared the basement. The hall sloped downhill and was lined with small rooms. Some of those rooms were very tiny and in another age, when smuggling and speakeasies were the norm, he knew they'd been used for the storage of liquor.

Reaper blocked out the men behind him. Savage would have their back trail, knowing Reaper would be alert to anything in front of them. His senses were finally honed and he used every one of them. It was rare for both Czar and Steele to go on the same mission together. That way, if one was killed, the other was still there to lead.

According to Anya's floor plans, they would need Steele when they got to Hammer's woman. Reaper's sinking heart and that faint smell of blood told him they might need Steele's healing skills even more.

Her name was Maria, and Reaper had seen it on Hammer's face—that overwhelming emotion he was practically choking on, even when he was determined to hide it. Hammer thought the world revolved around that woman, just as Reaper did with Anya. He had a bad feeling, and he didn't want to bring a dead body home to the president of the Demons. She had to be a good woman if the man looked as he had when talking about her disappearance.

He halted, one hand raised in the air, fingers closed in a fist. There were narrow rope lights strung overhead along the sides of the ceiling. Those lights were fairly dim and his men were silent when they walked. They had a lot of practice in that as well. He'd learned to walk over broken glass barefoot without uttering a sound—or allowing his weight to crack a piece of glass. He'd been beaten repeatedly for allowing twigs and branches to snap under his feet, or disturbing a rock when he hadn't felt the object with unfamiliar shoes on.

He signaled for Player to check the other rooms while he moved forward. Straight ahead, at the end of the hall, he could make out the large cage with metal bars from ceiling to the floor. The scent of blood grew stronger and he could hear her now, those soft moans and pitiful crying. He'd rip out throats if Anya was lying on that cold stone in her own blood. Whatever they had done to the woman, he knew it was bad.

He was in full-blown assassin mode as he moved toward the room just off the dungeon. He'd spent his entire childhood in a dungeon. The bathroom for all of them was the corner. Every now and then they had been given buckets to clean up.

They had no clothes, little food and there were endless beatings that brought blood. Blood attracted insects and rats. There were chains to lock them to the wall while men and women brutalized the younger ones and whipped them front and back. Yeah. He knew about dungeons and the kinds of vile monsters who shoved women and children, those weaker than them, into prisons so they could do their worst.

He'd been weak when he was four. He'd started striking back at five. By the time he was ten, he was lethal. Scary. But he'd had to hide it. They'd all had to hide what they'd been becoming in order to survive.

Reaper tried to pull his mind away from those memories. When they'd taken him to torture him, raping and beating him repeatedly, burning him, slicing him open with knives, all to make him tell who the ringleader was. Then they'd brought Savage and done the same to him in front of Reaper. He'd remained silent. So had Savage. They hadn't looked at each other for a very long time after that, too humiliated and guilty to look each other in the eye.

Now the odor of blood was a stench in his nostrils. He paused at the door of the room where the guards were playing cards. He heard them, their laughter, the murmur of their voices. All five of them.

Pool table. Four doors down, right side. Two men. Player took them out, Transporter informed them.

Reaper ignored that. He locked eyes with the woman. Her face was bloody and swollen. She wore the remnants of a top and nothing else. There was blood on her arms, long ugly streaks. More on her thighs and dripping from under the shirt. There was even more blood between her legs.

Fuck. Fuck. Fuck. Those guards were going to die hard. Seeing it coming, hurting every second. Reaper raised his finger to his lips and mouthed, *Hammer sent us.*

She nodded and continued that soft moaning. Occasionally she added a hiccupping sob. She was smart and quick. Most people tortured like she'd been would have reacted before they thought. She didn't, and she tried to keep up the illusion that she was alone.

He deliberately stepped into the doorway. The five men looked up. One actually had enough time to throw his cards before Reaper was on them. The card thrower would have done better to pull his gun. Reaper's blade sliced through an artery in the closest man's thigh; the knife continued in an upward motion and sliced through the artery under the arm of the second man. The third took it in the right-side carotid artery. The fourth across his throat, a pretty slash from left to right. The fifth man got it in the gut, his intestines spilling out.

Get her out of there, Czar, and don't let her see this mess.

Reaper was already on the table to avoid the worst of the spraying blood. It was going to be a bloodbath in there. He kicked a gun away from the one with the blood pumping out of his thigh.

"You're going to die," the one with his underarm spewing blood stated and then coughed, blood bubbling through his mouth.

Reaper shrugged, not saying a word. What was there to say?

"Ghosts everywhere," the one with the thigh slash added.

The two with throat and neck wounds were already slumping unconscious. Two minutes down, two more to go and they'd be gone. The leg might take a little longer, but it was pumping like mad. The armpit was a kill almost immediately. The man just staggered as he tried to stand and then crashed to the floor, unconscious. Thigh wound went next. The man holding his intestines took the longest. He just stared at Reaper, too dumb to know he was already dead.

We got to get her out of here now. Czar made it a command. *Put a bullet in their fucking heads if you have to, but don't leave any of them alive. She's in bad shape, Reaper. Bad.*

Steele had come prepared. He had his medical kit. He'd

do his best as soon as they got her in the van. Reaper had the feeling that the urgency was because they were afraid they were going to lose her, not because someone else might come down and realize their prison was under attack. Reaper watched the fifth man fall forward, right out of his chair, face-first, into a pool of his own blood and intestines. He wasn't checking pulses, he knew dead men when he saw them.

Reaper stepped out of the room and shut the door, falling into the front of the line to lead Czar and Steele out. Savage took up the rear, and Player stepped in front of Savage. Czar carried the woman. Her eyes were closed and she held herself rigid, as if afraid to move, that her rescue might not be real. Savage had covered her with his jacket. None of them exposed Czar or Steele to cameras if it could be helped. Mechanic had shut down everything for two blocks, but that didn't mean cell phones weren't around, so neither man could give up his hoodie.

As they approached the end of the hall, Reaper stopped abruptly. The hall branched here. One way went up toward the casino, the other toward the outside to the basement steps that led to the alley. Two men rounded the corner. Reaper was on them instantly, breaking the closest man's neck and slamming his shoulder into the second as he shoved the first man's body off him. He drove the second man into the wall. Player was there instantly, gripping the man's head, locking it to him and turning so the body hung over his shoulder. He jerked hard and the crack was audible.

They were out fast, up the stairs and through the alley. Transporter was there with the van, both doors wide open. The woman was handed in gently and laid down on the mat they'd brought, Steele on one side, his medical bag there. Czar on the other to assist him. Player took up a guard position in the front with Transporter. Reaper and Savage stayed in the back where they could better protect the president and vice president of their club.

Let's go home, Transporter said. *Mechanic, Keys, pick up Preacher and get out of there. Lana, Alena, make your exit. Watch each other in case they try to put a tracker on you. We'll sweep the cars at the rendezvous point.*

They've already given us a VIP card that allows us back here as well as into any of their other clubs. They want to recoup their money, Lana said smugly. *So many people won tonight, not just us, that they can't conceive that we might have cheated, although I'm certain they'll review the tapes. They just won't find anything to make them believe we weren't just lucky.*

~

Anya wandered around the outside of the clubhouse. She had a couple of hours before work and she was bored. She was looking at the flower beds, all in bad shape, when she stumbled right into what felt like an oak tree.

Hands caught her arms, steadying her. "Be careful, woman."

She looked up to see Ink. He was covered in tattoos from his neck down. They drifted under his shirt and down where it was impossible to see, but she wanted to look because the tattoos were so intriguing.

"What are you doing?"

She gestured toward the flower beds. "They're dismal and need work. I was going over a mental list trying to figure out what I'll need to bring them back." Farther out, someone had planted a lot of wildflowers in the meadow, but the beds were a mess.

"Don't wander off. Stay in the compound," he cautioned and started to walk away.

"Um. Ink." Her heart went crazy. She was out of her mind to ask, but asking didn't hurt. When he turned back, she held up her wrists. "Is it possible to tattoo Reaper's fingerprints on my wrists? You know, like a bracelet."

Interest blossomed. He stepped close and took her hands, turning them over to inspect her inner wrists where the faint smudges of Reapers fingerprints remained. "I have his prints."

Her stomach dropped. "You do? Why would you have his prints?"

He shrugged. "When we go out on a job, we don't use our own prints. I make them up for the brothers and their prints are always in the various projects I'm doing." He turned her hands over again. "What about across the top of your wrist, a fine gold chain, and under across the tender part of your wrists, the fingerprints. I can see the marks on your skin so we'd know the exact placement on both hands. You really want to do this?"

Anya nodded. "I want him to know I'm not going anywhere. When he . . ." She broke off. Even to his brother, she wasn't going to disclose private information about Reaper. Maybe they already knew. Maybe he'd told them what issues he had and they knew even more than she did, but that didn't matter. Reaper was hers to protect now and she was determined to do it. She had no idea what being an old lady entailed, but she was going to find her way and be the best old lady any man could have. "It will be a reminder to me too, when I lose my temper."

"Let's do it now."

"Right now? I have to work in a couple of hours. Preacher isn't here so Maestro is filling in. He doesn't exactly like to bartend and he isn't fast at it."

Ink shook his head. "That dog. He could be fast if he wanted to be, he's doggin' it so no one asks him to fill in." He turned and started walking to the front of the compound and then on past it, continuing down the road.

Heart doing triple time, Anya followed him. Who got fingerprints tattooed on their wrist? She had to be out of her mind. The tattoo parlor wasn't that far and it felt good to stretch her legs and be out of the confines of the compound. It looked like a fortress with its high chain-link fence, a place bikers might make their last stand.

She rubbed her wrist. "What if he gets into trouble and they want his fingerprints and he isn't around and they find his real prints on me?"

"Anya, Torpedo Ink doesn't take a job and then use their own prints. We have an entire library of prints. They peel them off after and get rid of them. They're very small and thin. Once off the warmth of the finger and put in water, they'll dissolve. They wear thin gloves over those and, of course, they don't ride with their colors. Few, if any, on a job see their faces."

She found herself in a good-sized room with two cubicles. There was a long, padded table and several low chairs with backs that were at an angle.

Ink gestured toward the heavily padded, more conventional chair. "Have a seat."

Was she really going to do this? What if she broke up with Reaper? What if it just didn't work? He had so many issues, and she didn't know enough about him. He was violent. He pounded his fists into the wall, but what if he ever turned that fury on her? With great trepidation, she watched Ink washing his hands, sterilizing them and then laying his equipment out. There were needles.

"You ever get a tattoo before?"

She shook her head. "No, but I always wanted to get one. I had this life plan. Tattoo was step four, after I made it and had a healthy bank account. I was well on my way."

"Money's still there."

She shook her head. "It isn't. Somehow, they were able to drain my accounts. Even my savings are gone."

He shrugged. "No worries, Code will get it back for you with interest." He took her wrist and laid her arm straight on the surface, wiping it down with alcohol. "So, you like to sketch. Did you sketch your own tattoo for when you made it?"

She shook her head and watched as he quickly sketched her a thin chain. It appeared fragile. Delicate. As if it could be broken easily. She shook her head again. "Not like that. I want something strong. Unbreakable. A reminder to both of us."

Ink's gaze moved over her face with something like respect. He nodded his head, just a jerk of his chin, but she could tell he was pleased with her. He tossed the piece of paper and sketched another chain. This one had thick links. Not gold. Titanium was silver, and when he drew the bracelet part, he based the links on that alloy in its raw form. There were little jagged bumps along the line of the chain. She loved it.

"We'll do this in a charcoal silver effect." He turned her hand over and took the carefully prepared paper with copies of each fingerprint. He placed them over the smudges on her wrist and left the distinct imprints. He tatted those first in black, carefully following each whirl until she had the imprint of four fingers spread across each wrist. He did a print of Reaper's thumb on top of her wrist, right where his thumb had pressed into her. Around the top of her wrist was the chain.

There was no wasted motion with Ink. He was skilled in his chosen art and it showed in every move, every clean line he tatted onto her wrist. The chain was going to be gorgeous. She could see, even though she wanted strength, something unbreakable, he gave it beauty. Her heart hurt as he slowly, with painstaking care, brought the chain around to touch the first and last of Reaper's fingerprints on each wrist.

Ink didn't talk much while he worked, but she didn't want him too. She was too busy thinking about the enormity of her decision. She didn't know for sure if Reaper was serious about having his prints on her, but she liked the idea the more she thought about it. She loved the way the two brace-lets looked around the top of her wrists. The silver gleamed in places.

Ink gave her all the necessary care instructions and cov-ered the tattoos, telling her to keep them covered for two to four hours. She asked if she could keep them wrapped through her shift. He said he'd stop by and put the cream on it before covering it with a thin, light bandage. She went to work with both wrists wrapped. It looked almost like she had tried to off herself. She got lots of questions and even more tips and just told them she'd gotten tattoos. Everyone wanted to see but she just shook her head. She wanted Reaper to see first.

She was halfway through her shift when Jonas Har-rington, the local sheriff, and Jackson Deveau, his deputy, walked in. She had the hardest time with cops. Both men were nice, very polite, she couldn't fault them on that, but she was always afraid she was going to say or do the wrong thing.

"It's Anya, isn't it?" Jonas asked with one of his smiles. His eyes were on her wrists. Jackson had frozen, his face very still.

"It isn't what it looks like," she assured, not waiting for the inevitable question. "I got tattoos a few hours ago. I could take off the bandages, but think it would be more sanitary to finish my shift first. What can I get you?"

Maestro moved over next to her, smiling at the two cops. "What's up, man? Haven't seen you for a long time. More than a year." He nodded toward Betina. "She's got three needing drinks, Anya." He turned back to Jonas. "I detest bartending. Don't know the drinks. She not only knows the drinks, but she remembers what everyone is drinking. What can I do for you?"

"It seems we have more disappearances. Still have noth-ing on the three we asked about yesterday. Now we've got three more. It hasn't been a full twenty-four hours yet, but they didn't return to their motel rooms last night and their families are worried. We were told all three of these men were in the bar the other night."

"You're asking the wrong man," Maestro said. "I don't have a clue what you're talking about. I'm never here. Wish I wasn't now." He raised his voice. "Anya, they need you here. Are you finished with those drinks?" He added the last on a hopeful note.

She laughed at him. "You make the *worst* bartender. Preacher needs someone else to come in on his days off." She leaned against the bar, trying to look nonchalant instead of as if she might faint any moment. "What can I do for you?"

"The three we asked about last evening, did they ever come back in?"

She wrinkled her nose. "Nope. And I'm glad. One of them in particular was a pain. This is a biker bar, I get that some of the customers are going to harass us, but I didn't much like his names for me. They left, though, and were heading in the direction of their bikes. I wasn't paying attention. I was with Reaper, and I tend not to pay attention to anything or anyone when I'm with him." She blushed, because it was true.

"Reaper?" Jonas's eyebrow nearly went through his hairline. "You were with Reaper?"

She nodded. "We're living together." She might as well have dropped a bomb. There was satisfaction in telling them the truth. She had been with Reaper and that meant if anything had happened to those three men, no one could blame him.

"What about these men? Were they in here?" Jonas asked. He spread three photographs onto the bar.

Anya glanced around the bar as if to make certain no one needed a drink. Maestro hovered, ready to protect her, she was certain. She tapped Thomas Randal's picture. "They were in the other night when you came in. They sat together. Very quiet. Kept mostly to themselves. I think this one talked to Alena, but only briefly. I'm not sure, it was busy that night. They seemed nice enough. They definitely aren't bikers, and they didn't pretend to be like some people do when they come in. I pegged them for businessmen."

"That was the last time you saw them?"

"The last time I saw this one. The other two came in the next night, had one drink and left. They didn't talk to anyone."

Jonas turned his head to look at Jackson, who nodded slightly. She was certain Jackson was the lie detector, although Jonas might be as well. Both men were certainly shrewd, sure of themselves, very confident.

"I'm sorry I'm not more help."

"It's strange that six men have come to this bar and no one has seen them since." Jonas made it a statement, his eyes unblinking on her face.

She stared down at the pictures to avoid that penetrating gaze. "I don't understand. Do you think something happened to them when they left here? Like what? The first three might have been drunk and they could have done something stupid. I wasn't about to ask them for their keys because Preacher had already left. I cut them off just before closing when I realized how awful they were acting, but the other three barely drank. One, maybe two drinks at most."

She decided sticking as close to the truth as possible would be best. It would be unusual for three bikers to drive off a cliff, but it could happen if they were drunk enough. That wouldn't explain the other three men though.

Jonas gathered up the photos. "I don't like having to contact wives and tell them there's no trace of their husbands or their children's fathers."

She shook her head. "How awful for you. Let's hope it doesn't come to that."

Maestro bumped her hip. "Seriously, she has to get back

to work. Preacher will be here tomorrow. Maybe he can give you something else. I need her now."

Customers were stacked up. Anya sent the two cops a small smile and turned back to making drinks, working fast to catch up. She just wanted the night to end. Mostly she worried about Reaper and what was happening.

FIFTEEN

It was four in the morning before Reaper pulled up on his Harley to the house on the cliff. He sat, straddling the bike, staring at the large two-story, nearly completely glass structure. Fortunately, the glass was mostly on the ocean side, so it would be difficult to come at him through those long banks of windows. Still, he'd have to do something to make the place more secure. He had to appreciate the architecture though. The house was designed to take advantage of the views.

He turned his head as a motorcycle started up. He lifted a hand to Fatei. "Thanks, man," he said. Meaning it. Fatei was on his way to being a fully patched member of their club. The man never shirked his duty, in fact went above the call. A second motorcycle started up and Maestro rode over to where he was parked.

"Escorted your woman home," Maestro reported. "Everything go okay tonight?"

"They fucked up that woman. Hammer's got a long road ahead of him," Reaper said. "Lana, Alena, Keys and Mechanic made the club a butt-load of money. Seven dead."

"Cops came around tonight, questioned your woman again about that douchebag Deke and his friends. Brought up the Burrows brothers and Randal. She handled it like a pro. She's going to be a good old lady."

Reaper was certain she would be. The moment he'd laid eyes on her, he'd known she was the one. He'd prepared for it, sending away for the patches for her jacket. He wanted that shit all over her. *Property of Reaper.* He wanted everyone to know, when they went on runs with the Diamondbacks or any other club, she was off-limits. "Thanks for looking out for her."

"No problem, Reaper. Get some sleep."

Reaper waited until the bike was making its way along the curves in the road leading back to the clubhouse before he slid off his motorcycle and walked to the front door. Every muscle in his body hurt. Every joint. His knuckles ached. Mostly, he was bone-tired. None of that mattered. He knew she was in the house. Anya. His Anya. She had to be, or Maestro or Fatei would have told him. It didn't matter that he knew, he still had to see her to believe it.

He walked into the entryway, the large foyer with floor-to-ceiling mirrors and gleaming white marble on the floor. Two steps into the great room and he stopped dead. The blankets were downstairs, the fireplace on low. She lay on her stomach on top of the blankets, naked, her long legs sprawled out. Her arms lay casually at her sides, fingertips nearly touching her hips. Her hair was in the inevitable braid she seemed to prefer to sleep in.

She killed him. She looked like the sexiest angel he'd ever laid eyes on. She hadn't gone to bed upstairs—a place he wasn't certain he'd ever be able to sleep in. She'd made up the bed in front of the fireplace and gone to sleep there waiting for him. He pulled off his boots, looking at her the entire time, wondering how he'd manage to get through the night, now early morning, without making a mistake that would get her hurt.

Upstairs, he took a long, hot, much-needed shower, tossing his dirty clothes in a corner. The water felt good, cleansing him of the images of Hammer's wife, Maria, covered in little slices, her body bruised and swollen. If he'd been Hammer, he would have gone on a killing rampage.

He pressed his forehead to the cool tiles, allowing the hot water to run down his back. He'd thought that once they were out of the prison, away from what he considered the worst of human beings, they would discover people like Maria, like Anya, but they kept running across vile, ugly excuses for men and women, those who preyed on the weak. He was tired. Tired of killing. Tired of seeing. Tired of being Reaper. He wanted to be normal so he would deserve Anya. With him, she was never going to get easy.

He shut off the water abruptly. The alternative was to let her go. From the first moment he'd laid eyes on her, he'd known he was going to keep her. He'd made small attempts to save her, but deep down, he knew, even if she'd left, he would have gone after her.

He went down to her naked. Clothes still felt heavy on his body. He was afraid they always would. He lay on top of the blankets next to her, breathing her in. His Anya. Naked, just the way he preferred her. He ran his hand down her back, from her neck to the dip just above the rise of her ass. She had a beautiful ass. He stroked his hand over that curve, feeling possessive.

He leaned into her and used his teeth, taking a bite. Her breath hitched. Her entire body shuddered. He moved over her, his legs trapping hers. He'd taken his time exploring the front of her, claiming every inch; he was going to do the same to the back of her. He kissed his way back up her spine to the nape of her neck.

"You're okay?" She whispered it.

"Do I feel okay?" He used his hands to shape her body, memorizing her form, secretly worshiping her the only way he knew how.

A faint smile was in her voice. "More than okay. I was dreaming about you."

He liked that a fuck of a lot. "Tell me about your dream." He loved the drowsy note in her voice. Sex and sin. It was there, sliding over his skin.

"I dreamt you walked up to the bar when I was working and you kissed me like you do."

"Like I do?" he echoed. "How do I kiss you?"

"Like fire. Like lightning. A storm of fire and lightning."

He liked that a fuck of a lot too. His hands kept stroking, finding her curves, sliding over them. His mouth followed. Kissing her soft skin. Tasting it. He savored the slow burn building inside of him. Coming together with her was usually a firestorm, hot and wild. This was good too. Gentle. Relaxed. He was beginning to think he couldn't survive without her.

"That was your dream? Me kissing you?"

Her mouth curved more. That lower lip made his cock jerk hard against the back of her thigh. He dropped his hand to his aching flesh and fisted it. He could just make out her face turned to one side, looking back at him over her shoulder. He did a slow, lazy pump of his shaft, watching her face, wanting to take her in so many ways, but loving the easy burn growing between them.

"You kissed me over and over until I couldn't think. Then you sat me on the bar and you ate me, pulling me right into your face. It was the most decadent thing ever. I don't know how you got all my clothes off, but you did."

"Were we alone?"

There was a small silence. Her teeth sank into her bottom lip, and he found himself holding his breath, waiting for her answer, his fist tighter now, sliding up and down his cock in earnest. His other hand went between her spread legs and found her slick and hot. He curled one finger into all that heat.

"Anya? Were we alone?"

"No. There were others in the bar, but I couldn't see how many or who. Your mouth drove me wild. I threw back my head and screamed when you made me come."

"I like when you lose control." He pushed a second finger into her tight channel. Her small muscles bit down. That made his cock pulse with need. "Then what happened?"

"You laid me down on the bar. Right on top of it. Your face was shiny and wet and you knelt over me and told me to lick you clean. I did. I couldn't help myself. You looked so sexy. Then you kissed me again, and I could taste myself."

"I love how you taste," he said. He could spend a lifetime devouring her.

He pulled her hips back until she was on her knees, her ass in the air. He put his mouth between her legs and licked at that sweet nectar. His. She gave him everything he asked for. His finger swept between her cheeks, and then his tongue followed. She didn't pull away from him. She pushed back into him.

"Tell me more, baby," he whispered. He put his mouth over her and suckled. Strong. Pulling out the liquid with his tongue, running it up and down her body, claiming every inch of her, inside and out.

"You pulled my legs around your waist and then took me harder than you'd ever taken me, face-to-face, your eyes staring into mine. The bar was hard, and when you pounded into me, you pressed my body right into that rigid slab so I felt every inch of you. It was so beautiful. So perfect. I loved it. I love everything you do to me."

He hoped so, because he had a lot of things he wanted to do to her. He wiped his face on those ass cheeks he was in love with and without waiting, entered her. It didn't matter that he'd gone slow, taken his time, let that burn build. She was hotter than hell, surrounding him with a scorching hot silken fist, gripping him hard, squeezing down until that fire rushed up his spine and spread like a wildfire out of control.

"I can't tell you how many times I sat in the bar, thinking about doing just that, stripping you naked and throwing your ass on the bar. I think I took you a dozen ways. Your mouth. Your pussy. Your ass. All on that bar."

"Were there people in the bar?" Her breath came in ragged little bursts. Hitches. She moaned in between each word.

"Hell if I know. Once my cock was in you, I couldn't see beyond that. I was feelin', baby, not thinking."

He couldn't think anymore. He began to move in her harder, searching for the lightning. Feeling it streak through his body. Long strikes of electricity. Flames danced over him. A thousand tongues licked up his shaft with heat. He held out as long as he could, driving her up three times before he couldn't hold back, his release explosive, his hot seed splashing those sweet walls, triggering dozens of after-shocks.

She collapsed back onto the floor, breathing hard. He lay on top of her, crushing her into the blankets with his heavy weight, but she didn't complain. She reached back and found his hand. "I don't like going to bed without you."

"You don't like going to bed without my cock," he corrected.

"That too," she agreed. "I've got something to show you, but I'm too tired to move."

"Tell me then." He didn't want to move. He liked holding her down. Feeling her under him, knowing she wasn't going anywhere.

"I asked Ink to tattoo your prints on me and he did."

Her voice was so muffled by the blankets scrunched up around her, he didn't believe what he heard at first. Her declaration penetrated slowly and something broke in his chest. Just fragmented and left him unable to move or speak.

Anya squirmed under him. "Reaper? Are you upset with me?"

He slid to the floor on his side, keeping one leg over her thighs so when she turned onto her back, he was still pinning her down. It hurt to breathe, his lungs burning for air. His throat felt raw. "You did what?" The words were a whisper because his voice couldn't go above a thread of sound.

She held up both hands. His heart thudded in his chest. He caught her forearms and brought her hands in close so he could look at her wrists. Silvery, dark chains bound the top of her wrists. He could make out the dark whorls of his thumbprints beneath the chains. He turned her hands over. There were his prints. Marking her his. Declaring to the world she belonged to him. She'd done it. For him. No one had ever, in his entire life, given him a gift. Not once.

This wasn't just a gift. This was . . . enormous. He couldn't move. Couldn't think. She was killing him. Taking him to uncharted territory. He didn't know what to do with the feelings pouring into him, or the intensity of those feelings. A man like him didn't feel. She'd opened some floodgate, and now he knew she wasn't ever going to be free. Not ever. No matter what happened, she was going to have to bear the consequences of her actions. Of giving him her, because he was taking her and keeping her for eternity.

He stared down at the prints. Cleared his throat of the large obstruction there. "Gettin' your prints tatted onto me." Was that even his voice? Shit. He was losing it.

Anya touched his face, her fingers gentle. His heart slammed hard against his chest. "I'm glad you like it. I love the chain. I wanted something unbreakable."

He fucking loved that. Or her. Maybe he fucking loved her. He didn't know what love was, but it might be whatever was killing him inside.

"Next time he puts my prints on you, I want to be there."

She frowned, and he found that adorable. Sickening. He had it bad. He waited and wasn't disappointed. "More of your prints?"

He nodded. "Want them on your ass. Thought about putting a handprint there too, but my fingers will do."

"I'm not going to let Ink tattoo my ass."

He ran his hand down her belly to stop right over her mound. He laid his palm there. "Your body is mine, Anya. I want my prints on it, you'll have my prints on it."

"So, if I want mine all over you, I suppose you'll get them?"

"That's a fuckin' dumb question. Do I belong to you?"

Her lashes swept down. Back up. Exasperation warred with pleasure. "Yes." That was decisive. "You belong to me, although half the time I want to kick you."

"Love that you put my prints on you, baby," he said softly. The weird lump in his throat and the burning behind his eyes were finally gone and he could speak without worrying he was going to blow it. "I've never had anyone give me a gift before and this one is the most . . ." He broke off because the lump and the burning were back. The pressure in his chest increased.

"I'm glad you like it," she whispered.

Her voice wrapped him up. Reaper could only take so much. He leaned over her, deliberately running his fingers over the curve of her breast. "Can't decide whether to tattoo my prints on the curve here, so when you wear a tank everyone can see them, or here." He ran his fingers under the soft mounds, stroking caresses over that soft skin. "Only I would see them."

"Do I get a vote?" Amusement lit her voice. Her eyes.

All that green shone at him in the early morning light. Erased images from the night before. Took him to a good place. "Nope. This is all mine." Lifting his leg, he caught her arms, rolled her over so she was on her belly and then trapped her again by lowering his leg over her thigh. She giggled. It was soft, but he heard it and he found himself smiling. So, this was what fun was. Teasing his woman. Having her give it right back to him.

He smacked her butt because he loved to see his hand-print glowing on her pale skin. She turned her head to glare at him. "Ow. Stop that."

"You like it."

"I do not."

He slid his hand between her legs. "Wet. Slick. Hot as hell. Yeah, baby, you like it." He rubbed out the redness and then repeated the action, spreading more heat across her ass. Playing was fun. He hadn't been taught that. He hadn't been taught that a man and a woman could enjoy each other without the end result being blood and death.

She wiggled her butt at him. "Maybe I do, but only because you make everything sexy." She acted as if she was giving him a great concession.

He spread his hands over her cheeks, pressing his fingers into that firm muscle. "Prints might look nice here." He pressed harder so there was a faint indentation when he lifted his hand. It faded quickly. He bent, swirled his tongue and then bit down. She yelped and glared at him again. "Just checking. I thought maybe my bite mark, but it's not nearly the right thing."

"I think you're obsessing over my butt."

He was. He swatted her again. Studied his handprint. "I like my hand there. I'd have some fun watching Ink tatt your ass. I could swat you a few times, get you hot and bothered, fuck you and then let him ink you."

"Fuck me? In his shop?"

"Right there, baby. Bend you over that chair and take you. Looking at this very nice ass. Gives me all sorts of ideas." He ran his finger between her cheeks. "Like the idea of fuckin' your tits. Want to claim every part of you. Want to fuck your ass. And then there's the possibility of trying something else."

He dipped his fingers deep and then stroked the slickness between her cheeks. He pushed his cock in that warm crease, caught two fistfuls of her buttocks and pressed her cheeks together around him. He moved, sliding his cock through that warmth.

She lay still, her hands cradling her head, face turned to

the side to watch him, those green eyes never leaving his face. She looked utterly relaxed, at peace. That struck him. He could use her body and she let him, liked it. Wanted whatever he did to her. He couldn't fuck her mouth, not yet, but he was determined he would find a way.

"Want you to swallow me down, babe. Want you bathing in my seed. Cover your body in me, so I can watch those long ropes trickle down."

"That can happen." Her voice was soft and amused.

He loved the idea of her covered completely in him, creamy rivers dripping off her. "I'll cover you, wait till it starts to drip off you and take pictures. Blow the best one up, or maybe all of them. Frame 'em. Put them up on the walls and when you're not around, I can jerk off looking at them."

She laughed. "You're so crazy. You getting yourself off now?"

He was pushing his cock between her cheeks, pressing tighter and tighter. His talk was getting him off. The idea of coating her in him. "Yeah, baby, I'm going to get off, so turn over." He backed off her, his heart beating hard again.

She rolled over, looking up at him. He wanted that mouth so much it hurt. "Put your hands above your head. Stretch them out high." Neither could make mistakes. His heart beat so hard he felt it in his cock. He had to be so careful, but even the fact that he was on dangerous ground excited him.

She touched her tongue to her bottom lip, and he groaned. His cock jerked hard and more drops leaked. Good. He needed that. He coated his fingers with more of her slick heat and then rubbed it all over his shaft. He straddled her, sat back down on her belly and pressed her breasts around his cock.

Her chest rose and fell. Her eyes never left his face as he began to fuck her breasts. It was hot watching his shaft sliding between those curves. Watching that broad head slide closer and closer to her mouth. His balls grew tight. Excitement coursed through him.

He was close. Just thinking about it, he was that close. "Open your mouth but keep your head still."

Her long lashes fluttered. Her lips slowly parted. She opened her mouth wide. Just the sight set him off. Fire rushed up his spine. Coiled in his belly. Roared through his groin. He let the first spurt fall across her face, but then he pulled away from her breasts and kept pumping, aiming for her mouth. Left his seed on her tongue. Triumph burst through him. He was in her mouth. *In her mouth.* He hadn't tried to strangle her, or slit her throat. The sight of his seed in her was so erotic the eruption kept coming, ropes of long white cream he wanted to feed to her.

"Swallow. Swallow me." He wanted to be inside of her. Deep. Where she could never get him out. Where she wouldn't care how fucked-up he was and she'd have to stay because her need was as great for him as his was for her.

He aimed the last few eruptions across her breasts. He loved looking at her covered in him, but it was her mouth, her throat, he couldn't take his eyes from. She didn't once look away. She did what he said, slowly swallowing him down. Her throat worked.

"Open your mouth." His heart was going crazy now.

She did. Very slowly. First her tongue slid around her lips as if to get every drop of him then she opened her mouth. His seed was gone. She'd done exactly what he'd asked. That was the exact moment he knew what love was. He knew he was so in love with her there would never be any other woman. Ever. It was Anya or no one.

"Keep your hands there, baby." Now his voice was husky. "You look so beautiful."

"You're a little crazy, Reaper." She said it, but she smiled at him.

"I know. Can you live with my crazy?" He ran his finger through the ropes of cream on her breasts. Rubbed the liquid around her aureoles and nipples. Pinched. Wrote his name. Collected the seed on his fingers and pressed it to her lips. She opened her mouth, and he slipped his fingers in. She sucked. Licked his fingers clean. She was fucking perfect.

"You know something, baby?" He bent his head to kiss her, uncaring that they were both sticky. That she tasted like him.

"I can't wait to find out."

"I'm going to fuck you on that bar. I've fantasized about it so much and knowing you have, I've got to do it."

She laughed, the sound happy. "Please make sure the customers are gone first."

"I'll try. Won't be as much fun without you shrieking, all embarrassed. Gonna fuck you in Ink's shop too. Want him to ink where I spank you. My hand on your ass."

"I might have to draw the line there, Reaper."

"Draw away, baby. I'm fuckin' beat. Have to go to sleep now."

"I have to take a shower."

"You leave me on your skin tonight. Wash me off in the morning." He fed her more of him. He loved watching his fingers disappear into her mouth. The feel of her tongue sliding around and between his fingers, cleaning them, drove him nuts.

She studied his face as if she was thinking of protesting, but in the end, she nodded. He slid off her, rolled her to her side away from him and curled his body around her. He locked his arm under her breasts and buried his face in her hair.

"Did you bring that woman home safely?"

"She's home," he said. "She's alive, and we're not talking about it. I just fucked you, feeling good, babe, don't want to relive that fucked-up mess."

"It's okay, Reaper. Go to sleep. I'm just glad you're home. I was a little scared something might happen to you."

He thought about that as he drifted off. Anya afraid for him while he went off to work. Had anyone been afraid for him before? Czar maybe, but if he was, he hadn't voiced it. Anya was giving him things he didn't know how to process, but they were good things. Everything about Anya was good.

~

Reaper drifted in an erotic tangle of fiery heat. He had Anya on her knees, her face turned up to his, eyes locked on his, his cock, thick and hard, shoved deep down that hot wetness. Para-fucking-dise. He held himself there, savoring that feeling, the power, the sheer submission in her eyes as she gave him whatever he demanded. This wasn't for her. Not at all. This was all for him. She didn't know. Only he knew. She would serve him. Do exactly as he wanted. Hold his cock down her throat until she couldn't breathe, until her eyes went wide with fear and tears formed. Until she saw the blade coming at her throat, but couldn't do a fucking thing about it.

Fists pounded on his thighs. He heard sounds. Muffled screams. That face. That ugly, disgusting excuse for a human being at him again. Using him. Forcing him to do whatever she wanted. Her partner whipping him, pounding on him with his fists. Her laughter echoed in his ears as his partner rammed into him, as pain exploded in his belly. He struck over and over again at that face. Wanting to kill her. *Needing* to kill her. He *would* kill them both.

His eyes snapped open as he reached blindly for the knife he kept close. He realized he had his fist buried in thick hair and he was jerking Anya's head back. His cock was down her throat and his fist hit her cheek, knocking her back and away from him. She crawled like an animal away from him, gasping for breath.

He stared at her in horror, saw droplets of blood on the carpet leading away from him. A single sound escaped his throat. He looked around frantically, for the first time in his life praying, begging whatever powers there were, that he hadn't had a knife. He couldn't move. Couldn't go after her.

He was frozen, just standing there, helpless, silent screams
tearing his throat apart.

~

Anya made it to the wall and pulled herself into a sitting
position, her lungs on fire, her throat raw and sore. The left
side of her face felt mangled, swollen, on fire to rival her
lungs. She turned terrified eyes on Reaper. He let out a howl,
like a wounded animal. Then he was pounding the wall,
over and over, roaring with pain.

Seeing his pain, his hopeless fury, was the worst thing
she'd ever witnessed in her life. She was terrified for him,
not herself. She knew this was the thing Reaper had most
feared would happen. He'd been afraid of killing her. She
didn't know what the trigger was, or why it was a trigger,
but she recognized that there had been one. He'd tried so
hard to keep this from happening, and now, when he knew
he'd hurt her, when he knew he could have killed her, she
was afraid of what he'd do to himself.

His boots were just a few feet from her and next to them
were his neatly folded colors and his phone. She couldn't stop
Reaper from hurting himself, his problems were so far out of
her realm, but she knew there was someone else who could.
She stretched her arm out, not taking her eyes from him.
Blood trickled down her cheek. Her left eye was swelling
shut. She hurt, especially her throat, but it wasn't the physical
pain that was her undoing. Her heart was in a panic. How did
she bring him back from this? How did *she* come back from
this? She would be afraid to go to sleep, and so would he.

Her fingertips caught at the phone and she dragged it to
her. Her throat was so raw and bruised she doubted she could
talk. She wouldn't know what to say to anyone. His phone
was pass-protected, but she'd watched him punch in the
numbers more than once. She did it, scrolled to Czar's name
and hastily typed in: **911 need help with Reaper. Hurry. It's
bad.** Surely Czar would know what to do.

She drew her knees protectively to her chest, tears running unchecked down her face. He had to stop. He was mangling his hands, punishing himself. She wanted him to stop, but she knew he'd leave if he did. He dropped his hands suddenly and turned to face her. She'd never seen a face more ravaged.

"Anya . . ." He broke off, shaking his head. "Baby. I wouldn't hurt you for the world. You have to know I wouldn't ever do anything . . ." He broke off again.

Her heart broke into a million pieces. Reaper. *Her* Reaper. Strong. Invincible. He was crushed. Broken. Tears trickled down his face, and she knew he wasn't even aware of them. He didn't come to her. He just stood there, blood dripping from his knuckles onto the floor.

"I'm leaving, Anya. Just know, in my fucked-up way, I love you. I've never said that to another human being. I love you. I'm sorry for this." His hand started to gesture toward the bed of blankets, but then turned to sweep down his body. "I knew I was fucked-up. I should never have taken a chance on your life." He looked around the room, realized he didn't have his clothes and turned away from her.

She had to stop him. Had to find a way. "Reaper."

He stopped moving, but he didn't turn around. Just shook his head. "No, baby. We don't get past this one. I'm not taking a chance with your life, and I don't think I can live without you." He started back up the stairs.

She knew it. She knew what he was planning. He was going to ride his motorcycle right over a cliff. She'd known he would do it the moment she woke up with his hand in her hair, yanking her to her knees, shoving his cock down her throat. Reaper was rough, but he never hurt her. Never. There had been a difference in his touch. He hadn't been the same man and she knew she was in trouble. She also knew she would recover and get past it, but he wouldn't.

She glanced down at the phone she still clutched in her hand and typed in another message. **I can't stop him by myself.**

If you don't get here, Reaper won't survive. She didn't want Czar to think she was afraid Reaper would leave her. He had to know that Reaper would end his life.

Even as she finished typing the last word and hit send, she heard the sound of bikes. Not one. Several. She took a deep breath, praying the locks wouldn't stop Reaper's family from coming right in.

Reaper was halfway down the stairs when Savage, Ice and Storm came striding in the front door. Absinthe, Steele and Preacher came through the kitchen into the great room. All scanned the room, took in Anya's huddled figure with her swollen face, Reaper's ravished features and mangled fists and then it was Savage who moved first. He walked over to the bed, ripped a blanket off the floor and took it to Anya. He knelt beside her and gently tucked it around her.

"Do you need a doctor?"

His voice was so gentle, tears blurred her vision all over again. She shook her head. "Don't let him go. He'll do something crazy. Please don't let him go." Her voice was a thread of sound and every word hurt.

"Take care of her," Reaper said and came down the rest of the stairs.

Savage regarded his brother as Reaper caught up his boots and sat down to yank them on. "Czar's on his way. Wait for him."

Reaper gestured toward Anya. "I did that. Didn't know what the fuck I was doing and nearly killed her. You think anything Czar says to me, you say to me, or any of you says, including her, will have me takin' that chance again? Not fuckin' likely."

"Reaper, please," Anya said, brokenly. She knew it was a mistake immediately. Her voice was husky, her throat raw and burning, and it showed in her tone. She couldn't speak above a whisper even if she tried.

"Baby, I'm not takin' chances with your life and I'm not fucking living without you."

Czar strode into the room. He looked larger than life. Anya couldn't believe how relieved she felt, as if somehow he could work a miracle when no one else had a clue what to do. He took in the scene, and she saw knowledge on his face. No one had to explain to him what had happened or what Reaper intended to do.

"Everyone take a breath. Reaper, stop scaring her. You haven't lost her. She's not the one threatening to leave. That's you. There's always a solution. Your way is bullshit and you're not going there. One of us might not be able to take you, but there's seven of us here and I can call for reinforcements. Go over there and sit your ass down so I can think."

Anya drew the blanket closer around her. She couldn't stop shaking. Now that help had arrived, shock was setting in. She couldn't stop the burning tears no matter how hard she tried. She also couldn't look away from Reaper, silently begging him to listen to Czar. She hoped that childhood faith would kick in.

Reaper hesitated, looked around at his brothers and then walked over to her. Anya watched him come, shocked, as he got closer, at the lines carved deep, the unchecked tears spilling over. He didn't notice them, he didn't even wipe at them. He slid down the wall right next to her, defeated. His shoulder touched hers. His thigh. She was very cold and her body welcomed the heat radiating off of his.

He sat beside her ramrod stiff and then he slid his arm around her shoulders and pulled her close. "Baby, stop shaking. You're going to break bones shaking like this." His mangled knuckles slid down the side of her face, moving gently over the swelling bruise there.

"Ice, see if you can find water in the fridge for Anya. Steele's going to take a look at your eye and cheek, Anya," Czar said.

She shook her head. She didn't want any of them to look too closely. She didn't want them judging Reaper.

"Yes," Czar said. "Reaper, control your woman."

She opened her mouth to protest and then realized Czar was making Reaper responsible for her. Giving him something to think about other than walking out and driving off a cliff.

"He's right, baby, Steele needs to look at you and see if there's any permanent damage. I don't remember hitting you, but I remember the dream and I was fighting for my life." Again, his knuckles slid down her cheek.

Anya's heart turned over. She leaned her head against Reaper's shoulder. "Don't leave me," she whispered. "We can work through this, I know we can."

Steele knelt in front of her, his hands gentle as they moved over her face. She kept her eyes glued to Reaper's face. He didn't look away from her. Not once. Steele sat back. "No broken bones. You were lucky. The angle probably helped and it looks like you were pulling away from him. Let's get some ice on that."

Storm went into the kitchen just as Ice emerged, handing Anya and Reaper both a bottle of water. Reaper set his on the floor, took Anya's, unscrewed the cap and handed it back to her. She was afraid to take a drink. Her throat felt swollen. It felt as if only a little air could get through at a time. Still, she sipped a little experimentally. It was wet and ice-cold, feeling good on her burning throat.

"Thanks for the rollout," Reaper said. "I'm not crazy now." He started to pull his hands away from Steele, but Czar made a noise in the back of his throat and Reaper subsided, allowing the VP to examine his knuckles.

"You sending us home?" Absinthe asked.

"Trying to. Got some things to work out with my woman," Reaper said. "Czar's right. There's always a solution. I've been thinking on it and I think I've got an answer."

"You want to share?" Czar asked.

"Not likely," Reaper said.

Anya knew he wasn't about to tell them he couldn't tolerate her hands or mouth on his cock. At least, she was positive that was the problem. He hadn't exactly talked to her about it. He'd given her an order not to touch him unless he said it was okay and she hadn't. He'd been the one to touch her. She hoped he'd share his solution with her, because neither of them was going to get much sleep until the situation was resolved.

She pressed the ice to her cheek while Reaper did the same to his knuckles. The club members talked back and forth, mostly she knew to assure themselves that Reaper was in a much better state of mind. Somewhere along the line she drifted off, her head on his shoulder, while the talk swirled around her.

When the club members left, Reaper carried her up to the bathtub, but he didn't tell her what his solution was.

SIXTEEN

Therapy. It wasn't a word bikers threw around, and if they did it, they sure weren't going to talk about it. It had taken him a couple of weeks to work up the nerve to talk to Ice and Storm. He couldn't bring Savage in on his plan because a younger brother had to look up to his older brother. He was the fucking enforcer of the club. Talking therapy with any of them was a risk. They could hold it over his head for the rest of his life.

He knew he had to do something. Two weeks of not sleeping in the same room with his woman was enough to make a man crazy. Worse, it was making her moody. She was doing her best, trying to make herself into the best possible old lady imaginable, but Anya had a temper on her, and the edges of that sweet nature were becoming frayed.

He took her furniture shopping. He bought a washing machine and dryer. He went grocery shopping with her. He insisted she buy a new car. He went with her and, in the end, bought one far out of her price range and paid for it outright. Nothing she said could convince him not to do it, and in the end, she gave in because she knew he was still very upset over what had happened. Yeah, he'd played that bullshit pansy card to make certain she had a safe vehicle.

Preacher refused to allow Anya to work until the swelling went down and the bruising eased. He said it wasn't good for customers to see her face like that in a biker bar. They'd jump to the wrong conclusion. Reaper was happy about the decision. He didn't want people to know he'd struck the woman who meant the most to him in the world. Preacher's decree left her planting flowers in the yard—something Reaper noticed the minute he got home. He stared at them a long time and then smiled at her. A real smile. Those flowers meant something to him. She was planning on staying no matter what. She was making a home for them.

She baked bread. Loaves of it. She braided the bread and made cinnamon loaves. She tried out recipes she thought were kick-ass. Reaper ate the food whether it was great or not. He helped with dishes. He noticed when she did the laundry. Sometimes he was gone with the others for hours, but he never told her what he was doing and she didn't ask, especially if his face was grim.

Their make-out sessions were long and the most amazing thing Reaper had ever experienced, other than sex with her. The sex was wild, but she was always on her hands and knees, facing away from him. He was inventive in that position, in every position where she faced away from him, but after a while he wasn't satisfied and he knew she wasn't either. He wanted to look into her eyes. He wanted to hold her, fall asleep with his body wrapped around hers.

She didn't say anything about the sex, but she was upset that she was upstairs and he was downstairs. He didn't like Anya upset over anything. So . . . he had to find a way to fix it. The idea sickened him, but it had to be done. For her. Ice and Storm agreed. Ice read everything. He read up on the various therapies, and they'd discussed what to do over and over. The twins urged him to get moving on their plan, but he'd been putting it off, reluctant to go through with it. The idea made his skin crawl. He had nightmares every night, and just thinking about it made him break out in a sweat.

Reaper tossed back his third whiskey, let it burn down his throat, hoping it would dull the edges of his mind. He couldn't put it off any longer. Every time he saw his woman, even if she was across the room, like now, he was as hard as a rock and he needed to be normal. To be like other men so he wasn't afraid he'd kill the woman he loved just because she touched him. Preacher had allowed her to come back to work. Reaper had taken Anya to Santa Rosa to get clothes and she was wearing one of the kick-ass outfits. The jeans were straight-legged so she could wear the soft leather boots he'd bought her.

He especially liked her in those jeans, because she'd worn them a few days after they bought them and he could barely peel them off of her when they were frantic to get at each other. They'd ended up together on the floor laughing. He'd actually laughed. The woman could tame the devil if she was in the mood. He couldn't help thinking about what had happened after he'd gotten the jeans off of her.

He took another sip of whiskey, his eyes on Anya. He knew she was watching him. Ice and Storm had joined him—a rarity. He was drinking hard alcohol, something Anya had never seen him do. She was worried, and he couldn't blame her. He sat back, studying her through half-closed eyes. She was so beautiful she could take a man's breath. Her hair, usually worn in a high ponytail for work or a braid, was pulled back with a thick clip at the back of her neck so the silky mass fell in waves to the middle of her ass. Every man in the room was looking every time she turned her back to grab a bottle.

"You got to get this done," Ice said. "You're like some edgy beast, Reaper. What's the big deal? We'll be there to make certain nothing bad happens."

He wasn't going to discuss his feelings with Ice or Storm.

The two of them sat there, putting away nearly as much whiskey as he was, and they weren't the ones who had to get therapy. He winced at the word. How did civilians do that sort of thing? He wasn't spilling his guts to some bored idiot who would be all superior and lord it over him that he was so screwed up he couldn't let his woman blow him.

He closed his eyes, groaned and pressed his whiskey glass to his forehead. He could have sworn Storm snickered, and his eyes snapped open and he glared. He'd threatened the twins with death by the worst torture imaginable, but even then, the look they exchanged alarmed him. Now, it was ten times worse. They knew he was fucked-up. They didn't know why and he wasn't telling them. He wasn't telling anyone. Certainly not a therapist. Still, he had to do something before his woman ran out of patience with him.

"Don't be such a pussy, Reaper," Storm said. "What's the worst that can happen?"

"I kill someone?" He snapped the question right back, but that wasn't the worst. Not for him. The thought of another person anywhere near him. A woman not Anya. He rubbed the glass across his forehead again. He had to do this. He had to go through with it. He'd do anything for Anya—even this.

"We're not going to let that happen," Ice said.

Reaper swung his gaze to Ice's face. Studied it. There was no trace of amusement anywhere on his tough features. Not in his eyes. He was serious, and he wanted Reaper to know it. The twins might give him a hard time, but they were in this with him, fully committed.

"Don't like the idea, but I know I gotta do it," he said and tossed back the entire contents of the glass.

"You should be lookin' forward to it," Storm said. "Getting blown can take you to another planet."

Ice scowled. "Are you out of your fuckin' mind, sayin' something like that? You've been watching too much porn."

"Maybe we ought to film Reaper getting his rocks off,"

Storm continued. "It could inspire him when he needs a reminder."

Fury burst through him. Sweat broke out and trickled down his body. "Fuckin' shut the hell up, Storm," Reaper snapped. "I'm going to pound you into the ground if you don't."

"And I'll help," Ice said.

This was worse than Reaper thought it was going to be. Feeling eyes on him, he looked up to see Anya staring across the room, her green gaze speculative. Yeah, now there was real trouble, because his woman was smart. She figured things out fast. They had to go. Get this over. He stood up abruptly. It was now or never.

He didn't wait for Ice and Storm. He strode to the bar, beckoning to Anya with his finger. She came straight to him, ignoring the calls for drinks. He caught her under her arms and pulled her up onto the bar. She scooted on her butt around, dropping her legs over. His hands went to her waist and he lifted her down to the floor, set her on her feet, and took her mouth all in one motion.

The moment her lips parted for his, that familiar fire swept through him. She just had a way of lighting that stick of dynamite. His heart contracted when she gave him everything. Right there. Right in front of the world. She didn't care if the world was watching. She let them know she belonged to him.

"Honey, you going to eat me out right now in front of the world?" she whispered. "Sit me up on the bar and go at it?"

"Would you let me, baby?"

She smiled at him. "I'd let you do just about anything."

His chest exploded. He could do this for her. He *had* to do this for her. He wrapped his arms around her and held her tight, burying his face in her neck, breathing her in. He needed the comfort. He needed to know why he was doing such an asinine, very risky thing. It was for Anya. For his woman and he could do anything for her.

"Honey."

Anya's hand slid up his back. Rubbed. Went to the nape of his neck. Massaged. She knew how to make him feel good. Special. Like she cared about him. As if he was the only man in the world for her. She was a great old lady. The best a man could have. He had to step up and be that man for her. He was determined to work through his problem no matter what it took or how long.

A shudder of revulsion went through him. She felt it. How could she not? She tried to pull back to look at him, but he refused to allow it. She saw too much. She always did. He wanted to tell her he loved her, but the feeling was too overwhelming and choked him.

"Goin' to the clubhouse. If I'm not back to walk you to your car, or take you home on the bike, have Fatei or Preacher get you safely home." His voice didn't even sound like it belonged to him. It was gruff. Impersonal. He still couldn't look her in the eye so he gave the order into her neck.

Abruptly, Reaper put her aside, turned on his heel and left the bar. Ice and Storm nearly knocked over chairs in their haste to follow him. He went straight to his Harley and forced himself to head toward the clubhouse when he wanted to go home. To smell Anya, pull her deep into his lungs. He wanted to put her on the back of his bike and go for a long ride. A road trip. Somewhere safe for both of them—but there was nowhere Anya was safe until he got a handle on his trauma.

He fucking hated the word *trauma*. Blythe liked to use it to describe what her kids had suffered. *Trauma*. What the fuck did that even mean? That he couldn't sleep? How did that word describe what had happened to him? To any of them? Or the end results. They were fucked-up. *Trauma* was just a word people used to soften the blow. He was damaged. Broken. Couldn't be fixed.

How the hell could therapy fix him? Nothing could ever fix him. He was that fucked-up. He got off his bike and stood beside it, looking at the clubhouse. Ice came up on one side of him. He took a breath and shook his head.

"Feels wrong, Ice. It isn't going to work. Something bad could happen here. What's the difference between someone you call a surrogate and the bitch from hell getting her rocks off on torturing kids?"

"Surrogate's tryin' to help you get over the bitch from hell. You read the article. She stands in for Anya, trains you not to have triggers that bring up traumatic events." Ice quoted the article. "Plus, this way, you're not takin' any chances that you clock Anya again. You can't go to the real thing, so this is the next best thing. It can work, just let it."

Reaper's stomach lurched. The moment he had been fully awake, when he knew he had punched Anya, worse, he'd violated her, he'd been sick to his stomach. That feeling hadn't diminished in the last two weeks. There was no other word in his vocabulary for what he'd done. He knew she hadn't consented. He'd been exactly what they'd made him into. He'd been forced to repeat their words over and over, thousands of times, those lies, telling him it was his right to take by force whatever he wanted from a woman, a man, a child. They had been determined to shape him into one of them. He had become that very thing he despised with the woman he loved.

It could never happen again. *Never*. He'd endure anything to ensure Anya was safe from him. He'd walk barefoot and naked into the flames of hell. Letting another woman touch him? His entire body shuddered at the idea. His stomach rolled again.

"Maybe I should talk to Anya about this. Make sure she's okay with it." But he knew what she would say. What she'd already said, over and over. It didn't matter. She could live without ever going down on him. She would be careful, follow his directions. She wanted to sleep with him. She'd be careful not to touch him.

He wasn't certain she had touched him first. *Fuck*. Why was he so screwed up? Why couldn't his woman be all over him the way he was all over her? Why couldn't he shut out those fuckers' voices? Why couldn't he forget the things they'd done to him? The things they'd forced him to do to others?

Anya. Her laughter turned his world around. She made him better. He had no idea why, other than when he was with her, those demons receded. They were pushed back so far he could almost close that door in his head to keep them locked away. He was afraid if he couldn't keep bolts on that door, he would lose her. He would hurt her again, and he'd never forgive himself. Never. That wasn't the worst that could happen. He could kill her.

He touched his heart with shaking fingers. He'd done exactly what he'd told her he would. Ink had taken Anya's fingerprints and tattooed them over his heart. He'd added the unbreakable chain right over them, weaving her name into the links. He'd done the same on his left wrist, the chain forming a bracelet just like hers, with her prints on his inner wrist. He looked at it, needing courage. Reminding himself why he was putting himself in this position.

"Man up, Reaper," Storm encouraged. "This is for your woman."

Reaper swore. He was sweating and he wiped the beads from his forehead. Some ran down his face. A few more trickled down his chest. He went into the clubhouse, clenching his teeth, knowing it was a bad idea, but not knowing what else to do. His head hurt so bad that every step pounded through his mind like a jackhammer digging at him relentlessly.

"You sure you two can stop me if I try to kill her?" he asked. "It's a very real possibility." He was already feeling a little murderous toward the woman. His mouth was dry. So dry he could barely get words out.

"There's two of us. You don't have any weapons, right? No knife?" Storm inquired, suddenly looking worried.

Reaper stopped in the middle of the common room. "For

fuck's sake, Storm. Don't act like we didn't go over this a million times. Can you stop me?" His heart raced hard, putting so much pressure in his chest he thought he might be having a heart attack.

It was Ice who answered. "We can stop you. All it's going to take is to drag you away from her. The moment either of us puts our hands on you, you'll go after us. A few punches and you'll know who you are and who we are."

The confidence in Ice's voice steadied him. Reaper took another deep breath. "What did you tell her?" God. *God.* He couldn't do this. He couldn't let another woman put her hands on him. No one touched him. No one but Anya.

"I was bringing a brother for a birthday surprise. I told her I wanted her to give you the best blow job of your life, but to do a lot of hands-on stroking. That you like that. Told her to blow your mind. Of all the club girls, she's got the best mouth."

Reaper didn't want to know that. He didn't want to have her hands on him, let alone her mouth. He swore, his stomach in such tight knots he was afraid he'd vomit all over the woman.

"Think in terms of her helping you get over this," Ice encouraged. He urged Reaper into the hallway leading to the rooms.

Just knowing the woman was in his room made Reaper feel sick. Angry. Tense. Hell, he didn't know what he was feeling except this was all wrong. He stopped again, just outside the room. He was never going back in there knowing this woman had invaded his territory. He'd make Czar assign him another room.

"Wait. Really. I think I should talk about this to Anya."

"She'll say no and you'll be back to square one," Storm pointed out.

"Anya could do this. With you two there, there's no way she could get hurt." Reaper backed a few steps from the door. "I think I'll wait until I talk it over with her."

He couldn't breathe anymore. Tremors ran through his body and that blinding rage was close. So close he could taste it. Metallic. Like copper. Blood. Blood in his mouth from biting down, trying not to feel. Trying to go someplace in his mind where he could block out pain and humiliation.

The door to his room opened, and one of the club women was there. He couldn't remember her name, but she liked to be with more than one man at a time. He couldn't—or refused to—focus on her, so his vision remained blurry. She was indistinct, just like Helena. Even remembering the bitch's name struck him like a blow. The woman in front of him became even more indistinct.

Somewhere he heard Ice hissing at him to use his discipline, and knew he was supposed to force his body to cooperate, but for the first time in his life since he'd been trained, he couldn't. His cock refused to get hard. He didn't want this woman to touch him. She wasn't Anya. His body wanted one woman. He couldn't do what he'd been trained to do. He stepped back away from her, shaking his head.

"Reaper." She was practically purring. She went down to her knees in front of him. "I didn't think I'd ever have a chance with you. I'll make this so good for you, sugar. You're going to feel so good."

The more he backed away, the more persistent she became, shuffling forward on her knees, her fingers busy at his belt. He felt them, but they didn't seem real to him. It was as if she had faded so far into his past he was in two places at the same time. He stepped back a second time. Bumped the wall. He half turned to face the attack coming at him from the rear.

The woman shuffled forward on her knees again. Caught at his zipper. He had nowhere to go. He shook his head, sweat pouring off him. "No." He said it distinctly. He screamed it over and over in his mind. No. He didn't want anyone touching him. Then. Now. It was his body. His right to say no. He said it. He meant it.

The hands stroked at the front of him. Greedily. He felt that greed. His body shuddered again, revulsion so strong he knew the woman had to die. He knew the attack would come from behind him, the blows that would bring him to his knees, the shove that would force him into her ugly mouth. The whip striking him over and over. Pain blossoming through his body, the threats, the burns. The worst.

Dimly, far away, he heard Ice. "Tawny, stop. He said no. Something's wrong."

"Get away from him." That was Storm.

"I'll make him feel so good," the woman insisted.

He had to stop her. She couldn't put her hands on him. He reached for the knife he kept close. It wasn't there. *It wasn't there.* The roaring in his head grew louder. Fingers touched his skin and the well of rage deep inside him opened up to allow the monster out, the monster that would defend him. The one that protected him and protected all the others. He would snap her neck. He reached for her head, grasped her hair.

"You lying, cheating bastard."

The voice broke through the veil. Her voice. Anya. He hadn't caught the actual words, only her voice. It was like a clear wind blowing through the past, pushing it back so he could slam that door closed. So he could draw in air. Find breath. He turned his head and she came into his line of sight.

There was horror on her face. Knowledge of betrayal. Pain. The pain was plain, there for him to see, for everyone to see. He realized he still had the woman's head gripped in two fists. Her fingers had brushed his cock. His stomach lurched. He stumbled sideways and back, away from her, dropping his shaking hands. His muscles hurt, felt cramped. Locked. Hurting almost as bad as that terrible look on Anya's face.

"It isn't what you think," Ice said.

"Anya, just listen." Storm took a step toward her, his hand outstretched pleadingly.

"Anya . . ." Reaper couldn't get his mouth to work. He was frozen. In shock. His body didn't feel as if it belonged to him.

"Fuck you, Reaper. She can have you. Don't worry, I won't cry or whine. I'm gone." Anya spun around and ran from the room.

Ice let out a long, high-pitched whistle of warning to anyone in the clubhouse. Storm was on his cell group-texting the others. Reaper tried to go after her, but his pants were down around his knees and he stumbled and went down.

"Fuckin' stop her!" he yelled to the twins. "Don't you let her go!"

Ice broke into a run while Reaper fought to get his jeans up. He was still disoriented, but he knew that he'd just made the worst mistake of his life.

~

Anya still had her car keys in her hand, which was a good thing since her vision was blurred from the tears she'd told Reaper she wasn't about to shed. The pain was visceral. Gutting her. She bent over, clutching her stomach, afraid her intestines would spill out onto the ground.

Tawny. Anya didn't hang around the clubhouse, but in the weeks she'd been there, Tawny had come into the bar and was all over the men. She'd made it clear she thought the men were hers. All of them. She even went after Czar a few times, although he'd shut her down hard. It was rumored she wanted every one of the members of Torpedo Ink, and she was willing to take them a few at a time, or all. Of all the women he could have chosen to cheat with . . .

Anya had lied her ass off. She was sobbing so loudly she wouldn't have been surprised if she scared off all wildlife in a hundred-mile range. She actually tripped, unable to see where she was going because her vision was so blurry.

She yanked open the door to her car. Someone took the keys right out of her hand. She whirled around, prepared to fight, afraid it was Reaper with some lame excuse she'd probably be too weak to ignore. It was Lana.

"Honey, whatever is wrong, you can't drive a car in that state."

"I've got to get out of here," Anya said. Crying. Sobbing. Wiping viciously at the tears. "Right now. I have to go."

"Then we'll go. Get in the passenger side. I'll drive."

Anya did what Lana said because she couldn't bear to face Reaper and he might appear any moment. Or maybe he wouldn't. Which would be worse? She hated him. *Hated* him. "What's wrong with me, Lana?" She covered her face with her hands.

Behind them the doors in the back opened and two men slid in. Ink and Absinthe shut the doors and ignored her when she turned to glare at them. It was hard to maintain an evil eye when she couldn't stop crying like a baby.

"Get out. Men aren't welcome."

"Lana, drive," Ink said softly. "We're a family, Anya. Whether you like it or not, you agreed to be part of us. We took you in. That means when you're hurting, we look after you."

Lana didn't wait for another invitation. She put the car in gear and drove away from the clubhouse. "Where do you want to go?"

"The house. I have to get my things. My cash."

Lana glanced in the rearview mirror as three Harleys fired up. Maestro, Keys and Player swung in behind them.

"Darlin'," Ink said gently. "Tell us what happened."

"You didn't see? You didn't see Reaper's jeans around his butt and some woman on her knees, her hands all over his cock, mouth wide open? Because, let me tell you, it's burned into my memory forever."

There was silence in the car, other than her wild sobbing. Anya tried desperately to get herself under control. She should have known letting herself believe she had a home and family would be her downfall. It was a huge one. She'd invested her heart. All-in. Everything. No reserve. She hadn't seen this one coming. She believed it would be impossible not to trigger Reaper's memories of the traumas he'd suffered. She was prepared for that. She would have fought for him, fought beside him, done anything necessary to stay with him and find a way to work it out.

Another woman. A club woman. *Tawny.* One who went from man to man. He'd thrown her away for casual sex. Not a love affair, not a woman he met and fell for, but a woman who would give him a blow job and turn and give one to Ice and Storm immediately after. He didn't care about that woman. He didn't want a relationship . . .

Her wild thoughts settled. He didn't want a relationship. All along he'd been stumbling, trying to tell her, and she just didn't pick up on the clues. She stared out the window, forcing great gulps of air into her burning lungs to get herself under control. Women all over the world had this happen to them. The love of their life didn't love them back. They survived. She could survive.

She pressed her fingers to her trembling mouth, aware Lana, Ink and Absinthe were shocked at what she'd told them. The silence was awkward, but she wasn't going to fill it.

"Let's drive around first," Lana suggested. "Just until you're not so upset. We can go sit at the headlands or go to one of the parks. The ocean is always soothing to me when I'm upset."

Anya tried to force a smile, but she just couldn't make it. Inside, she felt smashed. Fragmented. Alone again. So alone. She shivered and wrapped her arms around her middle. Holding tight. She just had to hold on tight.

"I just need to get back to the house, Lana. I don't want him to show up and give me some lame-ass explanation. If I had a gun, I'd shoot the bastard."

Lana glanced at Ink in the rearview mirror. He gave her a small shake of the head, mouthed, *Blythe,* and went back to his phone, trying to get a reasonable explanation for why Reaper would do such a thing. Anya turned around.

"You better not be talking to Reaper," she said. Her heart accelerated again. "Ink, I need you to put away your phone or get out of the car."

Ink put his phone down immediately. "A man like Reaper doesn't tatt you into his skin, Anya, not if he's going to throw you away," he said softly. "I know what you think you saw, but there was more to it than that. There's an explanation."

"I don't want to hear it," Anya said. "I told him if ever there was another woman, *any* woman, we were done. We both laid the rules down, and we both knew what they were. He chose that woman. *Chose* her instead of coming to me."

She was crying all over again. She'd been so stupid to believe Reaper could fall in love with her. Men like Reaper didn't fall in love. They used women for their purposes and threw them away. He'd even warned her. Right up front. When he was done, it was done, no crying and whining to him. He wouldn't get that. She might not be able to stop sobbing, but she wasn't doing it in front of him. Not. Ever.

She had to go back and get her things. Fuck him, she was keeping the car too. He might have paid for it, but it was in her name. She was going to get out of there, drive so far away from him that she could never go back because she wouldn't have the money. Alaska was looking good. A cruise ship. She could work a cruise ship, they always needed bartenders, didn't they?

"You're getting a little crazy," Lana said. "A cruise ship?"

She'd said it out loud. What else was she saying? Anya pressed her fingers over her mouth. She had to get out of there.

"I was texting Ice, Anya. He was there. I was just trying to get a sense of what really happened so we could talk this out. You can't just go home, get your things and drive away."

It was taking too long. They should have been at Reaper's house by now. She glanced out the window through blurry eyes and saw they were on the highway. She knew immediately where they were taking her. Czar and Blythe. The go-to couple. The problem solvers.

"They can't solve this one," she murmured aloud.

Lana didn't need an explanation for her fragmented conversations. "They don't need to solve anything, Anya. You're hurting, in no condition to drive, that means we take care of you. Blythe can do that better than anyone else."

"I need my clothes."

"We can get them later. Just let us take care of you." She turned off the highway and drove between the gates leading to the farm Blythe owned with her five other "sisters." Women she'd chosen as family.

So this was what it was like to have a family. To have people who surrounded you when things had gone horribly wrong. It was annoying as hell. She *had* to leave. She felt almost desperate to get out of the area. She couldn't be anywhere she and Reaper had been together.

"You have to tell Czar I'm quitting. I'm sorry about not giving notice." She burst into a fresh flood of tears. Of course Czar would know. All of them would know Reaper had cheated on her. They texted one another constantly. It was utterly humiliating to know Blythe stood outside on her porch waiting to comfort her because she knew already, before Anya had the chance to tell her what a complete and utter bastard Reaper was.

Lana parked the car right in front of the house. Anya just sat there, even when motorcycles swept into the yard behind them. At first, there were only a couple, but then it seemed as if the entire yard was full of the big machines. She buried her face in her hands. She *had* to stop crying. She'd told Reaper she was a big girl. When it was over she'd walk away and never contact him again. There would be no crying and whining. No begging him to take her back. No jealousy that he had another woman.

She wanted to scream to the heavens. *Screw him.* The least

he could have done was act like a man and tell her straight up it was over. That's what a real man would have done.

"Anya." Ink opened her door and reached in for her, his hands gentle as if she were the most fragile creature alive.

She was acting exactly as she'd promised herself—and Reaper—she wouldn't. "I'm fine, really, Ink. It was just such a shock. I was worried about him. He'd been drinking heavily and he doesn't do that. I asked Preacher to let me off early because I thought I should take him home. How stupid. I was worried about him."

How many times had he snuck off to get blow jobs from someone who wasn't her? She wanted to pound him into the ground. Ink was urging her out of the car, his hand around her biceps, tugging. She didn't want to get out and face everyone. She just sat there, staring down at the fingerprints on her wrists.

She looked up at Ink. Blinked away the tears until he came into focus. "Can you get rid of them for me? I don't think I can look at them for the rest of my life."

"Sure, honey. Let's get you out of the car."

He agreed so readily she didn't believe him, but she got out of the car because she knew she'd never get out of there until she pulled herself together. She straightened her shoulders, took a quick look around and saw the various members of the club were scattered around the yard like silent sentries. It was dark. She couldn't make out their faces, but she knew them. She went up the stairs, and Blythe put her arm around her shoulders and took her from Ink.

Ink stayed outside. Anya was grateful for that. She didn't want him to witness whatever was said between Blythe and her. Czar wasn't anywhere in sight, and she was grateful for that as well. She didn't want to talk to any of them. Not even Blythe.

"I've got the kettle on," Blythe said. "I don't know why, but whenever there is a crisis of any sort, tea always seems to make it better. Do you drink it?"

Anya nodded. "There was an older gentleman who would occasionally come to the shelters when I was a child. Everyone knew he didn't belong there. He was class, pure class."

Blythe took her through the house to the kitchen, and Anya found a small comfortable chair she could curl up into while Blythe made the tea. She was grateful Blythe hadn't asked about Reaper. Not yet. She needed time to gather her composure. Blythe seemed to understand that.

"His name was Chandler Barret. He talked about his mother making tea the proper way. He said she used the ritual to calm everyone down if they'd had a bad time or were angry." She lifted her gaze to Blythe's. "I think this qualifies for both, don't you?"

"Absolutely it does," Blythe answered. She looked up from where she was putting together a tray. "There's plenty of tissue right there. And if you need to scream, do it. Just please don't smash my dishes. These are the ones I never use around the children."

Anya found herself capable of a small smile and that amazed her. Astounded her. Maybe Blythe really did work miracles. "Why do they all think you can fix anything? Even before Reaper, when I first was bartending, and around the others so much, I heard them talking about you like you could walk on water."

Blythe sent her a small smile in return as she poured boiling water into the teapot. "Czar thinks I walk on water and can fix anything, so he convinced all of them. He brought me the three girls: Darby, Zoe and Emily. The club brought me Kenny. I expect there will be others."

"Do you mind?"

"The children? No, I love them. I won't mind more if they need a home and family. We'll give it to them. I can't give birth to children, and I've found it doesn't matter, although I would have loved to have a little replica of Czar running around." She gave a little laugh. "Kenny might just be that. He walks like him and talks like him. He does all the little things that Czar does. He worships that man."

"They all do."

"He saved them. Well, he taught them how to save themselves by banding together. Each had specific roles and carried them out. He saved their lives, and he's expecting me to save their souls. That's what he says anyway." She picked up the tray. "Let's go into the other room. The chairs are comfortable in there."

Anya thought the chairs were comfortable enough in the kitchen, but she followed Blythe into the spacious great room and waited until she put the tray down. No one else appeared to be in the house. "Where is everyone?"

"The children are sleeping. Anya, it's two in the morning."

Anya was used to the night hours. She glanced out the window into the darkness. She hadn't heard the motorcycles start up. In fact, she'd heard a few more arrive. "Of course. I work at night, so I lose track of time. Why don't they all go home?" She waved toward the outside.

Blythe understood her gesture. "You're family and you're hurting. That means they hurt. I hurt. None of us likes it, Anya."

Anya's hands were shaky as she accepted the teacup. She wrapped both hands around it, needing the warmth. "Reaper cheated with some club woman. I've seen her around." She ducked her head and forced air into her lungs. "I was willing to do anything for him. He has so many issues and it isn't easy being with him, but I thought he was worth it."

Blythe stirred a spoonful of honey into her tea. "He does have issues," she agreed. "All of them do. Still, like you, I believe they're worth it and whoever has the courage to stand with them will have someone who will love and care for them all the way to the end. I believe Reaper is like that, Anya. I don't know how this all came to be, but I do think you have the right to know. You have the right to look him in the eyes and demand an explanation."

"I thought I'd do that," Anya admitted and took a small sip of the hot tea. She needed it. She was shaking with cold. Or shock. It didn't matter which it was. The heat of the tea seeped into her chilled cells, trying to warm her. "But then I realized an explanation didn't really matter. I saw him with my own eyes."

"What did you see?" Blythe asked. "Every detail. Tell me."

"I was worried so I got off early and went to the clubhouse," Anya replied in a little rush to get it over with fast. "He wasn't in the common room so I went to the back, going down the hallway. I could see him standing in front of his room. The door was open and the woman—Tawny—was on her knees with her hands on his cock. She had her face upturned toward him and her mouth wide open as if she was just about to take him in her mouth." Her stomach lurched. "I can't talk about it. I'll be sick."

"What was he doing?" Blythe persisted. "How was he acting?"

Anya shook her head, tears starting all over. "I wasn't focused on him. The moment I saw her, she was all I could see. That woman with the man who was supposed to belong to me."

Blythe indicated her tea. "Don't let it get cold." She waited until Anya took another sip before she spoke. "You can't expect any of them to know the right thing to do in a situation. One that calls for action, this crew is the best, but regular everyday matters? No. They haven't a clue. Someone with a deep sexual issue? Absolutely not. They might be silly enough to listen to one of their brothers who read an article in a magazine about using a surrogate for sex. They might be so desperate to keep their woman that they allow their brother to talk them into trying to use a surrogate to overcome whatever the problem is."

Anya put down her teacup. "It doesn't matter what the reason was, Blythe. Would you live with Czar after he let some other woman do that to him?"

"She didn't actually do it," Blythe pointed out. "You don't know what would have happened had you not arrived. He might have stopped her. From the two thousand texts I'm getting, there appears to be more to it than met the eye."

"I only know I saw her there on her knees. He let another woman do something he would never let me do." She put her hands flat on the arms of the chair and pushed herself up. "Thank you for the tea, Blythe, but I can't stay. I know what you're trying to do, and I'm grateful. Believe me, I am. I've never had caring before, and this felt like it. It's just that I'm not strong enough to keep going back to get kicked in the teeth. How does one recover?"

Blythe stood up too. "I don't know, Anya, but I do know, if you can do it, it would be worth it. At least listen to him. Hear him out."

Anya shook her head. It wouldn't matter what he said. Her more than healthy dose of self-preservation was kicking in, stronger than ever, and telling her to run like hell as far and fast as she could.

SEVENTEEN

※

Blythe stood up as well and hugged her. "I hope you find peace, Anya."

That brought a fresh flood of tears. Blythe brought her peace. She probably brought it to Czar and any of the others that stayed around her. "I'll miss you," she said softly. "I wish I had more time to get to know you."

"I wish I could persuade you to stay."

Anya clung for a minute, wishing the same, but she knew she had to go. Deep inside there was a blaring warning signal that wouldn't leave her alone. It was telling her she had to leave immediately. To run. Her clothes and money were back at the house. She just had to get them and get on the road.

Blythe went with her to the porch. Motorcycles were parked all over the yard. Some were behind her car. Anya went straight to the two sitting on them. "You're going to have to move."

"Where you headed?" Maestro asked.

"Back to the house. Would you please move?"

Both men nodded. "Didn't mean to park in the wrong spot. I think Czar needs to paint stripes for designated parking."

"Yeah," Player agreed. "Might have to suggest that to him." He leaned down and fiddled with something on his bike.

Anya heaved a sigh and walked around the bikes to get to her car. The men waited to move until she had turned on the engine. She hadn't spotted Lana anywhere, but when she started up the car, she was suddenly on the porch, Ink and Absinthe beside her. She could see them in her rearview mirror. Lana swung onto the back of Ink's bike, and Absinthe got behind Maestro, further delaying her as she had to wait for Absinthe, who sauntered down the porch stairs over to Maestro, had a small exchange before he climbed on the back and the motorcycles backed up and then swung around to leave in front of her.

She wanted to scream at them to hurry up. When they turned onto the highway, in the direction she needed to go, trapping her behind them, she sighed and decided to use the time to plan instead of raging. She needed to know exactly what to do. She was a planner, and until she got things settled in her mind, chaos would rule her head.

The motorcycles didn't turn off to go to the clubhouse, but led the way to Reaper's home. Thankfully, she didn't see his motorcycle. She parked the car, waved the motorcycles away and ran into the house. She took the stairs two at a time, dragged her old duffel bag from the closet and tossed it on the bed. Her cash was stashed in her duffel bag. She threw two pairs of jeans, several tees, sweaters, socks, and underwear into it. She hesitated. She didn't have a picture of Reaper and knew that was a good thing. Her sketch pads were covered with him. Still, she reasoned, knowing she was lying to herself, she needed the sketch pads. She could always throw away the drawings of him. They went in her bag, and then she ran down the stairs.

She nearly ran right into Reaper. He caught her by the shoulders to steady her. Anya jerked away instantly. "Don't you touch me," she hissed, pulling back so hard she stumbled.

"Anya, you have to listen to me."

"No, Reaper, I really don't," she said. "Get out of my way."

He shook his head. "No. You're going to listen."

She stepped toward the door. He glided between her and her way out. He did it easily, as if he hadn't drunk all the whiskey in the world.

"Get out of my way."

"I said no. You're going to listen to me. After that, if you still want to go . . ."

He hadn't said he'd let her. Desperation set in. Reaper could talk her into anything. She'd looked once at his face. Her heart had stuttered. Butterflies had taken wing in her stomach. He looked as destroyed as she felt, and that worthless part of her that needed to fix him, that couldn't stand him hurt, had risen up to try to comfort and save him. Not her. She wasn't going to be that person.

She swung the bag at him. Hard. He dodged it and when she tried to get around him, he blocked her way again.

"Just calm down and let me talk to you. I can explain what happened."

"I'm sure you can, Reaper. You always have an explanation for everything, don't you? I don't want to hear this one. I'm done. I'm all explained out. I was patient. I gave you every opportunity to talk to me, but you chose not to. You made your choice with Tawny. Hell, you gave your cock to her. That was more than you ever did for me." He winced, and she hated herself for being a bitch.

"Baby."

She dropped her duffel bag and pushed at him. Hard. Both hands on the wall of his chest. He didn't even rock back. He just caught her hands in both of his and pulled her in close. She was waiting for that. She knew him, she knew he'd take advantage. She brought her knee up hard between his legs. He howled. Let her go. She whirled around, caught up the duffel bag and ran out of the house to her car.

It wasn't there. She looked around blankly. Shocked. Of all times for a car to get stolen, this was the worst ever. She dropped the bag, fished around until she got her bankroll, shoved it into her pocket and started up the drive at a jog.

Ice moved out of the shadows into her path, forcing her to stop. "Can't let you go, honey," he said. "Go back into the house."

Club members moved then, coming out from cover of darkness, surrounding her. She caught sight of Maestro and Player. They'd been stalling her. Waiting for Reaper to get home. What had taken so long? Had he stayed to comfort Tawny? Let her finish the job? Her mind just couldn't go there, but it did, and it wouldn't stop, looping the two scenarios in her head, over and over.

"All of you?" She turned in a circle. "Lana? Even you?"

"For you, Anya," Lana said. "Just listen to him. After, if you're certain you want to leave, I'll help you."

"You'll do what's best for her and Reaper," Ink said. "Just like all the rest of us."

"You don't get to make that decision," Anya said. "I have rights as a human being."

"Those rights include fucking up?" Ice asked.

"Yes, as a matter of fact they do," she snapped back.

"Too bad, honey. We don't want you fucking up," Storm said. "I think Ice and I have taken the cake in that department. Someone has to have some sanity. That someone is you. Go in and listen to him. As crazy as it sounds, every word is the truth."

Czar stepped out of the darkness. "Anya, I stayed back when Lana took you to Blythe, so I could talk to Reaper. That's where he's been. That's where Ice and Storm have been. If I didn't believe their idiotic explanation, I wouldn't have agreed to holding you here to listen. Reaper swears he'll tell you everything. Not just what they were attempting, but why he believed it to be necessary. If you want to leave after that, I'll personally escort you off the property."

They weren't giving her any way out. She looked around her. In the dark, it was hard to distinguish features, but those she could see held regret and upset. No one appeared to like what they were doing, but they were resolved to continue with their actions.

They weren't giving her a choice. She marched back up the pathway leading to the front door, refusing to look at any of them, or give Czar the dignity of a reply. Reaper stood in the doorway and he stepped back as she approached. She blew right past him and flung herself into the armchair closest to the door, crossed her arms over her chest and stared straight ahead. He could talk until he was blue in the face. It didn't mean she had to listen.

Reaper closed the front door slowly and turned back to face her, leaning his back against the door. "First, before anything else, Anya, I have to apologize to you."

"Don't bother. I know Czar told you to, and I don't want your apology." She snapped it at him, furious again. Wanting to cry again. Apparently sitting in silence wasn't her forte. He'd uttered two sentences and she was already snapping at him. She was supposed to keep her mouth shut.

"Why would you think Czar would tell me to apologize?" He sounded genuinely puzzled. "Czar has nothing to do with this. I made a terrible mistake and you had to see it. It was humiliating that I ever put either of us in that position. It hurt you—really hurt you—and that would be the last thing in the world I ever wanted to do. More than anything else, I'm sorry for that."

"Okay, you've apologized." She waved her hand at him. "I accept, Reaper." Her voice cracked and she inwardly cursed. He had to know, by the redness of her face, how swollen it was, that she'd been crying. Still, she didn't want to cry in front of him. If he had an endless line of exes crying over him and begging him to take them back, she didn't want to be one of them. "This is done."

He shook his head. "It isn't done. We had a deal. It was done when I say it's done, and I never said that. I never thought that. Not for one moment."

"It was done the moment you put your hands on another woman."

"I never touched her."

She wanted the frying pan. The urge was so strong she nearly got up to get the weapon so she could knock sense into him because he wasn't making any. "So sorry I used the wrong part of your anatomy," she said as sarcastically as humanly possible. "Please allow me to rephrase. It was done the moment you put your cock in her mouth."

"Damn it, Anya, I would have broken her neck if you hadn't walked in and yelled. That's what was in my head. Ice and Storm were there to make certain it didn't happen. I left all weapons in their rooms, but they would have been too late. I would have fuckin' killed her, and all because she wasn't you!" He shouted it at her. "I said no. I told her no. I said it over and over in my head. I tried to move, but I was frozen there."

He looked as destroyed as she felt and she froze. There was no denying the ring of absolute truth. "You were going to *kill* her? What are you saying, Reaper? I don't believe you're a sociopath. I just don't believe that."

He paced across the floor, and Anya watched him, for the first time allowing herself to see the image that was in her head, replaying the incident, all of it, not just seeing the parts she remembered for Blythe. She tried to focus on Reaper, not Tawny. He'd been sweating. She had seen the beads tracking down his skin. He hadn't looked as if he were in the throes of ecstasy, or even in anticipation; he'd looked . . . destroyed, just like he did now.

Nothing made sense. Not his disturbing confession. Not

the way he'd looked when she'd walked up on them. Not the way he was acting now, or the way his brothers and sisters had acted. She forced air into her lungs. She had to be calm because Reaper wasn't calm. He was highly agitated.

"All right. I'm listening. You'd better tell me what happened." God. God. What *had* happened? Even now he looked so ravaged, so beyond grief. Sick even. As if he was running a temperature. He kept rubbing his chest, right over his heart. Her tattoo was there, and it was still new. He shouldn't be pressing so hard, but she knew he wasn't even aware of doing it.

"I'm going to tell you everything. I haven't even told Czar all of it. Not Ice and Storm. I told them part, but not all. I already feel like I've lost you, so it's a huge gamble, telling you the truth, but you're leaving me because I was so fuckin' stupid I took the easy way out."

She frowned. She was so lost, feeling like she'd come into a story halfway through it.

"That woman, whatever her name was. Tawny. She would have been the easy way, and I fuckin' couldn't stand her near me. She made my skin crawl and every nightmare I've ever been through came screamin' back. Telling you all this is the most difficult thing I've ever done. When you look at me, Anya, you look at me in a way no one ever has. Like I'm someone special. Like you see inside me to some part of me everyone, including me, gave up on before I was ever born."

That right there was what she'd feared if she let him talk to her. He got to her heart every time.

"You don't see me covered in dirt. In filth. You see something else. Something even my brothers and sisters don't see. The sun shines in your eyes when you look at me."

That was true. More than true. He was everything to her and she didn't even know how he'd gotten in so deep.

"No man wants his woman to know another man put his hands on him. It happened, over and over. It was ugly and brutal. But there were women there too. Women who liked to hurt children. Liked to see them hurt. One of the women, her name was Helena, was assigned to help us learn discipline and control of our bodies." His voice cracked.

He turned his back on her, paced across the room and returned. "She was the worst, Anya. No demon from hell could rival her. She always brought her male partner to the sessions. She would go down on me, and he would whip me, or slice into me with a knife. Sometimes he would burn me, and always, always, he raped me. They started when I was ten and kept at me until I was fourteen."

Her mouth went dry. There was something in his voice, a note that warned her. When he was talking about the man torturing him his voice was matter-of-fact. Whatever was coming, in his mind, was even worse. She didn't want to know worse, but at least she understood his aversion to having anyone go down on him.

"One day Helena introduced something new into the mix. God knows, it wasn't sick enough already for her. She brought a young girl with her, one of the newer ones. The girl had been brought in a week or so earlier and was very submissive. She was so scared she did anything they said. We couldn't work with the new ones, not until they got past that stage. It was too dangerous for us. We had to know they weren't plants so Sorbacov couldn't figure out how we were killing the instructors, or even if it was us. By that time, he suspected us, all the instructors did as well, but they couldn't figure out how we were doing it."

"At fourteen, you were still under their control?"

He nodded. "By that time, we were being sent out on missions. If I went, Sorbacov had Savage locked up with the worst of them. The faster I returned, the quicker he was released. And vice versa. He knew with each of us who to threaten. Czar had it the worst because Sorbacov was certain he was the glue, keeping us all together and being the brains behind the killings, and he wanted to break him."

Reaper stalked across the room to the small bar they'd

set up at the far end. He poured a small amount of whiskey into a glass and tossed it back. She almost asked him for a drink herself, but figured one of them had better stay focused, sober and calm.

She wanted to put her hands over her ears. He'd been a child, and he was talking so easily about killing. About being sexually assaulted repeatedly.

"Helena brought the girl with her and told her she had to keep me aroused while Helena's partner tortured me. Of course the kid had no idea what she was doing, and I was supposed to try to resist. I figured it was an excuse to hurt her, but . . ." He cleared his throat, his hands going to his eyes. His throat worked. A hard swallow.

Anya braced herself.

"She slit the girl's throat. Right there, with her kneeling in front of me. Mouth still on me. Blood was everywhere and that bitch laughed and smeared it around, pushed the body aside and I swear to God, she took the kid's place. I just lost it, Anya. I grabbed the knife out of her hand and killed her just the way she'd killed that girl. Mouth still on me. Then I turned and stabbed him. I don't even know how many times. I don't remember much of it, although I have nightmares all the fuckin' time."

Both hands raked through his hair. His blue eyes met hers. His were tortured. Tormented. "That's what happened that night. My dreams of you, of you loving me, turned into a nightmare of Helena torturing me. God, baby. I'm so fuckin' sorry. I'm so fucked-up and there's no way around it. None."

"Reaper." She didn't know what she was going to say. What she could say? Tears trickled down her face, and this time they were for both of them. For Reaper because he was right, there was no way to undo that kind of severe damage. That kind of trauma. And for her, because she loved him with everything in her and she didn't see a way through this.

"There's more. I'm going to give it all to you."

How could there be more? She wasn't certain her heart

could take any more. She felt paralyzed with grief for him. Her chest hurt there was so much pressure.

"Just say it, honey," she whispered.

"When Sorbacov was told, I expected him to kill Savage or at least me. I should have known better. He was devious, the sick kind of man who loved psychological torture as much as physical. He had Savage so he knew I'd do anything to keep him safe. Pay any price. His price was to send me out to kill. I was his assassin. We all were, but I was his prized one. He wanted me to duplicate the kill over and over. Seduce the target and kill her the same way. I refused to kill an innocent. I wouldn't trade Savage's life for a woman who hadn't done anything wrong. I honestly don't know whether or not they manufactured evidence against women, but over the years, when it was a female target, Sorbacov sent me after her."

"And you . . ." she prompted, feeling sick.

"Repeated the killing in exactly the same way. Sorbacov made me record it and bring him the evidence. If I didn't hand the recording over, they didn't release Savage. I always knew I was working against the clock. He was in bad, bad shape when I'd get him from them. Sometimes we discussed killing ourselves like some of the other students had done."

She felt sick for all of them now. Every club member. Whatever was being done to Savage while Reaper was on his missions was clearly horrifying. All of the members had suffered unspeakable crimes.

"I'm so in love with you, Anya. I didn't want to take chances with your life. After what happened, I had to find a solution. I talked to Ice and Storm. I didn't give them details, just told them I was having trouble in that department and that I didn't want to hurt you. They knew about the instructor, but she worked with all of them. They didn't know I killed her or why. Czar knew that part. I didn't tell Czar or anyone else, not even Savage, what I had to do to keep Savage alive after that." His eyes met hers again and then he looked away, shame on his face. Guilt.

She knew he was expecting her to condemn him. She cleared her throat so she could speak, swallowing the terrible lump there. "What was the solution you came up with?"

"Ice read this story about sexual surrogates. I can't talk about killing multiple people to a therapist. I can't talk about things the club does now. I can't explain why I won't let the love of my life go down on me even though I want it more than anything. I told Ice finding a sexual therapist wouldn't work for all those reasons. He said we didn't need a therapist, only a sex partner who knew what she was doing."

Anya groaned and hit the back of her head against the chair several times. Of course they'd think that. "Honey, surrogates are trained."

"Well, yeah. So is Tawny so to speak, at least that's what Storm said and he had a point."

She was going to strangle the twins with her bare hands. She couldn't think too much about what he'd revealed. That would take a long time to process. She just had to keep her mind from screaming and screaming in rage and heartache for him.

"Keep going," she encouraged.

"They convinced me. I knew I'd have to be drunk, but I couldn't drink enough to make it all right. The thought of anyone touching me but you . . ." He broke off, shook his head. "I kept trying to tell Ice and Storm I needed to talk to you first. Ask what you thought, but they said you'd object."

"They were right, the blockheads," she muttered.

"I couldn't go into the room. I didn't want her in there. While we were arguing, she came out and right away started. I couldn't move. It was like it was happening all over again. That woman. I couldn't stand her hands on me. Touching me. She wasn't you and I couldn't get back to reality. I don't know what happened."

He pushed both hands through his hair and paced away from her. She could see his hands were shaking.

"I said no. I remember saying it. Then I was thinking it, like I did back when I was a kid. Screaming it over and over in my mind. She just kept coming at me, and when she touched me, I went crazy. In my head, it was Helena all over again. I wanted my knife but it wasn't on me so I grabbed her head in my hands. Anya, if it wasn't for your voice, for you walking in . . . she'd be dead, baby. If it was that close with her, no way can I take a chance on hurting you again, let alone killing you."

She bit down hard on her fist, fighting to keep from crying again. Crying for both of them. How did one fix this? She couldn't think with all the things he told her running around in a mad circle in her mind. He was having flashbacks. Of course he would. He was traumatized as a child. It didn't matter that he was a big badass biker, a trained assassin, he couldn't escape the past any more than a rape victim could. He *was* the victim of rape. Repeatedly. He was having posttraumatic stress episodes. She didn't know that much about it, but she'd certainly seen some of the soldiers in the shelters.

"I know I have to let you go, but I couldn't let you go thinking I'd betrayed you. I didn't. I wouldn't have gone through with it. Even without that reaction, Anya, I wouldn't have gone through with it. You have only my word on it, but I felt like you deserved the truth."

He stood, head down, waiting for her to say something. Anya pressed her fingers to her eyes. She didn't know what to say. The idea of leaving was horrifying. If there was one person in the world who needed her, who needed understanding and love, it was Reaper.

The idea of staying was equally as terrifying. She knew his problems were going to be problems for life. They wouldn't go away just because she loved him. Not. Ever. No matter how long they were together, even if they had children, his past would torment them, and that was if they could get past this.

"Say something," he snapped and stalked back to the bar.

"Stop drinking. The last thing we need is for you to have any more alcohol."

He spun around. "I'm going to need it to watch you walk out that door, and Anya, unless I'm dead, there's no guarantee I won't come after you."

She knew that. The moment he'd declared his love aloud, she knew there would be no way he would let her go without a fight. Maybe not this minute when he was feeling raw. Guilty. Humiliated. Maybe not now, but later, he would wake up one morning, get on his Harley and ride after her. She knew that with the same certainty she knew the sun would rise in the morning. She pretended she didn't know.

"You might be ready to give up on us, but I'm not quite there yet. I have to think things through. My mother may have chosen drugs and shelters for us, but she said a lot of very intelligent things and one was, when you don't know what to do, stand still."

Reaper turned to more fully face her. "What do you mean, you aren't so certain? Do you have any idea what I just told you I've done?"

"Reaper, don't talk to me right now. Go tell the family to go away. We need to figure this out between the two of us. *If* we stay together we'll figure out how between us, not with the others. If I'm leaving, I'll go say good-bye to them in the afternoon. And grab my duffel bag while you're at it." She tried to sound matter-of-fact when her heart was beating out of control and her lungs felt as if they were desperate for air.

Reaper stood in front of her, staring at her as if she'd grown two heads. She held his stare through sheer will-power. She was a shelter girl and she was strong. She'd pulled herself out of that life and created another one for herself. All of those fighting skills, the will of iron she had, her ability to plan, it all had to be for a reason and she suspected that reason was standing in front of her, so no, she wasn't about to flinch. Or give up. Not until she'd exhausted every possibility.

Reaper turned and stalked outside. His head was up, not down, and that was something. She put her head between her knees and fought for air. Was she strong enough to stay? If she stayed, could they have any kind of a life the way Czar and Blythe had—with children? She wanted children. Did Reaper? If he did, was he willing to work in order to have them, because there would be work involved. And he'd have to let her talk to someone if they couldn't figure it out on their own.

What was she thinking? Committing to a life with him? Knowing the things he'd told her? Was she out of her mind? She should be running. If she had one ounce of sense she'd already be gone. She remained seated. Her mind went over those things. Everything he'd said. Right in the beginning, before anything else, he'd said, "I would have fuckin' killed her, and all because she wasn't you."

He hadn't said he would have killed Tawny because she'd put her hands on him. Or her mouth. It was because she wasn't Anya. He may have thought that was what he meant, but it wasn't what he'd said. Later, he'd repeated something very close to that a second time. It would be dangerous, but could they work through his problem? She had to look up PTSD and figure out Reaper's triggers. More, they had to find out how others handled nightmares and how they kept their partners safe. Reaper and she couldn't be the only ones in a dangerous situation.

She straightened slowly, seeing not the room, but the look he'd had on his face. Destroyed. He'd been destroyed when Sorbacov had his parents murdered and he'd been taken from his home and thrown into the school. He'd been destroyed yet again when Sorbacov's criminal friends had murdered his sisters. So many times that destruction had happened, over and over, and yet, Reaper remained standing. He'd built a life for himself with his brothers and sisters.

Anya saw now why they were so interdependent on one another. She'd known what they'd been through was bad, but she'd had no real idea of the horrific extent of their suffering. They had brought Blythe into their circle, making her part of their club, making her voice count. They had shown a willingness to extend that invitation to Anya as well. Neither woman would have a vote in club business, or even know most of what went on, but they had much bigger roles in Torpedo Ink.

Reaper returned, carrying her duffel bag. He set it to one side. "I want you to know, they probably put a tracker on your car. I did when I bought it, just so if something happened, I could always find you, but they would have tonight for certain."

"You're telling me this because?" she prompted.

He remained by the door, leaning against it, studying her face. Looking for something. She didn't know what it was. Reassurance maybe? She couldn't give that to him. Not yet.

"I'm telling you this because if you have any brains in your head you'll leave and try to hide from me. You won't find the trackers, either one of them, so you'll eventually have to get rid of the car. Still, Anya, most likely, I'll track you down." His voice dripped with tears, although there were none on his face. "I want you to have a decent chance to escape all of us."

"You're pulling out all the stops to get rid of me. How 'bout you call Czar right now and tell him I want Tawny gone. I never want to see her around the bar, the compound or anywhere else I might run into her. She knew you were trying to get away from her and she refused to stop. Just you saying no should have been enough. She also knew you were mine. She doesn't get to stay. If Czar chooses to allow her . . ."

"He won't. He already gave that order, baby, when he was trying to snap me all the way out of it. Not to mention, he bit the heads off the twins and reamed me up one side and down the other."

"Don't call me *baby* yet. I'm not ready for it. This was one of the stupidest things you've ever done, Reaper. I hope you know that. Not Ice or Storm. You. You belong to me, not them. It was up to you to come to me with all of this. You needed to share why you didn't want to be touched. Why you were afraid to sleep in the same bed."

He nodded. "I'm well aware of that, Anya."

"That frying pan is looking better and better to me," she muttered under her breath. "I think we're going to have to hang one on the wall in every room, both here and at the clubhouse."

He slid down the massive front door to the floor, as if his knees had buckled and refused to hold him up anymore. He drew up his legs and put his arms around them, holding tight, holding himself together. "You shouldn't stay, Anya."

"You think I don't know that? You think I don't know it's absolute madness to stay with you? I want a home. A family. A man devoted to me. Not only do I want those things, Reaper, I deserve them."

"Absolutely you do."

Those compelling blue eyes never left her face. She couldn't look away from him. "The thing is, Reaper, you deserve them too. And I'm in love with you. Not just falling, I'm in all the way. Gone. Totally gone. Don't let admitting that to you let you think you're off the hook—you're not. I want a family. Children. I want to sleep with my man. I want it all. We have to find a way for that to happen."

He shook his head and dropped his face into his hands. "It's never going to happen, Anya. I can't take a chance with your life. I'm not willing to do that with you."

"There's two of us in this relationship, Reaper," she pointed out as gently as she could. She wanted to go to him and shake him. He was willing to try some lame-ass, harebrained scheme his brothers came up with, but wouldn't explore any ideas with her. "You don't get to make those kinds of decisions alone."

"Anya."

"Reaper." She stared him down, uncaring that those blue eyes slashed at her, fury beginning to build. "If the roles were reversed and I'd been the one traumatized . . ."

"*Don't* use that word. I fuckin' hate that word."

Anya stayed very still. There was something here she didn't understand. "Why? Why would you hate the word? It's just a word describing the results of a childhood of rape and torture."

"No, it isn't. It's a word people toss around when they don't have the least idea what the fuck they're talking about." He ran his fingers through his hair repeatedly. "I'm a man. A grown man. I keep my shit together, and it isn't supposed to leak out and hurt the woman I fuckin' love more than life itself."

She opened her mouth twice and then closed it on the things she wanted to say. She recognized she had to choose her words carefully. "We're all products of our past. Me included. All of us have triggers. We used various things to cope with whatever ordeals we went through as children. That's normal, Reaper. *Traumatized* is just a word to describe those things, it isn't a judgment."

She desperately wanted to go to him, to hold him. Comfort him. She couldn't do that, not until she knew he would accept the things she said to him.

"I know you love your brothers and you respect them. That's normal as well. You had to grow up with a much tighter bond than most people, certainly more than I ever had. But, honey, you have to know the way you grew up wasn't normal. You were given educations in very specific areas, and in others that education was neglected. Going to Ice or Storm or any of them for something that belongs to you and me was wrong."

He kept pushing his hands through his hair over and over.

Twice he pressed his fingers into his eyes as if they were hurting. He didn't move from the door, and it occurred to her that he was blocking it at the same time he was telling her she had to go.

"I know that. I get that. I got that almost right away, Anya. The fact remains we can't sleep in the same bed. You can't touch my cock or put your mouth on me."

"You don't know that because we haven't tried. The bed is something we can figure out. The other might never be worked out, but we could have fun trying. We can also get real help, not some horrible woman who knew, who *knew*, Reaper, that you're mine."

His entire body shuddered. "She touched me. I almost killed her, Anya." His hands went to his face again. "It was close. So close. If you hadn't come when you did, Ice and Storm could never have stopped me."

"Like I care," Anya muttered under her breath, but she did care. Tawny deserved to be kicked out, she didn't deserve death. She wanted to punch the woman in the face for touching Reaper after he'd clearly said no. If nothing else his body language had said no.

"The point is, we can get legitimate help."

He lifted his head. "Babe, you know we can't go spill our guts to some fuckin' counselor who will be required to tell the law that I confessed to slitting Helena's throat."

"Why didn't you go to Czar?"

He went silent. Staring at her. Giving her nothing. She didn't back down. She kept looking at him. Waiting. Eventually, and it felt as if he took forever, he looked down at his hands. "He wouldn't have been satisfied with me telling him about killing Helena. He knew that. He would know there was more, and I was ashamed. I didn't want him to know."

Czar was father, brother, friend, guardian angel all rolled into one. Still. She kept looking at him. His blue eyes shifted from her face.

"He tells Blythe everything if she asks, and she would

because she always knows when it's about one of us. Don't want her to look at me any different. She's like you, not as bright for me, but she still looks at me like I'm worth something—like we all are."

"Does she look at the children any different because of what happened to them?" She leaned toward him, her eyes once more meeting his. "Reaper, what happened to you was beyond your control."

"Not killing those others, not when Sorbacov sent me out and told me precisely how I had to do it. Czar worries there are videos of us as children—I know no one will ever be able to identify us, but Sorbacov liked his snuff films. I did my best to keep the camera off me, but when I was young, I was terrified. I could have made mistakes. What if the woman was . . ."

"If a woman touched you when you were a child, Reaper, and that includes your teenage years, she was a pedophile. She wasn't a good woman. I don't know about those tapes, or films, but I do know, you should have trusted Czar. You've always trusted him. There was no reason for you to be ashamed. You told me they held Savage . . ."

"What I didn't tell you is that when a woman touches me like that, the first thought in my head isn't pleasure," he burst out.

"Okay. That's fair. But you should have told me. You could have given me the opportunity to work through it with you."

He scrubbed his hands through his hair for the millionth time. "Are you going to stay, Anya? I'm terrified you'll say yes. I'm equally terrified you'll say no."

"No more secrets." She took a deep breath and stepped off the proverbial cliff. "We talk things out, and we're going to Czar and Blythe together when we need to. That's the price for me to stay. There's no reason to stay otherwise because we'll never work."

He stared at her so long she thought he'd never speak.

Once again, she thought she caught the sheen of tears in his eyes but he pressed his fingers tightly over them. "Anything, Anya."

"And you touch another woman or let her touch you, I'm going psycho on your ass."

"Understood," he agreed.

EIGHTEEN

"I've been thinking about ways you can comfortably have me touching you when you want me to," Anya said softly. She got up and stretched, arms overhead, her body beautiful there in the moonlight spilling through the windows. "I've been giving it some thought for some time, long before this, when I first realized you didn't want to have sex facing each other and you didn't want my hands on you." She took a breath and kept her back to him, looking at him through the reflection in the window. "Or my mouth."

"I always want your hands or mouth on me, Anya," Reaper admitted softly. "I think about it constantly. I'm always hard." His hand dropped to the front of his jeans and he rubbed over the bulge at the crotch. "Can't look at you or think about you without getting this way, baby. You're so fuckin' beautiful. Inside and out. I want your hands on me, but the idea of me hurting you is so strong, I don't see how that's going to happen."

"When you were telling me about Tawny putting her hands on you, you kept saying you were upset because she wasn't me. You didn't say you wanted to hurt her because *no one* could touch your body. You said because she wasn't me. You said it more than once, Reaper."

Anya needed to touch him right then far more than she'd ever needed to before. She wanted her hands on him, showing him she loved him. Caring for him after all the trauma. She wanted to reassure him—and herself—that they would find a way. That they were worth fighting for. Reaper was more into a physical, hard and fast cementing of their relationship. She was thinking slow. Easy. Take her time.

"I did? It's the same thing." He rubbed at his eyes again.

She knew he was hurting. His body aching, reacting to the trauma. She wanted to word what she had to say carefully. She didn't want him to think she was going to keep at him, but she had several ideas on how she could touch him to both of their satisfaction. If she blurted that out, he'd think she was still reprimanding him for not coming to her first. She'd said her piece on that. He'd suffered more needless trauma, put a woman's life in jeopardy and nearly lost her. That was consequence enough.

"It's not the same thing, honey." She kicked off her shoes and walked across the room to the corner where she'd rolled up the blankets he'd slept in the night before. There was going to be no more of that. She felt as if she'd run a marathon, and she couldn't imagine how he was feeling. "I think there's a huge difference, and we'll get around to that in a little while. Right now, I want to get you relaxed so you can sleep. Do you want a shower?"

He stared at her a long time before he nodded. She nearly sagged with relief, but she forced a smile. "Good. I'm going to get things ready here and then I'll take my shower."

"What are you planning, Anya?"

He sounded wary. She couldn't blame him, but she wasn't going to have him so wound up and worried about her ideas that he couldn't relax. "Not a thing, honey. Go shower. It's late, and we both need to just let our minds go blank for a while. I'm showering down here, so you can have the master bathroom."

"Babe, the master kicks ass. I consider it yours."

"I consider it ours and I want you to have it tonight. Take your time." She needed time to mentally prepare herself. Her idea had come slowly, before Ice, Storm and her man had come up with their seriously idiotic plan to "cure" Reaper. There was no cure. She hadn't known what she was dealing with, but even then, when she realized he had a problem with her putting her hands—or mouth—on his cock, she'd begun to think of ways to make it happen.

Leslee, the woman she'd first met out at the Egg Taking Station, was a massage therapist. She was good at her work and proud of it. She'd talked about her work when they'd first met and then again when they were in her truck riding out to the Egg Taking Station. Lana mentioned that Blythe owned a gym, that she'd recently bought it, but that her work was mainly in massage therapy. That both women did therapy through massage got her thinking about whether or not something like that would help Reaper get used to her hands on his body.

She set out to read about it. And ask questions over the phone of both Leslee and Blythe. Not questions so they could figure out what she was using it for, just saying she wanted to surprise Reaper with a really good massage. Leslee had offered to show her. So had Blythe. She hadn't had time to avail herself of the opportunity, but she'd studied techniques on YouTube and read about them in books.

Anya relaxed into the hot water pouring over her. She hadn't realized she was so stiff. Every muscle seemed locked and tight, like giant knots. She couldn't imagine how Reaper felt after all he'd been through. She should have told him she was working out an idea. She was every bit as guilty as she accused Reaper of being with her lack of communication.

She knew just giving him massages wouldn't solve all their problems, but she just wanted the building blocks, even small little stepping-stones to help.

She hoped Czar and Blythe had some suggestions as well. She was well aware the members of Torpedo Ink would never go to a therapist, but they would trust whatever Blythe said, and she had access to all kinds of therapists. If she didn't know them, she knew people who did. Blythe was fighting for all of them. Anya knew Czar's wife had to feel like she was battling uphill and alone some of the time, and she was determined to join her.

She toweled off the droplets of water and then tamed her hair, drying it, which she rarely did, and then braiding it before pulling on her favorite shirt—Reaper's flannel. She left it unbuttoned and didn't bother with panties. Her massage was supposed to be intimate. Sensual. She wanted that for him.

Anya had been angry at Ice and Storm, but she realized they were victims of trauma just as Reaper was. They hadn't had the education or the experiences of most people so they solved their problems within the limited experience they did have. She would always have to remember that and make allowances for them. She had to be more like Blythe and try to gently guide them in the right directions.

They were men. Intelligent men. Traumatized men. They were also very good at what they did, and what they did was kill enemies. They fought. Had sex. Fought more. Took jobs that risked their lives, but they remained a closed society. She could be a part of that and one they listened to, or she would have to leave.

She wanted Reaper. She found she also wanted the rest of them. She lit candles. Lots of them. Groups of citrus-smelling candles. A few vanilla. Mostly soft essentials because when she'd asked, Leslee'd said most men didn't like florals but were good with citrus. She wanted Reaper as comfortable as possible.

The room was ready for him when he came down the stairs. As usual, he was deliciously naked. Sometimes, she thought he was more comfortable out of clothes than in them. He always walked with confidence. Gliding. So fluid. She couldn't help but watch him as he came right into the room, looking around him, and then his gaze flicked to her.

"Why are you wearing clothes?"

Of course he would ask about the clothes and not about the candles or the way she'd set up the bed.

She waved toward the blankets, taking a step back as he was coming at her aggressively. With purpose. "I'm going to give you a massage."

He stopped in his tracks. Ran a hand through his hair. "Baby."

"Yes." She pointed to the blankets, trying to look confident when inside she was shaking. "The point isn't sex. We're not having sex. This isn't about that. You know my body, Reaper, but you don't know my hands. I'm going to start giving you massages. If they don't work, we'll stop, but in the meantime, you might actually like them."

"Baby."

"You said that already." She tilted her head and deliberately challenged him. "You said you were willing to do anything, to try anything. Try this."

"I could hurt you."

"You're naked, honey. No weapons."

He stepped closer. Right into her space, forcing her to tilt her head just that little bit, which intimidated her. "Anya, I *am* a weapon."

"Then lie facedown, your hands under your head. If you start to get squirrely, you just have to say something."

He stared down into her face for a long time. Long enough to give butterflies a chance to take off, wings brushing like mad against her stomach. One hand came up to cup the side of her face. His thumb slid over her lips. "You're something else, Anya. I don't know what I ever did that allowed you to walk into my life."

He took a breath and abruptly did as she asked, lay facedown in the middle of the blankets, his head resting on his arms. His face was turned to the side so he could watch her.

She straddled his back and lowered herself slowly, giving him time to get used to the idea of her weight on him. The oil was special, something Blythe had gotten from a woman named Hannah Drake Harrington. She was the wife of the local sheriff, but she made all kinds of special soaps, oils, and bath salts, along with natural healing lotions. This oil was not only good for the skin, but edible. Sometimes, according to Blythe, that was necessary in a good massage with one's man.

"I haven't had time to learn a lot of techniques," she admitted, feeling a little nervous as she poured the oil into her hands. The bottle had been sitting in hot water to warm it. "But I think you'll like this. And it will get you so you know how my hands feel on your skin. If you know my touch, hopefully, as years go by, even in your sleep, you'll recognize the difference between my hands and someone else's."

"Is that what you think?"

She put her hands very gently on his neck and began to rub, fingers digging into the tight muscles she found there. "It's what I hope. It may never happen, but think of all the great massages you'll get night after night."

His body had been tense, but as her hands and fingers worked the muscles of his neck, she felt him begin to relax.

"Gotta admit, baby, that feels fuckin' great."

Anya couldn't help but smile. It was a relief that he hadn't thrown her halfway across the room. Hearing what he'd told her about his life had been hard, and it had taken a lot of courage to continue with the plan she'd devised over the last two weeks.

"You've got great hands, Anya," he murmured a few minutes later when she was working the muscles of his back.

"I'm glad you like it, Reaper. Just close your eyes, honey, listen to the music and drift. I want you to always associate my hands with something good. Something positive."

"Something beautiful," he added. "You're so fuckin' beautiful, Anya."

His voice turned her heart over. She knew he wasn't talking about her looks. He liked the way she looked, but it was really about so much more. She'd never had the kind of compliments Reaper gave her.

She worked her way slowly down his back, exploring the muscles in between his ribs, trying to do what the massage therapist in the video had done. She was getting nervous again as she approached his buttocks. She was sliding over him, sitting on the backs of his thighs, her heart pounding.

"You feeling good, Reaper?"

There was the tiniest of hesitations. Her heart sank. "We can stop, if you need me to," she whispered. "Seriously, I'm so proud of you and pleased that you let me get this far. I loved it, and I feel like I've mapped out your back. I loved having the chance to explore."

She'd taken her time, worshiping every muscle, recording every scar in her mind. She'd kissed those scars. Licked over them, tracing them with her tongue as well as her fingers. She'd claimed them. Claimed his back. She was patient, she could wait to claim the rest of him.

"I'm feeling very good, Anya. My dick is so fuckin' hard it hurts. You put your hands on my ass and start working it the way you did my back, my cock, for sure, is going to be cuttin' a hole in the floor."

She couldn't help but smile. "I'm going to put my hands on you now, and I want you to feel me. Know it's me, Reaper. Know I'm just making you feel good." She massaged the small of his back, tracing the roots of the tree that was tattooed on his back. The piles of skulls rolling among the roots. So many. Some of the roots had grown through the skulls. "Tell me about this tattoo." She wanted him a little distracted. She kept kneading his muscles, her hands moving lower, beginning a deep tissue massage as best she could on his buttocks. He was tight, very tight, sculpted, as if an artist had designed him with loving care.

"That trunk is Czar, holding us together. Seventeen branches, the seventeen survivors. Crows represent the ones that didn't make it. Our loved ones are there, the ones we couldn't save. So many we couldn't tatt that many birds on us. Skulls are the fuckers we killed to survive. Or to avenge the fallen. The others are the ones we had to take for our country or to save someone. Ink's going to have to tatt a few more on there for me."

His voice was gruff as he explained. She looked at that tattoo with new eyes. It was the same as the patch he wore on his jacket.

"Why Torpedo Ink?" She was really massaging him now, fingers digging deep, her hands all over his butt. He wasn't fighting her. He wasn't tense. He hadn't once tried to jerk away. So many scars. His buttocks, the back of his thighs. She couldn't resist kissing them.

"We were kids when we called ourselves that. The name grew up with us, as did the tree. Ink tatted us, and he's damn good. *Torpedo* is used for *hit man*. We were all raised to be just that. You send us after someone and we lock on like a torpedo and stay locked on until the job is done. We thought we were clever to use INK instead of INC. You have to remember we were in our teens when we thought that shit up."

He groaned as her hands moved to his lower thighs, just under his buttocks. "You're fuckin' killin' me, baby. Seriously. I'm going to come all over the blankets. Gotta turn over."

She slid off him immediately. She loved the sexy, gravelly note in his voice, the one that told her he was about to take command of the situation, but she didn't want him taking over. Not yet. She had one more thing to try.

With another groan Reaper turned over. His cock was thick and hard, raised along his stomach, and there were drops of pearly white all along the velvety head. She forced her gaze from that delicious treat and began working on his legs, fingers digging into tight muscles. She could feel his eyes on her. Both his hands went to his cock, fisting there.

"You like this," she said softly, keeping her attention on what she was doing.

"Yeah, baby, you could say I like this."

"You like my hands on you."

"I have to admit, I do."

She moved up his leg to his thigh. "That's good, Reaper. I'm hoping if I can do this most nights before you go to sleep, you'll eventually get so used to me touching you, that even if you never let another adult put their hands on you, you'll crave mine." She glanced up at him from under her lashes, a small smile on her face because that idea really was her goal. "I see you're really enjoying this."

"Come up here. I'm going to have you sit on me."

Her heart stuttered. She wanted that, but she wanted something else more. "I have another idea, Reaper. I'd like you to let me try."

"Tell me." His voice was low. Sexy. Full of sin.

He wanted her and he was going to have her. She knew that because she wanted him just as much, if not more. How could she touch him, all those scars down his back, the burns and whip marks on his buttocks. Down the backs of his thighs. The burns on his inner thighs. He'd been beaten front and back. How could she touch all that, and not want every inch of him? He was hers. She didn't necessarily want him able to stand any other person's touch. Or their lips or their mouth.

She scooted up his legs, straddling him, settling over his thighs. She poured more oil into her palms. "I'm going to put my hands on your shaft, make a tight fist, and you're going to put your hands around mine so you're controlling everything. But I get to touch you, and you'll feel my hands on you for the first time. If you hate it, you just take my hands away. If you like it, you control the action. If you want my mouth on you, you control that too. I'm going to turn all control over to you."

He studied her face for a long time. Too long. Her heart began to pound. He was so beautiful lying there, his hands fisting his cock, his body laid out beneath her, so perfect, so scarred, his mind so damaged. She'd thought him broken, but he wasn't. He hadn't let them do that to him. Damaged, yes, broken no.

"All right, baby. If you have that kind of courage, the kind that will face a monster, I have to have it too. You fuckin' terrify me, woman."

Anya smiled at him, trying to convey confidence. Her heart hammered at her, so loud she was afraid he could hear, but she didn't hesitate. She held out her hands. He curled his around hers.

"Look at me, baby. Keep looking at me. I need that."

She couldn't have looked away. His blue gaze was locked on her, just like the torpedo he described. His hands took hers and brought them to his cock. She curled her fingers around his shaft. Velvet over steel. He felt beautiful. Hot. Hard. His body shuddered under her, but his gaze didn't waver and his hands tightened around hers, forcing her fist to tighten around his shaft. He pumped. Slowly at first, the warm oil making it easy to slide up and down. She wanted to memorize every part of him. That part of him.

"Anya." He breathed her name. "You're a fuckin' miracle."

"I was thinking the same of you," she admitted.

He threw his head back, exposing his throat, but his eyes stayed on hers. "Now, baby. Look at us." Very slowly, almost reluctantly, his gaze slid away from hers, dropping lower.

She did the same. Her breath caught in her throat. Her hands surrounded his cock. Fisted him. His hands guided hers. Each pull, the slide of that smooth, hot velvet had her sex clenching. Her inner muscles spasming. Needing.

"You're touching me and I want it, Anya. I want to feel your hands on me like this. I didn't know it would feel like this. So good."

"Thank you for taking the chance with me," she whispered. "If I never get the chance again, I'll always remember this." She would. Straddling him, sitting on his thighs, face-to-face, her shirt open, breasts heaving with every panting breath, her hands tight around his cock, feeling that thick, hard length sliding through the oil in her palms. She loved that his hands surrounded hers, holding her fists tightly around him. That felt . . . intimate. More intimate than if she'd been giving him a hand job on her own.

One of his hands came up to her hair, fisted at the back. Tightly. His fingers next to her skull. There was a small bite of pain she barely noticed because her eyes were on the beauty of that broad head sliding through her fists. It was gorgeous. Temptation.

Reaper began to put pressure on her, bending her down toward his cock. Her heart pounded as she understood what he was doing. She relaxed completely, giving herself to him. Letting him have complete control, just as she'd promised.

"Tell me what you want," she whispered.

"Nothing. Not yet. Just your breath."

She kept her fists tight, working him. Increasing the speed because he was increasing it. Holding him tighter because his hand was nearly crushing hers. He brought her mouth within a breath of his cock, and she inhaled, taking the musky scent of him deep, exhaling need and hunger out of her lungs, over that broad, velvety head with the tempting droplets. More leaked as she watched.

"Touch me with your tongue. Just touch, Anya. Don't try anything else."

She wasn't about to try anything else. It was terrifying, yet she found it sexy as hell to have him forcing her head over his cock, his hands forcing her fist to work him fast. If anything, his cock was harder and thicker than it had been before. He kept her head just out of reach, so all she could do was flick her tongue gently across that surface, swiping up a couple of the drops spilling out.

His body shuddered and he jerked her head back. The flash of pain through her scalp was nothing like the piercing pain shooting through her heart. He didn't yank her up, so much as just lift her head an inch from him. He breathed deeply.

"Holy fuckin' hell, woman. That was like a lash of fire."

Her heart settled back to a hard pounding. She kept forcing air through her lungs. "You taste good."

"Yeah? Want more?"

"Yes," she whispered. "If you can give it to me."

"Don't fuckin' run off again, Anya."

"Don't let another woman touch what's mine," she said, refusing to take the blame for the mess he'd created by not talking to her.

"I didn't allow her to touch me."

That was true. He'd never consented. "I'm going to punch her right in the face," she said. "But right now, I'm feeling like I need another taste."

"Yeah? Not hearin' you say it, baby."

Was he teasing her? Her hands around his cock, her mouth inches away? Was that happiness in his voice? Teasing?

"What do you want me to do?"

"Ask nice. I'm giving you something special, baby. Something no one else is ever going to get."

That was true. At least she hoped it was. She hoped it was only *her* hands he could take. Her mouth. "I would very much like another taste, Reaper. Please." She used her best manners, trying not to laugh when she was so happy. This could go wrong at any time. She wasn't stupid, she knew it could, but right now, she had this with him and she'd always cherish this moment. She also knew this might be her only time like this with him and it would have to be enough for both of them, but she was going to enjoy every minute and hope there would be more.

His hand bunched her hair tighter and he put pressure on her head, pushing her down over him. "Just your tongue."

She was closer this time and she lapped at him, took those drops, now leaking over and over, into her mouth. "Your taste is addicting." Her mouth was so close that when she spoke, her lips whispered over the broad head.

Again, his body shuddered with pleasure. He didn't lift her head away from him. He pushed her down a little closer. "Open your mouth, Anya."

Heart racing, she did as he said. Instinctively she knew not to close it. His cock pushed against her tongue. She let it slide there, over and over, before she tentatively curled her tongue around him, danced it over him and then slid it up that long prominent vein. He pulled her head back, just an inch, that pain biting into her scalp. She was so elated she didn't care.

Reaper was breathing fast, his hips moving now, a subtle push, building a rhythm. "Suck this time. Hard. I want to feel it. And tighten your fist."

She did what he'd commanded with her hand but waited for him to push her head down on him. The moment he did, she closed her mouth over him, letting her own fist push him deep while she hollowed her cheeks and suckled hard. His breath exploded out of him. He swore, pushing her head down more, pulling her hands off him so his hand took their place at the base, guiding his cock into her mouth.

"Cup my balls, Anya. Gently. Be gentle."

She knew he gave her those instructions because others hadn't been gentle. She was. Mostly she concentrated on the way he felt in her mouth. She wanted to be good for him. The best. She wanted him, at the end, to want more with her. She hoped that he would grow to know her hands and mouth and that he would crave them on him.

His hands gripped her hair harder and he yanked her off

him. She let him, reassuring him that he had complete control just by her compliance. He didn't push her away, but just breathed deeply, his hand working his cock.

"Roll them, baby. I want your mouth there." He pushed her head down so she was level with his heavy sac. She used her tongue to lap, her mouth to suckle and her hands to gently roll his heavy balls around. Then he was dragging her head up again, and forcing her mouth over his cock.

"Fuck me with your mouth."

She did, keeping the suction strong, using her tongue, letting him guide her head up and down. Then he took over completely, and she had to use every ounce of courage and trust she had. He held her head down, forcing her to take him deep, forcing her to breathe through her nose as she suckled him.

The breath hissed out of his lungs. His hips bucked into her. She felt him hit her throat and she fought for air. He pulled her off of him immediately, his hands going to her waist. "Guide me into you. I need to be in you, baby. Face-to-face, just like this."

Elated, she sank down over him, letting him fill her. The feel of him was insane. So tight. Like he was never going to fit. Her body would never give in to his invasion. And then he was there, part of her. Exquisite. Perfect.

"Scorchin' hot, Anya. You're always like a fuckin' furnace, surrounding me with your fire." He began to move, surging into her, pulling her down over him.

Anya caught his rhythm and helped, riding him hard. Feeling the burn running up her spine. She pushed off the shirt, and then brushed her hand down his chest, watching those sensual lines in his face, carved so deep with lust. The blue of his eyes darkened with desire—for her. She rode him for as long as she could, while the flames licked at her thighs, danced down her breasts into her belly and that coil deep inside wound tighter and tighter.

"Honey, I have to let go."

"No." He was firm. "Not yet. Don't want to come yet and you'll take me with you."

She bit her lip and pushed down into each stroke, arched her back, but that only added to the friction. His fingers were on her nipples, pulling and tugging until the breath hissed out of her and her entire body felt as if it might implode if she didn't let go.

"I have to let go. I need to."

"No. Not yet. A little more time, Anya." It was a plea, but it was also a command. "Fight it for me, baby. I promise it will be worth it."

Her breath hitched. She tried to pull back, but he didn't. He kept slamming deep, sending those streaks of fire rushing through her. It felt like whips of lightning crept in. Then his fingers left her breasts and slid down her belly to the junction between her legs.

"Paradise right here, baby. Love your mouth. Love your sweet pussy. Love that you're all mine." His finger slid between them and circled her clit.

She gasped and caught at his wrist. "I won't be able to hold back."

"I want to see your hands on your tits, Anya. I love how you look right now. So needy. Desperate. You want what I can give you, don't you?"

"Yes." She nearly sobbed it, riding him hard, trying not to think about his finger flicking at her clit, torturing her with sheer pleasure.

"So fuckin' beautiful, baby. I could look at you all day like this. Now, baby, give it to me now."

He flicked her clit hard, and she screamed. A sob escaped as her body fragmented, burst into a million rocketing pieces. Colors gathered behind her eyes, sparkling and shifting, her body dragging at his, gripping, the muscles clamping down and milking hard. His fingers bit deep into her hips, her wild orgasm forcing the seed from him. Each hot splash set off a chain of reactions, shock waves going through her, rippling through every cell so that her body kept clamping down again and again on his.

She finally slumped forward, burying her face in his shoulder, fighting for air. He held her tightly. So tightly, she feared she'd never breathe again, and that he was going to break every rib she had, but she didn't move. She remained still, pressed against him, his body buried deep in hers.

"I got to put my hands on you, Reaper. It was so wonderful. So perfect." She felt tears burning in her eyes and she wiped them on his bare shoulder. "Thank you so much for trying with me."

"You know I loved every second of that. And I got your mouth. You gave that to me, Anya. You let me be in complete control, and I liked it. There wasn't a moment of hesitation when you handed control over to me. Not only are you the most beautiful woman there is, but you're the smartest and the bravest."

She laughed, because the relief was so tremendous. She knew they would have problems. Always. It wasn't going to end, but they'd found a way for at least this time. She hoped it was the start of many times. "Loved giving you a massage, Reaper. I'd like to continue that practice often. When we do, I'm hoping you'll get used to the feel of my hands. Any time you want my hands or mouth on you, you take complete control."

He stroked her hair. "You good with that, Anya? Giving me control like that? I could have shoved my cock down your throat. Felt that fuckin' good."

"I'm sure it did, but you also know I'm not ready for that. You can give me instructions. I kind of get off on that. I trust you to take care of me."

"You can, Anya. I'll always take care of you. You're worn out, baby. Why don't you go upstairs and get some sleep?"

"I'm not going upstairs. I'm sleeping with you," she said stubbornly.

"Anya." His voice was pure warning. "That's not happening. I hit you."

"You didn't hit me. You knocked me off of you." She tried to make a joke of it. "My hair assaulted you."

"Not happening," he repeated.

"You're going to hold me until I fall asleep and then you're going to put a barrier between us so I can't roll over and take advantage of your body in my sleep."

He leaned down and bit her shoulder. Hard. She yelped, pulled back and glared at him.

"That was mean."

"I'm mean. You knew that when you took me on. You're getting bossy, woman. Just sayin'." The teasing note left his voice. "Not takin' a chance with your life. I couldn't live with myself if that happened."

"It isn't going to happen. We might never make it upstairs to an actual bedroom, Reaper, and I'm fine with that. We might never get to the point where I can touch you on my own, or put my mouth on you on my own, and I'm really okay with that because it's hot as hell the way we did it tonight, but I'm not okay with not sleeping with you. I know you won't fall asleep before me, so you can have the task of rolling blankets or getting pillows and putting as wide a barrier as you think you need between us."

His gaze moved over her face. Moody. Hooded eyes. Sexy. She held her breath. He didn't move.

"I need this, Reaper," she whispered, telling him the truth.

"I ought to lock you up at night, you're that dangerous. Have me turnin' into a fuckin' pussy. Don't talk to me like this in front of my brothers."

Elation swept through her. She smiled. Big. She couldn't help it. She wrapped her arms around his neck and kissed him. "Thank you, honey."

He kissed her back. Over and over. Then he rolled her over and took her body hard and fast a second time. She didn't mind at all that she was on her elbows and knees. Fire was fire, and she'd had him face-to-face. He could exert dominance any way he wanted. He'd given her everything she'd asked for and more tonight. And he gave her a hell of another orgasm.

Blankets spread on the great room floor, Reaper held Anya until she fell asleep exactly as she'd asked. He couldn't believe she'd touched his cock. He really couldn't believe her mouth had been on him. He hadn't had one adverse reaction. Not one. Not a twinge. She'd given up all control, trusted him completely, and they'd done it. He couldn't wait to try it again. Every fuckin' night.

He swept his hand down her hair. All that glorious hair he loved to see spread on his pillow. That was coming next. He wanted it all with her. He knew he was being a little greedy, but he believed in her. In the two of them. They were a long way from fixing his issues, and he was certain they never fully would, but she'd found a way to work on them. Work around them.

He loved that she wanted him to recognize her hands. He lifted one into the air and stared at it in the light streaking through the windows. His thumb slid over her palm. Once. Twice. Her hands were little in comparison to his, but they wielded such power over him. So much. He knew his body would recognize her touch, but he wasn't going to tell her that. A nightly massage, a blow job, his cock buried deep in her, he was okay with all of that. For the first time he had hope. He brought her hand to his mouth and brushed kisses over it. Hope was a fragile thing and he was determined he'd keep it alive for both of them.

He carefully slid away from her, tucking rolled blankets at her back, grateful for the little murmur of protest she gave. He knew it was going to be a while before he drifted off and he paced for a long time, wishing he smoked. He'd never taken up the habit because he was a hunter. He often followed his prey by the scent of their cigarettes. It was even easier if his target smoked weed.

He was still shaken at the idea that he'd nearly killed a woman. He knew the experience was too close to take the chance of lying next to the woman he loved and falling asleep close to her. He could have nightmares and she would be at risk. He stared out the window, noting, if they were going to continue to sleep in that room, they'd need heavy drapes. She was a bartender and up half the night. She'd need to sleep in.

Anya had faith that they could overcome the problems they had. Now, with her new idea of getting him used to her touch, he was beginning to share that same faith. He paced some more and then stood by the bank of windows staring at the ocean. It was raging in the early morning hours, the wind kicking up white crests, the water dark, murky, very choppy, reflecting his own mood.

He turned back to look at the woman sleeping on the floor. On the floor. Not the comfortable bed upstairs, the fucking floor because her man couldn't stand sleeping with four walls so close. She'd just laughed and told him she didn't care where she was sleeping as long as she was with him. The hell of it was, he knew it was the truth. Anya would go with him anywhere. If he said he had to leave, to just ride, not knowing where he was going, she'd get on the back of his bike in a minute.

She was beautiful. Far more than he deserved. She deserved the world and yet she was choosing him, knowing all his problems. Could he really be a husband and father like Czar? He'd scoffed at the idea because he'd known it was impossible, but now . . . He shook his head and sank down into the chair next to her so he could look down at her face.

He'd once asked Czar how he thought he could be a father to the children they'd taken in. His reply made sense. He was good at protection. He could provide for them. He could help Blythe with discipline and talking to them, loving them. He would count on her for the bulk of knowing what to do in situations he didn't comprehend. Czar believed he learned fast and would know the next time the same thing came up, so he could be of even more help.

It was really all about total commitment. Being all-in. Reaper leaned down and caught Anya's long braid in his hand. He had to make up his mind to cut her loose or keep her. If he cut her loose, he couldn't go after her later—and he knew he would. He wasn't strong enough to stay away from her. He needed her brightness. He needed to see himself the way she did. He could be that man because she believed he *was* that man.

So, total commitment. He could do that. He felt he already had. If she was willing to find a way for them to be together even at night, if she was willing to risk that, he had to be right there with her—even if that meant confessing to Czar. If she wanted children, he'd provide them and follow her lead on what to do with them. The club would help, not that they knew anything more than he did, but they'd help.

"Reaper?"

The long lashes fluttered and then he was looking into her eyes. His breath caught in his throat. She was drowsy, unable to mask her true feelings, and he could see the way she looked at him. He knew the love of his brothers and sisters. He knew the fierce loyalty they shared. Anya's love was soft. Protective. Sexual. Comforting. It was all kinds of things, but mostly it was that look on her face. The one that told him he was her man and she didn't want any other.

"Go back to sleep, baby. You have to work tonight, and we've got things to do later." He didn't know what they were, but he wanted her asleep so he wouldn't get any ideas. Already his cock was acting like a monster, the way it did anytime he was close to her. And he'd had her twice.

She smiled and her lashes fell. She went back to sleep

with that smile on her face. He watched. She went to sleep confident in him. Confident in them—that they could find their way together. So, he was going to be that as well. Confident in them. He stretched out beside her, on the other side of the rolls of blankets. All weapons were across the room. He could get at them fast if need be, but there would be no accidental mistakes. The rolled blankets would ensure if he turned over, and she did as well, she wouldn't be touching him and playing into his nightmares.

Reaper reached over the blankets and wrapped his arm around her. He knew he shouldn't, not until he had a handle on his bad dreams, but touching her soothed him. He slid his hand under her breasts, spreading his fingers wide to take in as much territory as possible. He wanted to feel her heart beating into his palm, but he kept his hand low, on her rib cage, just below her breasts, listening to her soft breathing.

"Do anything for you, baby," he whispered. "Anything at all." He meant every word.

NINETEEN

They came in just after midnight, seven members of the Diamondbacks. They didn't come in noisily. They were quiet, looking around, faces grim. They went to tables at the back of the room, directly across from the bar, looked at the occupants, who vacated immediately, and sank into the chairs.

It was slow on Tuesdays. One waitress. One bartender. Preacher had gone to some big meeting Czar had called at the clubhouse. Reaper was there as well. Fatei was on as bouncer, but no way could he take on the Diamondbacks if they got ugly. She'd forgotten Absinthe sitting just down the hall, watching the monitor. The club took the security of the women seriously. He came sauntering out, reached around her to casually push the button that was hooked into the clubhouse.

"Should have done that yourself, darlin'," he said softly and moved around her again to the hinged slab of bar that lifted.

Anya watched as three more of the locals left their drinks

right on a table and got up and left. She heard more Harleys. Big ones. Powerful. She lowered her lashes and settled her accelerating heart. She was a damn good bartender. Fast. Efficient. She could bullshit anyone. She glanced at Betina, who nodded and followed Absinthe directly to the table.

"Nice having you here," Absinthe greeted. He didn't smile, because he wasn't a man who smiled much, but he did manage to sound welcoming. "Drinks are on the house. Just let Betina know what we can do for you."

"You can introduce me to the bartender," one said.

Absinthe didn't so much as change expression. "Anya? She is gorgeous. She's Reaper's old lady."

Betina flashed her high-wattage smile at the group. "What can I get for you?"

As she asked the question, seven more Diamondbacks entered. Anya's heart sank. No way would that many come in just for fun without someone warning them. She didn't know much about club life, but when the Diamondbacks were on the move, everyone knew about it. This run wasn't advertised.

Absinthe and Betina stepped back as the Diamondbacks pushed tables closer to accommodate the new group. Absinthe and Betina helped with the chairs.

"Czar around?" one asked. His patch proclaimed him the Mendocino chapter president.

Absinthe nodded. "He'll be here in a few minutes."

Betina came back with their orders, and Anya lost herself in fixing the drinks fast. She put them on trays and Betina swept them away. She served the men and returned, leaning across the bar, looking as if she was showing off what was under her short skirt, but mostly she wanted to be close to Anya.

"If they start trouble, get out fast. Don't try to help." Betina kept her voice low. "These guys play for keeps. And while I'm at it, I just want to warn you that Tawny's seriously pissed. Lana and Alena paid her a visit, and it didn't go well for Tawny. They apparently didn't like that she kept at Reaper when he'd told her no. She didn't look good when she left town. Before she left, she had a lot to say, and she's very vindictive. Just watch your back from here on out."

Anya wasn't certain if Betina had switched the conversation to really warn her, or if she'd done it because a couple of the Diamondbacks hadn't sat down with the others and were wandering around and the waitress didn't want to get caught talking about them. Anya nodded, just to show she was listening, but already she could hear the motorcycles arriving. She recognized the various bikes now. Reaper's was among them.

Reaper and Savage entered through the front door, paused the way they always did and scanned the room. Reaper noted that one of the two Diamondbacks wandering the room was close to the bar, close to Anya. He flicked his gaze toward the middle of the bar where the hallway would have her back, indicating he wanted her in that position. Anya patted Betina's hand, gave her a small smile and moved to the middle of the bar where Reaper wanted her to stay.

Maestro came up behind her and took his position behind the bar. "Sorry I was late, Anya, had a little trouble with a tub of ice cream."

"You have such a sweet tooth," she fired back. He was lying his ass off, but if he could, so could she.

The door opened and Lana and Alena came in, walking together, looking good the way they always did. The two of them drew the eye; man or woman couldn't help but look. Lana's dark hair curved at her chin, calling attention to that elegant detail. Her mouth was lush, her dark eyes framed with long black lashes, making her look exotic and mysterious. She had curves and she knew it, showing them off with her tight jeans and tighter tank. Her clothes screamed biker babe, and her looks screamed sheer elegance.

Alena's platinum hair was thick and wild, falling down her back and around her face in untamed waves. Her ice-blue eyes were striking. She was average height, but there was nothing average about the way she wore her clothes. Like Lana, she wore jeans that hugged her butt lovingly, and her breasts threatened to spill from the red bra that seemed part of the black tank.

Anya had no idea how they did it, but the two women commanded the room. The air went electric, and they had the attention of everyone. Neither looked around; they came straight to the bar, smiling at her.

"Hey girl, missed you," Alena said. "You doing all right?" She slid her butt onto one of the stools and put her elbows on the bar, leaning into Anya's space.

Anya felt the butterflies settle in her stomach. Alena and Lana always exuded such confidence. In themselves. In the club. Whatever was happening, they would help take care of things. She was determined to learn, so she could be more of an asset in any situation.

"Great, Alena. I'm doing great. Things are good," Anya said. "You want a drink?"

Alena nodded. "Make me something. I'm in *such* a mood tonight."

Lana slipped onto the stool beside Alena, making a show of settling herself, shifting from hip to hip, mesmerizing the men in the room who had eyes on her butt. "She is, Anya. Fix her something refreshing."

"And strong," Alena added, stroking a red-tipped finger along the bar as if it was skin and she was caressing it.

Anya glanced up just to catch a glimpse of Reaper. She blinked. He wasn't there. Neither was Savage. They had faded into the darker corners of the bar, places the light didn't quite reach. No one had noticed, especially the fourteen Diamondbacks sitting together at the table, eyes on the women at the bar.

"I'll make you a mojito. A strong one. The mint will refresh you, Alena. Who upset you?" She reached for a bottle.

"Do your thing," Lana encouraged. "You promised you'd show us."

Anya knew they'd never ask her if they didn't want her providing a distraction. Alena and Lana had gotten Reaper and Savage in position. She knew Preacher would be up on the roof outside, waiting to cover the Torpedo Ink members if they needed to retreat. She was slowly learning how they did things.

Anya flashed a quick grin, caught up a napkin, her thumb on the crease facing away from her, spun it like a frisbee, caught it on the back of her hand, turned her hand over and dropped the napkin in front of Alena with a flourish.

Alena laughed. "Nice."

"Easy," Anya said and reached for the bottle of vodka. She did the move she liked, one she'd practiced an insane amount of time. It was merely a stall, the bottle coming to rest on the back of her hand, staying there a moment and then she did a slight toss, caught it and in one motion pushed it toward Alena, tipped it to pour into the glass before it could spill. The "stall" was one of her favorite moves. It was small, didn't slow her down, but effective.

"Awesome," Lana said.

"Feel better already," Alena agreed.

Ice and Storm came up behind Anya from the hallway. Evidently, they'd come in the back way. Czar walked right behind them. Behind Czar were Master and Player. They were moving from behind the bar into the main room before anyone had noticed. Anya hadn't heard them come up behind her.

Czar smiled and walked right up to the table of Diamondbacks. "Nice to see you again, Plank." He addressed the man with the patch on his jacket proclaiming him president. "Absinthe said you're looking for me."

Absinthe hadn't left the bar. He hadn't spoken to anyone.

Anya glanced at the camera over the bar. There were dozens of them, most hidden from view, but every angle of the bar was seen in the monitors. There had to be audio as well. She made a note to be aware of that in the future when she was talking to customers. Many of them told her all kinds of personal things.

"Need to talk," Plank said. He nodded to the second table of Diamondbacks. They immediately stood. "Clear the room."

"Betina, you're off," Ice said. "Bannister. Call it an evening."

The older man at the bar glanced at Anya. "You going home? I can escort you."

"She stays," Plank said.

The moment the president of the Diamondbacks decreed one of the Torpedo Ink women had to stay, the tension in the room went up several notches until it was stretched out to a screaming point. Bannister didn't seem to be affected. He slid off his stool without looking at the Diamondbacks. "Be outside if you need me," he said to no one in particular and sauntered out.

Ice followed him and locked the door. He turned and leaned against it. Storm took the opposite side of the room. Czar slipped into a chair one of the Diamondbacks had vacated. Master and Keys sat on either side of him.

Lana reached across the bar to Anya. "This goes bad, hit the floor," she said softly. "Don't look if you can help it."

Anya wasn't about to argue. She didn't like the fact that Plank had insisted she stay. None of the Torpedo Ink members liked it any better. She'd heard more bikes minutes earlier. She knew the members of Torpedo Ink in the bar weren't the only ones around. The others were just out of sight. Waiting. Waiting for everything to go bad.

"You sent us word that a group of men had gotten together and formed some kind of club calling themselves the Ghosts," Plank stated. "What do you know about them?"

Czar nodded. "Code, our resident hacker, came across them. They were extorting money from another club that had asked us for help. When Code looked into the Ghosts, it was made up of several corporate men, very wealthy with ties to gambling in both Vegas and Reno. They play for keeps, Plank. They have no problem slicing up women and children if their demands aren't met. We saw that firsthand."

"Mafia?"

"Ties to it for sure. I think a couple of sons of owners in Reno started with an idea to target MCs because they figured we couldn't go to anyone for help. They start small, use computers to find members with gambling problems. Target them first, get them hooked, in deep, needing to pay off a large debt, and they flip them."

Plank stirred. Looked around the table at his men. "You're saying someone in my club fed them information on us?"

Czar nodded. "The Ghosts don't give a damn about the gambling debt. They want information on the club's activities. If you're running drugs through a pipeline, they want a cut. They want to use the pipeline to move their money around. They need to know what you're doing and how you do it. What kind of money they can get. Once they have that information, they go after the club president's wife. That's why we gave you the heads-up. Your wife was on their list. We sent the proof, the pictures they had of her taking her yoga class. Running up by the dam. Picking up your kids from school. She was a definite target."

"Do you know who the mole is?"

Czar shook his head. "I don't. Code might be able to find out for you. He's good at what he does."

"I had her guarded night and day. Locked her away. She was pissed too. Sent the kids to her mother's, just to be safe. Had my men guarding them. They still got my wife. Knew right where she was. Killed two of my men." Plank glanced at Anya. "Took her right out from under us. My. Wife."

Czar's fingers tapped on the table restlessly. "I'm sorry, man. These fuckers don't play around, Plank. You have to get her back or pay their price, whatever it is."

Lana stood up casually and walked around the bar. Instantly there was a stir, the seven Diamondbacks moving to cut her off. She gave them a small smirk. "Bathroom. Come with me if you want, boys." She kept walking to the door marked "Women" and disappeared inside.

Alena leaned across the bar to Anya. "Checkin' on Blythe," she mouthed.

Anya's nod was barely perceptible. She realized that Plank was vaguely threatening her by insisting she stay. She knew the members of Torpedo Ink had gone on alert, but she hadn't realized she was the cause, that they were really threatening her. She had been identified as Reaper's. Uneasy now, she began taking care of all the empties behind the bar.

‎ ‎‎‎➛

Plank's enforcer, Jiff, had been identified by the patches on his jacket. He was a big man. Big to be intimidating. Reaper watched him move around the room, a deliberate act to show the members of Torpedo Ink that he was watching them. He never spotted Reaper or Savage. He hadn't even noticed they'd disappeared.

The real threat came in the form of a slender man, one not noticeable. He was quiet, leaning against the wall, arms folded across his chest, almost as still as Reaper was being. That man had noticed they'd lost eyes on two of the Torpedo Ink members, and he continually scanned the room, searching for them. His patch declared he was a road captain named Pierce. Reaper knew that was bullshit. Or if he was, he was also Plank's greatest protector. He had draped himself against the wall behind Plank, in a position to cover him, take him to the floor if necessary. He was a man few would notice. Most wouldn't even mark him as a threat.

There were fourteen Diamondbacks in their space. Three

prospects outside. Another two actual patch members pacing the parking lot. Preacher would take out the two patch members and all three prospects if it came to that. He'd kill at least three outright before anyone realized the threat to them. The fourth would go down trying to return fire. The fifth might be a problem.

He'd marked the road captain, enforcer and Diamondback nearest the president, the one on his right, in that order. Savage would take three more at the table. Czar would kill the president before he went to the floor. Ice and Storm would each take out two. Lana and Alena had indicated their targets. Master and Keys would take out the rest. The moment Plank had not so subtly threatened Anya, Reaper considered him a dead man. Even if he didn't kill him tonight, he would pay the man a visit.

"Your man, Code. Can he find where they're keeping her?" Plank persisted.

"Maybe. When we went after the wife of the president of the Demons, we took out their sanctuary. I didn't think they could regroup that quickly." Czar didn't point out that they'd offered to help protect his wife and track down the threat to her. Plank had been close to rude, stating they could handle their own shit.

"She's not here, is she?" Plank came right out and asked.

Czar sat back in his chair. "Seriously? That's fuckin' messed up. We bring you the word that you're going to take a hit, offer to help, without askin' for anything back, just out of respect and you accuse us of takin' her?"

"Not accusing you. Just asking you. She's been gone eight hours. Tried to find the son of a bitch that helped them, but have no clue."

Czar lifted his hand, and Absinthe, who had returned to his position behind the bar in order to help Maestro protect Anya, went down the hall to get Code. Reaper had no idea if Code could figure out where they'd taken Plank's woman, but no matter what, he knew the club was in trouble. The

Diamondbacks had chapters all over the world. They were a big club, had no problem using violence to get what they wanted, and they had long memories. Torpedo Ink had made certain to show their respect so they wouldn't have problems with the club.

"You meet Reaper?" Czar asked, holding Plank's gaze.

Plank shook his head. "No." He sounded annoyed.

"I think it's necessary that you do."

Plank shrugged. "Bring it."

Reaper moved then, coming out of the shadows as if a part of the dark wall had come to life. His face was scarred. Blank of all expression. His eyes were dead. Not just ice, but flat and glacier cold. He turned those eyes on Plank and let him see that his days were numbered and Reaper would cut his fuckin' heart out for threatening his woman.

"Reaper, Plank, president of the chapter in Mendocino," Czar said. "Reaper's our enforcer. One of two. His brother is around here somewhere."

The big man, the one wandering around, came at Reaper, stood close, too stupid to know Reaper would kill him in seconds. The man made it easy and seemed to be asking for it.

"Reaper." Czar kept his voice low.

Reaper didn't move. Didn't look away. These men had threatened Anya. Savage would be tracking the other one now, Pierce, the road captain who was no longer lounging so casually against the wall. Lana emerged from the bathroom right into the middle of the men waiting outside for her.

Plank studied Reaper's grim features and then leaned back in his chair, his eyes on Czar. "You son of a bitch." There was respect in his voice. "You really don't have her."

"No. We gave you the information and offered to help," Czar reiterated.

Reaper was very aware the president of the Diamondbacks was president for a reason. He was intelligent, just like Czar. He could read men and situations. Plank waved the enforcer away. "Stand down, Jiff."

Jiff continued to glare at Reaper. Plank sighed. "Are you crazy? Reaper, we're not a threat to your old lady. I don't wage war on women. Jiff, I told you to move on." The man poured steel into his voice.

Reaper barely nodded. He stepped past Jiff as if the man was beneath his notice. He was making an enemy, and they'd worked hard to stay off the Diamondbacks' radar. They'd tried to do something good, to save Plank's old lady, and now they'd brought hell down on their heads. Fuck them. He'd go at them one by one. Take them out when no one suspected them.

He glanced again at the president of the club. He'd suspect. He was too smart. He also recognized Czar had them boxed in. If push came to shove, they were all going to die.

Code came out of the back with his computer. "Got something, Czar. Don't know if it's the place where they're holding her, but found another club. They like to hide in plain sight. This one is in Marin. It's smaller, and as far as I can tell, no underground tunnels . . ."

He walked right past Anya, seemingly so intent on his computer and the information he'd come up with that he didn't notice the standoff in the room. Reaper knew better. Code was extremely lethal. He'd studied the monitors before he'd come out and he knew the position of every Diamondback in the room. He already had his plan of kill, just as Reaper did. Just as they all did. Reaper also didn't doubt that Code legitimately had information that would help find the Diamondback's woman.

Code bumped casually into Anya as if he hadn't seen her. "Sorry," he muttered.

Reaper saw Anya's eyes go wide and knew Code had shoved a gun into her hand. He was proud of her. She hadn't so much as flinched. She was very pale, but she kept it together. She stepped away from Code, toward the bar, where she could place the weapon on the shelf below the bar for easy access.

"No problem. I hope you can help them, Code." There was sincerity in her voice. She had seen the work of the Ghost hit men.

Code made his way to the table and plopped his computer between the two presidents. He leaned in between them, his body blocking Plank from Czar deliberately. No one had liked the idea of Czar exposing himself to danger. As long as he was in such close proximity to the president he was vulnerable.

"They have a small club in Marin. No underground, and the layout of the club doesn't leave a lot of places they could hide her. But if they took her fast, they'd have to have her close," Code said. "I've got my girl fishing right now. She can hack anyone. If she gets a nibble, she'll find your old lady."

"Your girl?" Plank raised an eyebrow. "If they think we're going after her they'll kill her. I had the feeling they wanted to kill her. Make us all think they can get to us any time."

"Don't know her name or where she is," Code admitted. "She's an elite hacker. We met online several years ago and struck up a friendship. We help each other out occasionally. She won't get caught. I've tried tracing her and can't find her."

Czar had been studying the layout of the club. Reaper saw him nod. Code was right. There didn't appear to be a place to hide a prisoner. "Anya, you ever work at the Ghost Club in Marin?"

Anya leaned her elbows on the bar. Reaper guessed her legs were shaking and she didn't want to draw attention to that fact. "I subbed in a few weeks when one of the bartenders was really sick."

"What comes to mind? Take your time and think it over."

Anya bit her lip, frowning a little. "The club is the draw for the big spenders, Czar. All their clubs are."

"How many do they have, sweetheart?" Czar asked.

"In the Bay Area? Just the two. They're very popular. Marin and San Francisco. In San Francisco, the casino is underground, but in Marin, it's at the round tower building. Big complex. A few condos. It's about six to ten miles from the club. The club owns the building. The casino takes up the entire second floor. Security is particularly tight because they need time to hide the equipment from the cops if a disgruntled loser is ever stupid enough to turn them in. So far that hasn't happened because they play rough."

"She's got to be there," Code muttered. "I was already searching for properties owned by the club. It would have come up eventually, but Anya got us there faster."

Plank started to rise. Anya's breath hissed out of her lungs. "No. Stop." She held up her hand. "You can't go after her. Not if she's there. Not like that." There was real fear in her voice, and for the first time Reaper was torn between his duty to protect Czar and to get to his woman, who was clearly afraid.

To Reaper's shock, Plank lowered himself back into the seat, looking at Anya. The president of the Diamondbacks beckoned to Anya. "Come here, sit with us. Why can't we go after her if we know where she is?"

Anya hesitated. The enforcer for the other club made a move toward her, and Reaper came out of the shadows. Every member of Torpedo Ink stood up. Lana slid between the enforcer and Anya while Alena positioned herself directly in front of the road captain, a faint smile on her face.

"Did I ask you to escort Reaper's woman over to me?" Plank demanded. "Go outside and take a breather. I know Sylvia is your sister, but she's my wife. I'll get her back."

That put things in perspective for everyone. Jiff was strutting around trying to make something happen. Anything. Just to bring his sister home safely.

The enforcer stomped to the door but didn't go through it. Instead, he turned back toward the table, arms folded across his chest, a stubborn look on his face.

Reaper held out his hand, gesturing once toward the table, and Anya immediately came out from behind the safety of the bar. Alena glided away from Pierce, giving him her sweet smile. He grinned and shook his head. Lana followed Anya, making certain to stay close enough that Anya might feel safe, but enough of a distance that she could fight if need be.

Keys vacated his seat to allow Anya to sit beside Czar. She did so reluctantly. Plank leaned close. "Why shouldn't we go after her?"

Anya took a breath, touched her tongue to her lips nervously and then glanced first at Czar, and then Reaper. Czar nodded. "Tell him, Anya." His voice was very gentle.

"They'll kill her before you could ever reach her, and they'll be gone like smoke. That's why they call themselves ghosts. You can identify the main players by the little gold cuff links they wear. They're in the shape of a ghost. They dress in suits, and if they do ride, they only ride to try to fit in. That building is very secure. Cameras, audio recorders, guards at every entrance. On every floor. At the elevators. I was taken there several times in the weeks I was subbing and worked the bar at the casino. I had to be escorted in and out. If they think you know where she is, they'll slice her into little pieces just the way they did my roommate."

Plank went silent. He sank back in his chair, staring almost uncomprehendingly at Anya. Reaper couldn't blame him. The Diamondbacks were considered one of the most powerful and dangerous clubs in the United States. Few crossed them. No president of a chapter would ever think someone would have the balls to kidnap his old lady. It just wasn't done. The entire club would hound you for the rest of your days. No one would stop until you were dead. If the Diamondbacks went after Plank's wife, they would do so in force and she'd be dead before they got to her. That was plain to the club president.

"We got out Hammer's old lady," Czar said. "We were

able to use blueprints of the tunnels and plan each move carefully. You know we're originally from Russia. Taking back people and things was sort of our business over there."

"Why'd you leave?" Plank asked.

"It got a little hot for us. Don't worry, we're legitimate here." Czar glanced at Code, who flashed a brief grin that failed to light his eyes. "The point is, that's our area of expertise, if you care for help in planning."

That would be a big one for the club president of the Diamondbacks to swallow. On the other hand, Plank was a very intelligent man. So far, Torpedo Ink had been respectful, even when they made it clear they would be willing to fight if the Diamondbacks tried to take Anya from them. Plank was smart enough to use every resource available to him.

"Do your thing. I have to make a couple of calls."

"Plank, it's your call," Czar said, "but I'm warning you, the more people who know you're going in after her, the less her chances are. Let's find your mole, figure out how to get her back and then make any necessary calls."

Plank put his phone away. "How can you find the member betraying us? I would stand behind every member of my chapter. They're brothers."

Code's fingers were flying on the computer. Data was moving across the screen fast. Almost too fast for the human eye. Plank craned his neck at first trying to see what Code was accessing, but it was almost impossible from his angle. Code continued for a few minutes. In the silence, one could have heard a pin drop. He sucked in his breath and turned the screen toward Czar. While he did, his fingers tapped on the table. The sound was barely perceptible.

Reaper read their code. Few things shocked him. He moved ever so slowly. A soft glide on the floor. Staying in the shadows, trying not to bring attention to himself while he made his move, stalking his prey from the darker corners of the room. Ice, already with his back to the door, shifted subtly as well.

Czar turned the screen toward Plank. The financials were there in black and white. The wins and losses. The losses piling up until the amount was obscene. Plank stood up, pushing back his chair slowly so the legs scraped over the wooden floor.

"Anya," he said very gently. "I would very much like you to go to the back room for just a little while. I need to chat with Czar."

Anya glanced at Czar, who nodded. Reaper appreciated that Plank realized Anya was new to the life. She got up without a word and turned toward the bar. Instead of going to the hinged slab that Reaper expected her to go to, she went around the bar toward the door that led to the back. To do that, she went dangerously close to the Diamondbacks' enforcer. Jiff reached out with both hands and yanked her hard against him. One hand held a knife and he locked Anya to him, the blade of the knife against her throat.

"Anya. Baby." Reaper spoke gently. No alarm. No expression. "Don't move until I say to move. Give me your eyes." He stepped in front of the Diamondback enforcer, right under a light so that it spilled down on him, bathing the lines and scars carved deep into his face with a yellowish, malevolent glow.

Anya's gaze jerked to his, went wild in alarm and then settled. He willed her breathing to do the same. The Diamondbacks surrounded Reaper, but he didn't back off and he didn't look at them. Only Anya. Keeping her grounded to him.

"What's the problem, Hogan?" Plank asked, calling the man by his legal name instead of his road name.

Plank walked through his men to stand beside Reaper, something Reaper would never have allowed Czar to do, and he hoped like hell that Ice and Storm or someone would prevent Czar from making that mistake. Out of the corner of his eye, he saw Alena moving through the Diamondbacks, coming in from the left. Lana was taking the right. Jiff didn't bother to look at either of them. No one could ever conceive of the two women being a threat. The truth was, they were every bit as lethal as any of the male members of Torpedo Ink. They'd had the same training in every way to kill another human being.

Jiff shook his head. He was sweating. "Step back. All of you need to step back. I'll slit her fucking throat if you get any closer."

Anya made a soft sound of distress that crawled right down Reaper's throat and hit him in the heart, piercing deep, settling in his belly. She was pale, so pale her skin looked almost translucent. He took a deep breath. He would have to move fast. The knife was too close, skimming her flesh, a thin line of red appearing.

"Hogan, take the knife from her throat. What the fuck is the matter with you? You've already cut her. We need their help in getting your sister back. You don't want to get them all riled up so we go to war and don't have time to bring Sylvia home."

"You know. I know you know," Jiff blurted. His eyes were wild. He was going to kill Anya. Reaper could see he'd made up his mind that he had nowhere to go. He'd double-crossed his club. He'd traded his sister's life for his own. He'd betrayed their code. Plank wouldn't forgive him. They'd kill him, and if they did it fast it would be a miracle.

"What do I know?" Plank asked softly. Making him say it.

Jiff threw his head back and howled. "I owed them hundreds of thousands of dollars. If you'd just let them run their fuckin' money through our pipeline, they would have backed off, but you said no. I had to give them Sylvia. I had no choice. They were going to cut me up."

"Who?" Plank prompted. "Who threatened you? If you'd come to the club we would have protected you. Taken care of it for you. That's what we do."

Hogan had not only given up his sister, two Diamondbacks had been killed when she'd been taken. He knew, no matter what Plank said, he was a dead man. Jiff shook his head, his eyes wild with fear. Reaper could smell his terror. He'd smelled it enough times. With each back and forth of his head, the knife slid lightly over Anya's throat in a sawing motion. Blood trickled down her throat onto her chest. Reaper's gaze followed the drops.

"Czar, when I kill this douchebag are we going to war?" It was a warning to them all.

"No war," Plank said.

Reaper didn't wait. At the same time, Alena went in from one side, Lana from the other. Lana sliced right through Jiff's arm, the one holding the knife, cutting up, not down, going through the under part of his arm, the blade continuing in one motion right under his armpit where she slammed it deep.

Alena simultaneously yanked Anya free as Jiff's arm lowered just enough to get his victim out of the way. Alena pulled Anya with one hand and went up under Hogan's other arm with her blade, twisting back to slice deep under the arm and then shove the knife all the way into the armpit.

Reaper went straight into the man, blurring fast, one, two, three seconds and he was stepping back. Jiff stood absolutely still, shock and horror on his face. Reaper's blade had sliced him up the middle, sliced open his belly and twisted through his heart in one continuous stroke. Reaper didn't wait for the enforcer's brain to acknowledge death. He stepped into Anya, facing the Diamondbacks, sweeping her behind him with one arm.

"You okay, baby?" he asked without looking at her. He was already feeling in a murderous rage. He wanted to carve a few of the Diamondbacks up. They'd come with their show of force, threatened Anya and then tried to act as if they should help with the president's wife.

"Reaper." Czar's voice cautioned him. "Plank gave you the go-ahead. Anya's okay. Take her into the other room and clean that up. It's a knife wound. Infections are the worst."

Plank kicked the body. Blood pooled on the floor around and under it. It was going to take a hell of a lot to clean that shit up. Reaper didn't do as Czar commanded. Alena pulled Anya to her, circled her shoulders with her arm and took a step toward the back. The Diamondback road captain was blocking her way.

"Nice moves," he said softly. Admiringly. "You got a name?"

Alena's chin went up. "Alena. Sometimes my brothers call me Torch."

"I'm Pierce."

"She's bleeding, Pierce," Alena said.

"You got a man?"

She didn't answer for a long minute and then she shook her head.

He stepped out of the way slowly. "Be back this way sometime soon." He turned, caught Reaper's eyes, shrugged and stayed where he was.

"We've got work to do," Plank said. "We need that girl to talk us through the building."

"I've got my girl on it," Code said. He wasn't about to give up the name she went by on the Internet, not to the Diamondbacks. "She's hacking into security while I'm working on getting the entire layout of the building and parking garage."

"I want this piece of shit out of my sight. Buried deep. Hell, feed his ass to the sharks if you want, just get him out of here," Plank said. "He's gone, and as far as Sylvia has to know, those fuckers who took her killed him. You understand?" He looked around at his brothers. "She doesn't ever know her brother betrayed her."

TWENTY

The Marin Ghost Club was a small little building sand-wiched between two other buildings right on the edge of the water. The views were beautiful, and a long deck allowed those in the club to spill outside when it was too hot inside. The club was immensely popular with the wealthy, celebri-ties often visiting. Just as in San Francisco, the cars were assessed along with clothes and jewels, the valet radioing the managers of the club to let them know of potential play-ers for the casino.

Lana and Alena had already been given the VIP card from the San Francisco managers, and they were recog-nized. It had taken them exactly four and a half minutes to be approached by the manager of the Marin Ghost Club, and another seven before he offered them the card that would get them into the casino. The manager made it very clear they were welcomed back. They stayed another half hour, flirting and laughing with him. Alena danced with him twice.

Keys and Pierce entered, each man dressed in a suit

worth well over two thousand dollars. Pierce glanced at Alena as they found a table. "You always have your women do your dirty work for you?" he asked Keys.

Keys shrugged, gave his order to the waitress and looked across the table at the Diamondback enforcer. No one had bought his road captain patch. "First, Alena is a fully patched member of the club. Both Lana and Alena grew up with us. They have a full vote in everything we choose to do, like running this little errand."

"You're still pissed because Plank insisted I come along."

"This is what we do. We count on one another. You're an unknown, and that could get one of us killed."

"I can hold my end up. You have any idea how difficult it was for Plank to turn this job over to you in the first place? Don't worry about whether or not I can take care of business."

Keys didn't say anything for a long time, but watched as Pierce stared across the room at Alena laughing up at the manager. "You did hear me when I said she was a fully patched member of Torpedo Ink, right?"

Pierce shrugged. "I heard you. You do understand that I'm a fully patched member of the Diamondbacks, right?" That was pulling rank. Blatant pulling rank.

"Exactly," Keys said, not in the least disturbed by the reminder. He tilted his head and gave another female manager his megawatt smile as she approached their table. He was happy when Pierce did the same.

The woman made it clear she was all over Keys, and he asked her if she had time for a dance. Pierce waited for the music to start and then he sauntered across the club to Lana and Alena's table, bending close to be heard above the nightclub DJ and the pounding beat he provided.

"Dance with me." It wasn't a request. He knew he was pulling rank a second time. His club held jurisdiction over theirs. He wanted to make that very clear to them.

Alena tilted her head to look up at him, her eyes searching his. With a small, rather haughty nod that made him want to smile, she stood, and he didn't hesitate, taking her into his arms. She felt as good as she looked. She had curves. The kind he liked. Her full breasts pressed against his chest as he whirled her deeper into the shadows. His hands slid down her back, following the curve to that sweet, round ass he'd been thinking about since he'd first laid eyes on her.

"You shouldn't have come with us."

It wasn't what he wanted to hear, but he'd take it. Her eyes were on his face, all blue. A deep, ice-blue. Gorgeous. "Where the hell did you come from?"

"Russia." She knew what he meant, but she deliberately misunderstood him.

She made him want to smile. He hadn't felt like smiling in a very long time. His hands curved over her ass, pulled her closer into his body. Fit her to him. She fit perfectly.

"Russia's loss," he murmured, his mouth against her ear. His teeth closed over that little lobe and bit down.

She didn't try to move away, her hips swaying into his rhythm. "Seriously, Pierce, we do this kind of thing all the time. We're good at it. You could get one of us killed."

He didn't like her thinking that. "I spent my share of time in the SEALs, baby, I think I can keep everyone alive. I don't make mistakes."

"Then why are you dancing with me?"

Pierce knew she was right. He shouldn't risk it, not with the stakes so high. Keys had been right as well. He couldn't be interested in a fully patched member of another club. "Your club accepts female members?"

"Obviously."

The tone of her voice dripped with haughtiness, and it made him smile. She was perfect. Everything he'd been looking for, but she wore another club's patch. "You ever think of ditching your club?"

"Never."

That was firm. He knew it was a waste of time. She was

used to being heard, having a vote, knowing what the club was doing and participating. She wasn't the type of woman to be happy in a relationship with a man who wouldn't give her that.

"We'd be good together." He persisted, knowing she was lost to him.

"I know. Chemistry is a bitch, isn't it?" She smiled up at him.

The song was ending and he'd have to let her go. He wanted to kiss those perfect lips, but they were working and he'd pushed his luck as far as it could go. In any case, tasting paradise and walking away wasn't his idea of smart. He walked her back to her table, noting that slight little limp she had and wondering why it turned him on and made him feel protective at the same time. He left her there and made his way back to Keys.

"Manager told me about their casino. It's not located here, just like we thought. The casino is in the building the corporation running the clubs owns. It's located about seven miles from here, just like Anya said. Another drink and we can go. I want to wait until Lana and Alena are safely out of here."

Pierce was happy Keys didn't say anything about his dancing with Alena. Technically, he was there to oversee the rescue—or kill them all. Those were his orders. Things went south, he was to put a bullet in each of their heads. He didn't think that was going to be as easy as Plank had made it sound. In fact, watching them work together the night before was an eye-opener. Torpedo Ink wasn't an average club. They might be small, but they were lethal. He was certain Plank recognized it in Reaper, but unsure if he'd noticed it in the others.

"The girls are making their move now," Keys reported.

Pierce was very aware of Alena standing with Lana, both shaking their heads when two men approached to ask them to dance. They appeared to be two carefree women moving across the dance floor toward the door, bent on having a good time at the casino.

He didn't like that Alena was involved in any way in this business, but he had to get his head in the game. There were a lot of lives at stake.

<hr>

Reaper stared up the side of the building. It was a strange, square tower rising up four stories where the rest of the building was only two, plus the parking garage. The two women, dressed in their slinky dresses, dripping diamonds and rubies, walked right up to the front door, completely confident in their spike heels. Both waved a card at the doorman, smiling at him, Alena tossing her platinum hair over her shoulders, all flirty.

They're in, he reported.

Having the time of our lives, Lana said.

Reaper could see them through the glass making their way to the elevator where the guard there looked at their card for a second inspection. Alena had tripped slightly on the carpet just past the doorman. She bent to check her heel, running her hands down one silky leg. The doorman looked at her, not to the front. Lana flirted outrageously with the guard at the elevator, distracting him while Mechanic cruised right in, disrupting all cameras with the energy radiating from his body. He wore an elegant suit and continued across the floor without pausing to aid Alena as she stood up slowly.

Mechanic avoided the elevators. He went directly to the first door to the left of the elevators, opened it and disappeared inside. *In position.*

Lana and Alena entered the elevator, rode up to the second floor where their card was checked a third time. They were let through the double doors to the much larger casino. It was in full swing. And crowded. The Ghosts were making money. The two wandered around as if looking for the right game to play.

We're in. Cameras everywhere. Can you take them down from there, Mechanic?

I can shut down the entire building. Mechanic was matter-of-fact. *We can't tip them off. Play a little. Have fun.*

Reaper watched as Keys and Pierce presented their card to the doorman. Keys was the number one player they needed inside. His gifts held the key to their success, which was how he'd gotten his road name. Reaper detested that it was Pierce with him. Keys needed backup he could count on. They'd argued long into the night and most of the next day, but Plank had insisted Pierce accompany them into the club and then into the building where they were positive Sylvia, Plank's wife, was being held.

"Nice building," Keys commented to the doorman. His voice softened. He looked directly into the man's eyes. "I've put up a few, but this design is incredible. Any chance I could look around on this floor before going up?"

The doorman hesitated. Couldn't look away. He shrugged. "Knock yourself out. It's all offices down here. They've all gone home for the night." He pointed to a security guard standing at the end of the hall, and the man jogged to him. "Show them around the floor."

The guard nodded. Clearly, he'd been bored, and showing two wealthy strangers in dark suits around was better than standing there trying not to fall asleep.

Keys walked slowly, making a show of looking up the walls to the ceiling every few feet while Pierce engaged the guard in small talk. They made the entire circuit of the lower floor before the guard escorted them to the elevator.

Keys stepped inside. *She's not in the parking garage or the lower floor. She won't be on the casino floor, but I'll make the circuit just to be safe. I'll have to get up to the third floor.*

He and Pierce circled the outer rim of the gaming tables. They spotted Lana at the card table and Alena at the slot machines. Both appeared to be winning small pots, nothing too big yet. They couldn't draw undue attention until—and if—they needed the distraction.

She's not on the second floor. I need to get up to the third.

Reaper and Absinthe approached the building. Absinthe smiled at the doorman and showed him a map as if lost. The two talked for a moment, and then the doorman nodded several times, took the map and left the building, going straight to his car. Absinthe could plant ideas as well as extract information.

Now, Mechanic. Start shutting things down, Czar ordered from his vantage point across the street. He was up high, running the mission like he normally did, Preacher stretched out with his rifle, ready to protect his crew from a distance.

The lights in the building flickered. Came back on. A few seconds later they flickered a second time and then dimmed. *Cameras off,* Mechanic reported. *I'll take out the elevators after you're up to the third floor, Keys.*

Copy that, Keys said and sat down at a slot machine next to the elevator.

"What the hell are you people doing?" Pierce demanded. He sat at the machine next to Keys. "I thought we were looking for Sylvia, not playing games."

The dimming of the lights hadn't slowed down those in the casino. Alena was moving to the craps table, and Lana was sitting in on a high-stakes card game.

"Be patient. An operation like this takes time. We're getting into position and spreading out, looking for her. If you're having too hard a time, you can wait outside."

Pierce glared at him. "I can't see that you're doing much beside wandering around," he said. "You might clue me in."

Keys sighed. "I know she's not on the lower floor, the parking garage or here on this floor. Mechanic is messing with the lights and shutting down the cameras a few at a time so they think the glitch is in the wiring. Absinthe and Reaper will be taking the elevator with us to the third floor. We're waiting for them."

"Every door on the first floor was closed. How do you know she isn't down there?"

Keys shrugged. "I don't know how to explain it. It's what we do. We . . . sense . . . things."

"You did this in Russia?"

"We were schooled in Russia, trained. Since we were children."

Pierce studied his face for a long time. Then he finally nodded. "What's next?"

"They're on the way up now." Keys rose casually, collected his money and sauntered toward the elevator. Pierce kept pace with him.

The doors opened and Keys and Pierce stepped inside. A roar went up in the casino, Alena's laughter contagious. A crowd rushed to the tables where she was winning throw after throw. The guard turned his head toward the sound of the crowd and the elevator doors closed, taking them up not down. The arrow on the outside of the door simply didn't light up, nor did the numbers above the elevator.

Reaper regarded the two men. "Mechanic's keeping the pressure on. Lights, cameras, things moving on and offline. We have to hurry though. Someone's bound to call it in soon and we can't take the chance that anyone holding the woman gets nervous."

"I can sweep the third floor fast. Just watch my back, I won't be scanning for trouble."

"I've got you," Reaper assured him. He didn't look at Pierce. He knew why the man was there. He'd been in Pierce's position all his life. He was there to kill them all if things went bad. Savage usually guarded Czar if Reaper didn't, but Ice and Storm were outside keeping all escape routes open and guarding their president. Savage was tracking Pierce, his entire focus on taking him out if the man made a move against any club member. Pierce hadn't spotted him, not with Reaper so close.

The doors opened, and when Pierce went to step out,

Keys held him back, shaking his head. Absinthe stepped out while Reaper kept the doors open. A security guard turned toward them in surprise and Absinthe spoke to him very quietly. The man handed over his gun and pointed toward a door. Absinthe walked him to the door, spent a few moments there and then closed the door, leaving the guard inside.

Keys stepped out and started down the hallway, doing just what he'd done when he'd been on the first floor, looking at each closed door, his gaze going from floor to ceiling. It took time to clear the floor, but he shook his head and they were back in the elevator.

No luck on the third floor. We're in the elevator. Lana, you're up for the distraction. Mechanic, we're headed to the last floor, Keys reported in.

I've got you. Cameras are off. No lights. The lights up there are so dim, they'll be lucky to see you step out, Mechanic assured.

Czar, Alena won a shit-ton of money. Do we get to keep it?

What do you want it for? There was suspicion in Czar's voice.

Lana's laughter was a bright spot in their grim world. *We're getting you and Blythe another child for your birthday, Czar. You need another little boy running around giving you fits. And I can't wait to see Blythe's face.*

You can't buy children, Czar said, relief pouring into his voice.

There was silence. Not one of the members of Torpedo Ink addressed that. Reaper pressed his lips together. Trust Lana to bring it up when they were running a mission.

Lana? Suspicion was back. *The rest of you are in on this. What the hell is going on?*

No one spoke for another few seconds so Reaper stepped up. *An Internet sale of a young boy. Code stumbled on it. We bid on him. Can't track him. Code and his friend are*

*on it, but so far, the signal is bouncing all over Europe and
the United States. We want to get the winning bid, get the
kid free and shut them down.*

Czar growled, letting them all know he was going to kill
them when they got home.

The elevator doors opened and this time Pierce stayed to
the back, allowing Absinthe to step out. Reaper was ready
with his gun, as was Keys. The first moment when a guard
saw Absinthe was the most dangerous. He went straight to
the guard, striding with great authority and confidence. This
guard was more resistant to Absinthe and in the end, the
Torpedo Ink assassin slit his throat and gently lowered him
to the floor.

Keys hurried out of the elevator. *She's here somewhere.
There's tension on this floor. Fear. I can feel all of it.* He didn't
wait for the others, he simply hurried down one side of the
floor, his gaze moving from floor to ceiling. He stopped
abruptly and pointed down a hallway. *She's there. On the left,
third from the last room.*

Reaper moved close to Keys and signaled to Pierce to
take the other side. Weapons were drawn. Reaper wished
they'd brought Steele with them. He was a good doctor and
if the woman was in bad shape, he could fix her up fast
enough to get them out of there quickly.

*Guards in both rooms on either side of her and one room
across,* Keys reported.

How many?

Keys paused just to the left of the first room. He held up
four fingers and pointed to the first door. He looked at the
door across from the woman's room and held up five fingers.
The room on the other side had three men in it. The woman's
room was last. He stared at the door for a long time. He held
up two fingers.

*They're raping her. She's bleeding. Cut up. She's fighting
though.*

Reaper stood in front of the room with the five men in it.

He was going to have to be accurate and fast. They didn't want to tip off the men holding the woman hostage. Absinthe took the room with three men in it. Keys, the first one with four. Pierce went to stand with Reaper. Reaper indicated he take the left and Pierce go right. Pierce nodded he understood.

Three. Two. One. Reaper counted off for the others, pointed to Pierce. They went in together, using silencers. Reaper shot three of the five. Pierce shot the other two and managed to get a bullet into one of Reaper's men before he hit the floor. They heard the sound of bodies falling from the other rooms, then silence.

"You're efficient," Pierce commented. "I'll give you that."

Took out their guards. Going for the woman now, Reaper reported.

Hurry. Mechanic can't hold them off forever. Lana. Alena. Be ready, Czar said.

Reaper didn't wait. He went through the door, gun out, firing almost before he saw the exact position of each of the two men. He did it instinctively and took the man in front of Sylvia through the back of his head and the man behind her through his left eye. He fired a third and fourth time, taking the one in front through the base of his skull and the second man through his throat. He'd fired all four bullets before either man could recognize they were already dead.

"Don't let her scream," he told Pierce.

There was so much blood on the woman from the tiny slices the two-man hit team had made in her skin. *Same exact MO as the men comin' to cut up the Mayhem president's wife. What the hell, Reaper? Did we miss a school somewhere, because what are the odds that these men all use the same method?*

To her credit, Sylvia didn't scream or make any sound at all. Her gaze jumped to the men and then to Pierce. He wrapped his jacket around her and then lifted her into his arms. She was slippery with blood, but he held on to her. She gasped in pain, and her entire body shuddered.

"I'm sorry, Sylvie," Pierce whispered. "We have to go now. Fast. I know it hurts, but we don't have a choice. We're taking you home, honey," he said softly.

She nodded, buried her face in his shoulder and tried to make herself smaller.

"She good?" Reaper asked. "We've got to move."

"She's good. She's Plank's old lady," Pierce stated firmly, as if by declaring that, it would tell Torpedo Ink she was good to go.

Have the package, we're on the move.

They formed a tight group with Pierce and Sylvia in the center, hurrying toward the elevators. Mechanic had the door opened from his position on the first floor and they all pushed in together.

We're in. Lana, Alena, be ready. Reaper all but shoved Pierce toward the back of the elevator, so that they formed a solid wall of protection in front of the pair.

In position, Lana said.

In position, Reaper reported.

The elevator doors opened and both women stepped inside, turned and rolled small devices that had been put together hastily from the contents inside their purses onto the casino floor. They'd already positioned more of the small devices throughout the entire floor as they'd walked through it.

The elevator doors shut and they were heading down fast to the first floor. They exited the elevator as the first explosion shook the building. Screams came from up above them.

"Mostly smoke," Keys assured Pierce. "We go out together. Stay in the middle with her. Steele's in the van. He's a doc. He'll tend to her there."

As they made the exit, Lana and Alena peeled off to get their car in the parking garage. Keys went to the right to hop into his car. He was picking up Preacher, who would leave last. Ice, Storm and Czar were in the truck. It was just at the entrance to the parking garage, in position to cover them if something went wrong. Steele was already in the van waiting. Doors open. They leapt in and moved away to give Steele and Pierce privacy to work on Sylvia.

Transporter was at the wheel and he had the van moving before the doors were all the way shut. The truck fell in behind him. Lana and Alena's BMW followed behind the truck and Keys took up the rear with Preacher.

"Nice operation," Pierce said to Reaper, once Sylvia had been convinced to take the pills Steele had provided. He kept his eye on the Russian doctor, but the man seemed to know what he was doing and handled Sylvia carefully.

"Not our first," Reaper said.

"I noticed. Where did you learn your skills? I've got training, but you were practically going in blind. You still hit your marks, kill shots, every fuckin' one."

"You killed the two you had."

"I took a little more time," Pierce said. "Where'd you train?"

Reaper shrugged. "Russia. We went to the same school."

"Must have been a hell of a school. Military?"

Reaper stayed silent for a long time. Pierce looked at him steadily through the silence, clearly expecting an answer.

"You could say that." It said nothing, yet said volumes.

Pierce got it. He nodded slowly. "All those scars, you get them in that school, or after?"

"Both." Now they were getting into territory Reaper didn't want to discuss. Pierce was Diamondback. Their club was the top club and all the smaller clubs in their territory—and it was very large—deferred to them. Torpedo Ink had been careful to fly under their radar. Men like Plank and Pierce were smart. They saw things. They sized up anyone who might be a potential threat to their club. It would be impossible for a man like Pierce not to see that every member of Torpedo Ink was deadly. Knowing they were trained assassins probably didn't sit well with the enforcer. His president had gone into the bar with complete confidence that they had the upper hand, when in fact, they were surrounded by men already planning out how to kill them.

"Alena and Lana train there as well?"

Reaper turned his gaze fully to Pierce's. Let him see what was coming at him if the man went after either woman. "Yes." He kept his tone terse. Ice dripped. He wasn't alone. The other men in the van turned toward Pierce, and, Diamondback or not, the threat was very real.

Pierce was a man who would recognize the threat, but he didn't react. He didn't look uncomfortable, he just nodded. "They were . . . extraordinary. At the bar. In the nightclub. I would have liked to have seen them in action in the casino. No one would ever suspect them."

Reaper was impressed in spite of himself. Few men outside his circle impressed him. Czar's brothers—but they'd gone to different training schools in Russia, suffered at the hands of sadistic instructors—and strangely, Jonas Harrington, the local sheriff, and his deputy, Jackson Deveau. Those men had earned his respect. Pierce joined that elite realm. Because he was beginning to like the man, he warned him off.

"She's beautiful, but she's also a fully patched member. We have two women in our club for a reason, Pierce. Blythe and Anya are under our protection, but that means under Alena and Lana's protection as well. She'll never switch to another club. Never. She's got our colors on her back, the same as all of us. She's sworn to protect every member and she would never break that vow. Don't go there."

Pierce flashed a grin. Reaper noted it didn't light those deadly eyes. He shook his head. He'd given the warning. If Pierce chose to ignore it, that was on him. Alena was Torpedo Ink. Pierce was Diamondback. There was no mixing those two. Even if she dated him, she would wear her colors with pride, and sooner or later another Diamondback would get ugly. She'd kill him, and the war would start.

The ride home was mostly silent. Sylvia slept and Steele

stayed close to her, washing each of the lacerations on her arms and chest and then along her legs and torso. A few he closed with butterfly stitches. A few he glued. He was gentle as only Steele could be. Reaper watched the care on his face. He was very impersonal with the way his hands cared for her, yet the personal was on his face, the flashes of anger as he moved to her lower body.

"Was she . . ." Pierce wanted it confirmed, but Sylvia was a friend and he couldn't say it aloud.

"Yes, she was raped. She has tearing." Steele swore softly, his hands still closing cuts. "She needs antibiotics. I can prescribe them. And Plan B, the morning-after pill. She's a fighter. Her hands are bruised, knuckles torn. She has bruises all over her. They worked her over pretty good. You have good doctors in your club?"

Pierce stared out the window. "Some. Not close, but we can send for them. Plank may ask you to help out until we can get someone from one of the other chapters."

Steele nodded. "I can do that. I've had a lot of experience with this . . ." He broke off and shook his head.

Reaper felt for the man. He'd been the one to care for all of the girls when they'd come back broken and bloody to their disgusting, germ-ridden dungeon. Too many. Too many times. Over and over. Helping Sylvia had to bring back those nightmare days.

Pierce glanced at Steele and then his gaze jumped sharply to Reaper's face. Reaper gave him stone. What they'd all suffered was private. Alena and Lana had a past that belonged only to them, not to anyone else. If they chose to share it, as he'd shared his with Anya, that was their prerogative. He wasn't about to confirm or deny what Pierce was thinking.

It moved through Reaper's mind that someday he might have to kill this man. It was the reason he never got close to anyone. There was always that possibility. He didn't let himself like Pierce, but he wanted to. The man was solid. He was the kind of man Reaper hoped Alena and Lana would find someday. But not a Diamondback. Neither woman would ever fit into a club where the women had no say, no vote, and came second. Not only would Alena hate that and refuse it, her brothers—Reaper included—would never allow it. They'd fought too hard to keep Alena and Lana alive and give them freedom. Two women out of so many.

His eyes met Steele's over Sylvia's head. They'd seen this hundreds of times. They had experienced it. The pain. The humiliation. The guilt. The horror. Life went on, but the victim wasn't the same. They would never be the same. They didn't know Plank. They didn't know if Sylvia's husband was a good man, one that would take his time and allow his woman to process in her own way. They had no idea if he would allow her to work things out slowly, to come back to her life and grieve and be angry. To go through the gamut of emotions not once, but over and over.

"You have someone she can talk to?" Steele asked. "She'll need someone."

Pierce's expression shut down. "We don't go outside the club."

It wasn't exactly what Steele asked, but it still said a lot. The men looked at one another and then out the window, memories far too close.

Plank waited at a house on the outskirts of Ukiah, a town an hour and a half from the coast. The president of the Diamondbacks had an army with him. The van had to go through two checkpoints before they made it to the drive in front of the house. It said something about Plank that he ignored the men guarding him and leapt forward even before the engine had shut off to jerk open the double doors of the van. When he saw his wife, he turned away, a loud groan escaping before he swore violently.

Pierce jumped out first. "We got her back. The ones who did this are dead, but they have an operation going, Plank. A big one."

Plank turned back to his wife, hearing nothing, seeing nothing but her bruised, swollen face. He reached for her. Steele gathered her up and gently placed her in her husband's arms. Pierce covered her with his suit jacket once again.

"I'll want a report," Plank snapped, his voice thick with emotion. "Who was taking care of her?"

Steele jumped out of the van and stretched. "I'm a doctor. That would be me."

"Come inside with me. And Czar as well."

Reaper stepped out of the van. "Czar's inside, so am I." He said it to Pierce. It occurred to him that the Diamondbacks' president might not want others to know his wife had been raped. What better way than to wipe out the Torpedo Ink club. They were small in numbers, and right now, the Diamondbacks had the vehicles surrounded. The vehicles were armed with all sorts of weapons, but the Diamondbacks had no idea of that.

Pierce glanced back at him, gave him a curt nod and then followed his president into the house. Reaper watched Lana and Alena take up their positions. They were still dressed in their slinky, formfitting, low-cut dresses and both made a show of moving around their little car, bending to look in the mirror, checking makeup and generally keeping all eyes on them.

Pierce came back out of the house as Czar and Reaper approached, but his gaze was on the two women. He shook his head. "I see they know exactly what they're doing."

Reaper didn't react. As far as he was concerned, Pierce was on his own figuring out what Czar's crew was doing while Plank's men were watching the Alena and Lana show. He flanked Czar, Savage moving into step beside him. His brother had come out of nowhere. Pierce's sharp gaze jumped to his face then to Reaper's. Neither man looked at him. They weren't going to explain where Savage came from, not when he had to have ridden in one of the three vehicles to Marin and back.

Pierce shook his head again. He knew now just what kind of men and women Torpedo Ink was composed of. They'd wanted to keep that secret, especially from other clubs, but they'd blown it when they'd decided to help Plank get his wife back. Now, it was up to Pierce whether or not he decided to share that information and start a war, or just tuck it away for future use, if he ever needed it. Either way, Reaper didn't like that he knew.

Plank carried his wife straight to the bedroom, glancing over his shoulder at Steele. "In here," he said unnecessarily. "Why won't she wake up?"

"I gave her a mild sedative. She was in a van surrounded by men she didn't know, no clothes, and I had to work on her. I didn't want her more uncomfortable than she needed to be. She'll wake up soon. She's been showing signs of coming around for the last few minutes. If you talk to her, that will help. She'll need to take a couple of pain pills in the next twenty minutes. I want to keep her as comfortable as possible."

"Before she wakes up," Plank said, staring down into his wife's bruised and swollen face, "I want you to tell me everything that happened to her. Don't leave out one detail."

Steele told him everything he knew about the multiple attacks on Plank's wife. "They had to have intended to kill her, because they would know if they gave her back in this condition, you'd retaliate."

"I would have retaliated anyway," Plank said. "We're already preparing to take down their club and the casino."

Steele shrugged. "I don't care what you do, but I do care that your wife recovers. To do that, she needs her man."

"I get what you're saying." Plank walked him out of the bedroom and pushed open the door next to the room. "You can stay in here." He wasn't asking.

Steele stood for a moment then looked past him to Czar. Czar nodded slowly. Steele shrugged. "I'll need my equipment." He walked around Plank, heading for the door. Two

Diamondbacks stepped in front of him, preventing him from leaving.

Pierce shook his head, went straight to his president and lowered his voice so no one else could hear him. Reaper was on the side of Czar closest and he shifted, gliding silently so he could get into position to hear what the enforcer said to his president.

"Plank, this club risked their lives for Sylvia and you. They pulled the rescue off like clockwork. Precise. It was a thing of beauty. Not once have they shown disrespect toward us, but every time they turn around they're met with suspicion and hostility. You've got to tell the boys to stand down."

Plank shook his head. "It's Sylvia."

"I was there when Reaper shot the bastards. He killed both of them before they could even register we were there. There was no risk to Sylvia, and the moment they got her out of there to safety, Steele began working on her. She was treated with respect at all times. I didn't have to make sure of it, or remind them who she was. They just did it."

Plank nodded his head and waved the guards from the door. "I wanted to kill those fuckers myself, Pierce. Sitting here, waiting for word on my wife while another club rescued her, made me feel like a pussy. I should have taken the boys and stormed that place."

"They would have killed her before you got to her. The place was a fortress. Security that tight. It had to be a small force going in undetected to get her back. It was the only way, and you did the right thing. Torpedo Ink is affiliated with us. They came to us and asked to be in our territory. We agreed. They might be small, but they have their uses. Seriously, Plank, I watched them work. They were like a machine. If you want my advice, I would tell you to form closer ties with them. They definitely have their uses."

Plank regarded him for a long moment and then nodded. "We'll do it right, put it to the members and bring them in closer."

Pierce nodded. Reaper thought the enforcer was a crafty, seriously intelligent son of a bitch that he was going to have to watch night and day because the man was up to something. He hoped he didn't have to kill Pierce, but there was a glimmer of dread forming in his gut that told him that possibility was growing. He glanced at his brother. Savage was looking at Pierce and thinking the same thing, Reaper could tell by the ice in his eyes.

TWENTY-ONE

The Demons arrived late evening. Czar had invited them for a meeting and a party after. Reaper knew they needed allies. The Diamondbacks had made vague overtures after Steele had returned, but Czar was reluctant to be too close to them. In the end, that club tended to swallow the smaller clubs. None of them could give up the freedom they'd finally found after years of being "owned."

Hammer brought a small contingency of twenty with him plus three prospects. Torpedo Ink had enough room to host the bikers and the women they brought along with them. Hammer's wife didn't come. He claimed she was still recovering, but Reaper was certain she didn't want to see the men who had rescued her quite yet. He didn't blame her.

Reaper and Savage stayed close to Czar at all times. The meeting went well, with the two presidents, vice presidents and their top people hammering out details of what they were willing to do and the cut each side would have. Czar insisted that anything running through their territory had to be reported to the Diamondbacks and a deal struck before it went through. Hammer agreed to allow Czar to do the negotiations, but he wanted to be there.

The party was already under way by the time they adjourned. Drinks flowed freely, along with food from the barbecue that had been going most of the day, slow roasting a quarter of a beef and enough chicken to feed an army. A couple of hours later, the fire pits were lit and the music was cranked up.

The Demons weren't any shyer about snagging a woman and letting her have her way with them. Tops were coming off and women were dancing on tables by the time Reaper could leave to go get Anya. He'd wanted her there for the barbecue, before things got crazy, but he couldn't keep his eyes on her while the meeting was taking place and he didn't trust the Demons that much—not with his woman.

The party had completely taken off by the time they arrived, and Reaper snagged a blanket, bottle of whiskey and a couple of glasses. He took Anya outside where the fire pits were lit and the music was loud. They talked to several of his brothers as they passed them, but the men were already occupied with the women who had come to the party to try to snag one of the club members. Snag them or have wild sex, it didn't matter, they wanted to have fun.

He claimed a spot out of the light, spread the blanket, and set the whiskey and glasses down so he could dance with his woman because she liked that. After a while, he wasn't going to be able to do that with her body sliding against his so seductively. She knew how to move. She wore a low-cut camisole with no bra, because he'd asked her to, and her breasts pushed against the stretch lace, demanding to be freed. Her jeans hugged her body and when his hands slid over the curves of her ass, she didn't reprimand him, just moved in closer, pressing against his fully aroused cock.

Reaper took her back to the darkest corner of the large fenced-in area where one of the three fire pits burned. They sat together on the blanket, back to the fence, her between his legs, the whiskey burning pleasantly down his throat as music pounded around them, adding to the frantic beat of his heart. Women danced, pulling their clothes off as time went on, and the alcohol kept flowing. Some of them crawled over to one of his brothers' laps and went to work.

Reaper caught Anya's chin and turned her face around to his, settling his mouth there because he needed it. He kept kissing her because Anya's kisses were like the whiskey, fire in his belly, in his veins. In his groin. He let it happen, that slow burn that built and built until he was so hard he thought he might cut right through the material of his jeans. His hands dropped to his lap, and he unzipped his pants, allowing his thick cock freedom.

"Your glass," he whispered in her ear, pushing aside the stray strands curling around her face. She didn't argue, just lifted her glass. He knew her eyes were on the women kissing another brother, taking turns, their hands all over him. He remembered worrying that she wished she could just touch him whenever or wherever she wanted. Now, they experimented every night. They both looked forward to the massages, and he especially looked forward to her hands on him, and sometimes, when it worked, her mouth.

He poured the whiskey into her glass and then set the bottle aside. She rested her back against his chest as his hands went to the front of her camisole, finding the laces. She lifted the glass to her mouth, tasting the drink, letting the whiskey slide down her throat. He opened the laces, allowing her breasts to spring free. He loved her breasts. The soft weight of them. The firmness. The way they were high and jutted out just perfectly. Her nipples.

"Someone will see." She put her hand up to cover them.

He pushed her hand down. "We're in the dark, away from the fire. And who gives a fuck? They won't bother us. They're occupied with whatever they've got going on." He was already tugging at her nipples, pinching and rolling. Giving her that little bite that always made her squirm. The tension went out of her and she eased her body back, arching just a little to give him more. He liked to play and he did, squeezing, kneading, stroking. All the while his mouth was on her neck, kissing, sucking, teeth scraping and then biting. Her earlobe. That sweet spot where her neck met her shoulder. She squirmed.

"You getting wet for me?" he asked, his lips against her ear.

"Yes. Always."

Her voice was breathless, and he recognized that need. She was close to where he wanted her. The place he loved to get her, where nothing mattered to her but him. But his body. His mouth. His hands. What he could do to her.

"Did you do what I asked? No panties?"

"Yes."

"Unzip your jeans." He whispered the command into her ear, his hands working her breasts, his mouth on her neck. He was harder than ever.

She put down the drink, and he noted her hands were shaking as she slowly pulled down the zipper. He turned her face toward him again and kissed her. Over and over. Deeper. Harder. Rewarding her. Claiming her. Happy as fuck that she was his and she loved his body as much as he loved hers.

He lifted his head and looked into her eyes. "Slide them down over your hips, baby."

She glanced out toward the fire. The bodies swaying in the darkness. Dancing. Kissing. Fucking. Some women on their knees. Others drinking and laughing.

"Fire's glowing hot, baby. No one can see us. Give me that sweet body." His fingers slid down her belly. Lower. Curved into her, making her gasp. Her hands went to the waistband of her jeans, she lifted up and shimmied. He kept his fingers buried in her. When her jeans were down to her knees, he pulled his fingers free of her sweet pussy and licked them. She tasted like heaven. That aphrodisiac he craved.

"Take them all the way off. I want you facing me, knees up, legs apart." He watched her hesitate, need warring with old rules. Need won. *He* won. He lifted the whiskey glass to his lips, unable to take his eyes off her as she turned around, slipped off her jeans, scooted toward him and leaned back on her elbows, knees up and wide apart.

His breath caught in his throat. She was the sexiest thing he'd ever seen. He swallowed down the whiskey and took another slow sip, enjoying the view. Enjoying the knowledge that she was really his. That she gave him herself. Her body. Any way he liked. Any time he liked.

"Closer, baby. Scoot right up into me. I want your ass on my lap, legs on either side of me, feet planted on the ground."

Her eyes went wide. Her tongue touched her lip. She complied again, this time more slowly, making a show of it. The firelight spilled across her body, her breasts gleaming at him, the liquid gold between her legs glistening an invitation. He waited to put down his glass until she'd straddled him, once more lying back onto her elbows, legs wide, feet planted, her body open to him. Her eyes never left his face.

The beat of the music pounded through his veins. Tripped his heart. He caught her ass in both hands and lifted her to him, just as if she were a glass of the finest whiskey. His tongue swiped across all that gold. Her body shuddered. He looked down at her and smiled. He felt that smile rolling through him. It felt beautiful. His mouth clamped over her and he suckled, his tongue flicking her clit hard.

Her hips bucked. He held her and feasted. Ruthlessly. All for him. Letting her taste drive him as wild as the music. Watching her head thrash, her body undulate. Felt the first rush hit her hard and more of that aphrodisiac poured into his mouth, onto his tongue. He stroked and caressed. He used his fingers, his thumb, he smeared the liquid all over her and lapped it up, biting at her thighs, licking caresses to ease any sting. He devoured her.

She let out a small sound, the air leaving her lungs in a rush. The music started again, another wild, pounding beat. Her little keening wail added to the pulsing rhythm. He kept his eyes glued to his woman. Her face. The beauty there. In his wildest dreams, he'd never imagined he would have everything all wrapped up in a woman. Anya. Everything.

The orgasm rushed over her, strong, rolling through her in waves. He could see it, moving up her belly, her breasts, settling as a scream in her throat. She tried to suppress it, but she was losing all inhibition, uncaring where they were, her entire being centered on him. He fucking loved that. His little angel, Anya. He corrupted her occasionally and it felt like a gift.

The third one had her reaching for him, trying to get his mouth off her sensitive clit, even as the orgasm tore through her body, spilling more gold aphrodisiac into his mouth. He lifted his head, his gaze burning into hers. "Lift up, baby. Need to get rid of my jeans."

Her back was to the fire, the darkness, the others dancing and playing, and she didn't hesitate. As she got to her knees, he pushed his jeans down around his thighs. He caught her hand and brought it to the thick base of him as she once more straddled him. He loved the feel of her fingers wrapped around him. It was a kind of secret paradise to have that. Others might take it for granted that their woman could fist them, or put their mouth on them, but he never would. Never.

He gripped her hair and began pushing her head down over him.

"Are you sure?" Anya's voice was hesitant. "I'm wild for the taste of you, Reaper, you know that, but we've only managed to do this a couple of times, and we're surrounded by others."

He couldn't tell her that was part of the reason he knew

he wouldn't freak out. He was that fucked-up. "Need this, baby. Right now. Need your mouth."

She gave him the control the way she always did. She let him push her head over his cock. "Open your mouth, use your tongue." He shuddered as she complied. The heat. The fire. "Suck, baby. Suck hard."

She obeyed, hollowing her cheeks and sucking him deep. Her tongue lashed and stroked. Danced around and over him. She did something with her throat and then swallowed so that she seemed to massage him with her mouth. He let her breathe, although it was hard to think of that when she was taking him right off planet Earth.

He tightened his fingers in her hair, using both fists, holding her there while every stroke of her tongue sent flames licking up his shaft. He'd never enjoyed having a mouth on him until Anya. Each time they managed to go a little further, making some progress. He found he was becoming as addicted to her mouth as he was to her taste and her pussy.

His hips moved, almost of their own volition, thrusting gently into the scorching hot depths of her mouth. He was thick and he loved the way her lips were stretched to accommodate his girth. He liked the way the firelight played over her face, highlighting her mouth on him. It was becoming more difficult to think. For the first time, with her mouth on him, his balls grew tight and hard. He felt his seed boiling, desperate for release.

Movement caught his eye and he lifted his head. Anya started to lift off him as Player approached their spot, but Reaper refused to allow her to stop. He couldn't let anything stop her. "Harder, baby. Take me there. Swallow me down." He whispered the entreaty. A command really, since he wasn't allowing her head up other than to breathe.

She looked up at him, her mouth working him, each beat of the music, driving down on him until he knew he was there, right at her throat. He held her there, his heart pounding. His cock swelled and triumph burst through him. Player grinned at him and caught up the woman he was with, taking her out farther, away from the firelight, leaving Reaper alone with Anya.

He stared down at her. He loved the sight of her, those eyes staring up at him, that mouth, hotter than hades, those lips, stretched wide to accommodate him. He let her breathe and pushed her down, deep this time, felt her throat. Felt her swallow. Muscles squeezed. His balls felt like they were on fire, a scorching inferno to match her mouth. Then it was there, pulled from him, jetting up like magma, pouring down her throat.

Lightning streaked through him. Pure lightning, zigzagging through his body, ripping down his spine, licking along his belly, roaring through his groin. He clamped his hand around her throat, feeling her swallow, feeling his cock jerk. The sensations were unlike anything he could have imagined. He threw his head back and roared with the flames. They'd done it. That mouth of hers. He loosened his hold on her, but didn't let her head up all the way.

"Don't stop yet. Gentle, babe." He couldn't let it be over. He never wanted it to be over.

She obeyed him, her tongue licking along his shaft, under the broad head, over it, lower, to the base, catching every last drop. He let her up because he had no other choice. Her eyes nearly glowed, showing she was as elated as he was. Elated, but she still was dripping for him. He handed her the glass of whiskey so she could take another small sip.

"Fuckin' beautiful, Anya," he said. He reached out, used his thumb to take the last bit of evidence from the corner of her lip, pressed it to her mouth and waited until she licked his thumb clean. "Put the glass down. We're not finished."

She glanced at his cock. "You're finished."

He shook his head. "No faith, baby." No way was he finished, not after they'd actually had the first success they'd ever had with her mouth on him. His cock was already thinking about coming back to life just at the thought of his plan. "Straddle me like you did before and lie back, legs apart, knees wide, feet flat on the blanket."

Anya complied without hesitation. He reached down and rubbed between her legs. "Love this sweet little pussy, baby. Hot as hell and so fuckin' tight I think you're going to kill me sometimes."

Her hips followed his fingers and she gave a little moan of disappointment when he took his hand away. "I really want you, Reaper."

"I can see that. I want to watch you get yourself off."

"I can't do that in front of you." She sounded breathless, and he saw the fresh flood of liquid seep along the junction exposed to him.

"Yes, you can."

"Not here, Reaper." But her hand slid down her belly.

"Pinch your nipples for me first." He loved her tits. Fucking loved them. He wanted to do a little sucking of his own.

She laid her head more comfortably on his legs, both hands going to her breasts. He watched her fingers on her nipples. Occasionally he reached to rub between her legs, or circle her clit. Once he pushed a finger deep, curled it to brush her most sensitive spot, but pulled away when her hips bucked, trying to allow her to get off.

He poured himself whiskey. "Use your hand like I did. Let me see you, Anya."

He sipped, letting that burn reach his stomach as her hand disappeared between her legs. She began fucking herself with her fingers. The sight was hotter than hell and his cock reacted, just as he knew it would. He reached out to help, flicking her clit hard, watching her face, that beautiful flush, her breasts rising and falling as her breathing deepened.

"Stop, baby."

"Reaper!" She wailed his name.

"Sit on me. Slow, baby."

She didn't want slow and her breath came out a hiss of

protest, but she was Anya and she lowered herself onto him, letting him fill her. Letting him stretch her. She was hot as hell, an inferno surrounding him, burning him alive. That sweet pussy of hers was going to be the death of him. He felt those tight muscles giving way with great reluctance to encircle him like a scorching hot, silken fist. He threw his head back, savoring that sweet death she always gave to him. That all-encompassing fire that ran through his body like a volcano erupting and spreading hot magma until he almost couldn't breathe.

"Your top. Take it all the way off." It was the only thing left on her. The material had been framing her breasts, but now he wanted it gone.

No hesitation this time. Anya was already lost in him and she pulled the camisole completely off and dropped it to the side. She tried to move. To ride him. He held her down, hands on her hips, pinning her there. Her gaze jumped to his face.

"Cup your tits, Anya. I want you squeezing and kneading them."

"I need you to move."

"We'll move when I say. Do it, baby. Hands on your tits."

He watched her hands come up under her breasts, and his entire body gave a little shudder of anticipation. Fingers worked that soft flesh. His mouth watered. Fuck, he loved that sight. He bent his head. "Feed it to me."

She did without hesitation, raising her right breast to his mouth. He sucked that mound in hard, his tongue lashing her nipple. His teeth were next, biting down harder than he normally did. She cried out but he didn't release. He pulled his head back, stretching her nipple taut, eyes on her face. The heat there, the flush of need, how could he ever have lived without it? How could he ever survive if she was gone?

He let go of her nipple and raised her hips, then brought her down over him in a slow slide. He had to clench his teeth it was so good. So perfect. "Work your tits for me, baby,"

Reaper said and went still again until she put her hands on her tits and began massaging and kneading them, until she began pinching her nipples, rolling and twisting to his satisfaction.

He forced her to ride him slowly, staying in control, letting the need envelop both of them. Letting the fire build until it felt so out of control that it was going to leap through both of them, consuming them.

"Please." Anya sobbed the word, her hips squirming, spiraling, the last accelerant to those flames.

He shifted, holding her with one hand across her back, catching her leg to curl it around him. "Both legs," he grunted the command. "Lock your heels. Wait for me. Fuckin' wait."

He shifted, rising up to his knees, putting her back to the ground, ramming into her deep. Fuck. Fuck. That feeling of nothing but fire. Not nothing—he realized that as he looked into her eyes, as he hammered his body into hers, going deep. Needing deeper. There was love there, burning just as deeply between them. He felt that with every stroke.

He rode her hard. Over and over. Her breath whispered over him in ragged pants. Her eyes had gone dazed, shocked. Darkly sensual. He picked up the rhythm of the music, that beat that pounded through his body. The crackling of the fire. The moans. The soft laughter. He lifted his head, throwing it back to look at the night sky as he let the flames streak up from his cock into his belly.

Her pussy clenched at his shaft, squeezed the broad head until he thought he'd explode or lose his fucking mind. He glanced across the fire. Several others were closer than he'd realized, close enough that Anya might have objected had she been aware, but she was lost in him. He locked her tighter to him. It said something to him that *he* hadn't been aware of anyone getting that close. They were still on the other side of the fire, but he was just as lost in Anya as she was in him. He never had lost sight of where everyone was, no matter what.

"Honey." Her voice was a soft plea.

"No. Fucking no. You'll take me with you, and this isn't going to end. Not yet." He kept at her, holding her hips now, pistoning his body into hers. Burying himself deep.

She rose to meet each thrust, the breath rushing out of her, her breasts jolting with every thrust. He loved that. Loved watching her face. Her body. Loved feeling her surrounding him with the ultimate fire.

"Reaper." Soft. Entreating.

"No. Fuck no."

He pulled out, and she let out a wail. He flipped her over, caught her hips in his hands and yanked her up onto her knees, pulling her ass back to him. He knelt behind her, slammed home into that slick, hot inferno again. She cried out, the sound better than the music pounding all around him.

He caught her hair in his fist and pulled her head back, so her back was a beautiful line. So her ass was high and he could be even deeper inside her. He'd like to hit her belly. Claim that. Claim her fucking throat. He knew he was a little out of control, a little wild, but he didn't let go often and she gave that to him. She never protested. She rocked back into him hard, her tits swinging, her throat making sweet little sounds that just egged him on.

"Reaper. Honey, I have to let go."

He smacked her ass hard. Harder than he meant to. Liquid gold, hotter than hell surrounded him. Felt like heaven. He added more swats, keeping with the rhythm of the music, bathing in her scorching gold. Wishing he could eat her and fuck her at the same time. His cock was swollen to the point of no return. His balls were drawn up tight, hot and needing to explode. He forced himself to wait for her next plea. She'd waited for him. He could do the same for her.

"More," she whispered. "I'm going to go over the edge and I want more."

He knew what she meant. Her nerve endings were on fire, so sensitive that when he smacked her bottom, the heat spread like wildfire. He gave her more until she was sobbing with need, pleading with him, begging him to let her come.

"Now, baby. Give it to me now." He couldn't take one more second in that inferno.

Her body clamped down so hard on his it hurt, an actual pain that shimmered through him, adding to the promise of paradise. She gripped and milked and his seed exploded out of him, jetting from him in bursts, splashing the walls of her sheath, triggering multiple tremors, shocks that rocked both of them.

He collapsed over her, pressing her into the ground, his lungs fighting for air. He couldn't move. Couldn't think. The pleasure was too intense, shaking him. He'd had sex a million times, in a million ways, but nothing prepared him for the way it felt with Anya. He loved her beyond words. He hadn't known it was possible to love a woman, to love anyone that much. He fought for breath when his lungs seemed to have seized, refusing to work properly. When he could finally get some air, he pushed aside her hair and kissed the back of her neck. That vulnerable nape that sometimes drove him wild.

"You okay, Anya?"

"I don't know. What about you?"

"Same here. Not certain I'm really alive. Fucking hell, woman. You nearly killed me."

"I think that was all you."

"In case you didn't hear what I was just telling you, Anya, I love you." He hadn't thought he'd ever say that where someone might overhear, but he didn't care. He wanted everyone to know. He wanted them to know she belonged to him and that he loved her above all else. He needed them to know if one hand touched her, he'd kill for her.

"I love you too, Reaper," she returned softly and turned

her head to the side. "When you get off me, I'm going to be stark naked."

"I love you stark naked."

"I know you do, but I don't like being naked in front of another club. It's hard enough in front of your club, but I understand their penchant for being naked and they really don't pay attention. The Demons aren't your club."

He got her. He got what she was saying. He hadn't thought about it because he truly couldn't care less if they saw him naked, but she'd never once complained about anything and he was giving her this. He rose to his knees, pulled up his pants with one hand, the other on her back, holding her down. When she got the message, he zipped his jeans and moved around her, gathering her clothes. Once he was in front of her, blocking her from anyone possibly looking their way, he handed her the camisole and waited for her to put it on and lace up the front. Her jeans were next. She pulled them up her legs, lifted up and dragged them up her thighs.

"I'm a mess," she whispered, as if everyone might hear her above the music.

"You're beautiful."

"I mean with you in me."

"That's the best part. Love being in you, baby, it's fuckin' sexy."

She sighed, rolled her eyes and pulled her jeans over her butt, going up on her knees to zip them closed. He loved that about her, no argument, no protesting, just keeping him in her. Smiling at him until he thought the sun might actually pierce the darkness around them.

He dragged her to him and kissed that sexy mouth of hers. So sweet. Robbing him of his will, knowing she was wrapping him around her finger, she'd already managed to take his heart.

"More whiskey."

"Are you going to get drunk? My little angel Anya is being very bad tonight."

"Yep. You're going to get drunk sex when we get home."

"We might not make it home." He settled her between his legs again, her back against his chest. "I've already picked out the spot where I'm going to fuck you."

"Where?" She held up her glass.

He poured her more whiskey. "I'm going to bend you over the picnic table. Thought about that before I took you right here."

"There's people sitting on it," she pointed out. "Not a good plan, honey."

She drank. He didn't. He wanted drunken sex with her, and he wanted to make certain he could keep her safe. He studied the three men sharing a bottle of tequila. "I can take them easy. They're pussies thinking they're badass."

"I'm sure you could. But then their bodies would be laid out all around us. Might kill the mood."

"Or you'd think I was a great conqueror and you'd be all the hotter for me."

She reached behind her, wrapped her arm around his neck and pulled his head down to her, turning her mouth to him, kissing him, her lips soft and sweet, tasting of top-shelf whiskey, the best for his woman. He wasn't going to be able to wait until they got home.

"Where else?"

"Where else what?" He kissed her again.

"If not the picnic table and you don't want to wait, where else?"

"You got an idea?"

She took another long sip of whiskey, allowing it to slide down her throat into her stomach, clearly admiring the wave of heat. "I've given it some thought. You like open spaces much better than indoors, which also gives me another thought."

"Two thoughts?" His woman was already heading toward that drunk phase.

She gave him a look of pure reprimand. "Yes. Since you like sleeping outside . . ."

"And fucking outside."

"That too. But we could put a bed on the deck. The side overlooking the ocean. It's way wide, big enough, and we'd have the roof overhead if it rained or misted. What do you think?"

He thought it was a damned good idea. "I think you're fuckin' brilliant."

Anya looked pleased. "I am, aren't I?"

Reaper nodded. "You are. What's your idea on finding us a place to have drunken sex?" He poured another finger of whiskey into her glass.

"Standing? Bending over? Knees? Back? Which?"

"I want you standing but bent over. I'm going to do all sorts of dirty things to you first though. That's just a warning."

"Drunken, *dirty* sex?" Anya squirmed. "Love the idea. Okay, we have to find the perfect place." She turned back to survey the yard, glass to her mouth. One hand fiddled with the ties on her camisole.

He took over the fiddling just so he could brush his fingers over her tits. Over those nipples he loved to suck on and pull.

"Right there, Reaper," she said, excitement in her voice. "Look, honey, the perfect place." She pointed to the small bench someone had stuck out in the middle of the flowers in the meadow. Probably Alena or Lana. The girls had worked to plant flowers and trees around to make the compound seem nicer, although they hadn't gotten to the flower beds close to the building.

The bench was out in the open, but a good distance from the fire. The ocean was behind it. There was enough of a moon to light the surface of the water so that light reflected onto the field of flowers. It looked perfect to him. He would be able to see all that soft skin.

"The bench it is, baby," he agreed, and watched the happy smile on her face. He loved that smile, but not nearly as much as he did drunken sex when they got around to it.

━━━━━

The barbecue was in full swing. Reaper leaned against the wide porch column and watched his woman as she ran after Emily, her laughter filling the sky with warmth. He could listen to her laugh for the rest of his life. Beyond even. Each time he heard her, no matter what he was doing, he had to turn his head and look. Each time it happened, she took his breath away.

Darby, Czar's oldest, joined the chase, a streamer of colors, pink and green and blue swaying like a snake behind her as she ran. Emily's streamer was of red and pink and a second shade of red. The little girl loved red. Anya had a trail of colors, yellow, gold and white, all colors of the sun, streaming behind her. He loved that. Loved that her colors were bright and hopeful.

Storm came out of nowhere, lowering his shoulder and catching Darby right in her stomach, bending her over his shoulder. He stood and ran to the far end of the backyard, all the way to the fence, with Czar's daughters screaming with laughter. Just before he made it, Ice blocked him and he had to turn. He ran right into Maestro, who caught Darby and in one smooth move lifted her off Storm and onto him. He turned to run, and Anya and Emily tackled him. They all went down in a heap, a pile of bodies, laughter ringing through the yard.

Reaper sauntered over, taking his time, making it clear he wasn't part of their ridiculous games, but that he was enjoying watching. He reached down with one hand, pulled his woman up and locked her to him, while extending an unopened beer to Maestro.

Darby and Emily both pushed Maestro back so he was lying in the grass, the beer out of reach. "He lost us points," Darby proclaimed. "He doesn't deserve a beer."

"No, he doesn't," Emily declared firmly, echoing her sister's sentiments.

"Zoey," Maestro called. "Help me. They're being mean to me. I was following the rules."

Zoey stood on the sidelines, close to Blythe, watching, a smile occasionally flickering across her face. She was in counseling at Blythe's insistence, but the trauma she'd suffered prior to being with Blythe and Czar stayed with her.

Blythe leaned down, her arm around the child. "Are you going to help him? Whose side are you on?"

"Maestro's," Zoey replied firmly, shocking all of them. She rarely spoke. "He said he'd follow all the rules and if he remembered, he'd get me ice cream later. He remembered."

Rules were important to Zoey. Maestro broke the rules of the game often, and apparently, he'd bargained with Zoey, the rule keeper.

Blythe gave an exaggerated sigh. "You're the referee." That had been Anya's suggestion, trying to bring Zoey into the fun without making it too difficult for her to participate. "I guess you'd better go help him."

Zoey hesitated and then she put her chin up and marched over to the group on the ground. Reaper held his breath, his arm tightening around Anya, locking her to him. Zoey pushed her older sister off Maestro. Darby let her, happiness on her face and tears glittering in her eyes. Emily resisted, but in the end, Zoey was able to distract her enough that Maestro could lift the younger child off him, set her aside and let Zoey help him to his feet.

"Yeah, that's what I'm talkin' about," Maestro proclaimed. "Come on, kid, let's go make some music together." He swept Zoey up and transported her across the yard to the small deck where the band had their instruments.

"I love the barbecues," Anya said. "Almost as much as I love drunken sex."

Reaper laughed. "I'm going to turn you into a bad girl yet."

"Don't count on it. I didn't ask you, because I usually don't want to know, but is everything okay between Torpedo Ink and the Demons?"

"Yeah, baby, it's all good."

"I'm very glad the floor in the bar was replaced before we reopened. Saying we were doing renovations was smart. Jonas and Jackson came in the other day. They're still looking for the men they say disappeared."

"Sounds like harassment. How many times have they been in now?"

She shrugged. "I never handle it, that's all Preacher. They ask me a couple of questions and then they talk to him."

"If it bothers you ever, you tell me."

"I would. In any case, someone is always on the monitor, and most of the time you're there. You were in a meeting when they came in. That was last night."

The club meeting where they'd taken a vote on whether or not to try to find the boy being auctioned off by some slimeball. They took jobs, but most of the time, they hunted pedophiles. Of course they voted to locate the kid. They'd do it too. Code was already trying to find out any information on him available. Reaper wasn't about to talk to Anya about it. Not yet. She needed time before she realized they were never going to stop hunting. Never. They were predators and they needed the hunt, but more importantly, those children needed them. Someone had to find them. Someone had to help.

"Do you think the Ghosts are looking for us?" Anya asked.

Reaper glanced down at her. She sounded scared. He never wanted her afraid, not if he could spare her, but he was always going to tell her the truth. "We shut down their cameras. If they connect Alena and Lana, that might be a trail back to us, but no fingerprints. No faces. We have no connection to the Diamondbacks. The Diamondbacks destroyed their nightclub, burned it to the ground. They did the same with the casino. They left behind their calling card."

"A snake." She'd heard of that before. Everyone had. "Isn't that like asking the cops to come after you?"

"Anyone can leave a snake behind. No one saw anything. It's done, baby. I think we're clear of the Ghosts." He knew the Ghosts would come creeping back. They targeted motorcycle clubs. They knew their hit men and investigator looking for Anya had disappeared after being in the Torpedo Ink bar. The Ghosts were probably busy right now, refocusing, deciding what to do, how to handle their losses and the fact that someone had tracked them, but they'd come around again. As would the Swords, the motorcycle club whose leader Czar had brought down. They also had to worry about the Mayhems, who wouldn't take kindly to Reaper beating the shit out of their president, if they ever discovered who he was. Torpedo Ink had the Demons on their side and possibly the Diamondbacks, but they had to be careful. They were garnering too much attention too fast.

"Hey, you two," Czar called. "Stop gazing into each other's eyes and come over and help out. Need someone to flip burgers, Reaper."

Reaper kept Anya's front to his side as they walked over to the group of men standing around the barbecue. His brothers. They moved to the side to make room for him and his woman. He never thought he would have this kind of life, but she'd given it to him. His Anya. His everything.

TERMS ASSOCIATED
WITH BIKER CLUBS

1%ers: This is a term often used in association with outlaw bikers, as in "99% of clubs are law abiding, but the other 1% are not." Sometimes the symbol is worn inside a diamond-shaped patch.

3-piece patch or 3-piece: This term is used for the configuration of a club's patch: the top piece, or rocker, with club name; a center patch that is the club's logo; and a bottom patch or rocker with the club's location, such as Sea Haven.

Biker: someone who rides a motorcycle

Biker friendly: a business that welcomes bikers

Boneyard: refers to a salvage yard

Cage: often refers to a car, van or truck (basically any vehicle not a motorcycle)

Chapter: the local unit of a larger club

Chase vehicle: a vehicle following riders on a run just in case of a breakdown

Chopper: customized bike

Church: club meeting

Citizen: someone not a biker

Club: could be any group of riders banding together (most friendly)

Colors: patches, logo, something worth fighting for because it represents who you are

Cut: vest or denim jacket with sleeves cut off with club colors on them; almost always worn, even over leather jackets

Dome: helmet

Getting patched: Moving up from prospect to full club member (you would receive the logo patch to wear with rockers). This must be earned, and is the only way to get respect from brothers.

Hang-around: anyone hanging around the club who might want to join

Hog: nickname for motorcycle, mostly associated with Harley-Davidson

Independent: a biker with no club affiliation

Ink: tattoo

Ink slinger: a tattoo artist

Nomad: club member who travels between chapters; goes where he's needed in his club

Old lady: Wife or woman who has been with a man for a long time. It is not considered disrespectful nor does it have anything to do with how old one is.

Patch holder: member of a motorcycle club

Patches: sewn on vests or jackets, these can be many things with meanings or just for fun, even gotten from runs made

Poser: pretend biker

Property of: a patch displayed on a jacket, vest or sometimes a tattoo, meaning the woman (usually old lady or longtime girlfriend) is with the man and his club

Prospect: someone working toward becoming a fully patched club member

KEEP READING FOR AN EXCERPT FROM THE NEXT
GHOSTWALKER NOVEL BY CHRISTINE FEEHAN

COVERT GAME

AVAILABLE MARCH 2018 FROM BERKLEY

Zara Hightower stepped into the town car with its tinted windows, sliding along the leather seat, positioning her briefcase at her feet on the floor. She gave the man who slid in beside her a small smile and looked out the window, ignoring the way her heart wanted to accelerate. It was always at this moment, when she was so close to her goal, that her body wanted to betray her. She never let it. Never. She was very, very good at staying in control. Breathing. Keeping her heart rate perfect, adrenaline at bay.

The car moved forward and her head went up alertly. "Wait. I need my interpreter. She always travels with me."

The car kept moving. The man beside her, Heng Zhang, turned his head and gave her a small, polite smile. "Miss Hightower, you do not need an interpreter. I speak English."

"I'm aware that you do, Mr. Zhang, but I require my own interpreter. I made that very clear to Mr. Cheng when he invited me. I was given assurances when I agreed to speak with his people. I've turned down his request four times, and will do so this time as well if you don't stop this car immediately, turn it around and get her."

She kept her voice smooth and even. She had a certain reputation to uphold. She never lost her temper. She never raised her voice. She was always polite. She cut people down sweetly, so sweetly they almost didn't realize at first that she was telling them off. She was an expert at that as well. Seeing as how she was considered one of the leading minds in the field of artificial intelligence, those around her should expect that she could hold her own with anyone, but they always took one look at her and judged on appearances. Like now. Zhang made the mistake of looking her up and down, then gave her a look that said she was nothing in his eyes before turning away from her and staring out the window.

In her head she went through the moves that would end his life and then the driver's life. She would use one hard-edged chop to his throat, hard enough to drive through the trachea. Or she could just scratch his arm accidentally. Smile and apologize. Then when he slumped on the seat, for good measure, she could follow up by taking his gun and shooting the driver in the back of the head, shooting Zhang to be certain and then taking control of the car. One, maybe two seconds was all she'd need.

Zara sat very still, appearing as she always did. She looked like a beautiful model with her long legs, oval face, flawless skin, large slate blue eyes and long red-gold hair that fell down her back. It was thick and unusual, sheets of it falling below her waist, an attribute that most reporters ended up commenting on when they should have been listening to what she had to say. Still, her looks enabled her to get her work done. She shouldn't complain. It was her looks that often kept her alive.

She turned her head and looked out the window, resisting the impulse to kill Zhang with his smug, superior attitude. They probably had a camera on her. She let her mind drift, uncaring of the direction the car was taking her. She knew where Cheng's lair was. He was famous in the district, his building a fortress. The government tolerated him because he paid them well and gave them all sorts of reasons to keep him protected. Cheng bought and sold secrets and shared them often enough with the government to buy their protection.

Once at the facility, the car pulled into the underground parking garage, went through three guard stations and pulled right up to a private elevator. Zhang got out first and went around to her door. For a split second, Zara debated whether or not to have it out with them right there in the parking lot by refusing to move from the car. She knew they would force her, but she also knew they wouldn't kill her.

Cheng needed her. He wanted the information she had. He kept doubling the price each time she refused to come to his private facility to give her talk on the VALUE system, as she called her project, and its uses in the business world. He thought he had her bought with his more than generous offer, the one that would set her up for life—or get her killed—if she accepted it.

She slid out of the car without looking left or right, and followed Zhang into the elevator. Neither spoke as they were whisked up to the middle floor where she knew Cheng waited for her. She was stopped as she stepped off. Two guards with automatic weapons took her briefcase and pointed to a door. She stepped through it into a narrow cubicle. Immediately her entire body was scanned, looking for listening devices, weapons and cameras, anything that might harm Cheng in any way.

Zara knew Cheng was paranoid, and deservedly so. He had his hand in every criminal activity around the globe that had to do with running guns, drugs or political secrets. He had top minds working for him developing all kinds of weapons that he sold on the black market. What he didn't develop, he stole. She knew every paper in her briefcase would be scanned and copied before it was returned to her.

She'd come prepared for just such a thing. Those papers were "encrypted." No one could break the code because there wasn't one. In reality, the code was nothing but sheer gibberish, but it would give Cheng's people something to keep them busy.

She was taken from the cubicle and marched through an open floor where there were several desks leading the way to Cheng's office. He stood in the doorway, all smiles, as if she would be pleased to meet him after he'd broken their rules.

"Miss Hightower, how good of you to come," he greeted.

She stopped moving a few feet from his office, forcing Zhang and the two guards to stop as well. "My interpreter?" She didn't smile. She kept her gaze fixed on Cheng without blinking, something she'd practiced for a long time. She was very good at it.

"I'm sorry." Cheng didn't sound remorseful in the least. "You must understand I have many enemies. I don't, as a rule, allow any outsider into these facilities. There are always industrial spies. We won't need an interpreter."

Stubbornly, she didn't move an inch. "Don't you think you should have let me know that you changed the conditions? I'm uncomfortable without her. When I come to Shanghai, I always use her and have grown used to her."

Cheng stepped back to clear his doorway, waving toward his office. "Please come in, Miss Hightower. My staff has made you tea, which I believe is your favorite drink."

She stood for several seconds, letting them all worry. Zhang stepped close to her. "Miss Hightower." He waved toward the office.

She looked at him coolly. Haughtily. Every bit as arrogant as his boss. "I'm deciding. I added this additional talk onto my agenda, and as you both are aware, I've had a very tight and exhausting schedule. I did this as a courtesy. I don't need the money. To have your boss break his word so quickly is disconcerting to say the least."

Zhang switched instantly to his native language. "Do you want me to take her up to the interrogation room? Bolan Zhu can extract the information you require from her."

Cheng shook his head, a small, humorless smile on his mouth, one that reminded Zara of a cold-blooded reptile. "Don't be so bloodthirsty, Heng. She will cooperate."

"I apologize again, Miss Hightower."

"I dislike others to speak in their language when I can't understand," Zara said, still not moving. She had understood every word they said. In her résumé, it was never added that she was gifted in languages. That was kept a secret for just instances like this one. She admitted to knowing a few pertinent words in the languages of countries she traveled often to, but was careful not to let on that she understood without her interpreter. Her heart had jumped at the name Bolan Zhu. He was extremely good at torturing people.

"Zhang was only asking after your comfort. We knew you would have trouble without your interpreter, so we tried to think of other ways that would assure you would enjoy your visit with us," Cheng lied smoothly. "We thought a tour of our labs was in order. Understand, this is a great privilege, one not extended often."

As in never. A tendril of unease slid through her. He wanted her evaluation; she understood that. He wanted to hear what she was doing in her chosen field of expertise; she understood that too. She had the feeling that if he showed her his labs, especially his computers, the ones that stored all that data, all the secrets he blackmailed or paid others to get so he could sell out countries—including his own—to the highest bidder, she would earn a bullet in the brain.

She kept her eyes steady on Cheng's face. Zhang didn't matter. He would carry out his boss's orders, but he wouldn't act on his own. He didn't take her as a threat.

"Miss Hightower, I realize the circumstances are unusual, but if you would just come into my office and hear me out, I would appreciate it."

She felt Zhang stiffen beside her. He didn't like his boss asking. He was used to the man ordering others, and if they didn't obey, punishment was swift and brutal. The fact that she was a woman and an American probably offended Zhang even more. Deliberately she made certain to stand as tall as possible so she could tower over Zhang. He was particularly short and she knew it irritated him that she was tall. Cheng was the same height as she was in her heels.

Zara flashed Cheng a small smile and walked past him into the spacious office. She took the chair he indicated and sank into it, deliberately crossing her legs. Zhang didn't like her, but he appreciated her looks. Doing the leg thing always kept others from thinking she was brilliant. She'd found out that most people didn't think looks and brains could go hand in hand.

Cheng seated himself across from her, not behind his desk, clearly trying to create a much friendlier atmosphere. He picked up a file and scanned it quickly. "This is very impressive. I see you went to MIT as an undergrad and then got your PhD at Stanford in Computer Science. Your subfield is machine learning?"

He made it a question but Zara didn't respond. Instead she looked slightly bored. She was really good at that particular look. She'd perfected that as well as the wide-eyed innocent look she was certain she was going to need very soon.

"I see you teach at Rutgers University. Why not private business? You could make a lot more money."

She shrugged. "Money bores me. I realize it makes the world go around, but I don't spend much time in the real world, Mr. Cheng. My mind prefers other pursuits." Which she supposed was the strict truth. She didn't think about money because she didn't have to. She thought about other things like life and death. Like survival. "I spend most of my time working on things others don't understand and that's all right. My programs, hopefully, will be a contribution to the world."

"There isn't a lot here about your earlier life."

She frowned at him. "What does my earlier life have to do with my work?" She kept her voice mild, as if barely interested. She kept her heartbeat the exact same rhythm and that took just a little extra work, but she knew it was possible her vitals were being monitored just by sitting in the chair he chose for her.

"I like to know everything about anyone I do business with."

"I'm not a businesswoman, Mr. Cheng. I lecture. I get paid to lecture. I give talks on exciting new breakthroughs in the world of artificial intelligence. That's what I thought you wanted from me, and knowing anything other than my credentials is not really helpful. I can assure you, my credentials speak for me. I'm regarded as one of the leading experts in AI and machine learning. I thought you were aware of that."

"I'm very aware of that, Miss Hightower," Cheng assured. "It's just that you're far younger than I thought you'd be. I noted your age, of course, but thought it was a typo."

His gaze flicked several times to Zhang, and more than ever she was certain they were somehow determining if she was lying or not. She liked cat-and-mouse games. She was good at them. She was fairly certain his secretary, or whoever prepared the report on her, wouldn't dare give him a report with a typo. His secretary wouldn't survive the hour.

"My age does sometimes give people pause, but I graduated with honors, I assure you," she said with a small shrug as if she didn't care whether he believed her or not. She uncrossed her legs to switch them, drawing their attention immediately. Once comfortable, she moved her foot, clad in a sexy blue high heel to match the blue jacket she wore, around in lazy circles. That always seemed to mesmerize males. It worked with Zhang, but not with Cheng.

"You disappear for long periods of time."

He made it a statement so she smiled sweetly at him as if waiting for a question, making him ask.

He sighed. "Where do you go?"

She shook her head. "I don't really think what I do in my downtime is any of your business."

"You're more of a consulting professor for Rutgers. I want to know where you go, Miss Hightower. You're asking me to trust you around my researchers."

She stopped the lazy circles, planted both feet solidly on the floor and leaned toward him. "Let's get something straight, Mr. Cheng. I'm doing you the favor, not the other way around. I said no over and over. I made it clear I wasn't interested in your money. You may think I agreed to speak to your people because the money was too good to pass up, but it was because you intrigued me. You were that persistent. I thought the research mattered to you. If you keep insisting on playing this silly game, I would very much like you to ask your driver to return me to my hotel."

"Have I offended you with my questions?"

Zhang interrupted, once again in his language. "Let me take her to the interrogation room, Mr. Cheng."

"That's it." Zara stood up, glaring at Zhang. "I can't believe how rude you're being when you *invited* me here. Please return my briefcase and escort me down to the car."

Cheng stood as well. "Mr. Zhang will be leaving us. I'm sorry for his rude behavior. Mr. Zhang, send in Mr. Zhu." He indicated the door with a jerk of his chin and it said something for the fear his people felt, even those closest to him, that Zhang hastened toward the door.

"Please, sit, Miss Hightower. I'm used to people trying to spy on us, stealing what we've worked hard to develop. Just a few weeks ago, a spy escaped with valuable information. It set us back months."

Zara kept her heart from accelerating, but it was difficult, especially after hearing the name Bolan Zhu twice. She knew all about him. He was Cheng's right hand and probably far more feared even than Cheng. He was the interrogator sent in for difficult subjects. Most people never got near him. He was the man Cheng trusted more than any other. Little was known about Zhu until he served with the army.

Zara decided it was better to appear to cooperate than have Bolan Zhu threaten her. It was one thing for Zhang to do so, but Zhu was a different matter altogether. She sank into the chair and gave a pretty little moue with her lips. "I'm sorry. I think I'm being temperamental because I'm tired and your Mr. Zhang wasn't the most welcoming."

Cheng looked up as Zhu walked through the door. Bolan Zhu was tall and wore a very expensive suit in a dark charcoal. He gave Zara a small smile as Cheng introduced them.

"So nice to finally have you here, Miss Hightower," Zhu greeted. "Cheng has spoken of you often. He is a great admirer of your work."

Clearly the man was as charming as he was lethal. Her information on him included the fact that he enjoyed traveling abroad, and when he did, he visited clubs nightly. He was considered quite a ladies' man and Zara could see why. He was extremely handsome. She gave him a smile and sat a little straighter.

"That's nice of you to say so," she murmured, lowering her lashes. She felt rather than saw the two men exchange a look. They bought that she was a little affected by Zhu's good looks and charming manner.

"Miss Hightower was just going to tell me where she disappears to when she isn't at the university, which is often," Cheng said.

"It's a little embarrassing," Zara said, acting reluctant. She snuck a quick glance at Zhu as if talking in front of him was the reason she would be embarrassed. "I work very hard for long periods of time without sleeping or sometimes eating. I realize it isn't the best thing for my health, but I just can't remember to eat or sleep when I'm on to something. I've been known to wake up in the middle of the night and use my walls for paper to write on. I often take breaks, sometimes just a couple of weeks, but often longer, to regroup. I go on retreats where I don't have access to a computer, phone or television. I have to shut out the world entirely. Sometimes I sleep for twenty-four straight hours."

"That makes sense." Zhu jumped to her defense. "Cheng told me you were a child prodigy, one of the leading AI experts at a very young age."

"It's such a fascinating idea," Zara said, pouring enthusiasm into her voice, hoping neither man would realize she hadn't answered the question of where she'd been. Only what she'd been doing. "Artificial intelligence is a growing field, covering so many things that could be useful. People have the mistaken idea that it is just robotics—although that alone is amazing and forward thinking—but it's so much more."

"We spend some time and energy on robotics here," Cheng said. "You think that's a waste of time?"

"No, of course not. It's just that artificial intelligence can be used in a much broader scope. I don't want any student to get bogged down thinking in a box. Just thinking one thing. Already we have small examples of machines learning. They can help so many people. On a small scale, people stuck in houses can just ask their devices to order food or supplies for them. If an elderly man or woman falls in their home, they can call out to their device and have it call for an ambulance or family member. The possibilities are limitless."

There was genuine enthusiasm in her voice. She sat up straight and her face lit up. Her eyes did as well. She was very aware of the changes in her and allowed them. She wanted Cheng and Zhu to see she was exactly what she said she was, a very young professor who believed in exploring artificial intelligence.

"Why did you choose a subfield like machine learning versus something else, like robotics?" Cheng asked.

"I like machines. I like programming, not that I do much of that anymore myself, but numbers speak to me. Machines are logical." Her long lashes fluttered. "I get carried away when I talk about my work. Please forgive me. What else do you need to know before I give my talk to your people, Mr. Cheng? I don't want to take up any more of your time than I need to. It's getting late and I'm certain your employees need to get home."

"They would wait all night to get a chance to ask questions of you, Miss Hightower," Mr. Cheng said. "Your briefcase has few papers we can understand. Your code appears to be unbreakable. Did you devise it yourself?"

She burst out laughing. "The few papers you can understand are used for my talk. The others are sequences of numbers I put together when I'm working out a problem in my head. It soothes me."

"Hasn't anyone ever stopped you, believing it's a code of some kind?"

She shrugged. "It's happened, but eventually they realize it's nothing but me doing something repetitious that helps me think."

Cheng's brows came together and he regarded her with skepticism. "Didn't you have trouble coming into the country with those papers?"

"I only had a couple of papers with numbers at the time and someone assured those holding me that it's no code but random sets of numbers repeated over and over on several pages. That ensures everyone thinks I'm a little eccentric, which I probably am."

"That doesn't make sense," Cheng said, suspicion in his voice.

"It does if she's OCD," Zhu pointed out, looking straight at Zara. "Those random numbers are repeated in sets of three."

Zara didn't change expression and she kept her heart rate exactly the same—a nice steady rhythm, as if she didn't have a care in the world. As if she wasn't sitting in a room with two deadly vipers ready to strike at any moment. Zhu's answer meant he'd looked at those papers.

A timid knock announced the arrival of the tea. It was

Zhu who physically got up and opened the door. Zara found that fascinating. He didn't call out to the woman carrying in the tray, but he got up and took the tray from her. She never entered Cheng's office, and Zhu lowered himself to carrying the tea tray. He set it on the small table in front of Zara. She knew she was really in trouble. Zhu didn't care what others thought of him. He didn't stand on protocol or ego. That made him very, very dangerous.

Was Cheng so paranoid that he didn't allow anyone into his office? Probably, she decided. "I don't mind pouring the tea for everyone," she said, pitching her voice low, almost submissive. "I don't know if that would be offensive to either of you. I'm unsure of the custom when there is no other woman in the room."

She knew Cheng would never pour her tea. He'd already stepped far back as if that would save him from having to do such a menial task in front of her.

Zhu had no such problem. He simply smiled at her and shook his head. "We are very modern here, Miss Hightower. I have no problems pouring you tea." He suited actions to words, picking up the little pot and pouring the liquid into three cups.

She watched very carefully, making certain he didn't put anything in the tea. He poured quickly and efficiently, his long fingers looking incongruous on the small cups. He was mesmerizing. Frightening, but mesmerizing. Bolan Zhu was a very scary man. He appeared modern and sophisticated, very charming with his white teeth and startling green eyes. His shoulders were wide, filling out his suit beautifully, and when he walked, he seemed to glide.

She noted that he served Cheng first and her second. They weren't quite as modern as they wanted her to believe. She took the cup of tea, observing that Zhu's index finger touched the rim, sliding around it in one continuous motion. The drug was on the outside of the cup, not the inside, but it was where her lips would go no matter where she placed them. Zhu also took a cup and deliberately brought the tea-cup to his mouth and drank. Cheng also drank. Both watched her.

Zara had a couple of choices. She could drop the cup and "accidentally" break it, or she could drink it and hope they weren't trying to kill her. She suspected Zhu would inter-rogate her, and whatever drug he'd just introduced to the rim of the cup would compel her to tell the truth. She lifted the cup to her lips and sipped. She had to take the chance. She knew if she didn't, Zhu would probably incarcerate her and that wouldn't go well for her at all.

"Have you been taken around the city at all?" Zhu asked.

"No. I haven't had time. I've been here four times and mostly I see the inside of hotels or facilities where I've been asked to speak," Zara said, taking another sip. She looked at the liquid in the teacup. "This is exceptionally good. I don't think I've ever had this before and I order tea all the time."

Zhu sat in the chair closest to her and Cheng seemed to fade into the background. "All our teas are made from one single plant, did you know that? It's actually an evergreen shrub that can grow into a small tree and live over a hundred years. It grows in Southeast China and the leaves are har-vested year-round."

He watched as she sipped at the tea. She smiled at him. "Well, it's excellent."

"Why did you come here?"

"I was invited, of course. I don't like to travel that much anymore, so I only go where I'm invited." She frowned. Something was definitely working on her brain. She had to puzzle it out fast. "That's not exactly true. I turn down a lot of invitations as well. I travel to the countries I'm interested in. Ones that are beautiful, but then I don't get to see them because I'm working."

Was she babbling? It sounded like it to her, but the words just tumbled out. She had to rein it in. Think. Force her brain to process whatever it was and work around it. She was good at repeating numbers in her head. That would lessen the effect of the drug on her. She watched the reactions of the two men and realized they expected her to babble and blurt things out. Well, she could do that.

"You find our country beautiful?"

"Don't you?" she countered. "It's so *alive*. I love the people." She didn't have to lie about that. "There are so many things to love." She put her fingers over her mouth as if embarrassed. "I'm sorry. I don't usually carry on this much." She took another sip of tea, careful to keep her mouth in exactly the same place. She didn't need a larger dose of Zhu's truth drug. Was it a new strain? Something that didn't slow her mind? It had to be a new strain. This wasn't making her slow and sleepy. It wasn't slowing her brain at all. What was it doing to her? She continued to count sequences of numbers in her head and solve intricate problems. It helped to clear her mind of the effects of the drug.

Zhu leaned into her, took her teacup from her and placed it on the table. Very gently he turned her hand over and stroked her wrist once. Something slithered through her mind, something unsettling that coiled hotly in her belly. He was looking at her differently. Not with the eyes of a viper, but more like a predator—a wolf or a tiger, something with teeth about to pounce. Her heart jumped. Stuttered. His fingers pressed into her wrist, right over her pulse, and she forced calm when she felt more threatened than ever.

"Do you wish Mr. Cheng harm?"

Her gaze leapt to Zhu's face. "Harm? Of course not. He seems a very nice man. He asked me to talk to his employees. I thought perhaps they would benefit from my work." She needed to blurt something out. Something true. "You have a really beautiful mouth. I should know. I notice mouths all the time." That was a truth that seemed to come flying out. She put her hand over her mouth again and tried to pull her arm away at the same time.

Zhu smiled at her and clamped his fingers around her wrist, but so gently she almost didn't realize he was holding her still. "Thank you. I was thinking the same of yours. What is the true reason you've come to see us tonight?"

His voice was extraordinary. She almost told him so, but that calm she called on, the one that kept her heart from beating out of control, thankfully prevented her from blurting out that he was mesmerizing. Spellbinding. "I came to talk about a new project my team has developed to Mr. Cheng's chosen researchers, the ones he thought would be interested in my work."

Her eyelashes fluttered at him because she knew it was expected of her. She wasn't a flirt. She never flirted because it would be fruitless to flirt. She couldn't have a relationship with anyone. She was forever alone. Now that her best friends were gone, she was truly alone.

"You look sad."

Those long fingers stroked her arm, sending more ripples of awareness snaking through her. It was more unsettling to her than if he'd put a gun to her head. "Do I? I guess I was thinking sad thoughts."

"Tell me."

"I lost my best friends recently." She lifted her chin, making her eyes go wide in seeming surprise that she'd blurted out such a personal detail. "That's personal and not pertinent to what I need to be doing here. Please take me to this group. It's already late, and I'm getting tired." It wasn't the drug making her tired, but she knew it made her susceptible to Zhu and his mesmerizing voice. She could feel his pull on her. She kept up the numbers running in her head, combating the drug in the only way she could.

Zhu immediately pulled back and looked at Cheng, who nodded. "Mr. Cheng thought you might like a tour of the facility. He's very proud of it and the work environment he's created here. It's a haven of sorts for his people. They're very loyal to him. He provides apartments, day care and even exercise rooms." He stood up and gently tugged on her hand until she was up with him.

The touch of his skin on hers sent an electric current sizzling through her. What was that? She hadn't experienced it before. Not. Ever. The drug wasn't a date rape drug, but it was something that made her respond chemically to him. In her mind, she gave a delicate shudder. She knew such things existed and they could even be permanent, causing the woman or man to be obsessed with the person giving off the pheromones.

Zhu led her out of Cheng's office, one hand on the small of her back. She'd never been so aware of another human being in her life as she was of Bolan Zhu as he walked her through the facility. She noted that several floors were avoided and most of the people failed to greet Zhu; in fact, they kept their eyes downcast.

It was definitely pheromones. Some kind of drug that made her physically susceptible to him. His fingers burned through her clothing right into her skin. She snuck a glance up at him. His breathing was much better than her own but not quite normal. He'd had to touch the drug with his fingers before administering it onto the rim of the teacup. He'd drunk his tea. Had he touched his fingers to his mouth? She couldn't remember. Her body had grown hot. She was almost too uncomfortable to listen to the sound of his voice.

Zara managed to ooh and ahh in all the right places, but it was clear to both of them that she was struggling against her attraction to Zhu more than she was paying attention to the things he was showing her. After all, that was the point, wasn't it? She kept that uppermost in her mind, so she wasn't too ashamed of herself for the fight she had to put up to not give in to the drug's effects. And she kept solving number problems in her head.

Before her talk, she had him take her to the ladies' room. She threw up like she did every time before she gave her talk. From experience she knew, once she got started, she would be fine, but the idea of standing before colleagues, others interested in AI work, always made her feel incredibly sick. She knew if Zhu was aware she was ill, he would think she had something to hide. He would never consider it nerves. She carefully rinsed her mouth and ate the strong peppermint candy she always carried before rejoining him.

"I'd like to take you on a tour of our city," Zhu said as he brought her to the auditorium where they'd set up a podium for her. Her briefcase was there, sitting right beside the glass of water provided for her.

"I'd love that." She'd be long gone, thankful she'd escaped with her life.

He took her straight to the podium and Zara immediately slipped into her role. She hated everything about her life but this: talking about what she loved and believed in with those interested. That, more than anything else, always allowed her to escape the horrible shyness that made her the worst traveler ever. She had developed the character everyone saw and believed, and she hid behind her. Once she got past her nerves, she could settle into explaining the program and why it could be so helpful on so many levels.

Zhu stood to one side. Close. Beyond the lights she could see a half dozen men with automatic weapons at the entrances. She pretended not to, but it was a very definite fight to keep her heart rate normal.

At her introduction, conducted by another very charming man in a suit, the applause was enthusiastic. She wondered if Cheng had threatened all of them—applaud her loudly or my goons will shoot you.

"Good evening. My talk is called the VALUE System, the program you'd love to have as a partner. I think you'll see why in just a moment . . ." She trailed off and scanned her audience. She'd given her talk dozens of times already and knew it was cutting edge. They would be hanging on every word if they were really interested in artificial intelligence and what it could do for them.

She reached out to the machines on the first floor. The computers. Touching them with her energy, that psychic gift Dr. Whitney had so carefully enhanced. She could talk to machines and they listened with rapt attention just as these people were listening. She had the ability to serve as a wireless conduit between the remote computers and her wireless hard drive. She instructed the remote computers to transfer their data from every one of the computers, floor by floor, and store it in the PEEK-carbon nanotube hiding the SSD in her brain.

"Since the 1960s, AI game playing systems have been fixated on winning. Every twenty years there is a quantum leap in AI programs' ability to win. Arthur Samuel built the first self-learning program in 1959, a program that learned how to play checkers increasingly better over time. The program reached a respectable amateur level status of play by the 1970s. Fast-forward twenty years, and in 1997 you could watch the deep learning program, Deep Blue, beat the reigning world chess champion, Gary Kasparov—an amazing accomplishment! Fast-forward another twenty years, and in 2017 you see Google's deep learning program, AlphaGo, beat the reigning world Go champion."

It took time to transfer the amount of data stored in the computers in Cheng's facility. It would take as long to destroy every hard drive to ensure the man had no data on the GhostWalker program given to him by the treasonous Senator Violet Smythe. Zara kept her voice even and calm so that later, when Cheng and Zhu compared it with other speeches she'd given, there would be no difference. Inflections would be the same. She wasn't under undue stress. She couldn't possibly be the reason they lost the data on every computer. She was incredibly thankful for her mind's ability to work on solving number problems. In doing so, it had lessened the effects of the drug enough for her to control the systems in her body.

"But there's one thing we have yet to see . . . What about

a program that could learn to intentionally *lose* when playing a little boy, so that boy could experience winning? What about a program that could learn how to propose 'win-win' solutions for itself and someone else? What about a program that knows that 'you can't always get what you want' and learns how to 'get what you need' by making good trade-offs given limited, competing resources—time, money, people, materials, etc.?"

The idea had been talked about for years. For trade, such a program would be invaluable. It was expected that there would be a breakthrough sooner or later, but to be able to stand in front of them and announce it had been accomplished was exciting. Every. Single. Time. She had to be careful to never lose sight of why she was really there. She needed the information in those computers. She'd done this so many times, but she'd never had to destroy the hard drives. Most businesses or universities had no idea she'd taken anything out with her when she went because she only gathered information; she never left evidence that their computers had been touched. Destroying the hard drives of every computer in the building would definitely raise alarms.

"In this talk, I'm going to describe a program, the VALUE system, which integrates an entire suite of learning techniques, some old and some new, to do just that. The VALUE system integrates the inverse reinforcement learning techniques of Russell and Ng for learning the value of others, our earlier deep learning techniques for creating and refining negotiations and compromise in a two-party circumstance, and our new supervised learning techniques for reformulating design spaces based on human guidance with acceptable trade-offs."

She launched into her talk, trying not to get lost in the excitement of the artificial intelligence world and the endless possibilities that always consumed her mind when she allowed herself to become fully immersed there. She had a job, a much more important one in terms of serving her country, saving lives and getting out of there alive.

As each of the computers gave up its data, the hard drive destroyed itself, wiping out all documents, making certain no trace remained. It was a big facility and she was used to delivering her talks while making the data transfers. She was certain the flow of information to her would never be detected so she was never nervous. It was a matter of instructing the machines in any chosen building to cooperate. She didn't need to hack in or figure out passwords. She just needed a wireless environment. Destroying the hard drives after was a much riskier thing to do and she'd never done it before. That left footprints. No one could prove she had anything to do with the losses, but she was there. On site.

Zara let her enthusiasm for her work show, in her voice, her mannerisms, the way her face lit up. She wanted to be animated, and she was. Her mind had finally let go of her curious obsession with Bolan Zhu, the need to focus on her academia and the particular program she was spearheading overcoming the last remnants of the drug. This program was her "baby" all the way and she was totally immersed in that world, and had been for a long while, when the sirens blared loudly. Instantly, the room went electric. Zara stopped speaking to look around, allowing her heart rate to accelerate just as everyone's had to be climbing. Her audience stood up in silence and began filing out of the room like robots.

Zara gathered her papers and turned to Zhu. "What's happening?" Fear crept into her voice, just enough of a note that she hoped Zhu would think was normal under the circumstances. She had to keep collecting the remaining data and destroying the hard drives as she went. There was no protection from her unless the wireless was shut down. Only half a floor to go and she'd be finished. She had no way of knowing what data was in what computer on what floor, but even as Zhu reached her, gathering her into him, she kept up the transfer and destruction.

"We have to get you to safety and then I'll check it out," Zhu assured. "I can't imagine a drill being scheduled, so this is more likely a glitch in the system or someone left chemicals out when they shouldn't have. Don't be alarmed." He escorted her to a small room.

No windows, Zara noted. She heard the lock turn when he left her. She didn't bother trying the door. Sinking down onto the chair, she glanced at her watch, noting the time. She wanted to press the stopwatch, but she forced herself to leave it alone. She had time, but it would run out fast if she didn't get out of Cheng's facility. She knew his lockdowns could last a week or longer.

She told herself her mission was important to Whitney. He wouldn't allow her to die, not when what she had in her head was so valuable to him. Calmly, she finished the data transfers and destroyed all remaining hard drives in the building. She could be calm because she had something for her mind to work on, but the moment that was done, fear poured in and she rocked herself in terror.

#1 *NEW YORK TIMES* BESTSELLING AUTHOR

CHRISTINE FEEHAN

"The queen of paranormal romance...
I love everything she does."
—J. R. Ward

For a complete list of titles,
please visit prh.com/christinefeehan